Praise for When Darkness Descends
(The Relevation Trilogy: Book I)

"A fresh and intriguing fantasy...the author introduces an array of memorable characters... fantasy aficionados will...find themselves engrossed in the story from beginning to end."

'Get it'. Kirkus Reviews

"G. W. Lücke's *When Darkness Descends* is an engrossing addition to the high fantasy catalogue. Lücke's characters have a vivid energy; the land and people of Enthilen are illuminated with care and detail, and the plot runs at a tight, satisfying pace."

Indi Reader (Approved)

"Lücke's strength lies undoubtedly in his ability to build worlds with immense depth. With intriguing plotlines and continuously evolving character arcs, the story keeps the readers engaged and anticipating the next sequence of events."

US Review of Books (Recommended)

"The exquisitely created fantasy world of Enthilen, and a horde of twists and turns as Tom and Grin are put against a set of formidable enemies keep the pages flying. Lücke strikes a perfect balance between stunning worldbuilding and layered narrative as his hero struggles against powerful enemies while on a journey of self-discovery. Lücke is a writer to watch for."

The Prairies Book Review

"With dynamic characters, interesting histories, and compelling drama, When Darkness Descends is a new fantasy that is sure to suck readers in. Engrossing and immersive, Lücke's epic fantasy is filled with charming creatures and mesmerising landscapes. With a dramatic, irresistibly exciting cliff-hanger as its finale, readers will be locked to the page and left wanting more."

Book Review Directory

Praise for At the End of Everything (The Relevation Trilogy: Book II)

"A second fantastic dive into the realm of Ostamp. There are brilliant lines and passages peppered across this novel, some so good they'll force you back for another read, while the action sequences and magical exchanges are exhilarating — a one-two punch that is rare in the world of fantasy writing. Lücke demonstrates a masterful use of language, bursts of unforgettable prose, a rich tapestry of characters, and a penchant for mythical history in this remarkably good second installment."

★★★★½ Self-publishing Review

"This propulsive, gripping sequel focuses on a hero's quest to find personal justice. The riveting story is a sure-fire treat for Game of Thrones fans."

'Get it'. Kirkus Reviews

"Lücke is a master of the cliffhanger, which he skillfully utilizes at the end of each chapter. Readers will be captivated to the very end."

US Review of Books (Recommended)

"Darkly real but classically fantastical...Packed with thematic descriptions and evocative prose, this fantasy is engaging, with many inspiring characters to root for."

Publishers Weekly (BookLife)

SHE WILL RISE

The Relevation Trilogy:
Book III

G. W. LÜCKE

With Distinction Publishing

Published in Australia by With Distinction Consultants
PO Box 97, St Marys, Tasmania 7215
https://withdistinctionconsultants.wordpress.com/
First published in Australia in 2021

Book website: https://relevationtrilogy.com
Author Facebook page: https://www.facebook.com/GWLucke/
Maps produced under commercial licence by G. W. Lücke
using Inkarnate software https://inkarnate.com/
Cover design, typesetting: WorkingType Studio

The characters and events portrayed in this book are fictitious. Any similarity to real persons, living or dead, is coincidental and not intended by the author. **Content warning**: this book contains adult content that some readers may find distressing, including sexual assault, suicide, mental illness, drug use and violence.

A catalogue record for this
work is available from the
National Library of Australia

National Library of Australia Cataloguing-in-Publication Entry:
Creator: Lücke, G. W., author
Title: She Will Rise. The Relevation Trilogy: Book III.
ISBN: 978-0-6488207-4-1 (Paperback)
ISBN: 978-0-6488207-5-8 (ePub)

BISAC Codes: FIC009020 FICTION/Fantasy/Epic;
FIC009100 FICTION/Fantasy/Action and Adventure

For Gayle, my light, my life, my hope

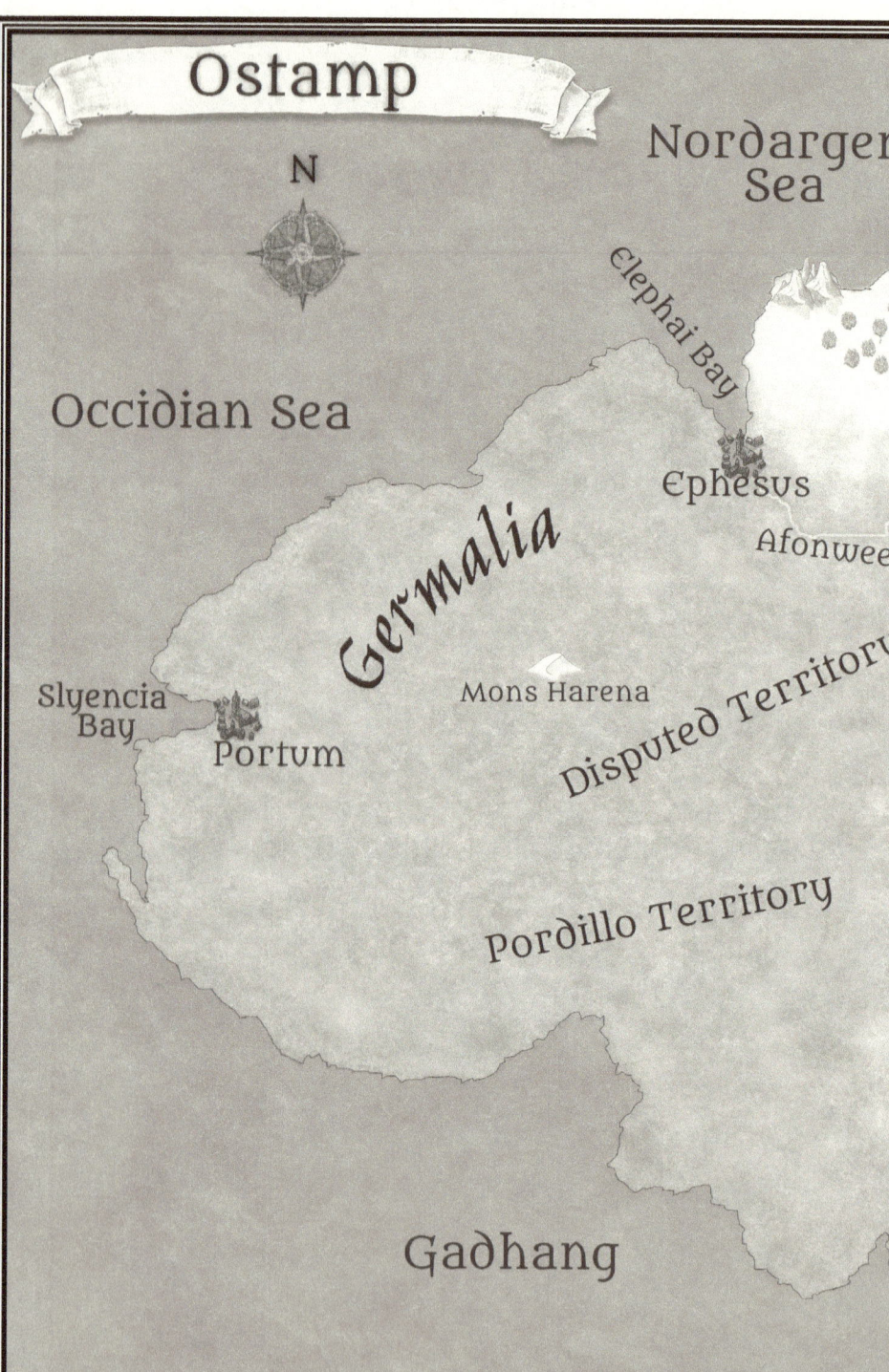

Hurst

Bay of Deception

Grauberge

Nordland

Thyatira   Revelé

River

Desolate Mountains

Sardis

Laodicea Traders Bay

Anchep River

Enthilen

Bagendon

Scaur Hills

Malang Gunya
(Pergamos)

Gestade

Veiled Occyan

Süden Forst   Dorfisch

Riverlands

Babir Birramal

Gügal

Bay of
Marrumin

Bindari

ENTHILEN

N

DESOLATE

THE FEIGN

SARDIS

ANCHEP RIVER

SLUMSTADT

RĀRIAN FALLS

GRŌZ WÜSTE

RIVERLANDS ESCARPMENT

BAGENDON

BREADELBANE

SCAUR HILLS

MOULDEWERP DWELL

BEITRAG

SÜDEN FORST

RIVERLANDS

GERMALIAN CAMP

FLÜSSE

ERSTÜRMEN CAMP

FARMERS' FORT

ANCHEP DELTA

GIIGAL

BAY OF MARRUMIN

MOUNTAINS

LEVIATHAN STATUE

DETRANTÉ

LOKAN

TRADERS BAY

LAODICEA

VEILED OCCYAN

SAND BĒĊE

ABROLOUS ISLES

RIVER LOUSSE

BAY OF FIRES

PERGAMOS
(MALANG GUNYA)

WALAR ROCK

GELIE BEACH

DAMBAY PLAINS

GESTADE

BRAMBLE ISLAND

DORFISCH

RUFOUS

GRIN'S MILBI

BABIR BIRRAMAL
(GRŌZ FORST)

DALMAN

BINDARI

GADHANG

GERMALIA

N

GRIFFIN ISLES

OCCIDIAN SEA

GRANTOU

WONCHULUS

M

SLYENCIA BAY

PORTUM

Nordland
Ephesus
Afonwee River
Waterhole
Wurloin Nest
Magna Avium (Grōz Wüste)
Pordillo Camp
(Qaysar Rais)
ns Harena
Pordillo Territory

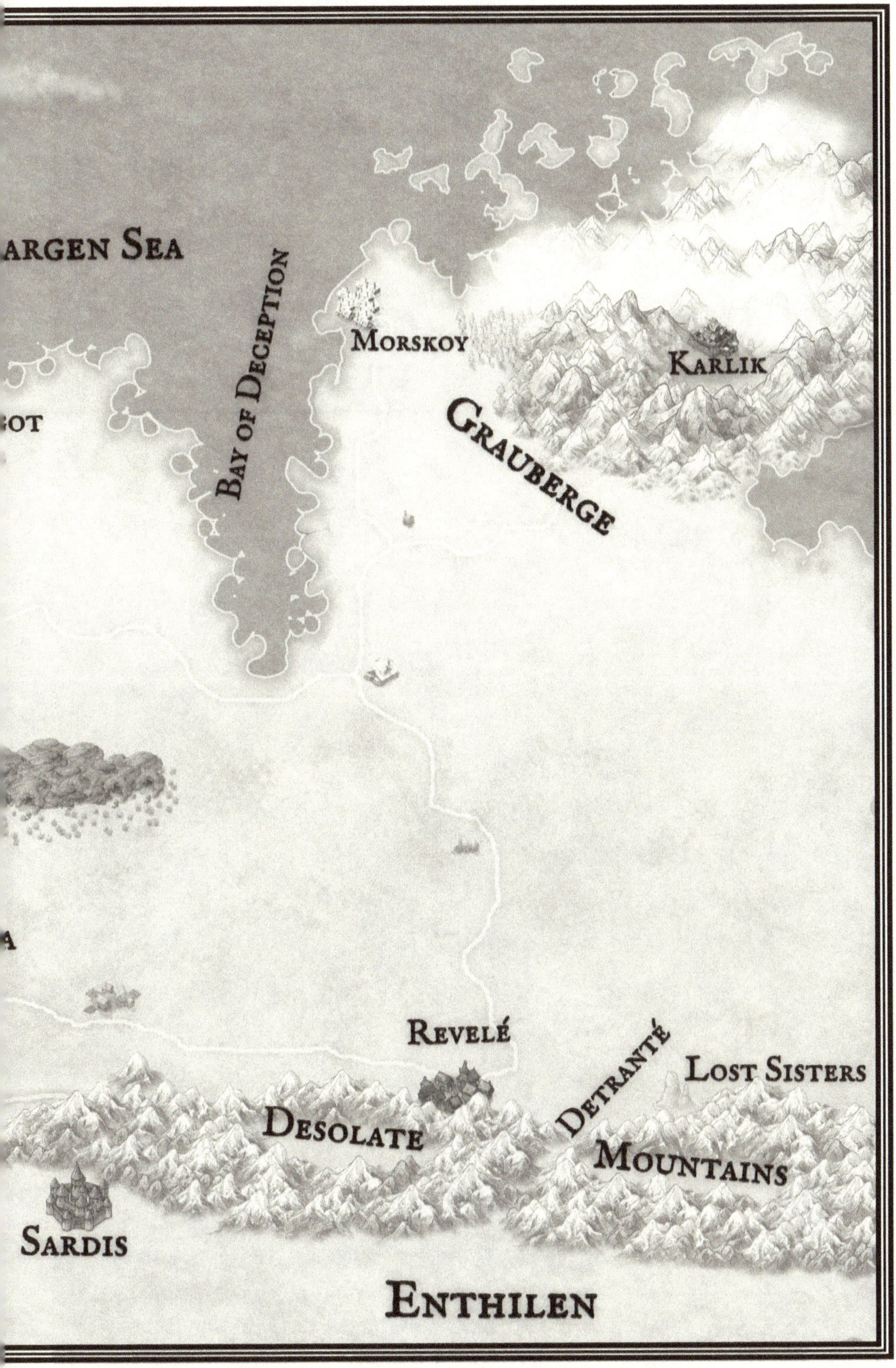

ARGEN SEA

BAY OF DECEPTION

GOT

MORSKOY

KARLIK

GRAUBERGE

A

REVELÉ

DESOLATE

DETRANTÉ

LOST SISTERS

MOUNTAINS

SARDIS

ENTHILEN

Rel`e*va"tion *n.* [*L. relevatio, fr. relevare.*]
A raising or lifting up.

And to the woman were given two wings of a great eagle,
that she might fly into the wilderness...
(Revelation 12: 14).

Note: A *Dramatis Personae* and Appendix
are included at the end of the book

~ What has gone before ~

Welcome back, my friend. You demonstrate a persistent fortitude I didn't think you had. I'll keep this brief, as I know you're itching to begin the final leg of our journey. In part two of our tale, Tom Anderson, Thaly and Grin escape Malphas by jumping off Hansen's Bluff in Laodicea and landing in Felsie, the pool of reflection. Saved from drowning by the shady Whibly, the skullard of the *Vulking*, the three companions fled Laodicea on the merchant ship, travelling into the Veiled Occyan towards Bramble Island. But an ugly tempest arrived, shattering the *Vulking* to pieces and separating Tom from his friends. He floated on wreckage for days before being rescued by Melinda, a fisher's daughter, who took him to Bramble Island. There, he recovered from the shipwreck and enacted his revenge on the *Vulking's* skipper, the unsavoury Captain Adcock. Tom returned to Enthilen with Melinda and her father, Jameus, and met their elderly weald-grell housekeeper, Annian. In a spot of coincidental good fortune, Annian was preparing to leave for the grell graveyard of Bindari, her final resting place, the exact location Princess Caeli told Tom he would find out why he'd been brought to Enthilen.

One morning, Annian disappeared, and Tom chased her, finally convincing her to lead him to the mysterious Bindari. There, inside a bleak house at the bottom of a gorge, he met the demented Widukind, Malphas' brother, and the draughoul Fullō, once Malphas' mother. After re-examining the First Scripture, words I wrote in my own blood generations ago, Widukind discovered that the only way Tom could foil Malphas' plans was to return to Earth using the throne of the dead, *my* throne, as a gateway. Then, Adalwolf couldn't steal Tom's soul with the eyes of lost souls and become immortal.

With Princess Caeli's help, Tom travelled to the ruined grell city of

Malang Gunya. Malphas and a newly crowned King Adalwolf were already there, preparing to resurrect the ancient city of Pergamos that lay beneath Malang Gunya's foundations. In Pergamos' throne hall, Tom confronted Malphas and Adalwolf. The meeting didn't go as Malphas planned, disrupted by a shaking, heaving earth that threatened to collapse the hall and kill everyone inside. Thanks to help from Dwarrow, Grin, Thaly and Caeli, Tom reached the dead throne, placed the eyes of lost souls in the eye sockets of the horned wolf that crowns the backrest, and sat in a place reserved *only* for me. The throne did as Widukind predicted, returning Tom to Earth. Twelve years later, he's still there.

What of the other players in our drama? Whibly saved Thaly and Grin from drowning in the Veiled Occyan, and the three companions rowed back to Enthilen. Arriving at the Erstürmen outpost of Gestade, Grin learned that King Adalwolf was leading thousands of citizens to Malang Gunya to tear down what remained of the grell city and rebuild Pergamos. He led Thaly into the vast forest of Babir Birramal, taking her to the sacred grell ceremony — the garrabari — where he hoped to convince the elders not to undertake the pilgrim march to Malang Gunya for fear the Erstürmen would attack. But Grin's pleas fell on deaf ears, and hundreds of grells, and their new mouldewerp allies, marched into Malang Gunya to honour their ancestors. In the calendar of life, King Adalwolf ordered the slaughter of the pilgrims. Grin lost his father and mother in the massacre, his conscience tortured by the decision to help Tom Anderson return to Earth rather than join his parents in the pilgrim march.

Thaly travelled to Malang Gunya with Grin, but Krieg, the red grell, kidnapped her, and Malphas imprisoned her, along with Princess Caeli, hoping to use them to bend Tom Anderson to his will. But Thaly and Caeli resisted Malphas' torture, Thaly risking her life to help Tom escape Enthilen, while Caeli forfeited her soul by stopping Adalwolf from stealing Tom's with the dark eyes. As Pergamos' throne hall crumbled, a wounded King Adalwolf fled with his mother, Romilda, thus becoming the 'absent king'.

In a Laodicea routed by barbarians, Lady Lily LáDown led war refugees to Gestade and took shelter with the kindly Commander Hartmut.

General Jurelle Stansfield rescued his wife, Genevea, and daughter, Saskia, from Sardis, taking them to the welcoming arms of the Germalians. Krieg arrived in Sardis and executed Master Hunfrid, an event exploited by the scheming Anselm and Rostard. In Bagendon, Emelin Wallace became the new Dobunni rebel leader, only to witness the town's devastation at the hands of Krieg and his grell soldiers, the Rephaim. Finally, a floundering Rosalie Barron abandoned her family in Sardis' fifth circle, fleeing to the poverty-stricken Slumstadt and straight into the arms of the beguiling Elmbray and the false comfort of the mind-altering substance, embruisia.

There you have it, my dear friend — the key events leading to this grand finale. The most important question is, of course, will I, Volerdie, finally return to Enthilen? Or will someone thwart Malphas' plans once again?

The east wind howled a buffeting harassment into Jurelle Stansfield's face as he steadied his courser. The Dobunni leader squinted against the onslaught of dust whipped along the road connecting the Riverlands Escarpment with Enthilen's royal city of Sardis. Behind him, the Anchep River plummeted over the escarpment edge and fell to a depth certain to kill anyone trapped in the tumbling waters of the Rārian Falls. Churning torrents of froth and wind melded into a raging dissonance as if nature warned Jurelle of a coming tumult.

Flanking him, Emelin and Thane Wallace straddled stout horses bred to navigate the steep, rocky paths of the Scaur Hills. Saddle cloths flailed in the wind, slapping the greaves covering the rebels' shins and knocking flecks of red dirt from the bottom of leather boots so worn, cord had been wrapped around the upper and sole to hold them together. The Dobunni fighters waited, rigid and watchful, exposed on the open road while their horses grazed on fresh grass growing in swales of alluvial soil.

The wind season will soon end, Jurelle thought. Let the expectant growth take hold.

Emelin faced him, her lips pursed and eyes cautious. "Are you sure about this? It could be a trap."

"King Ewald will expect the same," said Jurelle. "Away from his inner sanctum. Out from behind the veil of seven walls. If he comes with more than a handful of King's Shield, we'll escape into the hills."

"He's coming now." Thane pointed east towards the rising sun.

King Ewald's bannerman trotted around a bend in the road, bouncing atop a cremello mare and clutching the traditional Erstürmen banner; a rectangle of black cloth with the sigil of a two-headed, crimson serpent curled up into an incomplete circle, face-to-face. Behind the bannerman rode six armoured King's Shield led by their Umbo, Gerulf Heine, the king's brother. Sunlight filtered through the canopies of bullom trees lining the road, bouncing off the soldiers' pauldrons and illuminating dust particles that danced with the canter of hooves. The wailing wind carried the clink of scabbards' metal chapes as they knocked against polished silver cuisses.

King Ewald rode behind his Shield on a bay destrier, slouching low in the saddle. Jurelle pictured rolls of body fat squeezed and contorted to fit armour better suited to a leaner man. Catching the wind as if in flight, a black feather the size of a forearm fluttered from the peak of Ewald's spangenhelm. He claimed the feather had belonged to the griffin that spirited King Giltbert away during the barbarian assault on Nordland. Jurelle had no reason to doubt the story, though he expected no-one would see a griffin in Enthilen ever again.

At the rear of the royal party, two thick-set, piebald horses pulled a covered wagon. The elderly driver perched atop a wooden bench seat bounced along with every bone-rattling gouge in the dirt road, her convulsing body resembling a sack of chaff kicked by an ingratitude of children.

"Eight is more than a handful," muttered Thane. "Who knows what they've got in the wagon."

"We hold steady nonetheless," said Jurelle.

The King's Shield reined their horses to a stop within shouting distance of the Dobunni rebels. Behind the Shield, Ewald steadied his burdened steed, then heaved himself from the saddle. His spangenhelm almost toppled into the dust as he thudded onto the ground. He clutched for the chinstrap to avoid embarrassment, then removed the ill-fitting helmet and handed it to his brother, Gerulf.

Jurelle yelled into the wind, "Only the two of us, Ewald!"

Under a thick brown beard, sweeping down to mask the curled, two-headed serpent embossed on Ewald's breastplate, the king's face remained impassive, but his eyes flicked across the boulder-covered slopes on his left leading to the ridgeline of the Scaur Hills.

"He's scanning the rocks for an ambush," said Emelin.

"The king's paranoia runs deeper than the Anchep River," said Jurelle.

Ewald lumbered towards the rebels. Jurelle dismounted, handed the reins of his courser to Thane, then walked along the road to meet the king halfway.

"No ambush lies in wait for you, Ewald," said Jurelle. "And I assume none for me."

The king stopped, his hand clutching the pommel of a broadsword hanging from his belt. Jurelle wondered when Ewald last wielded a sword as his own hand moved to the waist of his tunic, where a long knife had been slipped underneath his belt. He took another six steps forward, then halted, face-to-face with the King of Enthilen. Although dressed for battle, the king's manner suggested a man who wanted no quarrel.

"Let's finish this as quickly as possible," said Ewald, his posture softening. "The world outside the inner circle becomes more deceitful with each passing moon."

"Take care your castle doesn't become your prison," said Jurelle, trying to suppress a wry smile.

Ewald grunted, then waved to the wagon driver. She climbed from her seat and limped to the wagon's tailgate before returning with a woman cradling a baby. They waited at the front of the royal party.

A breath caught in Jurelle's throat. "She's given birth?"

"Only a girl," said Ewald. "I offer my condolences."

Jurelle stepped towards his lover, Princess Genevea. Now the mother of his first child.

Ewald blocked his path with a bearish frame. "Temper your haste. I asked for this meeting to present my terms."

Jurelle expected as much; he wouldn't leave here without a forfeiture. "What are they?" he asked.

Ewald locked eyes with him. "You pledge fealty to me until your death, and I'll allow you to serve the Erstürmen Kingdom and marry my sister. The child, however, cannot stay. It is born of an illegitimate coupling. I won't condone an unwedded relationship between an Erstürmen princess and the Dobunni leader, consummated behind my back."

Jurelle raised an eyebrow. "What if I don't accept your terms?"

"Then the child dies, and Princess Genevea will be confined to Sardis' inner circle for the rest of her life. If she makes another mistake, I'll execute her. You *may* escape here alive, maybe not. My soldiers always yearn for Dobunni blood. I might even consider a major assault on Bagendon."

Jurelle shuffled his left foot behind his right, shoulder-width apart, and grasped the grip of his long knife with a tense hand. Can three rebels defeat half a dozen Shield? he wondered. Will Genevea abandon Sardis and follow him to Bagendon? How would the Erstürmen react to such treachery?

"Release your weapon," said Ewald. "Acceptance or death are your only options."

Jurelle relaxed, and the king beckoned to Genevea with a gauntleted hand. She left the safety of the royal escort and walked up to Jurelle and Ewald, embracing the newborn who'd been wrapped in a red and yellow silk throw adorned with embroidered griffins.

Genevea stepped past Ewald and stood before Jurelle, pulling the throw away from the baby's face. "She's beautiful," said Genevea. "She has your eyes."

Jurelle's chest swelled with adoration, his heart already captured by innocent brown eyes pleading for safe harbour. He brushed the cracked, dry tip of his index finger across the velvety cheek of his daughter.

Ewald broke the entrancement. "It's a simple choice. Serve me, spend your remaining days with my sister at your side in a legitimate marriage symbolising fealty to the kingdom, and the child lives. *And*, the Dobunni stronghold remains standing."

Jurelle longed for intervention from Genevea. An indication of what he should say. What he should do. Did she want him to leave the Dobunni behind forever and fight for the Erstürmen? He would become the most hated Dobunni leader in living memory. The child, though, was blameless and beautiful. She deserved to live.

The wind dropped as Jurelle spoke, "I accept your terms."

Ewald smiled, rising onto the balls of his feet. "Excellent."

Genevea's body slumped a moment before tears cascaded down her face like the Rārian Falls roaring in the distance. "I-I-I know it's...it's the right choice," she sobbed. "I know. B-b-but it's...so hard. Letting her go. Our firstborn."

"She'll never leave our thoughts," said Jurelle. He beckoned to Emelin, who dismounted and approached the couple.

A quaking Genevea handed the infant to the rebel fighter. "Please, take care of her."

Emelin smiled. "I will treat her as my own. Does she have a name?"

"Athalee."

* * * *

The tainted white hand of a stone-grell scraped at the dirt piled against a cave wall. Excavating rock and soil, he burrowed into a secret hole the length of a giant's arm. Trembling fingers, weakened by seasons of torture, fumbled around the bottom of the hole before grasping a treasure wrapped in torn canvas. Then the white grell froze as the flame of a lone candle flickered a warning. A waft of danger stalked the cave.

The grell quashed his fear, removed the treasure from the hole, untied the twine and folded open the mustard-yellow canvas. Enfeebled by this simple action, he slouched against the cave wall and pushed his naked back into the stone, trying to pierce the numbness wracking his body. The skin covering his cheeks tugged and stung, vandalised by scars that reminded him of the facial crest he once wore. Memories of another life and another name before the Worshipful Master ground those memories to dust and called him Eroberung.

But the tainted grell didn't accept the name. Although no longer the stone-grell of seasons past, he hadn't succumbed entirely to the Worshipful Master's authority. Yet.

With a delicacy belying thick, gnarled fingers, the white grell lifted a bauble, one of two, from the mustard cloth and held it next to the candle.

Inside the obsidian glass eye, a fiery pupil mimicked the flame dancing at the tip of the candle's wick.

Flattery through imitation, perhaps? Or mockery? The thought made him smile.

A spine-tingling gust of wind snuffed out the candle's flame, leaving only the dull light emanating from the two glass eyes with fiery pupils: the eyes of lost souls. The white grell cradled one of the eyes in his left hand, took the other in his right, then sat, legs crossed, palms facing upwards, balancing the dark eyes and meditating on Enthilen's fate.

Malphas, the Worshipful Master, now ruled these lands with absolute and undisputed authority. He'd rebuilt Pergamos after the destruction of Volerdie's Wrath twelve yarles ago, surrounding the city with a wall taller than six grells standing on each other's shoulders. Thousands upon thousands of soldiers filled Malphas' army. None in Enthilen could resist the threatening sweep of their swords. The vast forest of Babir Birramal burned, and dreams of peace blew away with the ash.

A distant snarl fractured the white grell's musings. Then another growl, closer this time. Weregrims hunted him. He closed his eyes, imagining viscid globs of saliva sliding down the stalactites hanging from the cave's roof as the tunnel transformed into the gaping jaw of one of Volerdie's hounds. The white grell had hidden the eyes of lost souls in a place few would search, but the guardians of this cave now came to tear him apart.

He had to flee. He had to take the journey fate demanded of him.

The white grell inhaled and wrapped his fingers around the glass eyes sitting in his palms. Amid the bitter scent of burning flesh from his hands, the cave shone with a swirling, pulsing illumination. A murder of weregrims emerged from the light, but they were too late to snatch their quarry. The white grell disappeared from Enthilen, tumbling into a vortex he hoped would take him to another world. Tom Anderson's world.

~ Chapter 1 ~

Ascorching, relentless desert sun burned the back of Saskia Stansfield's neck as she clutched at shifting red sands. With face and chest pressed into a sand wall, grainy avalanches cascaded past her like curtains descending after the final act, sliding into a black pit at the base of a funnel-shaped hole larger than a house. The Germalian soldier dug the toes of her sandals into the sand, pushing up towards the funnel's lip. But she lost traction and slid towards the pit, the entrance to a wurloin nest.

Almost at the point of no return, Saskia jammed her knees and elbows into the sand wall and held fast, teetering above certain death. Should she descend closer to the nest, she'd be eaten alive by a colossal, ravenous arthropod with toothed mandibles the size of a horse and an exoskeleton stronger than steel. Sweat poured off Saskia's brow and trickled down sunburnt cheeks into the thin, bone-coloured face scarf dangling around her neck. The peen block adorning the pommel of her cutlass dug into her hip, and she considered tossing the weapon away.

A sword's useless here, she thought. No blade can penetrate the wurloin's casing.

Saskia's kamel, Brower, trotted riderless and alone around and around the lip of the funnel, snorting and spitting, seemingly torn between loyalty to his rider and fear of descending into the wurloin's trap. A routine patrol of Germalia's borders in Magna Avium had taken a wrong turn, Saskia's turma ambushed by Pordillo insurgents who killed all the kamel riders bar one. Through good fortune, Saskia escaped, only for Brower to be spooked by a slider serpent, tossing his rider into the sandy red abyss.

The kamel stopped circling, craning his neck towards Saskia. He leaned in too far. The sand under the leathery pads of Brower's front feet gave way, and his knees buckled. A terrified bark shattered the desert haze as Brower plunged down the side of the funnel.

With a shriek, the wurloin thrust its head from the pit, razor-sharp mandibles gnashing and flailing. They latched onto the kamel and crushed its chest with enough power to split granite. Saskia shuddered at Brower's screams and the crack of splintering bones as he disappeared into the blackness, dragged to his death under the scalding, shifting sands of Magna Avium.

With her kamel's demise, exhaustion overcame Saskia. Let go, she thought. The end is here.

A moment before her surrender, a winged shadow swooped across the funnel and screeched its urgency into the sweltering air. Grains of sand swirled about Saskia like a tornado. She pressed her face into the wall of the wurloin's trap, suspended between despair and expectation. Punching through the sandstorm, a ribbed, medallion-yellow talon wrapped itself around Saskia's waist, and a griffin carried her into the blazing sky.

Saskia wiped sand grit from her face and flicked it into the buffeting wind. Silhouetted against the blinding sun, the griffin's rider tugged on the reins to guide the beast away from the wurloin nest. Light glinted off an amulet hanging from the rider's neck; a silver griffin. And tied around the rider's wrist, soiled from seasons of adventure, a white cloth with the letters 'T A' embroidered into the fabric flapped against the streaming air.

* * * *

Jurelle Stansfield stood atop a circular turret on Portum's east wall, pensive in the face of a dust storm brewing on the horizon. A billowing, air-borne rampart of red sand with a parapet of black cloud threatened to consume the Germalian coastal city. The sandstorm hovered above fields of wheat, barley and oats that stretched from the city's outskirts to the foot of dunes four times higher than Portum's walls. The roots of the sand mountains spread like probing tentacles, consuming Portum's breadbasket and depositing clouds of dust and grit onto its paved streets and terracotta roofs.

The city's residents will never escape the suffocating sands, thought Jurelle.

The once Erstürmen General and Dobunni leader struggled to reconcile the seasons of Germalia with those of his birthplace, Enthilen. Portum had only two seasons; a dry season and an even drier one. Sporadic and unpredictable rainfall sometimes interrupted the prolonged droughts, the downpours flooding the streets and creating swollen rivers of rusty-brown that gushed along irrigation channels, carrying precious topsoil into Slyencia Bay. But the occasional flood couldn't replenish the dwindling aquifers struggling to support the city's population.

Despite the approaching sandstorm, crowds wandered along Portum's broad avenues seeking goods and services, discussing city events or enjoying a stroll. Grand buildings with ribbed granite columns supporting friezes carved with scenes of oceans and deserts lined the boulevards. Under the shade of spreading polap trees, vendors sold blomgarnet fruit impaled on the end of wooden skewers, a sticky, sweet treat of translucent crimson flesh surrounding a white seed the size of a kamel's eye. In the city square, female scholars pontificated about Germalia's future or the meaning of life, capturing attentive passers-by with prophecies of doom or cornucopia.

In Portum's harbour, ships crowded bow to stern, carrying wares from lands never visited by Jurelle or most of his Germalian companions. While merchant seafarers from the Veiled Occyan, the waters off Enthilen's east coast, used whales to pull their ships, those riding the currents of the Occidian Sea relied on sails and the wind for propulsion. The Germalian navy, the classem, had the largest ships Jurelle had ever seen, each with a dozen sails attached to masts, sometimes reaching over ten stories high.

Classem ships dominated the waterfront, which the Germalians called The Hive owing to the constant busyness of merchants and seafarers clambering over wharves and decks trying to make coin or secure a favourable trade. Marble statues of twelve different animals representing the twelve Germalian factions had been perched on stone plinths overlooking the harbour. As part of his assimilation into this new culture, Jurelle had to memorise the faction names, representative colours and totem animals.

The centrepiece of The Hive, and, Jurelle soon learned, the most prized invention of his hosts was a giant clocktower standing taller than the masts of classem sailing ships. Unlike the Erstürmen or Dobunni, the Germalians recorded the passing of time with an intricate mechanism of clattering, whirling cogs and wheels. They divided each day into twelve lumina hours and twelve nocturna hours, based on initial observations from a sundial when day and night spanned equal periods. Although the sun may be in the sky for more or less than twelve hours, the clock never changed, its face ticking over each hour with a precise hand, and tollers in the tower ringing a bell to announce the time.

Starting at The Hive, the tree-lined avenue of Lata Via, wide enough to accommodate six horse-drawn carriages travelling abreast, dominated Portum, leading inland to the Pallaxium, a white building larger than a dozen classem ships and capped with a golden dome. There, Germalia's ruling conventus debated the future of this land and its people.

As the sandstorm towered over the Pallaxium's dome, Jurelle's anxiety curled in threatening waves. They need to return home soon, he thought. Don't want to be caught in that tempest.

His worry receded a little when a dot appeared in the sky, racing ahead of the storm. A griffin flew over the fields, farmworkers turning their faces skyward to catch a glimpse of the majestic animal. The griffin's rider, the Germalians called them wind-riders, swooped her mount past the spire atop the Pallaxium dome and skimmed over the rows and rows of tangerine roofs, circling Portum in an acrobatic flourish.

"She's showing off," Jurelle muttered, then trotted down the turret's spiral staircase to meet the returning wind-rider.

A griffin with alabaster and tan feathers layered over tawny fur alighted in the mounting yards of the Volatal Vexil, the Germalian army's flying fighters. Tall, pointed ears twitched, and gleaming, golden eyes watched the handlers who walked towards it. The griffin tossed its head as the rider jerked on the reins looped around its ivory-coloured bill.

Jurelle marched across the cobbled yard, catching his breath at the sight of a griffin up close. Bigger than four horses, he considered griffins regal but terrifying. Still, he celebrated with the rest of Portum when the Germalians discovered a griffin colony on an island in the Occidian Sea. Thought to be long extinct, the Stansfield family sigil experienced a dramatic and welcome resurrection.

After climbing from the griffin's saddle onto a dismount platform, Saskia trotted down the stairs and ran towards him.

"Dada!" she yelled, with a hint of mischievousness.

Jurelle laughed as his youngest daughter flung herself into his arms. "Oh, you're too grown up, and I'm much too old and frail for this."

"Surely, you're strong enough to catch a slip of a girl?"

"You're a woman now. Growing faster than I ever imagined."

Behind Saskia, the wind-rider gave the reins of her mount to a handler, then walked towards Jurelle.

He released Saskia and held his arms wide, ready for another embrace. "Both my beautiful daughters, safe home again. Welcome back, Athalee."

Thaly hugged him, then pulled away, tilting her head towards her younger sister. "This idiot almost got herself killed. *Twice.*"

Saskia's cheeky smile changed to a glower. "It wasn't my fault. A slider serpent spooked Brower, and he bucked me into a wurloin nest."

"You're lucky to be alive," said Thaly. "If I hadn't found you, those wurloin pincers would have munched you into a desert mash."

Jurelle rubbed his fingers across a furrowed brow. "What happened to your turma, Saskia?"

Darkness passed across his daughter's face. "We were ambushed by the Pordillo," said Saskia with hushed respect. "Everyone else is dead."

Thaly wrapped her arm around her sister's shoulder. "You're not at fault. I should have stayed with the turma instead of scouting further ahead."

"There are only a dozen griffins," said Jurelle. "Every kamel turma can't expect constant aerial support."

"Still, we lost nearly thirty fighters," said Thaly. "The Pordillo become more of a threat with each passing moon."

"How did you escape?" Jurelle asked Saskia.

"Brower panicked and ran off. I couldn't control him. His cowardice saved me from the Pordillo before he dumped me in the wurloin nest."

"Ladies," called Genevea as she strode across the courtyard.

When she joined them, Saskia embraced her mother, but Thaly hesitated, offering only a dismissive hug. Jurelle worried about the awkwardness, still evident after nearly twelve yarles since the family reunion. But he did what he'd always done and brushed the worry aside.

"Well," he said, "I'm thankful all the beautiful women in my life are together again."

"So am I," said Genevea, trying to catch Thaly's eye. "Another day later, and your father would have worried himself into the grave."

As the approaching dust cloud blocked the sun, a shadow passed over the Volatal Vexil mounting yards.

"We should get inside before the sandstorm hits," said Jurelle.

"I have conventus this evening at two nocturna," said Thaly.

"We know you've got important matters to attend to," said Genevea. "Let's hope the storm is over by then."

*   *   *   *

Thaly's thoughts drowned among the murmurs of two hundred and eighty-eight female senators bubbling under the Pallaxium's golden, domed roof. Dressed in robes of one of twelve colours, depending on which of the twelve factions of Germalian society they represented, the conventus' elected members milled about the foyer or ambled into the circular meeting room called the zōdiakos. A bellum cornu wailed, and the amble became a rush, past anitors holding open doors as thick as a torso, each carved from a single tree trunk. Thaly entered the meeting room last, stealing a kiss from her lover, Chloe — one of the anitors holding a door.

"Not at work," said Chloe, smiling wide-eyed as she closed the door behind Thaly.

Inside the zōdiakos, senators took their seats in a configuration of twelve, tiered, wedge-shaped galleries, one for each faction. Every faction had an identifying colour, an animal totem, and a name derived from ancient astrological signs of debated origin. In the conventus, an orator and a further twenty-three female senators comprised each faction. The orator acted as the faction spokesperson. Men were forbidden to stand for election to the conventus, although, theoretically, they could attend meetings in the zōdiakos by invitation.

The thin end of the equisized wedges met in the centre of the room, forming a smaller circle around a raised chair of cherry-red leather studded with gold. Here sat Charmion, the Sella — the conventus chairperson. Dozens of yarles confined to a wheelchair had withered Charmion's body to a shrivelled, delicate collection of bones dressed in dark, blotchy skin. But her physical stature belied her political influence. The only factionless member of the conventus, she dressed in robes of all Germalia's twelve colours, shimmering across the satin as one colour melded into another.

The pendulous sags of flesh under Charmion's arm shuddered as she thumped a malleus against a seasnail shell, the mollusc's discarded home larger than Charmion's chair. The oceanic chime echoed around the circular hall, silencing the senatorial babble.

Dressed in flowing green robes that swept across the tops of her sandals, Thaly inched along a row of seats to take her place in the Capri faction. In Germalia, everyone was assigned to a faction based on their birth day, with each yarle split into twelve, thirty-day periods. Thaly had been adopted into the Capri faction, green its identifying colour and the dune goat its totem animal, according to her approximate birth day. Actual birth days were never recorded in Enthilen, its citizens celebrating their birth on the first day of the harvest season. However, Genevea remembered that Thaly was born near the end of the wind season, which overlapped with the thirty-day period assigned to Capri.

As Thaly took her seat, she pulled a page of notes from her robe and glanced over them, jittery eyes failing to absorb most of the words. She would be called on to report to the conventus this eve, and she dreaded public speaking. Since arriving in Portum eleven yarles ago, she'd learned to read Erstürmen and Germalian but struggled with the language of her adopted home when nervous. Thaly's olive skin accentuated her unease. Like most of Portum's residents, every other conventus senator had skin of hickory brown or darker. The Stansfield family's lighter skin stood out like a red boil on a white cheek, forever reminding them that Germalia wasn't their true home.

As the gathering stilled, Charmion glanced into a convex mirror suspended from the ceiling above her head and winched her cushioned red chair around a circular running track to face an orator behind her who had raised their hand.

"The Sella recognises Zenais of Capri," said Charmion.

"I seek permission for one of our scouts to report," said Zenais.

Charmion nodded once. "Permission granted."

"Athalee Stansfield will report."

Already? thought Thaly, wiping sweaty palms on her robes and calming shallow breaths. She stood as Zenais turned in her seat and smiled, then turned back to face Charmion.

"My...myself," stuttered Thaly, slowly and purposefully, "and my... colleagues in the Volatal Vexil witnessed bands of Pordillo pushing further inland...breaching our borders to the southwest. Some have established temporary camps less than a day's flight from here, inside our territory. We expect more per...manent settlements will be built soon. A turma of kamel riders was ambushed two days ago. Only my sister survived. I should have protected the turma from attack, but I was s-s-scouting ahead for more encampments. I urge the conventus to view the Pordillo as an...im-im-imminent threat to peace in Germalia."

A hand raised to the left of Charmion. She turned the winch handle, moving her chair to face the orator. "The Sella recognises Sophia of Virg."

"It appears the Pordillo are receiving help from Enthilen," said Sophia.

"Weapons and food. Why might the Erstürmen seek an alliance with the Pordillo? How does this further the cause of the tyrant Malphas?"

Murmurs rippled across the assembly.

Charmion tapped the malleus on the snail shell. "Order. Is that the end of your report, Athalee?"

"Yes," replied Thaly, gladly retaking her seat.

Eutropia's hand shot up, crimson folds of linen cascading to bunch in the crux of her elbow.

Charmion nodded at her. "The Sella recognises Eutropia of Arie."

"I may be able to answer Sophia's questions," said Eutropia. "I've collated reports from our scouts inside Enthilen. I seek permission to present them to the conventus."

"Permission granted," said Charmion.

"I believe Malphas is using the Pordillo to distract our attention. He fears our military strength and knows if we're not fighting the Pordillo, we may turn our attention to him. And that is something we must do, to stop the threat...."

"Warmonger!" someone shouted, followed by a din of jeers from the opposed or cheers from the supporters.

"Order!" yelled Charmion. "Eutropia, this is not the time to discuss potential action against Malphas. Please, keep your comments focussed on the scouts' reports."

Eutropia scanned the room, nodded to the Sella, and then continued, "The destruction of Enthilen is almost complete. Sardis is ruined other than the Sunrise and Sunset Keeps still standing as part of the walled inner court. Atop the keeps, Malphas' servants watch their western border. Krieg's Red Shield rule Sardis, delivering judgement and execution to any challenger. On the banks of the Anchep River, destitute souls eke out an existence amid the remnants of Slumstadt.

"The Dobunni of Enthilen exist only as refugees at Gestade or small bands of raiders living in the Desolate Mountains. Alone and isolated, they're unable to challenge Malphas' will. Bagendon has not been rebuilt, and I believe it never will. The fire consuming Babir Birramal reaches almost to Giigal. A wild stone-grell is a rare sight. The weald-grells refuse to leave their city and confront the demon that seeks to eliminate them."

While Eutropia spoke, Thaly clutched the tattered white handkerchief tied around her wrist. The cloth she refused to discard. Her thoughts drifted back to her homeland, remembering friends lost and days long passed. Some recollections made her smile. The reunion of Grin with his family at the grell garrabari deep in the Babir Birramal forest. The antics of Dwarrow the mouldewerp and Thaly's brief friendship with Princess Caeli. Her mentorship of Tom Anderson, the young man who gave her his handkerchief to bandage the arrow wound on Thaly's arm.

Other memories caused her pain. The execution of her trainer, Jacob, by one of Malphas' tainted grells. Salacious seafarers raping her and Grin on the *Vulking*. The chaos that ensued in Pergamos' throne room when Volerdie's Wrath struck, and Tom Anderson disappeared from Enthilen without a trace.

The most valued memory was when her father, Jurelle, finally came for her. As she bled from the knife wound inflicted by Malphas, Jurelle carried her in his arms out of Pergamos' rubble. With Grin and Dwarrow's help, they escaped into Babir Birramal. There, grell medicine and her father's daily, attentive care saved her life.

After Thaly had recovered, Dwarrow left, determined to find Princess Caeli. Grin took up residence in his milbi to continue his vigilance against Erstürmen incursions into Babir Birramal. Thaly and Jurelle began the long trek to Germalia.

They travelled through the Scaur Hills to what remained of Bagendon. Thaly needed to see the ruins of her home to confirm the town no longer existed. Bagendon had been reduced to nothing more than blackened stumps. Jurelle and Thaly didn't meet a single Dobunni in the Scaur Hills. Not one. She accepted that among Bagendon's ash rested Emelin and Dayna, her adoptive mother and sister, and she erected a cairn of rocks in the centre of the derelict town to mark their passing.

Jurelle and Thaly rode weary horses down the switchbacks of an unguarded Riverlands Escarpment, over the dam wall at the bottom of the

Rārian Falls, and into the red desert called Groz Wüste by the Erstürmen, Magna Avium by the Germalians. They met a Germalian scouting party who guided them across the vast wasteland to Portum.

Eutropia finished speaking, and another orator dressed in ochre robes raised her hand.

"The Sella recognises Chariclea of Gemi," said Charmion.

Chariclea faced Eutropia. "What of Laodicea?"

"Our scouts speak of a timid, restless city," said Eutropia. "Citizens still trade or scavenge for resources, and merchants and barbarians from across the Veiled Occyan visit the Docklands' wharves. The black grell, Hunger, rules from the King's Quarter. He is Malphas' regent in the trading port."

"Any news from Pergamos?" asked Chariclea.

"We sent three scouts, one after the other. None have returned."

Zenais raised her hand, and Charmion glanced in the convex mirror before winching her chair around. "The Sella recognises Zenais of Capri."

"One of our scouts met a draughoul in Magna Avium. These creatures are often used as spies by Malphas, so I'm hesitant to trust her words. Nonetheless, our scout reported that the draughoul had a conviction unusual for such pitiful souls. She spoke of Malphas' growing power, ruling from behind a colossal wall surrounding Pergamos. While it appears he never leaves the city's confines, his legions of Erstürmen soldiers and Rephaim grells spread terror throughout Enthilen. He fixates on Volerdie's return to Enthilen, willing to do anything to achieve this end. Malphas' tyranny won't be confined to Enthilen's borders. I agree with Eutropia; we must counter this threat."

Malphas, thought Thaly. Would she never expunge his gloating face from her mind? The time she'd spent imprisoned in Pergamos felt like only yesterday, and Malphas' taunts continued to plague her nightmares.

In the faction adjacent to Thaly, the orator stood and tugged her bunched yellow robes towards her shins. She resumed her seat and raised her hand.

"The Sella recognises Melitta of Sagit," said Charmion.

"We have more important things to worry about than the distant threat of

Malphas," said Melitta. "Sandstorms increase in frequency, and our aquifers are almost dry. What is the conventus going to do about fresh water?"

"The seasons are changing," said Charmion. "What *can* we do? Even the conventus doesn't have the power to alter the sun and wind. To conjure up rain from thin air."

"We're isolated here," said Melitta. "Trapped between Magna Avium and the Occidian Sea. One day, merchant ships may stop docking at The Hive. We should reach out to our neighbours. Re-open trade with Nordland and the Riverlands farmers. Twelve yarles ago, we saved the Riverlands from Erstürmen invasion. They owe us their loyalty."

Sophia raised her hand. "The Pordillo raid the supply trains from the Riverlands."

"The Pordillo are stronger because of Pergamos' support," said Zenais. "This is why we must stop Malphas."

"Rubbish," scoffed Melitta. "Provide more warriors to protect the kamel trains. Use griffins if we must. That's the logical action."

"Order!" yelled Charmion.

But order dissolved in the night as mutters turned into catcalls and accusations. Thaly buried her head in her hands. Decisive action by the conventus often buckled under the weight of torturous bureaucracy. Major decisions required a drawn-out and convoluted voting process, sometimes corrupted by factional differences and in-fighting, and orators looking to advance their own agenda and become the next Sella.

Thaly endured the administrative annoyance. Better this than fighting for survival back in Enthilen, watching Malphas crush what little resistance remained. Portum offered safety and comfort, bound by the love of her family. And Chloe. Thaly wouldn't leave Chloe.

Maybe they'd marry one day? she dreamed. Adopt children.

The Volatal Vexil satiated Thaly's warrior desires, a way to honour the vow she'd made to Jacob and the Dobunni many seasons ago by fighting the enemies of those she loved. And the Germalians had promoted her to Legatus — leader of the wind-riders. She couldn't imagine this happening if she'd remained in Enthilen. The old homeland offered nothing.

~ Chapter 2 ~

In the city of Adelaide, South Australia, rain pelted down. Thunder hung in the black sky, roaring like a lion, and lightning flashed across the tops of skyscrapers. Gushes of water and rubbish raced along concrete gutters and clogged stormwater drains with debris, the overflow splayed by the tyres of rush-hour commuters. Tom Anderson cinched the hood of his raincoat tighter around his balding head and stubbled face. Wavering against the summer storm's onslaught, a gust of wind almost knocked him into the trunk of an oak tree, one of the dozens scattered throughout the inner-city cemetery. Tom thrust out a hand to steady his balance, the tree's rough bark pressing into the circular scar on his palm, reminding him of another place long ago. Wiping the rain from his face, he walked to a black granite headstone perched at the end of a grave covered in white pebbles.

In Loving Memory of Bert Anderson
12. 9. 1919 — 17. 12. 1993
Beloved Husband of Elaine, Father of Tom

Today was Tom's first visit to the cemetery since his dad's funeral two years ago.

I could have picked better weather, he thought, crouching and yanking dead flowers from the vase embedded in the grave. *Mum probably brought them. Who else would have?* He knelt on the concrete edging while rain dripped into his boots, soaking woollen socks.

His housemate, Max, ambled over to him. "Time to go? The weather's not gettin' any better."

Tom tossed a white pebble at the headstone. "I hated my father, but I

22

cried when I said goodbye in the hospital. He lay in bed dying, looking bewildered by it all. I kissed him on the forehead and lied. *I love you.*" He stood and faced Max. "I tried to make it from the room without breaking down. I sat at the end of his bed, bawling. Mum gave me a hug. 'You know we love you,' she said, thinking I was crying because dad never acknowledged my attempt at affection. But it wasn't that. I cried because then it hit me. This was the end of any chance I had for a relationship with my father. I cried for the lost opportunity. I cried for what could have been."

Max mumbled, clearly uncertain about the best response.

Tom forced a smile, not wanting to burden his housemate further. "Let's go. We need to return to the *Lame Brain* before nightfall. Otherwise, they'll send out the vampire hunters."

That evening, Tom sat alone on his single bed, a pillow propped behind his back, in the room he'd been allocated in the officially named 'Supported Living Environment'. Unofficially, the four residents called it the *Lame Brain*, a halfway house for those with mental health challenges. Tom thought of it as a kind of purgatory for misfits. Not a full-blown mental institution, but a place to keep the slightly unhinged away from the ordinary people of this world. Where society tossed its refuse; the loony bin.

Built in the early 1900s in the suburb of North Adelaide, the *Lame Brain* needed renovation. Tom had been here less than a month, but already the share-house walls closed around him like a trash compactor. Floral-patterned wallpaper and sickly cream paint blistered and peeled off the walls, unable to resist the rising damp from below. Crumbling cornices dropped flecks of white plaster along the top of lime-green skirting boards, the gypsum drizzle spilling over onto the grey carpet that adorned Tom's bedroom. Every time he stepped on the carpet, he expected to feel a squelch under his feet as moisture oozed through the cigarette burns and wine stains. From the ceiling, at the end of a cord, a lightbulb hung like a corpse in a noose, swayed by the breeze coming through the window that never shut properly.

Tom's handful of possessions filled the bedroom; a half-full wardrobe held together by duct tape, a bookcase he'd found discarded on the verge, a bedside table and a portable stereo. He couldn't afford much else. Twenty-eight years old, and he'd never kept a steady job. Never had a loving, meaningful relationship. Lost contact with most of his friends.

From the bedside table, he picked up his remembrance totem, a cylindrical, green-white softstone, no larger than a taper candle, given to him by his stone-grell friend, Grin, before they walked into Pergamos together to confront Malphas and King Adalwolf. Before Tom fled from Enthilen. He was supposed to etch his life story onto the totem's face, but he'd written very little, and the emptiness mocked him. The realisation that, since leaving Enthilen twelve years ago, nothing had happened worthy enough to fill some of the preciously small space. He rolled the totem around in his scarred palms, thinking of distant lands that still felt real.

Tom started when Max knocked on the door jamb.

"Your mum's here," said Max.

Tom nodded, returned the totem to the table and stepped onto the carpet, waiting for the always threatening squelch.

Wandering along the hall, he paused at the kitchen doorway to taste the aroma of fried eggs and bacon, then ambled into the visitor's room at the front of the house. His mother, Elaine, stood facing the window, the headlights of passing traffic framing her head and shoulders with an angelic aura.

She spun around and smiled. "Tommy," she said, extending her arms for a hug.

Tom embraced his mum. "Don't call me that."

Elaine pulled away, her smile turning mischievous. "Am I embarrassing you in front of your friends?"

"They're not my friends. We share a house. That's it."

Elaine sat on the brown vinyl couch, leaving the ratty paisley chair for Tom. He swivelled his bottom into place and sank low into the old seat cushion, tufts of wiry stuffing that resembled pine needles poking out through split seams.

Elaine reached into a plastic bag. "I baked muffins for you. Raspberry. It's a good season this year."

"You need to sell the house, Mum. The property's too big to look after by yourself."

"You'll be back soon. When you're better."

"I'm not coming home. I have to find my own place when I get out of here."

Elaine leaned forward and plucked a piece of lint from Tom's stubble. "Are you having nightmares again?"

Tom pushed his mum's hand away and turned his head.

"Did the GP give you a new prescription?" she asked.

"Yeah, we all love our meds here. Pills aren't the answer."

"Are you talking to Dr Hughes?"

"About what?"

"Everything. If you're still hallucinating...."

"They're not hallucinations." Tom pulled a strand of wiry stuffing from the chair and wrapped it around one of his fingers

"The psychiatrist said...."

"I don't care what she said."

Elaine sighed and leaned back into the couch. "I wish I could help, Tom. You can't keep dwelling on the past."

"I know it's hard to understand. *I* don't understand what happened when I disappeared. Where I went. But I have these visions. Memories of another place. Memories of friends with names. Grin, Thaly, Dwarrow. They're *real* to me. Well, they were real. Until I abandoned them. Now I live with the guilt. No pill's going to fix that."

"You didn't abandon them. It was only...a strange dream."

Tom held up his palms. "Then where did these scars come from? I travelled to another world."

Elaine shook her head and faced the window, maybe hoping the passing headlights could illuminate a new reality. Tom slouched back into the paisley chair, remembering the day the police picked him up twelve years ago, wandering the streets of Adelaide. A sixteen-year-old missing for six months.

'Another teenage runaway,' the police officer had said. 'Happens all the time.'

He couldn't explain where he'd been. Well, he could explain, but they didn't believe any of it. Neither did his mum. It sounded so crazy; Tom questioned it sometimes, thinking he must have imagined Enthilen.

When he returned home, he suffered from nightmares almost every night. Elaine said he talked in his sleep, babbling in a strange language like he was speaking in tongues. Once, his dad, Bert, got a priest to come and talk to Tom as if he needed an exorcism.

Bert grew tired of the stress and demanded Tom move out. Elaine couldn't convince her husband otherwise. Tom's life became a roller coaster of ambition and depression. Creative, hopeful highs plunged into bleak, crushing lows. After Bert's death, Elaine scraped together what money she could to help Tom, eventually securing him a place in the supported living environment. The live-in program of intense treatment and counselling was her last shot at helping her son manage his depression and anxiety.

Elaine faced Tom. "Keep taking your meds and make sure you attend the counselling sessions. Dr Hughes was adamant about that."

Tom rolled his eyes. "Yeah, yeah."

"I want you to get better, Tom."

"Do you understand this will be with me for the rest of my life? It's not the flu. It won't just *get* better."

"I know. Both of us must live with it. It's not easy for me, either."

Tom's heart sank. "I'm sorry, Mum. Sorry I'm like this. I wish I was different."

Elaine placed her hand on his thigh. "I don't want a different son. I want you."

After his mum left, Tom lay on his bed, eyes closed, visions of Enthilen so stark it felt like a movie projected onto the inside of his eyelids. Familiar yet unusual sights, smells and tastes punctured his mind. The botanical freshness of panalope leaves after rain. The confined mustiness of Dwarrow's dwell. The cloying burn of meduz as it trickled down his throat. The lurching stench of Captain Adcock. The coldness of Annian's dead body and the graveolent taint of a tortured Widukind. Princess Caeli's wide, smiling eyes. Thaly clutching his fingers and whispering her reassurance as Tom sat on the throne of the dead, Volerdie's throne, while Pergamos collapsed around him. Grin resting a giant hand on his shoulder and speaking in his deep, warm voice, 'A decision made with an honest heart....'

Enthilen refused to let Tom go. He'd departed that land, but the land had never left him. It seemed it never would. He had unfinished business there. To bring his grandmother's killer to justice. Malphas, the man who'd burst into Tom's bedroom twenty-three years ago to steal Nanna's soul with the dark eyes, making himself immortal and turning Nanna into a draughoul, her soulless, decaying body destined to wander Earth until her bones became dust.

Tom believed Malphas' consuming desire to resurrect Volerdie, the Divine Creator, would plunge Enthilen into an eternal tyranny. But who on Earth or Ostamp could stop the Worshipful Master?

~ Chapter 3 ~

The white grell sweated under the cowl of the torn, ill-fitting coat, the intense heat not enough to convince him to let his scarred face catch any breeze. Keeping out of sight took precedence over comfort. The horizon of a barren, empty landscape shimmered. Trees lamented the absence of rain with displays of dull, sage-green leaves. Flies buzzed around his nose as if they planned to lay eggs in his nostrils. One of the winged pests caught in his throat, sucked into the airway by a laboured breath desperate to draw energy from the smothering atmosphere. He spat onto the dusty ground bordering an endless ribbon of black used by the horseless wagons that screamed past at speeds unimagined in his world. Some wagons were so big they towered over even him. He sometimes wondered what moved them or how they stopped moving.

Since arriving in this new world, he'd counted the passing of dozens of moons. Only one each night, not the two moons of Seena and Bargan that floated in Enthilen's sky. In his search for Tom Anderson, he'd avoided the settlements full of people, staying undercover among what little vegetation grew within the large swathes of land stripped bare. Even with skin whiter than the salty crystals he sometimes found crusting the soil, he knew how to blend into his surroundings and disappear. He travelled principally at night, learning where to find food and water. Learning to stay out of sight of the people with their strange language and customs, enslaved by their machines.

The sun dipped below the horizon, and crimson clouds hung in the stifling air. Night would come soon, and the white grell could begin his search once more. He placed the tips of his fingers on the black ribbon that carried the whining, horseless wagons and recoiled from the heat.

The flat, smooth surface burned like a fire stone, but it was perfect for getting a bearing on his quarry.

From the inside pocket of his coat, he retrieved a vial of blood, and a solid gold pentagram with a pointed conical underside and a picture of a goat's head etched onto the top surface. The black magic of this blood compass would lead him to Tom Anderson. He uncorked the vial and let a drop of blood fall onto one tip of the five-pointed star. The plasma hissed and bubbled as the viscous liquid bound itself to the metal. With the bond again forged, the white grell balanced the blood compass, teetering on its pointed underside, atop the black ribbon roadway. The compass spun more slowly than before, then stopped; again, pointing west.

Tom Anderson is close, he thought.

Next to the road, a green metal sign with white writing creaked in the hot wind. The white grell couldn't read the writing, though he knew it conveyed the language of this place. A wail drifted in the air, and a horseless wagon appeared from the east. The grell snatched the compass and skulked into the littered wood beside the road, away from prying eyes. One day he expected to face the people of this new world, but he wanted to avoid that confrontation for as long as possible.

*   *   *   *

In the dead of night, driven by hunger, the white grell risked searching for food along the dark streets of a sparse settlement. He'd learned that food scraps could be found in the wheeled, green tubs lining the streets. Lifting a lid and reaching into a tub, he withdrew a soiled wrapper, stained magenta and covering partially masticated fare. He held the object to his nose and inhaled. Experience told him the wrapper wasn't edible. He peeled it back to expose the sustenance inside, sniffing the rations of different foodstuffs jammed between doughy brown circles that squished in his hands. Tearing off a strip of dough, he tossed it in his mouth.

How can something be tasteless *and* sweet? he thought.

Twigs and dry grass crunched under his bottom as he sat on the ground and pulled the doughy circles apart to reveal something wilted and green, covered in a sickly red juice and sitting atop a square sliver of bright yellow. He wrapped the two layers together and tossed them into his mouth, followed by three salty, acerbic, seeded morsels and a slice of sweet purple with concentric circles that reminded him of Sardis. At the bottom of the stacked food, he found what appeared to be cooked animal flesh minced into tiny pieces and mashed together in a disc.

The white grell held his nose and swallowed the flesh whole, retching from the sweetness and salt. He stood and walked further along the street until, at the edge of the settlement, he found a metal box large enough for a shelter. After lifting the lid, he climbed inside, nestling among split bags that spilled clothes and an endless array of trinkets that had no useful purpose as far as he could tell. For the first time since arriving in this strange land, he fell into a deep sleep.

Nightmares wracked his mind. He dreamt of feeling his way along a cave wall, the serrated rockface cutting into the palms of his hands and a smell of sulphur hanging in the darkness. A flash of screaming white lit up the cave, and from the floor, metal bars thicker than his forearm thrust upwards and surrounded him in an inescapable prison cell. In the shadows, an unseen tormenter cackled, their mocking echo bouncing from every wall. Into the light stumbled another grell, a slave with a familiar face, who placed a bowl brimming with murky stew at his feet. In the stew's reflection, a forest burned, scorched and shrivelled panalope leaves falling to the ground like an ashen snowstorm. Amid the carnage, the pale grell appeared, leaning on her sparth and offering the white grell a hand of liberation. She would save him, but for a price. Embracing death as the saviour always extracted a toll.

As he reached for the pale grell, the cave roof ripped open, and giant, clutching fingers wrapped around him and lifted him into black clouds. Among the fog, Malphas appeared, the face of the white grell's master unchanged since the day he first laid eyes on it. Could he ever escape Master's relentless, malicious desire? Malphas was closer now to achieving his dream than ever before. When the white grell found Tom Anderson....

He woke to sunlight pouring through a crack in the side of the metal box. People talked outside, yapping in the foreign tongue of this new land. Peering through the gap, he spied three strangers standing beside the box. Much too close for his liking. He planned to wait until they left before escaping, but something unexpected happened. The metal box lid creaked open, and a stranger screamed.

The white grell panicked. He sprang from his hiding place and sprinted across the street into dry, crackling vegetation that scratched his skin and crunched under his bare feet as he raced over the dusty soil. The screams behind him faded as he dodged between trees with oblong, muted-green leaves and bark shedding like snake skin and collecting in serpentine piles at the base of trunks. Birds with unfamiliar calls flushed from dense shrubs and flew skyward, while lizards scuttled under rocks to escape the white giant rushing through their habitat.

He burst from the woodland onto a dirt track and stopped, doubling over with exhaustion and sucking in morning air already hot and suffocating. No thudding, pursuing boots followed him, and his heartbeat calmed. But he remained wary. He always had to be cautious. Standing tall, he walked along the track, away from the rising sun. Around a corner, he stumbled upon a dishevelled old man sitting on a log eating food from a can. The man jerked upright, his mouth agape.

The white grell held up scarred palms to indicate he wasn't a threat, but panic writhed across the old man's face. A trembling hand reached for something unfamiliar leaning against the log. Fingers grasped a shaft of hollow metal bound with smooth timber like the handle of a halberd. The old man pointed the hollow end at the white grell and spoke in the foreign language. The grell tried to smile. Tried to reassure the stranger, who seemed to hunger for reassurance.

The man stood and spoke again, clutching the wooden sheath supporting the metal barrel with bloodless knuckles and pushing its butt end into his shoulder. The white grell stepped forward and raised his hands higher. But then, a crack like lightning splitting a tree shattered the dawn. The white grell could have sworn something exploded from the hole at the end of the metal barrel. Simultaneously, a projectile smacked into his chest next to his right shoulder. His body recoiled as if he'd been punched, and his flesh stung with a burning ache. He thrust his hand to his chest, where blood wept from a wound.

How? he wondered.

The old man yelled.

Yes, the land and people here were unfamiliar, but the white grell understood danger. He ran again, along the dirt track and away from the man with the thunder stick. The time remaining to find Tom Anderson had diminished. The pale grell's sparth, the blade of death, may indeed fall on the white grell before he could complete his quest.

~ Chapter 4 ~

Inside the Volatal Vexil barn in Portum, Thaly and Saskia stood in front of Thaly's griffin, Yagle, dwarfed by the regal creature. Around them, handlers scurried across the timber floor, bringing food to the other eleven griffins in their holding pens or removing manure to add to the dung heaps that sat fermenting beside the growing fields outside the city's east wall. Like most days in Portum, the air warmed quickly with the rising sun. Even under the tiled roof of the cavernous barn, sweat trickled beneath Thaly's green linen robes that hung loosely over her shoulders and arms, the attire impractical for working with griffins. On days like these, she missed the simple pants and tunic of a Dobunni rebel. But as a conventus senator, she was expected to dress and act a certain way in public.

Thaly scrunched the robes along her forearm and faced Saskia. "Don't rush him."

Saskia rolled her eyes and stepped towards Yagle. "I wasn't going to. I'm not stupid."

The griffin watched a jittery Saskia with a wary golden eye, ruffling his neck feathers to enlarge his presence, sending a clear message to the tiny human standing in front of him.

Saskia needs to control her nerves, thought Thaly, or this won't go well.

"Steady yourself," she counselled her younger sister. "Look him in the eye to make a connection, then hold out your hand and let him decide if he wants to come to you."

Saskia reached her fingers towards Yagle's bill. He swished his tail, the tuft of dark brown fur at the end smacking his side with a loud clack. Saskia jerked her hand away. Yagle turned his head to stare out the open barn door as if trying to mask his boredom or amusement. Thaly smiled to herself.

Saskia sighed. "This isn't working."

"Be patient. To be a wind-rider, you need determination, patience and understanding. Remember, Yagle's the boss. You can't simply jump onboard and fly off."

No longer interested in what lay outside, Yagle swayed his head, brushing the tip of his bill past Saskia's fingers.

Thaly rested a supportive hand on her sister's shoulder. "See, he wants to connect with you, but he's making you work for it. At least he didn't slice your arm off. I'll show you how to feed him. I've got a bag of rats here."

Saskia screwed up her face. "Rats?"

"What did you think griffins ate? Flowers?" Thaly pulled a grey rat from inside a canvas bag, grasping it by the base of the tail. It wriggled about in mid-air, squealing in protest as if aware of its fate. Yagle's eyes glinted, and he tilted his head towards the prey as Thaly held the rat at arms-length. In one fluid motion, Yagle swung his head and plucked the squirming rodent from her hand, swallowing it in a single gulp.

"Doesn't seem like much food for a griffin," said Saskia.

"He could eat twenty of these and still be hungry. Now it's your turn." Thaly handed Saskia the bag of wriggling rats.

She fossicked around inside the bag, then let out a yelp, "*Ow! One bit me.*"

Thaly placed a hand over her mouth to smother a laugh. "Look *inside* the bag first. Try to find a tail. The rear end is safer."

Saskia peered into the bag, thrust her hand inside and pulled a rat out by the tail. She held it towards Yagle, who tilted his head down and snatched the second morsel.

Saskia beamed. "Hey! I did it."

"Great work, Sas. He'll be your life-long friend if you keep bringing him food."

"What's next?"

"That's enough for today. The handler can feed Yagle the remaining rats." Thaly turned and called across the barn. "Puer!"

An old man shovelling griffin dung into a wheelbarrow jerked his head towards Thaly. He nodded, dropped his shovel and trotted towards her.

Thaly handed Yagle's reins to Puer. "Can you finish feeding him?" she asked.

Puer smiled and bowed, but stumbled as he grasped the leather straps, Yagle tossing his feathered head and shrieking in protest.

Saskia sneered at Puer. "Watch what you're doing, stupid old fool. Don't you know how to handle a griffin after all this time?"

Clutching the reins as if he might topple over at any moment, Puer bowed low. "Forgive me, Domina Stansfield. It won't happen again."

"If it does, I'll report you to the chief handler. You'll spend the rest of your days shovelling shit."

"Yes, Domina Stansfield. Please forgive me."

A flush of anger burned Thaly's cheeks as she pulled her younger sister towards the barn door. "It was an accident, Sas."

"So what? He still needs to understand his place. We must keep men subservient; otherwise, Germalia will end up like Enthilen."

"Do you consider our father to be lesser than you?"

"Well, no, but the Senatorial Dictum is clear about the role of men in Germalia. You should know that better than anyone, all the time you spend in the conventus."

Thaly frowned at her sister's petulance before leading her outside into the Volatal Vexil courtyard.

"A couple more days of on-ground training, and you'll be ready to take your first solo flight," said Thaly.

"*More* on-ground training? This is taking so long. I want to be flying through the clouds. I'm tired of kamels. They're stinky, grumpy and take forever to get anywhere. And griffins aren't going to tumble into wurloin nests."

Thaly wrapped her arm around Saskia's shoulder. "You must complete *all* the training to be a wind-rider, and even if you do that, I can't guarantee you'll ever get to ride your own griffin. All twelve currently have riders. Unless we bring more back from the islands, you'll have to wait until...."

"A rider is killed or too old to ride anymore." Saskia scuffed her leather sandals across the ground, flicking a puff of red dust.

"That's only the beginning," said Thaly. "Apprentice riders have to compete against each other in a gruelling examination of skill, stamina *and* patience. The Eligens."

Saskia rolled her eyes. "I *knowww*. I was there, remember? When Yagle chose you."

Thaly laughed and pulled her closer. "Even if you defeat the other apprentices, the riderless griffin might reject you."

Saskia stepped away. "Why would it reject me? I'm delightful." She beamed at Thaly. "I can't believe the conventus promoted you to Legatus. You're commanding a legion of fighters now." Saskia raised herself up on tiptoes and swelled her chest. "My sister, Legatus of the Volatal Vexil. Commander of all the wind-riders and their support forces. Father is so proud of you. And Mother, too."

A dull ache set in Thaly's bones, and she turned away at the mention of Genevea. Saskia's next question stung like an arrowhead.

"Why do you hate Ma?"

Thaly shrugged. "I don't hate her, but I can't forgive her for abandoning me."

"What else could she do? You've forgiven Pa."

"He didn't have a choice. Genevea could have escaped before Jurelle was ever put in that position. Taken me into the Scaur Hills to hide out with him and the Dobunni rebels. Instead, she became the bait to lure the Dobunni leader into the prison of the inner circle. To turn him into the Traitor General. It's hard to forgive her for that."

"You should try. All of it was Ewald's fault. He would have sent soldiers to hunt Ma down if she'd escaped. You don't know what it was like in the inner circle. More than one citizen would have gladly given Ma's secrets away to gain favour with Ewald. Nobody trusted anybody. Ma didn't have a choice. She loves you as much as Pa does. You need to love her back. When you brush her aside, I can see the hurt in her eyes."

Thaly rubbed the scar on her wrist masked by Tom Anderson's white handkerchief, where an arrow from the red grell, Krieg, had sliced open her flesh on Hansen's Bluff in Laodicea. Despite the edict dictating senator attire in Portum, Thaly refused to relinquish the reminder of lost friends and an abandoned homeland.

Saskia tugged at the handkerchief's frayed corner. "Why do you keep wearing this stupid cloth? One more wash, and it'll disintegrate."

"It reminds me of where I came from and who helped me along the way."

"Will you ever return to Enthilen?"

"Bagendon was razed. Emelin, Dayna and Jacob were murdered. There are no Dobunni rebels anymore. There's no reason for me to go back."

"The Pordillo keep invading our territory in Magna Avium. Will the conventus declare war?"

"Don't long for war, Sas. Be thankful if you never see one."

Saskia nodded, then placed her arm around Thaly's waist and squeezed. "Are you sleeping with Chloe this eve?"

A flush of self-consciousness spread across Thaly's cheeks like mulled vinum.

Saskia flashed a cheeky smile. "You'll have to tell Ma and Pa about Chloe soon."

"They're not going to be happy," said Thaly. "No grandchildren."

"Don't worry, I'll deliver enough for both of us."

"You don't have a lufu yet," said Thaly, but Saskia turned away too quickly, and Thaly guessed. "Or *do* you? What have you been hiding from me?" She grabbed her younger sister and tickled her.

Saskia giggled. "Alright...stop it! His name's Heron. He's a kamel stable hand."

"No wonder you hang around those stables so much."

"He's nothing special and has to do as I tell him."

"Love isn't about one person being in charge. It won't work like that."

"How should it work?"

"Men are not our slaves, though sometimes they're treated as such. I saw how the Erstürmen treated the grells. I don't want any part of that. Neither should you. Treat Heron as an equal."

"I'm so confused. I'm not sure I'll ever understand the Germalians."

Thaly and Saskia walked from the courtyard and into the bustling streets of Portum. Thaly enjoyed the Germalian city's energy. The busy hum of people living meaningful lives and contributing to the safety and comfort of all citizens, including those on the lowest rung of the social ladder. As a senator, she had certain privileges. Prime seats at Portum's theatre. First choice of freshly harvested food. The most elaborate housing. For Thaly, Germalia had become the land of good fortune, while Enthilen descended into chaos.

* * * *

Jurelle stood on the docks of The Hive in Portum as merchant ships bobbed about in a crowded Slyencia Bay. Sailors scuttled over the decks, loading supplies onto barges hitched to the sides of larger vessels or preparing rigging and harnesses for the next seaward journey. In the middle of the bay, the Germalian classem underwent battle-training manoeuvres. Ships with three masts and a dozen billowing sails, individually decorated with the twelve animal totems of Germalia, tacked into the wind to gain a better strategic position before launching sacks of coloured powder from catapults or ballistae at each other. While Portum hadn't been attacked for a generation, the Germalians considered the city most vulnerable to an assault from the ocean and invested substantial resources in maintaining the classem. The conventus believed the vast deserts of Magna Avium provided an almost impenetrable barrier to a land-based army large enough to threaten Portum.

Two dozen jetties protruded into Slyencia Bay like timber arms searching for whatever resources they could grasp. Teams of oarsmen moved heavily laden barges between the wharves and merchant ships, the barges' flat bottoms more suited to navigating the shallows of The Hive. Portum's burgeoning population, reaching into the hundreds of thousands, grew hungrier by the day, and the agricultural fields outside the city became less fertile as the sands of Magna Avium continued their march west. With aquifers struggling to serve thirsty residents, ships carrying fresh water had begun arriving in Portum.

Jurelle wondered about the sustainability of this city, trapped between the desert and the ocean. Thinning grey hair failed to protect against the stark midday sun scalding his head as his eyelids drooped closed amid a daydream. He started when the bell in the clocktower chimed seven lumina. The melodic clang pealed across The Hive, the toll announcing the virtues of hope or, thought Jurelle, warning of coming doom.

As the chimes ended, a familiar voice called out from behind him, "General Jurelle."

Jurelle spun on his heels and greeted the new arrivals. "Arve, Senator Zenais. Senator Eutropia."

"Have you been waiting long?" asked Zenais, swishing the hem of her green robe off the timber wharf.

"No. You persist in calling me General."

Zenais smiled and stood beside Jurelle, surveying the bay. "Old habits die hard. Does it bother you?"

Jurelle shrugged. "Thanks to you and Eutropia, I have a purpose in Portum. To offer my strategic knowledge to your military commanders so they can suck every drop before I die."

"I'm sure they appreciate your experience," said Eutropia, turning her back to the water to watch the crowds moving about the decked walkways of The Hive foreshore. "You could do a lot worse."

"Your advice to our commanders is much appreciated, General," said Zenais. "It's the first time on record the conventus has agreed to let a man hold a position of such authority."

"I've gained more privilege than most men in Portum. I sometimes wonder how that makes the rest of them feel." He faced Zenais. "Do they resent me?"

"Maybe," she said. "But they'd never speak it aloud in mixed company. You shouldn't worry about it. Do you have much experience fighting on the ocean?"

Jurelle turned back to the bay. "Never been on a ship. But I grew up on Enthilen's east coast at Sand Bēċe. During my time in Sardis, I often longed to be beside the ocean again. Breathe the salty wind. Take comfort from the constancy of breaking waves, and feel the sand through my toes. The Dobunni were renowned seafarers before they built Laodicea. Then our days of wandering the oceans diminished."

Eutropia leaned back and purred in Jurelle's ear, "It sounds like the wanderlust of your ancestors is still in your blood."

"Trapped behind the royal city's seven walls as Ewald's inmate, I desired many things I couldn't have. The absence of opportunity most likely drove the longing. I gather you haven't asked me here to discuss a land of hope and dreams."

Zenais sidled closer to Jurelle, and Eutropia resumed her crowd surveillance.

"You're comfortable speaking Germalian?" asked Zenais. "Or would you prefer Erstürmen?"

"Either," said Jurelle. "Though I imagine you want this conversation to attract as little attention as possible."

Zenais nodded. "A quiet word in Germalian, then. Do you remember our meeting in Flüsse? When you lost the Riverlands war."

Jurelle offered a wry smile. "After someone knocked me out while my back was turned? Yes, I remember. It's why my family ended up here."

"Eutropia and I have suffered an uncomfortable level of vilification from certain conventus senators for offering your family sanctuary in Portum. We accept it's for the greater good. Your skill as a military strategist was the defining factor swaying the argument in our favour. But we must take the next step in our plan."

Jurelle raised his eyebrows. "There's more to your scheming?"

"You make it sound very puerile," said Eutropia. "Surely a man of your background can appreciate a detailed stratagem evolving over many yarles?"

Zenais stepped closer, almost treading on Jurelle's sandals, but fixed her eyes on the ocean as she spoke, "We're here to discuss the defeat of Malphas. Some in the conventus believe the Worshipful Master is only a threat to Enthilen. That once Gestade and Giigal have fallen, he will be content to sit on his dead throne, waiting for the return of his beloved god.

We disagree. Volerdie will not return to Ostamp because Volerdie does not exist. He's nothing more than a figment of Erstürmen imagination. When Malphas' patience grows thin, where will his attention turn next?"

"Malphas won't sit idle for long," said Jurelle. "If he fails to fulfil his ambition of resurrecting Volerdie and leading the Erstürmen into paradise, he'll look for someone to blame. Search for another reason why the Divine Creator still forsakes Ostamp. Already, he purges Enthilen of unbelievers. The Dobunni and stone-grells are almost gone. The weald-grells will soon follow, and any Erstürmen refusing to kneel to his madness. Once the unbelievers are wiped from the landscape, if Volerdie doesn't appear, Malphas will seek others to punish, and the Germalians are a godless people. It will be easy for him to convince his followers that your existence is why Volerdie continues to forsake his home. Grōz Wüste, I mean, Magna Avium, won't keep his hordes from your doorstep."

"We couldn't agree more," said Zenais. "Our scouts report that Malphas supplies the Pordillo with food and weapons. We also believe he has corrupted at least one conventus senator."

"Is that why you called me here?" asked Jurelle. "To root out a traitor?"

"No," said Zenais. "We're more than capable of dealing with the deceitful."

Jurelle shook his head. "I don't know how to stop Malphas. He's immortal. I saw what happened in Pergamos' throne hall when marble and debris that would kill a giant grell tumbled down onto him, yet he walked away unscathed."

"Malphas may be immortal, but his army is not. They can be defeated. That must be our first objective."

"If you defeat Malphas' armies and throw him into a prison for all eternity, what then? The madman has stripped the land bare. Enthilen will be wracked by bitter feuds over dwindling resources and the clamour for power. In the absence of Malphas, the Erstürmen would try again to assert their authority and establish another brutal monarchy. The end of the Worshipful Master would create a vacuum sucking all into destitution; such is the irony."

Eutropia whispered in Jurelle's ear, "There are two alive who could stop it happening and offer a united future to all the peoples of Enthilen."

The pulse of air beating on Jurelle's eardrum started a headache. He knew what came next and didn't want to listen. Didn't want to accept the future Eutropia and Zenais planned. He'd tried to put it out of his mind. Never spoke of it to anyone, not even Genevea. But he expected the Germalian senators would continue to press until they got their way.

"I can see by the look on your face, Jurelle, you know of whom we speak," said Zenais.

"You've brought my family here under false pretences. This was your plan all along, to use my daughters to finish Malphas and save Enthilen."

"Athalee and Saskia," said Eutropia, taking her eyes from the passing crowd and searching Jurelle's face instead. Like most Germalians, she had deep brown irises, matching the colour of her flawless skin, dressed in red senatorial robes glimmering in the sunlight.

"Their mother is a member of the royal Heine family," continued Eutropia. "A descendant of an empire the Erstürmen admire and have followed for generations. And their father is a Stansfield. Long ago, before immigrating to Enthilen, the Dobunni were ruled by monarchs. The will of the people saw a peaceful transition from monarchy to democracy. But the last Dobunni king...."

"Was a Stansfield," said Jurelle. "I know what you think you're convinced of."

"King Leopart Stansfield," said Eutropia. "You're his direct descendent. Therefore, royal blood flows through your daughters' veins. Heine *and* Stansfield. Erstürmen and Dobunni; a blood mix that could unite and lead a liberated Enthilen."

"Even if the Dobunni believe all this, they'll never return to a monarchy."

"They wouldn't have to," said Zenais. "An accomplished leader with the necessary inherited authority could guide them along a different path. Once she has united the people, she could establish a diverse, representative ruling council, like the conventus."

Jurelle didn't bother to mask his sarcasm. "You mean a council excluding men?"

Zenais' face remained deadpan. "We do what we must. Regardless, Enthilen's new ruler would pledge to make themselves redundant once the initial task of defeating Malphas and uniting those left is complete."

"I refuse to ask Thaly or Saskia to accept such a challenge. I refuse to support it."

"You don't speak for your daughters, and your support is not essential, though we hoped you would see things our way and encourage Thaly to heed our request."

"So, you've already chosen your martyr?"

"Zenais and I have pulled many strings to ensure Thaly receives appropriate preparation," said Eutropia. "To become the leader her potential demands. Her position in the conventus is no accident. Neither is her place in the Volatal Vexil or her promotion to Legatus. You must have had an inkling, General Jurelle. You must have seen what was playing out around you."

"Are you saying Thaly obtained those positions only because of your intervention?"

"We lowered the bureaucratic hurdles, but Thaly's appointments reflect her skill and leadership qualities. We made sure such qualities weren't overlooked. Thaly's a natural leader, even if she and her father fail to recognise it."

"I won't put Thaly in harm's way," said Jurelle. "Despite being trapped inside Sardis' inner circle, I tried to keep her safe. Every time Ewald turned his thoughts towards Bagendon, I redirected them. Underplayed the town's importance. It took me half a generation to escape Sardis, and I lost a son to the Erstürmen. I found Thaly on death's doorstep among the crumbling ruins of Pergamos. I'm in no hurry to place her there again."

"Thaly's future is out of your hands," said Zenais. "She now has experience in politics, leadership and military strategy. When, not if we march on Enthilen, Athalee Stansfield is the best person to lead our army against Malphas. She knows the landscape and has fought the enemy before. She's the daughter of the greatest Dobunni leader that ever lived and has royal Heine blood flowing through her veins. It makes for a compelling case, doesn't it? The conventus won't be able to resist our proposal."

Jurelle's shoulders buckled with the weight of expectation. Zenais and Eutropia believed he had more influence over his daughter than was true. If Thaly wanted to return to Enthilen, she would go, regardless of what he said. Or she might dig her heels into Germalian sand if he urged her to lead an army against Malphas. Yet, if Thaly wavered in her decision, his advice could tip her one way or the other. The Germalian senators attempted to gain his favour to tie up this hanging plot thread.

"Whatever Thaly agrees to, you still must convince the conventus of your plan," said Jurelle. "Germalia will go to war only if all the factions vote in favour."

"Leave the conventus to us," said Zenais. "All we ask of you is to foster the promise of your daughter becoming the leader she was born to be."

"We'll talk again," said Eutropia. "For now, we'll leave you with your oceanic reminiscences."

Zenais and Eutropia nodded to Jurelle and walked off into the crowd. Dressed in the green robes of Capri or the red of Arie, they stood out amid the sailors, merchants, and labourers with their simple canvas pants and cotton shirts in shades of brown and white.

This was hardly a clandestine meeting, thought Jurelle.

The wind changed, and a cool sea breeze reminded him of his age, filtering through his shirt and caressing the ache of old bones and tired muscles that had forgotten the strength of youth. He'd never lead again, but it appeared his legacy would pass to Thaly whether she wanted it or not. It hurt to think about losing his daughter again, but it seemed inevitable.

~ Chapter 5 ~

O n Enthilen's east coast, south of Dorfisch, Adalwolf Heine trudged along the sandy trail from his beach shack to the road connecting Laodicea and Gestade. A bone-coloured tunic that once fit snugly now hung limp, flapping against his arms like a threadbare tapestry telling stories of hard times scrounging for sustenance and a glimmer of belief. Black boots stolen from a market stall in Dorfisch rubbed through thin leggings, swelling blisters on his heels that burst and wept like grapes rolled between stones. A prince for the first sixteen harvest seasons of his life, then briefly a king, Adalwolf's nobility hadn't prepared him for the travail of wringing meagre portions from a tired land. He'd never been taught to farm, hunt, or gather food from the wild. Never learned how to find water when streams ran dry or how to break a horse or forge a weapon. Wasn't trained how to mend clothes or build a shelter. He sometimes wondered what he did learn, all those yarles as an Erstürmen prince.

When a person falls into desperation, Adalwolf mused, privilege is a handicap difficult to overcome.

Yet, somehow, he'd survived for twelve yarles living like a peasant. Taught himself how to find nourishment when only emptiness confronted him, and how to protect himself from the elements when the land offered no shelter. Adapt or die — it was that simple.

The setting sun disappeared behind the crown of a lone bullom tree. Despite a familial urgency dragging his legs forward, one resolute step after the other, Adalwolf wouldn't reach the old Erstürmen outpost of Gestade until tomorrow. So, he gathered kindling for a fire and slinked into the wind-swept coastal vegetation beside the track. Although the growing season usually offered warm days, the east wind cooled the evening air, and the night threatened to send a chill through weary bones. Tangled with scraps of food that had escaped his hunger, a beard did little to protect Adalwolf's face from the cold.

After piling a cluster of dry grass under a pyramid of twigs, he took a fire striker, flint and char cloth from inside a shoulder satchel. To hold the flint and char cloth firm, he jammed them between a flat rock and his black boot, then threaded three fingers of his left hand through the oblong metal striker. Sparks flew from the hard rock as he smashed the striker against the flint with glancing blows until an ember caught in the char cloth. He stepped off the flint and carried the cloth to the dry grass, placing it carefully underneath, then puffed to coax the ember's glow to set the grass alight. A fire took hold, and Adalwolf crouched, blowing into the smouldering mat to nurture the flames.

He remembered the first time he tried to light a fire like this. It took most of the night. Managing anything with one hand — his less favoured hand — presented many challenges. But after seasons of practice, he'd reached a point where one hand was almost as good as two. Adapt or die.

With the fire ablaze, he unshouldered the satchel, slumped to the ground and pulled a soiled cotton cloth holding a piece of salted fish from his bag. He unwrapped the fish and shoved it into his mouth, flakes of tan-coloured flesh falling into his beard as he chewed, resting with the other morsels caught in the wiry growth dangling down to his chest. After washing the salty taste away with the last swig from his waterskin, he pulled his knees into his chest, stooping into the ill-fitting tunic.

He probably wouldn't sleep tonight. Fear of being discovered by a patrol from Pergamos usually kept his mind alert, though he doubted Malphas' soldiers would remember him as the one-time ruler of Enthilen. King Adalwolf the Redeemer quickly became Adalwolf the Absent King, his reign the shortest in Erstürmen history.

What did Uncle Gerulf say back in Sardis? thought Adalwolf. 'The eternal reign begins with you.' You, Adalwolf, will become immortal and rule for eternity. Could there be a more bitter irony?

Uncle Gerulf. Except, Malphas had told Adalwolf that Gerulf wasn't his uncle but his half-brother. Malphas fathered both of them. Then Malphas killed all his sons — Ewald, Hadufuns, Widald, and Gerulf. All except Adalwolf.

One day, he thought, Malphas will come for me, still fuming over what happened in Pergamos' throne hall twelve yarles ago.

When Adalwolf and Tom Anderson disappeared, it thwarted Malphas' plans to sacrifice an immortal Adalwolf on the throne of the dead to bring forth Volerdie. Adalwolf expected such a failure would plague Malphas for an eternity, the Worshipful Master refusing to abandon a chance at retribution. The reprisal, though, would be of a more traditional kind. Public execution, most likely. Adalwolf could no longer be used as the immortal sacrifice. Without a right hand, he couldn't steal Tom Anderson's soul with the dark eyes to gain the reward of eternal life. But Tom could capture Adalwolf's soul should the traveller from a strange land reappear. Then *he'd* bear the burden of fulfilling Malphas' fatal desires.

Though he had no reason to be sympathetic, Adalwolf didn't wish such a fate on Tom. He hoped Tom would die, as any ordinary person may die, and Adalwolf, his birth twin, would die with him.

* * * *

Adalwolf kept his chin down, his beard brushing the top of his stomach, and fixed his eyes on the dirt road to Gestade's main gate. The town surrounding the outpost bustled with life, and he withered under the pry of suspicious curiosity as the good citizens of Gestade passed silent judgement on the wretched man tottering past the market square. The stalls offered more food than he'd seen in yarles, and Adalwolf hatched a plan to secure his share, then dismissed it immediately when soldiers decked in the polished silver armour of the King's Shield marched towards him. He stepped aside, and they brushed past as if he were nothing more than a flap of curtain across a doorway. Once, they would have been *his* soldiers. *His* Shield. They would have stopped and saluted, thumping gauntleted right fists against breastplates to accompany the resounding proclamation 'Hail, King Adalwolf.' Once, this would have happened. Not anymore. Likely, never again.

Gestade's defences became more elaborate closer to the main gate. Every house lining the road had been turned into a small fortress — windows boarded up, sharpened timber spikes protruding from rendered clay walls, and arrow slits in doors from where archers could launch their projectiles. It appeared Gestade had been preparing for an attack from Malphas' army for many yarles.

The crowd walking with Adalwolf towards the outpost gate appeared wary and tense. People were on edge, waiting for the inevitable and wondering why it hadn't arrived. The attentive glanced over their shoulder again and again. Nobody laughed, not even the children, offering only murmurs of fatalism. Atop the outpost's crenellated east wall, cobalt-blue banners with the sigil of a white mongoose, Field Commander Hartmut's sigil, hung in sombre stillness. Hartmut led Gestade as he'd done for as long as Adalwolf could remember. And the commander clung to old loyalties, the traditional Erstürmen banner of black cloth with the red, two-headed serpent curled upwards into an incomplete circle, also flying proudly from the ramparts.

Faithful to the end, thought Adalwolf. At what price?

Wrapped in daydreams, he almost collided with an armoured guard who stepped into his path.

"Halt," snapped the guard. "State your business."

The guard wore the King's Shield breastplate, embossed with the insignia of the two-headed snake. Adalwolf pushed the stump of his right wrist deep into his pants pocket in case the handless arm drew the guard's suspicion. In case the guard put two and two together and realised the snivelling peasant before him, who looked much older than twenty-eight harvest seasons, was actually Enthilen's absent king.

"I need a healer," Adalwolf muttered. "For my mother."

"Where y'from?" asked the guard.

"We have a shack between here and Dorfisch. My mother is too weak to travel."

"If y'want a healer to make a house call, y'ull need coin, and ya don't look like y'have any."

Adalwolf rummaged around inside his shoulder satchel with his left hand until finding a cotton pouch with three coins jingling inside. Even with his eyes averted, he could sense the guard's inquisitive stare drilling into him, trying to see past the destitution masking a royal face. Adalwolf sucked a piece of salted fish from between his teeth, took a coin from the pouch and handed it to the soldier.

"I have more for the healer," said Adalwolf, briefly locking eyes with the guard but looking away just as quickly.

The guard wrapped his gloved fist around the coin and nodded. "What's yur name?"

"Fehler. I'm a fisher from the coast."

"Open yur satchel."

Keeping the satchel slung over his right shoulder, Adalwolf opened the flap with his left hand and turned side-on to the guard. The soldier peered inside, then used the tip of his halberd to push the satchel aside to check for weapons hanging from the rope belt around Adalwolf's waist. The guard flared his nostrils, seemingly repulsed at being this close to the unwashed. Yet, Adalwolf's repugnance kept the inquisition brief. The guard stood aside to let Fehler the Fisher into Gestade.

"Leave before sunset," ordered the guard. "Otherwise, y'ull be thrown in da cells."

Adalwolf nodded and ambled through the main gate, past walls ringed with palisades and reinforced with square stones the size of a wagon. Like the houses outside, every dwelling within the outpost's grounds had been fortified. Soldiers in the traditional blue and black tunics and silver armour of the Heine Empire, last used during Adalwolf's brief reign, mingled with the Dobunni who'd fled Laodicea after the barbarian attack. Towering above the crowd, a wild stone-grell carried a bag of grain on her shoulder, the black ink of her facial tattoo stark against pale skin. Adalwolf hadn't seen a wild grell since Pergamos when he ordered the slaughter of grell pilgrims in the calendar of life. Recalling the massacre turned his stomach, but at the time, he took pride in the victory, hopeful it would please his father, Malphas, and entrench the new king's authority over the Erstürmen people.

Now, Adalwolf cringed at his naivety, embarrassed his younger self had been so easily infected by the poisonous words dripping from Malphas' mouth. Pursuing power had tainted Adalwolf's mind, blurring the line between right and wrong. His mother, Romilda, exposed Malphas' true plans, but the revelation came too late. Everything fell apart when Volerdie's Wrath destroyed Pergamos.

Why *has* Malphas let Gestade remain standing all this time? wondered Adalwolf. Complacency? Recklessness?

Ignoring his pleading hunger, Adalwolf strode past a food stall and through the multifarious crowd as if quickening his pace would quell his grievances. He marched straight for the infirmary, a long, timber building with a white door painted with a red dove in flight — the bird of healing. From the infirmary's open windows wafted the desperate smell of death and decay, a fetid stew of blood, pus, urine and faeces. People flitted in and out of the front door carrying poultices, plants, toadstools or any concoction or implement that might be used for healing.

Adalwolf stopped at a puddle with two feathers floating on the surface, dancing together atop the ripples. He stepped over the puddle, so as not to disturb the feather dancers, and onto the infirmary porch, grabbing the arm of a plump woman carrying a jar of leeches.

"My mother needs a healer," said Adalwolf.

"You should bring her here," replied the woman.

"She's too weak to travel."

A scream burst from a window, yanking the woman's attention from Adalwolf. "We can't spare anyone at the moment."

"Some herbs or medicines then. I have coin." Adalwolf opened the flap of his satchel.

The woman turned to him again. "What ails her?"

"Fever, coughing. Cheeks flushed red. She can't keep food down. Can hardly swallow."

"We have others with the same symptoms and not enough medicine to treat them. I can't spare any for you. Best be on your way."

"What's the trouble here, Morgana?" asked a younger woman who strode across the grounds towards Adalwolf. She had a determined carriage and glinting eyes suggesting she wouldn't suffer fools yet would dismiss them with enduring kindness.

"This man wants a healer," said Morgana. "His mother's ill and can't travel."

"She's dying," said Adalwolf. "I need someone to ease her pain. Offer at least a little comfort for her final journey."

"Where is she?" asked the younger woman.

"We have a shack near the coast. I can take you there. Less than a day's ride on a strong horse."

"We already have too many patients." Morgana spun around and strode into the infirmary, yelling over her shoulder, "Don't succumb to his sorrowful eyes, Audie. You can't afford to adopt another stray."

Audie adjusted the white toque covering her silky black hair and smiled at Adalwolf. "Do you have a horse?"

"No," he said.

"Never mind, I can borrow two horses, but I must be back by tomorrow eve. What's your name?"

"Fehler."

Audie nodded. "Wait here. I'll gather medicines and return soon."

As she walked away, Adalwolf followed the dance of her ponytail, his brooding brushed aside by the swaying, rhythmic beauty of something so simple. He hoped he'd found a skilled healer. His mother, Romilda, deserved as much.

* * * *

Adalwolf and Audie rode all day, reaching the dilapidated fishing shack nestled among the dunes south of Dorfisch at dusk. During the journey, Adalwolf had deflected questions about his past, the fear of revealing his true identity overriding his urge to reciprocate Audie's kind attentiveness. They dismounted and tethered the horses to a post outside the shack. Adalwolf waited for Audie to gather potions from her saddle bag, and then they walked inside together.

On a cot made from driftwood and animal skins, and no wider than a horse's back, lay Romilda, once the Queen of Enthilen, then the Queen Mother. She'd covered herself with a quilt stitched with the scene of a king on a rearing white horse, his gold crown inset with gemstones of jasper, chrysolite and jacinth, brandishing his sword to slay a fiery red beast with two heads and a spurred tail. The vibrant quilt once hung in Sardis' throne room, but Romilda's devout possession had faded the colours and frayed the stitching. Her fingers, frozen in place, held the quilt edge up under her chin as if the blanket would shield her from any threat this dangerous world could conjure.

It seemed his mother hadn't moved since Adalwolf left her two moons ago. Had the quilt become her cerement? he wondered, until a quiet, feeble breath raised Romilda's chest.

Adalwolf dropped to his knees at the bedside, and Romilda moaned, forcing open weary, crusted eyes saddled with purple bags bulging with all the sorrow and pain of seasons past. Her greying hair sprawled dishevelled across a straw pillow, long ago rejecting the bejewelled crespine that had once pronounced a royal lineage.

"I've brought a healer," said Adalwolf.

Romilda attempted to smile, but it only accentuated the scar running from her forehead to the bottom of her left cheek. The wound Adalwolf inflicted as the cruel puppeteer Ende, the pale grell, pulled his strings at Malphas' command. It reminded Adalwolf of his mother's many sacrifices and how little she'd been rewarded.

Romilda brushed the back of her hand across Adalwolf's cheek, and he recoiled at the cold touch. "Thank you, Adalwolf," she whispered in frail adoration. "My beautiful boy."

"Can I look at her?" said Audie, standing behind Adalwolf.

He jumped up from his knees as his chest shuddered. Did Audie hear his mother speak? Did she realise who he was? "Y-yes," he stammered. "Of course."

Audie knelt and examined the patient, the healer's movements sure and decisive, not hesitating at the sight of the brutal scar.

She would have seen much worse, Adalwolf thought. Yarles surrounded by festering wounds and screaming victims had likely forged a resolve harder than the finest steel.

Her physical examination complete, Audie retreated to the koken table, took a mortar, pestle, and foliage from her backpack, and ground the plants together. "This potion should relieve your mother's pain. How long has she been ill?"

"Twelve moons," said Adalwolf. "At least twelve moons."

Audie splashed water into the mortar and mixed the concoction further before removing the pestle and stepping across to the bed. With Adalwolf standing beside his mother, holding her hand, Audie knelt again, placed one hand at the back of Romilda's head and with the other, tipped a few drops of medicine onto the patient's tongue. Romilda exploded in a coughing fit that shook the bed and rattled the scatter of utensils and fishing gear hanging from the wall.

Romilda squeezed Adalwolf's hand as Audie felt her forehead. The healer's apparent experience couldn't mask her concern; everything Adalwolf feared was written across Audie's face.

She stood, grabbed Adalwolf's arm and took him to one side, whispering in his ear, "I'm sorry. There's no more I can do. I'll leave the potion with you. Administer it again in the morning and evening until...."

The bed squeaked, and Adalwolf turned as Romilda raised her head from the pillow.

"Gestade, is that where you're from, my dear?" she asked.

Audie faced Romilda and grasped her reaching hand. "Yes."

"Is Field Commander Hartmut still there?"

Audie nodded and smiled.

"He's a kind man. Handsome and generous. I sometimes wish I married him instead of Ewald."

A clench of panic twisted in Adalwolf's chest. "Mother," he snapped. "No."

"Hush, Adalwolf. Our guest knows who we are. She's no fool. I saw her eyes widen at the sight of my scar. Here lies Romilda, the Queen Mother, on her deathbed, her faithful son by her side. Only her son." She collapsed back onto the bed, coughing.

Audie released Romilda's hand and went to gather her things. Adalwolf blocked her path and took a knife from the koken table.

Audie raised her eyebrows. "Are you going to stab me?"

"I can't let you reveal my whereabouts," said Adalwolf. "To anyone."

"I'm not in the business of exposing absent kings."

"It might slip out, even if you didn't mean it. I can't risk it. I can't risk anyone finding out." His arm trembled as he waved the dagger in Audie's face.

She didn't flinch, but her eyes betrayed an alarm that made Adalwolf nauseous. He didn't want to kill anyone, but he'd spent the last twelve yarles hiding. If Audie exposed him, those with evil intent would come looking. The Erstürmen of Gestade might consider him an enemy. Malphas still yearned to end his life. He needed to stay hidden. From everyone.

"Adalwolf," called Romilda. "Put the knife down. Come and sit with me."

Tears welled in Adalwolf's eyes at the distressing realisation this life, *his* life, wasn't worth living. Forever pensive, expecting enemies to crash through his door at any moment. Soon, his only friend, his mother, would die, and he'd be alone. This wasn't living; this was torture without end. Malphas had secured his victory after all.

Adalwolf released the knife, and it clattered to the floor. He stepped away from Audie and over to his mother, kneeling by her bed.

She brushed tangled black curls from his face. "You're the rightful king of Enthilen. Malphas stole that from you. Took something that didn't belong to him. Go to Gestade and claim your birthright. Commander Hartmut will listen. He's an honourable man. He'll see the value in resurrecting the glorious Erstürmen Kingdoms of old. You can stand together against Malphas. It's not too late."

Adalwolf bowed and wiped the tears from his cheeks with the soiled bed quilt. Romilda pressed her hand into his back with renewed strength, a clutch of determination flowing through her fingers. He lifted his head to face fiery defiance glowing in her eyes. She'd gathered the last bundle of kindling left in her body for a final act of ignition.

Romilda spoke over his shoulder to Audie, "Get me the parchment and quill, dear. They're resting on the shelf by the fireplace. Oh, and the royal seal next to them. Can you melt some wax for me?"

Adalwolf expected Audie to leave. To gather her things and rush back to Gestade to announce his presence. Instead, she followed Romilda's instructions while Adalwolf stoked the fire.

Romilda sat up in bed. Audie handed her the parchment and quill and placed a pot of ink on her bedside table. As the fire roared back to life, the Queen Mother scribbled on the parchment, then handed the letter to Audie.

"Use the royal seal to fix the letter closed," said Romilda. "Then take my son back to Gestade and give the letter to Hartmut. Make sure you deliver it straight to him."

Adalwolf turned away from the fire. "This isn't right."

"It's time to stop hiding, Adalwolf," said Romilda. "You can't go on like this." She shuddered in a coughing fit and sank into the sagging animal skins that barely held together the cot's timber frame.

Adalwolf approached his mother and clutched at the quilt's fraying threads. "Mother? Mama?"

"I go to wait with the other lost souls for Volerdie to open the door to paradise." Romilda's face turned scarlet. Breaths sucked through swollen cheeks wheezed with a screeching pain.

Audie stood beside Adalwolf. "The end is here," she said. "Hold her tight."

Adalwolf hugged his mother, then mopped the cold sweat from her brow. Marble-grey eyes rolled back in her head. Her spine arched, arms and legs tense as if fighting against the end. A staunch resolve, refusing to cede to the beckoning call of death. But, as always, death won, and Romilda's body relaxed. It rested in motionless suspense for a moment before releasing the odours and fluids that marked the beginning of its decay.

The haste of the final moment caught Adalwolf off guard, not ready to let his mother go. He stayed there, kneeling beside the bed and grasping her hand. Thoughts raced through his mind. Guilt at being an unworthy son. Never becoming the beloved king Romilda always dreamt of. Running away from Malphas, unable to gather the strength or courage to confront the old man. Romilda died in a tiny cot in a rundown shack, unable to escape her son's shame. There would be no ceremony for the Queen Mother. No majesty to herald her passing. No painted vase to hold her ashes and sit atop a pedestal in an Erstürmen throne room. Only Adalwolf's memory would mark her death.

The fire waned. Adalwolf lifted himself off aching knees and turned, expecting Audie to have already left. But she'd stayed, sitting at the koken table like a silent, divine sentinel, waiting for his remorse to abate.

"What should I do?" asked Adalwolf.

"Honour your mother's dying wish," said Audie. "Return with me to Gestade and help us face Malphas' hordes when they arrive."

"Why has he waited so long to attack?"

"Hartmut believes Malphas has been too preoccupied with rebuilding Pergamos. Swelling his armies and entrenching his power. But our scouts say he will come soon. Before harvest season ends."

Adalwolf sighed with recognition and sat at the table opposite Audie, running his fingers over the sealed letter Romilda had written as her final act. "I can't seem to escape my heritage. My ancestral expectation. I'm left to choose between king or martyr." His body slumped from exhaustion, but with it came the release of a burden as he accepted he could no longer flee. The demons waiting for him had to be confronted, even if it meant his death.

As the half-moon of Seena, and the quarter-moon of Bargan, rose outside, Adalwolf dragged himself from the wallow. "I'll burn her, as is the custom. Will you help me build a pyre?"

Audie nodded with sombre endearment.

"Then, in the morning, I'll ride with you to Gestade," said Adalwolf. "It's time to announce my presence to what remains of the Heine Empire."

~ Chapter 6 ~

Tom roamed among blackened skeletons of trees, smouldering roots sending bitter grey smoke up hollow trunks like fired chimneys. Gnarled, leafless branches reached into the begrimed haze, searching for a shard of sunlight. A sliver of life. Scorched stones, charred twigs and tendrils of burnt grass littered the black ground and crunched under Tom's bare feet as he walked through the desecrated forest. Nothing living stirred amid the carnage. Except, in the distance, the smoke swirled around an apparition coming towards Tom. Straight towards him. The dead trees offered no concealment. Tom's legs refused to carry him to safety as if the soles of his feet had melted onto the soil.

The apparition transformed into a creature walking upright on two sepia talons that clutched at the scorched earth. A raven's head swivelled atop a torso covered in wiry black fur with long arms like a spider monkey. And from the creature's back grew two giant, pale wings, the shoulders reaching above the raven head and the tips of the longest primary feathers stroking the bare ground. The creature prised the tip of its black bill into the crevice of a tree. Ran thin, elongated fingers over every scalded rock. It searched for something. A thorough, ceaseless quest. The creature stepped closer to Tom and halted in front of him, tilting its head from side to side as if appraising the human intruder. A piercing, soulless eye wrenched the air from Tom's lungs. He was unveiled. The creature reached out and grabbed his arm.

"Ahhh!" Tom sat up with a start, the bedsheet sliding to his waist, and sluiced the sweat from his forehead.

Only a nightmare, Tom, he thought. *That's all.*

He reached for a glass of water on the bedside table, gulping the last mouthful. As his bleary eyes adjusted to the dullness of the *Lame Brain's* bedroom, his door swung open. In the doorway, something big blocked the light from the hall. Something, *someone*, crammed underneath the door lintel and between the jamb.

The giant inhaled and spoke in a foreign but familiar accent, *"Tom."*
Shit! Shit!

Tom dropped the empty glass, sat up and pressed his back into the bedhead as if he might escape by dissolving into the timber. His body throbbed with adrenaline. The giant squeezed through the doorway and stepped into Tom's bedroom.

"Leave me alone," said Tom.

He turned on the bedside lamp, picked it up and waved it at the intruder like an incandescent sword. The tainted and scarred white face of a grell glared back at him. One word exploded into Tom's mind. *Eroberung.* He pinched his forearm, digging chewed fingernails into naked flesh until droplets of blood pooled on his skin, then released and squeezed again.

Only a dream. That's all it is. A hallucination. The psychiatrist said so.

The white grell swayed unsteady on the musty grey carpet, the peak of his hood almost touching the halfway house's flecked ceiling. A hoarse voice drew on a clearly dwindling reserve of energy to whisper, *"Tom, ist jun Grin."*

Tom whimpered. "No. No, you're not. You're somebody else; come to torment me. Come to kill me."

"Nuot. Kloss ai une dorsch."

"No. No." With his free hand, Tom rubbed the bedsheet over his eyes, hoping it might reveal a new reality. It had been a long time since he'd heard anyone speak Erstürmen, but he still remembered it. The language went through his head almost every day.

The white grell moaned, teetering under the glare of artificial light. Blood stained his coat between his chest and left shoulder. His legs buckled, and he collapsed face-first onto Tom's bedroom floor.

Max stood in the doorway. "What's all the commotion? Shit. Who the hell's that?"

"Do you see it too?" asked Tom.

"Well, it's pretty hard to miss. He's fuckin' huge."

"Oh, Jesus. I thought...look, please don't tell anyone."

"Is he alright? There's blood on the carpet."

"I think he's injured. I'll sort it out."

"You better do somethin'. They don't allow overnight stays."

Tom put down the lamp and climbed out of bed. "Shut the door. I'll deal with it. Please keep it between us."

Max nodded. "Not sure how long you'll be able to keep *him* a secret. Call me if you need help." He pushed the grell's bare white feet inside the room and closed the door.

Tom's bedroom door had a lock, but the *Lame Brain* administrators didn't allow the residents to have keys. They didn't bet on special keys. Tom had one of those, given to him by Dwarrow inside his dwell when they first met all those years ago. He grabbed Dwarrow's key from the top drawer of his dresser and locked the bedroom door.

That was stupid. I might have locked myself in here with Eroberung.

He stood at the door, listening to the wheeze of his visitor's breaths, until he found enough courage to kneel beside the white grell. Placing an arm underneath the grell's chest and waist, Tom heaved. The stranger rolled onto his back easier than Tom expected.

Grin? Is this you?

Almost invisible against tainted white skin, underneath raised scar tissue, Tom brushed his fingertip over the faint outline of a facial tattoo. The tattoo could have been a spider. Once. The ground spider, muwin. Grin's crest.

The white grell opened his eyes. Lilac eyes, like a wild stone-grell. Not the black eyes of a tainted grell.

"Grin?" said Tom.

"Tomtom Anderson," said the grell, his disfigured mouth twisting into a shape resembling a smile.

It is Grin. It has to be.

Tom's friend pointed at the bedside table, still smiling. "You kept your remembrance totem."

Like the ceiling in the throne hall of Pergamos during Volerdie's Wrath, the world inside Tom's head collapsed. Every memory of Enthilen rained down on him; good, bad, extraordinary, frightening. Days spent with Grin learning about the forest of Babir Birramal. Sacrifice and torture in Süden Forst. The relentless pursuit of Eroberung. A friendship forged in the Scaur Hills with Thaly and Jacob. The enigma of Dwarrow the mouldewerp. Sardis, Princess Caeli, the terror on Hansen's Bluff. Grin and Thaly rescuing Tom from Malphas. The *Vulking*. Annian weald-grell. Bindari. Widukind.

Everything and everyone flooded his mind as if the memories had been trapped behind a dam wall for twelve yarles, and the dam had burst. Grin's arrival had set them free. And they were *real* memories. Not hallucinations. Not fabrications or wild fantasies. Enthilen was real. Dwarrow's key and the remembrance totem were real. He'd brought them back from Enthilen, not picked them up in an op shop like his mother said. Grin was real. Right here, lying on Tom's bedroom floor.

Dying?

Tom caressed the loose white skin clinging to the back of Grin's oversized hands and winced at the blood oozing from his friend's chest wound. Grin clutched Tom's fingers and forced another feeble smile. For Tom, it all became too much. The flood of memories engulfed him, and he collapsed onto his friend's heaving chest.

*　*　*　*

Tom and Grin sat together the following morning, slouched against the bedroom wall. Grin had slept the entire night while Tom stayed awake, worrying. Occasionally, he mopped up the blood from Grin's wound with a pillowcase. As dawn filtered through the semi-transparent curtains covering Tom's window, Grin's condition improved. Enough for the reunited friends to talk in the language Tom thought he'd never speak aloud again.

"I thought you may have died, Grin. When Pergamos' throne room collapsed...."

"I escaped with Thaly and Dwarrow. Thaly's father came for her."

"Her father?"

"Jurelle Stansfield."

Tom recalled seeing Jurelle leading Erstürmen soldiers to war against the Riverlands farmers. "Thaly called him the Traitor General. The Dobunni leader who abandoned the rebels and pledged allegiance to King Ewald."

"Jurelle escaped Sardis and came for Thaly. To take her back to her family."

"Athalee Stansfield. I never would have imagined." Tom sighed. "The last thing I remember seeing is Malphas stabbing Thaly in the side."

"She was badly wounded. We took her to Babir Birramal, and there she healed. Then she left with her father to travel to Germalia. I do not know if they reached their destination."

"What about Dwarrow and Caeli?"

"Dwarrow never falters. I have not seen him for many moons, but I am here at his bidding. Even from far away, he directs my actions. Princess Caeli...." A shaft of morning sunlight through a gap in the curtains accentuated the sorrowful glisten in Grin's lilac eyes. "Caeli is a draughoul and spends her days wandering Enthilen in eternal torment. Adalwolf captured her soul with the dark eyes in the throne room."

"I saw it happen," said Tom. "How did *you* get the eyes of lost souls?"

"I rejected my culture. Although my father, Frennan, told me grells must never touch the dark eyes, I stole them from the throne of the dead in the chaos after your disappearance. Then I hid the eyes so Malphas would not find them. But he has punished me. He has punished me greatly." Tears trickled down Grin's cheeks, navigating the scars on his face like tiny, transparent mice trapped in a maze.

Tom placed his hand on Grin's shoulder. "I'm so sorry, Grin. I can't imagine what Malphas did to you."

"It is better not to try. The nightmares would never let you rest. But Malphas did not corrupt all of me. There is enough of the old Grin left to understand right from wrong. To know what I must do."

"The eyes of lost souls. Do you...."

Grin searched inside his coat, retrieving the eyes and placing them on the carpet.

Tom had hoped to never see the dark eyes again, but he couldn't turn away from the flaming pupils' hypnotic lure, glimmering inside the burnished obsidian. "You used the eyes to travel here. That means you won't be able to return home."

"The home I loved is gone. Malphas' servants burned Babir Birramal and destroyed the milbis. Drove the few remaining wild stone-grells from the forest. He hunted me, and I gave myself to him, hoping to stop the carnage. But I refused to give him the dark eyes."

Grin has sacrificed so much, thought Tom. *Every new revelation feels like someone tearing a sliver of muscle from my heart.*

"Malphas imprisoned me. I do not know for how long. With the cruel sorcery of a demon, he tainted my skin but did not break me. My mother...." Grin caught his breath and stopped, pain writhing across his face. "My mother, Mirrian, is trapped in Pergamos as Malphas' slave. I thought she had died in the massacre of Malang Gunya. But she suffered a fate worse than any death."

Grin sat in silence, and Tom adopted the pain coursing through his friend's body.

"How did you find me?" asked Tom.

Grin reached into his coat and withdrew a gold star with a sharp point on the underside and etching on the top. "A draughoul gave me this, the blood compass, and a vial of Adalwolf's blood, stolen by the draughoul and treated by the mouldewerps to stop it from drying. When I place a drop of Adalwolf's blood on one of the five points of this pentagram, the compass spins until it directs me to your location. The slower it spins, the closer you are. I watched this street from an abandoned building until I saw you."

Tom ground his teeth, plagued by what confronted him. The eyes of lost souls. The blood compass. Enthilen's black magic had arrived on Earth, and he questioned his longing to return to Ostamp.

"You said you're here at Darrow's bidding?"

"The draughoul, Fullō, came with a message from Dwarrow. The mouldewerp knew I had hidden the dark eyes and would never reveal their location unless...unless there was a chance to end it all. To end Malphas' reign of terror. Dwarrow said I must convince you to return to Enthilen."

Fullō. Malphas and Widukind's mother. Widukind, the strange, disjointed man who revealed Malphas' plans. Is Widukind plotting his own schemes? Is Dwarrow the instigator or the accomplice? Tom shook his head. "I'm not sure I want to go back, Grin. I don't even know if the eyes would take me there."

"Dwarrow was adamant they will. He believes the eyes' power to transport you between worlds was reset when you placed them in the dead throne."

"Where will I land? Last time, I almost drowned."

"I remember," said Grin, his eyes sparkling from the reminiscence. "I saved you from the stream. Our lives have changed so much since that day. The dark eyes will return you near to where I left."

"Where did you leave from?"

Grin fell silent, the gleam in his eyes fading as he faced the morning sunlight seeping through the window.

"Where, Grin?"

"A cave connected to Pergamos."

"Under Pergamos? I don't want to...."

"*Near* can mean anywhere within days of walking. It has taken me a dozen moons to find you. The dark eyes did not return me to the exact location from which you left twelve yarles ago."

Still, there's a chance I could end up inside one of Pergamos' caves. Or Malphas' throne hall. Or his private quarters. Tom's shoulders sagged from a growing burden. "I'm not sure I can face Malphas and Adalwolf again."

"Malphas has turned his attention elsewhere, and Adalwolf has vanished. You would be the hunter, Tom, not the hunted. You have the dark eyes and the blood compass. Your blood can be used to find Adalwolf."

Grin's insistence angered Tom. "Why should I find Adalwolf? I don't want to become immortal. I don't want anything to do with it. I'm here trying to get my life together. I can't return to Enthilen."

"You must. Dwarrow's message…Fullō was so burdened by its importance that she preached the words to me until I had memorised them." Grin paused for a moment, then whispered as if this message was the most significant secret anyone could keep,

"Blood and bone
Destroy the throne
Naevus and twin
Blood flows thin
Kindred lost souls
Here and there
Bones to crush
Dust laid bare."

Blood and bone. I've heard that before. "What does it mean?" asked Tom.

"The blood is your blood. Fresh blood that flows thin. The bone is her bone. You must bring them to Enthilen. They can destroy the dead throne and end Malphas' reign."

"Her bone?"

"Jean Anderson."

Tom's mind flashed back to the night in his bedroom twenty-three years ago, a five-year-old listening to his Nanna read him a bedtime story. Then the Bad Man burst through the door. Nanna stood up from the bed and faced the man. He spoke to her. 'I'm sorry, Jean.' That's what he said right before he attacked her. Right before he killed her. 'I'm sorry.'

"Jean Anderson is my grandmother's name. I don't remember telling Dwarrow that. Or anybody else in Enthilen, including you."

Grin turned away and stared out the window. "We are much older now. With age comes responsibility. New burdens for us to bear."

"Jean's a draughoul. The Bad Man, Malphas, stole her soul with the dark eyes."

"You must find her. She is the lost soul from here. Your kin. Fullō assured me only a fragment of bone is needed."

"I haven't seen Nanna since I first travelled to Enthilen." Tom pushed the tips of his fingers into his aching temples, trying to comprehend Grin's words. He recalled when he first held the eyes of lost souls. One in each palm. The old crone — no, draughoul, she was also a draughoul — who accosted him in the scrub had thrust the dark eyes into his hands. *No future here. Leave home. Paradise awaits.* She repeated those words over and over. He closed his fists, and the skin on his palms burned. As the world spun out of control, Jean Anderson appeared, reaching towards him.

"I know it is overwhelming," said Grin. "Focus on the now, Tom."

"I felt something. When I sat on Volerdie's throne, the moment the portal opened for me to travel home, something entered my body. My mind. Something chilling and evil." Tom faced his friend. "You've sacrificed yourself to deliver this message, haven't you? You can't return home. You're going to die here."

"I came because I knew my death would have meaning. I have faith in you, Tom. Now you must have faith in yourself."

Tom sat in his bedroom with Grin all day. They talked. Grin slept, and Tom thought. About the guilt he carried from the murder of his grandmother, Jean Anderson. He couldn't save her life and failed when he had a chance to deliver justice to her killer, Malphas. He thought about how he'd abandoned his friends in Enthilen. How his life on Earth had turned out; aimless, lonely, fragmented. He was always running away from something, never *towards* anything. He had no plans. No ambition. *No future here. Leave home. Paradise awaits. No future here. Leave home. Paradise awaits.* The draughoul's words mocked him, and the wallow of his life became suffocating. He could have drowned right then, sitting on the floor of his bedroom while a dying Grin lay beside him. Grin, who'd sacrificed so much because he had faith in the birraman. Tom *could* have drowned, but he didn't. A fuming resolve wouldn't let him. A spark set a fire in his mind, evaporating the drowning waters. A lick of flame grew into a vengeful inferno, forging a rod of steely determination.

When you hit rock bottom, you have two choices. Give up or fight. Dammit. It's time to fight.

By early evening, Grin's condition had deteriorated. Max came to the rescue, convincing the other housemates to join him for dinner at a local restaurant and lending Tom his van so he could drive Grin away.

"I should take you to a hospital — an infirmary," Tom said to Grin. "To a healer."

Grin winced as he sat up, placing his hand over the bloody wound on his chest. "What would they make of me?"

"I don't know, but I have to do something."

"I am beyond the help of any healer. Since I arrived many moons ago, I have done everything to avoid the people of your world. It is unwise for me to announce my presence here. To try to explain where I am from and why I have come. And I hear the ancestors calling me."

No. Not yet. "I could get medicine. Bandages."

Grin reached for Tom's hand and squeezed. "Do you remember our days in Babir Birramal?"

"Of course. I cling to those memories."

"Once, you told me about a place. A forest where you escaped from the pressing trauma of this world."

"The rocky scrub. It's not much of a forest."

"I would like to see it."

Sitting facing each other, Grin reached towards Tom and placed the tips of his fingers on Tom's cheeks. Tom reciprocated to complete the formal grell greeting. The reunited friends stared into each other's eyes.

"I am dying, Tom. A healer cannot help me. What I need most is a tree to sit beside. Show me one of your *eucalypt* trees. The ones you love so much."

Tom broke from Grin's touch and bowed his head.

"Much in your world is noise and chaos," said Grin. "Take me to a place of peace, where I can rest."

Tom's mind drifted back to his last moments with Annian, trudging up to Bindari bearing the weight of the dying weald-grell. He had accompanied one grell as she walked to her grave. And he would do it again for someone who'd been his friend since the day they met. Since Grin saved Tom from drowning in a stream and joined him in the search for Nanna's killer.

"I have one more favour to ask." Grin reached inside his coat and withdrew a remembrance totem. "This is my totem. When you return to Enthilen, you must take it with you and give it to my sister, Hannian. She is the bearer of our family totems."

"How will I find her?"

"When I last saw Hanni, she had joined a band of rebels living in the Desolate Mountains. Travel through the cursed wood of Lokan to the third valley east of Detranté. The valley goes deep into the mountains. At its end is a ruined monastery where the rebels live."

Tom sighed and stood, unlocking the bedroom door with Dwarrow's special key and gathering the courage to begin another journey.

"The birraman," said Grin. "The traveller. Such an apt name for you, Tom Anderson. Your journey is not over yet, but the day will come when it is time for you to rest. Now is the time for strength. To wash away the doubts. It is clear what you must do, and only you can do it. Find Jean Anderson, take a piece of her bone, and use the dark eyes to return to Enthilen."

*   *   *   *

Tom pulled Max's van into the driveway of his childhood home in Littlehampton, South Australia. Pale amber lamplight from the loungeroom window illuminated the shrubs underneath the sill, where rosebuds swayed among the night shadows like the nodding heads of ghostly children. Inside the loungeroom, behind a worn lace curtain barely clinging to its rings, Tom's mother sat in her favourite chair, captivated by televised colour and movement.

In the back of the van, Grin lay on the cold metal floor, curled up like a foetus, a piece of discarded rope tangled like an umbilical cord in a pool of blood next to him. Tom cut the engine and listened.

Still breathing, he thought. *Grin's alive. Barely.*

Tom stepped from the car and trudged up the front steps. His mother never locked the door, a habit born of life in the country, even though Tom's hometown had sprawled into something unrecognisable from his childhood. He entered the lounge, where Elaine sat beneath a flickering lamp, holding a framed photograph of her dead husband, Bert.

She looked up. "Tommy?"

"Hi, Mum." Tom sat on the footstool in front of his mother's chair.

She placed the photograph on the side table, picked up the remote and muted the TV. The sorrow in Elaine's eyes became so acute in the silence, Tom turned away to compose himself. He was all she had left, and now he planned to leave her again. Possibly forever.

"You shouldn't be out so late," said Elaine. "From the house. Isn't there a curfew?"

Tom faced his mother and tried to smile. "Don't worry about the curfew. I have to talk to you."

She gazed out the window, mournful eyes framed with worry. "Whose van is that?"

"A friend from the halfway house lent it to me."

"Why do you need a van? I could've picked you up if you wanted to come home."

Tom scooched the footstool closer to his mum's chair, reached across and cupped her swollen, arthritic hand. "Grin's here," he said.

Elaine pulled her hand away. "Oh, Tom...not this again...."

"I can show you. He's in the van. Asleep. But we must talk first.'"

Elaine turned a blank face to him.

"Please, Mum. Please believe me."

She smiled. "Tommy...."

"I'm going away again."

"What did the doctor say?"

"Forget about the doctors. This is something I have to do. My life here hasn't worked out. Not like I wanted. I must find a purpose. A place where I can make a difference."

"You've made a difference to me. I can't bear losing you again. Now that your dad's gone...."

Shit. This is going to hurt more than I hoped. "Grin said they need me. In the other world. Ostamp. Enthilen."

Elaine offered a doubting smile. "Which is it? Ostamp or Enthilen?"

"Ostamp is the name of the world. Enthilen is like a country. At first, I didn't want to go. But I've thought about it. I abandoned my friends once and carried the guilt with me for twelve years. I can't carry it for another twelve. You're the only person that means anything to me in this world. The only one I care about. I had to talk to you. I need you to understand."

"Are you taking your meds?"

"Yes!" Tom jumped up from the footstool and paced around the lounge room. "This isn't about my illness. Grin is *real*. Enthilen is real. They need me."

Elaine shook her head until it lolled onto the top of her chest.

"Damn it. Alright, please come and look in the van. Please." Tom clutched his mother's hand and dragged her outside.

He opened the van's back door. Inside, a bare-chested Grin snored and twitched, his skin almost invisible against the vehicle's white paint.

Elaine's eyes widened.

"Do you believe me now?" asked Tom. "This is Grin. I don't want to wake him. He's exhausted and wounded. He sacrificed his life to find me. To ask me to return to Enthilen."

Tom grabbed Elaine's shoulders and sought her eyes. "He's dying, Mum. I must...find a place where he can rest."

"I don't know who this is, Tom, but it's not someone from another world. Other worlds don't exist."

"Mum, I need you to trust me. Accept what I'm telling you. I have to find Nanna...."

"She's dead, Tom. You saw her die."

Tom stopped, overwhelmed by the bizarreness of this professed reality. He tried to justify his beliefs, as much for himself as his baffled mother. "I must go away again. I'm not sure how long I'll be gone. I wanted to see you before I left. I love you, Mum. You've been my best friend for my entire life. I wouldn't leave if I thought there was another choice. A choice where I didn't have to carry this burden for the rest of my life. A choice that quelled the demons prowling around inside my head. I must do this for my own sanity."

Elaine turned away from Grin and hugged Tom. "I love you, too. I've always loved you. I trust you'll do the right thing, whatever it is."

"I should get Grin...."

"Of course you should." Elaine pulled away and walked to the house, stopping at the front porch.

Tom rushed into the shed and collected a mattock and shovel. His favourite backpack hung in a corner, stressed black leather with red panels on the sides. The buckles had rusted, and the shoulder straps were frayed at the edges, but it would serve another journey. He unhooked the empty pack and brushed the dust and spiderwebs from the leather.

After placing the tools and the backpack in the van, he shut the door and approached his mum.

Elaine stepped from the porch and gave him another hug. "Travel safely."

"In the morning, ring the halfway house and ask for Max. Tell him I've left his van on Hansen's Rd, next to the scrub on Bald Hill. I'll put the keys inside the front bumper, where the dent is. Unless...unless you want to come with me?"

Elaine teared up and shook her head.

Too much to ask. "Don't forget to ring Max."

She smiled. "I won't."

Tom turned away and didn't look back. Enthilen waited to be saved.

Late in the night, he sat in the white van beside a rutted dirt road leading to the outskirts of the rocky scrub where he used to escape as a kid. The farm surrounding the scrub had been sold years ago and subdivided into 'lifestyle' properties. But the patch of bush remained, the land too steep and rocky to be worth much to a real-estate developer. Grin's snores echoed through the back of the van. He'd slept the entire way. Tom leaned back, sinking low in the grey vinyl seat, and closed his eyes. He'd face the future at sunrise. Grin and him together.

Despite all that had happened, Tom fell asleep. He woke to the carolling of magpies and the sun beaming through the windshield. His neck ached as he glanced over his shoulder into the back of the van. Grin wasn't there. Tom grabbed his backpack and opened the flap. Inside, Grin had placed the eyes of lost souls, his remembrance totem, and the blood compass. Tom tossed a jacket and a full water bottle into the pack, then searched the pockets of his shorts.

Dwarrow's key. My anxiety medication. What else do I need?

He took the keys from the ignition, opened the van door, jumped outside and shouldered his pack. The patch of bush wasn't large, the size of four cricket ovals at the most, and Tom soon found Grin standing beside a pink gum sapling, running his giant white hand over the smooth bark as if reacquainting himself with an old friend.

"This is a forest, Tom. What else could it be?"

"How are you feeling?"

Grin ignored the question and tilted his head to the warbles and whistles of the dawn chorus. "So many songs, all melding into one. What a wonderous place this is. So much life."

Tom's eyes darted back to the road. "We should probably move further into the scrub. In case...."

"Of course. Show me your secret hiding place."

"Should I get the...?" Tom stopped, dead, the finality of his thought terrifying him.

Grin put his hand on his friend's shoulder. "You must bring the tools for digging. It will soon be time."

Tom trudged back to the van, gathered the shovel and mattock, locked the doors and placed the car keys inside the hole in the front bumper, hoping his mum would remember to ring the *Lame Brain*, and Max would forgive him for the inconvenience.

The two friends ambled up the rocky ridge, Grin using the shovel as a walking stick. His wheezing breath bounced from boulder to boulder, the grell having to stop every few paces to rest and clutch at his chest. The bleeding lessened, but the wound had become infected. Tom blocked out the thought of what came next, forcing himself to focus on the now. Grasping his friend's hand, he led Grin to a shallow depression surrounded by granite outcrops and a grove of she-oaks protecting the site from prying eyes and ill winds. A serene place where the timber and stone battlements repelled the anxiety of the outside world.

"This is it," said Tom. "I would come here to escape from the world."

Grin slumped to the ground and rested his back against a she-oak. A light breeze wailed through the tree's needle-like branchlets that cascaded towards the ground like an exploded firework.

Grin lifted his face to the canopy. "The ancestors are calling me home." He turned to Tom. "Find Dwarrow. He'll be waiting for you in his dwell in the Scaur Hills."

Tom sat beside his friend and held his hand, running his fingers over the welt in Grin's palm where a dark eye had seared his skin. "Now you've got them too."

"A traveller's scars," said Grin. "Another birraman with a tale to tell."

A single tear rolled down Tom's cheek in a sad, soft caress.

"Do not cry, Tom Anderson. I am returning to the land that gave birth to all the life in this world, and from there, I am certain I will find my way home. Our worlds are connected, yours and mine. Earth and Ostamp. They always have been. Lifeforces united as one. Do you remember the picture on the blue book's first page?"

"Eyes joined by the sun."

"Not eyes. Two worlds, our worlds, *sharing* the same sun. The same lifeforce. I am sorry, Tom, I could not save the blue book from being burned when the Erstürmen raided our milbis."

"It doesn't matter. It's of little use to me now." Tom fought back further tears. "One day, we'll meet again, Grin. You and I together with the land."

"And together, we will bask in the crumble of soil through our fingers, the freshness of leaves after rain, the soar of an eagle, the scamper of a field mouse, and the pounce of a ground spider. I long for that moment to arrive."

Grin closed his eyes, and Tom squeezed his friend's hand tighter, sitting quiet and still, breathing together and drifting into the nature surrounding them. The wind calmed to a light breeze, but the wail of the ancestors through the she-oak foliage beckoned. A grey shrike-thrush sang as if heralding Grin's arrival into the circle of the departed.

*   *   *   *

Grin pushed his aching back into the tree's rough bark, his mind emptying all thoughts of dread and responsibility as it drifted through the cambium and sapwood. He counted the tree's growth rings, each marking the passing of time, right back to when the tree was a sapling, its roots reaching out into the soil to grasp whatever nutrients it could find.

Arriving at the darkness of the pith, Grin's mind turned skyward, floating towards a beaming light that illuminated the tree's heart. Up through the trunk and jumble of branches to rest high atop the crown. His mind explored the entanglement of embracing green strands.

There are leaves here! Tiny, like the teeth of a mouse, feeding on sunlight and encircling each joint in this segmented, green canopy.

Grin's mind chose a single branchlet reaching up to the canopy's pinnacle and crawled along the spine to the tip. It waited there for a moment, drinking in the scene around it. Trees of pale, smooth bark and sage-coloured leaves. Rocky outcrops reminding him of the stone shelter, the milbi, where he lived with his father, Frennan. Tufts of dry grass resembling the spines of a *ganyi*; Tom would say 'echidna'. Leaf litter. Moss clinging to a rock face sheltered from the burning sun.

Under the shade of a tree lay animals with grey fur, long tails and powerful hind legs used to spring across the earth.

Wambuwuny. Our worlds are connected....

Grin's mind conjured up the faces of his family. Frennan; stern, stoic, proud. Mirrian, his mother; loving, gentle, strong. Hannian, his sister;

determined, willing, naïve. Merran, the brother who sacrificed his life to save the stone-grells' forest home. Now, Grin followed in his brother's footsteps.

He saw his milbi, at the edge of the vast south forest of Babir Birramal, burned by the Erstürmen. He travelled with Tom to Laodicea to find a killer. Rode with Thaly on a ship that led to a place of sorrow and pain never forgotten. Danced at the garrabari with stone- and weald-grells before being initiated, then marching to Malang Gunya to honour the sacrifice of ancestors who failed to protect the city from Erstürmen invaders. Succumbed to the pursuit of Malphas, while his mother shattered like ice as her son transformed into the white grell.

The hate and anger buried inside Grin led him to Malphas. Hatred for the injustices he had to endure. The enslavement of stone- and weald-grells, and the massacre of those who refused to yield. Anger at the corruption of Enthilen. The indifference. The hostility.

The Worshipful Master used Grin's anger to his own advantage. Probed and prised. Twisted and exploited. 'If being repressed feeds your hate,' Malphas had said, 'then quell it by becoming the oppressor.' Grin had embraced his master's mantra almost completely.

His mind returned to the forest of Tom Anderson and melted into the sunlight to find a hand reaching for him. Grin followed the fingers to the wrist, along the forearm to the shoulder and neck. There, a tattooed face adorned with walga, the sparrowhawk, smiled and spoke an ancient language.

"*Ngali yanhagirri.*"

Inside his mind, Grin smiled back, took his father's hand and travelled with him to see the ancestors.

* * * *

Tom woke to a hot sun burning his balding head. He still held Grin's hand; his friend slumped low against the tree trunk.

Tom shook Grin's shoulder. "Wake up." But Grin didn't move or open his eyes. Or breathe. "Grin...?"

Tom staggered to his feet and picked up the shovel, anger hotter than the sun stinging his face. He slammed the shovel into a granite boulder. The metal rang across the ridgetop like the single toll of a bell, the wooden handle shuddering with grief.

"Fuck it." He fell to his knees, beads of sorrow and resignation dripping into his eyes.

Is this about you or Grin? thought Tom. *Don't feel sorry for yourself. Treat your friend with the respect he deserves.*

Tom stood, grabbed the mattock and began digging in a depression next to an undercut boulder. Sweat poured from his brow, every drop an exorcism, cleansing his body of doubt and worry. Grin had made his dying wish. Tom Anderson would return to Enthilen and finish what he started twelve yarles ago. Stop Malphas by whatever means necessary.

Tom dug until sweat soaked his shorts and t-shirt, his back ached, and the late afternoon sun dipped below the ridgeline of the rocky scrub. After excavating a shallow grave big enough to fit a grell, he knelt and braced the soles of his sneakers against a boulder, wedging his arms under Grin's back. Tom heaved, forearm muscles straining with Grin's weight, until the giant body fell into the grave, arms and legs landing akimbo against the bumpy, dry clay. Tom stepped into the hole, straightened Grin's legs and placed his arms folded across his chest, then reached for the dented shovel, clutching the wooden handle so tight his knucklebones threatened to burst through the skin.

He covered his friend's body with rust-coloured soil and bid farewell. "*Yanhanhadhu* Grin. Your sacrifice will be honoured. I'm not running away anymore. I'm going to fight with everything I have left."

Tom flattened the soil and scattered leaf litter and rocks over the grave to make it blend into the surroundings. As the sun set, he finished the last of his water, then fossicked inside the backpack until laying a hand on the eyes of lost souls. He set his mind on finding his grandmother. Jean Anderson, the draughoul.

Tom held the dark eyes aloft as if they might act as a megaphone, blasting out a call for Jean across the scrub and beyond. *It might work. Draughouls are drawn to the eyes.* He stumbled about in the waning light; his arm stretched high like an antenna. Climbed onto the most enormous boulder he could find. Walked further up the ridge. Thought about climbing a tree. Almost gave up. Until.

Near the stand of she-oaks where he'd buried Grin, a frail, flickering shape appeared. Tom trotted down the ridge, dodging among the boulders and trees until arriving back where he'd left the shovel and mattock. Nanna stood beside Grin's grave, waiting for Tom as if she'd always been there.

She turned her gaunt, ghostly face towards him. "The eyes, Tommy."

"Nanna?"

The sight of his loving grandmother turned into a draughoul tied knots of shame inside Tom's stomach. He had pitied Widukind's mother, Fullō, as she toiled amid the repression of the bleak house in Bindari, a draughoul servant waiting on her son's every need. Yet, Fullō had led Tom and Princess Caeli on a magical journey through stone and soil, forging a bond between him and Enthilen that could never be shaken.

A draughoul's life isn't always pitiful. Maybe Nanna can use secret paths to travel around this landscape like draughouls do in Enthilen?

Jean reached out her bony, translucent hand. "Let me hold the eyes."

Tom hesitated for a moment before placing the dark eyes in her palm.

She held them close, the flaming pupils' glimmer lightening the ridges of her wrinkled face. "So long ago," she whispered.

A mayhem of questions clattered inside Tom's head. "Why didn't you talk to me before? When I was younger. You know I saw you."

Jean never took her eyes off the obsidian gems sitting on her palm. "Too much to bear for a lonely child."

Tom clenched his jaw. "I could have handled it. You could have shown them...."

"What?" Jean lifted her face.

"That you were...*ah*, you're right, it would have made it worse. How could we explain any of it?"

She handed the eyes back to Tom, and he wrapped them up in his right fist.

A faint smile lifted the sombre folds of skin on Jean's face. "Poor little Tommy."

"Who did this to you, Nanna? Was it Malphas? He might have called himself Oldaric back then. When he burst into my bedroom right before he attacked you, I remember he said, 'I'm sorry, Jean.' He was remorseful. That doesn't sound like Malphas. And he knew your name. Did you know him?"

"Oldaric was not the man who took my soul."

Tom clutched his grandmother's hand. "Then who? I must know. I want to fix this."

Jean turned away as if trying to avoid Tom's questions. "Why did you call me here?" she asked.

"Blood and bone, destroy the throne. I'm supposed to...to take a piece of bone from you. Only a small piece. I need it to destroy the throne of the dead. To end Malphas' reign."

"Will it work?"

I don't know. Tom accepted what Grin told him and assumed Dwarrow would fill in the gaps. "All I have is the belief that it will."

Jean nodded, drifted over to Grin's grave, made the sign of the cross, and then grasped the mattock near the collar of the steel blade. Placing her free hand on a rock, index finger lying flat and extended, she lifted the mattock above her head. Jean wailed like a stone-curlew, smashing the blade onto her finger.

Crack!

Broken clean off, the digit rolled into the dirt. She dropped the mattock, crouched and collected her amputated finger.

"I have made my sacrifice," she said, handing the digit to Tom. "Now, you must make yours."

Grief, confusion and anger swirled around Tom's mind. "Tell me what you know."

Jean caressed his cheek with the bloodless stump of her finger. "Tommy, give love purpose." She turned away and vanished into the folds of dusk.

Tom called after her. "Wait! Don't leave. I still don't understand...I... still...I still miss you."

But Jean Anderson didn't return, leaving Tom alone to face the night. He placed the finger bone into his backpack with the other treasures, then shouldered his pack. He thought about getting water and food but worried that if he left this little patch of bush, he'd never travel to Enthilen. Never honour Grin's sacrifice. Never try to help the people he'd abandoned twelve yarles ago. The temptation to keep running away would be too great.

Tom took a deep breath and placed one dark eye in each hand, nestling the cold, black glass into the scars seared into his palms from the first journey to Enthilen. He clenched his fingers into a cage, but they froze as if resisting the final closure. As if understanding what this would mean — leaving home forever. He'd have to push through with every ounce of courage in his body to fight the doubt.

~ Chapter 7 ~

In Pergamos' throne hall, Mirrian knelt on the flagstone floor and scrubbed away the dirt between the joins with a brush made from coarse undred fur. Murky, tepid water oozed from the bristles, soaking through the hem of her dress and into the open sores on her knees. The bones on the back of her hands formed tired ridges under loose skin as she forced the brush back and forth. Eleven harvest seasons a grell slave; she didn't expect to see a twelfth.

Mirrian stopped for a breath and lifted her head to the throne hall's ceiling. One of the few underground rooms to be rebuilt after the devastation of Volerdie's Wrath, her pulse often raced inside the hall, waiting for a crack to appear in the plaster or a bust to begin swaying to and fro before crashing to the ground. The earth would quake again one day. She didn't want to be inside this room when it happened.

One section of the floor finished; Mirrian tossed the brush into a wooden bucket and tried to stand. Halfway up, a knot tightened in her chest as if someone squeezed her heart in their fist. As the room went black, she collapsed to the floor, but her mind fell further, tumbling into a hole with smooth sides like a well. At the bottom, Mirrian's mind reached into the darkness of her contemplation, grasping at a tiny creature lying motionless beside her. Cupping the animal in her hand, she brought it to her face as a light shone from above to reveal the mystery; the lifeless body of a ground spider perished in its lair.

Muwin, the ground spider. Her son Grin's facial crest.

This vision is an omen, thought Mirrian.

Except, she lost her son seasons ago. She witnessed his ruin. She *contributed* to it. The transformation of Grin into the white grell.

* * * *

"Keep stirrin', Slug," said Henruld. "Yur slower dan yur namesake."

Slouched on a wooden stool in the corner of the room, Henruld, Mirrian's overseer, scowled at her while she used a wooden paddle to stir a concoction of white liquid bubbling inside a cauldron perched on a nest of fiery coals.

"We gained favour with da Worshipful Master," said Henruld. "He don't just let anybody into his private chambers. If y'do a good job 'ere, who knows?"

The door to the room opened, and Henruld jumped to his feet. Malphas walked in holding a silver goblet in his left hand and grinning like a child who'd discovered a stash of sticky treats.

Henruld knelt and bowed his head. "Worshipful Master."

"Get up, Henruld," said Malphas. "Leave me alone with the slave."

"Right y'are, Worshipful Master. If dere's anythin' else...."

Malphas waved the overseer away before stepping towards Mirrian. "I've extracted the ölblut from the throne of the dead. Come see."

She rested the wooden paddle against the cauldron and faced Malphas. He tipped the goblet towards her. A thick, mahogany-coloured liquid resembling rancid syrup threatened to ooze from the silverware.

Malphas cackled. "It's amazing. I discovered the ölblut by chance. Stabbed the dead throne's armrest with my knife and out seeped this discharge. I guess you could call it the blood of the dead. I thought it was poison at first. But then... then I consulted the First Scripture and learned of its true power." Malphas held the goblet above the cauldron. "Take the paddle, Slug. Begin stirring, and don't stop until I say."

Mirrian grasped the paddle and swished the white into a swirling vortex.

Malphas' eyes widened as he tipped the goblet sideways and waited. "Very slow. Very slow. Here it comes."

The viscous liquid trickled from the cup and dripped into the seething white below, causing a plume of ashen-grey vapour to explode into the air.

Malphas shielded his face with his free hand. "The ölblut transforms the mixture's properties. When we apply the white paste to the skin, it will bind with the flesh. Become part of the creature's body. Forever taint it." Malphas placed the empty goblet on his bedside table, then flashed a cruel smile at Mirrian. "Keep stirring, Slug. Make sure the ölblut is mixed through the entire batch. We have a lot of grell to cover."

Bile rose in the back of Mirrian's throat. An acerbic reminder she was helping to make a potion to taint an innocent grell. To turn a poor soul into the next white grell. Her shoulders ached with the burden of complicity.

"What an honour this is for you," said Malphas. "Not only will you see the tainting of a grell, you will participate in the ceremony. And, Mirrian...."

She flinched at the use of her real name.

"...you will bear witness to the transformation of your own son."

Mirrian dropped the paddle and faced her tormentor. "Grin?"

Malphas smiled. "Not anymore. He will take the name Eroberung like his predecessor."

Inside the cauldron, a boil of white liquid exploded, spewing a stinging taint onto Mirrian's cheek. "No," she growled. "I will not let it happen." She charged at Malphas with a wild fury. Wrapping her arms around his chest, she lifted him from the floor and threw him onto the flagstones like a sack of grain.

He lay there, laughing. "You can't harm me. Don't waste your energy. We need you for the ceremony."

Mirrian sneered. "I will not help you. Free my son, or I will tear this kingdom apart."

"Don't be a fool, Mirrian. I have much grander plans for you." Malphas turned to the door and yelled, "Guard!"

A Rephaim soldier, a traitor grell, stepped inside Malphas' chamber.

Malphas stood, brushed the dirt from his robes, then addressed the guard, "Douse the coals and let the potion cool. Then we will be ready." Malphas faced Mirrian. "When did you last see your son, Mirrian? Before the massacre of Malang Gunya? Such a long time ago, and such painful memories for you. Your husband died in the massacre. Your daughter suffers the pitiful fate of all those who refuse to take shelter in Pergamos and worship the Divine Creator. Your son is all you have left. He is proving resistant, but I have almost broken him. He needs only a modicum of encouragement to make the final transformation. That's where you come in, Mirrian. What would Grin do to save his mother? I might allow you to apply the taint to his skin. What a proud moment that would be for mother and son."

* * * *

The smack of boots on flagstones woke Mirrian from her anguish. As two Rephaim marched into the hall, she sat up and began scrubbing again. Malphas followed the grell soldiers, pulling a two-wheeled, flatbed cart with the legless body of a draughoul perched on its tray. The soulless creature swivelled her head to gaze at Mirrian, then turned away as Malphas yanked the cart to the dining table. He balanced the cart handle on a chair, the draughoul taking her place as his macabre dinner guest for the evening.

Mirrian grasped the bucket's handle and stood, hoping to escape Malphas' attention by retreating to the slave quarters above ground. As she turned for the door, he cleared his throat.

"Mirrian," said Malphas. "You will join us this evening."

She halted so suddenly the water in the bucket sloshed over the side and spilled onto the flagstones. As she knelt to mop it up, Malphas stopped her again.

"Leave that," he said. "Another slave can deal with it. Come and sit with us."

Timorous expectation tingled across Mirrian's skin. Lately, for reasons she couldn't fathom, Malphas had taken an interest in her. Spoken to her more often and allowed her to forgo certain tasks. Gave her more freedom. Sometimes, even asked her opinion.

She placed the bucket on the floor, turned and walked to the table, standing beside the legless and soulless draughoul.

"Sit," said Malphas. "Please."

Mirrian pulled out a chair, solid timber carved from a panalope tree and polished to such a lustrous sheen the flames of the candles in the chandeliers hanging from the hall's ceiling sparkled across the mirroring wood. Sinking into the padded seat, she avoided Malphas' gaze and focussed her attention on the top of the dining table.

Two grell slaves lumbered into the room carrying trays of food and drink. Carian, a stern male stone-grell, and Julan, a kindly female weald-grell. Mirrian nodded an acknowledgement to her companions in bondage. She'd shared living quarters with them for many seasons. They were her friends.

Mirrian's mouth salivated at the aroma of stewed deer meat and freshly baked bread as Carian placed a tray on the table. Julan sat a silver goblet next to Mirrian and poured meduz from a pitcher while Carian arranged the place settings.

"No," snapped Malphas as Carian put an empty plate beside the draughoul. "Draughouls don't eat."

Carian bowed and placed the plate in front of Mirrian. She faced him and mouthed the words 'thank you' but shrank under the withering hate burning in his lilac eyes. Here she was, dining with the grells' most reviled oppressor. Here she was, another deserter twisting a treacherous knife into festering wounds. Her hunger abated as she devoured the guilt.

After serving Malphas, Julan slopped a scoop of stew onto Mirrian's plate, rested the empty ladle against the pot sitting on the table and stepped away. Mirrian picked up a spoon and dipped it into the stew.

"Wait," said Malphas to Mirrian before glaring at Julan.

The slave stepped forward, ripped a chunk of bread from a loaf and dunked it in Mirrian's stew. She never took her eyes off Mirrian as she placed the soaked bread into her mouth and chewed.

Poison, thought Mirrian. Julan, her friend, is testing the food for poison.

While it couldn't kill the immortal Malphas, it would undoubtedly end the life of a grell slave. Mirrian wanted to jump up and rip the bread from Julan's mouth, but the threat of Malphas' anger fixed her to the chair.

Julan stepped closer to Mirrian to make sure bearing the guilt of her death would be inescapable.

"We must wait for a moment," said Malphas. "Some poisons are slow to act. We can't use Mother to test for the venom of traitors. Poison doesn't affect draughouls."

Mirrian tore her eyes from Julan's damning stare and faced Malphas.

Mother? she thought. Is this draughoul your....

"Yes," said Malphas, tilting his head towards the legless torso. "This pathetic creature was once my mother. A queen of Enthilen no less. Queen Sigilind. She calls herself Fullō now. Well, she did. Until I cut out her tongue."

Mirrian thought she could sit here in silence until the charade ended. Endure Malphas' prattles and steal a few mouthfuls of food before returning to the slave quarters. But his revelations, as disturbing as they were, had a habit of drawing her in. Forcing her to engage.

Carian took a sip from Mirrian's goblet of meduz, saving Julan from further risk, then stood at her side, the two slaves bearing witness to this engagement.

Mirrian could have kept her tongue but decided to confront Malphas, attempting to save face with her friends. "How did a queen of Enthilen become a draughoul?" she asked.

He shrugged. "I doubt it will surprise you to learn that I did it. Captured her soul with the dark eyes."

Mirrian tried to snarl. "Why would you do such a thing?"

Malphas scooped up a spoonful of stew, hovered it near his lips to blow off some of the heat, then placed it into his mouth. "*Uhmm.* This stew is tasty. You know, Mirrian, an immortal doesn't need food to survive. Yes, I still hunger and enjoy the meal's social ritual, but I could learn to tame the impulses without consequence. Knowing those around you will perish while you live on is an odd burden. I can see how it would drive lesser men mad."

Mirrian wouldn't let the misdirection foil her. "Are you ashamed? Turning your own mother into a draughoul."

Malphas put down his spoon and took a sip of meduz. "Do you really want to talk about shame after what you did to your son?"

Anger seethed inside Mirrian's mind. You made me do it. You gave me no option.

Malphas waved Carian and Julan away, the pair staying long enough to expose an attempt to poison Pergamos' ruler, as futile as such an attempt would be.

The slaves strode from the throne hall. Mirrian would talk to them later. Explain herself and win back their trust.

As the throne room door closed, Malphas sought Mirrian's eyes. "My mother had four sons. Four chances to be the mother of Enthilen's next king. The two youngest, Alfwin and Colobert, were twins, both born with smiles and a gleam in their eyes. Mother doted on them as if she understood they would be the last of her offspring. Never left them alone for a moment. Forwent all her royal duties to raise them without the help of servants. You see, Mirrian, twins are cherished in Erstürmen culture.

"One day, my other brother, Widukind, succumbed to a crippling illness that saw him bedridden and teetering at the edge of his grave. The threat of Widukind's imminent death drew Mother away from the infant twins, her time spent sitting at his bedside. But she wouldn't agree to servants caring for Alfwin and Colobert. No, that responsibility fell to me, her eldest son. Eldest, but not old. I had seen only ten harvest seasons. Yet, Mother placed all her faith and hope in me, and I failed her. There was an accident...." Malphas fell silent and bowed his head.

Sitting opposite the old man, Mirrian couldn't avoid the grind of emotions spreading across his face. Something stirred inside her she never expected; sorrow for the Worshipful Master. Most frighteningly, the sorrow was blameless. Mirrian expected a reaction from Fullō, the draughoul. A trace of sympathy. But Malphas' mother stared straight ahead with a blank face. Mirrian wondered if Fullō could speak without a tongue and what she might say.

Malphas released a sigh of exaggerated burden.

Mirrian shook the sympathy from her mind. This is a ruse, she thought. A tale designed to elicit pity. Resist the deception.

"Two harvest seasons," said Malphas. "My twin brothers died after seeing only two harvest seasons. Mother blamed me for the fire, despite barely escaping the room with my own life. Why didn't she blame Widukind? After all, his illness dragged her away from those she loved the most. But no, I was the locus of her grief. The sacrifice to her anger. Widukind then became the only son she truly loved."

"That does not excuse what you did," spat Mirrian in a defiant burst.

Unexpectedly, Malphas acquiesced. "You're right. It doesn't. Though, if you understood the larger picture, you might decide otherwise. By taking my mother's soul, I became confident I could capture the soul of my birth twin. Not let indecision or pity stifle my actions. Quell the fear of the anguish that wracks your body and mind from such an act. When I found my birth twin in a world called Earth, I took his soul without hesitation and began the journey that will eventually see Volerdie return to Enthilen. So, Mirrian, Mother became a vital cog in a much grander ambition."

Fullō opened her mouth and tried to speak, but the words became lost in a jumble of defiant moans. Then, from the pit of the draughoul's throat came a haunting bawl that chilled Mirrian's bones.

When the cry ended, Malphas faced Mirrian again. "In the absence of affection, the mother-son relationship can be harrowing. You must understand this, Mirrian, having had a son of your own."

Mirrian shook her head. "You know nothing about my relationship with Grin. You could never know."

"Grin, *Eroberung*, has disappeared."

A lump caught in Mirrian's throat. Had Grin escaped? she wondered. Had he managed to avoid the fate Malphas planned for him? The unimaginable distress of being the next white grell.

Malphas picked a piece of gristle from between his teeth, then studied the morsel balanced on his fingertip. "Do you know where he is, Mirrian?"

She growled through gritted teeth, "I lost my son when you tainted his skin. I never spoke to him after that, but I hope he has fled, away from this evil place."

"*Hmmm*. I expect he may be hiding in what remains of that awful forest to the south. All the more reason to burn it down."

Mirrian thought back to her premonition; muwin, the ground spider, perished in his lair. If Grin had escaped Pergamos, she feared he may not have survived the journey to freedom.

Malphas sighed. "I have an ache in my mind, telling me Fullō's arrival in Pergamos is somehow connected to Eroberung's disappearance, and my pitiful brother, Widukind, is behind it all. Mother betrayed me at his command, and she refuses to divulge his secrets. However, Widukind wouldn't send Fullō into Pergamos unless it was critically important."

Why is Malphas telling me this? she thought.

"Now you have lost everything, Mirrian, I expect you wish you were dead. Anything other than serving me. I sometimes wonder why you haven't killed yourself already."

Mirrian glared at the old man. "It is against grell culture to take your own life."

Malphas scoffed. "How ironic. You refuse suicide because of your culture's dictates, yet your culture has died around you. The punishment of watching grell society disappear while you still linger must be a dreadful hardship."

Mirrian turned away and fidgeted with the sleeve of her slave dress, growing tired of the encounter.

Malphas gulped the remaining meduz from his silver goblet, letting the froth dribble from the crooked furrows at the corners of his mouth, then smacked the bottom of the empty cup onto the table.

Mirrian jumped, and Malphas caught her attention again.

"Ende is dying," he said. "She never fully recovered from the cowardly attack by the rebel woman when Volerdie's Wrath descended on us twelve yarles ago. To be honest, I'm surprised Ende has lasted this long. Her desire to remain my servant keeps her alive, but it won't be long before she takes her last breath."

Malphas stood and walked to the end of the table to stand beside Mirrian. He reached down and grabbed her wrist. She tried to pull away, but his fingers set like a steel cage.

"The pale grell won't see another harvest season," said Malphas. "I need a new confidant, Mirrian. A new Ende. I need you."

* * * *

Nettie Barron stood in line with her father, Yonna, waiting to enter the kirika in Pergamos. A hot, gusty breeze ruffled her hair, and sweat trickled between her breasts, forming damp, dirty blotches on the front of her tunic. The restless crowd behind her inched forward, forcing Nettie up against the back of a tall man who waited in front. She squeezed her torso from the crush to look ahead, past the hundreds of people lined up in front. The massive oak doors to the kirika remained closed. The building could seat a thousand, but Nettie worried she and Yonna might be too far back in the line to secure a place.

Should have arrived at dawn, she thought, jostling her way back to her father's side.

The line moved a few paces forward, and Nettie stepped into the shadow of the pyramid towering over Pergamos, giving her respite from the beating sun. Some said the stone-grells built the monument many generations ago when they called this city Malang Gunya. She'd always wanted to climb to the pyramid's summit. When she and Yonna first arrived in Pergamos, she was only six harvest seasons old, too young to tackle the three hundred giant steps to the top.

But I could climb them now easy enough, she thought, after sneaking past the guards watching the stairs day and night.

As if he'd read her mind, a soldier guarding the pyramid turned to Nettie and cast a gaze of statuesque judgement. He wore the Master's Shield armour; the traditional Erstürmen spangenhelm, pauldrons, rerebraces, tassets, cuisses, sabatons and gauntlets, all polished silver with black inserts. She knew the armour well, having helped Yonna make suits of it in the smithy. That's all he made now. Armour and weapons for the military. No jewellery or cutlery or brass lanterns. No trinkets. Only the chattels of war. Nettie had been his apprentice since her older sister, Rosalie, ran out on the family twelve yarles ago back in Sardis.

The soldier stepped towards Nettie, and the sun glinted off his breastplate, the metal embossed with the two-headed snake curled into an incomplete circle, a renowned symbol in Erstürmen history. Within the circle, a new insignia had been added; the image of a sun, its rays reaching out to touch two orbiting eyes with flaming pupils. Malphas, the Worshipful Master and ruler of Enthilen, had introduced the design. Only *his* Shield, his elite soldiers, wore this armour, and one of them marched straight for Nettie.

The kirika bell tolled from its tower, and the people around Nettie rushed forward, carrying her along like a twig in a river. She shrank into the crowd, thankful for inheriting her father's physique; short and slight — easy to hide from a soldier's searching gaze.

"They've opened the doors," said Yonna, flashing a smile.

Nettie glanced behind her and smiled, too, the soldier's threat drowning amid the flood of worshippers.

The line pushed forward. Nettie stepped from the pyramid's shadow and back into the harsh sun. She took a square of beige cotton from her pants pocket and tied it into a kerchief to protect her head and neck. The growing season's hot days would soon end as Enthilen moved into the milder climes of the harvest season.

Yonna's smile broadened as they approached the kirika entrance. "We'll get in. I wish they'd stop ringing that damn bell. There are already too many people here."

Nettie never begrudged Yonna his devout pleasures. Her father rarely smiled anymore. Yet, today his joy appeared to enliven the crowd as the kirika façade loomed ahead.

"Praise Volerdie," a woman near Nettie whispered, a tear trickling down her cheek.

"Blessed be the Worshipful Master," said a man. "Only he could build such a magnificent temple."

It is magnificent, thought Nettie.

Six sandstone spires topped with gargoyles, and resembling columns of twisted honeycomb, ringed an enormous belltower almost as tall as the stepped pyramid. An ogee arch shadowed the main doors into the kirika, its pointed top twice the height of a grell. Fired clay sculpted as stalactites lined the archway inside such that it resembled the entrance to a cave or the mouth of a voracious beast. The building fanned out left and right into identical half circles, with hundreds of windows resembling the scales of a serpent. Nettie had never heard of a kirika being built above ground, but the fear of another wave of Volerdie's Wrath meant Pergamos' citizens refused to worship in a place that resembled a tomb.

Nettie and Yonna stopped at the front doors and bowed their heads to the Heilig-jün, twenty-four old men dressed in white robes and holding a copy of the scripture verses at their waist, the holy book encapsulating the word of Volerdie. The Heilig-jün served Anselm, the Hoch-Vater of Enthilen, and, as far as Nettie knew, attended every homily held in the kirika's chapel. Sermons ran day and night, so no citizen could excuse themselves from the pontifications delivered by a growing lechery of curates. On special occasions, Anselm would deliver the exhortation, his voice booming through the chapel's pillars that held the vaulted ceiling aloft, embedding words of reverence and sacrifice into the minds of the faithful.

Yonna reached inside a satchel slung over his shoulder and withdrew bread, cheese and vegetables tied in a cloth. He placed the offering in a wicker chest beside the Heilig-jün.

"Let darkness descend," said one of the holy men.

"And engulf us all," Nettie replied. "For in the darkness, Volerdie will reveal his paradise."

Yonna grabbed Nettie's arm, disrupting her moment of thanksgiving, and dragged her into the narthex leading to the chapel.

"Find a good seat," he said. "Rumour is, Anselm will give the sermon today."

A special occasion indeed, thought Nettie. No doubt, the promise of Anselm's words fed the crowd's longing.

The chapel was already half-full when Nettie and Yonna stepped inside. He rushed her past rows and rows of empty pews into the middle of the cavernous room, as close as possible to the pulpit. They slid onto the end of a timber bench near the aisle, sitting beside a plump man and woman with spotless clothes of fine silk stitched with tight, perfect seams.

Residents of one of Pergamos' better neighbourhoods, thought Nettie. Inside the kirika, a person's origins or fancy clothes don't matter. Volerdie's paradise has room for all believers.

"Volerdie's mercy," said the man, tugging the cuffs of his preened white shirt towards soft, pale hands.

"Let the door to paradise open," replied Yonna.

As the chapel filled, Nettie focussed on the pentagonal floor tiles and began the silent prayer she always recited before the sermon. A prayer for her departed mother, Heady, and two brothers, Allum and Petas, all of whom died over ten yarles ago from The Ravage, a crippling disease that spread through Sardis and much of Enthilen. Allum died in their old home in Sardis' fifth circle, while Heady and Petas perished during the journey to Pergamos.

Nettie also prayed for her big sister, Rosalie. If she hadn't already succumbed to The Ravage or another misadventure, Rosalie would turn thirty on the first day of the coming harvest season. Now, more than ever, Nettie wondered what had happened to her sister. After attacking a soldier in Sardis, Rosalie fled from the fifth circle and never returned to her family. Nettie wanted to believe she still lived somewhere in Enthilen. Still thrived.

She reached inside the collar of her tunic and fingered the necklace of interlocking bronze circlets Rosalie had given her on the day she left Sardis. The rose-coloured glass set in the spiral pendant pressed against the top of her chest and cooled her skin.

Rosalie would hate all this, thought Nettie. She never liked chapel.

Shouts came from the back of the room as soldiers slammed the chapel doors closed despite the howls of protest from those locked outside. Every seat inside was taken, the crowd bubbling with virtuous energy. As far as Nettie knew, everyone in Pergamos attended chapel. She'd never met anyone who didn't or at least would admit to it.

Rosalie would hate Pergamos, too, thought Nettie.

Three levits, two boys and a girl, walked onto the stage. The girl placed candelabra on a table beside the altar while the boys put a dozen golden urns at the front of the stage. Then the levits disappeared behind black curtains, and the crowd stilled. The Heilig-jün filed onto the stage from a side door, chanting a prayer with every pious step. Twelve old men took seats at the rear of the stage while the other twelve collected the metal urns and walked into the crowd of parishioners. The Heilig-jün dipped their fingers into the open urns and dusted the gathering with ash, the cremated remains of people who had sacrificed their lives to entice Volerdie to return when darkness descended.

Nettie pulled the kerchief off her head and leaned into the aisle to make sure a Heilig-jün saw her when he passed. A hand disappeared inside an urn and reappeared above her, the holy man rubbing his thumb across his fingers, sprinkling ash onto her scalp. Nettie swore she felt every sacred particle landing on her skin and offered a silent prayer to the Divine Creator for his kindness, hoping the powder of the blessed oblation would show against her blonde hair to proclaim her devotion to anyone who cared to look.

With the urns empty, the Heilig-jün ended their chant, and the chapel fell silent, Nettie imagining Volerdie's murmurs of approval as he watched over proceedings. A hand reached through the gap in the curtains and pulled them across. The congregation stood as one when Anselm stumbled onto the stage and shuffled to the pulpit on bowed legs, his sangria robes trailing across the polished floorboards. Enthilen's Hoch-Vater appeared to have aged since last Nettie had seen him. Even from this distance, she could count the wrinkles on his withered face, framed by unruly wisps of grey hair extending past his shoulders. He climbed the stairs to the pulpit, the timber panelling at the front carved with a scene of prostrate worshippers bowing before Volerdie's merciful judgement, and placed a copy of the scripture verses atop the lectern. From Nettie's vantage point, only Anselm's forehead was visible above the pulpit. It looked ridiculous, and she masked a smile with her hand lest a zealot denounced her for heresy.

A levit burst through the curtains, carrying a tread board, and raced to the pulpit and up the stairs. After a brief ruckus, Anselm stepped onto the tread board to offer his face to the flock.

That's better, thought Nettie, welcoming the virtue in his eyes.

The Hoch-Vater cleared his throat and squawked, "Let darkness descend."

"And engulf us all," the congregation replied in unison.

"For in the darkness, Volerdie will reveal his paradise. Sit, please."

Everyone sat. A hopeful Nettie willed the curtains at the back of the stage to open again. She wanted the levits to return, carrying copies of the scripture verses to hand to the crowd so the faithful could follow the sermon. She'd heard the story from Sardis. Once, Anselm had allowed his congregation to read the scripture verses. Actually *read* them. Yonna argued it never happened, the story a lie. Only curates and the Heilig-jün were permitted to read the verses. Nettie hoped Yonna was wrong.

"As always, I begin my sermon by reading Volerdie's words," said Anselm, holding the scripture verses aloft. "Page one hundred and forty-four, verse six: six. Volerdie wrote, *Rid the land of non-believers. Scrub the unfaithful from the mountains and plains like dirt is washed from skin. Make clean my home before I return. No barrier should remain that blocks the door to paradise. No barricade to impede our progress. Dust from the bones of unbelievers will seal the path of our redemption as we walk together into a glorious future.*"

Anselm lowered the book and placed it back onto the lectern.

"Praise Volerdie," came a shout from the crowd.

Anselm held up his palm. "Praise him, indeed. In the coming days, we, the loyal citizens of Pergamos, will face many challenges. Heathens and unbelievers still poison Enthilen's soil, behind the walls of Gestade and in the slums of Giigal. They suck the life from our land as a leech steals blood. Only when the Worshipful Master has disposed of these vermin can we be certain of Volerdie's return. But the master cannot complete this task alone. We all must sacrifice to secure our place in paradise."

Nettie drifted with Anselm's words. In recent times, the curates' sermons followed a familiar theme, and the Hoch-Vater offered nothing different today. Always a new task needed to be completed before Enthilen would be ready to accept Volerdie again. The purging of unbelievers from Gestade and Giigal dominated the current discourse. Throughout Pergamos, printed notices had been pinned to walls and doors, proclaiming the danger emanating from the outpost of Gestade. Nettie expected Malphas' soldiers to soon march to war. Only together could the Erstürmen people hope to overcome the obstacles keeping paradise at bay. Attack or be attacked. Cleanse or be cleansed.

"Volerdie is almost with us," continued Anselm. "Can you feel it?"

"Yes," shouted some in the crowd.

"He observes every moment of our lives. Measures the breaths we take. Listens to every word we speak, judging our eagerness for his return. Our *worthiness*. Are we eager?"

"Yes!" cried Nettie.

"Are we worthy?"

"Yes!"

"Are we prepared to enter Volerdie's paradise?"

"YES!" yelled the crowd as one.

"We must prove it," said Anselm. "The temple is ready for another sacrifice. Who will offer themselves to Volerdie?"

Nettie started as people around her sprang to their feet in response to Anselm's request. Yonna jumped from his seat, waving and yelling, demanding the Hoch-Vater choose him as the next offering.

Sit down, thought Nettie.

Being chosen as Volerdie's sacrifice was a privilege, but she needed her father.

Anselm pointed into the front rows, and a Heilig-jün pulled an old woman from the bevy of willing parishioners. Delirious with gratitude, the woman howled and threw herself to her knees in front of the pulpit before the Heilig-jün guided her from the chapel. The sacrifice would occur outside, in the open, circular temple at the pyramid's base, so as many citizens as possible could witness the glorious aflammation.

Yonna slumped onto the pew, his face riven with disappointment.

Inside Nettie's head, her father declared, 'That's why we must sit closer to the stage.'

Anselm's sermon continued, but Nettie directed her thoughts to the upcoming harvest season. On the first day of the season, every Erstürmen would become a yarle older, this being Nettie's eighteenth harvest season. She worried Yonna may force her to marry. Expel her from their modest home to find a husband and start a family. Stop her from working in the smithy, as he'd done with Rosalie back in Sardis. None of this appealed to her, but she had no plan for a different future. No idea what she might do with the rest of her life other than forge metal.

The sermon ended. Anselm disappeared behind the black curtains, followed by his faithful Heilig-jün. Nettie and Yonna joined the other parishioners as they filed from the kirika. They stopped in the narthex as noise from a commotion outside filtered in through the central doorway. A woman bawled and cursed, followed by shouts from a male voice.

"We're taking him," said the male.

Yonna glanced at Nettie and frowned. "Nothing to worry about," he said. "Likely a blasphemous heathen."

They reached the front door where soldiers from the Master's Shield stood on either side as if farewelling the parishioners. Nettie's heart skipped when the guard who'd stared at her from the pyramid's base stepped in front of Yonna.

"Hail, Malphas," said the soldier.

"Hail, Malphas," replied Yonna, placing his right fist against his chest.

"Is this your daughter?" asked the Shield, tilting his head towards Nettie.

"Yes. She works with me as a metalsmith. We make armour and weapons for the Worshipful Master's army. I can't do without her."

"How old is she?"

"Eighteen this harvest season."

The soldier took his hand from the grip of his sheathed sword and grabbed Nettie's bicep, the leather on the palm of his gauntlet prickling her skin. "She looks strong. Can she wield a sword?"

"She's had no need to," said Yonna.

The Shield released his grip, and Nettie rubbed her arm, expecting a bruise to show.

"We have a need now," said the soldier. "She's coming with me."

He grasped Nettie's forearm and dragged her away. Behind her, another young man was pulled from the crowd, his mother begging the soldier to reconsider.

Nettie yanked back, pushing the soles of her boots into the flagstones. "I want to stay with my father. He needs me."

But the Shield was much too strong for Nettie to resist.

Yonna walked behind them, pleading his case, "The Erstürmen have never had female soldiers. It's against our culture."

"The Worshipful Master is building a bigger army," said the soldier. "Anyone over fourteen harvest seasons old is eligible to fight."

Yonna wrapped his wiry fingers around the Shield's vambrace and yanked downwards, momentarily freeing Nettie.

"Please, no," said Yonna. "She's all I have left. My only family. Please."

The soldier snarled and backhanded Yonna across the face, the slap of metal on skin ringing in the air. He grabbed Nettie again as another Shield stood in front of Yonna with a halberd clutched across his chest. Yonna dropped to his knees, tears flowing down his cheeks. Nettie had never seen her father cry, not even when his wife died.

"Papa!" she yelled, trying to pull back against the soldier.

The Shield kicked her legs out from under her and dragged her along the ground. "You'll have to put on weight before we march to war."

Yonna prostrated himself and lay his withering body over the flagstones. Nettie imagined his prayers to Volerdie, pleading for the Divine Creator to intervene and change the fortunes of two of his most devoted followers.

"Papa!" she yelled again, but he didn't look up, engrossed in his prayer.

They had only each other. Now they'd been torn apart, Nettie wondered who would die first. Who would succumb to the yearning caused by familial disintegration?

~ Chapter 8 ~

"I'm too old for this!" Bathed in sweat, Lily LáDown collapsed naked onto the bed beside her lover, Hartmut Adelmund, inside their private quarters in Gestade.

"Then we should do it as much as possible before our bodies give up," said Hartmut, his beaming smile framed with prickly stubble.

"How much energy do you have, Commander?" Lily laughed, sat up and straddled her lover's waist again.

Hartmut grasped Lily's hands. "I need at least a moment of rest. Otherwise, you'll kill me before Malphas' hordes ever arrive."

"Ha," said Lily, "a Dobunni finally ends the life of the famed Mongoose of Gestade. What then would your soldiers think of you bedding the enemy?"

"Consider our regular consummations as reforging the alliance between the Erstürmen of Gestade and the Dobunni of Laodicea. Enemies never again."

"If only other alliances were as easy and as pleasurable." Lily climbed off her lover and lay beside him, resting her head on the wiry hairs of Hartmut's chest and tracing her index finger along the scar running from the front of his shoulder to the bottom of his ribs. The remnant of a battle wound most men would have died from.

"How long can we go on like this?" asked Lily. "I mean, here, in this place. How long is it all going to last?"

"Malphas has busied himself with the destruction of what remains of Enthilen and let us be for twelve yarles. But his forces will amass at our walls soon enough."

Lily rested her hand on Hartmut's taut but aging stomach muscles. "We can't defend against the hordes. Not alone. I wonder if we should make our escape while we still can."

"We have no fleet of ships to travel the Veiled Occyan. The southern forest is almost gone, and the weald-grells of Giigal cower in their city, gates and bridges impassable to all. Where can we flee to? I've never run from a fight, and I won't start now."

Lily frowned. Hartmut's stubbornness could sometimes be a boon, other times a hindrance. He should have led an evacuation of Gestade yarles ago, but many Erstürmen residents refused to go, and he refused to abandon them. So, the commander would make a stand here, whatever the cost.

He brushed Lily's hair from her shoulders, tangling his fingers in the greying locks. "Do *you* want to leave?"

She sighed. "Merchant ships could take the children and elderly to islands off Enthilen's east coast. At least we could save them."

"That would cost coin, better spent on securing food for a siege."

"I've never regretted fleeing Laodicea after the barbarian attack. It was the right decision. But now…I don't know what to do." She sat up and pulled her knees into her chest. "I can't stand the waiting. Sitting here pretending our future will be the same as our past. Living a lie. Biding time. If we can't leave, we should ride out to meet the enemy when they come. Face death head-on. If the end is nigh, then let it be glorious."

Hartmut caressed the curve of her spine with a light touch. "I'm not convinced we'll find glory in haste. We should continue to hold fast behind our walls. Fight from a position of strength. There are enough stores for one or two seasons of siege if we limit the rations to one serving a day. Who knows how the future may unfold if we can hold out."

"We have no friends or allies to swoop down and save us. Where are the rescuers going to come from?"

Hartmut climbed from the bed, poured a tankard of meduz, then offered it to Lily, who shook her head. The Field Commander shrugged and emptied the mug in a single gulp. "I've sent an envoy to the weald-grells in Giigal, hoping to convince them to help us. After Gestade falls, Malphas will march his army to the weald-grell city. Nothing is more certain. If we could join forces…."

"When Giigal burns, the purification of Enthilen will be complete," said Lily. "Then Malphas will sit on his dead throne until darkness descends and the Divine Creator returns. The wait could last lifetimes."

Hartmut sat on the bed, sweat still glistening in the creases of his naked body. "All the while dealing judgement and death. Enthilen's people can't afford such a wait. Soon, they'll realise Malphas' promise of paradise is nothing more than a ruse designed to keep him in power."

"Too many Erstürmen have blind faith in the scripture verses. Why haven't you been afflicted by the same blindness?"

"I've never read the verses. Only curates are afforded the privilege. I can't trust something I'm forbidden to see. That I'm unable to interpret through my own eyes. Keeping the masses illiterate is a cornerstone of corrupt power. Ignorance begets compliance." He faced her. "Have the Dobunni ever fallen for such an elaborate diversion?"

"For the Dobunni, faith has always been a personal choice, never to be dictated by a single set of rules interpreted by others. Each person is free to find sanctity in whatever form fulfils their need for peace and prosperity. To worship any of the Gods providing guidance on the trials of life — fear, jealousy, greed, love, humility, among others. The Erstürmen never understood this. They considered us heathens."

"You're the most desirable heathen I've ever met," said Hartmut with a cheeky grin.

A warm blush spread across Lily's face, but her prurient thoughts soon turned serious. "What about the Germalians? They turned the tide in the Riverlands War. We could send someone to Portum to ask for help."

"The Riverlands War was nothing but a skirmish compared to what will rain down on us, and it's a long way across Gröz Wüste or by ship. I would send an envoy if I thought we'd receive a fair hearing and a chance of their support. But I would expect neither."

Hartmut stood, opened his closet and pulled out clothes while Lily lay back and sank into the mattress, lounging with restless thoughts. Atop the bedhead, a fly wriggled and squirmed inside the webbed sheath of a wolf-spider as the hairy arachnid spun ever tighter strands. The spider scuttled off, but Lily knew it would be back to slowly suck the life from the hapless fly. In such circumstances, she expected death was a welcome release after the anguish of the wait. The agonisingly slow demise of hope.

Gestade's people, the refugees from the barbarian attack on Laodicea and the gracious citizens who'd taken them in, had waited twelve yarles for Malphas to arrive at their gates. Lily couldn't remember a day when she hadn't thought about leading her people elsewhere. But Hartmut wouldn't abandon Gestade, and Lily had fallen in love with him.

How much does that cloud my judgement? she wondered, longing for a pragmatic voice to help make decisions. A voice like Dealhia Rossingbird, her dear friend who'd died by the roadside with an Erstürmen crossbow bolt sticking from her chest.

Dressed in supple black leather, Hartmut stepped across to the bed and kissed Lily on the lips. "We should prepare for the Leadership Council meeting this afternoon," he said.

Lily smiled and nodded as Hartmut left the room.

Above the bed, the wolf-spider returned, sooner than Lily expected, bared its fangs and thrust them into the writhing fly.

*   *   *   *

In the Commander's Hall of Gestade, Lily sat at an oval-shaped table with Hartmut and Lieutenant Roben in the meeting room. Hartmut drummed his fingers on the dark, polished timber, frowning the whole time, while Roben slouched, gangly arms and legs spilling awkwardly outside the confines of the padded chair. The Lieutenant had long dispensed wearing armour to these meetings, instead donning cotton pants and a shirt. Roben preferred action over talk, telling Lily if he had to endure endless meetings, he might as well be comfortable.

She stood and strolled around the room, stopping at a shelved display of weapons, maps and other trophies secured from vanquished enemies over the outpost's long history. Is it too much to hope a trophy from Malphas might adorn the cabinet soon? thought Lily.

A rushed Yannus Rossingbird interrupted her melancholy, the stout man bursting through the door and tripping on a floor rug. An armful of parchments scattered across the woven scene of whales pulling a ship across the Veiled Occyan into a rising sun.

"Goodness, sorry," said Yannus. "Am I late again?"

Hartmut stopped drumming his fingers. "Yes, Yannus."

"There's never enough time to do everything."

Lily crouched and helped gather the parchments, smiling at Yannus and being struck at how much he resembled his mother, Dealhia. He'd inherited her physique, soft, round face and scruffy auburn hair.

"Find time for the most important things in life, Yannus," she said. "That's all that matters."

Lily and Yannus took their seats at the oval table.

Hartmut cleared his throat. "We'll start the meeting with word from Roben about our enemy's movements."

Roben nodded. "Thank you, Commander. Our scouts report an increase in military activity outside Pergamos' walls. Battalions of Erstürmen soldiers and Rephaim engaging in large-scale manoeuvres."

"Estimated numbers?" asked Hartmut.

"Twenty thousand men-at-arms, five thousand Rephaim...."

"Five thousand!"

Lily pulled the collar of her tunic away from her throat. "I didn't realise so many grells still lived."

"They'll be more," said Hartmut. "Malphas won't reveal all his forces until they're ready to march. These manoeuvres are for our benefit. He knows we're watching. He wants to scare us into submission."

"Malphas won't leave Pergamos undefended," said Lily. "We can't be sure how many soldiers he'll send."

"Enough," said Hartmut, running the thumbnail of his left hand across his lips, as he often did when in deep thought. "Continue, Lieutenant."

"Our scouts also counted an undred cavalry of over one hundred. Regular cavalry, two thousand, and war machines, the likes of which we've never seen before. Broad, flat wagons carrying trebuchets lined up three abreast, ballistae with winches that operate at lightning speed to reduce reloading times, and iron siege towers with room for hundreds of fighters. Malphas also has an enormous battering ram with a head of solid steel, fashioned as the twisted horns of a demonic goat. It swings inside a wheeled, metal frame with armour plating to defend the operators."

"Are our defences prepared for these machines?" asked Yannus.

"We've done what we can," said Roben. "Reinforced every wall. Encircled Gestade with enormous pitfall traps and trenches. Prepared trip wires."

"What about our own forces?" asked Lily. "How many can we arm to defend the outpost?"

"At a stretch, fifteen thousand. If we force the elderly and children to fight...."

Hartmut raised his hand, cutting Roben off mid-sentence. "We won't do that. Let it be known those unable or unwilling to fight are free to leave. Dorfisch is the closest town. They can take their chances there."

"Some...most won't leave their families behind," said Roben.

"Then they'll shelter here like the rest of us." A knock on the door interrupted Hartmut. He sighed and called out, "Enter."

A guard opened the door and marched into the room. "Field Commander Hartmut, a man and woman outside are demanding an immediate audience. They claim to have news of utmost importance."

Hartmut raised his eyebrows. "Who is it?"

"One of them is our cardinal healer, Audie. The other one wouldn't give his name."

Hartmut looked to Lily for guidance.

"I trust Audie," she said. "If she believes the matter is urgent, it probably is."

Hartmut nodded. "Alright, send them in."

The guard returned to the entrance hall. Lily recognised Audie's voice a moment before the healer walked into the room, followed by a man dressed in ragged clothes and reeking of tepid brine. Yet, despite the matted beard and weather-beaten face, his walnut-brown eyes glinted with entitlement.

Audie handed Hartmut a sealed letter. "I was told to give this directly to you, Commander. It's from Romilda Heine, the Queen Mother; may she rest in peace."

Hartmut's eyes widened as he rubbed his finger over the blue wax seal. After breaking the seal, he read the letter to himself, the room descending into silent anticipation. The bedraggled stranger rocked in place, almost falling over. Audie reached out and grabbed the stump of his right wrist to steady him.

The splitting leather of Hartmut's chair creaked as he leaned back and let a soft whistle escape his lips.

"Are you going to keep us in suspense all day?" asked Lily.

"The letter claims the man standing in front of us is King Adalwolf," said Hartmut. "It was signed by the Queen Mother and sealed with the royal seal. The seal and the signature appear genuine."

Roben stood, placed a hand on the pommel of his sword and faced the stranger. "Neither the Queen Mother nor the king have been seen in more than eleven harvest seasons. Some believe they were buried under the rubble of Volerdie's Wrath in Pergamos. This man is an imposter."

Maybe, thought Lily. The wavering, unkempt man standing before her *could* be Adalwolf. Why pretend to be the absent king? If...when such news reached Malphas, assassins would almost certainly be dispatched to end Adalwolf's life lest he claim Enthilen's throne. This man had placed himself in great danger.

"Do you have anything to say?" she asked the stranger.

He pulled away from Audie's supporting hand and stepped forward. "I am the deposed king. My mother's words, written on her deathbed, speak the truth."

"I can attest to that," said Audie. "I treated Romilda before the end."

Hartmut rubbed the stubble on his chin. "There is much devilry in this world. How can we be sure you haven't been deceived, Audie? Indeed, the deceit may continue now."

"No," said Lily. "I believe this man is Adalwolf."

Adalwolf held up the stump of his wrist. "My right hand was severed by a Dobunni rebel in Pergamos' throne room a moment before the world collapsed."

"That proves nothing." Roben widened his stance and gripped his sword tighter.

Hartmut stood. "I was at the naming ceremony for the infant Prince Adalwolf. I remember it as if it was yesterday. He had a mark on his left shoulder. A naevus shaped like a crescent moon."

Adalwolf swayed on unsteady legs again as if all the eyes trained upon him tugged his body to and fro.

Audie placed a hand on his shoulder. "I can help you disrobe."

He flashed a feeble smile, then held out his arms. Audie removed his woollen, black coat soiled with dirt and desiccated food. Lily placed her hand under her nose to block the less-than-regal smell wafting from the absent king's armpits.

"I can do the rest," he said. Adalwolf reached behind his neck with his left hand and pulled his tunic over his head.

Hartmut stepped behind the half-naked visitor. "The mark is here. This is King Adalwolf."

Adalwolf faced the commander. "I'm the rightful king of Enthilen. I have returned from exile to reclaim my throne."

~ Chapter 9 ~

Fastened to a saddle, leather straps cinched across her thighs, Thaly flew Yagle over the red sand dunes and swales of Magna Avium, keeping the griffin above the stratocumulus clouds to mask her presence to anyone below. The climate among the clouds contrasted sharply with the desert's stifling heat. Eddies of cold air ruffled Yagle's feathers and whipped against Thaly's face. She pulled a scarf over her mouth and nose, thankful the furred leather tunic and pants of the Volatal Vexil warmed the rest of her body.

Through gaps in the vaporous cover, glimpses of the ground below flashed past, reminding Thaly of how fast a griffin could fly. On the ground, griffins lumbered, the combination of talons at the front and lion's paws at the rear making for an awkward gait. But in the air, they spread their wings, the span wider than a Germalian classem ship, and soared the currents with no more effort than Thaly would exert strolling along a beach.

She tugged on Yagle's left rein, guiding him towards the desert oasis of Wonchulus, sometimes used by Germalian soldiers as a rest stop. Yagle tilted the shoulders of his wings down, and Thaly's stomach threatened to burst from her mouth as they plummeted towards the clouds before he regained his mastery of the air currents. The thigh straps fixed her to the saddle, but an unexpected uncoupling always played on her mind.

The clouds parted, and the tops of palm trees appeared, clustered at the bottom of a deep swale with a permanent water source fed by an aquifer. Thaly flew Yagle closer to the ground, keeping the rising sun behind them as they swooped over Wonchulus. Underneath the palm trees, at least a dozen tents surrounded a stone well the Germalians had built to tap the aquifer. Next to the tents, inside a holding pen cobbled together from wooden stakes and rope, four white khorsals milled, their stark coats reflecting the sunlight like milky quartz. The preferred mount of Pordillo insurgents, khorsals were bred by crossing horses with kamels. Their humpless back made for a more comfortable ride, and soft feet the size of dinner plates could easily navigate shifting sands.

A Pordillo camp, thought Thaly, less than three days' march from Portum.

Other than the khorsals, nothing moved within the camp. Thaly yanked on Yagle's reins and wheeled him away from the oasis in case hidden enemy soldiers spotted her. This close to the ground, sweat beaded under her metal skullcap and bulky tunic. She leaned forward and yelled in Yagle's ear, urging more speed. The griffin shrieked and increased the beat of his alabaster wings. From the north and south, two more wind-riders appeared, the morning sun glinting from the white-gold breastplates strapped across their griffins' chests. They joined Thaly, flying in a V-formation low over the dunes. She raised her hand, and the wind-riders drew close together, the tips of their mounts' wing feathers touching their companion.

Jayla, the oldest wind-rider in Portum, mounted on her griffin, Namu, called into the headwind, "Did you spot something, Thaly?"

"A Pordillo camp!" yelled Thaly. "At Wonchulus."

"How many?"

"Twelve tents and four khorsals. Couldn't see any fighters."

"We should alert the turma."

Thaly nodded, and the wind-riders broke formation, speeding west to find the Germalian kamel turma they were escorting.

*　*　*　*

Saskia flicked her heels into the flanks of her new mount, Nibloo. The kamel grunted and picked up his pace, sand splaying from broad toes, following the turma leader towards Wonchulus. Saskia bounced atop a cushioned saddle strapped to the peak of the kamel's hump. Fixed inside sheaths on either side of the saddle, two lances jutted past Nibloo's neck as if pointing the way to go. The traditional Germalian cutlass sat tight against Saskia's body, its sheath looped between a light tan robe and black waist sash, with a bow and quiver of arrows slung across her back. The morning sun burned her pale face, and she pulled a neckerchief up to the bridge of her nose to ward off the sun's biting rays.

At least there's no wind today, she thought, then groaned when a whirlwind sprang up ahead. She turned in the saddle to shield her face from the sandblast.

As the whirlwind passed, Centure Elpis, the turma's commander, raised her hand, and thirty riders stopped as one. To their left, three wind-riders swept their griffins over a ridge and into the swale, landing at the head of the column.

One day, thought Saskia, that will be me. No more riding lumpy barrels with legs that spit in your face and stink of rotting fruit.

Thaly walked Yagle towards Elpis, a tall, slender woman with luscious raven hair and perfect brown skin, who managed to look graceful even when riding a kamel.

Saskia smiled at her sister, glad to be among familiar company. After three days with this turma, she'd yet to find a friend among her new companions.

"Arve, Elpis," said Thaly.

"Arve, Legatus Stansfield," replied Elpis.

"Thaly is fine. The desert sun melts all formalities." Her face turned dour. "There's trouble up ahead. A Pordillo camp at Wonchulus. At least twelve tents, though I saw only four khorsals and no fighters."

Saskia walked Nibloo closer to Elpis and Thaly.

"We can take them," said Saskia.

Thaly shook her head. "Better to be cautious. I could have been spotted, forewarning the enemy of our presence."

"Only four khorsals," said Saskia. "We have over thirty soldiers and three griffins."

Elpis turned to Saskia and glared. "Leading fighters into the unknown is a good way to die. We'll scout the camp first."

Saskia flinched, Elpis' comment reigniting her shame at being the only survivor of a Pordillo ambush on her previous turma. One where she had many friends. Saskia set her mind to avenging the deaths of her companions. Routing a Pordillo camp would see justice served.

"The griffins need water," said Thaly to Elpis. "Grantour Waterhole is close by. Keep a watch on the camp and wait for our return. We'll decide what to do then."

Thaly whispered into Yagle's ear, and he took off, leading the other two griffins from the swale in a vortex of wind and sand. Saskia followed her sister's flight path as the wind-riders disappeared among the low clouds.

Centure Elpis faced the turma. "Once again, the Pordillo have breached our borders, disregarding the peace treaty they signed a generation ago. Let's see what they're up to."

By mid-morning, the kamel riders reached the base of the tallest dune on the eastern side of Wonchulus. Ten fighters, including Saskia, dismounted and climbed the dune while the others guarded the kamels. The dune's crest gave the Germalians a commanding view of the Pordillo camp, the sun at their backs masking their presence to the enemy. Lying on their stomachs, they searched for signs of activity.

"Legatus Stansfield was right," said Elpis. "But why only four khorsals in the holding pen? They'd need many more to carry all those tents and supplies. Your eyes are younger than mine, Kallisto. Do you see any Pordillo?"

Kallisto squinted as if it would improve her eyesight. "The camp looks empty...no, wait. I see guards. Three of them. The others could be asleep in the tents."

"Then where are their mounts?" asked Elpis.

"Isn't it obvious?" said Saskia, getting impatient. "The other Pordillo are on patrol."

Elpis shook her head. "This doesn't feel right. We should confirm our enemy's numbers. Kallisto, take Agatha and Saskia and scout the camp's perimeter on foot to see if you can spot more soldiers. Keep below the dune ridgelines and report back here. If you get in trouble, blow your bellum cornu."

Kallisto faced Saskia, who lay beside her. "Let's go, Greenskin."

Greenskin. Saskia hated the label given to the newest or most inept fighters. While she was new to this turma, she'd been in the military for nearly two yarles, the same as Kallisto. Both being pedites, basic infantry, Kallisto had no right to give Saskia orders. She raised her upper lip in a scowl, hoping Kallisto got the message.

Saskia, Agatha and Kallisto marched north, regularly stopping and peering over the crests of dunes to search for Pordillo soldiers.

"Keep *below* the ridgeline, but scout for the enemy," mumbled Agatha, a short, stocky woman with wires of frizzy hair poking from the gaps in her headdress. "We can't do both."

"We won't see anything," said Saskia. "Most of the Pordillo are on patrol. We should storm the camp, hide in the tents and launch a surprise attack when the enemy returns."

"Typical Tavr," mumbled Kallisto.

Saskia stopped dead. "What did you say?"

"Typical Tavr. You're all as dumb as your kamel totem."

"Shut up." Saskia puffed her chest towards Kallisto.

"Stop it," said Agatha. "We're here to fight the Pordillo, not each other."

"Centure Elpis placed me in charge," said Kallisto. "She gave an order, and we're going to follow it."

"If she ordered you to jump off the Pallaxium dome, would you do that too?" asked Saskia.

Kallisto smirked. "You'll never command a turma, Greenskin. You have no respect for hierarchy and discipline."

"I don't want to command a turma. I'm going to be the next wind-rider."

Kallisto laughed aloud. "I doubt it. Do you realise how hard it is to join the Volatal Vexil? Because your sister leads the wind-riders, do you think it gives you an advantage? You'd never complete the Eligens; even if you did, the griffin would turn its bill up at your unique *perfume*. Griffins can smell Erstürmen stench from here to Enthilen."

Saskia wanted to draw her cutlass and slice a cheek from Kallisto's smirking face. Instead, she clenched her fists. "Thaly is Erstürmen, and Yagle adores her."

"Your sister is Dobunni. You're not. Griffins can tell the difference."

"Why don't you just...."

"Enough," snapped Agatha. "We must concentrate on our task."

The three Germalian fighters continued walking. Saskia fumed with every sand-swallowed step, making sure the taller Kallisto walked between her and the Pordillo camp in case an enemy archer caught sight of them. Kallisto belonged to the Scorp faction, well known in Portum for its animosity towards Tavr, a legacy of a purported cheating incident. When Germalian explorers returned to Portum with twelve griffins, everyone assumed a wind-rider would be selected from each of the twelve factions. However, apprentice riders from Tavr claimed Scorp riders cheated during the Eligens. The judges decided in favour of Tavr, resulting in two wind-riders selected from this faction. Saskia knew Kallisto yearned to be the first Scorp wind-rider.

At midday, they stopped due west of Elpis and the turma, resting from the hot sun below a dune ridgeline. Saskia sat, unwound her headdress, squeezed the sweat from the single length of cotton, then rubbed the fabric over her face to wipe away the dirt and grit. She untied a waterskin from her waist sash, flushed out a mouthful of warm water, then flipped over onto her stomach and crawled up to the lip of the ridge to scout the Pordillo camp below.

"There are only three guards," she called back to her companions. "We won't get a better chance to storm the camp."

"Then what?" asked Agatha. "We should finish scouting the perimeter and report back to Centure Elpis."

"It's pointless," said Saskia. "There aren't any fighters lying in wait for us. No sign of the enemy nearby. We should surprise them now. Each of us can take out a guard. Then we signal for the turma to enter the camp. Elpis will be impressed with our initiative."

"Are all Erstürmen soldiers this stupid?" asked Kallisto. "No wonder we beat you in the Riverlands War. We're doing nothing unless I say so."

Saskia pushed aside the bow and quiver slung over her shoulder, then rolled onto her back, her face burning from more than the sun. "I'm *not* Erstürmen. I left Enthilen when I was six harvest seasons old."

"Your skin says otherwise."

"Look, this is the same band of Pordillo that attacked my old turma. I recognise their khorsals. We should avenge the death of my sisters."

One of the khorsals *does* look familiar, thought Saskia, but then again, it's almost impossible to tell one khorsal from another.

"We will," said Agatha, "after we report back to Elpis."

"It might be too late by then." Saskia twisted the cotton of her headdress until it resembled a corkscrew snake, then wound it around her head. After tying the waterskin to her sash, she turned over and rechecked the camp. "The guard watching our dune has disappeared into a tent. This is our chance."

"Stay here," hissed Kallisto. "Do as I com...."

Saskia didn't wait for the rest of Kallisto's order, scrambling onto her feet and lurching down the eastern dune face towards the Pordillo camp. Sand swamped her ankles and tugged at the straps of her sandals, almost causing her to topple over. But she pushed ahead, not checking if Kallisto and Agatha trailed behind.

At the bottom of the dune, she ducked behind a tent to hide from the other two guards. Saskia waited there alone, her heart thudding so loud she thought it might give her away.

Now what? she wondered. Now you're stuck here alone. Idiot.

She unsheathed her cutlass, preparing to dispatch all three guards herself, until a hand clutched her shoulder.

"We can't be here," whispered Kallisto.

"We must go back," urged Agatha.

As Agatha spoke, the third guard reappeared from the tent and resumed his watch.

"Too late," whispered Saskia. "He'll see us climb the dune."

Kallisto dug her fingers into Saskia's shoulder. Saskia wriggled out from under the angry grip and crept around the side of the tent behind the guard.

For my sisters, she thought, tiptoeing to the guard and slashing the cutlass across his throat.

With a muted gurgle, he collapsed dead on the sand. Saskia pointed Kallisto and Agatha towards the guards north and south of the well while she planned to search the tents.

The first tent she looked in sat empty, except for six sleeping mats on the floor. The second tent was the same as the first.

As expected, thought Saskia. The other soldiers are on patrol.

Agatha and Kallisto disposed of the remaining two guards, then searched the other tents. Saskia sheathed her cutlass and waved her arm towards the turma stationed at the dune crest, signalling for them to enter the camp. They didn't move, and Saskia grew impatient, yanking a Pordillo flag of black cloth with a red scorpion sigil from the ground and flailing it above her head.

Kallisto trotted up to Saskia. "What are you doing?"

"I'm signalling for the turma to join us. There's nobody here, right? We should prepare for the return of the remaining Pordillo."

"We shouldn't be here. I only came down to save your stupid Erstürmen skin."

"Well, we're here now."

Kallisto rolled her eyes, "I need a drink," then walked to the Wonchulus well.

Saskia waved the flag until Centure Elpis led twenty soldiers down the face of the east dune and into camp.

The Centure's face flared an angry, ruddy-brown as she confronted Kallisto. "Did you not understand my order?"

Kallisto stiffened. "It wasn't me. Saskia kept pressing."

Elpis spun around and glared at Saskia.

Saskia shrugged. "I saw an opportunity to storm the camp while our enemy's defences were weak. Now we're here, we can hide in the tents and...." She stopped short as a shout echoed across the swale.

A Germalian fighter pointed to the dune Elpis and the turma had descended. Waterfalls of sand cascaded down the face as if a dam wall had burst, red waves tumbling one over the other. Beneath the waves, shapes appeared. Indistinct at first, then morphing into the blockish front of three timber containers with doors as tall as a kamel.

Elpis squinted as the sand settled. "What's this?"

The creak of clogged metal hinges pierced the quiet tension as the containers' doors dropped open. Mounted on white khorsals, out galloped dozens of Pordillo fighters dressed all in black with only the slits of their eyes showing from between strips of cloth wrapped around their heads and necks. They brandished spears, bows and swords and howled like a desert sandstorm as they raced towards the stunned Germalians.

"It's a trap!" yelled Elpis, her face riven with panic. "Get in formation!"

Backs to the stone well, the Germalians formed two circles and faced their attackers. Twelve fighters knelt and thrust rectangular shields into the sand in front, jabbing javelins through the gaps in the shield wall. The other eleven, including Saskia, unshouldered bows and nocked arrows, then waited for Elpis' command.

"Fire!" she screamed.

The Pordillo riders encircled the Germalians, galloping around and around the well and launching spears and arrows that sailed above the shield wall. Next to Saskia, Agatha fell with a spear embedded in her back.

Elpis yelled, "Raise your shields! Get in tighter around the well."

Saskia released arrow after arrow, chiding her stupidity with every twang of the bowstring. The Pordillo had the upper hand because she'd led the turma right into the middle of a trap. Another Germalian fighter collapsed to the ground, and Saskia almost cried aloud. She aimed ahead of a rider, hoping he'd gallop his khorsal into her line of fire, but she mistimed the shot, and the arrow thudded harmlessly into the trunk of a palm tree.

The Pordillo never stopped moving, a blur of white and black creating a storm of dust that choked the Germalians. Saskia lost track of the enemy, unable to tell if any of the riders had fallen. Panicked, she thought about escaping into the well. Instead, she cowered behind a shield, searching her quiver for another arrow. The last one. She nocked the arrow and raised her shoulders above the shield wall, clenching her jaw as she fired the shot. A Pordillo rider screamed as her arrow pierced his black robes and lodged in his chest. But it wasn't enough to stop the enemy assault from overwhelming the Germalians. Saskia drew her cutlass and prepared to charge into the stampede of khorsals.

*   *   *   *

Thaly kicked her legs, whacking the stirrup tread into Yagle's side to urge her griffin over the dune west of the Pordillo camp. Behind her, the other two griffins shrieked, trying to keep up as they raced towards Wonchulus. Thaly pulled a lance from the saddle holster and launched it at a Pordillo rider like a lightning bolt. It impaled his chest and thrust him backwards off his khorsal. On her griffin, Namu, Jayla flew up to Thaly's side and hurled another lance, slicing through the neck of an enemy khorsal. The creature toppled forward.

The Pordillo attack on the Germalian ground forces faltered, the griffins' arrival causing a moment of chaos among the enemy riders. But they soon regrouped, sending a hail of arrows towards the aerial threat.

Thaly ducked an arrow, then skirted around the well at Wonchulus, grimacing at the sight of dead or wounded Germalian fighters littering the sand. Yet, Elpis stood firm, raising her cutlass and leading the soldiers in a charge against the enemy. Saskia followed Elpis, running straight into the maw of danger.

Thaly yelled in Yagle's ear, and the griffin hovered close to the Pordillo, beating his wings to whip up the sand and create a storm of confusion. The combined assault shifted the battle's momentum. A handful of Pordillo broke from the main group and galloped from the camp. Yagle swooped on one of them, wrapping his talons around the long neck of a khorsal and ripping open its flesh. Thaly launched another lance, cursing when it missed the target.

The remaining Pordillo riders fled, their resistance seemingly over. However, one rider stopped and fired an arrow towards Jayla and Namu. The arrowhead lodged in Jayla's chest, and she doubled over, still clutching the reins of her mount. The Pordillo archer yelped a vengeful cry and galloped off into the wasteland.

Thaly guided Yagle next to Namu and yelled a command into the female griffin's pointed ear. Together they glided into Wonchulus and landed beside the well while the third wind-rider, Beatrice, continued to circle the camp atop Alesha to keep watch.

Unbuckling herself from Yagle's saddle, Thaly climbed onto Namu's back to check on Jayla, whose body had slumped forward. After pulling Jayla upright, Thaly checked where the arrow had pierced the thick leather of the Volatal Vexil uniform. Dark blood seeped from the wound, and Jayla's chest remained still, her nose and mouth failing to draw a breath. Thaly held the sorrow at bay with gritted teeth while she strapped her dead friend to Namu's saddle. When done, she climbed back onto Yagle and ordered him to dip his shoulders to the ground so she could dismount.

Thaly marched towards Centure Elpis, stepping around dead or injured Germalian fighters. "What happened?" she snapped. "I told you to wait for us."

"We walked into a trap," said Elpis, the tan cloth of her robes splattered with blood. "They had shelters buried in the sand."

"Why did you enter the camp? I gave you clear orders."

"I sent a reconnaissance group to scout the perimeter and look for signs of more insurgents. The group were supposed to report back to me, but they decided to enter the camp. Alone." Elpis flicked accusing eyes at Saskia.

Thaly strode over to Saskia and grabbed her forearm. "Did you ignore orders?"

A glisten of regret lined the bottom of Saskia's eyes, her chest heaving with the exertion of battle and, maybe, the pain of liability.

"I thought," stumbled Saskia, "...the camp looked empty. I thought we could secure it...wait for the enemy to return. Surprise them."

Before losing control, Jurelle's voice came to Thaly to cool her anger. 'Stay calm, no matter the circumstance. Belittling soldiers won't make them better fighters or better people.'

She released Saskia and plucked an enemy arrow from the ground, examining the stained metal tip. "These arrows are poisoned, almost

115

certainly from the glands of a slider serpent. Anyone hit is going to die before sunset. Saskia, you're in charge of caring for the wounded. I trust you'll provide their final comfort."

Elpis led Thaly to three containers resembling rectangular caves embedded in the side of the sand dune.

"They were hiding in here," said Elpis.

Thaly scuffed the toe of her boot against the wooden door half buried in sand. "The Pordillo couldn't have hidden these crates by themselves. They had help." She walked around to the side of a container. "There are burrows near the doors. Holes like dreadwerps make."

Elpis joined her, eyebrows raised. "Dreadwerps?"

"The Pordillo have more friends than we realised. The Erstürmen supply them with food and weapons, and dreadwerps help them build traps. Our enemy has suddenly become a lot more dangerous."

Screams from injured fighters shattered the Wonchulus oasis as the Pordillo poison took hold. Thaly raced back to the well where Saskia had set up an infirmary, assigning healthy soldiers to tend to the injured fighters by providing water, herbs, and ointments to numb the pain.

A quick death would be more merciful, thought Thaly. But she couldn't bring herself to give the order. To ask the remaining fighters to slit the throats of their companions.

Walking among the dead and dying, she recalled something Zenais had said, 'The sand of Magna Avium is red because of all the blood spilled defending Germalia.'

When will the sacrifice end? wondered Thaly. When will we grow tired of war?

* * * *

Jurelle sat at a table with Genevea outside a taberna on the cul de sac of Postremus Stabit in Portum, drinking white vinum and picking at a platter of mussels, scallops and fried seagrass. A band played in the street, the beckoning, light-hearted call of a panpipe contrasting against the almost baleful cry of a cithara, a stringed instrument resembling a lyre. A third band member kept time with a gentle beat from a hand drum as he walked among the diners, nodding and smiling whenever someone placed a coin into the cup attached to his belt.

Male servants scuttled around the dozen tables, delivering food and drink and cleaning away empty dishes. Most diners were women, the taberna being a favourite among the conventus senators. They sat in their coloured robes, resembling a fractured rainbow fallen to the earth, deep in conversation about matters Jurelle had little interest in. Unless it involved his daughters going to war.

"Are you enjoying the music?" asked Genevea.

Jurelle nodded and forced a smile for his wife.

"Worrying won't change anything," she said. "All we can do, is hope Thaly and Saskia are safe."

Jurelle leaned in. "It's much harder being left behind. Waiting for them to return."

Genevea rubbed his forearm. "Now you know how I felt. All those days trapped inside Sardis' inner circle, waiting for you to return from your latest campaign. Wondering if you were still alive. Dreading the moment when a messenger from the battlefront arrived at my door to announce your demise. Thaly and Saskia are women now, not children. You can't protect them from the world."

"It seems I can't protect them from our heritage either," said Jurelle.

Genevea puckered her face with curiosity. "What do you mean?"

"I met with Zenais and Eutropia four moons ago. They want Thaly to lead the Germalian army into Enthilen to defeat Malphas. All they must do is convince the conventus to declare war."

"Is that what you've been mulling over these past days? Why didn't you say something before?"

"Guilt. The senators chose Thaly because of who we are."

Genevea clutched Jurelle's hand, the fog of confusion clearing from her eyes. "The child of an Erstürmen royal and Dobunni leader. A perfect choice to unite Enthilen's people against Malphas."

"There's more to it. A long time ago, the Dobunni were ruled by monarchs. I'm descended from the last Dobunni king."

Genevea's eyes grew as wide as her smile. "You never told me that."

"I never considered it important. The Dobunni rejected the monarchy many generations before we settled in Enthilen. Now, our ancestry puts Thaly in the gravest danger." Jurelle pulled away from Genevea's grasp and wiped the sweat from his brow. "Not sure I'll ever cope with this infernal heat. Even at night, it's uncomfortable. How do those senators wear such bulky robes?"

"They're used to it. Born into this world."

"This place isn't *our* world, our language, or heritage. We're foreigners here."

The music stopped, and the crowd outside the taberna applauded, raising their goblets in a toast to the musicians. Life continued in Portum as it had done for generations while Thaly and Saskia risked their lives in the desert to protect this foreign land.

Culpability plucked Jurelle's conscience like a cithara as the furrows on Genevea's brow cast shadows across her skin.

"I shouldn't burden you with my worries," he said.

"These are burdens we share. I would have discovered the Germalians' plans to send Thaly to Enthilen eventually."

Jurelle reached for her hand again. "I'm scared. For Thaly and Saskia. For what they will be asked to do."

A servant arrived to fill up their goblets and bring another plate of food, cheese made from kamel's milk, a skill closely guarded by the Germalians. Jurelle enjoyed the taste and texture of the creamy white portions, but his appetite had deserted him.

"Listen," said Genevea. "What do you hear?"

The citharista played again, plucking strings with a deft touch so one note blended into the other, creating an ethereal harmony that floated into the night sky to escape with the stars. Cutlery clinked on plates. People smiled and talked. Two lovers strolled by, arm-in-arm, laughing at a group of children chasing an unruly cartwheel along the street. In the distance, a dog barked. A hawker spruiked his wares outside a haberdashery. A woman sang from a balcony, heralding the quarter moon of Seena and its absent companion, Bargan.

"Life," said Genevea. "*Peaceful* life, one worth fighting for. Something we never had in Enthilen. Our days in Sardis' inner circle weren't filled with culture, art and music. They were scarred with suspicion, horror and death. While Malphas rules Enthilen, its people will never wake from the nightmare. I don't want to lose my daughters, but if they're the beacon to guide the resistance, then so be it. I long for their safety, but I will honour their sacrifice. If the Germalians asked you to lead their army into Enthilen, would you?"

Jurelle scoffed. "Men aren't allowed to hold a kitchen knife, let alone lead an army."

"But if you *could* lead an army, I know you'd want to save Enthilen for the sake of all the innocent people trapped there. We escaped, but they cannot. Thaly could liberate them."

Yes, thought Jurelle, she could liberate them or die trying. He knew Zenais and Eutropia longed to protect Germalia from Malphas as much as they wanted to save the people of Enthilen.

"Whatever you do," said Genevea, "whatever you say, Thaly will listen to you. She and I can't seem to...." Genevea's eyes glistened as she stared past Jurelle, almost weeping with the pain Thaly's lack of forgiveness caused.

"She'll understand one day," said Jurelle. "How hard it was for you to give her away. How a peaceful life can still be burdened with difficult choices."

~ Chapter 10 ~

Tom stood surrounded by the vast Dambay Plains in Enthilen, rolling, shallow hills covered in tall grass swaying to the baton of a swirling southerly breeze. He inhaled, expecting the ambrosial scent of a world yet to embrace the mephitis of industrialization. Instead, his nostrils stung with the fetor of charred timber and scorched ground. From the south, smoke plumes drifted up from the horizon to swell a russet haze, hanging in the air like a funeral shroud suspended above a corpse. The forest of Babir Birramal burned, as Grin said. Malphas had set fire to the lungs of Enthilen.

Tom flexed his aching hands. The dark eyes had left new marks over the old. Another layer of tissue scarring his palms. The journey from Earth to Enthilen had summoned nausea and exhaustion, and Tom had passed out for, well, he didn't know how long. Yet, despite the physical jolt of the displacement, he had enough energy to start walking.

Am I getting used to the travel? he wondered. *At least the eyes didn't return me to the cave from which Grin fled.*

Tom half expected the dark eyes not to return him to Enthilen. But Dwarrow was right. Again. Placing the eyes in the throne of the dead must have renewed their power of transportation.

'Blood and bone, destroy the throne.' If I ruin the throne, I'll be trapped here for the rest of my life, won't I?

Slipping his thumbs underneath the straps of his leather backpack, Tom walked west, keeping the smouldering Babir Birramal on his left. The cool, smoky air tousled the flowerheads of pink and yellow plains daisies, knocking them against Tom's white sneakers. Bees climbed among the flower stamens searching for pollen and nectar in the late afternoon sun. He leaned down and ran his fingers across the flowers, realising how much he'd missed this land. The land that gave birth to everything.

Our worlds are connected. "You and I, Grin, together with the land," he said aloud, shifting into the Erstürmen language without hesitation.

He wouldn't travel far before Seena and Bargan decorated the night sky. Or only one of the moons. Or maybe none. He'd rest then, under the blanket of darkness. For now, he chased the setting sun, the only thing marking the western horizon, hoping he would soon see the Scaur Hills rising from the plains like the humps of rocky camels.

'Find Dwarrow,' Grin had said. 'He'll be...waiting for you.'

In the mouldewerp dwell in the Scaur Hills, remembered Tom. He hadn't been to the hills since his first days in Enthilen when Thaly and Jacob helped him and Grin escape Eroberung. He rubbed his hand across his t-shirt, over the raised, diagonal scars on his chest marking his allegiance to the Dobunni rebels. Scars inflicted by the Dobunni leader, Ryder, during the Pledge Feste in Bagendon.

Tom stopped and unshouldered his pack, the dark eyes clinking against Grin's totem and the blood compass as he laid the bag on the ground. After uncinching the pack, he searched inside, finding his jacket and empty water bottle: cheap plastic with a leaky lid, but he could refill it if he found fresh water. Not bringing food made him realise how unprepared he was for this journey. Grin's death, saying goodbye to his mum, and the encounter with Nanna had muddled his thoughts.

After unzipping the backpack's side pocket, he discovered another treasure; his own remembrance totem, a handful of words etched onto its surface.

Grin must have put it there. The gesture struck him with a gut-wrenching finality. Grin knew Tom wouldn't be able to return to Earth. Only here in Ostamp could Tom inscribe his life story on the totem.

He shoved his hand inside the left front pocket of his shorts where Nanna's amputated finger rested beside Dwarrow's key. Tucked away in his back pocket was his anxiety medication, seven tablets sealed inside their foil homes.

He considered using the blood compass. *Not even sure how to use it.*

"I need a water diviner, not a stupid bloody compass."

Tom shouldered his pack and walked on until dusk, stumbling into a shallow depression to rest for the night. He retrieved the eyes of lost souls, marvelling at the fiery pupils that flickered and swayed, casting a dull-orange glow across his blemished palm.

How many souls do I hold in my hand? He pictured his grandmother, Jean Anderson, materialising within the obsidian and repeating the words she uttered in the rocky scrub; 'Oldaric was not the man who took my soul.'

Oldaric, once an Erstürmen king, now called himself Malphas. Tom believed that twenty-three years ago, Malphas had burst into his bedroom and murdered Jean. Captured her soul with the dark eyes and turned her into a draughoul. But Nanna's words shattered any certainty.

Then who was it? Who attacked Nanna all those years ago, and why?

He sighed, tossed the dark eyes back into his pack, and lay in the grass to wait for darkness to descend. Behind closed eyelids, Grin appeared in his mind, standing inside the milbi, cooking a forest feast on the hot stone. Phantom smells wafted into Tom's nose; roasted *wadhu-gung* and crushed mopoke berries. He smiled at the memory. Grin had made the ultimate sacrifice for Enthilen. Gave his life for the land he loved, and it seemed only Tom had the power to honour Grin's gesture.

* * * *

The morning sun warmed Tom's body as he marched west across the plains, head up, trying to remember to scan every horizon for signs of danger. Around midday, he found a shallow pool of muddy, tepid water, collapsing to his hands and knees to lap up the moisture like a thirsty dog. Next to the puddle, orange flowers bloomed at the end of long, thin stalks. Tom dug into the grey soil underneath the spreading rosette supporting the blossoms, uncovering a swollen, yellow root.

"A yirany." He brushed the dirt from the tuber and bit into its crunchy rawness. Hardly bothering to chew, jagged lumps of starch lodged in his throat, so he revisited the dirty water to wash it all down. The inconvenience didn't deter him. He dug up and ate another tuber, and then another.

After filling his water bottle, Tom walked on, every new vista looking almost identical to the previous one. A mix of smoke and cloud drifted across the sun's face, hiding Tom's principal means of navigation. An anxiousness bubbled inside him. He took the anxiety medication from his shorts' pocket.

Don't leave home without your meds.

The thin foil crackled between his fingers as he counted the number of tablets.

Seven tablets. Take one now? No, wait. You might need them later.

The sun peeked through the murky clouds, and Tom continued west until dusk. Tossing off his pack, he collapsed into a clump of tall grass, wrapping the stalks around his body like a blanket. Despite being exhausted, an aching stomach made for restless sleep.

Deep in the dark night, only the quarter moon of Seena accompanying the stars, Tom woke with the ground beneath him quaking. He sat upright among the grass stalks and sniffed the air. An awful stench polluted the darkness, the scent resembling a rotting carcass ripped open by scavengers. Murmurs rippled through the night, guttural voices cursing on the breeze. A horse snorted. Tom dropped to the ground, hiding among the tufts of tall grass.

Over the rise of a rolling hill, silhouetted in Seena's pale moonlight, came giants sitting astride monstrous beasts; grell soldiers, Malphas' Rephaim, riding undreds. Each undred, twice the size of a regular horse, had a single curved horn protruding from its forehead. Longer than a spear, the horn could impale a skinny man from Earth like a steel rod through a watermelon.

Tom hoped the Rephaim would pass by, but they didn't, stopping their undreds a stone's throw from his hiding place. He pressed his body closer to the ground until the thud of his heart made the grass tremble.

"What is it, Mammon?" asked a soldier.

The largest Rephaim, Mammon, wearing a grilled helmet spiked at the top, leaned forward in his saddle. "The undreds sense something. An unusual scent."

"Wild grell?"

"The wild grells have vanished, thanks to the Worshipful Master. But there is something strange nearby. Fear hides under the veil of darkness. Maybe we can flush it."

Six Rephaim fanned out in a line and held their undreds to a walk, black hooves pounding the soil as they pressed on towards Tom. The beasts' bloodshot eyes flashed into his mind as he remembered a time long ago when he'd faced undreds up close, trying to distract Erstürmen soldiers while Grin rescued prisoners tied to the undreds' saddles. A female stone-grell and her child lost their lives that day, and Tom ran and hid while the soldiers dragged Grin to Süden Forst and tortured him. For Grin, that point marked the beginning of his end, brought on by his friendship with Tom, the birraman.

Mammon yanked on the reins of his undred, halting the beast a few strides from Tom's hiding place.

"We are close to where the fear resides," said Mammon to his soldiers. "The tension of the undred is coursing through my thighs."

Lying on his side, Tom drew his legs into the foetal position, preparing to roll onto his knees and then jump to his feet. He couldn't outrun the undreds, but he would try.

A moment before he sprang from the grass, a hiss pierced the night, racing across the plains. Almost hidden in the darkness, a sibilating shadow glided towards the Rephaim, causing startled undreds to snort and stamp. One of the beasts tossed its head, chomping on the bit between its teeth until spit foamed across its mouth.

Mammon turned his mount to face the menace. "Who is out there? Show yourself, lest you be skewered before your next breath."

The apparition materialised into a ghostly-looking woman, a cadaverous draughoul, the hem of her torn dress grooming the sleeping heads of plains daisies. Wrinkled, coriaceous skin clung to the bones of a gaunt frame as if age had descended with unnatural haste and set itself to linger forever. But from the weary face, hazel eyes still sparkled with a glint that refused to fade. Tom caught his breath and fought back tears. Despite the scars of a soulless life, he recognised the draughoul's face. Princess Caeli had come to confront the terror he couldn't.

Caeli spoke to the soldiers in a scolding wail, "Rephaim. Demons on demon mounts."

Mammon's undred reared, almost tossing him onto the ground. "Who are you?"

"I am not what I once was," said Caeli, "and never will be again. But you should fear what I have become."

A soldier mounted beside Mammon recognised their accoster. "It is a draughoul. One of the few things undreds are scared of."

Mammon held steady. "Keep your distance, else we crush you into dust. What are you doing in the middle of nowhere?"

"Nowhere?" asked Caeli. "This is my home, as it is yours. I wander the hills and plains to pay my respects and keep my covenant with the land."

"The land is dying," said Mammon. "I do not mourn its loss. Our Worshipful Master prepares to lead us into a paradise only revealed when this old land is forgotten."

"Malphas' paradise is not for grells. He lied. The Rephaim have given away so much to become what they are. You and I are not so different. Both of us have lost our souls." Caeli drifted closer, and the undreds whinnied in terror.

Tom pulled his knees into his chest, making himself smaller in case the undreds stampeded.

"Stay back!" yelled Mammon to Caeli. "One step closer, and I will smash your bones with my axe."

"We should move on, Mammon," said a soldier. "Leave the draughoul to her miserable wanderings."

Mammon nodded. "You are right. We have more important matters to deal with." He turned to his riders. "Move out. We continue our patrol."

As the Rephaim departed, Caeli drifted into the tall grass and stood beside Tom.

"Tom Anderson," she said. "You don't have to hide any longer."

Tom stood to face the woman he hadn't seen in twelve yarles. He thought she tried to smile, but it resembled the scowl of a peg-toothed crone.

"The boy has become a man," said Caeli.

Tom reached out to hug an old friend, but she stepped back.

"I have no need for affection," she said. "And your embrace would cause us pain."

"H-h-how did you find me?" asked Tom.

"The eyes of lost souls have drawn me here. Show them to me."

Tom winced. "Don't torture yourself, Princess."

"Show me," she shrilled.

Tom's shoulders slumped. He gathered his backpack from the ground and retrieved the dark eyes, placing them on the palm of the princess' bony hand.

She held the eyes to her face. "I can see my soul dancing among the flames with all the others. Held captive in this obsidian prison."

"Caeli...I...I'm sorry about what happened...."

"Draughouls can travel, you know. With the eyes. Not only through rock and soil but between worlds. Would my life be better in your world?"

Tom shook his head. "You'll still be a draughoul. Your soul won't find restitution there."

"Yes, you are right, Tom Anderson. I must remain here. There is much to do." Caeli held the dark eyes towards him. "You keep them."

He took the eyes and returned them to his pack. "It's so good to see you." Despite Caeli's warning, he grasped the princess' hand, flinching at her ice-cold skin.

"So much has changed since you left," said Caeli. "But you will help us regain what is lost. Come now, they are waiting."

"Dwarrow?" asked Tom expectantly.

"Dwarrow. Of course. He is a constant among the tumult. Follow me to the hills. I know a path to hasten our progress."

Tom shouldered his pack and followed Caeli into the night, chasing the flap of her torn dress as it caught the breeze, trying to reconcile his memories of the princess with what she'd become. Memories of the woman he first met, locked in her room atop the Sunrise Keep in Sardis, yet still bubbling with a stubborn effervescence. Her remote sadness when she appeared at the door to her father's house in Bindari, yearning to discover his love once more. The arresting strength she'd shown leading Tom to Malang Gunya, then offering herself to Malphas and Adalwolf in exchange for Thaly's life. And, finally, the sacrifice she'd made to stop Adalwolf from stealing Tom's soul with the dark eyes.

Tom expected the last memory to haunt him until his death. Every moment Caeli spent in the lingering, detached existence of a draughoul would remind him of the cost she bore to save his life.

*   *   *   *

The loose stones of the Scaur Hills slipped under the worn tread of Tom's sneakers, aching knees jarring with each misstep as he climbed towards a ridge top. Following Caeli on secret paths, they'd been travelling for over two days, leaving the Dambay Plains behind a day and a half ago. Tom had asked Caeli if she could take him through solid rock using the eyes of lost souls, as Fullō had done in Bindari. 'Draughouls can only travel through stone when there is a path,' she'd said. 'The path is there, though you cannot see it.'

Caeli found Tom food and water, hidden in crevices and under rocks, while leading him through caverns and tunnels appearing from nowhere. They talked little, and she sometimes disappeared during the night. Caeli's captivating virtue resurfaced in one brief, unexpected moment, filling Tom with joy. He hoped remnants of a soul still lingered inside her decaying body, refusing to succumb to the lure of the dark eyes or let the smother of this failing world crush the beauty of the inner child.

In the late afternoon, they reached the eastern ridgeline of the Scaur Hills.

Tom slumped against a rusty-orange, sandstone boulder. "I have to rest, Caeli."

She nodded and drifted on, scouting for the quickest path forward. She did that a lot. Never tiring. Never eating or drinking.

The sun disappeared behind a rocky outcrop, draping the hills in a blanket of soft half-light. No wind whistled through the gaps between the boulders or rustled the prickly blemmel bushes. Tom sat alone among the stillness, content to be travelling once more towards a destination of certainty.

So different to the aimless wandering of my life back on Earth. Not different, better. Much better.

A loud snuffle interrupted his thoughts. He reached for the foil packet of anxiety pills in his pocket. *Could be a boulder lion? You'll need more than pills.* He snatched a rock from the ground to use as a weapon. *Where's Caeli?* Standing, he raised his arm, ready to throw.

"Tom Anderson," came a voice. "You're not going to batter me with that rock, are you? I mean, we haven't even said hello."

Tom recognised the voice. How could he ever forget it? "Dwarrow."

The little mouldewerp toddled out from behind a boulder, clutching his walking stick, a satchel slung over his shoulder and a dozen pouches bouncing from the twine belt holding up his cut-off britches. He tilted his salmon-coloured, echidna-like face towards Tom and sniffed the air.

"Well," said Dwarrow. "You certainly don't smell any better."

Tom laughed aloud, stretching the corners of his mouth with a beaming smile, then dropped to his knees and hugged the wiry-furred mouldewerp.

"I've missed you so much," said Tom.

"Of course you have," said Dwarrow. "Affection grows in hearts held apart, or something like that. I don't know what took you so long to return. Never mind. You're here now and not a moment too soon. Not a moment at all!"

Tom pulled away from Dwarrow, and his smile faded. Grief came with a chaotic, churning rush, like an avalanche of rocks tumbling down the face of a scree slope. He curled up at Dwarrow's feet and sobbed, a five-year-old again, hiding under the bed while the Bad Man murdered his grandmother. A nervous teenager, quivering inside a rotting log while Erstürmen soldiers captured Grin. A man for whom others had given their lives. A man unable to make peace with his past and still frightened of the future.

The dry red soil of the Scaur Hills wicked away Tom's tears as Dwarrow rested a clawed hand on his shoulder. Tom lifted his head, hoping to find solace and forgiveness inside Dwarrow's squinting eyes.

"Grin's dead," said Tom. "He sacrificed his life, so I could return to Enthilen."

Dwarrow sighed, resting his walking stick against a boulder. "I hoped Grin would find peace in your world. I tried to convince myself the hope wasn't foolish. It was my idea to send him to fetch you, knowing he would never return to Ostamp. His death is a guilt *I* must bear, Tom Anderson. You are not to blame."

Tom steadied his emotions, stood and dusted himself off. "I've brought my grandmother's bone, but I don't understand how we'll destroy the dead throne. Can't we simply smash it to pieces with a hammer?"

"No," said Dwarrow. "The throne is made of things that can only be unmade in a certain way. But let's not worry about it now. He will explain everything."

He will explain everything. The words stung like a wasp. Tom had been thinking about what Grin said before he died. *How did Fullō know Nanna was a draughoul and her name was Jean Anderson? How did Fullō discover the means to destroy the throne of the dead?* There was only one answer, of course. All paths led back to *him.*

"It's Widukind, isn't it?" said Tom. "He's the one behind all this."

Dwarrow nodded. "The other elders didn't want to let Widukind hide in our dwell, fearing it would lead only to disaster. But without him, we can't defeat Malphas. Widukind has had important dealings. Even more important than me."

Tom wrestled with unruly thoughts. "Widukind knew about Jean Anderson. He discovered how to ruin the throne and knew the dark eyes would bring me back to Enthilen."

"Hoped rather than knew. You returned to Earth through the portal that opened at the dead throne. Widukind believed this method of travel would re-establish your connection with the eyes of lost souls so you could use them again as if it was your first time. And he knew the eyes would return you close to where Grin left this world. That's how they operate, mostly. Or so I've been told. We sent Caeli to find you, knowing the dark eyes would draw her close."

"Well, I'm here, but don't expect me to save everyone from the end of the world."

With a wave of his clawed hand, Dwarrow beckoned Tom down to his level. Tom crouched in front of the mouldewerp and counted the creases snaking across the werps' pink brow. Age had descended on Dwarrow in a rush, the black fur ringing his face streaked with grey.

Dwarrow pressed his face close to Tom's and whispered, "This isn't about saving our world from its end; it's about avoiding the start of an awful world that may last forever." He pulled away and sputtered, "And it's already late. Late indeed! We must hurry."

Dwarrow grasped his walking stick and scuttled off into the dusk.

"What about Caeli?" asked Tom.

Dwarrow called over his shoulder, "She's probably already at the dwell. Those draughouls move fast, you know. Follow my nose!"

As dusk turned to night, Tom followed Dwarrow to the mouldewerp dwell hidden in the Scaur Hills. Unlike Tom's first visit, Dwarrow didn't attempt to mask the dwell's location, expediency trumping secrecy in a time of dire need. Dozens of furry werps, no taller than Tom's knee, stood in front of their burrows, sniffing the air with wandering, black-tipped noses and whispering behind open hands as Tom passed.

Dwarrow led Tom to the dead tree in the centre of the dwell where the werps had bound Grin while deciding on his fate twelve yarles ago. Caeli stood beside a dishevelled man. Even after all this time, Tom recognised the man's face. It hadn't changed one bit. Widukind. Caeli's father. Malphas' brother.

A hot wind gusted through a gap in the boulders and flung grit into

Tom's face. He rubbed the sting from his cheeks as thoughts smashed against the inside of his skull, like death-row inmates trying to topple prison walls in a desperate bid to escape. A frantic, searching hand dove into the front pocket of his shorts.

No. Back pocket, idiot.

Tom pulled his anxiety medication from the back pocket and burst open a foil seal, popping a green and white capsule into his mouth. The pill sat on his tongue until his mouth mustered enough saliva to slide it down his throat.

It'll take a while. Stay calm. Stay calm.

But anger that had been simmering for days boiled over. Tom needed answers to the questions plaguing him since he was five, and he'd force Widukind to tell all if it was the last thing this pitiful man did.

Tom unshouldered his backpack and dropped it on the ground, then marched up to Widukind, clenched the pleats of his tattered coat, and screamed at him in English, *"You fucking prick! Tell me what you know. Blood and bone. How did you know my grandmother was a draughoul? How did you know her name was Jean Anderson? Tell me!"*

An impassive Widukind stared over Tom's shoulder into the fading light and spoke as if to himself, "I've been waiting for this moment. It's been plaguing my mind for more than half a generation. I'm relieved it's finally here so I can end the burden. Release me from the torment I've endured all these seasons."

"That you've endured? *Fucking arsehole. Fuck you!*"

Tom shoved Widukind in the chest. He was as tall as him now and strong enough to deliver a brutal beating. Widukind staggered backwards, clutching Caeli's arm to steady himself, then slumped against the dead tree trunk and buried his face in gloved hands.

Tom stepped forward and spoke in Erstürmen, "Don't try to confound me with your misery. I want the truth."

Caeli ran her fingers through her father's matted hair. "It's time, Papa."

Widukind's shoulders rose and fell with a resigned sigh. He smiled at Caeli, then faced Tom. "Yes, Tom. You deserve the truth. All of it."

Widukind pulled his knees into his chest and stared at the ground as if he'd transcribed his confession in the red dirt. "I loved my brother. Once. Idolised him. Before he became Malphas, Oldaric Heine was a wise and charismatic man. I know that's hard to believe, given what he's become. Enamoured with my older brother, I'd do anything he asked. Believe anything he told me. Imagine my astonishment when he announced he'd discovered the First Scripture, the eyes of lost souls, and the path to eternal life. That I could follow the path too, and, together, we would usher in a new era for Enthilen. The Divine Creator's resurrection."

"So, you *were* Malphas' servant," said Tom.

"I followed the brother I once had, not the madman he became. It's true, though; Oldaric seduced me with the promise of immortality."

"You travelled to Earth and killed your birth twin."

"Yes. I'm immortal. I would give anything not to be. Oldaric lied. About many things. Said he wanted us to rule together. Promised we would share power for eternity and witness the Divine Creator's second coming. Not only witness it; make it happen."

"That's what he told Adalwolf," said Tom.

"Indeed. The same lie for the same purpose. Like I said back in Bindari, Malphas needs an immortal to sacrifice on the dead throne. An eternal vessel for Volerdie's soul to occupy when he returns to Enthilen. Without this, the Divine Creator may never rule over us again. Adalwolf was to be sacrificed. That was Oldaric's plan from the beginning. To my shame, I agreed to play my part. Believed such a sacrifice would be a glorious end for the young prince and elevate him to the status of a deity.

"However, when I returned from Earth as an immortal, Oldaric changed. He became more secretive, keeping his plans to himself. Locked me in a dungeon underneath the Desolate Mountains and buried my dreams of eternal rule. Under the guise of Oldaric's servant, my mother, you know her as Fullō, started to undermine his plans. One night, she came to my cell and told me Oldaric had gone to search for the one thing consuming his every thought: the throne of the dead. When he found it, *I* would be the immortal he'd sacrifice on the throne, not Adalwolf. I would be the vessel to entice Volerdie to return.

"When confronted with this reality, I found the promise of a glorious end much less appealing. Mother freed me and handed me a gift; a copy of the First Scripture. I clutched the parchment and ran. Ran and hid. For season after season until you found me in Bindari."

Tom's thoughts focussed as the anxiety medication cleared his mind. "Your absence forced Malphas to return his attention to Adalwolf. To find another immortal to sacrifice on Volerdie's throne. Because you hid, I was taken...."

"Yes," said Widukind. "After Adalwolf stole your soul, he would have had a brief life as an immortal; such is the irony."

"When Grin delivered his message, a memory flashed into my mind. I'd heard...seen the first couplet of that poem before. *Blood and bone, destroy the throne.* I couldn't remember where I'd seen it until I arrived in Enthilen and walked the Dambay Plains, thinking. Then it dawned on me. I saw it scrawled on one of your books, scattered over the floor of that dark room in your house like litter. Grin's message, delivered by Fullō, came from you. Why didn't you tell me all this before?"

"Because before, I didn't know. Part of me never expected you to arrive at my door in Bindari, beneath the graves of the wild grells. I had long abandoned my study of the First Scripture. You must understand, Tom, it's a complex thesis, its true meaning hidden behind pages and pages of symbolism and obtuse messages. Then, I was confronted with your innocence and desperation. Blame forced me to return to my study. Day and night, without sleep. Finally, I uncovered a path I hoped would lead you home. But I also started to decipher something else."

"How to ruin Volerdie's throne."

"A glimpse. That's all I had when you left my home with Caeli. It took many seasons before I uncovered the complete picture, each of the poem's words buried under layers of obfuscation. My guess is someone other than Volerdie inserted the text into the scripture. Why would the Divine Creator include a recipe to destroy his own seat of power?"

Tom shook his head. "I still don't understand. How did you know my grandmother's name was Jean? Or that she was a draughoul? I never told anyone...." An awful realisation stopped him mid-sentence as the final unspoken fragment of Widukind's confession revealed itself.

'Oldaric was not the man who took my soul.'

Nanna's words hung in the night, and there, in the flames of a cresset reflected in Widukind's pupils, Tom saw the Bad Man clearer than he'd ever seen him before. The man who murdered his grandmother, landing on the floor of Tom's bedroom as he threw Jean Anderson to the ground. The terrified, confused killer staring at little Tommy hiding under the bed. The Bad Man stealing Nanna's soul.

The Bad Man. Widukind.

Confirmation appeared as Widukind rolled up the cuff of his right pant leg to reveal a pear-shaped naevus on his calf — the same birthmark as Jean Anderson's.

"I killed her," whimpered Widukind. "I'm sorry, Tommy. Forgive me."

Tom clenched his fists and screamed. Anger, loss, and remorse; all rolled into a single, brutal emotion. He wrenched the cresset from the ground and wielded it like an axe, swinging the flaming weapon onto the quivering Widukind. It smashed into his body and set his hair and clothes alight. Widukind wailed and rolled across the dusty ground, trying to extinguish the flames. No-one moved to save him. They didn't have to.

The arsehole is immortal. Tom gasped, dropped the cresset and collapsed to his knees. "W-why...why did you kill her? Why...like that?"

Widukind doused the last of his burning clothes with handfuls of dirt, then crawled to Tom, clutched at the leg of his shorts and pleaded with desperate frailty, "Oldaric had it all planned, Tommy. I couldn't resist him, lest all I loved was lost." He glanced at Caeli before continuing, "I had to travel to your world and find my birth twin, Jean Anderson. Take her life with the dark eyes to become immortal and return home to rule at Oldaric's side. But there was more. I needed to leave something for Jean's grandchild. A book with a blue cover. To prepare the child for his own journey to Enthilen. To bring you here so Adalwolf could steal your soul, and we could use the young prince as the eternal sacrifice."

"You're sick," snarled Tom. "All you wanted was immortality. To be the same as your brother."

Widukind pawed at the dirt with ratty gloves. "My mind oscillated with the choices before me. You, of all people, should understand. You abandoned your friends when you used Volerdie's throne to travel home to Earth. You left Grin, Thaly and Dwarrow to face Malphas alone. Was that the right choice? Your absence fuelled Malphas' wrath."

"Don't put this on me. I've been a pawn in all your schemes." Tom slumped to the ground, exhausted.

Widukind slithered closer and placed his hand on Tom's shoulder. "It shouldn't have happened like it did, Tom. I panicked. When your mother and father left the house, a window of opportunity opened, and I decided to take it. I didn't realise Jean would be in your room. When she saw me, it was too late. I had to...complete my quest. When the transfer ended, and I'd trapped her soul in the dark eyes, I felt no joy or satisfaction. Only emptiness and repentance. From the first moment, immortality became a curse. Shame has wracked my mind and body ever since. Now, I have an opportunity to find redemption."

Leaning on his walking stick, Dwarrow stood beside Tom and spoke with the resonance of understanding,

"Blood and bone
Destroy the throne
Naevus and twin
Blood flows thin
Kindred lost souls
Here and there
Bones to crush
Dust laid bare."

"What do you want from me?" asked Tom.

Widukind replied, "This is what I believe. To ruin the throne of the dead, we need drops of fresh blood from you and Adalwolf. *Naevus and twin, blood flows thin.* And we need the dust of crushed bones from two lost souls, one from Ostamp and one from Earth. *Here and there.* But not any lost souls — kindred. Ones related to the birth twins. Family of you and Adalwolf."

"Jean." Tom's eyes drifted to the princess hovering beside the dead tree. "And Caeli, Adalwolf's cousin."

"We have almost all we need, Tom," said Dwarrow. "To destroy the dead throne and stop Malphas. Only one thing is missing. Adalwolf's blood. We must find the absent king."

"How do you know it will stop Malphas?" asked Tom. "Even if we smash the throne, his eternal reign may continue."

"I've deciphered another passage," said Widukind.

"Every lost soul
Trapped in glass
Again, made whole
Free to pass
One birth twin
Immortal no more
Repent the sin
Live as before

"I believe the draughouls will be released from their suffering when you shatter the throne, and Malphas will no longer be immortal."

"Are you sure?" asked Tom.

"There is no certainty in life," said Dwarrow. "Only hope."

"Don't you *want* Volerdie to return?" Tom asked Widukind. "He's your God. Your Divine Creator."

"Not like this," said Widukind. "Not with a madman by his side. Part of me wonders if such a creator ever existed. So far, Malphas' failures have resulted in suffering beyond imagination. What future will there be for Enthilen if the Divine Creator never returns? If Malphas can never fulfil a desire that has consumed him since childhood? How might his bitterness curse our lives?"

"Did you bring the blood compass?" asked Dwarrow, holding his hand towards Tom.

Tom uncinched his backpack and searched inside, retrieving the gold pentagram and handing it to Dwarrow. "Where's Adalwolf?"

"He disappeared," said Dwarrow. "After the throne room in Pergamos collapsed. But we found him again."

"Grin had Adalwolf's blood," said Tom. "He used it on the compass to find me."

"Yes, Fullō tracked the absent king to Enthilen's east coast. There she stole his blood and brought it to us. We treated it to stop it from drying out."

"Why can't we do that again? Steal another vial of his blood."

"No," said Widukind. "It must run straight from your veins onto the throne. I'm certain of this. We must convince Adalwolf to join us. Then you and he will shed droplets of fresh blood over the throne."

Tom pushed his fingers into aching temples. "This sounds like madness." He faced Widukind. "You left a lot to chance. What if I never came to Enthilen in the first place?"

"When I betrayed Oldaric, I knew he would focus all his attention on Adalwolf's birth twin. I'd backed him into a corner. And with the dark eyes in his possession, Oldaric had the means to send someone to Earth to find you."

"Did you tell him where I lived?"

"He already knew. Before he sent me."

"How?"

"Oldaric's birth twin was Jean's brother."

"Great Uncle Henry? He disappeared in the desert, Mum said."

"Oldaric stole your uncle's soul and turned him into a draughoul. But before that, he met you. Little more than a baby. He saw the birthmark on your shoulder, the same as Adalwolf's, and his plans began to form."

Tom rested his chin on his knees and counted the stones on the ground.

"It's not uncommon for Volerdie to mark more than one family member," said Widukind. "Oldaric didn't know your grandmother was my birth twin, but he guessed it might be one of your family members. The blood compass did the rest. It wasn't hard for me to find you both."

Caeli stood close to Tom and lifted the hem of her tattered dress to expose a birthmark on her emaciated stomach. "I am marked, Tom, like you."

"After you became immortal, you could have killed Oldaric and ended all of this," Tom said to Widukind.

"The dead throne would still exist," said Widukind, "as would the risk of someone else falling under its spell. I could have faltered. Even if I defeated my brother, the temptation to become the next Malphas would have devoured me."

Tom herded his thoughts to another conclusion. "Wait. You needed me to return to Earth to collect Jean's bone. You said it was my only escape from Malphas, but you had another motive."

"Selfish or selfless," said Widukind. "I have always battled with duality."

Dwarrow thrust the heel of his walking stick into the stony ground. "Blame has been apportioned. Time to move on. Widukind and Caeli will search for Adalwolf. You and I, Tom, must prepare for an attack on Pergamos. Malphas' defences are strong. He has collapsed all the old dwells and gathered forces never seen in Enthilen. We'll need to assemble a formidable army to breach Pergamos' walls and reach Volerdie's throne."

"How will we do that?" asked Tom.

"First, we travel to Giigal to see if I can't get those indolent weald-grells off their backsides and ready to fight."

"I must go to Lokan."

"The cursed wood. Whatever for?"

"Grin told me he last saw his sister, Hannian, in a valley of the Desolate Mountains above Lokan. She's with a group of rebels held up in an old monastery. I promised Grin I'd take his family totem to her. I'm going to honour the promise even if it kills me."

Dwarrow's long nose twitched and buckled as if a mucus of thoughts bounced around inside and would suddenly burst from his nostrils in a triumphant sneeze. Then his squinty eyes grew wider than Tom had ever seen before.

"*Hmmmm*," said Dwarrow. "A wild stone-grell. Not many of those around anymore. Not many at all. Hannian lived with the weald-grells if my memory serves me correctly. A known acquaintance. Friend, even. Fluent in Grellian."

"What are you scheming, Dwarrow?" asked Tom.

"She'd be a perfect travelling companion for our mission to Giigal."

"You can't expect her to help us. Not after I've told her, Grin is dead."

"Sacrificed his life to defeat Malphas. If Hannian is with a band of rebels, I imagine she's also fighting Malphas. She'll jump at the chance to help us."

Tom rolled his eyes. "Dwarrow, you can't...."

"Yes, I can," interrupted the werp. "I can indeed!"

Dwarrow scuttled off, leaving Tom alone with the man who murdered his grandmother. Widukind took a white-veined leaf from his coat pocket and popped it in his mouth. Tom remembered the foliage from Bindari. The tang on his tongue and the feeling of euphoria when he chewed the leaf. He didn't know whether to hate Widukind or pity him, but Tom expected he'd never deliver justice to this man for Nanna's death.

And yet, 'One birth twin, immortal no more', recited Tom inside his head. Does that mean both Malphas and Widukind will become mortal if I destroy the throne of the dead?

The justice Tom longed for, and the righting of all the wrongs inflicted on Enthilen's inhabitants hinged on the throne's destruction.

"What happened in Bindari?" Tom asked Widukind. "Why aren't you still there?"

Widukind's sorrowful eyes glinted in the light cast by a ring of cressets. "It was ruined by Erstürmen soldiers. They slaughtered the miyans and shattered the monoliths into pieces. So much history. So many stories lost forever. The grells won't forgive me. If I hadn't used Bindari as my refuge, the terror of Malphas wouldn't have come."

Annian's grave. Gone.

Caeli floated to her father's side, reached into her mouth and extracted a tooth as if she was picking berries.

"Another one has fallen out, Papa," she said, cradling the tooth in her palm.

"I'll put it with the others." Widukind retrieved a leather pouch from his pocket, untied the drawstring, reached up and took the tooth, then dropped it into the bag.

Tom smiled at Princess Caeli, wondering if he would ever get used to the blighted smell of lingering death. She'd been trapped again, trading Sardis' prison keep for a soulless existence of enduring decay. As if the daughter paid the penance of the father.

Tom closed his eyes and ruminated on what lay ahead. *First, find Hannian and hope she doesn't blame me for Grin's death. Then, begin to build a resistance to challenge Malphas. One step at a time. Focus on the now.*

Ostamp was a confusing, messed-up world, but Tom accepted it as his world. He never fit in on Earth. Never had a purpose or clear destination. But here, he had friends who needed him and the means to smash Volerdie's throne, saving Enthilen from Malphas' tyranny and finally finding justice for Jean Anderson.

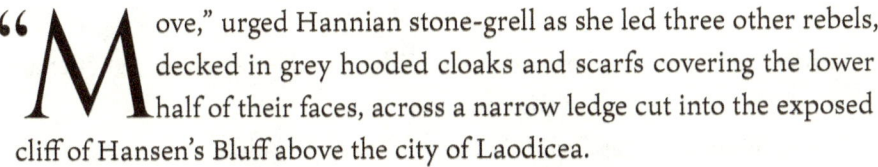

~ Chapter 11 ~

"Move," urged Hannian stone-grell as she led three other rebels, decked in grey hooded cloaks and scarfs covering the lower half of their faces, across a narrow ledge cut into the exposed cliff of Hansen's Bluff above the city of Laodicea.

Despite the black night, only Seena's quarter moon visible, a person below could spot them before they reached the safety of the outcrop. Erstürmen soldiers forever walked the stone battlements surrounding the city, watchful for incursions. Their master, Hunger, the black grell, allowed little to escape his notice. Laodicea, once a bastion of cultural diversity and Enthilen's busiest trading port, had become a prison under Hunger's rule. The city also had the largest stockpile of food, weapons and other supplies outside of Pergamos. Rich pickings for bold raiders.

Carrying near-empty backpacks, Hanni and her friends clambered onto a rocky shelf with an overhang, keeping them hidden from below and above. Quenan unshouldered her pack and, with the long, sinewy fingers of a weald-grell, undid the buckles and searched inside, withdrawing looped metal bolts to hammer into the rockface. Tilly, a refugee from Slumstadt, dropped coils of rope from her shoulder onto the ledge.

After checking for soldiers, Hanni faced Quenan. "There is no-one on the street," she whispered. "Nevertheless, try to do it quietly."

Quenan nodded, slotted a looped metal bolt into a crack in the limestone, then took a wooden mallet from her pack and hammered in the bolt. Hanni started with every strike, hoping the noise wouldn't draw the attention of an Erstürmen guard.

Sonya, a Dobunni refugee from Laodicea who knew the city better than the other rebels, kept watch, lying flat on the ledge and craning her neck over the lip. "We must go soon," she whispered from behind her mask. "Before the next patrol."

With speed and deftness, Quenan hammered another looped bolt into the rockface, then threaded the rope through the loops, tying it around her waist. "Ready," she said.

"Tilly, you go first," said Hanni. "You are the lightest and can test the bolts."

Underneath the hood of her cloak, Tilly raised an eyebrow as Quenan handed her the free end of the rope.

"The bolts are in deep," said Quenan. "They will hold even a stone-grell."

Tilly cinched the shoulder straps of her empty backpack tight, then tied the rope's loose end around her waist while Quenan took up the slack.

"We will keep watch while you descend the rockface," said Hanni, pondering a way to distract her friend's mind from the height of the ledge. If the bolts failed, only Quenan's strength and reflexes would stop Tilly from plummeting more than six stories to her death on the cobbled street below.

Tilly looped the rope under her arms, faced the sheer side of Hansen's Bluff and nodded to Quenan. The weald-grell slackened the rope, and Tilly stepped off the ledge, falling back and twisting mid-air. Her thigh slammed into the point of a sharp rock, pain writhing in her eyes.

Please do not scream, thought Hanni. Please.

Sonya turned to Quenan and hissed, "Hurry."

Tilly adjusted her mask and nodded to Quenan again, who released more rope.

She is small and slight, thought Hanni. The bolts will hold.

Tilly pushed away from the cliff with her feet, descending towards the street below.

Peering over the ledge, Sonya whispered, "She's almost there. Almost there. Yes, she's reached the ground. Wait." She raised her hand.

Hanni tensed. "What is it?"

"Nothing," said Sonya. "She's untied the rope." She faced Quenan. "Quickly."

Quenan tugged on the rope, then looped it around her giant hand and elbow, pulling the loose end up to the ledge.

"You go next," Hanni said to Sonya. "I will keep watch."

Sonya, a stout, thickset woman, tied the rope around her waist while Hanni kept her keen lilac eyes focused on the streets below and atop the wall protecting Laodicea's western boundary. An Erstürmen soldier stepped from behind a turret and looked up at the face of Hansen's Bluff. Hanni pulled Sonya down onto the ledge and held her there, hoping they hadn't been seen, then peeked over the lip of the rock shelf. The soldier turned his back and disappeared through a doorway.

"Go now," whispered Hanni.

Sonya slung herself over the lip of the ledge, and Quenan fed the rope through the metal loops to ease the stocky rebel to the ground.

Hanni faced Quenan. "You must watch the guards atop the walls and feed me the rope at the same time."

Quenan nodded, then pulled up the rope's loose end.

Hanni tied a double knot around her waist, threading the cord between her cloak and tunic and under her armpits. Adrenaline rushed through her body as she turned her back to the empty night and braced the soles of her bare feet against the rock shelf's edge.

"The bolts will hold, Hanni," said Quenan. "I promise."

Hanni pulled her cowl down to her eyebrows and dropped over the side of the ledge. Quenan's shoulder muscles bulged under her tunic as she struggled with the weight of a massive stone-grell dangling from a rope. She jammed her feet into a crevice and released some slack as Hanni descended into the city.

The cobbled street below Hanni marked the boundary between the Terraces and the King's Quarter of Laodicea. The rebels had entered the city this way before. But only once. While Laodicea held many treasures, stealing them was fraught with danger. Hunger ruled every one of the city's four quarters. The Terraces had been converted into a storage depot for food and weapons, protected by stone walls, metal barricades and watchful soldiers. The rebels couldn't breach that quarter's defences, and poverty and misery cast a burdened shadow across the Southern Vale and Docklands. Those quarters had little worth looting.

So, the rebels would try the King's Quarter again. The Master's Hall within the quarter housed grain, flour, cured meat, preserves, weapons, and likely other riches. Hanni had seen grell slaves carrying supplies into the hall the last time the rebels raided Laodicea, and she couldn't resist returning. Her group grew desperate, hidden behind the veil of the cursed wood of Lokan in a valley stretching deep into the Desolate Mountains. Poor hunting in the mountains meant two dozen rebels risked dying of starvation.

This raid must succeed, thought Hanni.

The cobbled street loomed towards her feet.

Made it easily, she thought.

Snap!

The rope above her broke clean through, and Hanni fell backwards, landing plumb on her buttocks in the gutter. The mask bridging Tilly's nose didn't disguise her amusement.

"Are you alright?" asked a chuckling Tilly.

"*Yesss*," said Hanni. "I did not fall far. Although, the pain in my bottom thinks otherwise."

"Let's go," urged Sonya.

Hanni stood, pushed her empty backpack under her cloak, untied the rope and hid it in a drain. Quenan had a spare rope on the ledge and would wait until the rebels returned. Sonya led Hanni and Tilly into the dark alleys of the King's Quarter, past the path to Felsie, the pool of reflection, the lake now so polluted as to reflect only wastage and apathy. The stocky rebel had grown up in the Southern Vale when the Dobunni and Lady Lily LáDown ruled the quarter. But Sonya told Hanni she knew the streets of every quarter, her family responsible for delivering barrels of meduz to the many taverns and inns dotted across Laodicea.

Despite being burdened with the stature of a stone-grell, Hanni hoped the grey cloak, tunic and pants would help her melt into the city's dark recesses as the rebels dashed along the empty streets of the King's Quarter.

Around a corner, two guards approached, and Hanni, Tilly and Sonya ducked into the shadows of a portico. The guards wandered past the three raiders and apparently failed to notice anything.

Signalling with her hand, Sonya led the others to the square at the front of the Master's Hall. They crouched in the shadows, and Hanni silently assessed the hall's defences. Erstürmen soldiers dressed in the basic armour of men-at-arms milled around the front door. Their spangenhelms protected the head, but they didn't wear a gorget or chainmail beneath the breastplate, leaving the neck exposed. Rephaim, the traitorous grell soldiers, watched the stables and other outbuildings, their armour sparser than the men-at-arms, comprising a grilled helmet, plackart to cover the stomach and a spiked pauldron on one shoulder. Hanni preferred to avoid the Rephaim's hooked broadswords; the traitor grells much harder to bring down than regular soldiers.

Three guards marched past the front door of the Master's Hall, then disappeared around the corner, seemingly encircling the building at regular intervals.

Regular and predictable, thought Hanni.

"We can't breach the front door," whispered Sonya. "We must go around the back."

Hanni and Tilly followed Sonya along a side street and past a row of houses, creeping up another alley to the rear of the Master's Hall. Hiding under the shadows of the eaves of a two-storey house, the raiders surveyed the hall from a safe distance and planned their assault.

"Two guards on the back door," said Tilly, pressing her hand onto her thigh where blood had seeped into her pants.

"Your leg is wounded," said Hanni.

"Stupid rock cut me when I climbed down. I'll be alright."

"The roaming patrol should appear again soon," said Sonya. "We'll wait for them to pass before we attack."

She unsheathed a throwing knife. Hanni did the same as the three soldiers they'd seen at the front of the hall, rounded a corner and approached the guards watching the back door.

One of the soldiers called to a guard, "Ho, Bron! Dey got ya on guard duty again? Yur eyes are too old to see the enemy comin'."

"I can see well enough, Hul," replied Bron. "And I can still ride an undred better dan you."

Hul and his two companions stopped at the back door. "We'll see about dat," said Hul. "Let's have a race. Next few days."

"Forget about racin' and keep ya wits sharp," said Bron. "Dark tonight. Perfect time for an attack."

"Who's gonna attack us? No Dobunni left. No wild grells either. Grōz Forst is all gone from what I heard. Malphas burned da weeds and killed da pests."

Bron leaned his halberd up against the back wall. "Keep movin'. Y'ull face Volerdie's Wrath if anyone gets inside dis hall. Da black grell will kill ya nice and slow. I might even come to watch."

"Yar, yar," said Hul. "Yur as cheery as ever. We'll see ya on da next pass."

The three soldiers ambled into the darkness and around the corner of the hall, leaving the two guards alone.

Hanni whispered, "On the count of two. One...two."

Two throwing knives thrummed through the night, piercing the throats of Bron and the other guard watching the rear door. A gurgle of bubbling blood disturbed the stillness as the rebels raced across the open court between the houses and the Master's Hall and pressed themselves against the back wall.

Sonya retrieved the throwing knives, handed one to Hanni, then tried the door. "Locked."

Hanni wiped the bloody blade across her thigh, sheathed the knife, then searched the guards, pulling a set of keys from Bron's belt. She tried each key in turn until she found one that unlocked the door. Tilly unsheathed a long knife as Hanni nudged the door open, but no soldiers waited inside, only musty darkness. The rebels dragged the dead guards into the hall before locking the door behind them.

Confronted with pitch black, Hanni opened a pouch tied to her belt and withdrew a handful of light. A giba, the luminescent stone prized among grells.

"Crates and chests stacked to the ceiling," said Hanni, sweeping the giba through the darkness.

The rebels unshouldered their empty packs. Sonya prised open a crate with her knife, then cut into a canvas bag, grain spilling at her feet. She nodded to Hanni and Tilly as she shoved two bags of grain into her pack.

"There are weapons here," whispered Tilly, filling her pack with arrows.

Hanni shoved a sword under her belt, gave another sword to Sonya, then loaded three bags of flour into her pack.

"We need more food," said Sonya.

She took a single step towards another crate then stopped dead. Someone outside thudded against the back door. Almost slipping from Hanni's sweaty fingers, the giba irradiated the panic in Sonya and Tilly's eyes. Erstürmen soldiers had already discovered the missing guards. Any moment, they'd break the door open.

"Push crates against the door," hissed Tilly.

"No," snapped Sonya. "We need to get out of this room. Otherwise, we're trapped."

"The guards at the front might be drawn to the rear of the hall," said Hanni. "We could try the front door."

As she spoke, another door to the storeroom creaked open. Hanni shoved the giba in her pouch and hid behind a crate with Tilly and Sonya. An Erstürmen soldier holding a flaming torch stepped into the room and searched among the containers. As he approached the rebels' hiding place, they sprang from cover. Tilly slashed her knife across the soldier's throat and rushed the door, followed by Hanni and Sonya. The three of them burst into a passageway lit by tiered chandeliers. Two more guards stood at the base of a staircase leading to the second floor. They spun around and shouted in surprise before being silenced by Hanni's flailing sword. However, the call of the guards raised the alarm, and three more soldiers brandishing halberds rushed in through the hall's front door.

We can dispatch these soldiers, thought Hanni, then run straight out the door.

The rebels' gasping breaths bounced from the passageway's timber-panelled walls as they stood and waited for the guards to advance. But the soldiers didn't move, instead casting their eyes up the staircase behind Hanni. She turned as a rumble of lumbering footsteps grew louder, resembling the thud of an axe as it severed a tree from its roots. Hunger appeared on the landing above the stairs, the tainted grell's naked ebony torso dressed in a sheen of sweat glistening in the candlelight. He tapped the blade of a frightful broadsword, curved and notched at the tip, against a leg as thick as a barrel. A malicious grin sprang from his dark face when he spied Hanni.

Does he remember me? she wondered. The last time she'd seen Hunger, the only time before this, was when he hunted her brother, Grin, in Lokan's cursed wood. Hanni and Grin had reunited for less than a day. Exchanged stories and hope before the black grell and his soldiers crashed through the forest of dead trees.

'Run!' Grin screamed.

And she ran. On young, quivering legs, she sprinted off into the forest, too scared to fight beside her brother. Too frightened to wait for him. When she stopped and turned, Hunger had already cast a net over Grin, trapping him as a hunter traps a deer. Hanni gathered her courage and her spear and started back. With Hunger in her sights, she launched the spear. The black grell swayed like a ceremonial dancer at a garrabari, the spear whistling past his chest and thudding into a dead tree. He smiled at her then, too, the same evil smile plastered across his face now. As the seasons passed, the memory of Grin faded, but she could never forget Hunger's smile.

The black grell marched down the stairs. Tilly threw her knife. It sliced across his scarred cheek, but he didn't break stride. Didn't even flinch. Hanni wondered if he could feel pain as her thoughts sent her legs numb.

'Run!' Grin screamed. *Run.*

Sonya leaned into Hanni and Tilly and whispered, "There's an open door on our right leading to a window. We can run for the door, then jump through the window. It's our only chance."

Hanni and Tilly nodded as one. The black grell had almost reached the bottom step. Against every instinct churning inside, Hanni turned her back to Hunger and faced the open door about halfway along the hall.

"Now!" yelled Sonya.

Hanni and Tilly rushed for the side door. Sonya didn't follow. Hanni stopped at the door jamb and spun around to find Sonya lunging at the black grell with her sword.

"Sonya?" said Hanni.

"Go!" came Sonya's reply. "Run!"

Tilly latched onto Hanni's forearm and dragged her to the window. The young rebel threw a chair through the glass and then jumped after it, rolling onto the brick pavers outside. Sonya screamed in the hall. Not the cry of a victorious warrior felling the enemy. An agonizing bawl. A scream in the throes of death. Hanni had to leave Sonya behind like she'd abandoned Grin. She had to. Otherwise, all three of them would die.

She sprang through the window to find Tilly surrounded by soldiers. Hanni rose up and swung her sword with manic fury, cutting a path through the enemy. Then she and Tilly ran, leaving their friend to Hunger's malice.

Tilly's injured leg and the weight of the full backpacks slowed them down, the soldiers gaining with every laboured footfall. Hanni tucked the sword under her belt, reached down and scooped Tilly up like a child, clutching the scrawny woman to her chest. They raced for Hansen's Bluff, back where Quenan waited. Back to their only chance of escape.

As they approached the rocky overhang, Hanni yelled, "Rope! Drop the rope!"

Quenan peered over the ledge, then threw a rope down the cliff face.

Tilly stood, favouring her good leg, while Hanni slung the rope around her own waist and under her arms, then tied it tight. "Both together," she said.

Tilly's eyes grew wide. "Quenan can't pull us both up."

"She has to. No time to wait." Hanni reached for Tilly and yanked her close, then tugged on the rope.

The rope tensed, strands of fibre straining and contorting with the extra weight. Hanni could almost hear Quenan groaning under the burden as the weald-grell lifted her companions into the air. Could almost see the metal bolts creeping dangerously from the rock crevice.

Along the street came the enemy's racing boots, slapping the cobblestones with the urgency of avoiding the punishment for failure, sure to be dealt by the black grell.

"Fire!" yelled a soldier on the west wall.

Crossbow bolts cannoned into the cliff above Hanni, their metal tips pinging on hard stone, wooden shafts shattering with the impact. Dangling in mid-air, she clutched Tilly to her chest and hunched her body over, trying to shield her friend. Quenan had pulled them halfway up.

Not fast enough, thought Hanni as she dug her toes into a crevice, trying to find purchase to lever herself to the ledge.

Erstürmen soldiers howled in an angry chorus. From the west wall and below Hanni, arrows and crossbow bolts flew like a cauldron of swarming bats.

Only a matter of....

Hanni's thought ended when an arrow lodged in her shoulder. She kicked her legs, scrambling and flinging toes into rocks to try to clamber up the cliff face. Quenan kept the rope taut, and finally, Hanni and Tilly climbed onto the ledge and rolled to safety.

Quenan sat there, her chest heaving and her face mask drenched in sweat. She drew a knife, cut the rope and tossed it over the edge.

"Now what?" she asked.

"I can run," Tilly said to Hanni. "You can't carry me with a wounded shoulder."

"We run together," said Hanni. "As fast as we can."

The companions looked into each other's eyes for reassurance, gathered their courage and scrambled away from danger along the narrow ledge, dodging arrows as they went.

* * * *

Rosalie Barron walked a winding path towards her home, a crumbling monastery snuggled in close to a cliff face in a hidden valley in the Desolate Mountains above the cursed wood of Lokan. Tan-coloured tufts of highland grass poked through drifts of melting snow piled up against boulders. Next to mountain pools fed by snowmelt, white and yellow meadow daisies decorated the dull and bleak landscape with a floral tapestry unfurled over shallow soil. The flowers' petaled heads bobbed in the wind that forever whistled through the narrow valley bordered by rugged, snow-capped mountains.

The monastery housed two dozen rebels fighting against Malphas. Once, when its stone walls stood solid, protected by a slated roof and shuttered windows, the building sheltered devote seekers who'd excluded themselves from society and dedicated their time to pursuing spiritual awakening. They followed no formal, organised religion. Worshipped no gods, their mind's eye always focused inwards, looking for inspiration and salvation from within, hoping it would lead to the betterment of self. The occasional goat herder who grazed their flock in the meagre grasslands near Lokan told Rosalie stories about the seekers of the monastery. Yet, no herder could explain the seekers disappearance. When or why it happened, or where they disappeared to. If it wasn't for the dilapidated, dissolving shell of a building the rebels now occupied, the seekers' presence in the mountains would be marked by nothing more than the fading memories of old men and women herding goats.

The monastery's sandstone walls were built into the rock as if the structure had grown from the mountainside. It resembled one of the many rocky outcrops dotted along the valley, its presence masked by mountain shadows. The rebels had fashioned doors and window shutters from thatch and scraps of timber that had been exposed on the valley floors by retreating glaciers. The coverings trapped the warmth of a modest fire forever burning inside the main room. However, the roof opened to the sky in a handful of places and couldn't be mended, meaning the new occupants were almost always cold, even during the warmer growing and harvest seasons.

At the building's rear, inside a shallow cave near the back wall, Rosalie forged weapons and tools from scraps of metal scavenged from herders and travellers using the road between Sardis and Laodicea. The simple furnace, crafted from crudely hewn stone, offered few options for smithing. A primitive dagger now and then. A hoe to till the rocky soil. To make these basic items, Rosalie had to draw on all her skills, learned long ago as an apprentice to her father, Yonna Barron, once renowned as the best metalsmith in Sardis. That was another time and place. Rosalie had swapped family life in Sardis' fifth circle for a meagre existence in the Desolate Mountains, trying to sting the hide of the tyrannical regime that ruled Enthilen like a flea may bite a tufted goliath.

Rosalie's muscles tensed as she approached the front door to the monastery. Raf, a Dobunni rebel, leaned against the door jamb.

"Hey, Rosy," he said with a smile spoiled by stained yellow teeth, making him look older than the forty-four harvest seasons he claimed to have seen.

Don't call me Rosy, she thought.

"Hey," she replied, deadpan, wondering if she should walk right past and continue up the valley. But she didn't.

Raf reached an arm around her waist and pulled her close. "You been avoiding me?"

"No."

"Seems like it. We've been having fun, ain't we?"

Well, yes, thought Rosalie, the sex *is* good. Everything else, not so much.

Rosalie and Raf had been lovers off and on for three yarles. A Dobunni soldier in Bagendon before the town fell to the Erstürmen twelve yarles ago, Raf's lean, muscled torso had enough allure to keep Rosalie coming back. She could do worse, Rosalie often tried to convince herself. She could do better, too, if she had a choice. The monastery's other male occupants were too young or too old — a legacy of yarles of fighting between the Dobunni and Erstürmen taking men and women in their prime. Rosalie was thankful she'd survived for this long. She sometimes wondered how Raf had managed the same.

He leaned in and smothered her mouth with his, prising his tongue between her lips.

The stink of decaying teeth turned her stomach, and she pulled away. "I'm going to make weapons."

Raf whispered, "I've got a dagger ready to go right now. If your forge is hot enough, I could thrust it...."

"Get away," said Rosalie, rolling her eyes and shaking her head as much at her own untameable desires. Soon, the lure of sex would again override her reservations about Raf.

Vlostak, a brawny Nordman almost twice Raf's height, interrupted the awkward courtship by pushing past the wooing couple. The olive skin under Vlostak's hairy torso gleamed taut with the cold mountain air. Even in the bleak of the long dark, he rarely wore a tunic, saying the bitter chill taught him how to endure pain. Half a generation ago, Vlostak had hiked through Detranté to seek work in Enthilen. He ended up herding goats in The Feign and never returned home, preferring the life of a drifter. His wandering ways eventually led him to the rebel hideout, where he decided to rest his aging, weary legs.

"Did you see the raiders?" Vlostak asked Rosalie.

She shook her head. She'd been on watch at the foot of the valley, waiting for the raiding party from Laodicea to return. Tilly was with them, the little girl Rosalie had saved from a burning Slumstadt. But Tilly wasn't little anymore. She'd turn eighteen this harvest season, the same age as Rosalie's sister, Nettie. In many ways, Tilly had become the younger sister Rosalie left behind when she fled Sardis.

"I'm worried," said Rosalie. "They should have returned by now."

"We need the supplies," said Raf. "These damn mountains give us nothing. Goat herders don't come around no more, and the cursed forest is only good for firewood."

"We should send scouts," said Vlostak. "Check other paths through the mountains."

A yell echoed up the valley. Rosalie spun around. Through the hazy dusk light, two grells and a slight woman with blonde hair, Tilly, hobbled around an outcrop of rocks.

Bion, Sonya's son, emerged from the monastery, brushed past Rosalie and sprinted towards the returning raiders. As he approached the rebels, his pace slowed.

"Tilly, Hanni and Quenan," said Rosalie. "Where's Sonya?"

Bion wavered in front of Hanni for a short while as she spoke with him. Tilly put her hand on his shoulder, but his legs failed, and he collapsed. Hanni crouched beside him as Rosalie and Vlostak walked down to meet them.

"Where is Sonya?" asked Vlostak.

"She didn't make it," said Tilly. "She sacrificed her own life to save ours. Sonya is a hero."

Bion rolled onto his back, his chest heaving, face as stony as the mountain peaks. Only fourteen harvest seasons old, he'd lost his father and now his mother to the Erstürmen. He had no other family. Like Tilly. Like Rosalie.

Rosalie reached for Bion, but he rolled away, staggered to his feet and ran up the valley.

Vlostak knelt and placed his hand on Hanni's bloody shoulder. "You're wounded."

Hanni grimaced. "The arrow is out, but we cannot stop the bleeding. Tilly's leg is also cut."

"We'll treat the wounds inside," said Vlostak.

Tilly faced Rosalie. "We breached the Master's Hall. Found food and weapons, then got trapped inside and had to fight our way free. Hunger came for us. Sonya faced him alone."

"We'll honour her bravery tonight," said Rosalie.

She led the group up the valley to the monastery. Raf came to meet them with half a dozen other rebels. With Sonya's death, the group now numbered twenty-three. One of the few pockets of resistance standing against Malphas and his tainted grells had diminished, Rosalie accepting their task had become much harder. Raids into Laodicea to find supplies were too risky, and travellers on the Dambay Plains' northern roads too few. If Erstürmen soldiers didn't come for the rebels, starvation soon would.

"Sonya?" asked Raf.

Rosalie shook her head.

"Supplies?"

Anger prickled Rosalie's skin. Is that all you care about? she thought.

But without supplies, this group was doomed. Raf knew it, and Rosalie knew it. Sonya's sacrifice would mean naught if the group dissolved.

Inside the monastery, Vlostak took Hanni and Quenan to the healing room for treatment while Rosalie and Tilly warmed themselves beside the fire built in the centre of an ample, open space used for communal living. Most of the group slept on the cracked stone floor. It didn't rain much in the mountains, but it often snowed, especially during the long dark. Snowflakes would float through the holes in the roof, draping the rebels in white blankets that provided little comfort. The relative warmth of the late growing season had kept the snow and rain at bay for many days.

The harvest season must be close, thought Rosalie, often losing track of time in the mountains. Seasons progressed differently here compared to on the plains. It stayed colder for longer, and little grew in the shallow, rocky soil. Rosalie had tired of eating cliff rats and lichen scraped from the rocks. Snow rabbits disappeared seasons ago. A boulder lion hadn't been seen for yarles, and Lokan's cursed wood had finally scared the goat herders away.

Rosalie had to ask. "How much food?"

"Three bags of flour," said Tilly.

"Is that all?"

"Sonya had the grain. We have new weapons. Daggers, swords and arrows."

What good will they do? Rosalie wanted to say but bit her tongue. "Your leg is wounded," she offered instead, tilting her head towards the blood-soaked thigh of Tilly's pants.

"I'll be alright," said Tilly.

Although short and slender, Tilly could match any rebel in fortitude, her early yarles in Slumstadt preparing her for life's most demanding challenges. Rosalie had lived in Slumstadt for only a short while, and it almost broke her. The crush of poverty pushed her into the waiting arms of a sage called Elmbray, who provided comfort and escape via the mind-altering substance embruisia. When Slumstadt burned to the ground twelve yarles ago, the temptation of embruisia burned with it, and Rosalie led Tilly to a different life. They drifted across the Dambay Plains, from village to village, accepting whatever work they could find. They met Raf in the town of Hahndorf, near Laodicea. Poor, hungry and begging on the street, Rosalie and Tilly thought living with a group of strangers inside a crumbling monastery in a bleak valley above a cursed wood sounded like a good idea.

Back then, thought Rosalie, it *was* a good idea.

She left Tilly to the fire and shuffled to a room off the communal living area, one of the few still wholly intact. Inside the room, on a bed made from sheaves of straw bound together and covered in woollen blankets, slept Emelin Wallace, the group's elder, almost seventy-six harvest seasons old. Her body bore brutal reminders of the battle for Bagendon; a missing left leg severed below the knee and replaced by a wooden peg strapped to a wearing stump, and a scar running from her forehead to chin, across a blind right eye.

However, the most painful wounds would never heal. The death of Dayna, Emelin's birth daughter, cut down by Krieg, the red grell, as he butchered his way through the Dobunni rebels. And the loss of Thaly, Emelin's adopted daughter, last seen travelling west to Germalia, according to Hanni's brother, Grin.

Emelin snored, shallow, soft wheezes passing through cracked lips. Rosalie turned from the doorway to leave her in peace, but the old woman sat up with a start.

"Sonya?" said Emelin, scratching at the scar on her face.

"Don't get up," said Rosalie, stepping into the room to sit on the bed. "Sonya didn't make it."

Emelin may have been sad, but she didn't show it. She rarely showed any emotion Rosalie could discern.

"What about the others?" asked Emelin.

"Hanni and Tilly are injured, but they'll recover. Quenan is unharmed."

"Poor Bion," said Emelin, her left eye drifting towards the shuttered window.

"He's run off into the mountains," said Rosalie.

"He'll come back. When a parent dies, you lose some of your past. When a child dies, you lose...."

"Your future," finished Rosalie, reaching along the bed to grasp Emelin's frail hand. "And you've lost two children."

"I hope Thaly is out there, somewhere. She wasn't mine by rights, though I loved her as much as I loved Dayna."

"You've been like a mother to many of us."

"I often wonder what would have happened if I didn't find this place. After Krieg razed Bagendon, the mouldewerps healed me and offered a home in their secret dwell in the Scaur Hills. But I needed to find people like myself. Werps are kind and generous, but they're not my kin."

A burden of responsibility welled a sadness in Rosalie's mind.

Emelin noticed it. "What troubles you?"

"Now Sonya has gone, the others will look to me to lead. I'm not sure I can do it. Where will I lead them too? We can't live here for much longer."

"Stay true to yourself and remember, you're not in this alone. You have friends to lean on. Tilly, Hanni, myself."

"I sometimes wonder if a better life lies north."

"Through Detranté, to the Nordmen, is that where you would lead us?"

"What do we have to lose? Hunger will find us eventually. He'll double the patrols after our raid on Laodicea. We could seek sanctuary among the Nordmen."

"Malphas built an iron gate across Detranté, and his soldiers watch the pass day and night. We can't escape through there, and I'm too old and broken for the long journey to Nordland." Emelin squeezed Rosalie's hand. "I wish I had a simple answer for you. The right answer. But the future is dark to me also. We're in a holy place. We should turn our eyes inward to seek salvation."

We don't need salvation, thought Rosalie. We need food.

"If travelling north is your decision," said Emelin, "then others will follow you."

"It can't be only my decision. We'll vote for a new leader, then decide our future together."

Emelin nodded and smiled, released Rosalie's hand and slumped back into her bed. She closed her left eye, but the blighted socket of her butchered right eye kept its sad, grisly watch on the world. Once the Dobunni rebel leader, Emelin now spent most of her time resting, waiting for death to come. Rosalie could hardly blame her, but she'd grown tired of waiting for death or salvation, or whatever else might creep up their dead-end valley. This life, Rosalie's life, needed a purpose other than stealing from the rich. At the beginning of the harvest season, she'd turn thirty. An appropriate time to reimagine a new life.

That night, Raf came to her, reeking of meduz. Despite living in scarcity, he always managed to conjure another barrel of intoxication to indulge in. He made the mixture himself, but Rosalie dared not ask from what. They had sex in the communal living area next to the other sleeping rebels. That's how it was here. There were few secrets. Few moments of privacy. The sex was lustful, awkward and over before Rosalie climaxed. Raf slept beside her, draping his arm across her breasts. This token of intimacy was the best she could hope for. The only affection to be wrung from this desolate place.

~ Chapter 12 ~

Mirrian held her breath as she took the chamber pot from under Ende's bed. Beneath the quilt, painstakingly stitched with the image of a castle rising up from a forest surrounded by clouds, the pale grell lay still, barely breathing. Ende's body appeared to be shrinking a little each day. Mirrian tried to imagine the strong, female stone-grell Ende must have been before Malphas turned her into his hireling of death. Now, she'd become a faded shadow of even that abominable mantle. A giant wilted into a decaying runt, unable to deposit her own waste in the chamber pot without Mirrian's help, let alone wield the glittering sparth leaning against the mantle above the fireplace. The weapon forever used by Ende to dispatch Malphas' enemies and annoyances.

Mirrian placed the chamber pot outside the door to Ende's quarters on the floor of the passageway connecting Pergamos' underground rooms. Only Ende, Malphas and his guards lived underground. Malphas held court in the throne hall, and servants like Mirrian came and went. But the pulse of Pergamos was above ground, where most believed they could avoid being entombed by rock and earth should Volerdie's Wrath ever descend on the city again.

Mirrian turned back into Ende's room and gagged at the stench of rotting flesh, the wasting of a pale grell impatient for her demise. From the corner, Mirrian took a broom and swept the flagstones, collecting dirt and dust in a pile to be tossed into the fire. Despite being late in the growing season, Ende's fire always burned, fighting against the chill of Malphas' subterranean kingdom. Resting the broom against the mantle, Mirrian crouched and placed another log onto the fire, stoking the embers with a metal poker fashioned as a serpent with a forked tongue. Sparks wafted up the chimney, escaping the dank, buried world. She placed the poker on the hearth's edge and stood, blindly reaching for the broom. Instead, her fingers wrapped around the wooden handle of Ende's sparth. Mirrian lifted the weapon, assessing the blade's weight and balance, then ran her thumb along the edge and winced as blood oozed into her palm. The conveyance of so much death hadn't dulled the blade's keenness or dimmed the polished silver glinting in the candlelight. Mirrian gripped the sparth with both hands, holding it across her chest and imagining the power she could wield.

The macabre courtship ended when Malphas walked into the room. Mirrian swapped the sparth for the broom and continued sweeping, wondering if the Worshipful Master had seen her. He dragged a three-legged stool to Ende's bed and sat beside the pale grell. He spent a lot of time there, Mirrian often finding Malphas asleep, still sitting on the stool, with his head resting on Ende's mattress.

Malphas whispered something to his servant, and she rolled towards him, bringing a frail hand out from under the covers. Taking her hand, he grimaced as if the pain she must be feeling had entered his own body.

"How are you?" asked Malphas.

Ende tried to sit up. He grabbed two feather pillows from the floor and propped them behind her back as she rested against the headboard and wheezed, "Worshipful...*cough* Worshipful Mas...*cough*...."

"Water, Mirrian," snapped Malphas.

Mirrian dropped the broom and poured a cup of water from a pitcher on the bedside table. As she went to hand it to Ende, Malphas snatched it from her grasp.

"Here, Ende," he said. "I have water for you. It will soothe your throat."

She sipped from the cup, then handed it back to her master.

"Has the healer seen you today?" he asked.

"No, Master."

"He should have been here already. I'll send a guard to find him. If he dallies again, we'll dispense with him and find a new healer."

"A healer...a healer cannot...*cough*...save me."

Malphas leaned forward. "Don't say that. Our most glorious days are ahead of us."

Ende shook her head. "When the pain is too much to bear, will you...." She pointed to her sparth.

A frosty shade of terror glazed Malphas' face. "It won't come to that," he said. "Distract your pain with the paradise awaiting us. My army prepares to march on Gestade and rid Enthilen of the Dobunni dregs and the Erstürmen traitors housing them. Then we'll route the weald-grells. Once that is done, Volerdie will return and open the door to his paradise."

Ende's black eyes grew wide, and she sat forward. "I could lead the attack on Giigal, Master. As my final act of devotion."

Malphas guided her back down to the pillows. "No. You must rest. Your brothers Krieg and Hunger are willing servants. They can lead my armies. I need you here, by my side as always."

Ende nodded and closed her eyes.

"Are you dreaming?" asked Malphas.

"I see Volerdie's paradise, Master, as you described it. A land forever bathed in sunlight. Water springs from the ground, and food grows before your eyes. Men, women and children...*cough*...live in peace, in blessed worship...*cough...cough*...."

Mirrian crouched and picked up the broom. "Grells are not welcome in Volerdie's para...." She caught her foolishness too late.

Malphas stood, stormed across the room, flung his arm above his head and slapped her cheek. She cannoned into the wall as the broom clattered to the floor.

Malphas pressed his face up to hers and sneered. "*I'll* decide who enters paradise." He dragged her into the passageway. "Don't bother Ende with your witless ramblings. Your job is to take care of her until death."

Mirrian nodded a drooping, submissive head. "Yes, Master."

He stepped closer, his resigned whisper echoing along the passage, "She grows weaker with each passing moon. We must provide her with every comfort until her last breath. I need you here, Mirrian, watching over Ende. You can sleep on the floor in her room. Gather your bedding from the slave quarters. Tell Henruld he is no longer your overseer."

Malphas returned to Ende's bedside, leaving Mirrian alone. A draft whisked along the passageway and raised goosebumps on broken skin that had almost forgotten the sun's warmth. Malphas had kept her underground for the last seven days, allowing her to return to the slave quarters only after nightfall. By the time she'd climbed the stairs and walked to the quarters, Henruld and the other slaves were already asleep. Mirrian hadn't been able to speak with Julan and Carian since her invitation to feast with Malphas. She hadn't been able to explain to her fellow slaves she had no choice but to sit with the Worshipful Master. The accusations on Julan and Carian's faces as they served Mirrian food and drink still haunted her. She had to atone before being confined to this underground prison forever.

Mirrian trudged up the stairs, past the Rephaim guards watching the entrance to Malphas' miserable home. The sun set, painting clouds in the western sky tangerine and cherry. The old grell city of Malang Gunya glowed like gold under candlelight. The Erstürmen called this place Pergamos, but to Mirrian, the settlement would always be Malang Gunya, built by her ancestors many generations ago. She imagined the city as it used to be, underneath the shroud of Malphas' urban resurrection. The precincts devoted to education, healing, culture and nature study, each with grand, multi-storey buildings decorated with archways and balconies and light-filled rooms illuminating the thoughts of grell scholars. The arboretum, an expansive, rambling parkland that wound through Malang Gunya and celebrated the diversity of life found throughout Enthilen. The amphitheatre in the culture precinct used for ceremonies and performances. The library of oral history in the education precinct, where elders would tell stories of days long passed. Mirrian tried to picture it all, pasting collaged images into her mind, pieced together from stories her mother and father told her. Tried to remember the ancient past, thinking she may be the last grell in Enthilen to ever conjure such memories.

Malphas hadn't completely desecrated Malang Gunya. The pyramid stood, three hundred steps climbing to a lookout among the stars. It overshadowed the calendar of life, the open, circular temple ringed by white marble columns fashioned as the trunks of panalope trees, its floors once painted with scenes of grell culture.

As Mirrian lumbered past the calendar of life towards the slave quarters, her legs almost faltered at the memory of the massacre that unfolded in the calendar twelve yarles ago. King Adalwolf oversaw the slaughter of hundreds of grells who'd made the last-ever pilgrimage to honour the fallen defenders of Malang Gunya, cut down by Erstürmen invaders two generations past. For Mirrian, the massacre of pilgrims marked the end of a life worth living and the beginning of a survival she stubbornly endured. Marked the moment when her husband, Frennan, died in her arms, and the last time she would embrace her children.

Dusk settled in the still night as Mirrian weaved her way through the crowded streets to the front door of a brick storeroom with a thatched roof, where Henruld's twenty slaves would sleep head-to-toe, crammed into a space large enough to house two or three horses. She hoped to duck inside, gather her bedding, and flee before the other slaves returned from their daily chores, avoiding the afflictive explanation of why she'd been chosen to care for Ende. Avoiding the condemnation of her companions.

Her eyes adjusted to the half-light inside the empty storeroom, and she located her bed, where a blanket covered a tatty pillow resting on a pile of straw. Kneeling, she picked up the pillow and reached inside a hole where the seam had split open. Her fingers wrapped around a cylinder of softstone, no larger than a knife handle, and withdrew the secret treasure. Resting in the palm of her giant hand, the stone looked so small. So insignificant. She'd found it underground, in one of the dark passages of Malphas' kingdom, and stolen it away to be her new remembrance totem. To etch on its smooth surface the story of her life.

So small. So insignificant.

Mirrian hadn't written much yet. But she would, one day. She'd have wondrous tales to tell, written on the totem for all to see.

"You have hidden that well," came a male voice behind her.

Mirrian spun around. Carian stood in the doorway, his giant grell frame stopping all but a sliver of dusk light from entering the storeroom.

"The same way you have hidden your devotion to Malphas," said Carian.

"No," said Mirrian, standing, clutching the totem like a dagger and preparing to fight her way past Carian. "I am forced to serve the master."

"Yet, Julan and I served *you* as you sat at Master's table, feasting on delicacies the rest of us can only dream of. Unmoved, while Julan and I tested the food for poison."

"I can explain," said Mirrian. "I can explain it all."

Carian stepped into the room. Mirrian reached down and grabbed her blanket, planning to wrap it around his head and run. Though an emaciated slave, Carian was still a hulking stone-grell. Mirrian wouldn't win a fight against him, but she could flee, through the streets and down the stairs into Malphas' waiting arms.

"Where are you going, Mirrian?"

"To find new bedding. I will return."

"Liar!"

In the encroaching darkness, Carian's hand struck like a venomous snake, smacking the remembrance totem from Mirrian's palm. The softstone landed on the floor, shattering into a dozen pieces.

"No," said Mirrian, kneeling to gather the fragments of her life. "Please, no."

A bony, bare foot thundered into her ribs, stealing the air from her lungs. Mirrian curled up into a ball, preparing for the onslaught.

"What's goin' on 'ere?" Henruld stood in the doorway, his other slaves lined up behind him, their chains clinking with the slightest movement.

Carian faced his master. Mirrian took advantage of the distraction. Still clutching the blanket, she jumped to her feet and rushed outside, pushing Henruld to the ground and forcing her way past the coffle of slaves.

Mirrian ran. Away from the ancestral stories of Malang Gunya. Away from the salty wind of Giigal, where she lived with her daughter, Hanni. Away from the enormous panalope trees of Babir Birramal she climbed as a child. Away from the garrabari's joyous dances and the memories of a loving family.

Mirrian ran to Malphas, and she hoped no-one stopped her.

* * * *

"What's your name?" asked the chubby young man sitting on the cot beside Nettie's.

"Nettie Barron, daughter of Yonna Barron, the finest metalsmith in Pergamos."

"I'm Erwin Brotmacher, son of Wilfred and Adelina Brotmacher. Not sure if they're the finest bakers in Pergamos, but they make a tasty honey devil-kuchen."

Nettie nodded, imagining Erwin had probably eaten more than his fair share of sweetcakes.

"How long have you been here?" asked Erwin.

"Seven moons. Not that I'm counting."

Well, thought Nettie, I *am* counting. She hadn't seen her father since the Master's Shield pulled her from the crowd leaving the kirika. Yonna would come soon, she told herself, to take her back home. The army had made a mistake picking her for one of its soldiers. She'd be lucky to skewer a potato without stabbing herself.

Nettie collapsed onto her cot, the woven strands of willow bark rubbing with a creak against the timber frame. Around her, the long tent buzzed with the chatter of dozens of young men and women returning from another day of training. Under a regime of strict and judgemental faith enforced by a growing military strength, Pergamos had become more of a dormitory for soldiers than a royal city.

Soldiers? thought Nettie. Most in her barracks hadn't seen eighteen harvest seasons by the looks of them. She doubted many had held a sword or fired a bow before being conscripted. More than a dozen had already died in mock battles. The cot Erwin now claimed once belonged to a young girl who copped an arrow through the throat yesterday. Nettie couldn't remember her name.

"They pulled me from the line to the kirika this morning," said Erwin. "Before the sermon and everything. When will we go home? Tomorrow's the first day of harvest season. I don't want to miss the celebrations. It'll be my fifteenth harvest season."

Nettie propped herself up on her elbows. "I don't think we'll be home in time for harvest season."

Erwin's rosy face turned pale. "I can't be a soldier. I want to be a baker and make delicious honey devil-kuchen and sourdough bread."

Nettie slumped back on the bed. "Tough. We're soldiers now."

"Doesn't the Worshipful Master have plenty of soldiers already? I mean, he's got Erstürmen Shield and Rephaim. Men-at-arms and every kind of war machine you could imagine. I've seen some of those grell soldiers riding undreds. That would be enough to scare the wits out of our enemies."

"You should rest," said Nettie. "Before training tomorrow."

"We won't be training tomorrow, will we?" asked Erwin. "I mean, being harvest season and all. We should be feasting and...."

Nettie rolled onto her side and growled, "I'm trying not to think about it. My father will come and get me soon. Until then, be thankful you've been chosen to fight for Volerdie's paradise."

"Is he watching?"

"Who?"

"Volerdie. If he isn't watching, how will he know I'm worthy to enter paradise?"

"If you're a true believer, you won't be left behind. When paradise is revealed, Ostamp will wither in the darkness, and the unbelievers will wither with it."

"Wither with it," repeated Erwin. "That's hard to say. Wither with it. Wither with it."

"Acht!" came a yell from the front of the dormitory tent.

The murmuring troops snapped into silence. Nettie sprang up and stood to attention by the side of her bed. She glared at Erwin, who sat there looking bewildered.

"Get up," she hissed.

Erwin stumbled to his feet as Lieutenant Berard strolled along the aisle, followed by the snivelling Sergeant Weedle. Not a single strand of the lieutenant's silver hair out of place, he cradled his spangenhelm under his arm and inspected every soldier. The curled, two-headed snake on Berard's breastplate, bordering two eyes on either side of a golden sun, marked him as an Erstürmen Shield. Master's Shield, an elite soldier in Malphas' army.

Now women fought in the army, thought Nettie, maybe she could become a Shield? Don't be stupid. Papa is coming to get you.

With fear-breeding slowness, the two commanders finally reached the middle of the long tent where Nettie and Erwin stood waiting. A nervousness pecked at the back of Nettie's mind, telling her the commanders would linger here.

The longer the delay, she thought, the worse the outcome.

Berard stopped and faced Erwin, who shook inside his ill-fitting boots like a spoon rattling around a cup.

Nettie tried to project her thoughts into Erwin's mind. *Don't speak. Don't say a word. Stand there as still as a rock and hope.* But it didn't work.

"Hail Malphas!" cried Erwin, slapping his right fist against a breast that jiggled underneath his cotton shirt.

Berard raised his eyebrow, "Hail, indeed," then faced Sergeant Weedle. "Is he new?"

"Brought in dis mornin', Lieutenant."

"*Hmmm.* Seems we're getting desperate."

Weedle sniggered as Berard unsheathed his sword and held the hilt towards Erwin. The young man glanced at Nettie, but she tried to pretend he wasn't there.

"Take the sword," ordered Berard.

Erwin nodded, his trembling fingers reaching for the grip. As Berard removed his supporting hand, the sword tumbled into the dust. Erwin went to pick it up when Weedle sprang from behind the lieutenant and slammed his hob-nailed boot down on Erwin's hand.

"*Ahhh!*" cried the young man.

"Never drop y'weapon," snarled Weedle. He removed his boot, and Erwin clutched his hand to his chest, sobbing.

"Pick up the sword, soldier," said Berard.

Erwin bent over, keeping tearful eyes fixed on Weedle, grasped the sword, then stood, the blade hanging loosely by his side.

"Have you wielded a sword before?" asked Berard.

"No, Sir," said Erwin.

"Any weapon?"

"My Ma says I'm handy with a bread knife."

Nettie groaned, expecting it wouldn't be long before the bed beside hers would be empty again.

"Sergeant Weedle is your mother now," said Berard. "The soldiers in this tent are your brothers and sisters. If you can't handle a weapon, then they die."

"Yes, S-s-sir," stammered Erwin. "But...you see...I think there's been a mistake. I shouldn't be here. I should be baking cakes and buns and...."

"Shut it!" yelled Weedle. "Answer da lieutenant's questions. Otherwise, keep yur mouth shut."

Erwin nodded, stepping back, away from Sergeant Weedle.

Berard held out his gloved hand. "Before you faint, I'll have my sword back."

Erwin returned the sword.

"Training will sort the flesh from the peel," said Berard to Weedle.

The commanders walked off, continuing their inspection of the remaining troops, then exited the dormitory.

Nettie swore everyone inside the tent sighed with relief.

"Does that happen all the time?" asked Erwin.

"Inspection every evening," said Nettie. "To find the weak ones."

"What happens when they find one? A weakling, I mean."

"They deal with them."

Erwin sat on the edge of his cot and rubbed his pudgy fingers over a dejected face. Nettie pulled the blanket back from her pillow, readying the bed for the night. The evening meal would be served up soon, then straight to sleep. Sleep, eat, fight, eat, sleep. That had been the last six days of her life. It might be the rest of her life until an enemy soldier or one of her new companions stuck a blade in her chest.

Erwin sobbed again. A part of Nettie pitied him, expecting he wouldn't survive the training. 'Better that,' Lieutenant Berard would say, 'than risking the lives of fellow soldiers during battle.'

Erwin looked up. "W-w-when do w-w-we eat?"

"Any moment, they'll call for supper," said Nettie, her stomach grumbling. "You should get hold of yourself."

"I'm not a soldier, Nettie."

"None of us are. But we have to be."

Bullwork, a recruit who'd been here longer than Nettie, walked up to Erwin and tossed an empty bucket at his feet. "Go clean the privy. It's 'round the back."

Erwin stared at him with pleading eyes. "I haven't eaten all day."

Bullwork smiled. "I'll keep your portion under me bed. It'll be waiting for you when you return."

No, it won't be, thought Nettie. If Bullwork managed to get an extra portion, he'd clean it up before reaching the dinner table. She could try to stop him, but she had no authority or will to make things right, and Bullwork was twice her size.

Erwin looked at Nettie, but she turned away, pretending to tidy her bed. The sullen young man walked off towards the privy as the cook called for supper. The recruits lined up and marched from the tent to the mess hall.

Nettie wondered what Yonna would be eating tonight. How his withering body coped with the burdensome work of forging metal, now he'd lost his apprentice. Did he think about her? Has he tried to find her? He'll come, she tried to convince herself. Papa will take me home. And yet, maybe this is all part of Volerdie's plan? The Divine Creator needs young men and women to fight for him. To fight for his paradise. Volerdie needs *me.*

Tomorrow, she'd turn eighteen. A girl no longer. A woman and a soldier in Malphas' army. No, *Volerdie's* army. If she trained hard, she would become a warrior, prepared to give her life for the Divine Creator.

~ Chapter 13 ~

A clear, crisp morning dawned in Gestade, and preparations to celebrate the first day of the harvest season began. Unable to sleep from the excitement, Lily bounced around the outpost grounds, greeting everyone she met. Despite Malphas casting an endless shadow over Enthilen, Lily refused to let the threat of war dampen her enthusiasm for this most joyous and important time in the cycle of the six seasons.

"Bountiful harvest, Master Lily," said a vendor, walking a wheelbarrow full of ripe, red cherbuls through the main gate.

"Bountiful harvest," replied Lily. "May I?" she asked, pointing to a cherbul.

"Of course. Wonderful season this yarle. Best ever by my reckoning."

Lily grabbed a cherbul and bit into the skin, a flush of juicy yellow flesh spilling onto her tongue and out the sides of her mouth. "*Mmph...* goodness, they are delicious."

The vendor tipped his straw hat. "Thank you, Master Lily. I got plenty more where these came from."

"I'll send everyone to your stall," said Lily.

She turned and trotted up the wooden stairs to the top of the east wall, knocking the dirt from the soles of her polished boots as she went. Atop the wall, a group of six Dobunni soldiers, refugees from the war in Laodicea, stood at the parapets, waiting for the enemy to come. The rebels turned on their heels and snapped to attention as Lily approached, clutching glaives in firm hands as if she'd arrived to give the order to attack.

"Bountiful harvest," said Lily with a beaming smile. "You can relax."

The soldiers stood at ease and replied in unison, "Bountiful harvest, Master Lily."

Lily stood beside her companions to continue the watch. In the distance, the sun rose above the Veiled Occyan like a fiery leviathan, sending white-capped waves of glistening chartreuse towards Enthilen's eastern shore. Ocean birds hung in the breeze, specks of grey dotting the dawn horizon. Outside the wall, in the village surrounding Gestade, citizens stirred from their evening slumber and loaded baskets of food or barrels of meduz onto carts to bring into the outpost's main grounds. The harvest feast would be inside the walls, as it had been for the last twelve yarles, in case Malphas launched a surprise attack.

We'll squeeze everyone in, thought Lily, planning where the tables and benches would fit, where they'd erect the stalls and the dancefloor, and light the bonfire. Already Lily had the feeling today's celebration would be the greatest ever.

She faced the oldest Dobunni soldier. "How many harvest seasons today, Cor...."

"Callam, Master Lily," replied the soldier, his blue eyes twinkling under a veranda of unruly grey hair. "I'm proud to say this will be my seventy-fourth harvest season."

"My, that is something to be proud of. If I recall, weren't you a guard at the Master's Hall in the Southern Vale?"

Beneath a well-worn tunic, Callam swelled his chest. "That's right, Master Lily. I was honoured in the duty."

"How many harvest seasons for you, Master Lily?" asked a woman with long, flaxen hair that had a youthful shine.

Lily searched her memory. "You're Orella?"

Orella nodded and beamed.

"It'll be my sixtieth," said Lily.

Orella's eyes widened. "That's a real special anniversary, that is. *Real* special. I doubt I'll ever see sixty harvest seasons. I hope they have a grand celebration planned for tonight."

Lily nodded and smiled. "I'm sure Field Commander Hartmut will do his best."

"How many harvest seasons for the commander?"

"Forty-eight."

Orella flashed a cheeky grin. "Oh, he's quite a bit younger than you, Master Lily."

Lily laughed. "Are you saying an old doe like me shouldn't bed a younger buck?"

Orella blushed, then blurted, "No, yes, well, I mean…no…*ah*…you can have any man you choose. Any man at all."

"If only that were true," chuckled Lily.

Standing beside Orella, a young man, little more than a boy, stepped closer to Lily, the hem of his chainmail suit clinking across his kneecaps. "We've heard rumours, Master Lily. The enemy are already marching."

"I don't know your name."

"Landon."

Lily nodded. "We have spies inside Pergamos' walls and lookouts stationed across the Dambay Plains between Gestade and the enemy strongholds. We'll know when Malphas marches his army. There's been no news as yet."

"My father told me what happened to Laodicea when the barbarians came," said Landon, bowing his head.

Lily placed a comforting hand on Landon's shoulder. "How many harvest seasons?"

Landon faced Lily. "Today is my sixteenth. I was only four when we fled our home."

"We were vastly outnumbered in the battle for Laodicea, yet every Dobunni man, woman and child fought with bravery and honour. I expect nothing less this time." She huddled in close and wrapped her arms around Landon and Orella's shoulders, then locked eyes with each of the six soldiers in turn. "Before the enemy arrives, embrace those you love and look into their soul. There, you will see what we're fighting for. When the battle commences, stand shoulder-to-shoulder with your brothers and sisters. Peasant or noble. Dobunni, Erstürmen or grell. We're all fighting for what we cherish. Love, peace and freedom. And when the battle ends, the one thing of which I'm certain is that I'll never be prouder to be a Dobunni."

A single tear slinked down Orella's cheek. Lily wiped it away with the tip of her finger. "Today, we can forget about battles," said Lily. "Today, we celebrate the bounty and beauty of Enthilen and the bond the Dobunni forged with this land generations ago."

Lily broke from the group and walked down the stairs into the main grounds, dodging past people moving long tables and benches into place or stacking wood for the bonfire. Across the grounds, Hartmut weaved through a cluster of Erstürmen soldiers who thumped their silver breastplates with a clenched right fist to hail his presence. He responded in kind, Lily understanding how much Hartmut valued preserving tradition. Within the grounds, men and women built a temporary timber podium, ready to support the stomping feet of hundreds of dancers as they jumped and twirled to the jaunty melodies of a dozen minstrels. Next to the platform, a local puppeteer had erected a tent, large enough to house one person standing, with a hole and stage at the front. The puppeteer's head peaked over the top of the stage, in the middle of a line of puppets she would use to enact her captivating tales throughout the day and night.

Hartmut stopped in front of the tent and greeted the puppeteer. Lily snuck up behind her lufu and blew into his ear.

He spun around, and a weary face lightened with a wry smile. "You're up early."

"It's the first day of harvest season," said Lily, kissing him on the cheek. "In case you didn't notice."

"We're all another yarle older and none the wiser."

Lily placed her hand in the crux of Hartmut's elbow. "You're such a curmudgeon." She faced the puppeteer. "Bountiful harvest."

"Bountiful harvest," replied the woman.

"What stories will you be telling?" asked Lily, trying to identify the characters lined up along the stage.

"The collapse of Pergamos' throne hall always goes down well."

Lily nodded, recognising puppets of Malphas and Adalwolf, wooden figurines dressed in minute royal robes. The puppeteer also had figures for the red grell, Krieg, the pale grell, Ende, and Queen Romilda. Lily had seen the performance before. In the end, Malphas died beneath a pile of rubble, and Adalwolf became king, uniting all the peoples of Enthilen.

Of course, neither is true, thought Lily, but why ruin a happy ending?

She and Hartmut bid the puppeteer goodbye, then strolled arm-in-arm across the grounds in comfortable silence. Citizens stopped to acknowledge them with a smile, salute or nod. Lily remained cheerful, but Hartmut's feet soon dragged as if a clutch of stones had been piled into each of his boots.

"What are you thinking about?" she asked.

"For so long, Gestade has remained distant from the rest of Enthilen, almost as if the Dambay Plains were a vast ocean no-one would ever cross. But now, with Adalwolf's arrival, the future stands at our gate, and there's no way to keep it at bay."

"Gestade continues to be a harbour for absent royalty. First, Prince Hadufuns, now Adalwolf."

"I'd almost forgotten about Hadufuns," said Hartmut. "Do you think Adalwolf knows the prince survived the assassination attempt in Laodicea?"

"It might be best to keep that to ourselves," said Lily. "Hadufuns disappeared twelve yarles ago and hasn't been seen since. If he's not dead, I expect he doesn't want to be found. Will you cede command to Adalwolf?"

"He has no experience in war. At the time of greatest need, it would be a cruel blow to our people to put a failed king in command."

"He may come in useful, though. The Erstürmen will rally if they see a future similar to their past."

"Adalwolf needs to display a bravery that appears lacking."

"I don't understand why he chose now to announce himself."

Hartmut sighed. "Romilda had a strong hold over the boy. Without a caring father, I warrant she was the only place he found love and affection. Yet, she appeared to use that devotion to meet her desire of having a son rule Enthilen. Indeed, such was her desperation for an heir to the throne; she risked death by being unfaithful to Ewald."

"So, you believe the rumours?" asked Lily. "That Adalwolf is Malphas' son."

"It makes sense. Ewald dead at the hands of tainted grells. A young, confused boy thrust into power, ripe for a puppet-master to pull his strings."

"I don't understand why Malphas wanted Adalwolf to take the throne. The Worshipful Master quickly seized power when Adalwolf disappeared."

"The coronation of Adalwolf was a ruse to placate the masses until Malphas could entrench his authority. The Erstürmen would only march to Pergamos behind their new, legitimate king. Malphas always wanted the Erstürmen to rebuild the lost city, but Adalwolf had to lead them there."

"Is that all he needed Adalwolf for?"

"I don't know."

Lily squeezed Hartmut's arm. "Adalwolf could enlighten us."

Hartmut scoffed. "I doubt it. We've confined him to the command hall for nine moons. His patience grows thin. He wants to announce himself to the people, but I've forbidden it. A Field Commander giving orders to a king is unheard of. Adalwolf isn't likely to grant me any favour."

"Rumours are already spreading about the absent king's return. We can't keep Adalwolf a secret for much longer. Whatever Malphas desired from him, we could use it to stay our enemy's hand."

"For how long, Lily?" Hartmut shook his head. "It's unwise to play a game when you're unaware of all the cards in the deck. Better Adalwolf stays under close watch here in Gestade. Or disappear from Enthilen forever."

A rider galloped her horse through the outpost's east gates, bursting through the crowd preparing for the harvest festival and riding straight to Hartmut and Lily. The horse skidded to a halt as the rider caught her breath.

"Com...com...mander Hartmut," she gasped. "Word from our spies in Pergamos. Malphas will march his army tomorrow, east to Gestade. They come for us."

* * * *

175

Adalwolf slouched in Field Commander Hartmut's chair in the windowless meeting room of Gestade's main hall, picking at the worn cow-hide cover with dirty, broken fingernails. Roben, Hartmut's lieutenant, guarded the door. He'd been standing there since dawn, in full armour, gauntlet resting on the hilt of his sword, and his eyes not wavering from Adalwolf for a moment.

What does Hartmut fear? wondered Adalwolf.

He'd been held captive in this room and the adjacent private quarters since he arrived. Always with guards watching over him, bringing him food and disposing of his waste. Hartmut had the sole window in the private quarters boarded up from the outside, signalling that Adalwolf's claim on the throne of Enthilen threatened not only Malphas.

Adalwolf turned his attention to the wall-hung tapestries depicting notable events in Erstürmen history, one tapestry catching his eye; King Faramund leading scores of Erstürmen refugees from Nordland through Detranté and into Enthilen.

It's a lie, thought Adalwolf. The Erstürmen didn't invade Enthilen through Detranté. The Dobunni always watched the narrow gorge breaching the Desolate Mountains in the north, ready to thwart the advance of an invading army.

Malphas had told Adalwolf a draughoul led Faramund and the refugees along a secret passage under the mountains. A path likely to never be found again. Emerging on the south side of the Desolate Mountains, King Faramund marched his army to Laodicea and defeated the Dobunni with a surprise attack, enshrining Erstürmen reverence for their king. He'd rejuvenated a vanquished people expelled from the north by wild Nordmen after the defeat of King Giltbert. Yet, the victory in Laodicea wasn't absolute. The Dobunni resisted Erstürmen dominance. Faramund secured a truce, dividing Laodicea into quarters, the Erstürmen taking the King's Quarter as their own, with the Dobunni confined mainly to the Southern Vale.

Faramund then turned his attention west, taking Erstürmen settlers to the fishing village of Iglund, perched on an island in the middle of the Anchep River. The king recognised the importance of Iglund's watchtower, Al Mōr Sŭrl, the towering stone turret with commanding views over Enthilen's western border. Despite the difficulty of the river crossing, Erstürmen soldiers overran the Dobunni villagers and secured the tower. Faramund drafted plans for a royal city, laying the inner circle's first stone to mark the heart of Sardis.

Faramund's wife, Queen Ida, gave birth to two daughters and a son, Alaric, who became king at twelve yarles of age when Faramund died. Adalwolf had been told Alaric was a brutal ruler who ground his subjects into despair and poverty as they worked tirelessly to build the walls of Sardis' seven circles. Yet, Erstürmen dominance over Enthilen reached its peak under his rule; Adalwolf's grandfather responsible for finally routing the stone-grells from Malang Gunya, setting the Erstürmen on the path to rediscovering Pergamos under Malang Gunya's flagstones.

Adalwolf groaned as he stood from the commander's seat. The stiff, dutiful Roben stepped further into the room, but Adalwolf waved him away and walked to another tapestry hanging near a cabinet full of parchments. Time had yet to dull the bright colours of the woven picture or fray the cotton threads at the tapestry's edges. He cupped the stump of his right wrist in his left hand behind his back and leaned forward to examine the weaving's intricate details. The absent king stood face-to-face with a younger version of himself carried on the dead throne by four grell pole-bearers. In the picture, Adalwolf towered over the crowd crammed into the square in front of the Master's Hall in the King's Quarter of Laodicea. All raised their arms as one in a salute to the new king.

Adalwolf didn't remember it like that. His memories were a warren of dismay and guilt, undermining any sense of entitlement he had to claim the throne. Yet, in a dark, lonely corner of the burrows, a covetous longing hid, waiting for the right time to again seek the sunlight. On her deathbed, Romilda had rekindled Adalwolf's desire to be king, and he'd announced as much to Commander Hartmut. Now, he fought to suppress the apprehension and overcome Hartmut's reluctance to allow Adalwolf to re-join his subjects. To rule over them once more.

At the bottom of the tapestry, someone had scrawled a title in fading ink: *The coronation of the thief.*

Not every Erstürmen citizen would welcome Adalwolf reclaiming the throne. He jumped when someone knocked on the door.

Roben turned on his heel and opened the door, his armoured frame blocking Adalwolf's view. A brief, quiet conversation ensued until Roben stepped from the room, and Audie stepped in, closing the door behind her.

"Bountiful harvest," said Audie.

Adalwolf half-smiled. "Is it harvest season already? I've lost track of time, trapped in this room."

"The harvest festival has begun. The commander might allow you to attend."

Adalwolf shook his head. "When it comes to important decisions, Hartmut is renowned for taking his time. Roben likely has orders to cut me in half should I try to leave. Even the window in my sleeping quarters has been shuttered tight. The commander isn't ready for his people to reacquaint themselves with their king."

"I wanted to speak to you about that. May I sit?" Audie stepped forward and grabbed the back of a chair.

Adalwolf raised his eyebrows. "You have time to speak with me? I thought you were too busy with the ill."

"There are more ills than those of the body," said Audie.

"Yet those of the body are more easily treated." Adalwolf beckoned Audie to sit.

She pushed a black cotton skirt up against the back of her bare thighs and sat with a graceful finicality.

Adalwolf returned to his seat on the opposite side of the map table to Audie.

"I know Romilda wanted...."

"You shouldn't assume to know anything about my mother," interrupted Adalwolf. "Having shared her company for a fleeting moment."

Audie sighed, then set her face like stone. "I could see she wanted her son to be a great king, but you don't have to be king to lead."

"Without the throne, I'm just a pauper, and the Erstürmen won't follow a peasant."

"Show them leadership by your actions, not the fulfilment of your own desires."

"Who are you to question my desires?" snapped Adalwolf.

Audie flinched, setting a pang in Adalwolf's chest. The kind of regret a child may feel after hurting his mother.

"Queen Romilda's dying wish was for me to reclaim the throne," said Adalwolf. "How can I forsake that after everything she did for me?"

Audie sat tall, pressing the fold of her blood-stained apron into her stomach. "The outpost of Gestade isn't much of a kingdom."

"Better this than nothing."

"Help Hartmut fight Malphas and put aside talk of who is the rightful ruler."

"I'm the rightful ruler!" Adalwolf smacked his hand down on the map table, knocking a cup of meduz onto the floor. The frothy liquid invaded the cracks between worn timber floorboards, and he slumped back in his chair, rubbing his left hand across a furrowed brow. Audie glared at him, declaring her disapproval.

Why should he care for this healer's approval? thought Adalwolf.

"If you throw your support behind Hartmut," continued Audie, "it will serve as a beacon of hope to rally the soldiers."

"We can't defeat Malphas. Nobody can."

"Then Malphas will always rule Enthilen."

Adalwolf clenched his jaw, then sneered. "He isn't the king. He's a usurper and a liar who uses faith in the Divine Creator like a sword to wield his power. Piety is the armour shielding him from scrutiny. Malphas promised me immortality, yet I escaped Pergamos barely with my life."

"Where did you go?"

"Mother arranged for loyal King's Shield to take us to Bramble Island, where we lived in hiding, eating fish and brambleberries for yarle after yarle. When Romilda fell ill, she demanded to return to Enthilen. To die in her homeland. By then, I looked nothing like my younger self, and

Mother kept her scarred face hidden. Both of us wore a veil of shame and secrecy, lest Malphas' spies came looking."

"Rumours abound that Malphas is marching his army to Gestade tomorrow. Soon, there will be no place to hide."

Adalwolf scratched his fingernails into the table, his thoughts drifting across the lands and oceans drawn on the parchments spread over the table's surface. "When I was a child, King Ewald, the man I thought was my father, used to bounce me on his knee, sitting up at the map table in Sardis. He'd tell me stories about the lands of Ostamp; Oder, Sexton, Feyerlund, Morund, Brucht, Nordland, Germalia. I dreamed of travelling to those regions. One day, ruling all of them.

"When I grew too old and heavy to sit on his knee, Ewald dismissed me and concerned himself with more important things. Servants taught me how to dress, how to ride a horse and wield a sword. Mother taught me everything else, forever relishing the day I would take the throne. Ewald resented the attention Romilda gave me, threatening to keep the throne for himself even after he reached the age of succession. To not step aside for his eldest son, his *only* son, despite Erstürmen tradition demanding it.

"Then, when I was sixteen yarles old, Malphas revealed himself, claiming to be my real father and wishing to place me on Enthilen's throne immediately. Can you imagine, Audie, how entranced I became with this revelation? As the days passed, I embraced a new dream formed in someone else's mind. And I sat at the centre of it all. *I* was the fulcrum of Malphas' plans. He said he wanted me to reign forever; 'the eternal reign begins with you.' King Adalwolf the Redeemer, ruling side-by-side with the Worshipful Master, preparing our people for the Divine Creator's return. When Volerdie returned, all three of us would lead the Erstürmen to a better life in paradise."

"Do you believe any of that now?" asked Audie.

"Not a word of it. After we arrived in Pergamos, Mother learned Malphas had more sinister motives for shaping my future. He wanted me to become immortal only so he could sacrifice me on the throne of the dead to entice Volerdie to return to Enthilen. My empty body would be the eternal vessel to house Volerdie's soul."

Audie narrowed her eyes as if much of what Adalwolf said made little sense.

"Some of us have birth twins," continued Adalwolf, "who share the same birthmark. Tom Anderson is my birth twin. If I'd captured his soul using the dark eyes, he would become a draughoul, and I would be immortal. I had a chance. On Hansen's Bluff, overlooking Laodicea. But I couldn't go through with it. As I clenched the dark eyes in my right fist and thrust it against Tom's chest, such a pain coursed through my body I thought my heart would explode. Tom felt it, too, the agony scarring his face. I pulled my hand away and collapsed to the ground. Malphas thinks I was thrown backwards by the shock, but I ended it. I stopped the transfer of souls.

"In Pergamos, Mother convinced me I would never be free of Malphas unless I dispatched him myself, and the only way to do that was to become immortal. One immortal can kill another. I had to steal Tom Anderson's soul before confronting Malphas. There was no other way to set myself free." Adalwolf held up the stump of his right wrist. "Now, that path is no longer available to me."

"Then forge an honourable future," said Audie. "One to make your mother proud."

Adalwolf slumped back in the chair and fell into wavering thoughts. After twelve yarles of hiding, the past had caught up with him, and Romilda wasn't here to provide a guiding hand. He vacillated between Romilda's dream of him reclaiming the throne and Audie's advice to cede to Commander Hartmut and stand by the commander's side when Malphas' army arrived. Adalwolf was sure of only one thing, he couldn't stay trapped in this building with the enemy marching towards him.

* * * *

Lily shimmied the flowing red dress of seamless silk over her naked body and tied her long greying hair into a ponytail. She dabbed two drops of lavender scent behind her ears before slipping on a pair of soft, black shoes, perfect for dancing. The dress' hem brushed against her knees as she rushed outside into the comforting warmth of a calm night. The bonfire had been lit, and Gestade hummed with a radiance of people singing, dancing and feasting. It would take Malphas' army at least five moons to march from Pergamos to Gestade. Lily refused to let the approaching threat dampen her enjoyment of the harvest festival. She danced and sang, laughed at the antics of the royal puppets, feasted on roast plainalope deer, and drank too much meduz. Late in the night, she and Hartmut rode to Gelie Beach, made love on the sand, then lay there staring at the stars twinkling above a gentle ocean.

The joys of life will push back the darkness, thought Lily, as she rested her cheek against the scar on Hartmut's chest. They have to, or else nothing will remain.

~ Chapter 14 ~

W*hy are these ceremonies always at night?* thought Tom, fighting to keep his eyes open. *Do it for Grin's sake.*

On this evening, all the mouldewerps of the Scaur Hills gathered to honour the passing of Grinnian stone-grell. According to Widukind, today was the first day of the harvest season, but the werps had little interest in celebrating such a milestone. They considered honouring the life of a defender of Enthilen's natural world much more important.

Dwarrow had spent the last three moons preparing for the ceremony, leaving Tom to rest and explore the hills. He'd avoided Widukind as much as possible, fearful of what he might do to Nanna's killer. Though immortal, Tom could still inflict psychological pain on Widukind by stoking the pathetic man's feelings of shame. But that would do nothing to allay Tom's own hurt. So, he busied himself by helping to find and prepare werp food, unique delicacies he'd grown to enjoy. And after every meal, he dug a hole and returned food scraps to the soil that yielded Enthilen's bounty. Grin had taught Tom to do this during their first days together in Babir Birramal. A long-ago world, now as foreign as Earth was to Ostamp.

Tonight, under a sky dazzling with thousands of stars fighting to shine the brightest, the crowd stilled to breathless silence. Mouldewerps crammed atop the boulders surrounding the dwell, peered out from burrows or between shrubs, or balanced on each other's shoulders to watch proceedings. Dwarrow boasted he was responsible for such a large turnout. In seasons passed, he would sit beside the dead tree, Tu'sok, telling stories of Grin's bravery and kindness and the sacrifices the grell had made trying to save the land they all loved.

The steady *clack, clack, clack* of two music sticks clapping together drifted over the gathering. Atop the largest boulder, a shaman raised her arms skyward and wailed, serenading the quarter-moon of Seena and the half-moon of Bargan with a song resembling the baying of a wolf. Marching in time to the clacks, Dwarrow led five other elders through the crowd. They encircled Tu'sok and thrust wooden staffs into the ground beside a ring of burning cressets, set aflame for the benefit of Tom, Widukind and Caeli. The ocular designation between light and dark mattered little to the werps. Using olfactory senses honed over generations, they could navigate in pitch black as if it was bright sunlight. Tom recalled his first visit to the dwell with Thaly, Jacob and Grin. The werps had caught them sheltering in one of their sacred caves and took the intruders prisoner, holding Thaly and Jacob in a rocky gaol and tying Grin to Tu'sok while the elders debated the future of the unexpected visitors. Dwarrow made sure Tom wasn't harmed. Even back then, at their first meeting, the secretive werp recognised the importance of Tom Anderson, the birraman from another world. He also understood the worth of Grinnian stone-grell.

The echo of the music sticks faded, and the shaman fell silent. A campfire burned beside Tu'sok, sending amber spectres skipping across the dead tree's ashen-grey bark.

Dwarrow stepped forward, turned his salmon-pink face skyward and called into the night, "Moobok, moobok, moobok."

The burgeoning crowd waited. Widukind and Caeli stood together on the opposite side of Tu'sok from Tom. He glared at Malphas' brother, anger simmering in his mind, then pictured himself thrusting a sword into Widukind's heart.

Won't do any good. Arsehole is immortal.

Shouts came from the werps standing on the boulders. As Tom turned towards them, a gust of wind rushed past his face. An enormous owl, taller than an adult werp, alighted on the highest branch of Tu'sok. White, speckled feathers protruded from its crown like bull horns, and yellow eyes set in tawny facial discs swivelled around the gathering as if searching for the one who had dared mimic its cry.

Dwarrow called again, "Moobok, moobok, moobok."

The owl fixed its gaze on him and replied, *moobok, moobok, moobok.*

Dwarrow raised his staff to the bird and chanted. The owl nodded its head, then plucked a feather from its chest, letting it float to the dead tree's base. Dwarrow ended his chant and stepped back into the line of elders. The owl called one last time, then flew silently into the night.

Another elder stepped forward, placed a clawed hand on his stomach and bellowed a growl that resembled the rumbling of stones sliding down a mountainside. As one, the entire crowd sniffed the air as if a threatening scent stained the night. A commotion behind Tom made him turn on his heels. Beside a blemmel bush, a kerfuffle of werps shrieked and fussed before scuttling apart to allow a clear path into the circle of elders. Down the path sauntered a male boulder lion, half the size of a horse, a mane of black crowning the cream fur of its head and shoulders. With a knowing swagger, the lion walked up to Tu'sok, turned to the growling werp elder and roared a thunderous, ferocious bawl that sent the younger werps cowering behind the legs of their guardians.

The boulder lion sniffed the dead tree's base, then held his front paw up, broke a claw from his toe with his teeth, and dropped the nail next to the owl's feather. The werp elder stopped growling and smacked the heel of his staff into the dirt three times. The lion surveyed the crowd as if selecting his next meal, much to the terror of the werp youngsters, then shook his mane and ambled away from the dwell.

A female elder stepped forward, pursed a leaf horizontally between her lips and blew. Tom strained his ears but couldn't discern a sound. Yet, from the sky, a cloud of bats appeared above the dwell, careering and hurtling in manic flight around the heads of ducking werps. The elder continued her silent symphony, stamping her feet to a rhythm apparently only the bats could hear. A handful landed on Tu'sok, defecated over the owl feather and lion claw, then flew into the night on silent, membraned wings.

Three more elders each summoned an animal. A rock wallaby left behind a tuft of rufous fur, a cave python donated a flake of shed skin, and a golden moth dusted powder from its wings onto the collection beside Tu'sok. Then Dwarrow stepped forward again, knelt and thumped his fist on the ground as if knocking on a door. Near the tree's base, a hatch of dirt the size of a fingernail popped open and out crawled a plump spider.

Tom caught his breath. *Muwin. The ground spider. Grin's facial crest.*

Muwin scurried over all the animal offerings piled at the tree's base, spinning a web to join them together as one. Entranced by the diligent arachnid, Tom stepped closer, more acutely connected to his memories of Grin than ever before. Each new strand of web bound Tom's heart and soul closer and closer to Enthilen.

Job done, muwin returned to its underground home while Dwarrow dug coals from the fire with a metal trowel, shovelling them into the hollowed-out surface of a rock. He placed the webbed package onto the coals, and another elder covered the smouldering collection with panalope leaves. Dwarrow took the stone in his hands, carrying it like a serving tray among the crowd of werps. As mesmerising tendrils of white smoke wafted into their nostrils, the werps reeled and swayed. Then, one by one, they fell to the dirt and curled up like unborn babies.

Dwarrow waved the smoke into Tom's face until his nostrils stung with an aroma resembling burnt eucalypt leaves. The stars in the clear sky spun until their singular luminescence melded into a blur of streaked white. Drowsy, knees buckling, Tom fell into nothingness and kept falling. His mind inhabited the horned owl. In a dreaming twilight, he flew over mountains, rivers and plains, gliding above the canopy of Babir Birramal, where a young Grin pulled a drowning birraman from a stream. Tom followed the forest edge, skimming across the roofs of Süden Forst as a band of escapees ran to freedom. Flying back into the Scaur Hills, the owl showed him the Dobunni, dancing and singing at the Pledge Feste in Bagendon. Following the Anchep River, Tom arrived in the royal city of Sardis and perched on the sill of a barred window in the inner circle's Sunrise Keep. Inside the keep, a lonely Princess Caeli lay on her bed reading a book about a land she'd never visit.

A westerly wind carried Tom from Sardis, then up over the cliffs of Hansen's Bluff above Laodicea. He travelled across the Veiled Occyan, following the wash of the *Vulking*, where a crippled seafarer limped across the ship's deck to stand at the helm beside his captain. A storm brewed above the ocean, sweeping Tom south to treacherous cliffs covered in mist and an army of stone monoliths standing to attention. He swooped low over Bindari before racing towards the Dambay Plains, where the colossal pyramid of Malang Gunya appeared on the horizon. Tom alighted on the pyramid's zenith while rivers of blood flowed down its steps, pooling in the calendar of life among masses of dead grells and werps.

The horned owl then carried Tom's mind to places the birraman had never been. Across a red desert with dunes and swales in endless rows like ripples on the bed of an immense ocean. Over shining cities with golden domes and carefree residents. To tall spires of rock rising from the sea and bleak lands covered in snow and ice. The owl barked and pecked at something tied to its tarsus, a tear of white fabric flapping in the wind. A handkerchief. The one Tom had carried with him on his first journey to Enthilen. The one he'd given to Thaly.

The owl wrenched Tom's mind from this memory and swooped through a narrow chasm and back into the Dambay Plains. In the centre of the plains, surrounded by a wall as tall as a panalope tree, the city of Pergamos reared up like a rapacious bear.

As Tom flew past a turret, a lance exploded from the battlement and hurtled straight towards him.

* * * *

The midday sun evaporated Tom's dreams, and he woke curled up in the dirt beside a smouldering fire with werps snuffling in the distance. Sitting up, he leaned against Tu'sok, pressing his spine into the dead tree trunk and wondering when its roots last drew sustenance from the shallow, rocky soil atop the Scaur Hills. Widukind appeared, crawling from a dwell and then staggering to his feet. He nodded at Tom and ambled towards him, Tom's disdain growing with each step bringing Nanna's murderer closer.

"How are you feeling?" asked Widukind.

"Fine."

"Did you have any dreams?"

Tom shrugged, hoping Dwarrow or Caeli might appear soon.

"The smoke causes visions," said Widukind. "Real or imagined pasts and futures. I became a moth, hiding in a room while an old woman suffocated in the strangulation of a snake. Then I crawled across the face of a monolith inscribed with the life story of a grell called Annian. Around me, Bindari collapsed, gravestones splintered, the ground uprooted, and skeletons scattered across the misty hills like twigs after a flood. All the visions came from my past. The moth showed me nothing of the future."

Tom stood and brushed the dirt from his shorts. "I must find Dwarrow. Change these clothes and prepare for our journey to the Desolate Mountains."

Widukind grasped Tom's hand. "Wait. Please. I know there's nothing I can say to repair what I've done. I accept you'll hate me until the end. I deserve it. But this is also my chance for redemption. To make something good from the evil I did. And you must feel...."

"Feel what? How the *fuck* would you know how I feel?"

"Angry. Frustrated. Remorseful. Confused. I tried to hide from those feelings. In that hole in the bottom of the gorge in Bindari. I tried to absolve my sins and begin a new life."

"You don't deserve a new life," said Tom. "You're a liar and a murderer. You could have admitted your guilt when I first met you."

"If I did, would you have listened to anything I said beyond that?"

Tom's shoulders slumped, accentuating a sigh of resignation. "I hate you, but I hate myself more for not realising sooner you murdered Nanna. Her killer was contrite. 'Forgive me,' he said before leaving my bedroom. Malphas wouldn't have said that. You knew about the blue book. One of its secrets revealed the combination to unlock your front door in Bindari. And those gloves you always wear hide the scars on your hands from using the eyes of lost souls to travel between worlds."

Widukind nodded.

"Caeli spoke *English*," continued Tom. "You taught her because *you* had to learn the language. All these clues I missed, my thoughts blinded by consuming revenge focused on the wrong person. Malphas."

"Malphas is our adversary now," said Widukind. "The enemy of a peaceful Enthilen."

"You brought me back here because you're too afraid to face Malphas yourself. You used Grin to persuade me."

"Grin made his own choice. Either he travelled to Earth to find you or became Eroberung, the white grell. Grin's last action was to trust in you. To have faith you would save Enthilen from an awful future." Widukind placed his hand on Tom's shoulder. "Where did Grin find you?"

Tom pulled away. "What?"

"When he arrived on Earth, where did he find you?"

"In my room. In a...you wouldn't understand."

"In a place you didn't want to be in? Wallowing in a life going nowhere? No purpose. No reason. Is that where you would have stayed until the end?"

"I was making progress." Tom reached for the back pocket of his shorts. The foil packet crunched under his fingers, and he counted six tablets.

Widukind looked on with cheerless eyes. "I made a terrible mistake, Tom. An awful mistake. If Malphas doesn't end my life, I'll live with the pain for eternity. Can you think of a worse punishment? I know you want me to suffer. I *am* suffering. There's nothing you can do to make it worse." Widukind grasped Tom's shoulders with prising, grappling fingers. "All I had left was Caeli. She was the only thing making my endless life bearable. Now, look at her. Look what my daughter's become because of you." Widukind's face swelled with crimson fury. "Caeli's a draughoul because she saved you!"

Tom wrenched himself free of Widukind's grasp and stepped away, bracing for an attack. Widukind was right; if Caeli hadn't wrestled Adalwolf in Pergamos' throne room, the king would have stolen Tom's soul. Tom yanked a cresset from the ground to use as a weapon, but the rage in Widukind shrank as quickly as it had arisen. The tortured man went to walk away.

"Wait," said Tom. "I know you have reason to hate me, too."

Widukind shook his head. "I don't hate you. When you arrived in Bindari, I saw a frightened boy who wanted to find his way home. But now you've returned of your own free will, and the boy has become a man. I know you struggle with the thoughts inside your head, but I also feel a growing strength. A growing sense of purpose. You faced Malphas when I never could, and you've returned to face him again. Your presence quells my anxiety and gives me hope that we can rise to this challenge together."

"And if Adalwolf and I destroy Volerdie's throne, you'll be an immortal no longer. Your endless penance will cease."

Widukind nodded. "It's true. When I'm mortal, you will finally be able to inflict the punishment on me you've so long desired."

Tom shrunk away. "I won't do anything. I can't carry more guilt."

Widukind embraced Tom, nearly knocking him over, then whispered in his ear, "Malphas has to be stopped. It's all that matters."

"Get this blasted bird away from me!" yelled Dwarrow as he trotted towards Tom and Widukind, closely followed by a dodo who pecked out strands of fur from Dwarrow's greying crown.

Tom stepped away from Widukind and smiled. "Mr Prickles is here."

"Yes," said Widukind. "Mr Prickles is more resilient than most of his kind. He escaped Bindari with me."

"Widukind," cried Dwarrow. "What *is* this infernal bird doing? It seems to be trying to build a nest with the only thing keeping me warm. You should control your pet."

Widukind laughed. "He's never done this before. It appears he's taken a fancy to you, Dwarrow. You're about his size."

Dwarrow stood beside Tom, trying to swat Mr Prickles away. "I don't have time for misbegotten courtships. I have important dealings to attend to."

Widukind lured Mr Prickles to the side with an apple.

Tom faced his werp friend. "When are we leaving?"

"Soon," said Dwarrow. "I've called up Xaviary." He pointed to a clump of thorny blemmel bushes at the dwell's edge, where a horse-sized lizard plucked rust-coloured berries from the ends of branchlets with its mouth.

"Are we riding that?" asked Tom.

"Of course we're riding her. We're not going to eat her."

"I need different clothes," said Tom. "Tunic, leggings, boots, a coat."

"Yes, yes, yes. Wirrikow is gathering your supplies now."

"Who?"

"My son, Wirrikow."

"I didn't know you had children. Or a partner. Do male werps have wives?"

"Didn't need one. I gave birth to Wirrikow myself. Before the change."

"Ah...but...you're male, aren't you?"

Dwarrow huffed. "It seems you're as ignorant of werp biology as the rest of Enthilen. Werps are born one gender, then change to another gender later in life. It helps us better appreciate the world's complexities. I was born female. Gave birth to Wirrikow with my male partner before he died, and I changed. My partner's death triggered my transformation." Dwarrow tilted his head and sniffed. "Ah, here's Wirrikow now."

Another werp, younger and shorter than Dwarrow with dark fur and a peach blush to the skin on his face and stomach, emerged from a dwell carrying clothes and a backpack.

Tom leaned down towards Dwarrow. "Does he speak Erstürmen?"

"Of course," said Dwarrow. "I haven't raised a halfwit."

"Hello," Tom said to Wirrikow as the younger werp dropped the clothes and pack beside Tu'sok.

"Greetings, Tom Anderson. It's a pleasure to finally meet you."

"Likewise."

"You have a momentous journey ahead, but you do not face the future alone."

Dwarrow rolled his eyes. "No need to be so melodramatic. I have no idea where you get that from."

Wirrikow looked at Tom with squinty eyes, a faint smile curling up underneath his long, pliant nose, then pointed to the ground. "I've gathered a canvas tunic and pants, a woollen coat and socks, a belt and a pair of old boots borrowed from a Dobunni rebel. In the pack, I've put Grin's totem and yours, the blood compass, a waterskin and food."

"Werp food?" asked Tom.

"Oh, yes," said Wirrikow. "Grated ravens claw fixed in a block of solid toad fat. A jar of slitherweed and bile from the stomach of...."

"Any pickled lizard?" interrupted Dwarrow.

Wirrikow nodded. "No quest is worth undertaking without pickled lizard."

Dwarrow swelled his chest. "That's my boy."

"I've also taken the liberty of grinding your grandmother's finger bone to dust and mixed it with bone dust taken from Princess Caeli. I've placed the mixture in a pouch you can tie to your belt." Wirrikow held the pouch towards Tom.

Dwarrow snatched it away. "I'll be keeping that."

"Why?" asked Tom.

"Make sure it doesn't get lost. You're already burdened with too much responsibility. As the most accomplished adventurer in Enthilen, I must play a major role in this mission."

Tom crouched and sifted through the pile of clothes. "No weapons?"

"I have my walking stick," said Dwarrow. "It's the deadliest weapon in all of Enthilen."

"Nevertheless, I'd feel better with something to defend myself."

"I'll swap my dagger," called Widukind from the edge of the group.

"For what?" asked Tom.

Widukind patted Mr Prickles on the head, then approached Tom. "A vial of your blood and the blood compass. It's the only way we'll find Adalwolf."

"Maybe I should come with you," said Tom. "The blood will get old. Dwarrow can take Grin's totem to Hanni."

"No," said Dwarrow. "We have other important things to do. Crucial things."

"The werps can treat the blood to stop it from drying out," said Widukind. "And I'm Adalwolf's uncle. I have the best chance of convincing him to help us shatter Volerdie's throne."

"Caeli will go with Widukind," said Dwarrow.

"Where is she?" asked Tom.

"Wandering again," said Widukind. "Even with the dark eyes close, the wanderlust pulls her away. But she'll return."

Tom took the eyes of lost souls from his front pocket. "What shall I do with these?"

"Keep them close," said Widukind. "Don't show them to anyone. Since your last visit to Enthilen, stories about the dark eyes have spread far and wide. Others saw what happened in Pergamos and didn't keep their tongue."

"Come on," snapped Dwarrow. "No time for chit-chat." The werp marched off towards Xaviary.

Tom gave Widukind the blood compass, changed his clothes and shouldered the pack; a simple animal-skin bag that wouldn't attract the same attention as the red and black leather backpack he'd brought from Earth. He held his scarred palm towards Widukind and turned away, wincing when the dagger sliced open his finger and blood drained into a vial the size of two thimbles.

Dwarrow returned riding Xaviary.

"How do I get up there?" asked Tom.

Dwarrow tapped Xaviary's scaly head, and the lizard swung her tail down to form a ramp. Tom slipped Widukind's dagger under his belt, then clambered up the tail, as thick as his own thigh, to sit behind Dwarrow and the frills poking from the nape of Xaviary's neck.

"No saddle?" queried Tom.

"Clench your bottom cheeks together," said Dwarrow. "You'll be fine. We'll head for The Feign first, then into the valleys of the Desolate Mountains towards Lokan. Are you ready, Tom Anderson?"

"Yes."

"Excellent. Then it's time to follow...."

"...my nose," finished Tom.

"*Hmph.* It seems I'm becoming predictable."

Widukind, Wirrikow and dozens of werps lined the path from the dwell to bid Tom and Dwarrow goodbye. Sun beat down on Tom's thinning hair, sending rivulets of sweat along the furrows of his brow. The parching stillness of the Scaur Hills sucked the moisture from his mouth. He longed to drink from his waterskin but decided to ration the supplies, not knowing when they'd next encounter fresh water. The last werp shaded her eyes from the sun as she closed in behind Xaviary's tail, blocking the path back to the dwell.

No going back now. Another journey had begun. Tom didn't know exactly where this one would lead or how long it would take, but worried it may be his last. Somehow, he had to find the throne of the dead again. He and Adalwolf. Find it and destroy it.

~ Chapter 15 ~

Thaly brushed a stray hair from Chloe's face and kissed her cinnamon lips. Chloe opened her mouth, and the two lovers tangled moist, searching tongues. Sinking into a mattress stuffed with the fleece of creatures living far across the Occidian Sea, Thaly rolled Chloe onto her back and pressed her thigh between her lover's long legs. Enveloped between silk sheets, two naked bodies shuddered together in lust. Thaly dropped her head and brushed her tongue along the length of Chloe's neck, her skin tasting as sweet as caramel, then lingered over pendent breasts, teasing taut, puckered areoles with gentle bites, before disappearing under the sheet towards the foot of the bed.

Chloe arched her back, pressing her groin against Thaly's penetrating tongue and moaning a desiring ache. She pulled the sheet away and rested her hand on the back of Thaly's head, guiding her lover's exploration. Outside, the bells of Portum's clocktower pealed, announcing two lumina in the morning. As the peal reached a crescendo, Chloe clutched a pillow and folded it over her face, biting into the cotton-covered plumage. Despite the smother, her moans of climax drowned out the city's noise.

She pressed down on Thaly's shoulders and whispered, "Enough... enough."

Thaly kissed Chloe's wetness, then raised her head and smiled. Chloe pulled her up and kissed her mouth, forcing her tongue between Thaly's pursed lips.

Thaly pulled away. "It's alright. We should get ready for the Eligens."

"Are you sure?"

"You can owe me."

Thaly stood and opened the burgundy curtains to the only window in Chloe's room, then shielded her eyes from the morning sunlight reflecting off the Pallaxium's golden dome. As a senator, Thaly could request more elaborate accommodation than the single room Chloe lived in. Her lover's employment as an anitor attracted a modest wage, enough for a room in a townhouse with communal bathing and cooking areas. Senators commanded private, multi-room houses with servants for cooking and cleaning. Thaly wasn't ready for that yet, still dividing her time between her parent's apartment and Chloe's room.

One day, Thaly thought, she and Chloe would move in together.

She turned from the window to let the morning sun highlight Chloe's buxom curves dressed in chocolate skin, making them look even more enticing. Her lover's supple comfort was a welcome contrast to Thaly's athletic leanness, forged by yarles of training and battle. And Chloe's ambivalence towards the military redirected Thaly's thoughts to matters of greater importance than defeating enemies.

Chloe rolled onto her back. "Bountiful harvest. Is that what you say?"

Thaly smiled. "You remembered. I *think* this is the first day of the harvest season. Sometimes I lose track." She sat on the bed.

Chloe reached across and curled a lock of Thaly's hair around her finger. "Wait. What's this? Is this a grey hair?"

"Ha, ha. I'm not much older than you."

"But today, you're a yarle older, right?"

Thaly nodded.

Chloe leaned across to the opposite side of the bed and reached underneath the mattress. Her hand reappeared with a small timber box resting on her palm.

"Open it," she said.

"What is it?" asked Thaly, taking the box and turning it around in her fingers.

"A present. Today is your birth day. Your thirtieth harvest season, right?"

Thaly nodded.

"It's a special day. We should celebrate."

Thaly prised open the box's tiny lid to reveal a pearl ring snuggled inside red velvet. As she plucked the ring from its nest, specks of light resembling salt crystals dotted the air, powered by the morning sunlight streaming through the window.

"It's a friendship ring," said Chloe. "I'm not asking you to marry me. Yet."

Thaly held the ring to her eye, marvelling at the perfect circle of radiant white. "It feels stronger than steel. Who made this? How?"

"I can't give away all my secrets. Put it on." Chloe sat up and rested her back against the cedar headboard.

"Which finger? Is there a tradition?"

"Forefinger. It'll fit. I already measured."

Thaly raised her eyebrow.

"When you were asleep," said Chloe, smiling.

Thaly placed the ring on her index finger and held her hand to the ceiling. "It's beautiful. Thank you." She leaned across and kissed Chloe on the lips.

"Now you can't avoid it anymore," said Chloe.

"Avoid what?"

"Introducing me to your parents. I don't know how you've kept our relationship a secret for so long."

"When I'm not home, I tell them I sleep in the Pallaxium, or with the griffins, or have a night patrol."

"Such elaborate lies, Athalee Stansfield. Today is the day to face reality. Everyone will be at the Eligens to see Saskia become the next wind-rider. It's the perfect time to introduce me."

Thaly sighed, then turned her attention to the paintings hanging from Chloe's sandstone wall. "I know you're right, but...."

"You have told them, haven't you? That you prefer women?"

"Yes...and no. I mean, not directly. My parents believe I'm married to the military and don't have time for a relationship, and my father's still hoping for grandchildren."

"He has another daughter. Saskia can be the dutiful offspring and deliver grandchildren to the mighty General Jurelle Stansfield. She's already chasing a kamel handler named Heron."

"How do you know? I found out only recently."

Chloe tapped a fingertip on the end of her button nose. "Anitors see and hear all." She grasped Thaly's hand. "Love, in all its forms, is nothing to be ashamed or embarrassed about. We must embrace what we have. Celebrate it, and let others share the celebration. Too soon, love can disappear." The morning sun evaporated Chloe's smile. She released Thaly's hand and slouched back against the headboard, looking glum.

Thaly swung her legs onto the bed and sat beside her lover, caressing Chloe's thigh with her fingers. "What's wrong?"

"I hear what goes on in the conventus. I know some senators want to fight a war against Malphas in Enthilen. If we vote for war, then...."

"Don't think about it," said Thaly.

"How can I not? Already you're flying into Magna Avium to fight an insurgent Pordillo. I can't help but worry that you won't return one day."

Thaly wrapped her arm around Chloe's shoulder and pulled her to her chest.

"I'm never going back to Enthilen. You shouldn't fret."

"You might not have a choice." Chloe pulled away, reached across the bed and took Thaly's tattered white handkerchief from the side table. "Why do you keep this? It's almost falling apart."

"It's a reminder of someone I cared about a long time ago. A young man."

Chloe rubbed her finger across the embroidered letters in the corner of the cotton fabric. "What are these?"

"His initials," said Thaly. "T. A. Tom Anderson."

"Did you love him?"

"I cared about him. He needed protection."

"From what?"

"It's a long story. Tom's life was tangled up with the insanity gripping Enthilen. He came from another place, far away, and then disappeared, leaving behind chaos."

"Where did he go?"

"I'm not entirely sure. I didn't believe everything he told me, though he seemed sincere. I know *he* believed it. It's all in the past; my future is here with you."

* * * *

Thaly walked hand-in-hand with Chloe into Portum's main stadium to watch the Eligens — the choosing of the next wind-rider. Underneath curling, dark clouds trapping in the heat, the burgeoning crowd hummed with energy and excitement. Such an event had happened only once before, three yarles ago when the original twelve riders were selected after the Germalians discovered a colony of griffins on a remote island. Thaly remembered it well; she became a senator and a wind-rider in the same yarle.

Around the sandstone amphitheatre, thousands of people stood or sat on tiered levels underneath twelve banners pulsating with the wind like the sails on a classem warship. Each flag had a different colour and a unique animal totem representing the twelve factions of the Germalian people. The crowd's clothing reflected the occasion's importance. Long, flowing robes of cream and tan, cinched around the waist with tasselled cords spun with silver thread, and circlets of fabric draped around the neck and extending to the small of the back, representing the colours of each faction. Thaly wore the Capri faction's green circlet, and Chloe wore the indigo circlet of Pisce. Almost everyone in the crowd, including Thaly and Chloe, wore a broad-brimmed hat pulled low over the brow to protect against the harsh sun. Though now, clouds had drifted in off the Occidian Sea, and Thaly thought it might rain, an event in Portum almost as rare as the Eligens.

As she navigated through the crowd, Thaly surveyed the red sand of the empty playing field inside the stadium, visualising Saskia sitting triumphantly on the riderless griffin, Namu. Thaly's younger sister hadn't trained hard enough, and she likely wouldn't be selected, but Saskia had a habit of delivering surprises, welcome and unwelcome.

Thaly led Chloe to a spot underneath the Capri faction's green banner with the totem of a white dune goat. Jurelle and Genevea were already there, waiting. Thaly's father hadn't cinched his robes properly, and the Libr faction's orange circlet hung low down his chest instead of his back where it should be. In a rare occurrence, Jurelle looked awkward, uncertain and nervous, unlike Genevea, who presented as the stately Erstürmen princess whatever the situation. Among a crowd of dark-skinned, plump-cheeked Germalians, Genevea's angular, pearl-white face made her look like a marble statue, as if a sculptor had fashioned her features there on the spot.

"Your palms are sweating," said Chloe as they approached Thaly's parents.

"It's so humid today," said Thaly. "Can't you feel it?"

"Are you sure that's all it is?"

Thaly faced Chloe with a nervous smile, then approached Jurelle and Genevea. "Pa, Ma, this is Chloe."

A beaming Genevea placed the palm of her hand on her chest. "Arve, Chloe."

Chloe copied the greeting and replied, "Bountiful harvest."

"Yes, I think you're right." Genevea faced Jurelle. "I told you this was the first day of harvest season."

Jurelle's back stiffened as he nodded towards Chloe.

Genevea appeared to scowl at him before resuming pleasantries. "Jurelle's so old, he'd rather forget the passing of harvest seasons. We'll celebrate this eve. It's Thaly's thirtieth harvest season and Saskia's eighteenth. You'll come, won't you, Chloe?"

Chloe faced Thaly, her eyes searching for guidance.

"We have other...," started Thaly.

Genevea reached across and grabbed Chloe's forearm. "You must come. It will be so nice to have the family together. We hardly see Thaly anymore. She's always so busy with conventus and the Volatal Vexil."

"We'll be there," said Thaly, realising her protests wouldn't prevail.

"Is this your first Eligens, Chloe?" asked Genevea, flicking her long, tawny hair from under the violet circlet around her neck, the colour of the Scorp faction.

"Yes, Domina Stansfield...I mean, Princess...*ah*...."

"Call me Genevea. Despite the clouds, it's still a lovely day for it. Now the wind is abating."

"Yes, lovely. I don't get outside much."

"Where do you work?"

"In the Pallaxium. I'm an anitor for the conventus."

"Is that where you met Thaly?"

Chloe smiled. "Yes, she was running late, and I had to lock her out. We talked for ages. I fell for her...."

Jurelle narrowed his eyes. "Her what?"

Chloe blushed and dropped her gaze to her sandals.

"Don't be a buffoon, Pa," said Thaly.

"Thaly can be very engaging when she wants to," said Genevea to Chloe. "She takes after her father. I fell for his doleful brown eyes during a forbidden courtship."

Thaly groaned. "Ma, not this story again. Chloe doesn't want to hear it."

Chloe raised her head. "It's alright. Go on, Domin...Genevea."

"Well, Thaly's probably told you, Jurelle used to be the Dobunni rebel leader, and me, an Erstürmen princess. Sworn enemies who became lovers. If anyone in Sardis discovered our secret trysts, I'd be executed. I had to sneak from the royal city at night to meet him in the woods across the Anchep River."

"How did you first meet?" Chloe asked.

"He tried to kidnap us."

"That's not true," said Jurelle.

"Well, it's a matter of debate," said Genevea. "The rebels ambushed our carriage on the way to Laodicea. Thieves and vagabonds, every one of them. Wounded some of our Shield and held the others captive at sword point. I cowered inside the wagon with my cousin, Princess Caeli, and our handmaidens. Then a brute flung the door open."

"We only wanted food," said Jurelle. "The gluttonous citizens of Sardis left little for anyone else."

"That's probably why you gained so much weight inside the inner circle." Genevea patted Jurelle's stomach. "Dobunni rebels were the least of our worries. From the Desolate Mountains came wild mountain men, screaming a portent of death. Erstürmen and Dobunni fought side-by-side that day. Jurelle stood at our carriage door and thwarted every attack. Who would believe it? A Dobunni saving Erstürmen royalty. I fell in love with him right there and then. Whenever I rode near the Scaur Hills, I felt him hiding among the rocks watching me."

"You rode there because you knew the rebel outpost was nearby," said Jurelle. "You were looking for me."

"Don't flatter yourself."

"Ma, Chloe's bored with this story," said Thaly.

"No, I'm not," said Chloe. "It's fascinating. I want to know more about... well, everything. Thaly never talks about herself."

"They're here." Jurelle pointed to the arena of sand.

Trumpets blared. A draconarius marched in first, bearing the Volatal Vexil standard, a red and yellow flag with a polished silver griffin perched at the top. Behind her came five women dressed in short tunics and sandals. The crowd rose as one to applaud their arrival. Saskia's honey-coloured hair, tied in a ponytail, stood out among her raven-haired competitors. The women had passed the first vetting of potential wind-riders. Thaly's pulse raced, recalling how she'd felt marching into the stadium, hoping a griffin may select her to be its rider.

Chloe waved at the riders. "Arve, Sas!"

"How well do you know Saskia?" asked Jurelle.

"We've met a few times, General Stansfield."

"When you say *met*, what exactly...."

Thaly rolled her eyes. "Oh, for goodness' sake, Pa. Chloe's not sleeping with Saskia too."

"*A-ha*. So, she is sleeping with *you*."

Genevea tugged on Jurelle's sleeve. "Saskia likes that kamel stable-hand. What's his name?"

"Heron," said Thaly. "You also knew about him?"

"Of course." Genevea smiled at Jurelle. "See, General Stansfield, there's still a chance we'll have grandchildren."

Jurelle lifted his chin and raised himself up onto the balls of his feet as if the first grandchild had been born this morning.

"Let's hope they don't inherit his narrow-mindedness," said Thaly, lifting her fingers to her lips.

"Are you biting your nails again?" asked Chloe.

"No. I have dry skin on the tip of my finger."

"She always bites her nails when nervous," said Genevea. "And she gets sweaty palms, like her father." Genevea's eyes grew wide. "Oh, where did you get that gorgeous ring, Thaly?"

Thaly lowered her hand, hiding it and the pearl friendship ring into a fold of her robes. "Chloe gave it to me."

Jurelle frowned. "Must be serious. Such an expensive gift."

"Pa."

Jurelle leaned closer to Chloe. "What do your parents do?"

"They have passed."

"Oh, sorry. I didn't mean to intrude."

"There's no need to apologise, General Stansfield."

"Call me Jurelle."

Thaly smiled at Chloe, then faced the arena. "They're getting ready for the first challenge. Saskia is lucky to be here. She disobeyed orders at Wonchulus, costing the lives of ten Germalian fighters. Elpis was going to report her to the turma Legatus. I advised against it. I know Sas wants to be the next wind-rider. The misstep at Wonchulus should have cost her that chance, but I buried the mistake."

"You're becoming a true politician," said Chloe.

"Thaly grows more like her father every day," Genevea said to Chloe. "For him, family always comes first." She grabbed Jurelle's hand. "You're pacing again."

Jurelle raised an eyebrow. "I'm standing perfectly still."

"You're pacing inside your head. I can see it on your face."

"I'm nervous for Saskia."

"All that matters is Saskia does her best. If she becomes a griffin-rider, you'll only divert your worries to her falling from the sky."

"It's *wind-rider*, Ma." Thaly turned from her parents and caught Chloe's beaming smile, enjoying the exposure of Thaly under the probing light of family ties. With the advantage of personal distance, Genevea recognised the similarities between Jurelle and Thaly more than Thaly did herself. And Thaly understood Genevea worked hard to forge a stronger bond between mother and daughter. To allay the regret she carried for abandoning Thaly as a baby. Somehow, sometime, Thaly needed to acknowledge the effort.

But now, she turned her focus to Saskia, who had a one-in-five chance of becoming the next wind-rider if she could control her recklessness and emotions.

* * * *

Oh my, thought Saskia, look how many people are here.

The vast crowd sucked the air from Saskia's lungs as she marched into the stadium with the other four budding wind-riders behind the draconarius carrying the Volatal Vexil banner. Rills of hot red sand, warmed by the morning sun before a bank of clouds drifted in off the ocean, sifted through the openings in her leather sandals, burning the tops of her feet. She curled her toes, aching to plonk down and deal with the discomfort, but thousands of pairs of eyes yearned to pass judgement, and she hadn't even begun the first challenge.

On a platform within the arena, seated in her wheelchair, Charmion waited for the hopeful riders. Testament to the occasion's importance, only the conventus Sella could oversee proceedings. Walking towards Charmion, Saskia tightened the mustard-coloured sash tied around her waist, identifying her as a rider from the Tavr faction, and scanned the crowd for her family. One distant face blended into another until the gathering resembled a collage of dark skin, cream cloth and circlets of rainbow colour.

Behind Saskia marched Kallisto from Scorp, the only faction without a wind-rider. And Jayla, the deceased wind-rider, was from Tavr. If Saskia won the Eligens, Tavr would again have two wind-riders, further fuelling the feud between Scorp and Tavr.

Saskia expected this to work against her. Moreover, Kallisto had trained with Namu, the riderless griffin, as Jayla's apprentice. During the Eligens, Kallisto couldn't complete any riding challenge with Namu. Nevertheless, should Kallisto win the Eligens and be presented to Namu as her potential rider, the griffin would almost certainly select someone familiar. Kallisto would have considered all the permutations. Saskia had seen her working with other griffins in the holding pens, hedging her chances.

I'm so dumb, thought Saskia. Should have trained with griffins other than Yagle.

The competitors stood at attention in front of Charmion. The Sella raised both arms skyward as the clouds parted and sunlight bathed the stadium. Thousands of onlookers stilled as one, only the flapping of banners buffeted by a gust of wind breaking the tension.

Charmion called down to the hopeful contestants, "At ease, fighters of Germalia. You have passed the first hurdle by being accepted into the Eligens. Now, inside this arena, you will face seven demanding challenges. The winner of each challenge will receive a griffin feather they must carry with them until the end. After completing the tasks, the three competitors with the most feathers will proceed to the next stage atop their assigned griffins."

Charmion waved her hand, and the haunting wail of a bellum cornu filled the arena. Male servants sprinted over the ground preparing the equipment for the first challenge, a tower at least five stories high with an enormous cushion at its base.

Damn, thought Saskia, not fond of heights. Stupid phobia for someone who wants to ride griffins.

She walked to the tower's base, realising too late the other four competitors had held back. A servant at the top of a timber ladder beckoned her to climb. She grasped the ladder rails and pulled hard, testing they'd been tied securely to the tower's struts.

"What are you waiting for?" asked Kallisto. "Scared of heights? You realise griffins fly, don't you?"

The other competitors tittered, and Saskia's face burned with unease. "Shut up," she growled, shaking out the sand trapped inside her sandals and stepping onto the first rung.

Kallisto prised her fingers under Saskia's sash and held her back, whispering in her ear, "You better concentrate, Greenskin. Last time you made a mistake, ten soldiers died."

Saskia pulled away, wanting to spin around and slap Kallisto in the face. But she kept her composure.

Deep breaths and don't look down, she thought as she ascended the ladder.

Reaching the top platform, the wind picked up, nearly blowing her off the edge. She clutched at a handrail with her left hand.

The servant gave her a lance. "Jump from the tower and throw your lance at the target." He pointed to a bulging sack with a bullseye painted on it, hanging from gallows near the arena's edge. "Don't release the lance before you jump; otherwise, you'll be disqualified. And make sure you land on the cushion. Otherwise, you'll die."

Holding the lance in her right hand, Saskia released the handrail and crept to the platform's edge to check the cushion's location. On the ground, the cushion looked as large as a house, but up here, it appeared no bigger than a saddle blanket on a kamel. She balanced the lance on her shoulder.

"Jump!" yelled the servant.

Alright, don't rush me, thought Saskia.

She gritted her teeth, raised the lance and pushed her arm back, preparing to throw. In a blur, she took one step from the platform and panicked, launching the lance much earlier than planned. Hair slapped her face as she plummeted to the ground and landed on the cushion with a whoosh. She jumped to her feet and checked the target on the sack. Her lance had pierced the bullseye.

Done it! she thought, turning to the crowd to bask in the adoration.

A judge, a senator from the conventus dressed in red, raced over to Saskia and screeched, "Disqualified! Your foot was still touching the tower when you released the lance."

"What? How can you see from down here? What a load of...."

"Disqualified," snapped the senator. "No argument."

Saskia bit her tongue, scuffed the sand with her sandals, then stormed off to watch the other competitors.

Two more hopefuls jumped, threw their lance and hit the edge of the target. The third competitor missed the sack completely. Kallisto came last and hit the bullseye.

Of course she did, fumed Saskia, crossing her arms as Kallisto accepted the first feather from the judge.

Through the entrance to the arena, handlers led in five young male kamels, the beasts grunting and spitting foam. Heron struggled with the first kamel, yanking on its reins to guide it towards the middle of the arena. The sheen of the young man's muscled arms glinted in the sunlight as he pulled the reins tight. Heron smiled at Saskia, but the acknowledgement didn't put her at ease, her mind already churning with thoughts of the next challenge.

"This task will test balance under duress and the ability to build a connection with an animal," said Charmion. "You must ride your kamel six laps of the arena. The first to finish will receive a feather. If you fall, you will be disqualified."

Great, thought Saskia, they've chosen the most cantankerous kamels they could find.

Heron led his kamel towards her. "You've got this," he said, guiding the kamel onto its knees so Saskia could climb into the saddle.

She paused to admire Heron's clean, boyish face, then stroked the kamel's neck and hummed a lilting tune in its ear before gripping the pommel and swinging her leg over the seat. Heron brushed his fingers along her bare forearm before handing her the reins, further stoking her nervous energy. The kamel rose to its feet.

"What's his name?" asked Saskia.

"Iratus," said Heron, trying to hand her a crop.

She pushed it away. "No. Kamels hate them."

Iratus swung his head about, moaning and thrashing saliva into the air. Saskia leaned forward and rubbed his flank, trying to keep her muscles loose and her thoughts calm. Iratus' head stilled, and his body stopped quaking.

In front of Saskia, Kallisto teetered in the saddle while her kamel kicked at the handler. Kallisto tried to control her mount's outbursts with a crop, smacking the leather whip against the kamel's neck. That angered the beast further. He spun around in circles until Kallisto crashed into the sand, rolling away from the kamel's stamping feet.

A judge from the Sagit faction, dressed in yellow robes, approached Kallisto. "Disqualified," said the judge.

"I didn't get a chance to race," said Kallisto.

"Only one chance," replied the judge. "Fall off. Disqualified."

Saskia tried not to smile, but she couldn't help it.

The four remaining riders moved up to the starting line to prepare for the race around the arena. Every apprentice wind-rider could ride a kamel. Victory would be hard fought.

Before the riders settled, the bellum cornu wailed, and the sprint began. The crowd's roar swamped any chance Saskia had to soothe Iratus with her voice. Instead, she kept her body loose and supple, trying to move in concert with her mount. They stayed at the rear of the pack, using the other kamels to reduce headwind resistance. Iratus was the largest kamel, built more for short bursts of speed than distance running. Saskia planned to conserve his energy as much as possible before launching a decisive sprint near the end.

They kept pace with the leading pack for five laps. At the start of the sixth lap, Saskia moved Iratus to the outside of the group and yelled into his ear as if a band of blood-thirsty Pordillo were on their tail. Iratus threw his head back and kicked forward, flying past the third-placed rider as if she stood still. Then he passed the second rider.

With half a lap to go, Saskia bore down on the front runner, Iratus' head now level with the leader's tail. As they rounded the last bend, Saskia leaned forward, preparing to yell a final encouragement to Iratus. Then the leader veered off course, and her kamel crashed into the railing separating the arena from the crowd. The rider flew from her saddle and cannoned into a group of spectators. Saskia focussed straight ahead, turning into the home straight and racing over the finish line in first place.

She tugged on Iratus' reins and sat tall in the saddle, basking in the crowd's cheers. As she bounced atop the trotting kamel during a victory lap, she passed the fallen rider who sat with the crowd while being treated by a healer. Saskia guided Iratus over to the rider.

"She's alright," the healer said to a judge. "But she can't continue the competition."

One down, thought Saskia. Four left.

The remaining competitors completed another three physical tasks, shooting arrows at moving targets, racing each other on foot, and high jump. At the point of exhaustion, Charmion introduced the final two challenges to test mental acumen; a game of latrunculi against a seasoned opponent, and organising miniature soldiers into the correct hierarchy of military ranks.

At the end of seven challenges, Kallisto held three feathers, Saskia two, and Helena, the oldest in the group and representing the Leo faction, also had two. Saskia won the kamel race and running race but competed poorly in the mental challenges, which Helena won. Without any feathers, the remaining challenger left the Eligens.

A trumpet blared, and handlers led three griffins into the arena, the animals having to duck their heads to fit underneath the entrance archway. Puer, the old man Saskia had berated in the mounting yards, led Yagle.

Saskia's hopes lifted. Please, please, please, she thought, match me with Yagle. Completing the next tasks on the only griffin she'd trained with would give her an advantage over the other competitors.

As if her thought had been a command, Puer stood beside her, bowed his head and offered Yagle's reins. A flush of remorse stung Saskia's face as she recalled how rude she'd been to the griffin handler.

"Arve, Puer," she said, placing her palm against her chest.

He responded in kind. "Arve, Domina Stansfield."

"Look, I'm sorry about yelling at you the other day."

"My clumsiness deserved to be reprimanded, Domina Stansfield."

No, it didn't, thought Saskia.

Yagle crowed and pushed his bill into Saskia's back. She turned and smiled. "I don't have any rats for you."

Charmion descended the platform's ramp, using the spoked handwheels attached to the armrests of her wheelchair to propel herself forward. A bare-chested man with muscles resembling sculpted slabs of granite draped in ebony skin, met her at the bottom of the ramp, then helped Charmion push her wheelchair through the arena's sandy soil.

She approached the three riders. "Congratulations, Germalian fighters. You've proven yourselves worthy to face the penultimate challenge." She pointed skyward, where paper lanterns filled with hot air floated above the stadium, hoops, flags and targets hanging beneath them. The clouds had drifted away, and a blanket of blue sky draped over Portum again. "Above you," said Charmion, "awaits an airborne obstacle course. You must navigate your griffins through this course to score as many points as possible. A point is awarded for every flag you gather. They are limited in number. Two points are awarded for every hoop you fly through, and each hoop can only be flown through once, so don't waste time approaching a hoop another rider has already conquered."

"How will we know?" asked Saskia.

"The judges will keep track, and so must you. This challenge is not only about your skill as a wind-rider. It's also about your awareness of fellow riders. Wind-riders often travel together and must know where their companions are at all times. Finally, there are two different types of targets floating above you. Seven targets are for your arrows. You will score three points for every bullseye, and you may shoot at any target until your arrows are spent. Three targets are for your lance. There are six lances, two for each rider. You will score five points if you hit a target with your lance. Once a target has been hit by any rider, no points will be scored if it is hit again. At the end, when the bellum cornu blows, the two riders with the most points will proceed to the final challenge. Do you understand?"

Saskia twisted her sandals into the sand, trying to process everything Charmion had said. She'd practised with the lance, but so had Kallisto and Helena. Saskia needed to get to the lance targets first; they yielded the most points.

"Good luck, Domina Stansfield," said Puer as he turned and walked from the arena.

Saskia faced the sky and mentally mapped each target's location. She then joined Kallisto and Helena in leading the griffins to a mounting platform that had been wheeled into the arena. Kallisto ascended the stairs first and climbed into the saddle of her griffin, Lien. Helena followed, mounting Chirité.

How much training have they done with these griffins? wondered Saskia. Not as much as you and Yagle, she tried to convince herself.

Yagle yanked on his reins and crowed, impatient to fly.

"Alright," said Saskia. "Don't be in such a hurry." She climbed the stairs and then checked everything on the saddle and harness, like Thaly had taught her, not wanting a faulty piece of equipment to be her downfall. The lances could be reached easily, and their sheaths loose enough for a fast withdrawal. Saskia took a bow and quiver from the platform, slung them over her shoulder, then climbed into the saddle, looping her legs through the harness and cinching it tight across her thighs.

She whispered into Yagle's ear, "We can do it, boy. Thaly's watching us."

Despite her words of reassurance, dread hit Saskia like a punch to the chest. She'd never flown on Yagle alone. Always with Thaly. Her muscles tightened. The sweat damming on her brow burst its furrowed banks and drenched her face. She sluiced it away and tried to steady the tremor in her arm. Yagle's body shuddered underneath her.

'Griffins can sense your emotions,' came Thaly's voice.

Stay calm, thought Saskia. For goodness' sake.

The hopeful wind-riders settled, and Charmion waved her hand. A male servant standing atop the platform blew into a bellum cornu until a wail echoed around the stadium, and the crowd cheered.

Saskia's mouth turned as dry as the deserts of Magna Avium. She leaned into Yagle's twitching ear and yelled above the crowd, "Let's fly!"

With a shriek, the griffin trotted away from the mounting platform, then flapped his mighty wings until the momentum sent him airborne. As Saskia took to the sky, onlookers removed their neck circlets and waved them above their heads in a multicoloured blur of celebration and encouragement. The wind rushed past Saskia's face and tangled her sweat-sodden hair, the cuffs of her cotton tunic slapping bare arms with a sting.

Atop Yagle, Saskia's fear of heights dissolved amid her complete trust in the griffin's abilities. She guided him to the first lance target, unsheathed her weapon and flung it at the bullseye. *Strike!* She turned for the second target, but Kallisto had beaten her to it, and Helena secured the third. The points tally would be close. Saskia unshouldered her bow and set her sights on the arrow targets.

* * * *

Above Thaly, three griffins swooped and whirled among broken clouds. People gasped and cheered when the competitors took a flag, threaded a hoop or hit a target with an arrow or a lance. Thaly urged Saskia on, picturing herself in Yagle's saddle and willing the griffin to fly towards victory.

"She's going for the arrow targets," Thaly said to Chloe. "It's not the right strategy. She should fly through the hoops first, then collect as many flags as possible. The arrow targets are open to anyone for the course duration."

Jurelle cupped his hands around his mouth and yelled skyward, "Hoops, Sas! Go for the hoops!"

"She can't hear you," said Thaly. "You can't hear anything up there except the wind whistling past your ears."

Around the perimeter of the aerial course, four judges mounted on griffins tracked the competitors' progress, tallying the scores and watching to see if any rider should be disqualified. Thaly waited for a judge to fly to Saskia and bar her from the course for an error. But the moment never came, and the bellum cornu wailed sooner than Thaly expected.

The three apprentice riders landed their griffins within the arena while Charmion conferred with her judges.

Thaly yanked on Chloe's arm. "How many points did Sas get?"

Chloe smiled. "I don't want to ruin the surprise."

"You'd have to know everyone's points to determine if Saskia won," said Jurelle.

"She knows," said Thaly. "It's written in her smile."

Chloe's smile widened. "I've counted the points for all the riders. I know who won."

"That's impressive," said Genevea.

"I'm used to keeping track of two hundred and eighty-eight senators. Scoring points for wind-riders is like crumbling a cake."

"The judges have separated," said Jurelle.

Charmion's hulking male servant wheeled her up the ramp onto the podium. The bellum cornu blasted to quieten the crowd.

"I'm not going to hear this announcement," said Jurelle. "The crowd's making too much noise. Thaly, can you hear?"

"If you be quiet," said Thaly.

Charmion took a deep breath and yelled her pronouncement, "In second place, with twenty-six points, is Kallisto Stratus."

"What did she say?" asked Jurelle. "Who?"

"Kallisto came second, Pa," replied Thaly.

"Does that mean Sas won?"

"We don't know yet. Someone must've done well to beat a tally of twenty-six points."

"*Sssh*," said Chloe. "Here comes the announcement of the winner."

"In first place," cried Charmion, "with thirty points, is Saskia Stansfield."

Thaly and Chloe jumped up and down, then hugged each other.

"Did she say Saskia?" asked Jurelle. "Genevea, did you hear?"

Genevea placed her arm around her husband. "Yes, my dear General, our daughter is the winner."

Jurelle swelled his chest and beamed a smile at the crowd around him as if they'd erupted into spontaneous congratulations.

Thaly pulled away from Chloe. "We can't get too excited yet. The final and hardest challenge is ahead, and even if Saskia wins that, Namu may reject her, and they would continue the Eligens without Sas."

"So, if she beats Kallisto in the final challenge, it could all be for nothing?" asked Genevea.

"The riderless griffin must accept the new rider to complete the Eligens."

"The other griffins didn't have a problem allowing the three challengers to ride them."

"Almost anyone can *ride* a griffin, but the animal will bond with only one wind-rider, and they will be inseparable until one dies or can no longer fly. If Namu deems Saskia or Kallisto worthy, the griffin will bow before the rider, dropping its head and shoulders to the ground so the rider may mount. If Namu deems the rider unworthy, she'll turn away. In the first Eligens, the griffins rejected two winning riders, and the process had to begin again with all the initial competitors. It can take days for the final selection to be made."

"Why don't we ask the griffins first?" said Jurelle. "It would save a lot of time."

"It's not that simple. The griffins communicate with each other. I've watched them. They're making judgements about each rider as we speak. They want to understand the rider's skills and temperament. When Namu is brought into the arena, the other griffins will approach her with their verdict."

"Yagle wouldn't...I mean, he likes Sas, doesn't he?"

"It won't sway his judgement. He's thinking of Namu's future and safety. Griffins are highly intelligent. Most people don't understand this. I only hope Saskia does."

*   *   *   *

A servant ran to Saskia and placed a bundle of clothes at her feet. "You must wear these," he said. "For the last challenge."

She picked up the Volatal Vexil leather coat and threaded her arms through the long sleeves, pulling it over the short, thin tunic she already wore. The servant tied the laces at the front of the coat as Saskia began to sweat with the slightest movement. The thick, furred leather would protect her from the elements when Yagle flew into the clouds, but they made life on the ground a sweltering puddle of discomfort. The servant helped her pull on leather pants and replace her sandals with knee-high boots. Finally, he squeezed a metal skullcap onto her head and cinched the chin strap.

"No weapons?" asked Saskia.

The servant shook his head, then walked off.

Both in Volatal Vexil garb, Saskia and Kallisto approached Charmion.

The Sella wheeled her chair to the platform's edge and addressed the competitors, "One challenge remains before you are presented to Namu for consideration. It is the hardest challenge, pushing your endurance and patience to the limit and testing your bond with the griffin to its utmost."

Charmion nodded, and a servant stepped from the platform and handed Saskia and Kallisto a parchment. "Each of you has a different map," said Charmion. "Marked on the map is the location of an object. Find the object and bring it back to the stadium. I won't tell you what the object is, but it must be returned in the exact state in which you find it. The first competitor to return will be placed before the riderless griffin. Mount your animals."

Saskia faced Kallisto, expecting a final taunt from the Scorp rider. But the tremble of Kallisto's hand as it clutched the parchment set a lump in Saskia's throat. The games had ended. The danger of the Eligens' final stage confronted them.

Saskia returned to the mounting platform, climbed into Yagle's saddle, then cast her eyes over the map. It depicted the topography of the desert surrounding Portum but not place names. She'd have to use landmarks to navigate. The target location, marked with a cross, looked familiar. Saskia thought she'd been there before, but not on a griffin.

Charmion waved her hand, and the herald blasted a call on the bellum cornu, stilling the crowd.

"The riders begin their final challenge," yelled Charmion. "Bid them farewell and a safe return." She faced Saskia and Kallisto. "Now, fly!"

The cornu wailed, and Yagle took to the air. Saskia lost sight of Kallisto as soon as they left the stadium. She soared above the tangerine roofs of

Portum and into low clouds sitting over the ocean, taking Yagle north along the coast. Sooner than she expected, riding a griffin became comfortable and familiar. The sweat on her body cooled, and she nestled her backside into the padded leather seat, checking the harness buckles fixing the lower half of her body to the saddle. Two yarles ago, an apprentice rider had failed to secure her harness correctly and fell from the saddle, her body plummeting onto the Pallaxium dome and shattering bones with a deathly thud.

Saskia yelled in Yagle's ear, fighting the whoosh of the rushing wind. He dropped low, skimming over the dunes of Magna Avium where they met the sea before turning northeast and inland. As they left the coast behind, Saskia checked the topography. Over the point of her right shoulder, Mons Harena, the tallest dune in Magna Avium, appeared on the horizon, afternoon sunlight illuminating its peak.

Must return to Portum before nightfall, thought Saskia; otherwise, navigation will be more challenging.

She bit her lip, resisting the urge to push Yagle harder. A misdirection could cost her the Eligens or her life. If they had to camp in the desert at night, so be it.

The sun sank towards the western horizon as Saskia flew over a dune's crest and down into her target, Wonchulus, the site of her recent and costly brashness. Yagle hovered above the abandoned Pordillo camp. Elpis had burned all the tents and crates that housed the Pordillo riders. Piles of ash littered the waterhole, ringing the stone well. Saskia closed her eyes and saw Agatha's face, frozen with the shock of sudden death. People had died because of Saskia's stupidity. She wondered if she deserved to be the next wind-rider.

Yagle must have sensed her tension, turning his head and cooing.

"Don't worry, boy," said Saskia. "I'll get you back home to Thaly safely. Let's find our object."

Yagle landed beside the well, allowing Saskia to climb from the saddle and onto the stone wall. She searched among the camp's burned remains in the dimming light, kicking ash across the sand. "How are we supposed to find something if we don't know what it is?"

Yagle crowed.

"Sorry. I should've given you some water first. It's stifling today."

Saskia pulled up the rope hanging over the well's edge. Instead of a bucket, she found a terracotta pot full of water. Inside the pot, a black mark indicated the waterline.

"Is this it? Is this the object?"

Yagle cooed and thrust his bill into the pot.

Saskia yanked it away. "We should keep the water at the mark. If it's below, then we might be disqualified."

Yagle twisted his head to the side quizzically.

"Alright. Take a drink. I can fill it again."

Yagle and Saskia drank from the pot before she lowered it carefully back into the well and drew it up again, brimming with water.

"We'll keep a bit extra in case we spill some."

She strapped the pot to her saddle, tying a leather patch over the top to act as a lid. The sunlight disappeared, and the first stars shone in the cloudless night.

"It's getting late. We must find the western star. Otherwise, we'll get lost."

Saskia waited with Yagle at Wonchulus until the night had become dark enough for the western star to appear. She expected Kallisto had found her object and was homeward bound or already back in Portum. The honour of being a wind-rider mattered little now. She concentrated on keeping Yagle safe and ensuring they didn't get lost. Yagle lowered his body to rest on his stomach. Saskia sat beside him, leaning her back into his furry hide.

"Oh well, I was a wind-rider for a day at least."

You should not give up so easily.

Saskia jerked her head around to face Yagle's bright golden eye, shining in the moonlight.

"Did...did you talk to me just then? Inside my head?"

Yagle didn't blink; Saskia's stupefied face reflected in his cornea.

"Did you?" she persisted.

Yagle crowed and ruffled his feathers.

"I understand. You're eager to go home."

The western star shone brighter than Saskia had ever seen before as she climbed into the saddle, buckled the harness and grasped the reins. "Alright, boy, let's fly."

Yagle launched himself out of Wonchulus and flew west, guided by the stars. Shadows cast by Seena's quarter-moon and Bargan's half-moon draped across the sand dunes, but Saskia didn't fret. Between her and Yagle, they'd find their way home.

When they reached the coast, she guided Yagle below a bank of sea mist to follow the beaches south back to Portum. Even at night, sweat pooled underneath her clothes, the air humid and close. Yagle struggled with the smother, the pulse of his wing beats slowing with each passing moment. Saskia tried to encourage him higher into cooler air, but he shrieked in protest, not having enough energy to make the ascent or worried the gathering mist might disorient them.

"You need fresh water," said Saskia, "but there's none between here and Portum."

She pushed on, lanterns from ships sailing to Portum's docks appearing on her right.

"Almost there."

Yagle dropped his head, pausing between each slow beat of his wings.

Saskia whispered in his ear, "Land here, boy. On the beach. You're struggling."

He dropped from the sky and alighted among the ocean's shallows, cooling his talons, paws and underbelly in the surf. Saskia unstrapped the terracotta pot, removed the makeshift lid of torn leather, leaned across Yagle's feathered neck and held the pot near his bill.

"Drink this. We must get you home safely. That's more important than anything."

* * * *

A ring of cressets burned around the stadium, lighting up the terraces like a tiered, fiery waterfall. The wind had dropped, the still night air hot and balmy. Half the crowd had already left, probably believing the Eligens wouldn't finish tonight. Thaly refused to go. Saskia could return at any moment, and she'd be here waiting.

Jurelle yawned and stretched his arms above his head. "This is ridiculous. I'd forgotten how long these Eligens can take. We won't be having a harvest season celebration tonight. I'm ready for bed."

"Are you too old and tired to wait for our daughter?" asked Genevea.

"I didn't say I was leaving. Only commenting on the absurdity of it all."

From the night sky, a lone griffin flying slow and erratic circled around the Pallaxium's golden dome and descended towards the stadium. The murmur in the crowd grew louder in anticipation.

"Is it Sas?" asked Jurelle. "My eyes aren't what they used to be."

"I'm sorry, General Stansfield," said Chloe, "it looks like Kallisto."

Kallisto and her griffin, Lien, alighted within the arena, the griffin standing awkwardly on three legs, holding a glass bauble the size of a human head aloft in his left talon. Kallisto jumped from the saddle and took the bauble, sprinting towards the podium where Charmion waited. Behind her, Lien collapsed to the ground, exhausted, as handlers rushed to his side.

Kallisto marched up the ramp to the platform, handing the bauble to Charmion. The Sella held it aloft, running her hand over its surface.

"What's she doing?" asked Genevea.

"Checking for cracks in the glass," said Thaly. "The target object is often something delicate. It has to be in perfect shape for the task to be deemed a success."

Charmion nodded. "The object is complete!" she yelled to the crowd.

Kallisto raised her arms in triumph as people cheered and clapped.

"I hope Saskia's alright," said Jurelle. "I should climb the clocktower to look for her."

"Have faith," said Thaly. "She's trained hard, and Yagle will protect her."

"Yes. I suppose you're right." Jurelle paced up and down the terraces.

A servant walked through the crowd, balancing cups of water, vinum or meduz on a silver tray. Another came with salted slivers of pig hide burned to a crisp so they'd crunch between the teeth like ice. But the salt made them tasty, and Thaly grabbed a handful to share with Chloe. Genevea took a cup of vinum, but Jurelle pushed the servants away, seemingly unable to stomach sustenance amid the nervous churn.

Thaly, Chloe and Genevea sat together on the terrace's hard stone.

"The waiting is the hardest part," said Genevea before sipping the white vinum.

Chloe leaned towards her. "You must have missed Thaly. All those yarles apart."

A fragment of burnt pig hide caught in Thaly's throat.

Why talk about this now? she thought. Had the tiresome day made her lover delirious? She glared at Chloe, but Chloe focussed on Genevea.

Genevea took another sip of vinum, then stared off into the night. "You can't imagine how much it hurt, Chloe, giving her away. I've paid a penance every day since."

I'm sitting right beside you, thought Thaly. Talk to *me* about it. But not here. Not now.

"Is she named after anyone?" asked Chloe, persisting with the futile, painful examination of the past.

"Athalee is an ancient Dobunni name," said Genevea. "The name of a Dobunni queen. Princess Caeli had a book about her."

"You gave birth to a boy, too? Thaly's brother."

Genevea nodded. "Jürgen. He died in Sardis' inner circle, killed by Erstürmen traitors. Then, all I had left was Saskia."

Genevea turned, flames from the cressets catching the sliver of tears welling in her eyes. Thaly wanted to reach across and hug her mother. Longed for it so much. But her backside clung to the stone seat like a mussel on a rock, pain ebbing through her like salt water through gills. Anger and regret coursed around her body, seeking an outlet. A way to reconcile the past and shape a better future for her and Genevea, building the bond they always should have had.

"There," cried Jurelle, pointing at the sky. "Another wind-rider. Saskia."

The crowd cheered again as Saskia and Yagle appeared from the stars and flew towards the stadium.

* * * *

The Portum stadium resembled a fire ring from above, with Saskia flying into the middle. Smoke caught in her throat as she guided Yagle towards the arena. The crowd had thinned from when she left, and she wondered how long she'd been gone. By how much Kallisto had defeated her.

Saskia landed Yagle beside the dismount platform. Handlers rushed to the griffin with food and water while Saskia unstrapped the empty terracotta pot from the saddle. She nodded to Puer as she passed, carrying the pot across the arena. Off to the side, Lien, Kallisto's griffin, lay on his stomach, panting heavily, surrounded by handlers trying to keep the griffin cool by bathing him in fresh water. Saskia trudged up the ramp to the podium, where Charmion and Kallisto waited for her.

The Sella took the pot and looked inside. "It is empty."

"I failed, Sella Charmion," said Saskia. "Kallisto is the winner."

Saskia left the podium and returned to Yagle, helping the handlers remove his saddle and harness.

"Bring in Namu!" yelled Charmion.

A line of musicians entered the arena. Women with drums strapped around their waists banged on taut hide with sticks, the thud echoing through the stadium. Hornblowers followed, trumpeting a mighty tune that would have been heard all the way to The Hive. The band marched around the arena's perimeter as scores of people filed into the terraces, the news of Kallisto's return and the raucous music likely raising them from their slumber.

Then the procession's luminary emerged; Namu the griffin adorned with tassels and saddle-cloths decked in the colours of the twelve Germalian factions. She strutted into the arena, seemingly aware of the need for pomp. A mustard-coloured plume fluttered from Namu's crown in honour of her fallen rider, Jayla, from the Tavr faction. A handler led Namu around the arena's circumference as the crowd showered the griffin

221

with dried yellow daises.

Kallisto waited on the winner's podium beside Charmion while Saskia scrubbed Yagle's hide with a kamel-hair brush to remove the sand grit.

"He needs more water," she said to Puer.

Puer bowed, "Yes, Domina Stansfield," picking up a full bucket and holding it near Yagle's bill.

Lien lifted himself up and stumbled towards Yagle. As Namu passed, she tugged on her reins and pulled the handler across to the two male griffins. Amid coos and squawks, Namu and the male griffins nuzzled each other, rubbing feathered necks together and clicking the tips of ivory bills.

Saskia wondered if the encounter would continue all night until Namu broke from the engagement. The handler led the griffin to the podium to stand in front of Kallisto and Charmion. When he dropped the reins and stepped aside, the crowd hushed.

Charmion wheeled herself from the podium, leaving Kallisto alone to face Namu's judgement. The clocktower on The Hive foreshore pealed through the night, heralding seven nocturna. Namu turned her head, a gleaming golden eye with a sharp black pupil examining the hopeful wind-rider. The griffin stepped forward, and Kallisto smiled in triumph. Many in the crowd removed their coloured circlets, preparing to twirl them above their heads in celebration.

This is it, thought Saskia. The moment Namu chooses Kallisto.

But the griffin turned away from the podium, and the crowd gasped. Namu walked towards the mounting platform where Saskia still tended to Yagle.

Kallisto called to Charmion, "What is the beast doing?"

Charmion's gaze followed the griffin. Namu stopped and faced Saskia.

Still brushing Yagle's flank, Saskia pointed to the podium with her free hand. "I didn't win, Namu. Kallisto's over there."

Namu shrieked. A loud, piercing screech that reverberated around the terraces. She fluffed her feathers, tassels and bells flapping with the disorder, then dropped her head and neck onto the ground, bowing before Saskia.

Saskia stopped brushing and stood motionless, mouth agape, wondering what to do.

Kallisto stormed from the podium and confronted Charmion. "This isn't right. The griffin can't choose someone else. I won the Eligens. It's either me or no-one."

Helped by her man-servant, Charmion wheeled away from Kallisto to the judges at the arena's edge. They consulted in whispers, Saskia straining her ears, hoping to catch a word or two. Namu seemed content to wait, her feathered upper body pressed to the ground, raised hindquarters saluting the crowd. Saskia swivelled her head between Namu, the judges, Kallisto and the gathering, hoping her family were still there to provide reassurance when the time came, whatever the outcome.

The judges broke from their meeting, and the brawny helper wheeled Charmion up the ramp and onto the podium.

The crowd's murmur stilled again as the Sella raised her arms and yelled, "Namu has spoken. The new wind-rider and twelfth member of the Volatal Vexil is Saskia Stansfield."

What? thought Saskia.

Kallisto stormed from the arena in fuming silence.

Namu squawked and tossed her head towards Saskia.

She wants me to climb onto her back, thought Saskia.

She obliged, still in disbelief, then nestled into the ceremonial saddle, made from the softest and shiniest leather she'd ever seen and carved with scenes of wind-riders flying among the clouds. Namu stood and trotted ahead, preparing to launch. Saskia grasped the reins. Her griffin, her *companion*, took flight, wings beating with strength and majesty. Together, they circled above the crowd, a few onlookers ducking their heads to avoid a pair of dangling talons and tarsi decorated with a ring of bells.

For the first time, among the thousands gathered, Saskia spotted familiar faces. Her mother, Genevea, and her sister, Thaly, stood together, hugging each other. *Hugging* each other. And Saskia beamed.

~ Chapter 16 ~

In the late afternoon sun, Rosalie rested her back against a tree trunk in Lokan's cursed wood, a stone's throw from the road into Laodicea. Her head throbbed, the after-effects of consuming too much of Raf's secret meduz brew the night before. The rebels had celebrated the first day of harvest season, though their harvests had grown thinner recently. Nevertheless, every Dobunni and Erstürmen now counted themselves a yarle older, and Rosalie wanted the milestones to be recognised. She'd turned thirty, Tilly nineteen, Raf forty-five, and Emelin seventy-six. Hanni and Quenan joined the celebration, despite measuring the aging process differently from everyone else. To stone- and weald-grells, time had a circularity Rosalie found hard to comprehend.

'Age is not a number but a collection of thoughts and feelings,' Hanni had told her. 'Everything that once was will be again and again.'

Rosalie imagined seeing her midday meal again soon if her stomach continued to churn. Hurling a vomit of rock-rat and yam stew didn't sound very appealing.

At the beginning of every harvest season, Rosalie took a moment to remember her family. Her father, Yonna, would now be fifty-eight. Her mother, Heady, fifty-three, and Petas, her brother, twenty-six. And the twins, Nettie and Allum, would be eighteen, the same age as Rosalie when she fled Sardis' fifth circle and left her family behind. The last time she'd seen Allum, he lay on the fifth circle's cobbled streets, his tiny, withered body stricken with The Ravage. Yonna planned to take Allum to the curate to save his soul before the disease finally claimed the boy. Rosalie tried to stop her father, attacking an Erstürmen Shield in the process, leading her to flee Sardis lest her family be punished alongside her. She expected Allum died before receiving the curate's blessing. The last she heard, Yonna had taken the family to Pergamos. Rosalie hoped they found peace and a brighter future in the resurrected city.

A hot wind gusted from the west, sweeping the split ends of Rosalie's hair across her face. Little else moved among the gnarled trees of Lokan other than a whirlwind of dust and a scattering of leaves clinging to entangled, spindly branches with a grimness apt for such a place. Dead, crownless stags stood resolute against the wind, refusing to yield roots from the soil until rot and decay made their stance impossible. The Desolate Mountains' guardian wood had not always been so bleak. Raf told Rosalie that Lokan once offered a bounty of fruits, meat and lumber few forests could match. But the forest spirits punished Laodicea's greedy citizens by poisoning the soil and water. Raf occasionally hunted here, willing to risk eating one of the few animals still living in this place. However, most people avoided Lokan, making it the perfect screen to mask the valley higher up in the mountains where the rebels had their hide-out.

A flux of vomit caught in Rosalie's throat, and she swallowed it back down with a groan. She wondered about her companions' alertness as they waited for a wagon to pass on the road to Laodicea. It was foolhardy to attempt an ambush with minds still dulled from overconsumption of meduz. Yet, such an opportunity couldn't be missed. Quenan had spotted the wagon while scouting; the carriage stopped at the last coach house before Laodicea so the travelling party could feast on midday fare. The weald-grell raced back to the rebels, urging them to prepare for an ambush.

'The wagon carries padlocked wooden chests strapped to the roof,' she had said. 'And is escorted by six riders from Malphas' Shield. Its cargo must be valuable.'

The news shook the rebels from their alcoholic slumber. The promise of treasure had a way of focusing the mind.

Rosalie had been joined by seven other rebels to form the raiding party. Behind a tree to her left sat Tilly, who'd embraced the rebel life better than Rosalie ever could. The little girl Rosalie had saved from Slumstadt's sewers twelve yarles ago taught Rosalie that living poor meant adapting. Fighting your oppressors meant sacrifice. Stealing and killing to survive meant taming your conscience. Rosalie struggled with an impoverished life, relying on memories of happier and wealthier times with her family in Sardis' fifth circle to escape.

To the right of Rosalie sat Raf, her ephemeral lover. He'd worked his way back into her desires. She enjoyed the momentary rapture of sex with the older rebel. It reminded her of a hit of embruisia, the mind-altering substance she'd been introduced to in Slumstadt and grown to crave. Beyond the fleeting euphoria, Raf had nothing to offer Rosalie. Sometimes, she pitied him. He deserved love like anyone else, but she couldn't provide it. Circumstances had pushed them together, and Rosalie found it hard to push back.

"Wagon!" yelled Bion, jolting Rosalie from her daydream.

Hanni and Quenan crouched behind a boulder, trying to hide their giant grell bodies as they scouted the road. Tilly and Raf drew their swords; Tilly's a keen, glinting blade that Hanni had stolen from Hunger's stores in Laodicea, and Raf's a rudimentary weapon of rusty metal with a cloth handle. Rosalie had made it for him. Not her best work, but he refused to use another.

Tormil, the oldest male rebel in the group, unshouldered a bow and nodded to his younger cousin, Ermer, who clutched a dented glaive as if it might draw lightning from the sky. Rosalie fumbled for her own weapon, a long knife of polished steel with keenly honed edges, a gold-plated quillon block, leather-bound grip and a pommel carved from the tusk of a tufted goliath. She'd made no finer weapon in her yarles of smithing but recognised her battle skills failed to honour the artistry. The knife, most suited to close, hand-to-hand combat, should belong to someone who could fight.

What good is it in the hands of a drunken fool confronting the armoured might of Malphas' Shield? she thought. *As good as it gets around here.*

She stood and faced the road, keeping her body hidden behind the tree trunk. In the distance, a plume of dust billowed behind an armoured metal wagon pulled by eight horses and escorted by six Erstürmen riders wearing the silver and black armour of Malphas' Shield.

A heavy load to warrant such horsepower, thought Rosalie.

Raf crept across to Rosalie's tree, placed his hand on her shoulder and whispered in her ear, "The wagon carries something important, to need all them swords as protection."

In Rosalie's mind, the wagon's promise morphed into a herald proclaiming a change in fortune for the rebels.

Bion and Tormil nocked arrows in their bows. Hanni and Quenan trotted up a slope among the trees, cleared of all rocks and dead brush. At the hilltop lay a tree trunk, twice as wide as Rosalie's arm span, wedged in place by timber poles levered over stones. The trunk had been stripped of bark and branches and hewn into a smooth cylinder. Ropes tied to the free ends of the poles led off to the sides of the trunk. One tug on those, and a hefty push from two huge, burly grells, would send the tree hurtling down the slope and onto the road. The impact depended on the timing.

Rosalie took it upon herself to give the signal, raising her hand to hold her grell friends in place as the wagon lumbered towards them. She'd target the horses pulling the wagon. The sleek, beautiful horses, their muscles rippling under coats of glistening brown and black. Their flowing manes flapping in the wind like royal flags. She'd aim to break their legs. Cripple all of them in a single, devastating strike. She couldn't risk the wagon driver taking off and leaving the soldiers behind to fight the rebels. Couldn't risk targeting the wagon and missing everything completely. Desperation had turned Rosalie into something she despised.

Better than going hungry, her mind snapped at her.

The jangle of the wagon harness grew louder. The snorting of galloping horses echoed through the cursed wood, and the plume of dust drifted up slope to where the rebels hid. Rosalie dropped her hand. Quenan and Hanni yanked on the ropes to remove the wedges holding the tree trunk in place, then rushed to the side of the trunk and pushed, their shoulder muscles bulging under animal-skin tunics. The tree began to roll, turning slowly at first, like a hog on a spit roast, before gathering pace to skip and bounce down the cleared slope. The escort of Malphas' Shield galloped along the road, right below where the rebels hid. Then, after an unexpectedly long moment, leading Rosalie to question her judgement, the first horses of the wagon team appeared.

The colossal trunk hurtled now. Careering downhill with a fearsome speed, setting Rosalie's pulse racing with it. At the road cutting, the tree exploded into the air and collided with the train of horses, right on target. Rosalie's desperation had been deadly. She'd never heard horses scream so loud. A forest of legs tangled with the harness, bones snapping like dry twigs. The lead horses collapsed, and the following six fell on top of them, mouths frothing with panic. The wagon's momentum carried it forward, the wheels crushing the pile of horses until it flipped onto its side and ploughed into the dirt in a cloud of dust.

Malphas' Shield wheeled their mounts around the same time Bion and Tormil loosed the first arrows. A soldier fell, an arrow lodged in his cheek underneath the rim of his spangenhelm. The Shield commander yelled orders, but Rosalie couldn't hear over the horses' wail or see much with the dust stinging her eyes. Behind her, Hanni and Quenan flung primitive spears, little more than slightly bowed branches and a flint of stone bound into the tip with twine made from goat stomachs. Yet, in the hands of a grell, the simple weapon had lethal effect. Each spear pierced an Erstürmen soldier's throat in the gap between the top of the breastplate and the spangenhelm. Quenan's spear lodged in place, while the force of Hanni's throw was so strong the soldier's head rolled to the side, and blood spewed over his silver armour like a fountain of red wine.

We should advance now, thought Rosalie. Three enemy soldiers down, the remaining three in disarray.

She stood and raised her long knife, preparing to rush at the Shield commander, but Bion sprinted past her, yelling with maddening anger fuelled by grief. He tossed his bow aside, the quiver on his back now empty, jumped from the road cutting and knocked the commander from his horse. Both fell into the dirt in a tangle. Bion found his feet first and unsheathed a short sword, smashing it into the commander's breastplate, right between the embossed insignia of the curled, two-headed snake. The commander flailed his gauntleted hand and knocked Bion's sword to the side. With his free hand, he drew his own sword and, still lying on his back, lunged the weapon up and into Bion's chest. Rosalie gasped as if the blade had pierced her own flesh. Bion staggered backwards, and the commander clambered to his feet, ready to strike again.

Rosalie searched for bravery while her feet remained pinned to the ground as Bion died in front of her.

"Come on," urged Tilly.

She pushed past Rosalie, brandishing the finely crafted, stolen sword with the keenness of a seasoned warrior.

Yes, thought Rosalie, come on.

She joined Tilly, and the two rebels hunted the commander from either side, Tilly with her perfect sword and Rosalie with her long knife, entirely unsuited for such an occasion. Rather than launching a strategic, graceful attack, they opted for a tempest of crashing and bashing into silver armour so polished Rosalie could see the blood rushing to her cheeks. Tilly knocked the commander's spangenhelm off, exposing a fatal weakness. Rosalie didn't hesitate, plunging her knife into the side of his face. She'd made the knife so well, sharpened the blade so finely, it sliced through the soldier's cheek, ground against teeth and bone, and severed the joint connecting his upper and lower jaw.

He won't be issuing any more orders, thought Rosalie.

As the commander clutched his bloody face, Hanni came up from behind and smashed a boulder into his skull, ending the linger of pain.

"The other soldiers are dead," said Hanni, her chest heaving amid snatches of air. "Wagon driver died in the crash."

Raf crouched over Bion. "He's dead, too. Probably for the best. He weren't coping too well with the loss of his mother."

Quenan moved among the horses, those not dying or galloping away, and whispered a Grellian incantation to calm their stamping feet and still the shuddering muscles of their flanks. Rosalie hoped the rebels might gain at least five horses from this raid, and new weapons from the defeated Shield, if nothing else.

Tilly marched to the overturned wagon and used her blade to hack through the leather straps fixing four wooden chests to the wagon's roof.

"They're all padlocked," she said.

Hanni walked over to a chest, wrapped her hand around a padlock and yanked the metal hinge from the timber. The lid opened, and out spilled coins. Hundreds and hundreds of coins.

Tilly's eyes shined with greed. "There's more than we could ever carry." She plucked a coin from the pile and held it to the sunlight, "It's a silver tausen," then crouched and took another handful of clinking bounty. "They're all silver tausens, with the head of King Adalwolf. These must be the rarest coins in Enthilen. We've struck riches beyond measure."

"If they're rare, how come there's so many of them?" asked Raf.

"Don't you understand?" said Tilly. "This could be the entire collection. Every coin ever made with the image of the absent king. Black marketeers would kill for this treasure."

"I thought six Shield was overdoing it," said Tormil. "Seems the opposite is true. Riches like this would normally command an army for an escort."

The hairs on Rosalie's neck prickled. "Something's not right here."

The hinge on the wagon's door creaked, and Rosalie clutched the leather-bound grip of her knife tighter. Hanni spun around, swooping down to collect a spear in the same motion. The door swung open, groaning with the protest of indented metal.

"Show yourself," said Hanni.

From the wagon, trembling hands appeared; fingers pointed skyward. A tall, thin man followed, dressed in a frilled white shirt and red cape embroidered with gold thread. A hawkish nose protruded from a gaunt face, wrinkled, it seemed, from yarles of worry.

Rosalie caught her breath, recognising the face but failing to recall who it belonged to. "Who are you?" she asked.

"Someone unable to serve your needs," replied the man.

"We'll decide that. You were important enough to warrant an armoured wagon and an escort of Shield."

"Important men may dress only in a diaphanous veil of self-esteem, while the pauper adorns armour thicker than buffalo hide."

Raf whispered in Rosalie's ear, "He's speaking in riddles. I don't trust him."

"You're in no position to play games," Rosalie said to the stranger. "You're alive only through our mercy."

The man gave a wry smile. "There's little mercy on display here. You ambushed my wagon and killed my guard without provocation."

"Where are you going with all this coin?"

"To Pergamos. To lay the treasure at the feet of our Worshipful Master."

"I don't believe him," said Raf to Rosalie. "The wagon was heading to Laodicea. Either he's in leagues with Hunger or seeking a ship to escape Enthilen."

"Has he stolen the coin?" whispered Rosalie.

Raf nodded.

"Then whoever he's stolen it from will send more soldiers to look for it. We can't stay here much longer."

"We could hold him for ransom. He's of noble blood, no doubt. Peasants don't dress like that."

Arms still raised to a sky reddened by the sunset, the stranger scanned his surroundings as if looking for an escape. Rosalie searched her memory for a name. He turned side-on for a moment, and the recall hit her like a jolt of embruisia.

Rostard, she mouthed, then spoke aloud, "Rostard."

He jerked his head towards her, confirming the recollection.

"You were King Ewald's soothsayer," said Rosalie. "Then Hunfrid's Master of Executions in Sardis."

"That was many yarles ago. Enthilen has changed much since then." Rostard squinted, then nodded at Rosalie. "The branding tattoo on your forearm marks you as a resident of Sardis. The fifth circle, if I'm not mistaken."

Rosalie wrapped her left hand over her right forearm to mask the brand of a sword crossed with a hammer seared into her skin.

"You're an Erstürmen like me," said Rostard, "and yet, here you are with these worthless rebels killing and stealing from your own."

231

"We should end this now," said Raf, raising his rusty sword. "Bion's dead. A fair trade, the boy's life for this snivelling coward."

"Rostard has always been a lackey to those in power," said Rosalie. "He may hold valuable secrets about our enemy's weaknesses."

Rostard lowered his hands. "I have no secrets worth risking your life for. Once news of this ambush reaches Pergamos, Malphas will seek his revenge. If you let me go, I can walk to Laodicea and raise the alarm. Tell the black grell, Hunger, that Nordmen snuck through Detranté and raided the wagon. It will divert attention away from you. All I ask is for you to spare my life and share the bounty you are about to plunder."

Quenan approached Rosalie, holding tight to the reins of five horses. "Even with the horses, we cannot carry all the coin."

Rosalie considered her options, recalling the last time she'd seen Rostard, leaving Elmbray's house in Slumstadt. The soothsayer had been there to get embruisia. She waited on the porch for her turn to buy a drop of the mind-altering substance. Her turn to twirl cerulean honey around the tip of a needle and jab it into her arm until the poverty of Slumstadt disappeared, and the dreams of children filled her head.

A craving corner of her mind wondered what Rostard hid in the pockets of his satin trousers. A vial of embruisia, perhaps? Did the soothsayer still slaver for the fantasies spawned by the viscous blue liquid?

"How do you serve Malphas?" asked Rosalie.

"I'm nothing more than an errand boy, running messages between Pergamos, Laodicea and Sardis. The Worshipful Master could easily replace me. Not so the coin you are about to steal. You will only get away with it if I help you. Concoct a story to misdirect your pursuers. And trust me, the pursuers will be many." Rostard pointed into the Desolate Mountains. "I imagine you're hiding in one of the valleys of those wretched mountains. Is it the one where the ruins of an old monastery stand?"

An ache of worry set in Rosalie's chest, but she kept her face blank. Rostard knew where their hideout was. Of course he does, thought Rosalie. He's a *soothsayer*, able to conjure visions at will of people he's never met and places he's never visited.

Tilly stepped across to Rosalie and whispered, "He knows where we are. We can't let him go. Either we kill him now or take him with us and decide later. We could force him to reveal visions of our own future. Use his skills to warn us of an attack."

"Malphas will send Rephaim to find you," called Rostard. "I've already seen it in my dreams. They'll search every valley until all of you are dead and the coin retrieved. I'm your only chance at survival."

"He's lying," hissed Raf.

"We'll take him prisoner and decide later," said Rosalie. She called to Hanni, who watched Rostard, "Bind his hands and put a sack over his head. We're taking him with us."

"You're making a mistake," said Raf before walking off.

It might be a mistake, thought Rosalie, but it's mine to make if you want me to lead.

She expected Rostard kept many secrets. He may know how to breach the walls of Pergamos and find Malphas' lair without needing an army. Rostard could lead Rosalie to the Worshipful Master, and she would cut the heart from a tyrant's chest, immortal or not.

~ Chapter 17 ~

The harvest season celebration faded in Lily's memory; over the last six moons, she'd turned her attention to the coming attack from Malphas' army. Sitting at the foot of a staircase leading to the battlements surrounding Gestade, she scuffed the heel of her knee-high leather boot across the peak of an ant mound. Thousands of angry, red ants poured from a mesh of holes, swarming over the ground in search of their attacker. Lily dropped a twig into the chaos, and panicked soldier-ants bit and stung the intruding object. She took another stick and dug a channel next to the ant nest. The defenders formed an entanglement of tiny bodies and limbs, bridging the depression with a living structure to allow others to storm across. A lone beetle strayed into the path of the marauding ants. Gnashing mandibles ripped it to shreds.

Scouts had confirmed the arrival of Malphas' army to the east coast of Enthilen. Around twenty-five thousand enemy soldiers camped less than half-a-day's march from Gestade at Walar Rock, a plateau formed by sheets of stone with waterholes hidden among the caves. Krieg, the red grell, led the army, the same tainted monster who'd attacked Laodicea with hordes of barbarians. This time, Krieg had brought Erstürmen Shield, Rephaim, men-at-arms, a cavalry of undreds, and war machines the likes of which Lily had never seen.

And women, thought Lily. *Malphas has conscripted women into his army.*

She'd never heard of Erstürmen women fighting before. But the present and past had diverged so much in recent yarles, she failed to recognise the Enthilen she once knew. With such a host waiting to test Gestade's walls, she doubted the outpost would stand for long. But stand it must, lest all hope for Enthilen be lost.

"Master Lily," yelled Roben from atop the east wall.

She jumped to her feet and raced up the stairs. Dark clouds drifted in off the ocean, trapping the morning heat. The humidity raised a sweat on Lily's brow as she reached the top of the wall. Roben pointed to the road leading to Gestade's eastern gate. Past the houses lining the road, two undreds pulled a chariot carrying a massive, brutish grell with black pauldrons shadowing a blood-red torso, his face masked by a grilled helmet crowned with a spike. Lily didn't need to see the face. Krieg had arrived to begin his war.

Villagers collecting water from a well scattered as the red grell urged his undreds along the road. Fixed to the chariot's rear, two banners adorned with Malphas' sigil slapped the heavy air. White banners stitched with an image of the red, two-headed serpent curled face-to-face in an incomplete circle around a golden sun bordered by two flaming eyes. Tacked to the chariot's sides in neat rows, a dozen scalps of tangled flesh and hair bounced and flopped with every rut caught by the wheels. Krieg had dispatched Gestade's lookouts before they could raise the alarm and kept trophies of his conquest.

"He's heading for our gate, Master Lily," said Roben.

"He can't take Gestade all by himself," said Lily, forcing her gaze from Krieg's grisly trophies to meet Roben's concern. "I'll wager he's come to present his terms of surrender. Tell Commander Hartmut we have a visitor."

Roben nodded and bounded down the stairs as the red grell pulled his chariot up to the east gate. Soldiers atop the wall nocked arrows and drew the strings of their longbows.

"Hold steady," said Lily. "We should hear what Krieg has to say."

Boots smacking timber stairs echoed behind her, Lily swearing the stone wall shook with the moment's urgency. A breathless and crimson-faced Hartmut arrived at her side and leaned over the parapet.

Krieg stilled his undreds and lifted the face cover of his spiked helmet. "Field Commander Hartmut," he said, with a voice like the roar of wildfire through a dead forest.

"What do you want?" replied Hartmut, the dread in his eyes betraying any pretence of bravery.

"I have come with a message from our Worshipful Master."

"Malphas may be your master; he's not ours," said Hartmut.

"He is the master and ruler of all Enthilen. He sits on the throne of the dead and prepares for darkness to descend."

"Darkness is already here. Filled with soulless ghosts and pitiless creatures unable to recognise the value of peace."

"You are Erstürmen, Commander Hartmut. You should rejoice in the Divine Creator's imminent return. Are you so lacking in faith your mind cannot see the undeniable? It is blasphemy to abandon your beliefs."

"Malphas' vision of the future is not what my ancestors hoped for."

"You have no time for the luxury of debate, Commander. The Worshipful Master offers this one opportunity to lay down your arms and abandon Gestade without incident. Save the lives of your people, and walk into paradise with the other believers."

"Are *you* a believer, Krieg?" asked Lily.

The red grell fixed his corrupted black eyes on Lily and tilted his head to the side as if he didn't understand the question.

"You may believe in Volerdie," she continued, "but neither the Erstürmen nor Malphas will welcome you into paradise. The grells will join the rest of us, suffocating on the dust of Enthilen's remains."

As Lily spoke, a clean-shaven Adalwolf appeared beside her.

Hartmut's eyes widened in alarm as he faced Roben. "How did he escape the command hall?"

"I...I left a guard to watch the door," said Roben.

"The guard fell asleep," said Adalwolf. "You've pushed your fighters too hard, Commander Hartmut."

With the arrival of Adalwolf, murmurs spread among the soldiers atop the wall.

"The stranger resembles the absent king."

"He's got no right hand."

"Severed when Pergamos' throne room collapsed like the stories told."

"It must be King Adalwolf."

An Erstürmen soldier faced Adalwolf and thumped his breastplate with a right fist. "Hail, King Adalwolf! Hail the king!"

His companions joined the accolade, their cries echoing around Gestade.

The commotion unsettled Krieg's undreds. They stamped and frothed around the bits in their mouths.

Adalwolf called down to the tainted red grell, "I see you're still a handmaiden to a madman, Krieg."

Krieg tugged on the reins shackling the undreds, his chest swelling like a dam wall ready to burst. Then a cruel smile split the scars on his face. "If I did not know better, I would say the coward king, Adalwolf, has returned. But it cannot be so. He fled his duty, clutching the coddling hem of his mother's dress. King Adalwolf is long dead, his bones rotting in the wilderness, picked clean by bloodied vultures."

"I *am* King Adalwolf, and I've come to reclaim my throne."

Krieg scoffed. "Truly? The absent child has wrenched his suckling mouth from his mother's bosom. Did you finally lose your appetite for her treacherous milk?"

"The Queen Mother is in a better place."

"She does not deserve one. Why show yourself now, Adalwolf? You have cowered for so long; I hardly recognise you. A young fool has become an older fool, but still a fool, nonetheless."

"I've returned to stand beside all those who revere the Erstürmen Kingdoms of old. I've come to defend the last place in Enthilen still loyal to the true king. To defend the memory of my ancestors who fell on the beaches of the Bay of Deception in Nordland, bravely facing the barbarian hordes. To honour the great kings like Giltbert and Faramund. I've come to fight you, Krieg. You and your master. I have come to fight and to win."

Soldiers close to Adalwolf raised their swords and cheered, "Hail the king! Hail Adalwolf!"

Krieg sneered. "Lay down your arms, Hartmut, and return with us to Pergamos. All Erstürmen will be given safe haven within the city's walls, preparing for Volerdie's return. This is my last offer."

Hartmut's stern face showed no hint of abandonment. No retreat. No surrender. He smiled at Lily, then faced Krieg. "Your master's offer is laced with deceit. I refuse it."

"Then war is upon you. Say goodbye to your loved ones. The stars you see tonight will be your last." Krieg slapped the reins on the sideboard of his chariot, and the undreds turned and bolted back along the road.

As Erstürmen soldiers milled around Adalwolf, his stature changed before Lily's eyes. A weary, broken man shook off the burden of despair and cowardice, revealing a vigour born from entitlement. For good or bad, Adalwolf had announced himself to the remains of the Erstürmen Kingdom he once briefly ruled. Lily wondered how the Laodiceans would react to the news of Adalwolf's return. The Dobunni and Docklanders. *Her* people.

Will the resurrection of King Adalwolf also bring them hope? she questioned. Will it spur them to defeat Krieg's army?

She'd have the answers to her questions tomorrow.

*　*　*　*

"We shouldn't be here," said Erwin. "I ain't had hardly any training. I've only been in the army for seven moons, *and* I missed harvest season celebrations." His face turned dreamy. "All that roast meat, berry pies, ca...."

"Well, we're here," snapped Nettie. "Forget about harvest season. We're fighting for our place in paradise."

"Why must we fight for it?"

"We weren't going to simply stroll into paradise. Something so precious has to be fought for."

Erwin uncinched the straps of his breastplate and let it fall to the ground. He sat beside it, leaned forward and rubbed bare calves. "My feet are aching. I never walked so much in my entire life."

Nettie believed it. Erwin was built for comfort, not exertion. She tossed her bedroll on the ground, plonked on top of it and undid the straps of her greaves, flinching when the leather brushed against skin rubbed raw. They'd been marching for six days, from Pergamos to Gestade, encamping on Enthilen's east coast in the shadow of a rock overhang jutting from the ground. Lieutenant Berard told Nettie the grells called this place Walar Rock. It looked as if a behemoth had tried to lift the lid of an enormous chest that had jammed halfway open.

Underneath the overhang and scattered across the cropped grass of an open plain, Malphas' army rested, waiting for the order to attack. Rows and rows of round, beige tents dotted the landscape, full of the bustling energy of twenty-five thousand soldiers. Nettie and Erwin sat inside a tent with their squad; forty-eight Erstürmen citizens who looked the furthest thing possible from elite fighters. Most hadn't seen twenty harvest seasons. A few, like Erwin, had seen only fifteen. They had rudimentary weapons and armour. A halberd or sword each, chainmail hauberks for some, a breastplate or greaves for others. No-one had a complete set of armour except Sergeant Weedle and Lieutenant Berard.

Berard, the commander of a dozen squads, wore the Master's Shield armour. Nettie dreamt of donning the armour one day. Being covered head-to-toe in hardy, polished silver, the two-headed serpent embossed on her breastplate, and the Erstürmen spangenhelm sitting proudly on her head. No enemy sword or arrow would threaten her then. No weapon would reach her flesh beneath the cuisses, pauldrons and rerebraces. She'd be protected, no matter the opposition, and Yonna would be proud of his daughter. Nettie Barron, the first female Master's Shield.

Pa could make me a suit of armour, she thought, with the perfect fit.

"What are you thinking about?" asked Erwin.

"Nothing," said Nettie, untying her bedroll and laying the blankets over the thin, dying grass.

Sergeant Weedle had ordered everyone to sleep before the call came to assemble for the attack on Gestade in the morning. But Nettie's mind raced with every terrifying and adrenalized thought about the coming battle. She needed to do something to relax.

"I can't sleep," said Nettie. "I'm going for a walk."

Erwin jumped to his feet. "I'm coming too. Will I need my breastplate?"

Nettie groaned. She'd been unable to rid herself of Erwin since Pergamos. He'd latched onto her arm like a leech as if only she offered the sustenance for his salvation. She grasped the handle of her halberd to pull herself up and a splinter lodged in her palm.

"Ow!" she cried, dropping the halberd and pulling the cuff of her tunic up to wipe away a droplet of blood.

"Splinter?" said Erwin. "I got a knife." He fished down in his boot and retrieved a paring knife the length of his hand.

Nettie took the knife and pressed the tip into her palm, attempting to dig the splinter out. But the intruder had buried itself deep in her flesh, and she couldn't find the courage to slice her hand open. She shook her head and handed the knife back to Erwin. The splinter would have to wait.

They left their weapons and armour beside the bedrolls and stepped outside the tent. The sun had almost set, and sea fog rolled in from the Veiled Occyan, accompanied by a misty drizzle that drifted on the easterly breeze like tiny snowflakes.

Mizzle, thought Nettie, wiping a droplet from her cheek.

The wind scooted among the rows of tents, ruffling the canvas and carrying the snores of sleeping soldiers. But not everyone rested. Grell slaves fed and watered the horses, undreds and oxen. Burly men with muscled arms almost as thick as Nettie's torso checked the war machines, testing the tension on the ballistae, oiling the catapult cogs, or tightening the spokes on the siege towers' wheels. Around firepits, soldiers sat in groups of half a dozen, telling stories of glorious battles, hoping the courage of the past would fortify the present.

Nettie strode ahead, thinking she might lose Erwin in the maze of tents, but he trotted beside her like a faithful puppy. She didn't want to be near him when the fighting started. He could hardly hold a sword, let alone kill anyone, and he'd distract her with his constant nattering.

'Shut up and kill the enemy,' she'd have to tell him. 'Shut up or die.'

"Are you scared?" asked Erwin.

"Stupid not to be," replied Nettie. "But we'll enter paradise after we dispense with the unbelievers, regardless of whether we live or die. As soon as Volerdie returns, he'll guide all living and departed souls through the door. All the worthy ones."

"Have you ever wondered what it's like? This paradise."

"Don't you listen to the curates at kirika?"

Erwin shrugged.

"No wars in paradise," said Nettie. "No need for them. Everyone has more than they could ever want. Food grows everywhere, and clean, sparkling water springs from the ground. The sun always shines, and it never gets cold. We'll have no enemies. No heathens to stand in the way of our dreams. *Polus Sepcarture*, the scripture verses, describe it in detail."

"Will there be honey devil-kuchen in paradise?"

Nettie stopped walking and faced her companion. "Is that all you care about?"

Erwin licked his lips. "Ain't had a cake since we became soldiers. No honey cake, no plum cake. Only watery stew and dry bread. I'd give anything for slivers of roast deer smothered in mushroom gravy, followed by a slice of honey cake topped with cream."

As if Erwin had delivered a successful incantation, the smell of cooked meat wafted in the breeze. Nettie's mouth watered as she stepped between two tents, discovering a makeshift tavern set up within the camp; a pavilion large enough to house a hundred soldiers, with bench seats and tables inside and out, and a fire roaring in the middle of the gathering.

"Ever had meduz?" Nettie asked Erwin.

"Ma and Pa said not 'til I get older."

"Well, you're older now, and they aren't here. Let's go." She led Erwin to the tavern and sat him on an empty bench seat outside. "You wait here. I'll get the meduz."

"Don't you need coin for that?"

"I got coin," said Nettie, reaching into the pocket of her tunic to finger the only two coins she had left. She'd kept them safe since being taken from the kirika in Pergamos. Since the forced enlistment.

No point hanging onto them any longer, she thought. Spend the coin before it ends up in an enemy's purse.

"What about food?" asked Erwin.

"Don't have enough for roasted meat," said Nettie. "But I'll see what I can do."

She stepped inside the pavilion, her senses hit with the bluster of nervous laughter and the stench of sweaty soldiers who'd been marching for days and not bothered to wash. A handful of female fighters braved the tavern, sitting at tables surrounded by men with reddened faces and lecherous smiles. Next to the fire, a satch of twelve Rephaim stood, the tops of their bald heads touching the shelter's canvas roof. Nettie had never spoken to a grell soldier, too scared she might say something stupid and have her skull crushed by one of their massive hands. Yet, tonight, she vowed to stick close to the Rephaim when the fighting started. No Erstürmen traitor or Dobunni rebel could defeat a Rephaim. She'd be safe among the giants with the scarred faces and notched broadswords.

Nettie marched towards the bar inside the tavern, through a crowd of longing eyes stalking her every step. She stood beside an old soldier who draped over the bar's countertop like a wet blanket.

He turned and belched the stale odour of meduz into her face. "Some of us gonna die tomorrow."

Nettie nodded, fixing her eyes on the bartender, trying to get his attention.

"Would hate to die...*belch*...and not know what it's like," mumbled the soldier.

Nettie ignored him, hoping he might pass out on the stool, but the alcohol-fuelled ramblings refused to abate.

"Being in love. Hate to die and not...*burp*...not know what it's like being in love."

The bartender finally acknowledged Nettie. "What y'want," he said.

"Is two coin enough for two mugs of meduz?" she asked.

The bartender scoffed. "Two small mugs."

Nettie nodded. "That'll do."

The bartender collected two wooden cups, then filled them from the tap of a barrel of meduz. With his back to her, Nettie reached across the bar, grabbing a handful of salted crackers and shoving them in her tunic pocket. The old soldier beside her slid his stool closer, a concoction of meduz and body odour turning her stomach.

He won't tell on me, thought Nettie. Will he?

"I could...*belch*...show you," said the soldier. "What love is. You're too young to know...but I could show you tonight...somewhere private. Before you die tomorrow."

"I know what love is, well enough," said Nettie. "I don't need you to show me."

The soldier scowled and drained his mug, then grabbed her wrist. "You're lying. You ain't been anywhere near a man. I can smell it."

"Let go of me," said Nettie, trying to twist her arm away from the clutch of dirty fingernails.

He smiled and gripped tighter. "Not much to ya, is there? Such a dainty little thing, all alone here in this tavern. I've never been with a woman with flaxen hair. Bet it tastes like honey. I...*errgh*...promise not to hurt you. I know how to do it proper. Nice and slow."

"Leave me alone," said Nettie.

As she went to yell for the bartender, something flashed past the corner of her eye. The soldier screamed and pulled his hand away, Erwin's paring knife lodged between his knuckles. Behind Nettie, Erwin stood, quivering like a naked mole rat frozen to a sheet of ice.

Clutching his hand, the old man staggered along the bar until he collided with a group of sniggering soldiers who pushed him aside. From the crowd, Lieutenant Berard appeared, grabbed the man and yanked the knife from his hand.

"Get to your tent and sleep it off," ordered Berard, pushing the old soldier towards the entrance. The lieutenant returned the knife to Nettie and Erwin. "You should be resting."

"Couldn't sleep," said Nettie. "Thought a mug of meduz might help."

Berard nodded. "Only one, then back to the tent."

The bartender delivered the meduz, and Nettie handed over her last coin. She walked with Erwin back to the empty seat outside. They sat beside each other, and Erwin lifted the cup to his face and sniffed. Creamy froth stuck to the end of his nose, and Nettie giggled. He blushed and turned to her, his face resembling a snow-capped, scarlet peak.

She laughed aloud, almost dropping her mug. Erwin laughed with her.

"Thank you," said Nettie. "For helping me back there."

"That's what we're supposed to do, ain't it? Protect each other. Those in our squad."

"I guess you're right. Shall we try it?"

"I thought you'd already tried meduz."

"Didn't exactly say I had. I'll sip first." Nettie put the cup to her lips and tipped. The foamy, grainy alcohol warmed her mouth and set her tongue tingling before stinging the back of her throat with a milky, sour taste. The first mouthful didn't convince her to drink more.

"How was it?" asked Erwin.

"Good," lied Nettie, not wanting to discourage him.

He raised the cup to his mouth and gulped.

"Steady," said Nettie.

Erwin spluttered, slamming the cup onto the table in front of him. "*Errgh*. It's awful. Tastes like...like bubbly vomit."

"Yuck. Do you eat a lot of vomit?"

"*No*, of course not. Do you want the rest?" Erwin pushed his cup towards Nettie.

"We should both finish what we've got. It'll give us courage for tomorrow." She reached inside her pocket and withdrew the handful of salted crackers. "I got these, too."

Nettie and Erwin sat outside the tavern eating crackers, drinking meduz, and talking the whole time. When eyelids grew heavy, they stumbled back to their tent and flopped onto the bedrolls to sleep. Sometime in the night, Sergeant Weedle burst into the tent and stood there, yelling for everyone to wake up and prepare for battle. Erwin looked as scared as Nettie felt. They dressed in silence, then Nettie helped Erwin strap on his breastplate before fixing the greaves to her bare legs. Erwin had no scabbard for his sword, so he slipped it under his belt, Nettie worrying he would stab himself in the leg. She grabbed her halberd, then she and Erwin marched outside with their squad.

The mizzle had gotten heavier. Sheets of it floated down from the moonless sky, the sea fog shrouding the tents around Nettie and Erwin. On the plain, every soldier in camp lined up before a timber platform. Sergeant Weedle led the squad to the gathering. Nettie and Erwin joined the thousands of Erstürmen standing in almost perfect lines, facing the platform.

Riding a huge red horse, as large as an undred, Vater Krieg emerged from the darkness, tendrils of fog swirling around him like arms of the faithful reaching to embrace their protector. Their leader. He cantered his horse up a ramp and onto the platform, spinning the beast around to face the waiting throng. Krieg wore the Rephaim armour, shoulders protected by black pauldrons, a plackart covering his stomach, greaves over his shins, and pointed sabatons on his feet. He flicked the grill of his helmet up to expose a face with a scarred smile, then raised a gauntleted hand to still the gathering.

"Volerdie reserves an honoured place in paradise for those who forfeit their lives in his service," yelled Krieg. "A place to fulfil all your desires. Alas, you will never see such a place while unbelievers stand in our way. Deserters of the Divine Creator's teachings. Heretics and apostates. We must wipe them from the face of this land. Today you serve the Divine Creator and his voice in Enthilen, our Worshipful Master. Today you protect all that Volerdie promises. To follow what is written in *Polus Sepcarture*. To rout the traitors from Enthilen and smite the heathens."

Hundreds of soldiers raised their weapons and cheered. Others thumped breastplates with right fists. Nettie's halberd slipped from her grasp, her hand wet with rain. Erwin crouched, picked up the weapon, and gave it back to her. He tried to smile. Tried to put on a brave face. She sensed it, but the reality of the moment crashed down around both of them. War beckoned. They were going to start it. They were going to fight it. Almost certainly, they were going to die because of it.

Nettie still hoped the people of Gestade would surrender. Once they see the tens of thousands of soldiers standing at their gate, she thought, they will lay down their arms and walk away without spilling a drop of blood. It's the only sensible thing to do.

"They wait for us now," yelled Vater Krieg. "The vilest filth Enthilen has ever known. Dobunni scum from Laodicea. Erstürmen deserters who turned their backs on Volerdie. They cower behind Gestade's walls like frightened children. Many have already fled, scampering across the Dambay Plains in terror. Our assault will fall like an avalanche of boulders onto a pane of glass. When we return to the Worshipful Master, we will be showered with gifts, our victory celebrated in Pergamos' halls until darkness descends."

"Hail Malphas!" yelled the gathering.

"There is nothing in Gestade to defeat us," cried Krieg, his voice rising to a crescendo. "No-one to lead the fight against us. They are consumed by their fear. Paralysed by their weakness. Crippled by their lack of faith. Volerdie watches over us, fighters of Pergamos. Volerdie will guide us to victory. We fight for his blessing. For Volerdie!"

"For Volerdie!" replied the thousands, roaring like a wild ocean.

"For Volerdie!" urged Krieg.

"For Volerdie!" yelled Nettie, raising the tip of her halberd skyward.

Erwin drew his sword. "For Volerdie!"

"Onward, brave soldiers," screamed Krieg. "Onward to Gestade. Onward to victory. Onward...to paradise!"

"Turn and march, y'bunch of roaches," ordered Weedle.

Nettie and Erwin jostled their way to the front and followed Sergeant Weedle. Erwin's bedraggled hair stuck to his forehead, and raindrops dribbled down his cheeks. He smiled at Nettie and shivered.

We're Volerdie's soldiers now, she thought, our place in paradise already assured.

She smiled back at Erwin. Together, they marched to war.

* * * *

Adalwolf slouched his back against a timber beam jutting from the top of
Gestade's west wall and slapped his cheek, fighting against the annoyance
of mosquitos buzzing around his unmasked face. The early morning sun
fought to clear away the fog and drizzle, steaming the air with a tepid pall.
Below him, a bog bubbled and oozed black and grey mud, the stench of
rotting life climbing the walls and assaulting the nostrils of those who
stood guard atop the wall. Dressed in a short tunic and leggings, Adalwolf
had refused the offer of armour from Hartmut, not wanting to deprive
another of Gestade's defenders.

No enemy will attack from the west, he thought. The shifting mud can
swallow a horse.

Adalwolf expected Hartmut had asked him to lead the wall's defence
to keep him out of the way. He considered arguing with the commander
but soon accepted Hartmut had made the right choice. A long-absent
king with no military experience and only one hand was a liability on the
battlefront, despite some Erstürmen soldiers being buoyed by the return
of their monarch. Adalwolf welcomed their adoration, though a nagging
conscience reminded him he had no right to claim Enthilen's throne.

These defenders don't need to hear misgivings, thought Adalwolf. They
need a hero.

"Sire, you could be the catalyst to turn the battle in our favour," said an
archer.

Adalwolf pushed his back away from the beam and faced the soldier, a
young, thin man with a gaunt face covered by a thick brown beard.

"What's your name, soldier?" asked Adalwolf.

"Willamar, Sire."

"That's a traditional Erstürmen name."

"It means *the desire to be famous.*"

"Then you're our talisman for a famous victory."

A beaming smile parted Willamar's beard from his moustache. "The
men are hopeful, Sire. We all are. Your return was the first good news
we've had in yarles."

"More's the pity."

"Have you fought many battles?"

"None like this."

Willamar scuffed his boots and bowed his head. "May I ask, Sire...."

Adalwolf nodded. "Go on."

"Ah, well...ah...why'd you abandon us?"

"You're bold to question your king in such a way."

"Sorry, Sire. I didn't mean...."

Adalwolf raised the palm of his left hand. "No need for apology. I hope you show the same courage in battle. Truth is, Willamar, I had no choice. The lunatic who seeks to end all our lives now would have ended mine long ago. Malphas planned my sacrifice, and I didn't have the strength to defy him. A strategic *absence* became the only option."

"But you've returned to face Malphas. Your true bravery showed itself, Sire."

Is it bravery? wondered Adalwolf. Is that why I'm here?

He smiled and nodded at Willamar, not daring to speak his thoughts aloud. The young soldier returned to his post to stare at the bog and wait. Two dozen archers lined up along the west wall, the total force Hartmut agreed to commit to Adalwolf's service. Every other fighter, twelve, possibly fourteen thousand of them, Adalwolf estimated, watched the east, south and north walls, or waited in the fortified village next to Gestade to spring traps on unsuspecting attackers.

Better the fight comes here than at some rundown outpost like Süden Forst or Detranté, thought Adalwolf. If any place in Enthilen can withstand Malphas, this is it.

The sun rose behind him and cast an eerie sepia dawn across the putrid bog that stretched west, fed by the River Lousse, before drying out within the Dambay Plains. Dead, rotting trees resembled ligneous ghosts with floundering arms as if they had died upright, trapped in the murky sludge. Tufts of cutgrass and spiny sedges clustered around the tree trunks like children clinging to their mother's skirt. Bogworms, the size of a man's arm, slithered between the sedges, raising endless piles of churned mud as they burrowed underground. In the pools of charcoal-coloured slop, trails of bubbles breached the surface, tracking the progress of something moving under the water.

How can anything live in such a place? Adalwolf wondered.

He started when Willamar pointed at the bog and cried, "Movement! There, Sire."

Adalwolf leaned over the parapet, expecting it to be another bog-worm. "Where?"

"Near the cluster of tree stumps."

An arrow's flight from the wall, a dozen rotten stumps resembled a fussment of old people, hunched over and stuck in the mud. Adalwolf almost dismissed Willamar's concern when one of the 'stumps' unfurled and stood tall. Then another.

"They're not stumps," said Adalwolf. "The forever dying have made the bog their home. Draughouls are coming for us."

"What do they want?" asked Willamar.

"Malphas has many draughouls in his service. These will be no different. They come to test our defences. Take your positions and notch your arrows."

A dozen draughouls approached the base of the west wall, skating across the bog like mud skimmers. Dressed in frayed cloth barely clinging to ravished frames, some had only one arm or half a face, their bodies unable to resist the ruin of slow decay, as the dead trees couldn't resist the festering mud. He hadn't seen a draughoul since Pergamos, where Malphas had them chained to the wall until demanding their service. Adalwolf tried not to think of them. To think of how woeful their lives must be. Such thoughts tortured his conscience, reminding him of what he did to Princess Caeli — turning her into a draughoul when she stopped him from taking Tom Anderson's soul moments before Pergamos' throne hall collapsed. Adalwolf had transformed the woman he most desired into one of those hideous creatures now winding their way through the bog.

It was an accident, he thought. I tried to pull away. Tom Anderson caused it. It's his fault.

As the draughouls neared the wall's base, Adalwolf studied every face and torso, wondering if Caeli might be among them, unsure he'd recognise her.

"Should we shoot, Sire?" asked Willamar.

"Wait," said Adalwolf, wanting more time to identify the creatures. Arrows couldn't kill the draughouls, yet the thought of Caeli's body being pierced by a sharp arrowhead, the idea of her in pain, was something he couldn't bear.

The taut string of a longbow twanged. An arrow with red and black fletching flew from atop the wall, lodging in a draughoul's chest.

"Hold!" yelled Adalwolf. Please, hold. A moment longer.

The draughouls stepped onto solid ground beside the wall.

"They're right below us," said Willamar.

Dammit, thought Adalwolf. "Fire! Fire at will."

Arrows rained down on the draughouls. As arrowheads lodged in what remained of their flesh, they didn't flinch. Didn't even look up. Instead, they drifted towards the stone wall, thicker than six men standing chest-to-back, and walked through it.

Adalwolf's mouth dropped open. "They've...they've disappeared into the wall."

"How's that possible?" asked Willamar.

"*Why* is the more important question. Why have the draughouls come here?" He faced Willamar. "Where's the storeroom?"

"All our supplies are stored in the dungeon. It's the safest place. The old folk and children are sheltering there too."

"Select a handful of fighters and lead me there. The rest can guard the wall."

Willamar gathered five men, and Adalwolf followed them down the stairs to the dungeon. If the draughouls burned Gestade's supplies, the outpost would fall in days without a single enemy soldier having to breach its gates.

* * * *

After a sleepless night, Lily sat with Audie on a bench seat next to the infirmary inside Gestade, searching the morning skies for a glimmer of cheer. The drizzle and sea fog had cleared, but the radiant blue sky only illuminated the unease hanging heavy on the faces of the outpost's defenders. Dressed head-to-toe in armour, the weight of expectation pressed down on Lily's spine, forcing her thoughts to uncomfortable places. Hartmut had dispatched scouts to gather more information on Krieg's army, but none had returned, and Lily expected they never would.

Despite the imminent bloodshed, Audie's hope appeared undiminished, and Lily sat here, leaching strength from her friend. The healer had prepared the infirmary, made beds and stretchers, gathered potions, poultices, bandages and implements, and enlisted whatever help she could muster. Krieg's forces may overrun Gestade, but Audie was determined to give the wounded a moment of comfort before the end. To have someone stand beside the dying, hold their hand and offer words of compassion to counter the voices of hate and death.

Above the infirmary, Hartmut paced along the east wall battlements. He'd been there all night, and Lily worried he'd have no stamina for battle. Krieg would almost certainly focus his attack from the east, targeting Gestade's main gate, the weakest point in the outpost's defences. Hartmut refused to let Lily face that onslaught, asking her to defend the south wall.

"Will you marry him, Master Lily?"

Lily smiled. "You can dispense with the titles, Audie. Whatever future awaits, we face it together as friends, not master and servant. If my only worry was when Hartmut and I should wed, then I'd be a happy woman. We could have done it yarles ago."

"Why didn't you?"

"Truth is, I never thought I'd find love again after the death of my husband and children. Granted, I didn't go looking. Too occupied with the business of the Southern Vale and attending those pointless city council meetings where Master Sleame and Master Widald would talk endlessly about nothing much. And Dealhia...."

251

Audie placed her hand on Lily's cuisse. "Dealhia's spirit is watching, wishing she could face this battle alongside us."

Lily nodded. "Dealhia abhorred conflict but never shied from it when diplomacy failed. I miss her counsel. Death took her too soon."

"I'm glad you found love again."

"Hartmut and I talked about marriage. The time never seemed right, and it never mattered. A wedding would not make us love each other more than we do. What about you, Audie? I've never seen you with a man or woman."

"Dealing with so much pain and death is exhausting. When a spark ignites, I can't find the energy to set it aflame."

"Adalwolf's eyes shine when he sees you."

Audie laughed. "A king! I doubt a king would come courting a lowly healer." Audie's smile faded, and she shook her head. "I can't read Adalwolf. I'm not sure what goes on inside his head. Thoughts appear to flitter between kindness and selfishness. He loved his mother, but now, I wonder if there's any love left inside him." Audie scanned the east wall. "Where *is* Adalwolf? I thought he'd be standing beside the commander."

"Hartmut asked him to defend the west wall," said Lily. "Adalwolf is inexperienced in battle. Hartmut is trying to keep him from danger while giving the king a purpose and the men hope."

"Adalwolf still desires to rule Enthilen."

"I wonder if he would be any better than Malphas. Unfettered power breeds corruption, and the people suffer. The poor and the weak."

"I believe Adalwolf has a good heart. When the time comes, he'll act with honour."

"The time is coming soon, Audie."

"Don't give up hope. There is a light, somewhere, waiting to shine."

Lily removed her gauntlets. "Do you know the formal grell greeting?"

"I've never tried it," said Audie.

"I place my fingertips on your cheeks, and you do the same to me."

Audie nodded and faced Lily. The two friends embraced, a soft, loving, gentle touch. Lily held on, her eyes welling with tears and her throat dry and swollen. She didn't want to leave her friend. She didn't want to let go.

"Enemy!" came a yell from atop the east wall.

Together, Lily and Audie released their touch.

"You have an infirmary to tend to," said Lily.

"And you have a battle to win," said Audie.

Lily climbed the stairs of the east wall, lugging her armoured legs up one step at a time. When she reached the top, she shielded her eyes from the rising sun. Krieg had chosen the moment of his advance precisely, sunlight almost blinding the defenders as they tried to assess the approaching army's strength. Lily took her place beside Hartmut. They resembled twins, bedecked in the King's Shield armour. Hartmut insisted Lily wear the armour rather than the sparser attire of the Dobunni. She liked the Erstürmen spangenhelm sitting atop her tightly bound hair, but the breastplate, made for a man, squeezed her breasts so hard against her ribcage that she worried they'd never spring back into shape.

On the outskirts of the village surrounding Gestade, Erstürmen war machines pulled by teams of oxen, undreds and grell slaves trundled along the road. They brought iron siege towers as tall as Gestade's walls, filled with soldiers. Catapults loaded with boulders and ballistae with drawstrings winched tight and armed with tarred lances. At the foot of the machines, ranks and ranks of Erstürmen soldiers marched in formation. Men- and women-at-arms wearing slate-coloured armour. They came with halberds pointing skyward like a dense forest of saplings. Or swords, short, broad or great, glinting with a keenness for blood. Longbows and crossbows. Knives and daggers. A few carried triangular shields with tapered ends, a weapon to thrust into the chest of Gestade's defenders. Others wore leather gloves studded with metal spikes to damage the enemy in hand-to-hand combat. The roaring clatter of boots and armour thundered with a rhythmic *clomp, clomp, clomp* as the soldiers marched to the outpost.

Synchronised discipline, thought Lily. The hallmark of a well-drilled force.

"Some of them look to be no more than children," said Hartmut to Lily, his voice almost breaking.

Behind the iron-clad fighters stumbled crowds of people with scant armour and primitive weapons. Most wore little more than a short coat of chainmail or a tunic and carried a single weapon with a rusty blade. The bewilderment of youth adorned many faces, male and female. Young people who'd likely never experienced the carnage of war. The children of farmers, crafters, servants and peasants. Where the men- and women-at-arms had sharpened weapons and staunch discipline, those following them had almost none.

A wrenching tore at Lily's heart. "Why? Malphas' army is big enough to raze Gestade in less than a day. Why's he enlisted the fledglings of Pergamos?"

"Fodder for the battle," said Hartmut. "Use them to draw our fire and wear down our fighters. Save his elite soldiers for future wars. Malphas is thinking beyond the fall of Gestade. He's thinking on the fall of Enthilen and the defence of Pergamos from any who might challenge him."

Among the war machines, a bell tolled, swinging from a makeshift tower built atop a wheeled platform. It heralded the arrival of Krieg, sitting astride a red horse the size of an undred that trotted beside the belltower. Behind Krieg came scores of Rephaim, grell soldiers wearing black pauldrons and plackarts, armed with axes and notched broadswords, their faces masked by grilled helmets. The Rephaim towered over the rest of the battalion, Lily estimating the grell force to exceed a thousand. She wished then the dozens of wild grells that once called Gestade home had stayed, but most left long ago to defend the forest of Babir Birramal from Erstürmen incursions.

At the edge of the village, Krieg reined in his horse and raised his hand. The war machines and army stopped, and the bell went silent.

Around Lily, Gestade's defenders shifted on nervous feet.

"Hold steady, brothers and sisters," she said. "Hold steady for the love of all that's decent."

"What's Krieg waiting for?" asked Hartmut.

A soldier bounded up the stairs behind Lily. "South wall," said the soldier. "Enemy at the south wall."

Hartmut's eyes widened. "There's more of them?"

"They're at the north wall also," said the soldier.

Hartmut faced Lily with a desperate yearning. She had no words of consolation. Nothing to fix the pain of knowing this is the end. In what may be the last moment with her lover, she removed her spangenhelm, leaned forward and kissed Hartmut on the cheek.

"I'll go to the south wall," she said, turning to leave.

Hartmut grabbed her gauntleted hand. Their eyes met in a silent, final realisation, then he turned away from her to face the enemy.

Lily caught her breath as she stood atop the south wall beside hundreds of Dobunni fighters. The enemy before her appeared to outnumber those to the east. She shook the horrible idea from her head and unsheathed her sword. It slipped from her grasp, clattering onto the timber walkway behind the parapets. As she collected the weapon, six siege towers rolled forward, crashing through fences and flattening barley fields almost ready to harvest. The Erstürmen soldiers around the war machines marched past a cluster of farmhouses. Inside the buildings, dozens of Gestade's brave defenders waited to launch an ambush. Lily focussed on the house where Yannus Rossingbird, Dealhia's son, hid inside with a handful of fighters from the Dockland's Guard. The enemy walked right past the front door of Yannus' house, and Lily willed something to happen, anything to halt the advance and strike fear into Erstürmen minds.

Timber shutters covering the windows of the farmhouses flew open, and lances shot from ballistae cannoned into the enemy ranks. A moment of chaos ensued, Erstürmen soldiers stumbling about to draw weapons and form a defence. Two dozen poorly-armed young fighters stood frozen, clutching sickles, pitchforks or halberds and swivelling their heads as if searching for the next attack or waiting on an order from their leader. They stood above a trapdoor, Lily almost yelling for them to get off before...too late. The ground gave way under young, innocent feet, and the fighters fell into a pit filled with poisoned spikes. Over the noise and calamity of the surprise attack, the screams of children were so clear the victims could have been standing beside Lily on the south wall.

'No more than children,' came Hartmut's words inside her head. *Fodder.*

A Rephaim pointed at the farmhouses, and armoured grells responded to the order by ripping timber walls apart with their bare hands. From inside Yannus' house, the Dockland's Guard rolled flaming barrels filled with serpent oil into enemy ranks. Lances thrown from rooftops shattered the barrels, and a flood of fire spread across the yards and fields, lapping at the shins of panicked Erstürmen soldiers. For a fleeting moment, Lily thought the defenders had the upper hand, but the siege towers kept coming, dragged towards the south wall by dozens of oxen and undreds.

"Aim for the beasts!" Lily yelled to her archers.

A volley of arrows flew from the wall like a swoop of falcons. Those hitting the mark bounced harmlessly from the stitched leather covering the animals' heads and backs.

"It's no good, Master Lily," said Orella, the young fighter Lily had spoken to during the harvest festival. "The leather's too thick. Our arrows can't pierce it."

Lily gritted her teeth and thrust her arm into the air. When she let it drop, a defender launched a lance from a ballista hidden inside the southeast turret of Gestade's wall. The lance flew straight into the flank of an ox, piercing the leather sheath and shattering the animal's ribs. It collapsed, pulling three more oxen down with it and yanking the harness connecting them to a siege tower askew. The tower veered right, bouncing off an adjacent tower and crushing foot soldiers underneath the wheels.

Another lance flew from Gestade's southwest turret, piercing the iron plating of a siege tower and exposing the soldiers waiting inside.

Keep going, thought Lily. "Fire at the soldiers in the tower!" she yelled to her archers.

Rephaim unhitched the staggering team of oxen and tied the harness around their own waists, taking up the slack and lurching the siege tower forward. Arrows and lances flew at will, yet the enemy wouldn't relent, slinking towards the south wall like sap down the trunk of a wounded tree. Lily's hopes of stopping the attackers rested with the covered trench at the base of the wall. The enemy would be upon it soon, unknowingly poised above a deep chasm running the wall's entire length. The siege towers' weight would snap the network of branches supporting the clods of soil and grass that masked the trap's presence.

Any moment now, she thought, the towers would tumble into the abyss.

However, the wheels of the siege towers creaked to a stop. A dozen young soldiers, *fodder*, crept forward, crouching low and probing the ground with the tips of their halberds as arrows rained down around them. Many fell, arrows lodged in their shoulders or backs, and Lily almost ordered her archers to halt. Three enemy soldiers made it to the trench, the blades of their halberds disappearing into the ground below the covering. They signalled to their commander a moment before all three died with arrows in their chests, their corpses marking the edge of the trench.

Dammit, thought Lily.

Grell slaves came next, carrying logs made from panalope trees tied one beside the other in groups of six or eight. The slaves laid the makeshift bridges across the trench. Most died to complete their task.

Fodder.

The siege towers' drivers cracked their whips, and the beasts of burden lurched forward once more, carrying the bevy of waiting soldiers stacked inside the war machines. Behind the towers, catapults let fly, pelting Gestade with boulders that splintered timber and smashed stone walls. The breath exploded from Lily's chest as a boulder crashed into the southeast turret, sending the ballista and crew tumbling to the ground. Hooked lances on the end of chains sprang from the siege towers and landed behind the south wall parapets. Crews inside the towers tensioned ropes using winches and dragged themselves closer to their prey, rendering the beasts and Rephaim pulling the towers unnecessary. It didn't matter if Lily killed all the beasts. But she had a final option to halt the advance.

"Light the fire!" she screamed.

Archers shot flaming arrows into wells filled with serpent oil at the base of the wall. Flames burst upwards, engulfing the lowest level of the siege towers and the soldiers marching beside. Men, women, children and grells staggered across the ground, screaming with the sear of fire set in their flesh. The towers' lower doors opened, and out poured waves of sand to smother the flames. Simultaneously, grell soldiers collected the injured and tossed them into the flaming wells to smooth the siege towers' progress. Those sacrificed screamed as the towers' wheels crushed what life remained.

Lily covered her ears at the chaotic din of battle. She'd tried everything. Nothing remained other than to helplessly recoil at the madness and terror of it all.

With the fires extinguished, the siege towers abutted Gestade's south wall, the defenders atop the wall now face-to-face with Erstürmen drawbridges waiting to be dropped, unleashing the hordes lurking inside. Lily pictured the whites of the enemies' eyes, stained with slavish rage, huddled together on storied platforms inside the towers. A boulder flew over her head and smashed into the roof of her and Hartmut's private quarters. Their sanctuary. The place where love blossomed, reduced to splinters and rubble.

Swarms of enemy arrows, tips covered in tar and set aflame, thudded into the walls of the timber buildings inside Gestade. Defenders sprinted between the spot fires carrying buckets of precious water to douse the flames. The outpost burned, the amber gleam of terror skipping across the Dobunni fighters' faces.

"Prepare for the assault!" yelled Lily. "The drawbridges will be dropped soon. Make sure you're ready when...."

SQUEEEEEAAAAAALLLL.

The remaining words never came, drowned out by the shrill of a barbed metal lance, thicker than a tree trunk and attached to a monstrous chain, that flew over Lily's head. As the lance reached the back of the wall, Rephaim pulled the chain tight with devastating speed and precision. The barbs crunched into the stone at the top rear of the wall.

Orella wailed, her young, delicate body trapped underneath a chain link bigger than a wagon wheel.

"Cut the chain!" pleaded Lily. "Cut it!"

Men and women with battle axes pounded at the chain link, but the metal was as thick as Lily's arm. Orella's ribs cracked, and her chest caved in, the last light in her eyes calling to Lily for deliverance. Lily turned away, every skerrick of her being demanding she give up. Fall to her knees and cry as if each tear would exorcise the pain of defeat.

Rephaim attached the chain's free end to teams of oxen and undreds, then cracked whips across bare rumps. The startled beasts lurched forward, and the timber walkway wedged between the outer and inner south wall of Gestade groaned and splintered under Lily's boots. From inside the siege towers, metal chisels pulsed in and out, cutting into the front of the wall to create fissures in the mortar.

They're going to pull the wall down, thought Lily. Soon, she'd have nothing left to defend.

*　　*　　*　　*

In the village near Gestade, Nettie ducked as an arrow whizzed over her head. Erwin froze, wide-eyed and gasping for air like a stunned fish.

"Move!" urged Nettie, pulling him down behind a barrel.

Around them, arrows and lances flew from house windows. Nettie's squad had been trapped at the rear of the advance, unable to re-join the main battalion. Her strategy of staying with the Rephaim failed amid the chaos of battle.

"Draw your sword, dammit," she said to Erwin.

"Swords no good against arrows," he replied.

"They'll run out of arrows soon. Then we'll have to fight proper." She squeezed the shaft of her halberd and tried to remember the training; feet shoulder width apart, hold the halberd with your lead hand near the blade's base and lunge forward from the middle of your torso. Beside her, Erwin fumbled and flailed like a dying swan until finally pulling his sword from his belt. With both hands gripping the hilt, he held the blade above his head, ready to swing down, as if the enemy had already arrived.

"Lower your arms," said Nettie. "Save your energy for the real battle."

They didn't wait long. The rain of arrows and lances dried up, and enemy fighters dressed in leather breastplates and skullcaps spewed from the village houses.

They're too close for us to run, thought Nettie.

"Advance!" yelled Sergeant Weedle from behind her.

Nettie hesitated. Erwin whimpered.

"Move, you worms!" Weedle screamed. "Attack, attack, attack!"

On heavy legs, Nettie stood, stepped from behind the barrel and pointed the tip of her blade at the enemy. A fighter faced Nettie, a young woman about Nettie's age with blood already splattered across the boat insignia on her leather breastplate.

Her blood? wondered Nettie. Or someone else's?

Erwin's sobs grew louder, and Nettie wanted to yell at him to shut up. She jabbed with her halberd, stabbing the air as if it might deter the enemy. But the young woman stepped towards Nettie, slicing through the chaos with a polished sword glinting with spite. Nettie rubbed a sweaty palm on her tunic, then returned it to the halberd's timber handle. The woman ran at her now, racing to complete another murder. Nettie's head throbbed with panicked thoughts of what to do next. She flailed her leg and kicked the barrel over.

"What's happening?" cried Erwin, still cowering on the ground.

Nettie pushed the barrel towards the woman, rolling it into her path. But the enemy, fast, agile and terrifying, leapt over the obstacle without breaking stride. Without taking her eyes off Nettie. Without dropping her guard.

"Get up," Nettie said to Erwin.

His whimpering filled the lulls between the screams of battle. "I'm s-s-s-s-scared."

"Get up, or we'll both die."

The young woman loomed, a lithe, ferocious lioness. Erwin stood and raised his sword again. Nettie thrust her halberd forward from the middle of her torso as Sergeant Weedle taught her. But she moved too soon. The lioness swayed back, unharmed, her eyes a bloodthirsty red.

Heathen, thought Nettie. She blocks the path to paradise. Kill her. Kill them all.

The lioness lashed her weapon like a giant silver claw, knocking the sword from Erwin's hand. Nettie swung her halberd from right to left, smacking into the enemy's leather breastplate with the blunt edge. The lioness groaned and stumbled sideways. Nettie thrust the blade tip at the boat insignia. The lioness spun on her heels and whipped her claw-like sword across the halberd's path. The blow jolted Nettie's arms towards the ground. The lioness struck again, swinging her sword down across the shaft of Nettie's weapon. The halberd's timber handle splintered in two. Nettie was disarmed. The lioness would begin her feast. She lifted her weapon for the fatal blow.

A moment before Nettie's life would end, Erwin gathered his sword and sliced it across the lioness' thigh. The heathen beast screamed and fell to the ground clutching her leg.

A quivering Erwin reached for Nettie's arm. "We gotta get out of here."

Blood pulsed from the wounded lioness, spilling over her hand and pooling in the dirt. Around Nettie, fighters from both sides writhed on the ground, wailing and sobbing. Or still lunged and cut at each other in a macabre dance choreographed by fear. Communal death came with a smell Nettie expected to never forget. Meaty, salty, recently hewn slabs of flesh, and the rusting-metal odour of blood mixed with bitter urine and faeces.

On a house porch, Sergeant Weedle faced off against a tall, thickset man holding a scythe. As the Sergeant lunged forward with his sword, the man swung the scythe faster than a bolt exploding from a crossbow and took Weedle's head clean off.

No leader, thought Nettie. No-one to tell us what to do. "We should hide," she said to Erwin.

Still holding the broken end of her halberd handle, she grabbed her companion and dragged him into an empty house. It may have been a house once, but now the shutters over the windows had been smashed, half the back wall pulled down, the stone chimney cracked and broken, and the single room stripped of most of its furniture.

"Not many places to hide," said Erwin.

Nettie dropped to her knees and brushed the dirt from a metal latch embedded into the grain of the timber floorboards. "Cellar," she whispered, pointing at the floor.

He nodded and knelt beside her.

She teased out the latch and tugged. The cellar door didn't budge. Nettie took the broken handle of her halberd and threaded the end through the metal loop, then placed a stone knocked from the chimney underneath the handle to use as a fulcrum. With all her weight, she pushed down on the lever. The handle snapped again, but the trapdoor came loose.

Nettie peeled Erwin's trembling fingers away from his sword grip, took the weapon and lifted the trapdoor to expose a rickety staircase leading to darkness. She pointed the blade's tip into the abyss and waited for enemy soldiers to come pouring out like bees from a hive. But no-one came.

Outside, the clang of blades and the screams of men, women and children threatened to burst into the crumbling house and reveal the deserters before cutting them to shreds.

Nettie looked at Erwin. He nodded. She lowered herself onto the first stair.

The timber creaked under Nettie's boots as she crept into the shadows with Erwin clinging onto the back of her tunic. He shut the trapdoor behind them, plunging the cellar into darkness. Except, it wasn't as dark as it should have been. A hole the size of a dinner plate in one of the walls opened to the outside, letting in a shaft of sunlight.

Nettie descended the stairs, stepped into the cellar, then froze. From a dark corner came panicked breaths, tight and shallow. The enemy was here, after all. It wriggled underneath a pile of hessian sacks as if trying to hide from the marauding Erstürmen fighters. Volerdie's soldiers.

Nettie directed Erwin's attention with the sword tip, then faced the sacks again, moving her feet shoulder-width apart and into an L shape.

"Show yourself," she said.

The breathing stopped for a moment.

"I know you're there," said Nettie. "Come out, or I'll plunge my sword into your belly."

A hessian sack fell away, revealing the terrified faces of a young boy and girl. They raised unsteady hands and quivered at the corners of their mouths.

Heathens, thought Nettie. Kill them. Kill them all.

"They're only children," Erwin whispered behind Nettie. "Put the weapon down."

She hesitated. *Heathens. Kill them all.* Then relented, lowering the sword.

The girl sprang from the pile of sacks, bounded across the dirt floor on all fours and bit Nettie's calf between the leather straps of her greave.

"*Arrrgh!*" yelled Nettie, kicking the girl to one side.

"Stop it," said Erwin. "We don't have to fight."

"'Cept that's what you're 'ere for, ain't it?" said the girl. "You've come to hack us up and eat us raw."

"We're not going to eat you," said Erwin.

The little boy cried. Nettie waved her sword at the girl in case she lunged again.

"Why aren't you behind Gestade's walls?" asked Erwin.

The little girl sat back on her haunches. "Papa said it'll be safer 'ere. Erstürmen devils want to tear Gestade down stone by stone. They won't bother with a few houses."

Nettie squeezed the sword's grip, wondering if she could kill a child. "We're not devils."

"Ya...ya...yes y-y-y-you are," sobbed the boy. "Demons from a b-b-b-b-black pit."

"Do we look like demons?" asked Erwin.

"Papa said demons always come in disguise," said the girl. "If you ain't demons, then leave us be."

"We need somewhere to hide, too," said Erwin. "We're not trained to be soldiers."

The boy calmed his sobbing and pointed at Erwin's breastplate. "You got armour on." Then pointed at Nettie. "And she's got a big knife."

"It's not a knife," said Nettie. "It's a sword, and I'll slice you open with it if you try anything."

The boy sank back into the corner, pulling hessian sacks around himself like a shield wall. The girl shifted her feet, and Nettie spun around until the tip of her blade almost touched the girl's face.

The girl didn't budge. "I ain't scared of you."

Erwin tugged on the hem of Nettie's tunic. "Stop it." Then faced the girl. "We only want to hide. Until the fighting's over."

"You'll call more demons down 'ere," said the girl.

"No, we won't. I promise."

She waved her hand at Nettie. "What about her?"

"I won't yell if you don't," said Nettie, pulling her sword away.

"Alright." The girl crawled to the corner, squirmed underneath the sacks and hugged the boy.

"Why didn't you cover that window?" asked Erwin, pointing to the hole in the wall. "Much easier to hide in the pitch dark."

"My brother's afraid of the dark," said the girl.

"What's your name?"

"Lucy, and this is my brother, Armen."

"I'm Erwin, and this is Nettie."

"Don't say our names," hissed Nettie.

"Why not?"

"If we lose the battle, they'll tell their parents we tried to kill them or something. Then we'll be executed."

"Where *are* your parents?" Erwin asked Lucy.

"Mama and Papa are fighting."

"Yeah," said Armen. "Fightin' you demons."

"We're not demons."

"That's exactly what a demon would say," said Lucy.

Erwin sat on the dirt floor, loosened the straps on his breastplate and rested his back against the wall. Nettie squatted on a stool and placed the sword across her lap. Outside, the clang of metal on metal appeared to be dimming.

Everyone's dead or moved off, thought Nettie.

She sat in silence with Erwin and the enemy, wondering how long they should wait. On one of the cellar walls, timber shelves had been built, housing jars of preserved vegetables, dried fruit, bags of grain and a wheel of mouldy cheese. Sides of cured meat hung from metal hooks attached to a timber brace.

Nettie's stomach grumbled.

Arwen pulled a hessian sack up under his chin and shuddered. "Her... her tummy's callin' for us."

"I'm not going to eat you," said Nettie. "But we are hungry. Can I...." She caught herself. Why am I asking permission to eat the enemy's food? These are the spoils of war.

She leaned across, cut a sliver of dried meat with her sword, then tossed the salty treat into her mouth. Erwin glared at her. She shrugged and started chewing.

"May we take some food?" asked Erwin. "We haven't eaten properly in days."

"You got better manners than your friend," said Lucy. "It's alright, I s'pose. But don't eat all of it."

Erwin nodded, then stood to search the shelves. "I don't believe it. They got honey devil-kuchen."

"That's my favourite," said Lucy.

"Mine too," said Erwin.

"Mine too," said Armen.

"Mama baked it yesterday," said Lucy. "She said she didn't know how long we'd be hiding here."

"Can we?" asked Erwin, holding the round cake in both hands, his fingers glistening with sweet, sticky honey that oozed from the spongy base.

"Only if you share," said Lucy.

Erwin nodded, placed the cake on an empty stool, then took the paring knife from his boot. "Do you want a piece, Nettie?"

She shook her head, hungering for the cheese, not sweet cake. Erwin cut three equal slices of cake as if he was at a wedding, then handed a piece each to Lucy and Armen. He took a slice for himself, returned the cake to the shelf and sat on the stool.

"How long *have* you been hiding?" asked Erwin, catching crumbs in his hand as he launched into the sharp end of the cake slice.

"Stop with the chit-chat," said Nettie. "These people are the enemy. We sit here until...until...."

Erwin raised his eyebrows. "Until when?"

"Until it sounds like the battle's almost over. Then we can stumble from the house pretending we were knocked out and re-join our victorious army before going home."

"You already think you're going to win," said Lucy. "Gestade's defenders will squash your army like brambleberries under a hammer."

"Did your Papa tell you that?" asked Nettie.

"Mama did," said Armen through a mouthful of cake.

"Did you see our army? We've thousands of soldiers. *Volerdie's* soldiers. Erstürmen Shield. Rephaim. War machines you couldn't imagine. Gestade has no chance."

Armen shook his tiny fist at Nettie and yelled, "We'll crush you!"

"*Ssssh,*" hissed Lucy. "Mama and Papa told us to stay dead quiet. Better dead quiet than dead, remember?"

Armen nodded and continued demolishing his slice of cake. Erwin had already polished off his piece and was cutting another.

Nettie thought about her plan to re-join the army when the battle ended. She'd need a convincing story to avoid scrutiny by her commanders. She could knock Erwin on the head. Put a massive bruise on his skull, and nick his flesh here and there with the sword. *Erwin was attacked, Lieutenant Berard. He collapsed to the floor, and I fought off the enemy to protect his life. Then I nursed Erwin back to health.* She could cut her own arm to make it look more convincing. Not deep, mind you. Enough to draw blood, but not hurt too much.

Nettie's mouth watered as she turned her attention to the mouldy cheese. The saliva dried instantly when the trapdoor creaked open. Nettie and Erwin jumped to their feet at the same time. Erwin gobbled the last mouthful of cake, then reached for a clay pot, preparing to throw. Nettie raised her sword as a man tumbled down the steps into the cellar.

Arwen burst from the pile of sacks and cried, "Papa," then ran to the man who lay at the bottom of the stairs groaning.

Nettie stepped across and pointed the tip of her sword at the man's face. Blood seeped from his pants and tunic, his body covered in cuts and bruises.

No weapon, confirmed Nettie.

"Shut the door," gasped the man.

Lucy bolted up the stairs, closed the trapdoor, then ran back down. "You're hurt, Papa."

"I'll be alright, Lucy."

"Where's Mama?"

"She's gone. I couldn't save her."

"Dead?" cried Lucy.

Her Papa reached his arm up, and she fell onto his bloodied chest, crying. Armen dropped to his knees beside his father and sat quiet and still, looking miserable and lost, unable to comprehend how his world had changed.

Nettie stepped back from the reunited family, retreating into a dark corner with Erwin, unsure what to do. Wondering if Papa would recover his strength and come for them.

Eventually, Lucy raised her head, the sunlight through the dinner-plate window catching such fury in her eyes that it chilled Nettie's bones.

"You demons killed my mother," growled Lucy. "You dirty, stinking monsters came to our home and killed my mother."

Papa propped himself up on his elbow. "Who's there, Lucy?"

"Two filthy Erstürmen demons."

"No, we're not," said Erwin. "We came down here to hide. We're not soldiers. We don't want to fight."

"What about you?" asked Papa, staring at Nettie.

She gripped her sword, ready to attack. "I want to enter paradise when Volerdie returns. But we must cleanse Enthilen of the heathens first. Otherwise, he won't return."

"And we're the heathens," said Papa. "Well, here we are. Why don't you finish us?"

The straps and buckles of Nettie's greaves pinched her calves as she shifted on unsteady feet. Sweat beaded on her forehead, and the cellar walls closed in around her. "I've never killed anybody."

"We don't want to kill anyone," Erwin chimed in. "Really, we don't."

Papa collapsed onto his back and groaned.

Erwin faced Nettie. "We should help him. He's dying."

"No, he ain't," snapped Lucy.

"We should help him anyway," said Erwin. "You got any medicine?"

Lucy shook her head.

Nettie sighed, rested the sword against a stool, walked over to Papa and knelt beside him. Blood didn't bother her. Open wounds, raw flesh, none of it made her squeamish.

She reached a hand towards Erwin. "Give me your paring knife."

He handed it over, and Nettie sliced Papa's bloodied tunic down the front, trying not to grimace at the wounds. But it was instinctive, and she hoped Lucy or Armen didn't notice.

Across their father's stomach, deep gashes had been inflicted by a sword or halberd, the flesh exposed and resembling red leaves from a blood tree. He also had a shoulder wound, possibly from an arrow, and chest bruises that might have been caused by a punch from a gauntleted hand or the metal toe of a boot. Blood oozed from the wounds; it didn't squirt. Squirting was bad. Nettie had seen it before when a butcher in Pergamos slit the throat of a deer. Blood spurted everywhere. *Bad.*

"We must stop the bleeding and dress the wounds," said Nettie. "I need fresh cloths and clean water. Do you have any herbs for healing?"

"Ryebal leaf," mumbled Papa. "On the shelf next to the cheese."

"Erwin, get the ryebal. Lucy, fetch cloths and water. We're going to save your Papa."

*   *   *   *

The well-worn stairs down to Gestade's dungeon spiralled around a stone pillar as thick as a castle turret. Adalwolf raced after Willamar and five other soldiers, the urgency in their footfalls bouncing from the stone walls. As they descended into the outpost's depths, the sting of smoke flared Adalwolf's nostrils, followed by a fog of acrid grey filling the air.

"Fire," said Willamar. "Someone's set the dungeon and our supplies ablaze."

The draughouls, thought Adalwolf. Almost certainly the draughouls.

He stopped on the bottom step, reached into his tunic pocket and withdrew a handkerchief. Holding the cloth in his teeth, he used his left hand to tie a knot, then pulled the handkerchief over his mouth and nose. He stumbled his way forward, following the cough and splutter of Willamar and the soldiers, searching through the smoke that had reduced visibility to a few steps ahead.

At the end of a corridor, the fumes glowed bronze behind a prison door of thick timber with a barred porthole.

Willamar turned. "It's the...*cough*...storeroom, Sire."

Why don't the people sheltering there flee? wondered Adalwolf.

He arrived at the door as Willamar tried to force it open.

"Who has the key?" asked Adalwolf.

"Inside," said Willamar. "We thought it would be safer if those taking shelter here held the keys and locked themselves away."

Safer? wondered Adalwolf. How?

Willamar called through the barred porthole, "Anybody...*cough*... anybody inside?"

No answer. The door remained shut.

Two soldiers slammed their shoulders into the black metal straps fixing the timber panels of the door together.

"You won't budge it," said Adalwolf, pushing the soldiers aside and pressing his face to the porthole. On the flagstone floor, in the clear air underneath the smoke haze, slumped old men, women, and children. "People still inside."

"Dead, Sire?" asked Willamar.

"Not...*cough*...not moving." He yelled through the porthole, "Open the door!" No-one inside stirred. Adalwolf faced Willamar. "How do we get this blasted door open?"

"I'll find a commander. Don't know...*hack*...who...."

As Willamar spoke, an apparition materialised from the fumes. Inside the storeroom, a male draughoul wearing the King's Shield breastplate approached the porthole. Once a protector of Erstürmen Kings, the draughoul appeared to relish his new charge as King Adalwolf's tormentor. In his right hand, the creature clutched the hair of a severed head. He raised the head up towards the porthole and grinned with a grisly madness that turned Adalwolf's stomach.

"Monster!" yelled Willamar, smashing his shoulder into the door.

No good, thought Adalwolf. The stores and people are gone. He went to pull Willamar away from the door when a scorching pain shot up his spine.

"*Arrrh!*" Adalwolf reached for the small of his back and spun around simultaneously. A female draughoul with a dagger stood there, preparing to strike again.

A soldier stepped between her and Adalwolf, taking the dagger in his throat. Another soldier unsheathed his sword and sliced the draughoul's arm in half, the severed hand holding the dagger still dangling from his companion's neck. The wounded soldier collapsed to the ground, blood spraying across his armour. Another draughoul appeared from the wall and swung an axe into a defender's spangenhelm, splitting the helmet and skull in two.

"We gotta go," urged Willamar, grabbing Adalwolf's arm and dragging him away from the door and back up the corridor.

Adalwolf's legs screamed with every footstep as he held his left hand to his back, blood weeping through his fingers. He and Willamar staggered up the spiral stairs, Willamar letting Adalwolf lean on his shoulder with the stump of his right wrist.

Emerging into the kirika chapel, Adalwolf whispered a prayer to Volerdie, "I beg of you, don't let my chance at redemption end here," then tried to walk without assistance.

He almost fell, and Willamar threw Adalwolf's handless arm around his shoulder. "We'll head for the infirmary. Stay with me, Sire."

Up more stairs and into a chaotic daylight; smoke, fire, boulders flung from catapults smashing through slate roofs, soldiers falling from walls with arrows in their chests, citizens trapped under rubble. Screams, panic, surrender. Stabled horses whinnied in terror, yanking on the ropes that held their bridles to timber posts. Kennel dogs howled. A woman knelt in the dirt, face in hands, hovering over a lifeless infant. Atop a crumbling south wall, Lady Lily LáDown marched among her troops, issuing orders with the wave of her hand.

Adalwolf fell into the dirt. Willamar crouched, heaved his absent king up into the crux of his arms, and carried him through the infirmary door. The loyal soldier dropped Adalwolf onto a blood-soaked cot, Adalwolf biting his tongue to quell a scream. The room faded to black, and an angel appeared, Adalwolf thinking he may already be dead. But the sunlight shone again, forming a halo around Audie's raven hair. Despite the pain, Adalwolf pulled down the handkerchief masking his face and smiled.

"Stabbed in the back," said Willamar

Audie rolled Adalwolf over onto his side and yanked up his tunic. "The wound must be stitched."

Adalwolf closed his eyes, and when he opened them again, Audie had disappeared. No, he thought. Please come back. Reward me with another moment in your presence. It may be my last. He squeezed his eyes closed again, hoping the magic might work in reverse. It did.

"Open your mouth, Adalwolf," said Audie. "Then bite on this cloth. It's soaked with boneseed oil. It'll dull the pain."

The slimy, bitter oil slunk down the back of Adalwolf's throat as he clamped the cloth between his teeth.

Another healer, *Morgana*, Adalwolf remembered, tugged at Audie's skirt. "I got a woman with an arrowhead buried in her neck."

"One moment," Audie said before returning her remedial gaze to Adalwolf. "Keep biting the cloth." She handed Willamar a length of fine yarn and a needle shaped like a crescent moon. "Can you thread this for me? My hands are covered in blood."

He nodded, removed his gloves, and slipped the yarn through the needle's eyelet.

How so assured? thought Adalwolf. How much death have you already seen to be so calm when surrounded by it?

Audie and Willamar rolled Adalwolf onto his stomach. "Even with the boneseed," said Audie, "this will hurt, but I must close the wound. You're losing too much blood."

Audie pressed her fingers around Adalwolf's wound, and he recoiled.

"Hold steady," she said. "Is there a breach on the west wall?"

"Drau...*ah!*" cried Adalwolf as the needle pierced his skin.

"Draughouls, ma'am," said Willamar. "Found the dungeon and burned the stores."

"We need every able fighter we have on the walls," said Audie. "I can finish here."

Willamar nodded, turned on his heels and marched from the infirmary.

"How long did you live by the ocean?" Audie asked Adalwolf.

What? he thought. Why ask me...*arrrgh*...another stitch.

"How long?" she persisted.

"Two...three yarles. Almost three yarles."

"All with Romilda?"

"Yes, she loved being near the ocean...*ahhh!*...damn...hurts."

"Kings must be brave. Set an example for your subjects."

"I'm no king, Audie, I'm...*ouch*...blasted, bugger...."

"Yes, you are. King Adalwolf the Redeemer. When this wound is stitched, and you've recovered from your injury, we can begin planning how to take Malphas' throne."

"You've lost your mind. No-one can defeat Malphas."

"The south wall is falling!" yelled Morgana before racing to Audie. "If this one's the absent king like you said, we should hide him. Quickly."

* * * *

Lily clutched at the parapet to steady her swaying body as the wall beneath her feet lurched forward, stone and mortar so thick she thought nothing would breach it. Nothing would see it tumble to the ground. But she'd underestimated the maniacal inventiveness of a despotic regime. Gripped by hooks larger than grells, embedded into the rock and attached to a chain pulled tight by teams of oxen and undreds, the south wall couldn't resist. Lily had to continue the fight elsewhere.

"To the ground!" she yelled to the defenders still standing. "Rally to me!"

She bolted down the staircase, planning to lead the fighters to the east wall and stand together with her lover, Hartmut. But the east wall was overrun. From inside iron siege towers or scampering up ladders, Erstürmen soldiers swarmed over the parapets. They resembled a clutter of voracious spiders descending on helpless prey. The fly they hunted was Hartmut, standing atop the wall in his dutifully polished armour, flourishing his sword like the beat of an insect's wing. *Slash*; an enemy soldier fell. *Thrust*; down went another. But the spiders never stopped, with their tangle of arms, legs and finely honed metal stings. Hartmut's arm tired with the weight of his sword. With the weight of futility. Lily expected to see him die atop the wall, but a Rephaim soldier came, pushed the other spiders away, and threw a net over Hartmut as easily as spinning a web.

Every muscle in Lily's body demanded she climb the stairs and rescue Hartmut. Die beside her lover. A cacophony of thoughts screamed for her to do it. But the voice of her departed friend, Dealhia, stayed her hand, begging her to lead the Dobunni in a final assault.

Lily stood frozen in the middle of Gestade as Erstürmen soldiers reached the inside of the east gate. They raised the portcullis and removed the braces supporting the timber. The gate swung open, and Lily gasped at the hordes waiting outside.

"To me!" Lily cried at the Dobunni fighters nearby. "Mount the horses."

She led them to the corral, where saddled horses waited for riders. The creatures stamped and whinnied; big brown eyes flamed with terror. Lily climbed onto the fence railing, grabbed the reins of the nearest horse and heaved herself into the saddle. Half a dozen Dobunni soldiers did the same, barely enough to bring down a single Rephaim.

As a handler unlatched the corral gate, Lily spun her horse around and caught the fearful eyes of her fighters.

"They come for us," she said. "Like they came for us in Laodicea. Like they came for our brothers and sisters in Bagendon. Yet, here we still stand. They come to erase the Dobunni from Enthilen. Yet, here we still stand! This day may be our last, but I will not wait for the end to arrive. I will go out and meet it. To fight against the end until my dying breath. Are you with me?"

The Dobunni soldiers raised their swords. "Yah!"

"Are you with me!" screamed Lily.

"YAH!"

She galloped her horse from the corral and led her fighters through the main gate straight into the merciless embrace of Malphas' army.

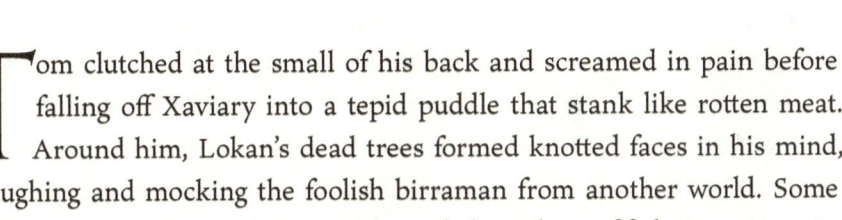

~ Chapter 18 ~

Tom clutched at the small of his back and screamed in pain before falling off Xaviary into a tepid puddle that stank like rotten meat. Around him, Lokan's dead trees formed knotted faces in his mind, laughing and mocking the foolish birraman from another world. Some wrapped spindly branches around gnarled trunks as if fighting to contain their mirth. Tom pawed at the ground, attempting to sit up.

Dwarrow called from atop his giant lizard, "Oh my. What's happened here? This is not good. Not good at all. Halt, Xaviary." The werp clambered down Xaviary's tail and ran back to where Tom wallowed in the salt-encrusted pool. "No time for sleeping, Tom Anderson. We're almost there."

Tom moaned, shielding his eyes from the mid-morning sun with his hand.

"I knew this wood was cursed," Dwarrow mumbled. "We should have gone around. Or further up into the mountains. It's this blasted heat. That's it. The heat's got to him."

Breathing fast and shallow, Tom rolled onto his side and reached for his back. "Pain...shooting pain...."

"Let me look," said Dwarrow.

Tom dragged himself from the puddle and flopped over onto his stomach.

Dwarrow removed Tom's pack and lifted his tunic. "Well, there are no arrows sticking from you. Or throwing knives. You probably landed on a sharp rock, though I can't see any bruises or marks. It's a long way to fall. Xaviary is taller than she looks. Rocks everywhere in this bothersome wood."

Tom grimaced. "My...back hurt...before the fall."

"*Hmph.* Very strange." Dwarrow hooked his clawed hands under Tom's armpits and heaved. "No. Too heavy. I can't lift you. I know; Xaviary can pick you up in her mouth." He sniffed the air. "Damn lizard, she's wandered off. The silly is becoming ridiculous."

The werp unshouldered his satchel and withdrew a strange-looking implement, a flat piece of wood rounded at both ends and covered in paintings of splayed lizards. Dwarrow unwound a cord from the implement's centre, tied to one end through a hole in the wood. The werp planted his stubby legs into the ground and spun the instrument above his head until a hum echoed through the trees and into a valley swallowed by the Desolate Mountains.

It's a bullroarer, thought Tom. Where'd he get it from?

"Xaviary will be back soon," called Dwarrow above the bullroarer's whirr. "Once she's heard the call."

Tom flopped onto his back, the roarer's thrum throbbing in his ears as clouds raced across the sky. He and Dwarrow had been travelling day and night, with Xaviary carrying the passengers on her back while they slept. Four days out from the Scaur Hills, they arrived at the lowest reaches of the Desolate Mountains after crossing the main road between Laodicea and Sardis. Another two days and they'd found the woods of Lokan. Tom had never seen a sadder place. What once must have been a lush forest had withered to a graveyard of trees, some fallen, others still defying gravity to stand as markers of what used to be.

Dwarrow stilled his bullroarer, rewound the cord, stuffed the roarer in his satchel and toddled over to Tom. "Xaviary will return soon enough. You're not going to die right now, are you? There are so many things to do."

Rain pattered on Tom's head.

"How can it rain in this heat?" said Dwarrow, tilting his nose skyward.

"Let's find shelter," muttered Tom.

He pushed his heels into the dirt while Dwarrow yanked on his shoulders. Half walking backwards, half dragging his buttocks along the ground, Tom followed Dwarrow until they reached the cover of a rock overhang.

He rested his back against a rock and sucked in deep breaths. *Maybe a wood-wright attacked me?* he thought. *Jabbed something into my spine, then disappeared. It felt like a knife or sword, but there's no blood. No wound. Only this burning pain. Wait....*

"Adalwolf's hurt," said Tom. "He must be. I'm feeling *his* pain. If he dies...."

"Let's not jump to the wrong conclusion," said Dwarrow. "Your hurt could be caused by, well, several things." He tapped his walking stick on the ground with stubborn impatience. "Where's Xaviary? The trip must have taken its toll. She hasn't slept, you know."

Loose stones falling from the lip of the overhang disrupted Dwarrow's babbling. He sprang into the rain and thrust his walking stick upwards. "Who's there? I can smell you. I'll knock you dead where you stand."

From above the overhang, a young woman dropped down in front of Dwarrow and Tom, her sword drawn.

"Don't think about using that," said Dwarrow, pointing his stick at the sword. "I can disarm you with my nostrils closed."

The woman smiled and sheathed her sword. "You don't look dangerous. Not in my wildest dreams did I believe I'd meet a talking goat."

Dwarrow furrowed his brow, pushing squinty eyes closer together. "Not a goat. Not a pig. Not a dog. A werp. *Mouldewerp.*" He trotted up to the stranger and brushed his nose over her hands and legs.

She jerked her arm away. "What are you doing? I'm right here; can't you see me?"

"Sight is an overrated sense. Smell is much more powerful."

"Sight's the most important sense," said the young woman.

"Not at all," said Dwarrow. "I can smell around corners or behind walls, where a silent, hidden enemy waits to slice you open. I would smell him there while you walk straight into his trap."

"You didn't smell me coming," said the woman.

"I was distracted."

"Do I smell like an enemy?"

Dwarrow shrugged. "I recognise a vile stench, reminding me of that run-down excuse for a town outside Sardis."

"Slumstadt. I grew up there."

"Yes, the odour of misbegotten youth never leaves your kind entirely."

"Who are you?" asked the woman, glancing at Tom but dismissing him as a threat.

"We'll provide our names once you've offered yours," said Dwarrow.

The woman shrugged. "That's no secret. I'm Tilda. I prefer Tilly. Is your friend injured?"

"Well, yes, he seems to be, but I don't know why. He fell off Xaviary and into a heap. No explanation for it. Says his back hurts."

"Is Xaviary your horse?"

"No. Liz-ard."

Underneath a fringe of matted, sandy-coloured hair, Tilly raised her eyebrows, then ducked under the overhang and knelt beside Tom. He flinched, unsure of what to expect.

"I won't hurt you," Tilly said before pressing her hand on his back.

"*Arrrh!*" cried Tom.

"Sorry." She lifted up Tom's tunic. "No wound. No bruise. Nothing. You must have hurt yourself falling off the giant...*lizard?*"

Tom yanked his tunic back to his waist. "Xaviary's real. And I hurt myself before I fell. Like someone stabbed me in the back." *Or Adalwolf.*

"They must have been using an invisible knife that leaves invisible wounds." Tilly stepped from the rock shelter and into a thinning rain. "Well, I'll let you two get on with it."

"Wait," said Tom. "We're looking for someone. You might know her."

"If you're asking for help, I'll be after those names you promised."

"I'm Tom, and this is Dwarrow."

"So, Dwarrow's one of these muddlewerps...."

"Mouldewerp," interrupted Dwarrow.

Tilly nodded. "And you, Tom, are...?"

Tom lay there thinking of a response. *If Tilly's from Slumstadt, then she's possibly Erstürmen. Yet, Lokan is a long way from Slumstadt. What's she doing here? Is she alone?*

He took a risk, sitting up and lifting the front of his tunic to expose the Dobunni pledge scars running across his chest.

Tilly didn't even blink. "Dobunni rebel, hey? How about that. Not many of your kind left. Bagendon?"

"I got the scars at Bagendon," said Tom, "during the Pledge Feste. But I haven't been back for a long time."

"Bagendon's not there anymore. The Erstürmen burned it to ash."

Dwarrow approached Tilly and sniffed at her hand again. "You're not living here alone. Other scents cling to your skin. A collection of different smells. Even," he screwed up his nose, "*grells*. The aroma of those bumbling giants will follow me to the stars. You've recently shared the company of a wild stone-grell *and* weald-grell. Very unusual. You don't smell them much anymore."

Tilly pulled her hand away. "How do you know all this?"

"We're looking for a stone-grell called Hannian," blurted Tom. "We need help. To fight Malphas."

"*Shoosh*," admonished Dwarrow. "Don't tell her anymore. She could be an enemy spy."

"I'm not a spy," said Tilly. "I'm not a fool, either. You can't defeat Malphas unless you've got an army in the tens of thousands."

"We're going to Giigal to get the weald-grells to help us," said Tom.

Dwarrow looked skyward. "Well, now you've told her everything. It will be on your head, Tom Anderson, if this woman hands us to the Erstürmen."

"We *fight* Malphas' followers," said Tilly, "not deliver them prisoners."

"A few smells on your skin; I'm certain I've met them before," Dwarrow said to Tilly. "Anyway, no more time for pleasantries. It seems Xaviary isn't coming back in a hurry. You must take us to your residence."

"How do I know I can trust you?"

"I'm Dwarrow mouldewerp, an elder of my culture. I am a friend to the Dobunni, stone-grells and any who fight against the nefariousness festering in Pergamos."

Tilly screwed up her face. "Nef-airy-whats-ess?"

"Never mind. I forged an alliance with the stone- and weald-grells at Dalman, served the needs of honourable Erstürmen who would never support the abomination of Malphas, and stood against the monster himself in his fetid lair. Are those qualities instilling trust?"

Tilly shrugged. "I guess so. Can Tom walk?"

"Yes," said Tom. "It still hurts, but...*ah*...how far?"

"Not far. We'll be there before sunset. I'll have to blindfold you, though."

"No point," said Dwarrow. "Mouldewerps use their nose to find their way. I'll smell and remember everything on the path to your hideout and be able to find it forever more."

"Then I should jam mud up your nostrils."

"You'll do no such thing. Nobody touches a werp's nose. Not unless they want to lose all their fingers."

Tilly looked at Tom and rolled her eyes. She had a young face, seventeen or eighteen harvest seasons old, and a lean body. Scrounging a living from the Desolate Mountains and Lokan's cursed wood couldn't be easy. However, Tom was convinced Tilly knew Hannian. Her eyes almost burst from their sockets when he mentioned the stone-grell's name. He would soon fulfil his promise to Grin, delivering Grin's totem to his sister. Then Tom could begin his mission to breach the walls of Pergamos and find Volerdie's throne.

*   *   *   *

Sitting atop a boulder overlooking the trail that led to the gorge hiding the rebels' monastery, Rosalie ran a whetstone along a dagger blade, honing its edge to lethal sharpness. Her metal-working skills were now more valuable than ever, forging and repairing weapons vital to the resistance. The scrape of stone on metal echoed through the valley as if signalling to anyone within earshot the resistance hadn't given up yet. Malphas' dominion wasn't absolute, and with the bounty gained from the ambush of the armoured wagon six moons ago, the rebels' future looked brighter than it had for many yarles.

A male crimson tweak, chest cherry-red and wings of raven black with white tips, alighted on the stone beside Rosalie and prised a moth from a crevice, holding it tight in his bill. He flew up to a ledge where a female waited, placing the prized morsel into her mouth. She shuffled her tawny wings and hopped across to a nest built of moss and lichen, pressed into the fork of two branches of a liebling shrub. After swallowing the moth, the expectant mother nestled into the nest, resuming the eternal desire to bring new life into the world.

The clink of loose stones shifting jolted Rosalie's attention away from the nesting tweak and back down the trail. Tilly rounded a corner, leading a slight man and a creature no taller than her knee with dark fur, who leaned on a walking stick. The man stumbled, falling heavily onto a pile of rocks. Rosalie sprang to her feet, placed the whetstone in her pants pocket and sheathed the dagger before sliding down the boulder's face.

She jogged up to Tilly and the strangers. "What happened?"

Tilly pointed to the man still lying on the ground. "Says he's hurt, but I can't see any wounds."

"Who are they?"

"The talking goa...I mean...the short, furry one is Dwarrow. A mouldewerp, apparently. This one's Tom. He's a Dobunni rebel. Showed me the scars. They claim to support the resistance."

"Why aren't they blindfolded?"

Tilly grabbed Rosalie's arm and dragged her away from the strangers. "The werp rubbed his wet nose all over me," she whispered. "He knows we have grells, where I was born, all sorts of stuff. They would have found their way here eventually. The man's looking for Hanni."

"Why?"

"He didn't say."

"Can we trust them?"

"We need more fighters, Rosalie. We've lost Sonya and Bion."

"The hairy goblin creature doesn't look like he could fight a cold."

"Erm-herm," said the mouldewerp. "While you bicker over there, my friend is writhing around in the dirt. Water, food and shelter would be nice if you can spare it."

Rosalie nodded to Tilly, then approached Tom. "Do you need me to help you up?"

"No," said Tom. "I can stand." He staggered to his feet and almost fell again.

Rosalie took his arm and flung it around her shoulder. "There's not much of you, is there? Maybe you're starving to death."

Tom faced her and offered a kind, open-hearted smile. "Thank you for helping us."

"Why are you looking for Hannian stone-grell?"

"Do you know her?"

Rosalie thought about avoiding the question, but Tilly had brought the strangers this far, and the rebels couldn't keep a stone-grell secret for long. "She's one of my closest friends."

Tom's muscles relaxed. Rosalie clasped his hand, worrying he might slide off her shoulder.

"I'm so glad we found her," said Tom. "I bring a valuable treasure from her brother."

"You know Grin?"

"He was one of *my* closest friends," said Tom, his voice breaking ever so slightly.

"Was?" asked Rosalie.

Tom turned away, and Rosalie didn't press further, drawing comfort from the fact Tom called a stone-grell friend and that he bore Dobunni pledge scars. He presented as an ally, not an enemy, and the rebels needed as many allies as possible.

They walked up the valley and into the monastery, Tom leaning on Rosalie the entire way. She helped him unshoulder his pack, then sat him on a bed cot while Tilly went to find Emelin. The group's oldest member knew more about healing than anyone else. If Tom needed care, Emelin would know how to provide it.

Dwarrow, the furred mouldewerp with patches of salmon-coloured skin on his face and stomach, and a mystery of pouches hanging from the belt tied around his waist, ambled around the ruin, sniffing every corner with his long, flexible nose. Rosalie had heard of mouldewerps but never seen one. Many had considered the werps lost from Enthilen until dozens of them arrived to fight alongside the grells during the massacre of Malang Gunya. The story of the killings, where King Adalwolf ordered the extermination of hundreds of grells and werps who'd marched to the city to honour lost ancestors, spread throughout Enthilen. After the attack, any werps still alive disappeared again, and Rosalie expected they'd truly been lost. She was pleased to be wrong.

She handed Tom a cloth soaked in glacial water. "Wash your face with this; you'll feel better. How did you get injured?"

Tom winched. "It might not have been...I mean, I don't know. I felt a sharp pain in my back, then fell to the ground."

"If you're getting injured when there's no enemy around, I don't like your chances when there is."

Tom sat up, smiled at Rosalie again and wiped the cloth over his face. "Damn! That's freezing."

Rosalie laughed. "You get used to the cold in the mountains."

Tilly returned, Emelin hobbling along behind and leaning on her crutch.

The old rebel leader stopped in her tracks and glared at Tom with her good left eye. "Who is this?"

Dwarrow spun around and sniffed the air. "*Aha!* There's a familiar smell I couldn't place before. Emelin Wallace of Bagendon."

Emelin squinted. "Dwarrow?"

"It's been many seasons since last we shared company."

Emelin smiled. "Yes, it has. But you don't forget a mouldewerp in a hurry. And I owe your kind so much after they saved me from Krieg."

Dwarrow pushed his shoulder satchel to one side, trotted to Emelin and titled his head up. "Your wounds are from the red grell?"

She nodded.

"He took your leg and an eye. At least he didn't take your nose."

"Who have you brought with you?" Emelin asked Dwarrow.

"You may remember him. Tom Anderson."

Emelin fixed her gaze on Tom. "Of course. You were much younger the last time I saw you, Tom. Much younger."

"Emelin...." Tom pushed his elbows into the cot and flung his legs off the side, trying to stand up. Rosalie grasped his hand and helped him to his feet.

"It's good to see you again," Tom said to Emelin.

She limped to him and stroked her fingers across the short, cedar-coloured stubble covering his chin and cheeks. "Many strange things have happened since you arrived in Bagendon twelve yarles ago. Many *horrible* things."

"Tom is not responsible for those things," said Dwarrow.

"*Hmmm*," said Emelin, her left eye clouding over to match the vacant expression from her right. She stepped back from Tom and lowered herself onto a stool, pushing her wooden leg out straight and resting her crutch on the floor. "All these yarles, unanswered questions have tortured my mind. You rode to war with Thaly, and I never saw her again."

"I believe Thaly is safe," said Dwarrow. "Her father took her to Germalia."

Emelin's eye drifted further away to another time and place. "Her father...I once met a masked man in the Scaur Hills asking after Thaly. Before Bagendon fell. I should have recognised him, but my thoughts were distracted by the threat to our home. Only later did I realise he was Jurelle Stansfield, Thaly's father. I was there when it happened more than half a generation ago. When Jurelle traded his loyalty to the Dobunni for his newborn daughter's life and the love of an Erstürmen princess. I adopted Thaly and promised to keep her ancestry a secret. I failed, and when the truth emerged, Thaly grew resentful, taking on the shame of her father."

"What about Dayna?" asked Tom.

Emelin offered Tom an acquiescent smile. "She died defending Bagendon. The red grell took my daughter and my hope." The moment of sorrow passed, and Emelin's face hardened. "How did you escape Sardis when all the other assassins fell?"

Tom baulked at Emelin's question, then sucked deep breaths while fingering something inside his pocket. Standing beside Tom, her hand on the small of his back to stop him from falling over, Rosalie absorbed the tremor of nervous energy flowing through his body. He appeared unsure, almost fearful. But his muscles tensed, and he stood straight, never wavering from Emelin's prying glare.

"I had help from Princess Caeli and Dwarrow," said Tom.

Emelin raised her eyebrows. "Caeli Heine? An Erstürmen princess?"

"An *honourable* Erstürmen princess," said Dwarrow.

"Honour is in the eye of the beneficiary," said Emelin. "It still doesn't explain what happened to the other assassins."

"An Erstürmen soldier called Jürgen dragged me from the needle before my companions freed themselves," said Tom. "I couldn't convince Jürgen to save anyone else."

"They died," said Emelin. "All of them, murdered in Sardis' inner circle for nothing. The plot to assassinate King Ewald and Prince Adalwolf failed long before it was hatched." Emelin undid the strap holding the wooden leg to her left thigh and scratched at the stump. "What part did you play in the loss of my adopted daughter?"

"Now, wait a moment," interrupted Dwarrow. "Tom didn't play any part in it. Thaly followed her own path, which led back to her father. It was bound to happen one day."

"You could be right, Dwarrow. But after all this time, Tom Anderson has appeared again out of nowhere, and I believe the gravest of troubles will follow him." Emelin cinched the strap of her fake leg, gathered her crutch, then pushed herself up from the stool. "I'm too weary to examine you now," she said to Tom. "I'm going back to bed."

"Wait," said Rosalie. "He's in pain and needs help."

"I'm unable to heal the pain Tom Anderson feels," said Emelin. "I expect only he can do that." She turned and hobbled from the room.

Rosalie patted Tom's back. "It seems you've led an interesting life."

Tom faced her. "I'd be happy to swap it for a more boring one."

"Well, you've come to the right place." Rosalie smiled, then removed her supporting hand. Tom sat on the cot while she took the stool. "Did you really make it into the inner circle of Sardis?" she asked.

"Yes, as an assassin sent to kill the king and prince. We planned to be captured by the Erstürmen and taken to the king as prisoners for execution, then escape when we reached the needle, the narrow corridor into the inner circle. Five of us made it to the needle; Ryder, Brynlee, another woman whose name I've forgotten, and a young man called Harris...Harris...."

"Snape," finished Rosalie, her heart throbbing from the hurt of a distant memory. "I saw you being led to the inner circle on a chain with Harris. He and I were lovers once."

Tom dropped his head. "Oh, I'm sorry, he died."

"It was a long time ago. Harris was one of my many mistakes."

"I've made plenty of those," said Tom.

"Do you want food?" asked Rosalie. "We don't have much."

"Do you have any pickled lizard?" asked Dwarrow. "We've eaten ours."

"I don't know what that is," said Rosalie.

"You should get out more," said Dwarrow.

"We have supplies to share," said Tom. "Slitherweed, yams, blemmel berries."

Rosalie and Tilly made a fire and sat with Tom and Dwarrow inside the monastery's main living area. As evening fell, other rebels came home to shelter, back from hunting or gathering food or scouting for intruders. Rosalie introduced the new arrivals to everyone, trying to make Tom and Dwarrow comfortable. The ice of suspicion thawed as those sitting around the fire swapped stories and shared food. Rosalie enjoyed the companionship. She hadn't been this at ease for many moons. Trouble may follow Tom Anderson, as Emelin said, but for now, an atmosphere of light-heartedness and hope filled the room. And something else; a stirring of warmth in the pit of her stomach, radiating across her skin and searching for an elusive sensation Rosalie hadn't experienced in many yarles.

*   *   *   *

As Rosalie sat with Tom beside the fire, an unexpected comfort flowed through him. The hard-to-explain tingling that sometimes appears in the company of endearing familiarity. Rosalie tied her long brown hair into a ponytail, accentuating soft, round cheeks, out of place amid the austerity of the rebel's hideout. Only partly roofed, the monastery sat atop walls of decaying mortar and missing stones, dozens of them strewn across the floor like broken shells scattered by ocean waves. The cold mountain wind whistled through a profusion of gaps. While the plains of Enthilen burned under the harvest sun, the Desolate Mountains clung to a chill reminiscent of the long dark.

Ngurung-ginya, Tom remembered. The grells would call the long dark ngurung-ginya and the harvest season gawimarra. Grin had taught Tom the grell words for all of Enthilen's six seasons.

Hanni, Grin's sister, hadn't appeared, and her absence fuelled Tom's worry about the message he came to deliver. About how she would respond to the news that her brother died far from home, away from his loved ones, so he could beg the birraman to return to Enthilen. Tom tried to dispel the concern by listening to the rebels' stories. Spirits were high owing to a recent raid netting welcome treasure, though Rosalie remained coy regarding the bounty's nature. One thing about the rebels struck Tom; no children. No sign this group had a future. Although now blessed with material wealth, the group suffered from a poverty of aspiration.

As Tom supped on the evening meal, a stew of mountain hare, yam-daisy roots, and dried beans, the group stirred when someone called a welcome from the front doorway.

Dwarrow inhaled with a snort. "Oh, a musty, malodourous malaise has wafted through the door. It smells like a grell. Two grells!"

Tom spun around to face the doorway as a stone-grell and weald-grell strode into the room. Both female; the stone-grell at least eight feet tall, muscled and athletic, the weald-grell a head shorter but no less intimidating. They wore tunics of stitched animal skins, the customary grell attire familiar to Tom, with cheeks and chins tattooed in black ink; the facial crest, displaying the plant or animal the grell had sworn to protect.

As they approached, Dwarrow stood, shuffled over and rubbed his nose against their bare shins. "This is strange. You *both* smell familiar. We've certainly met before."

"You are Dwarrow mouldewerp," said the weald-grell.

Turquoise eyes smiling, she knelt before Dwarrow and leaned down to place her fingertips on his cheeks. "I am Quenan weald-grell. First born of Turan and Primian. Protector of the resistance in the Desolate Mountains. I attended the garrabari when you begged for an alliance with the grells."

Quenan removed her fingers, and Dwarrow huffed, "Begged? Begged? If my memory offers the impeccable service I'm accustomed to, and there's no reason it shouldn't, it was the grells who jumped at the chance for an alliance. And rightly so. Rightly so, indeed." Then a smile flashed underneath his tentacle-like nose. "It is wonderful to smell you again, Quenan weald-grell. You carry the aroma of happier times."

"I was at the garrabari, too," said the stone-grell. "My mother, Mirrian, tattooed my facial crest."

"Gama, the spear fern," said Dwarrow. "You are Hannian stone-grell. Grin's sister."

Tom stood on shaking legs. "Hanni."

Hanni towered over him before grasping his left wrist and turning his hand palm up. She prised open his fingers to expose the scar on his hand, then her face hardened. "You are the birraman, Tom Anderson. Have you returned to rescue my brother?"

Air exploded from Tom's lungs as if someone had punched him in the chest. He stumbled, and Hanni grabbed his elbow, almost lifting him from the floor. Tom thrust his right hand into his pocket, fumbled around with the foil packet of anxiety pills until popping a rescuer from its cocoon, flung his hand to his mouth and threw the drug onto his tongue.

Five tablets left.

Hanni tightened her grip on his left arm. "Have you come to save Grin?"

Tom thought about looking away. Casting his eyes to the cold, stone floor to avoid this reality. A coward would do that. But he didn't want to be a coward anymore, so he swallowed the tablet and fixed his gaze on Hanni's lilac eyes.

"Grin's dead," said Tom. "He sacrificed his life so I could return to Enthilen."

Hanni dug her fingernails into Tom's skin and glowered at him. They stood in silence, Tom waiting for a slash of anger from Hanni that would end his own life. She could do it. One clutch from the hand of a mighty grell would snap his neck like a twig. But she didn't kill him, releasing his arm and marching from the building without another word.

Tom tried to go after her, but Dwarrow grabbed the hem of his tunic to stop him.

"The time will come when the reconciliation can begin," said the werp.

As the night wore on, Tom deflected questions about the appellation 'birraman', telling the rebels it meant someone who travelled long distances. Widukind's warning about the dark eyes played in his mind. *Stories about the eyes of lost souls have spread far and wide.* He didn't want to reveal too much until knowing more about the company he kept.

Supper over, those not on guard duty retired to their beds — little more than cots or blankets bunched over piles of straw. Dwarrow curled up near the fire while Rosalie offered Tom the bed that belonged to Sonya, a rebel fighter who died in a raid of Laodicea. He lay on animal skin with thick, soft fur stretched across timber slats perched above the floor on stone pedestals hewn in half. Rosalie disappeared into her private space, walled off by a dirty sheet, and Tom tried to sleep amid the restless murmur of a room full of resistance fighters.

But culpability stifled any chance of dreams, sleep replaced by the pain of losing Grin and the lack of opportunity to resolve the animosity expressed by Hanni. She hadn't returned to the monastery, but he needed to speak with her when his courage allowed.

* * * *

Dull morning light filled the living room of the rebel hideout, and people stirred, pulling on coats and preparing the fire for the morning meal. Rosalie tugged her privacy sheet along a metal rod hanging from the ceiling, then smiled at Tom, who still lay in bed.

"Are you feeling better?" she asked.

"Yes," said Tom. "My back has recovered."

Rosalie sat up and combed her fingers through knotted hair, her nakedness pressing against the inside of a thin undergarment. "*Hmmm. That is strange.* Last night, you said birraman is the grell word for...for...."

"Traveller. Someone from afar."

"How far?"

"It's a long story."

"I have time for a long story," said Rosalie, swinging her legs over the side of the bed and leaning towards Tom with intense curiosity. "There's not much else to do here in the mountains. Do you carry the eyes of lost souls?"

Tom's mouth turned dry. He shoved his hand into his tunic pocket and latched onto the dark eyes. *Keep them close. Don't show them to anyone.*

Rosalie's gaze didn't follow Tom's hand. Instead, she looked him straight in the eye. "Can I see them?"

Keeping his hand in his pocket, Tom sat up. Around him, the other rebels were engrossed in their morning chores. Bringing in wood for the fire. Grinding grains. Cooking breakfast. Tidying sleeping areas. Rosalie sat with her hands resting on her lap, moistening pale, alluring lips with the tip of her tongue.

"What do you know about the dark eyes?" asked Tom.

Rosalie shrugged. "I've heard a few stories. Not sure which ones are true. You could enlighten me."

Tom nodded and beckoned Rosalie over. She sat beside him on the bed as he took the dark eyes from his pocket. He wanted to keep them in his grasp, but she held open her palm, and he couldn't resist, tipping both eyes onto her hand. He then wondered if he'd made a terrible mistake.

"So," said Rosalie, "I could become immortal with these?"

"Only if you have a birthmark — a naevus — and a birth twin, born at the same time as you with the same mark."

Rosalie moved her hand up and down as if appraising the weight of the dark eyes, the clink of obsidian echoing around the room and sending Tom's pulse galloping with the fear of someone else seeing the eyes.

"I don't have a birthmark; my skin is perfect." Rosalie flashed a cheeky smile, then held the eyes close to her face. "Is that fire inside the glass?"

"Yes," said Tom. "Each eye has a flaming pupil."

"How...I mean...how is that possible?"

"I can't explain it. To be honest, I can't explain any of their magic."

"I used to believe in magic. Then it became an addiction that almost killed me. You can have them back." She handed Tom the eyes, brushing her fingertips across his palm, then stood and rinsed a cloth in a wooden bucket, rubbing the sleep from her face. "Some here say Malphas has seven heads and ten horns and breathes fire and ash. People wither just by standing close to him."

Tom placed the dark eyes in his pocket and yawned. "He's only a man."

"But he's immortal, right?"

"Yes. We might not be able to kill him, but we can smash the thing from which he draws his power. I faced Malphas on Hansen's Bluff and in Pergamos. Despite all his scheming, those encounters didn't go as he wanted. He may be immortal, but he's not invincible."

"What *thing* are you talking about?"

"Soon," said Tom. "We'll talk about it soon. Please don't tell anyone else I carry the eyes of lost souls. They're dangerous in the wrong hands."

Rosalie nodded, pulled a short tunic over her undergarment, slipped her feet into worn boots and walked to the fire.

After a meagre breakfast of oat mash and goat's milk, Tom, Dwarrow, and the rebels gathered in the monastery's main room, sitting on the floor around the fire pit. Dwarrow had called for a meeting, Tom unsure what plans the mouldewerp had cooked overnight. Hanni returned from wherever she'd been, standing in a corner and clutching a spear. Tom avoided eye contact with her, and she didn't look at him, the air inside the room laden with the weight of unspoken conflict. Emelin didn't join the group, the rebel matriarch wanting to rest.

Rosalie, who appeared to be the group leader, spoke first. "All of you have met our visitors, Tom and Dwarrow. They come seeking our help."

"Help with what?" asked Raf, a gruff man with weathered skin, scarred and gnarled like tree bark cut with a blunt axe.

"To defeat Malphas," said Dwarrow.

A few in the group scoffed. Others laughed aloud.

"That's impossible," said Tormil, an elderly Dobunni veteran of the battle for Laodicea. "A handful of weary fighters will never overcome Pergamos' defences. Malphas has countless legions at his command."

"You will not face them alone," said Dwarrow. "While the journey begins here, we have further to travel before confronting Malphas."

"Where do you propose to go?" asked Raf.

"We will travel south to Giigal and remind the weald-grells of the alliance they forged with the mouldewerps at Dalman. Their promise to stand side-by-side against the illness sweeping our land."

"It's many days ride to Giigal, and the Dambay Plains aren't safe," said Tilly. "Rephaim, Shield and draughouls patrol everywhere."

"We won't be travelling by land. The safest passage is by ship. Down the east coast."

"Even if you reach Giigal, the weald-grells will never agree to fight," said Quenan. "I know the disposition of my kin. Aggression is against their culture. The elders have never wanted to face Malphas. You embark on a futile mission."

"And yet, Quenan weald-grell, you are here, fighting," said Dwarrow. "To convince your kin, all that's required is a persuasive argument, and I'm a master of those. But I need an audience with the elders to present such an argument. Hence, I will take an aide. Someone to create the opportunity I seek."

"I cannot go with you," said Quenan. "I rebuked the elders of Giigal after they refused to help the stone-grells defend Babir Birramal. They banished me from the city."

Dwarrow smiled under the shadow of his long nose. "Oh, I won't be taking you. I was thinking of another grell."

"There's only one other," said Rosalie, turning to Hanni.

Grin's sister squeezed the shaft of her spear so tight the knuckles threatened to burst from her skin. At any moment, Tom expected her to raise the spear and thrust it into his chest. He pictured Grin dying at Hanni's feet on the monastery floor. Dying because of Tom.

"I am not going anywhere with the werp or the birraman," said Hanni. "I am staying here to fight beside my friends. It is pointless trying to convince those who cannot be convinced."

Dwarrow stood and leaned on his walking stick. "You lived among the weald-grells, Hanni. You know their customs, culture and language. And you are one of the last wild stone-grells. Your plea would not fall on deaf ears unless all compassion and sense of justice have shrivelled away among your kin."

"I will not abandon my friends," said Hanni. "Take the birraman with you. He is used to running away."

The spear had been thrown, one that hurt more than any blade of sharpened metal or stone. Tom bowed his head as the eyes of the resistance fighters peeled away the layers of his artifice. Inside his pants pocket, he popped an anxiety pill from the foil packet and brought his fingers to his mouth, surreptitiously delivering the medication.

Four tablets left.

"The weald-grells don't have enough fighters to defeat Malphas," said Raf.

"There is another army to consider," came a voice from the doorway leading further into the monastery.

Murmurs of surprise filtered through the group. Tilly jumped to her feet and drew her sword to confront a tall, spidery man with a hawkish nose and tired face.

"How did you break your bonds?" Rosalie asked the stranger.

He held up his clasped hands. "I am still bound, but the mortar in your walls is a little *friable*. The metal pole you tied me to came loose, eventually."

"Why didn't you run?"

"I doubt I would have gotten far among the rocks and ice. And truth be, I have nowhere left to run. I do not yearn to stumble around these barren hills until I starve. Being held prisoner for seven moons in your cold, cramped prison has weakened my legs to uselessness."

Rosalie faced Quenan. "Secure him again. Outside."

"Wait," said the man. "I overheard your deliberations. My counsel could prove valuable."

"I foresee no value in anything you have to say," said Tormil. "If you are indeed Rostard, as you claim to be, then you are a soothsayer, privy to events yet to pass. This puts you at a distinct advantage, able to twist our thoughts and actions to serve your own ends. And you remain a servant of our enemy."

Bound hands held out front, Rostard groaned as he knelt, then sat beside the fire. "What you say is true, though my service yields little reward. I'm nothing more than a guard watching over Sardis. Keeping the seat warm until Krieg graces the city with his presence."

"You still haven't explained where you were going when we ambushed you," said Rosalie.

Rostard flashed a wry grin but didn't answer the question.

"Fleeing Sardis," said Dwarrow. "Rostard seeks to leave Enthilen and escape Malphas' repressive hold."

"It seems I'm not the only soothsayer in the room," said Rostard. "Mouldewerps are renowned for their intuition. Although, it didn't save them from near obliteration."

"A canny nose is no match for rapacious grell hunters or cold-hearted Erstürmen," said Dwarrow. "What is this valuable counsel you offer?"

Rostard shuffled his bottom closer to the fire and held his bound hands next to the flames. "There are no armies left in Enthilen to challenge Malphas. However, one exists elsewhere, across the endless sands of Grōz Wüste. The Germalian army."

Germalia, thought Tom. *Thaly's there now, far away on the west coast of Ostamp.*

"The Germalians have no interest in Enthilen," said Raf.

"Ah, that is where you are wrong," said Rostard. "They keep a closer eye on this land than many realise. Our spies say the Germalian Conventus regularly debate declaring war on Malphas. Certain senators are very much in support of the declaration. Tipping the debate in your favour may require nothing more than a modest push."

Rostard fixed a cold, burrowing glare on Tom, who covered the pocket holding the dark eyes with his hand.

"What do you know, Rostard?" asked Tormil. "What visions have filled your vacillating mind? We could help you escape Malphas, but you must divulge everything."

As he spoke, Rostard never averted his eyes from Tom, "There is one thing that could sway the Germalian Conventus. A visit from someone who carries the eyes of lost souls. A man who is the birth twin of King Adalwolf. A man who has the power to ruin the immortal Malphas. Such a man could convince the Germalians to come and fight this war."

Shit. He knows everything. Shit, shit, shit. He could use the dark eyes to escape Malphas. To travel to Earth. He could stop me from finding the dead throne.

"That person isn't among us," said Raf.

"Yes, he is," said Rostard, smiling at Tom.

Every pair of eyes in the room turned to Tom and set hard like prison bars, foiling his escape. He had nowhere to hide. No hope of misdirection. Dwarrow twitched and shuffled, clearly distressed about Tom's secrets being exposed to desperate souls.

Can they be trusted? Any of them?

It didn't take a mouldewerp's nose to realise the atmosphere within the rebel group had changed. Suspicion and silent accusation assaulted Tom's senses until the tension became unbearable.

Tom went to speak, but Dwarrow interrupted, "If we divulge all we know," he said, "we place utmost trust in everyone here. It is a great risk to take in mixed company."

"You have nothing to fear from m...*urgh.*"

Rostard's words drowned in a bloody gargle. Emelin, standing behind him, had lashed a dagger across his throat. The soothsayer sat there, wide-eyed, blood spurting from his neck and spilling onto his fine clothes. As his skin turned bone white, no-one moved to help him. Emelin shunted him in the side with her crutch, and he crumpled to the ground, dead.

"Now, our company is less mixed," she said. "This soothsayer couldn't be trusted. Take his corpse outside for the vultures."

Two rebels wiped the stunned looks from their faces, stood and dragged Rostard through the doorway.

Emelin faced Dwarrow. "Time for your confession."

Dwarrow scratched the heel of his walking stick over the worn flagstones, then glanced at Tom, who nodded his agreement.

"We have the means to destroy the throne of the dead," said Dwarrow. "Volerdie's throne."

"What good will that do?" asked Rosalie.

"It will end Malphas' reign," said Tom. "Cripple his resolve, so he ceases the carnage. And it will remove the incentive for someone else to take his place. Also...." He paused, Widukind's voice seeping into his thoughts. *One birth twin, immortal no more.*

"Also?" asked Raf.

"When the throne is shattered," said Dwarrow, "we believe Malphas will no longer be immortal."

"Believe or know?" asked Emelin.

"Nothing is certain in this world," said Dwarrow.

"How will you destroy the throne?" asked Rosalie.

"Blood and bone," responded Tom. "My blood mixed with King Adalwolf's. The bones of my grandmother and Princess Caeli ground to dust. When we combine these ingredients and place them on the throne, that which Volerdie made will be unmade. Soon, we'll have everything we need to end Malphas' tyranny." Tom faced Hanni. "Grin sacrificed his life so I could return to crush the dead throne. For a final time, Grin showed he believed in me like he always has. I'm not going to let him down."

"You *are* King Adalwolf's birth twin," Tormil said to Tom.

Tom nodded, reached into his pocket, withdrew the eyes of lost souls and held them above his head. Almost everyone in the room gasped as one.

"Adalwolf and I share the same birthmark," said Tom, "immortality within my grasp should I capture Adalwolf's soul with the dark eyes. But I don't seek eternal life. I'm here to destroy Volerdie's throne. When I place the eyes in the throne, it will come alive. I've seen it. I've been *trapped* by it. It took me home twelve yarles ago, and the eyes have brought me back. When the throne comes alive, it's vulnerable. That's when we'll strike."

"All this talk of destroying thrones is pointless," said Tilly. "Nobody knows where Adalwolf is. He disappeared from Enthilen yarles ago. And we can't reach the damn throne; it's protected by walls thicker than three tufted goliaths and taller than a panalope tree."

"If we can convince the weald-grells *and* Germalians to fight, we might have a chance," said Rosalie.

"It'd take days and days of marching to reach Germalia," said Raf.

"Send the birraman and the werp," said Hanni. "Make *them* navigate the endless desert on a fool's quest."

Dwarrow shook his head. "On no, I'm not going anyway near that desert. Much too dangerous. Vagabonds, wurloins and worst of all, *dreadwerps*. Hideous, horrible things. They slink around under the sand and ride poisonous serpents larger than a horse. Venom oozes from the serpent's skin like pus from a wound. It's disgusting and deadly. The dreadwerps are immune to the poison, of course. They use it on their weapons."

"Are they not your relations?" asked Quenan.

"Distant relations," said Dwarrow. "Very distant. Sickly pale skin dressed in mangy white fur. *Errrk.* I can't bear thinking about them. If they caught a mouldewerp, well, I can't imagine what would happen to the poor soul. What would happen to me! No, my destination is Giigal. Definitely Giigal."

"Rostard may have spoken the truth," said Rosalie. "If Tom made a representation to the Germalians, it could sway their opinion in our favour."

"I agree," said Dwarrow. "But he'll need an escort. Someone to join him in the journey across the Groz Wüste to Portum."

Hang on, thought Tom. *Now I have to hike across some friggin' endless desert?*

"I'll go," said Rosalie.

Murmurs filtered through the group.

Rosalie stood. "Can't you see? This is the opportunity we've been waiting for. We can't spend our remaining days scratching a living from rocks, and we don't have the means to defeat our enemy. Sure, we have coin now. More coin than any of us have seen. But where can we spend it? Not in Laodicea. It would draw Hunger's attention. And not in Sardis."

"We could leave Enthilen," said Tilly. "Buy a ship and travel across the oceans to find our paradise."

"I won't leave my home to the desolation of Malphas' treachery," said Rosalie. "Our coin can't buy this land its freedom."

"I agree with Rosalie," said Emelin, leaning on her crutch. "The coin is not as valuable as our resistance. We should use the riches to bolster our efforts and nothing more. The return of Tom Anderson presents us with an opportunity to be seriously considered. A Germalian army marching on Pergamos could shatter Malphas' defences."

Emelin turned and hobbled back to her room. The group became restless. Hanni strode outside, and Quenan followed her. Tom pulled his knees to his chest, the ambitions of his hosts circling like a school of sharks. Any one of them could steal the dark eyes. If they had a naevus, the lure of eternal life would be too great. He scanned the skin of people beside him, hoping to spot any threat; someone with a birthmark. Other than Dwarrow and the grells, the only person Tom trusted was Rosalie. She'd already been tested.

The quest to ruin the dead throne had become more complicated than Tom had hoped. Widukind sought Adalwolf and would have to convince him to enter Pergamos with Tom so their fresh blood could be spilled on the throne. But entering Pergamos by stealth appeared impossible. An army was needed to breach the city's walls. An army likely bigger than Enthilen had ever seen. Tom had been chosen to travel the vast wasteland to enlist that army and convince them to fight a war. At least he controlled his own fate. Not in his hands was the search for Adalwolf and the absent king's response to Widukind's revelation.

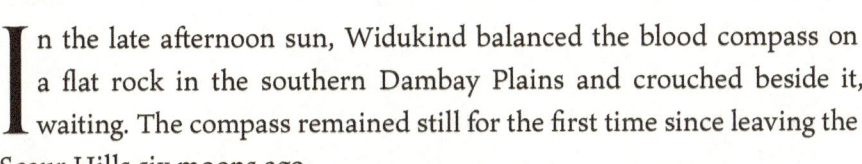

~ Chapter 19 ~

In the late afternoon sun, Widukind balanced the blood compass on a flat rock in the southern Dambay Plains and crouched beside it, waiting. The compass remained still for the first time since leaving the Scaur Hills six moons ago.

"That's odd," Widukind said, reaching out to collect the etched gold pentagram. "Blood might be too old."

He planned to add a fresh drop of Tom's blood to the compass and try again later. The vial of blood had enough reserve to last about twelve more moons. Although treated by the mouldewerps to extend its life, the blood became ineffective after two moons once bonded to the gold pentagram. With old blood, the compass spun haphazardly and pointed in random directions, thwarting any hope of finding Adalwolf. A compass that didn't spin at all, like today, could be caused by old blood or two other things; either Adalwolf stood beside Widukind, or the absent king was dead.

Widukind had battled internal demons for yarles but didn't believe he had such a flimsy grip on reality not to notice his nephew standing beside him. He didn't want to consider the other alternative. If Adalwolf had died, his search and the mission to destroy the throne of the dead was futile. Widukind's hope of becoming a mortal again and freeing himself from eternal torment would be dashed, and his dream of seeing Caeli released from her soulless misery crushed. Adalwolf couldn't die yet.

Old blood, he concluded. Must be old blood.

In an unrepentant corner of his floundering mind, Widukind had contemplated another path should he fail to find Adalwolf. He could stand at Pergamos' gates and offer himself to his brother, Malphas. Offer to become the immortal sacrifice Malphas so desired. Then, Widukind would be free of his perpetual cage, and maybe Volerdie *would* return to Enthilen to lead the Erstürmen people into paradise. *Maybe.* But Caeli....

Widukind collected the compass, slipped it into his coat pocket, and slapped his cheeks to dismiss wandering thoughts. The compass had spun yesterday, slow and steady. Adalwolf must have been alive then. When it stopped spinning, the compass pointed east. Always east. The absent king would be there, somewhere. He had to be. Widukind estimated it would take him eight moons to reach Enthilen's east coast on foot. The vial of Tom Anderson's blood would be almost empty by then.

Standing among the long grass of the Dambay Plains, he opened his shoulder satchel and retrieved a pouch bulging with dried leaves collected by the mouldewerps from the ha'nuk shrub growing on the eastern slopes of the Scaur Hills. Widukind loosened the pouch's drawstring, plucked out a leaf and tossed it into his mouth, mint, lemon and pepper flavours bursting onto his tongue. The medicinal plant, favoured by the werp shaman, helped smooth the oscillating thoughts bouncing around inside Widukind's head.

As the western plains swallowed the sun, he walked on, imagining Caeli appearing through the dusk haze. Emerging from the smoky veil tailored by the fires burning Babir Birramal to the south. Widukind often thought about Caeli, hoping his daughter would join him on this journey. He couldn't finish the task without her.

But as the dusk turned dark, he resigned himself to another night camping alone, stopping at a grove of shrubs forming a tight circle, unusual vegetation for the grassy steppes of Dambay. From his satchel, he took daisy yams, dried insects, and a rabbit he'd found lying in the grass, trembling as if afflicted with an illness. Even as an immortal, tainted meat could make him sick, delaying his search for Adalwolf. And Widukind didn't need sustenance but longed for the rituals of everyday life.

After collecting kindling of grass and dead, spindly twigs, he used a flint to start a feeble fire, gutted and skinned the rabbit, and skewered the carcass on a stick to dangle it over the flames. The rabbit would take a long time to cook, but he had all night. Sleep often eluded him, even at the best of times.

Widukind sat hypnotised by the pulsating yellow-orange flames, lost in his thoughts, until the smell of burnt rabbit wafted into his nose. He pulled the meat from the fire and set it on the ground to cool. Trepidation startled the butterflies in his stomach when four unexpected guests stepped from the darkness and into the campfire's amber hue; a man, woman, boy and girl. Widukind reached for a knife, thinking Malphas' servants, cleverly disguised as a peasant family, had found him.

"H-h-hello," said the man, holding up an open palm in deference. "No need for that weapon. Sorry to have startled you."

"Didn't expect to see anyone out here," said Widukind, clutching the knife's handle. "Other than Malphas' soldiers."

"We smelled the rabbit. Ain't had cooked meat in a while."

Widukind used his free hand to cover the rabbit with a dirty cloth, then frowned at the new arrivals. "It's only small. Not enough...."

"Oh no, we're not here to steal your food. We're looking for company, that's all. My children get frightened by the sounds on the plain."

"Your children are right to be frightened. Fiends from Pergamos patrol these plains. Satches of Rephaim soldiers. Howlings of weregrims, and other abominable creatures."

"We have food to share," said the woman, dropping a wicker basket from her shoulders and searching inside.

"We're marching to Pergamos," said the girl.

"Hush, Kurima," said the man. "The stranger isn't interested in our destination."

Widukind lowered the knife. "Why go there?"

"To obtain the Worshipful Master's blessing and earn our place in paradise."

"There's nowhere else to go," said the woman. "We abandoned our farm near Grōz Forst because the land is scorched. It grows nothing."

"Malphas cursed this land," said Widukind. "Now you go to worship at his feet?"

"The fire cleansed Enthilen," said the man. "Cleared away the pagans."

"A *cleansing*. That's a pleasant way to describe the desecration of a sacred forest."

"May we rest with you a while?" asked the woman. "The dark hides many terrors."

"How do I know you're not one of them, masked by deception?"

The man shrugged. "You brandished the knife. We take the same risk of trust sharing your company."

Widukind put the knife on the ground beside the cooked rabbit, then waved his hand, offering the strangers a place to sit.

"I'm Norn," said the man. "This is my wife, Fletta, my son, Stevan, and my daughter, Kurima."

"Is it true Pergamos is protected by a colossal wall higher than the clouds?" asked Stevan as he sat beside Widukind.

"A wall and an army," said Widukind.

"I've been assured believers can pass through the gates without trouble," said Norn.

"Assured by who?"

Norn half-smiled at Widukind.

Fletta sat and pulled beets from her basket, placing them next to her feet.

Kurima's face lit up. "We have bread, too."

"I baked it last eve," said Fletta. "It's still fresh enough to eat."

"Last eve?" queried Widukind. "On the plain?"

"Baked in a fire oven." Fletta heaved a lidded black pot from the wicker basket. "Flour, milk, salt and a dash of meduz. Cooked over the coals." She removed the lid from the fire oven and tore off a piece of brown loaf, handing it to Widukind.

He placed it in his mouth and chewed the dense texture. Salty but tasty nonetheless.

"I have...rabbit," said Widukind with a mouthful of bread. "A handful of daisy yams and...er...crickets. Not much to offer, I'm afraid."

"Don't concern yourself," said Norn. "We seek only shared company to calm our nerves. I'm sorry, but we didn't catch your name?"

"Murrigal."

"Murr-ee-gul. That's an unusual name. Is it Erstürmen?"

"The stone-grells gave it to me. A stranger who travelled to their land."

Fletta shivered. "Wild grells, how terrifying. Thank goodness the Worshipful Master cleansed most of them."

Cleansed, thought Widukind. That word again. It seemed slaughtered or enslaved meant cleansed to these people.

"Have you been to Pergamos?" asked Kurima.

"I'm not welcome there," said Widukind.

"Why not?" asked Stevan. "Are you a nonbeliever?"

"It depends on what you expect me to believe in."

"That Malphas will rule until the return of Volerdie, the Divine Creator. Then, together, they will lead us into paradise."

"Don't you want to live in paradise?" Kurima asked Widukind.

"I think our host has had enough of these questions," said Norn. "Let's be thankful he's willing to share his camp with us."

Norn's eyes betrayed his dismay. They twitched and flashed around the campsite, searching for a threat he might have missed.

A nonbeliever would be considered dangerous, thought Widukind. Norn may be planning to kill him. Or steal the rabbit.

"Are you travelling alone?" asked Fletta.

"I'm waiting for my daughter to join me," said Widukind.

"You're married? With children?"

"My wife is dead."

"I'm sorry." Fletta averted her eyes and stared into the fire.

"King Ewald executed her," said Widukind. "To punish me for supporting...."

"Who?" interrupted Stevan.

Widukind pulled his knees to his chest and hunkered into his dirty coat. "It was a long time ago. I made a lot of mistakes back then."

"We can atone for our mistakes in paradise," said Stevan.

"What was that?" Norn reached into a sack and withdrew a hatchet. "Something moving in the darkness, beyond the firelight."

"I can't see anything," said Widukind.

"I hear shuffling."

"Probably a wild horse or plainalope," said Fletta.

Norn stood and held the hatchet at arms-length, waving it towards the unseen. "A shadow stalks us." He glared at Widukind. "Have your pagan friends come to gut us and roast our flesh?"

Kurima shuddered. Fletta pulled her daughter close. Stevan stood beside his father.

"I'm not a heathen," said Widukind.

"Nor are you a believer, it seems," said Norn. "You must be one or the other. Either you follow Malphas, or you're his enemy." He fixed his jittery eyes on Widukind and stepped towards him. "What are those scars on the palms of your hands?"

Damn it, thought Widukind. Forgot to put on my gloves.

"Wounds from a pagan ritual," said Stevan. "Must be. Boiled the blood and brains of an innocent child, then scolded his hands on the feast."

"*Ewww*," said Kurima.

A faint, lilting voice drifted from the darkness, "Lower your weapon. My father is no threat to you."

Norn's hand shook as he chopped into the night. "Who are you? Show yourself."

Caeli stepped into the camp, and Widukind's mood turned as bright as the full moon of Bargan floating above him.

"A wraith!" cried Fletta. "She's come to devour us."

Norn lunged at Caeli, his axe cutting through the thin flesh of her left arm and striking bone. An ooze of blood darker than mahogany ran down Caeli's wrist. Widukind grasped a burnt branch from the campfire, jumped to his feet and plunged the fired end into Norn's side, searing his flesh through his shirt. The hatchet fell to the ground. Stevan reached for it, but Widukind pushed him aside and scooped up the weapon.

"Please," said Caeli. "We mean no harm."

Norn clutched his smouldering side. "Both of you are fiends. We were foolish to enter a monster's lair." He stepped back, looking as if the fight in him had dissipated.

Stevan remained a threat but seemed intent on protecting his father rather than launching an attack.

"The only monsters here are the ones trapped inside our minds," said Widukind.

Caeli wrapped the brittle, bony fingers of her right hand over the cut on her left arm to stem the bleeding. "We are father and daughter, not monsters," she said.

Fletta pulled Kurima to her chest. "The father of a wraith. I've never heard of such a thing."

"She wasn't always like this," said Widukind. "She was my beautiful daughter once."

"The Divine Creator made her a draughoul to punish your lack of piety," said Stevan.

Widukind gave a resigned nod. "Yes, you're probably right."

Still holding his side, Norn packed up the family's belongings. "We can't stay here and risk Volerdie's anger by sharing the company of heathens."

"The plains are dangerous," said Caeli. "Especially at night."

"We'll take our chances."

"You'll need this." Widukind gave the hatchet to Fletta.

"May the Creator bestow mercy on you and your daughter," she said.

"I've long given up such hope," said Widukind.

The family gathered their possessions and disappeared into the night.

Widukind retrieved a square of torn fabric from his satchel and held it towards Caeli. "Bandage your wound with this, Sweetness."

"The bleeding has already stopped," she said. "It never lasts long."

Widukind hadn't seen Caeli since leaving the Scaur Hills. He wanted to step across and hug his daughter, but the unresponsive slump of cold bones in his arms would only inflame his torment.

"Sit by the fire," said Widukind. "You must be tired after all your travels."

"I feel no weariness," said Caeli. "No ache. No joy. No loss. I am numb to the world."

A sob of blame caught in Widukind's throat. "All this is my doing. I've inflicted punishment on us more brutal than Malphas could ever devise. Me to live as an immortal, watching my daughter waste away for another thousand yarles. You to wander these lands, searching for the soul Adalwolf took from you."

"Your guilt makes the punishment worse. Please, Papa, let it go."

Tears welled in Widukind's eyes. "I can't, Sweetness. I'm clinging to one last hope both of us will be released when Volerdie's throne is gone."

"Adalwolf is east of us."

"You've seen him?"

"No, but I sense his presence. We formed a connection when Adalwolf stole my soul using the dark eyes. A bond exists between draughouls and those who turned them into the soulless. We will cross paths with him eventually. Keep walking east."

*   *   *   *

Next to Adalwolf's stinging eyes, a flame bee hovered on the coastal breeze. With senses inherited from generations of ancestors, the bee narrowed in on a single white flower fluttering like a flag of surrender, alighting on the yellow stamens and bathing in grains of pollen stuck to its legs and body. It unrolled its proboscis, searching for whatever nectar remained, and sucked it up as if gulping the last water from a well. At the foot of Adalwolf's prostrate body, a field mouse scurried among charred clumps of grass, devouring the corpses of burnt insects scattered across the dirt. Head down, nose twitching, it focussed on the easy meals, disregarding or unaware of how exposed it was on the barren field.

The peak of bravado is often reached the moment before a downfall, thought Adalwolf.

His prophetic musing came true when a plains kite plummeted from the sky and dropped onto the unwary mouse, piercing the creature's organs with razor-sharp talons. The bird wasted no time stripping the flesh from its prey with a deft bill. Hunting was good among the scorched, coverless earth.

With a screech, the kite became airborne, ascending on a thermal to glide among the throng of hawks, falcons and vultures circling above the spoils of war. Adalwolf had never taken much notice of the nature around him. But here, lying among the ash and ruins of Gestade, he couldn't escape it. The outpost may have fallen, the people cowering inside resigned to memories, but the ebb and flow of nature continued as if the terrors of war were simply another phase in the cycle of life.

The whinny of a lone horse drew Adalwolf's attention as it staggered among the carnage, the raw flesh of its flank charred and weeping. Then the mournful whimpers of undreds filled the smoky air, the once terrifying beasts reduced to nothing more than chunks of meat skewered on poisoned spikes protruding from the base of pit traps. A soldier with a missing leg crawled among the shards of shattered rock and splintered timber littering the battleground. Her companions and enemies lay dead or dying around her, entangled in the undiscerning futility of war.

She will soon follow them to the grave, thought Adalwolf, hoping future generations recounted stories of the bravery and resilience of Gestade's defenders.

Vastly outnumbered by the hordes of Pergamos, the defenders had given their lives for the sake of an Enthilen lost long ago. A better Enthilen. Though Gestade had been reduced to ash, Adalwolf longed for its memory to burn bright in the songs and stories of those searching for strength in the face of overwhelming odds.

Above him, Malphas' banner flew victorious from a vestige of Gestade's once proud walls, the white cloth adorned with the red, two-headed serpent and the sigil of two eyes orbiting a golden sun and joined together by the sun's rays. Adalwolf remembered the design. Malphas had shown it to him, claiming the image came from *Da Und Sepcarture*, the First Scripture. It represented how this world, Ostamp, was forever joined to Tom Anderson's world, and how decoupling the connection could disrupt the normal cycle of life and reward the fortunate and cunning with immortality.

Amid the moans of the dying, a timber wagon wheel ground against a metal hub, and the jangle of a harness drifted on the breeze.

A survivor? wondered Adalwolf. Or a war machine come to douse the last flame.

He lifted onto his elbows, determined to face damnation or salvation with open eyes. In the distance, a woman pulled a two-wheeled cart, navigating her way among the corpses. She wore a cream dress soiled with dirt and blood, the ragged hem flapping against her shins, and a toque and veil that teetered on straight, dark hair.

Audie, he thought. The healing angel still lived.

She marched towards him as if she'd decided his soul was the only one worth saving.

"You're awake," she said, resting the cart's pull bar on the ground and rubbing her lower back.

"You were here before?" asked Adalwolf.

"Don't you remember?"

"I remember being attacked by draughouls in the dungeon. Taken to the infirmary. You and Morgana. The south wall falling...."

Audie sat beside Adalwolf. "You've been drifting in and out of consciousness for two days. We hid you in a cellar underneath the infirmary and did what we could to save your life. There is a deep cut in your lower back, but it will heal if I tend to it."

Adalwolf sat up, reaching around to his back as skin tugged at the wound, threatening to open it again.

"Careful," said Audie. "The stitches may not hold."

"Any other survivors?" he asked.

"The infirmary was the last to fall. By that stage, most of Gestade's citizens were dead. Despite my protests, Morgana pushed me into the cellar and pulled a bed over the top to hide the door. The last thing I heard was her screams."

"We should treat the injured."

"I have little left to treat them with."

"But you've come to treat me."

The usual calm of Audie's face reddened with a stormy complexion. "I've chosen to save one life. It's the best I can do. The rest will have to survive on their own."

"Why bother saving anyone?"

The storm churned more. "Because I refuse to give up completely. If Malphas wants my last breath, he will have to wrench it from my lungs."

Adalwolf retreated, waiting for the tempest of Audie's emotions to calm. If he was going to survive this, he needed her stoicism. Her composed wisdom. He needed *her*.

Audie's face turned hopeful. "There's an uninjured horse nearby. I'm going to try and catch it. I can't pull this wagon myself." She tugged one of the few remaining clumps of green grass from the ground, stood and held the temptation at arms-length as she crept towards the saddled, black horse. "*Tsh. Tsh. Tsh.* Don't be scared, boy. I won't hurt you."

The horse flashed nervous eyes, its hide bathed in sweat and still trembling from the terrors of battle. It raised its head and stomped the ground but had little energy for fight or flight. Audie held the grass to its mouth, and it nibbled a blade through the bit of its halter but turned away at the rest. She took the reins and guided the horse to Adalwolf. When the horse settled, she tethered it to the cart.

"What do you have in the cart?" asked Adalwolf.

"Grain, waterskins, ropes, weapons, a handful of medicines. Whatever I could find and carry. I'll feed and water the horse, then harness it to the cart. It's only morning. We can travel until sunset."

"Where are we going?"

Audie shrugged. "I don't know. We can't go north, and there's no point heading to the coast unless a ship awaits to spirit us to safety. South? Some of Babir Birramal remains. We could hide there. Build a cabin in the forest."

"A cabin? You're delirious. Why do you hope for a future that can never be?"

"Hope is all I have left."

Adalwolf slumped to the ground. "Then leave me here to die. I will only be a burden."

"You can lie in the cart. I will tend your wound."

After feeding the horse, Audie fashioned a harness from rope and attached it to the saddle. She stroked the horse's flank and tried to soothe its nerves. "We should give you a name, boy. How about Girac? That was my father's name."

Adalwolf tried to stand, but pain shot down his spine, and his legs buckled under him. Audie came to his aid, looping his handless right arm around her shoulder and neck. Together they heaved until Adalwolf staggered forward, limping to the back of the cart and collapsing onto the tray. Squeezing between two bags of grain, he dragged his bottom along the worn timber, hoping to avoid any splinters, until, lying flat, his head rested against the front of the tray and the soles of his boots dangled off the end.

"Come on, Girac," said Audie.

As she led the horse away from Gestade and into the Dambay Plains, the desolation of war faded, and Adalwolf closed his eyes. Romilda came to him in his dreams, talking of love and marriage and the glorious kingdom he would rule. He didn't dismiss her this time, thankful for the mother's embrace he'd shunned as a young man.

When Adalwolf woke, the cart had stopped, and a campfire burned in the gentle dusk light. He dug the fingers of his left hand into the cart's timber slats and pulled his aching body off the tray, falling on the ground with a thud.

Audie stood over him. "You're stubborn; I'll give you that. And you're bleeding again. I should check the stitches."

She helped Adalwolf limp to the fire, sat him down and pulled his bloodied tunic over his head. From a satchel, she took a mortar, pestle, and a pouch of herbs and began grinding a mixture together.

"Will that help?" asked Adalwolf.

Audie smiled. "Do you have a better idea?"

Around the campsite, a dozen rotting tree stumps no taller than Adalwolf's waist but broader than his arm span stood as a sombre reminder of a long dead forest. Giants reduced to dwarf silhouettes. Adalwolf and Audie were too far north to have already reached the boundary of Grōz Forst, the southern forest the grells called Babir Birramal, so this area must once have been a grove of trees. A woodland outlier amid the endless plain.

Nothing moved as night enveloped the dusk. Not even a breeze across the plain to wave the grass stalks. The first star shone above Adalwolf. He smiled, then winced as Audie's fingers pressed into his wound.

"Sorry," she said. "I've mixed the herbs with honey. It's all I have. It should stop the weeping and heal the skin. The stitches are holding."

Adalwolf relaxed at Audie's soothing voice and knowing touch. He'd rarely been touched by a woman other than his mother. He met a young woman, Linza, on Bramble Island when he and Romilda hid there from Malphas. She had tan skin and sandy, sun-bleached hair. Adalwolf wooed Linza with lies about his reign as Enthilen's king. Stories of great conquests and generosity to his subjects. He lost his virginity to her, their consummations often awkward, nervous encounters, over too soon. Adalwolf had trouble controlling himself. Linza didn't seem to mind, infatuated with the idea of being the wife of a king. She'd make skirts from palm fronds, and tiaras from seashells and driftwood, and parade along the beach, calling herself Queen Linza.

Adalwolf and Romilda abandoned Bramble Island when Romilda fell ill, leaving Linza behind. Then he had thoughts only for his mother, already planning to seek treatment for her ailment in Gestade. Queen Linza and her dreams would have to wait.

Now, Adalwolf's fleeting chance of reclaiming the kingdom of Enthilen had been crushed under the boots of Malphas' marauding army. Only Audie's sanguine company filled the void of desire. Despite being surrounded by desperate horror, she carried on as if this was the life she would always lead. As if nothing could dent her optimism.

Build a cabin in the woods. He smiled at the idea.

"All done," said Audie.

She helped put Adalwolf's tunic back on, then made a bed for him from blood-stained blankets. They ate a mash of grain soaked in water.

"We must ration the supplies if we're going to make it," said Audie.

"Make it where?" asked Adalwolf.

She shrugged.

Adalwolf propped himself up against a tree stump. "Why don't you go home, Audie?"

"Home is far across the ocean. A land called Morund. Barbarians, thieves from Oder, raided my village, killed my family and stole me away." She soaked more grain in a cup of water. "We can have this in the morning."

"Malphas will hear about my appearance in Gestade. Without a corpse to prove otherwise, he'll assume I'm still alive and send soldiers to find me. It's not safe in my company."

"Others have said that to me. Why do men conclude I'm so weak, I can't face the same evil they must? Why do they feel a need to protect me from all that threatens them?"

"You're braver than I am, Audie. That, I will never doubt." Adalwolf pushed off the tree stump, leaned towards Audie and kissed her on the lips.

Eyes wide, she pulled back and slapped his face. "Is that all you care about at a time like this? Are you such a prisoner to your own desires?"

Adalwolf rubbed his stinging cheek and slunk away. "Forgive me. I...."

"Thousands of people are dead. Gestade is no more. And you...."

Adalwolf reached for Audie's hand. "Please. I'm sorry. I've not had much experience with women."

"No wonder if that's how you approach things." She tugged her hand away. "We've been forced together by circumstance, nothing more." Audie stood, walked to the cart and sorted through the supplies.

Adalwolf rested his back against the tree stump again and half-closed his eyes.

Is Audie's kindness towards him nothing more than a healer's burden? he wondered. Could the mature, worldly Audie ever fall for a man who still acted like a spoilt child? Is this...is this...hope? Did he have hope for a better world after all?

~ Chapter 20 ~

In the early morning, Tom shouldered his backpack and exited the front door of the hideout in the Desolate Mountains, away from snoring rebels, to breathe in the sunrise and brisk mountain air. A soft, almost honey-coloured light seeped down the sheer cliffs on either side of the valley, and plumes of tiny insects swirled up from tufts of grass like living whirlwinds. To the north, the valley narrowed into a sheer gorge penetrating the base of a snow-capped mountain. A cliff vulture glided across the mountain's eastern face at the snowline, searching for those already dead.

Tom walked south, away from the monastery and further down the valley, longing to stretch his legs. He'd been with the rebels for two moons, staying in camp to recover from the mysterious injury he'd received in Lokan. He concluded Adalwolf must have been wounded, and Tom had felt his pain. But the absent king hadn't died yet. The fact there were no physical signs of an injury made Tom the butt of jokes among the rebels, but also fed their superstition about the curse hanging over Lokan's woods.

He'd spoken with Rosalie, Emelin and Dwarrow about a plan to confront Malphas. The meeting with Rostard set them on a path from which there appeared to be no deviation. But Tom hadn't talked to Hanni other than telling her Grin had died. He still carried Grin's remembrance totem in his backpack, reluctant to give it to Grin's sister, knowing this would inflame her hurt and remind her of Tom's accountability.

As he rounded a corner, he came to a vantage point offering a commanding view of Lokan and, in the far distance, glimpses of a dirt road. *The road to Laodicea,* thought Tom, remembering the journey he'd taken with Thaly and Grin to join the rebel army led by Jacob in their defence of the city against a barbarian invasion. 'Bethesda,' Jacob would say. The original Dobunni settlers called the town Bethesda. Whatever the name, the settlement had become a shadow of its former self, according to the rebels.

To Tom's right, Hanni stood on a boulder, the grell as unmoving as a marble sculpture, surveying the woods and road. With her back turned, Tom wondered if she'd seen him. A rocky track led from the valley floor along a steep ridge to the west, ending at Hanni's vantage point. Tom shifted the weight of his backpack and climbed the narrow track, no wider than two feet side-by-side, with a sheer drop to his left. The toes of his boots kicked loose stones from the path. They fell over the edge, tumbling and clanking to the valley floor, a deathly distance below. Despite the morning chill, sweat pooled in the scarred palms of Tom's hands as they clutched the backpack's straps. The scars told anyone who cared to look, Tom Anderson was a birraman.

The sun rose over a saddle between two mountains and illuminated the boulder where Hanni stood. She'd turned now, clutching her spear and staring at Tom as he stumbled along the last section of track.

"You have made enough noise to rouse the black grell of Laodicea from his slumber," said Hanni.

"Sorry," said Tom as he stepped onto the boulder. "Hunger rules Laodicea now?"

"He has ruled the city since the barbarian invasion." Hanni turned from Tom to continue her vigil.

He stepped closer to her, an arms-length from the edge of a boulder taller than a three-storey house. One slip would end it. One misstep or a push from a grieving sister.

"Have you been on watch all night?" asked Tom.

"Tilly had the night watch. I have taken over from her."

"Do you expect an attack?"

"Expect or not expect, the watch must continue. In this new Enthilen, we must be prepared for anything."

Tom flicked his tongue around a dry mouth, hoping for any sign of a loosening in the tense muscles of Hanni's back. But she offered only a statuesque judgement as hard and cold as the stone under his feet.

"I'm sorry," said Tom, his voice breaking like a twig. "About Grin. I'm so sorry."

"Are you?" said Hanni.

"I would have helped him live in my world, but he was badly wounded. And, my people wouldn't have treated him kindly."

Hanni faced Tom. "Even if he lived in your world, he would still be lost to me. It makes little difference."

"I've come to honour his sacrifice. He wanted to free Enthilen of Malphas. That's what I'm going to do."

"If Malphas falls, who will replace him? More Erstürmen kings?"

The cliff vulture flew between Tom and the sun, casting a shadow across his face. *One slip, and....*

"I don't know," he said. "If the grells, mouldewerps and Dobunni come together, they could do something."

"What?"

"Form a leadership council. An assembly of elders. Whatever. I don't have the answer. It's not up to me."

"What part did the mouldewerp play in my brother's death?"

Probably, a significant part. But Hanni doesn't need to be angry with Dwarrow too.

"Dwarrow is trying to save Enthilen like Grin was. We all want a better future for this land. Along the way, sacrifices will be made." Tom's stomach buckled. His last comment sounded callous, and his temper had shortened. The vulture circled overhead.

Hanni stiffened. "Your sacrifice is yet to come."

Tom's heart thudded into a wall of fire, his chest burning with shame. "I'm ready to make it now," he pleaded. "I'm not running away or backing down. I will see this through to the end, whatever end that may be." *Please forgive me. Please.*

Hanni's arm muscles relaxed a fraction. Almost imperceptible, but not to Tom. He unshouldered his pack and reached inside.

"I have something for you," he said, retrieving Grin's totem, carried all the way from Earth. Nestled in the palm of his left hand, he held it towards Hanni, whose eyes glistened like morning dew on lilac petals.

"This is Grin's family totem," she said, plucking the sacred object from Tom's hand with trembling fingers.

"He made me promise to deliver it to you."

Tears welled in Hanni's eyes and slipped down her cheeks, wetting the fronds of the spear fern tattooed on her face. Tom couldn't recall if he'd ever seen grells cry.

"The black grell came for Grin," said Hanni. "We had been together only a day, hiding in the cursed wood. But Hunger and his underlings found us. Took both of us prisoner. I escaped. Grin did not. I watched Laodicea's gates for many moons, hoping one day, he would walk out. But Hunger did not take Grin to Laodicea. He took him to Pergamos. To Malphas." Hanni wiped the tears from her cheeks. "I do not have the other totems. The ones Frennan and Grin kept in the milbi before it was destroyed by the Erstürmen. My mother's totem is in Giigal. I hoped to return there one day."

"Now you can," said Tom. "Dwarrow is desperate for you to join him."

Hanni ran her giant finger over the words delicately etched onto the face of Grin's totem. "I miss the weald-grell city. The forest of Babir Birramal with towering panalope trees standing guard over all creation. Memories of those times have melted like snow under a blazing sun. I have spent too many seasons in these barren hills. I miss Grin. I can picture the last time I saw him as clear as you standing in front of me now. He was bold but fearful. Stern but joyful. Ready to protect the forest from all who may threaten her. That is how I will remember him. Not the broken creature who crawled from Malphas' lair and disappeared from this world only to die in another."

The cliff vulture landed on the skeleton of a dead tree, a stone's throw from Tom. It swivelled its head on a long, featherless pink neck and fixed its hungry gaze on him.

Pickings in the mountains and the cursed wood below must be slim.

Tom stepped closer to the centre of the boulder and took a deep breath, steeling his nerves for the final piece of news he had to deliver to Hanni. "Your mother, Mirrian. Grin said he saw her in Pergamos."

The vulture squawked.

Hanni's lilac eyes flared crimson. "What did you say?"

"When Malphas held Grin prisoner and tried to turn him into the white grell, Mirrian was there. Enslaved by the Worshipful Master."

"Why did you wait so long to tell me? I must save her." Hanni pushed past Tom, almost knocking him off the boulder with the shaft of her spear.

"Wait," said Tom. "A wild stone-grell has no hope of entering Pergamos alone. Grin told me the gates and walls are heavily guarded, and Dwarrow said all the secret entrances have been blocked."

Hanni turned on the heels of her bare feet and glared. "Why did Grin not save her?"

"By the time he knew she was there, it was too late. Malphas had too much of a hold over him. Grin came to me, Hanni, with skin already stained white. It took all his will to resist the final stage of transformation into a tainted grell and escape Malphas. Grin saw Mirrian only briefly. Near the end."

"He left our mother to rot in Malphas' dungeon to find you."

Tom gritted his teeth. "Because he knew it was the only way to save her. We have to raze the walls of Pergamos. Smash the dead throne. Then your mother will be free."

Hanni's shoulders sagged, and she bowed her head. "She may already be dead."

Tom rested his hand on Hanni's forearm. "Don't think like that. Hope is the only thing left driving us forward. Don't forsake it."

Hanni faced Tom. A tear fell from her chin and landed on the green-white softstone of Grin's totem as she read her brother's words. "Grin has written, 'Tom Anderson is with me as I prepare to join the ancestors. I am forever grateful for his friendship.'"

*   *   *   *

The wind howled through the mountain valley as Tom tried to sleep. The monastery did little to protect the inhabitants from the elements.

Window shutters made of timber scraps clattered against the crumbling stonework. Through the holes in the roof, grass and leaf litter rained down like botanical hail. The canvas sheet threaded along a rope next to Tom's bed, hung to create the illusion of privacy, billowed into his head, retreated, and came again. Over and over. Accentuating Tom's discomfort, Raf chose tonight to share Rosalie's bed. The closeness of Rosalie's sleeping quarters to Tom's meant he heard everything. The whispers and titters. Sometimes a laugh. Other times a scold. Then an awkward silence tugged at Tom's ears with a yearning he'd rarely experienced, followed by lustful breaths and moans rolling through the air and penetrating his thoughts. A gasp ended it. Then another silence. Raf left soon after, not staying to embrace the remainder of the evening with his lover.

Tom's anger...no, he amended, *jealousy*, kept him awake for most of the night as he tried to understand why such emotions had gotten under his guard.

By the following morning, the wind had abated. Rosalie pulled her sheet wall across, walked over and sat on the edge of Tom's bed like an old friend.

"Sleep well?" she asked.

"I don't know how you sleep with all the noise. Why don't you build separate shelters?"

"People are too scared to make this feel like a permanent home."

"How long have you been here?"

"Six yarles, but others have been here longer."

Tom sat up, resting his back against a wall of uneven stone. "I'd call that permanent."

"Did you leave family behind? In your world?"

"Only my mother. I worry the loneliness may kill her."

"I had a large family back in Sardis. Mother, father, two brothers and my little sister, Nettie. I think my father took them to Pergamos."

"You didn't want to go?" asked Tom.

"I abandoned my family twelve yarles ago. Ran away to Slumstadt and then here. Tilly is the closest thing I have to family."

"You have no children of your own?"

Rosalie smiled. "I have no husband, and who would bring children into this world?"

"Is Raf...?"

Rosalie's face set as hard as the stone wall behind Tom's back. "An occasional lover," she said. "Life is very long when you're lonely. We find comfort where we can."

Tom averted his eyes, not wanting to pry further.

"Sorry," said Rosalie. "I didn't mean to snap."

"It's alright."

"You must care a lot about Enthilen to leave your mother and your world behind."

"I'm running away from a failed life. Here, I have a chance to make a difference."

Rosalie smiled, placed her hand on Tom's knee and squeezed through the blanket. "We leave this morning for Portum. You, me, Raf and Quenan."

"It's been decided already?"

Rosalie nodded. "I will represent the Erstürmen, Raf the Dobunni, and Quenan the weald-grells. It's a good envoy." She stood. "Eat some breakfast. You'll need the strength."

Rosalie returned to her bed, pulled a tunic over her undergarment, and walked to the firepit where rebels gathered for the morning meal. Emelin hobbled from her room, and Tom tried to reconcile the strong woman he'd met in Bagendon with the frail person who limped to the fire. He climbed from the bed, put on pants, a short tunic, socks and boots, then walked over to Emelin, who leaned on her crutch beside the fire.

She smiled as he approached. "It's a good day for an adventure."

"Yes," said Tom. "My escort is ready, it seems."

"We met yesterday when you were exploring the valley."

"I'm sorry about what happened to the assassins in Sardis. If I could have saved...."

Emelin waved him away. "Don't fret about it. You were only a boy, and braver than most people to march into the inner circle bound in shackles."

"I can't prove it, but I think Brynlee was a traitor."

"You're probably right. When she arrived in Bagendon, Ryder let his penis make the decisions."

"The fall of Bagendon must have been awful."

Emelin nodded and stared into the fire with her good eye. "They made me rebel leader, a handful of moons before Krieg attacked. A poisoned chalice if ever there was one."

"Are you leader here?"

"I'm much too old." Emelin tapped her temple. "Mind not as sharp as it used to be. Sonya embraced the role. Now, most in the group listen to Rosalie, though there's been no formal vote." She leaned towards Tom and whispered in his ear, "She likes you."

Tom lowered his voice. "Her and Raf are...."

Emelin scoffed. "Raf's a pain in the arse. She's with him because she had no choice. Now she does."

"This quest will probably end my life. I can't get involved with anybody."

"Nonsense. Don't dismiss a chance at love because you fear death."

Hanni strode into the monastery, chased by Dwarrow.

"Don't walk away from me, Hannian stone-grell," said Dwarrow. "We must prepare for our journey to Giigal."

Hanni stood beside Tom. "Is the werp always this bossy?"

Tom tried to mask a smile. "Yes, I'm afraid so."

"Will you go to Giigal?" Emelin asked Hanni.

"She must," interrupted Dwarrow. "Too far for a tiny werp to go by himself."

"I have been thinking about what Tom said during the meeting," said Hanni. "Malphas can only be defeated by force, but there are not enough weald-grells to breach Pergamos' walls."

"They'll have the werps at their side," said Dwarrow. "A raging, ravaging horde. And now Tom's fetching the Germalians; it's vital the rest of Enthilen join them to confront Malphas."

"Fetching?" said Tom. "You make it sound like I'm going to pick mushrooms."

Rosalie joined the group. "What should we say to the Germalian council?"

"*Conventus*," said Dwarrow. "It's called the Germalian Conventus. You must get all the protocols right if you're going to get a hearing. No men are allowed inside the conventus except by invitation. Only women can be senators."

"Women are in charge of running everything?" asked Rosalie.

"Yes."

"Sounds like a great place." Rosalie smiled and elbowed Tom in the side.

"We can't dilly-dally here much longer," said Dwarrow. "Tom needs to reach Portum quickerty quack. Those Germalians can take a long time to make a decision. That conventus thingy of theirs, well, my goodness, I'm surprised they haven't starved for taking too long to decide what to eat for dinner."

After breakfast, Tom put on his woollen coat and filled his pack with whatever supplies the rebels could spare: six hand-sized chunks of dried, salted meat, a sack of rolled oats, and a waterskin. Rosalie gave him a sword she'd made in the monastery's smithy. 'One of the best,' she said. Tom thought it wasted on him. He threaded two scabbards onto his belt, sheathing the sword in one and the knife from Widukind in the other, then slipped the dark eyes into the front pocket of his pants beside Dwarrow's key and shoved his remaining anxiety medication in the other pocket.

Four tablets left.

Emelin held his hand tight as she said goodbye. "You place yourself in grave danger again. Let's hope for a better outcome this time, and if you see Thaly in Portum, please tell her I love her and miss her."

Tom embraced Emelin, then pulled away. "Will you keep something here for me?"

She frowned with uncertainty as Tom took his remembrance totem from the pack.

"Grin gave this to me before we faced Malphas in Pergamos' throne hall," said Tom. "I took it back to my world, and now, like me, it has returned. I can't carry it with me; I might lose it. Please, put it somewhere safe."

Emelin nodded and wrapped her fingers around the cylindrical softstone. "I'll ask Quenan to place it with her family totems."

Tom turned away and exited the monastery. Outside, Tormil, the old war veteran from Laodicea, led a horse down the valley with Hanni walking beside. Dwarrow trotted after them, finally convincing Hanni to travel with him to Giigal on a ship. This was a significant achievement, given that stone-grells feared water more than almost anything. Yet, Tom never doubted what Dwarrow could achieve, sometimes wondering if the little mouldewerp ruled Enthilen rather than Malphas.

Hanni stopped beside Tom, bent down and placed the tips of her fingers on his cheeks. He reciprocated to complete the formal grell acknowledgement of welcome or goodbye.

"Farewell, Tom Anderson," said Hanni. "I do not know if we will meet again."

"We will, Hanni. In the calendar of life, at the foot of Malang Gunya's pyramid. There, we will marvel at the history of grell culture and be awestruck at its promised future."

"Grin once said to me, 'There is something special about Tom.' My brother knew from the beginning. He embraced the expectation of the birraman who could change the world." Hanni lifted her fingers from Tom's cheeks and turned away.

Tormil mounted the horse, then held his hand towards Dwarrow. "You can ride behind me."

Dwarrow screwed up his salmon-coloured face. "Horses? No. Never ridden a horse. Not about to start now. I only ride grells or lizards. And since Xaviary has disappeared, Hanni will have to carry me."

Hanni rolled her eyes. "Really?"

"My legs are too short to keep up," said Dwarrow. "You can hide me in your pack."

"I will have to empty most of my supplies," said Hanni.

"Then hurry up," said Dwarrow. "We haven't got all day."

"We can fit more supplies in the saddlebags," said Tormil.

"I still have your key, Dwarrow," said Tom. "The one you gave me in your dwell when we first met. Do you want it back?"

"No need," said Dwarrow. "I have other special keys. Keep it safe with the rest of your treasures."

Rosalie, Tilly, Raf and Quenan led another six horses down the valley.

"How many horses do you have up there?" asked Tom.

"The raid on Rostard's wagon netted a fine bounty," said Tormil.

"We've selected our strongest horses," said Tilly as they approached.

"Why are we taking six?" asked Tom.

"I need one," said Tilly. "Dwarrow has given me an important mission. To travel into the Dambay Plains and find a hole in the ground."

"It's not a hole," snapped Dwarrow. "It's the entrance to the most hallowed dwell in mouldewerp culture. You should be honoured I'm letting you anywhere near the place, but we must get word to the elders and Widukind. And especially Princess Caeli. All will shelter there after they locate Adalwolf. Tilly is to deliver a message; Tom Anderson has secured the services of the Germalian army."

"Hang on," said Tom. "I might fail."

"You can't fail," huffed Dwarrow. "If you do, don't come back. You'd be better off boarding a ship and sailing into the sunset." The werp took a deep breath. "*When* you've convinced the Germalians to march their army east, they'll need a way into Enthilen."

"Something about a secret path?" said Tilly.

Dwarrow stamped the heel of his walking stick on the ground. "Right under our feet! A road beneath the mountains, from Nordland to Enthilen. Caeli will know the way. She's wandered more places than any draughoul I've ever met. Though, I haven't met that many. Tilly will tell Caeli to wait for the Germalians in Nordland. The entrance to the underground road is a day's march east of the town of Revelé."

Tom caught himself. *Revelé.* He remembered the word, written in the margin on page four hundred and sixty-two of the blue book, next to a drawing of a lemniscate. And 4-6-2 was the combination he used to open the locked door to Widukind's house in Bindari.

"I'll be going to Revelé?" asked Tom.

"Yes, yes, yes," said Dwarrow. "Please keep up. The Germalians will march their army through Nordland to reach Enthilen. You'll be with them, of course. A day out from Revelé, past the Detranté gorge, you will come to a cluster of stone pillars, tall and narrow like the trunks of panalope trees. The Nordmen call them the Lost Sisters. Caeli will meet you there."

"When?" asked Tilly.

"It will take many moons to travel from Portum to Revelé," said Dwarrow. "But for Caeli, the journey under the mountain can pass in less than a day. She will come and go, as is the want of draughouls, wandering to places rarely visited, but the eyes of lost souls will always draw her towards Tom Anderson. She'll know when they're close."

Tilly hugged Rosalie goodbye, then mounted her horse. "Don't worry, Dwarrow. I'll deliver the message. An Erstürmen princess will open the back door to Enthilen. Farewell friends. When next we meet, the Germalian army will be swarming over the Dambay Plains."

Tilly walked her horse down the valley towards Lokan.

Dwarrow tugged on Tom's coat sleeve, pulling him away from the group. "Keep the eyes of lost souls close," whispered Dwarrow. "We have shown our hand to these rebels, and I'm not sure I trust all of them. Anyone who is marked will be tempted to steal the eyes."

Tom stepped further away from the rebel group milling outside the monastery, wondering if anyone else had a birthmark and dreamt of finding their birth twin to secure immortality. Rosalie already told him she wasn't marked, and Quenan weald-grell would have no interest in the dark eyes. That left only Raf or someone else who may shadow the group travelling to Germalia.

Hanni approached Dwarrow, holding her pack open. "You will fit," said Hanni.

The werp peered inside the pack. "It looks like a tight squeeze. I think

I've changed my...." Before Dwarrow could finish his sentence, Hanni lifted him up, tossed him feet first into her pack, then cinched the drawstring. "Having trouble breathing," came Dwarrow's muffled voice seeping from the canvas.

Atop his horse, Tormil joined Hanni and Tom. "We head for the Docklands of Laodicea, my old home. I have enough coin to entice the most stubborn merchant seafarer to give Hanni and her little furry friend safe passage to Giigal. Beware the shifting sands, Tom."

Tormil tugged on the reins and pointed his horse down the valley. Hanni nodded at Tom, then followed Tormil, Dwarrow's cries of discomfort echoing up the gorge.

"The desert will not be crossed standing here," said Quenan, handing Tom the reins to a bay mare. "Saddle up. I will jog beside you. We will use the fourth horse to carry supplies."

"Finally, a decent adventure," said Raf. "I'm sick of being cooped up in this rotten building. I need to slit some throats."

He urged his horse forward, Quenan loping beside him with the pack horse in tow.

Perched in the saddle, Rosalie sidled up to Tom. "Let's ride together."

Tom smiled, welcoming Rosalie's friendship. But he worried about losing the dark eyes. Everything revolved around them. Convincing the Germalians to fight. Meeting Princess Caeli. Destroying the dead throne. If he lost the eyes, he lost everything.

Trust no-one.

~ Chapter 21 ~

Lying on a bed of straw and blankets tucked into the corner of Ende's room, Mirrian tried to remember the last time she'd seen the sun. Most of her life played out inside Ende's private quarters, beneath the streets of Pergamos in Volerdie's bitter kingdom. Living underground, the cold hounded Mirrian like never before. Shivering chills harrowed her breaths. Aching joints set hard like ice. Ende's fire provided respite, and Mirrian ensured it never died.

Malphas allowed her into the throne hall on occasion to sit beside him while he held audiences with those under his command. To sit quietly and watch while the Worshipful Master delivered fate and judgement from the throne of the dead, a mash of petrified bodies contorted together to form the gruesome cathedra. Atop the throne's backrest, the eyeless head of the horned wolf snarled its disdain. Sometimes, Mirrian pictured the throne coming alive. The hands of the dead clasping Malphas in place and the wolf leaning down to tear off Master's head with its ravening jaws.

Mirrian accepted the paradox of her new life. The underground rooms were her prison but also her sanctuary. Above ground, vengeful slaves waited for her. Carian and Julan would inflict their punishment for Mirrian's treachery. She saw them sometimes in the hallways of Pergamos tending to Master's needs. Mirrian avoided their wrath by escaping into Ende's quarters. No slave would confront her there and risk a fatal blow from Ende's sparth.

Mirrian rolled from bed and pushed herself off the floor to begin cleaning duties. Gathering a damp cloth from a wooden bucket, she rubbed the tear of fabric over the mantle above the fireplace, trying to scoop up every speck of dust. Behind her, lying on a straw mattress topped with goose down, Ende descended into a coughing fit. Mirrian worried she'd filled the air with tiny pinpricks of dirt, only for them to be sucked into Ende's throat. She dropped the cloth in the bucket, stepped to the bed and took a cup of water from the side table. Placing her hand behind Ende's upper back, she tilted the pale grell forward and rested the edge of the cup next to her bleak lips.

Ende stilled her coughing and took a sip of water. She looked at Mirrian with black, listless eyes that never exposed the weakness of emotion. Nevertheless, Mirrian convinced herself, at this moment, the eyes said 'thank you.' She turned away, and the pale grell did something unexpected, clasping frail, bony fingers around Mirrian's wrist.

"Sit with me," Ende whispered in a hollow voice as if it came from the grave. Then her grip fell away.

Mirrian placed the cup on the table and gathered a stool from the corner of the room, the one Malphas always sat on during his long vigils at Ende's bedside. She carried the seat to the side of the four-poster, cedar bed facing the doorway, prepared to jump to her feet and return to chores should Master visit.

Mirrian and Ende, once free, wild grells, waited together in their stone tomb in dismal silence. Mirrian wondered what reward or penance she'd garner for being the last soul to comfort death's servant. Malphas wanted her to replace Ende as the sparth's owner. Become the new pale grell, and furnish punishment at his command.

Reward or penance? thought Mirrian.

Eyes closed, the rise and fall of Ende's chest underneath the bedcovers gave the only sign the pale grell still lived. Mirrian leaned forward and pulled the quilt up towards Ende's neck. A hand fell from under the covers, and Mirrian reached down to shift it back in place, recoiling at the cadaverous chill of Ende's skin. Ende squeezed Mirrian's fingers.

Not a threat, thought Mirrian. An acknowledgement.

Ende opened her eyes and faced Mirrian. "How many moons...*cough*... have we spent...together?" she asked.

Mirrian concentrated. Wild grells didn't measure time in the same way as the Erstürmen. Grells considered time as circular, not linear.

Erstürmen days and yarles followed one after the other until forming a line stretching from Ostamp to the stars. Grells believed that past seasons and events would return in an endless cycle and that every action could disrupt the cycle's rhythm.

"I forgot," said Ende. "You would not...*cough*...not...have...*cough*...counted them. You are still...wild."

Mirrian flinched. Being called *wild* is an insult, she thought. Even as a slave, she'd procured a level of refinement. Hadn't she?

"I have...*cough*...counted them," said Ende. "I have counted...*cough*...the moons past...*cough*...since you...*cough*...*cough*...*cough*...."

Mirrian stood and walked to the other side of the bed, removing a dried sprig of yulumbang plant and a swatch of muslin cloth from the front pocket of her slave dress. A Rephaim guard had harvested the plant for her from a grove of shrubs growing on the Dambay Plains near Pergamos. Mirrian's mother would use yulumbang to remedy coughs and sore throats.

Keeping one eye on the door, knowing if Malphas caught her administering a heathen medicine she would be executed, Mirrian crushed the dried yulumbang leaves in her hand and wrapped them in the muslin before placing the concoction into Ende's cup. Tentacles of pickle-green snaked outwards as the sap from the leaves diffused into the water.

After soaking for moments that lingered threateningly, Mirrian removed the ball of muslin-covered leaves and tossed it in the fire. She placed her hand behind Ende's head, titled the pale grell forward and tipped the concoction into her mouth.

"It is bitter," said Mirrian. "But it may ease your cough. Drink all of it."

Ende drained the cup, and Mirrian swished water around the inside, tossing it in the fire before refilling the vessel to mask any trace of wild medicine. She returned to the stool to watch the door, listening to the wheezes in Ende's chest grow fainter as the healing began.

"Sixteen moons," said Ende. "Sixteen moons you have slept beside me."

"How can you tell night from day down here?" asked Mirrian.

"I feel it. When night falls, I know. You have served me for more than sixteen moons, and we have known each other much longer."

"Six yarles," said Mirrian. "Malphas took me into his service six yarles ago."

Ende smiled. "You *have* been counting."

"I should return to my cleaning." Mirrian went to stand.

"No," said Ende. "Wait. A moment...*cough*...longer. Your medicine...is helping."

Mirrian nodded.

"I have a secret," whispered Ende.

Mirrian leaned forward on the stool.

"Your son, Grin...."

Mirrian's thoughts sharpened to a pinprick. "What about him? Do you know where he is?"

Ende nodded. *Yes.* Mirrian swore the pale grell nodded.

"Where?" demanded Mirrian, clutching Ende's wrist. "Is he safe?"

"That, I do not know. But he can never return."

Mirrian stood, kicked the stool away, then dropped to her knees beside the timber bed, pawing at the covers. "Please, Ende. Please tell me."

Ende smiled. A rotten, haggard smile. "It pains you not to know."

"Yes. It hurts so much. I lost my husband and eldest son to the Erstürmen. My daughter, Hanni, I know not if she is alive or dead. Grin was all I had until Malphas tried to turn him into the white grell."

"The Worshipful Master did not succeed," said Ende. "Your son was too strong."

"Please tell me where he is."

"A favour offered. A favour returned."

Mirrian's thoughts fixated on Ende's desire. "What favour would you ask of a slave?"

"I cannot bear the pain much longer," said Ende. "Master wishes to keep me alive because it fulfils his yearning. But I have served him for many yarles, and I cannot serve any more. You must end my suffering, Mirrian. Kill me."

Mirrian's instincts screamed. *NO.* If Malphas discovered she killed his beloved pale grell...yet, Grin may have escaped Malphas' clutches.

And Hanni could already be dead. What did Mirrian have left to lose? Execution would be her punishment for killing Ende, but it would offer the freedom she craved.

"You are considering it," said Ende.

"Where is Grin?" asked Mirrian.

"Will you...*cough*...do it?"

"Is he safe from Malphas?"

"Yes. I doubt Master will pursue him."

Doubt isn't good enough, thought Mirrian. She needed certainty. "I will end your life. Tell me where my son is."

"He stole the eyes of lost souls and travelled to Tom Anderson's world."

Mirrian's mind spun. Had Grin become a birraman and journeyed to a strange world? Why? Was he trying to find Tom Anderson? Could Ende be trusted? If she spoke the truth, Grin would never return to Enthilen. He had disappeared forever.

"I have not told Malphas about your son," Ende said. "But I should."

"Is that a threat?" asked Mirrian.

Ende faced her and offered another haggard smile. "Favour offered. Favour returned."

*   *   *   *

Surrounded by impenetrable darkness, Lily couldn't see her finger touch her nose. Gravel scattered across the prison cell floor pressed into her bruised, naked body, biting and stinging with brutal indifference.

A prisoner in Pergamos? she thought, but couldn't be sure.

The charge into battle at Gestade didn't offer the glorious end she craved, felling the enemy with her mighty sword until they wrenched it from her cold, dead hand. The enemy had other plans, taking her prisoner and dulling her senses until she couldn't tell night from day, sky from earth, or love from hate. Lily's end hadn't arrived yet. She expected it to be without glory.

No surprise, she thought. Uncomfortable with the mantle of a warrior, why did she deserve a warrior's end?

She rolled onto her side and screamed as the sawtooth gravel pressed into a shard of broken bone in her right arm. Falling onto her back, she lay there and swallowed air as if it was one of Audie's healing potions. Inside her mind, she pictured the prison cell, unveiling every dark corner and the door leading to her escape. Her groping breaths stilled. Then Lily snapped her mouth shut. Another sound seeped through the darkness. A breath, not hers.

Her captor? she wondered. A ravenous animal? Another prisoner?

She pushed off the gravel with her left hand, sat up and sniffed for the scent of danger, the damp air rasping against the dried blood in her nostrils.

"Who's there?" whispered Lily.

No answer, but the breathing grew louder. The pointed stones jabbed and sliced as she pushed her heels into the floor and forced herself away from the threat of the unknown. Her back bumped into something, and she reached around to grasp the lip of a wooden container. A bucket. She leaned down and sniffed.

Water, thought Lily, dropping her head into the bucket and lapping her tongue like a dog, thirst overwhelming dread. She splashed water on her face and picked blood from her nostrils with an aching finger. Nose clean and soul watered with new courage, she sniffed toward the strange breathing.

Body odour, she thought. Human? Familiar.

"Hello?" said Lily expectantly.

Bottom fixed to the stony floor, she reached out front with her left arm and swung it side-to-side as if her hand could sweep away the darkness. It revealed nothing. She inched forward and swept again. Nothing. Again. Something. She touched something.

She yanked her hand back and clutched it to a thumping chest. Cold sweat dripped from her armpits and down her sides, making her shiver. The door she pictured in her mind would be here somewhere. She should find it and wait for the chance to escape. Forget about stirring the creature hidden in the darkness.

Instead, she reached out again and touched…skin. Warm. Damp. The foot of a person lying on their side. She traced her fingers across the toes, then up over the bulge of the ankle bone to the bottom of legs covered in thick, wiry hair. Her hand explored along the curve of a calf muscle, past the kneecap and onto muscled thighs.

Male, thought Lily. She confirmed it by slowly moving her fingers from the thigh to the groin until her knuckles rested against a flaccid penis.

The examination continued up a flat, smooth stomach to a hairy chest with muscles that would have bulged once but now sagged with age. As she tangled fingers in curly chest hair, Lily had a hopeful and devastating thought. Could it be?

She wouldn't speak his name; it might turn conjecture into fact. Yet, the duplicitous thought didn't abate, yearning for confirmation. She brushed along the outside right of the chest muscle and up to the front of the shoulder, searching with delicate fingertips until her ring finger found a line of raised skin. Scar tissue.

Fears and hopes melted into one and dripped from her eyes. Hartmut lay in the room with her. Prisoners of the darkness.

"Hartmut," she whispered.

His breath caught.

He heard me, she thought.

"I'm here," she said, scraping her fingers across the stubble on his chin to feel the softness of his lips. His eyes were closed, his brow pasty. She tangled her fingers in thick, damp hair, trying to picture the mane of silver strands she adored.

Hartmut moaned.

"Can you hear me?" asked Lily.

She searched his body again, looking for wounds. On his left side, her fingers dipped into a gash, warm and wet. Holding her fingertips to her nose, she sniffed blood.

"Hartmut?"

Lily stood and stumbled around the room until she found the door. Locked, of course. She pressed her ear to the timber. No noise from her captors.

Stay quiet, she thought. Take them by surprise when they next enter.

She crept along a wall, flinching at every saw-toothed stone cutting into the soles of her bare feet until she stumbled into a corner. Then another wall, another corner. Another wall, kicking the wooden bucket part way along.

Wash his wound? wondered Lily. What would Audie do? *Fight.*

Swollen, aching fingers dangling in mid-air for a moment, reached down, grabbed the lip of the bucket, then bashed it against the wall. The slosh of water and crack of wood bounced around the prison walls. Lily waited. No guards came for her or her lover.

A wooden stave in the bucket had worked free from the metal hoop. Lily bashed again. A splinter of timber the size of a paring knife broke off in her left hand. Clutching the makeshift weapon, she dropped to her knees and crawled back to Hartmut.

"Wake up," she said, shaking his shoulder. "I've found the door, and I have a weapon. When they come for us, we should rush the guard. Hartmut, wake up. Please."

He didn't stir.

"Please," whispered Lily. "I know you can hear me. Live or die together, like we always wanted."

He didn't stir.

Lily lay beside him, her thoughts oscillating between love and death. She pushed her naked body against his and hid the weapon between them. Draping her listless, broken right arm over his body, she covered the wound in his side with her hand and drew comfort from the rise and fall of his chest.

She'd almost fallen asleep when a key turned in the lock, and the door swung open.

* * * *

What a glorious day, thought Nettie, wiping sweat from her brow before waving to the tens of thousands of Pergamos' citizens who lined the boulevard to welcome home the victorious army from their triumph at Gestade. Sure, Nettie had done little to defeat the enemy. She even helped to save the life of one of them, the father of the two children she and Erwin found in the cellar. Nevertheless, Nettie marched with Erwin and the other peasant fighters across white cobblestones gleaming under a golden sun. They trailed behind thousands of Master's Shield, Rephaim and men-at-arms. Together, they were Volerdie's soldiers, celebrating a famous victory certain to push ajar the door to paradise.

Vater Krieg led them towards the centre of Pergamos, the enormous, magnificent blood-red General, riding high on his chariot, grasping reins with his left hand and holding a clenched right fist close to his heart. Pulling the chariot, the two undreds, draped with linen throws of red, black and white, seemed to revel in the pageantry, holding their heads aloft, sharp, curved horns piercing the blue sky. Rows of banners, white with the combined insignias of the red, two-headed serpent and the black eyes with flaming pupils orbiting the sun, flew above the boulevard and cast wavering shadows over the citizens lining the route.

As Nettie passed the banners, she followed Krieg's lead and thumped her chest with a right fist. Erwin did the same, then smiled at her. They'd re-joined their battalion after Gestade fell. With Sergeant Weedle dead, no-one questioned their disappearance. No-one knew they'd helped save the life of a Gestade defender and his children. Nettie made Erwin promise he'd never tell. They had enough scrapes and bruises to convince others they'd been fighting the enemy. Amid the joy of victory, no-one cared otherwise.

Marching towards the colossal pyramid in the centre of Pergamos, Nettie focussed on the crowd, hoping to catch a glimpse of her father, Yonna. She hadn't seen him since the army seized her from the front of the kirika twenty-two moons ago.

He'll be in the crowd, she convinced herself, not wanting to miss the celebration or the chance to see his daughter again. He'll forgo a morning in the smithy to honour her bravery and ensure she returned home safely.

Nettie had overheard Lieutenant Berard tell another commander the heathens of Gestade had wiped out half of Malphas' forces. She always believed the Worshipful Master to be invincible, his immortal power permeating into the blood of those who fought for him. Yet, despite the victory, the battle for Gestade had dented her confidence. Planted a seed in her mind threatening to germinate into the belief the Worshipful Master wasn't indestructible after all.

As the returning soldiers marched under the pyramid's shadow, women threw locks of hair tied with white ribbon onto the boulevard, a symbol of gratitude to the victors. A girl, half Nettie's age, ran into the procession and placed a lock of black hair at Nettie's feet. Nettie stopped and bent down to pick it up, clutching the treasure in a sweaty palm.

The girl smiled.

Nettie thumped her own chest with a right fist. "Hail, Malphas."

"Hail, Malphas," replied the girl before disappearing into the crowd.

Krieg stopped the procession at the calendar of life and stepped from his chariot.

"I want to get closer," Nettie said to Erwin.

He screwed up his pudgy face. "Closer to where?"

"The front. We can't see anything back here. Let's get near the calendar."

Nettie pushed through the peasant fighters, and, as always, Erwin followed her. Walking among the men-at-arms, the *real* soldiers, she pondered a way of separating herself from Erwin. When the next battle came, he'd be a liability, and she doubted they'd be able to hide a second time without being caught. Lieutenant Berard would appoint a new sergeant to replace Weedle. A new set of eyes to keep watch on those with weak wills. Erwin dragged Nettie down. She would drown with him if she couldn't peel away his desperate fingers.

Nettie dodged among the forest of Rephaim soldiers, tempted to reach up and run her hand over their swollen chests. The armoured giants' brutal power made her skin tingle with alarm and awe. Beside a stone pillar of the calendar of life, she and Erwin stopped and stood among the Master's Shield in front of the balcony partway up the pyramid's steps. At the bottom step, facing the pyramid, Krieg removed his grilled helmet, dropped to both knees, arms stiff and straight by his sides, and bowed his head. Nettie, Erwin and the soldiers around them mimicked the gesture. Only the Master's Shield guarding the crowd remained standing.

Through a tear in her pants, Nettie scuffed a bare knee on the flagstones, and blood trickled from the scrape. Gritting her teeth, she pictured the smile on her father's face when they reunited to celebrate a momentous victory. She planned to show him her new sword, the one she'd taken from the heathen lioness who died from the wound inflicted by Erwin. Yonna would be amazed at the craftsmanship of the polished blade, etched with images of seabirds suspended above a rolling ocean.

Silent anticipation descended over the submissive crowd. Erwin wiggled, clearly uncomfortable kneeling on the stones. Nettie wanted to punch him in the arm. The midday sun burned the back of her neck. Blood pooled around her knee. The silence stretched on.

Then boots, slapping the pyramid steps and sounding like a thousand washer-women beating wet clothes against rocks, sluiced away the silence. Nettie raised her eyes. From the bowels of the pyramid, scores of Rephaim soldiers marched onto the balcony, then partway down the steps to form a guard of honour. Following the Rephaim came a familiar face — Anselm, the Hoch-Vater of Enthilen and Malphas' personal curate. Anselm wore sangria robes that swept aside the impurity as he walked to the front of the balcony.

How fortunate she'd been, thought Nettie, to already hear a sermon delivered by Anselm. On that day, she was only one step away from the Worshipful Master. She'd never seen Malphas up close. He rarely made public appearances anymore. Yet, when Nettie and Yonna first arrived in Pergamos, Malphas held regular rallies. She remembered him as a powerful speaker. *Persuasive.*

'Volerdie will soon return to Enthilen,' he preached. 'The Divine Creator and Worshipful Master will lead the faithful into paradise.'

Nettie couldn't wait for the blessed day.

Standing on the front edge of the rail-less balcony, Anselm turned and bowed. Murmurs filtered through the crowd. The soldiers around Nettie swayed and shifted on compliant knees. Erwin looked like he might faint.

The idiot's going to miss Malphas, thought Nettie. On such a magnificent occasion, the Worshipful Master is bound to appear.

She didn't wait long. Sitting atop the throne of the dead, carried by four grell slaves, Malphas emerged from the pyramid dressed in robes that gleamed blinding white in the sun. The slaves lowered the throne onto the balcony and stepped back into the shadow of the pyramid doorway. Erwin joined Nettie in lifting his head, curiosity trumping subservience. She tensed, preparing to spring to her feet and proclaim aloud her reverence for the master. But she had to wait for the signal.

Sitting on the throne, Malphas turned his head left and right to survey the masses. He held them there, on their knees, before raising his hand. A hurna blasted from the podium at the pyramid's summit, where the trumpeter stood between two fluted columns under an imbricated slate roof. As one, Pergamos' faithful rose from their knees.

"Hail, Malphas!" acclaimed the crowd. "Hail, the Worshipful Master!"

The cries resounded across the city, reminding Nettie of a chorus of song-thrushes and grass robins heralding a new dawn. Malphas clutched the armrests of the dead throne and hoisted his body onto unsteady feet. It seemed immortality did nothing to relieve the aches inherited as a mortal old man.

Better to gain immortality while still young, decided Nettie.

The crowd stilled, and Malphas lifted his arms skyward. "Believers! We gather to honour our victorious forces."

"Hail, Malphas!" yelled the crowd.

"Gestade's pagans have been crushed by our devotion."

"Hail!"

"With their downfall, Pergamos grows stronger. Only one more barrier stands in our way. One more city to fall before we rejoice in the Divine Creator's return."

"Praise Volerdie!"

"The weald-grells hide in their island forest. Soon, we will march south and send their home tumbling into the ocean!"

"Hail, Malphas!"

"But such a challenge is for another time. First, we celebrate a momentous victory."

The crowd cheered. Malphas beckoned to Krieg, who bounded up the pyramid's steps, built by his stone-grell ancestors many generations ago. When the red grell reached the balcony, he dropped to both knees in front of Malphas and bowed his head. The Worshipful Master rested his hands on Krieg's broad shoulders, then bent forward and kissed the red grell on the forehead. Krieg stood and stepped behind the throne. Anselm came forward, and the kirika bell next to the pyramid tolled. The Hoch-Vater of Enthilen would deliver the victory prayer.

Nettie turned from the balcony. Among the crowd, on the other side of the boulevard, stood Yonna, crammed between a mass of citizens like a withered bush surrounded by tree trunks. From this distance, Yonna's face appeared more haggard than Nettie remembered; sunken cheeks and folds of skin hanging under glassy eyes fixed on Anselm as he delivered the sermon. Nettie had to speak with her father. Check on his well-being. Let him know she survived the battle for Gestade. Show him the ornate sword. Share the honour of being one of Volerdie's soldiers.

"Stay here and tell me what happens," Nettie said to Erwin.

"Where are you going?" he asked.

"To see my father."

Nettie snuck off, back through the Rephaim and men-at-arms. As she pushed past a group of peasant fighters, the crowd around Yonna closed in, and he disappeared.

"Pa!" yelled Nettie, shoving people aside.

A moment before she reached the spot where she'd last seen Yonna, a Master's Shield blocked her path.

"Where ya goin'?" he asked.

"My father's there," said Nettie, pointing into the crowd. "I want to celebrate our victory with him."

The soldier faced the crowd. "Show me."

"I can't see him now, but he was right there. Pa!" Nettie expected Yonna to be fighting his way through the crowd towards her, but he didn't appear.

"He ain't dere," said the soldier. "Get back to yur troop."

"He *is*," snapped Nettie. "I haven't seen him for twenty-two moons since I was enlisted. Pa!"

"Better to forget about him. Yur fellow fighters are yur family now."

Nettie stood trapped by the crowd, searching every face. Yonna had disappeared like a dream after waking. The guard forced her back into the lines of peasant fighters, but she set herself to sneak from the barracks one night and return home, if only for a moment.

*   *   *   *

Mirrian stepped onto the pyramid balcony wearing a new dress gifted to her by the Worshipful Master; folds of black satin and lace cascading to her ankles and along her arms to her wrists. A frilled collar brushed the nape of her neck, and pearl buttons glinted in the midday sun. She carried Ende's sparth in her right hand, squinting as the sunlight accentuated the sharpness of the silver blade.

Replenishing sunlight, thought Mirrian. The Worshipful Master had bestowed on her a generous gift.

She shuffled across the balcony to stand beside Krieg like family members at a wedding. Malphas' tainted children. Rephaim guarded the balcony, watching the crowd in case one of the faithful weakened to scepticism and launched an attack on Master. Or spies loyal to Gestade sought to deliver their vengeance. Or a weald-grell hid behind a Rephaim mask waiting to strike.

Master has many enemies, thought Mirrian, before relaxing with the realisation of her foolishness. Master is immortal. Nothing can harm him.

Anselm stood at the front of the balcony, pontificating to a congregation likely larger than he'd ever seen. Yelling his faith to the masses. Extolling the virtues of submission to Volerdie and reward in duty to the Worshipful Master. Mirrian wondered if those at the back of the crowd heard anything the curate said.

Her thoughts turned to the conversation with Ende. The pale grell's revelation that Grin had fled to Tom Anderson's world. Mirrian believed it. The dead ground spider she found on the throne hall floor confirmed Grin's fate. Her son would never return to Enthilen. But why did he leave? She kept a secret from Master, and the burden weighed heavier than a boulder. Ende threatened to expose her. Had placed Mirrian in her debt, demanding payment of a mercy killing. Mirrian had never killed anyone, but she might become a murderer to protect Grin. When Ende died, Malphas had no-one else to take on the mantle of pale grell. No-one except Mirrian.

Malphas leaned over the throne armrest and beckoned to her. "Come, Mirrian, stand beside me."

She stood next to the throne, wondering how long she could protect her secret.

"What a wonderful day this is," said Malphas. "Your brother, Krieg, has returned triumphant."

Your *brother*, thought Mirrian. *Your* brother.

"Nevertheless, our forces appear to have thinned somewhat." Malphas faced Krieg, who fixed his black eyes dead ahead.

"Gestade was well defended, Worshipful Master," said Krieg. "Erstürmen and the Dobunni from Laodicea. Among others."

Malphas rubbed the stubble on his chin. "*Hmmm.* How many of my soldiers did you bring home?"

"At least twelve thousand, Master."

"Twe...twelve thousand? That's less than half the force."

Malphas sank back into the throne and picked at the petrified limb forming the armrest. To Mirrian, it resembled someone peeling away the shell of a boiled egg. If Malphas kept digging, he might reveal the flesh of the contorted bodies trapped in stony suspension to form the throne. He could free the sacrificed, allowing their crooked limbs to disentangle into the living, breathing people they must once have been.

Would they pay homage to Volerdie? thought Mirrian. The Divine Creator who trapped them in this grotesque prison.

Krieg cleared his throat, a twitch at the corner of his mouth resembling a quiver of dismay. "There is something else, Master. Adalwolf was at Gestade."

Malphas stopped picking at the armrest. A red blush scalded his cheeks, and a swelling chest threatened to split open the front of his white robes.

"Is he dead?" asked Malphas.

"We could not find a corpse, but he could not have...."

"Silence!" Malphas snapped his head around to glare at the red grell. "You leave behind thousands of my soldiers, wasting on the fields of Gestade because of your incompetence, but the one corpse I long to see eluded you?"

Malphas faced Mirrian, and her naked body oozed sweat underneath the black dress.

"What do you think of your brother, Mirrian?" asked Malphas. "What do you think of his failures?"

Mirrian panicked. Was she allowed to...*think*?

"Well?" pressed Malphas.

Krieg stood on the opposite side of the throne to her, like an unwavering crimson idol. Yet, the corner of his mouth continued twitching, a nervous spasm underneath the web of scars marking where his facial tattoo would have been. His black eyes shifted to her, then back to Master. At that moment, Mirrian understood. Krieg didn't fear the Worshipful Master. He feared *her*.

She ground the heel of her sparth against the balcony stone as if squashing a red ant. "Failure must be punished, Worshipful Master."

"It must," said Malphas, "otherwise, it festers and poisons all of us. You will deliver Krieg's punishment, Mirrian."

Mirrian's heart lodged in her throat. The sculptured mantle of the red grell cracked as he turned to her. Krieg was a head taller than Mirrian and thicker in the torso and legs. She doubted she'd seen a larger stone-grell, and now, she'd been ordered to discipline him.

There are no secrets from the Worshipful Master, thought Mirrian. None.

Respite came when a draughoul appeared from inside the pyramid chamber, approached Malphas and whispered in his ear.

The birthing chamber, thought Mirrian. The stone-grells called the room behind the balcony the birthing chamber. How ironic a deathly lingerer should come from there.

Mirrian's mother had told her the story of the chamber, where the female grells of Malang Gunya would give birth on the altar inside after being carried up through the pyramid's internal passages to this sacred place. The guradyi, the shamanic healers who had long disappeared from grell culture, would present the newborn to the city, standing on the pyramid steps and holding the baby above their heads. Mirrian pictured them holding an infant Grin before he slipped from their hands and tumbled down the steps in a bloody heap.

The draughoul finished delivering her message, then slunk back into the shadows.

Malphas resumed picking shell fragments from the limbs of the twisted bodies comprising the dead throne. "This day grows steadily worse," he said, speaking into thin air. "Rostard has fled Sardis, and the Germalian menace stirs in the west. The very threat the soothsayer was tasked to monitor. Heathen Germalians and their dozen griffins. Women now ride what was once the right only of Erstürmen kings and princes."

"Griffins?" Mirrian dared to ask.

"Yes," said Malphas. "Who would have thought the creatures still survived?"

"Will the Germalians attack, Master?" asked Krieg.

"They spend most of their time bickering under jewelled ceilings. Only by a unanimous vote of their ruling conventus would the Germalians declare war on Enthilen. However, our spies say those in the conventus advocating for confrontation are growing in number and voice. We must distract their attention away from Enthilen. The Pordillo are bold and cunning; they owe us for sending them food and weapons. It's time we pressed the obligation. Convince the Pordillo to unite their forces and launch an attack on Portum."

"I could lead an envoy, Master," said Krieg.

Malphas shook his head. "No. You must return to Sardis and restore order." He fixed his eyes on the back of Anselm as the curate finished his sermon. "I will send Anselm to present our terms to Qaysar Rais of the Pordillo. Enthilen's Hoch-Vater has the necessary authority to negotiate a deal, and he's expendable should anything go wrong. He'll travel across the Grōz Wüste with a pledge of Erstürmen fighters to join the Pordillo attack on Portum."

The crowd roared their worship of Volerdie as Anselm reached his crescendo before stepping back from the balcony's edge to stand behind the throne.

Malphas stood with ease, his old body fortified with a new determination, and raised his arms to the gathering. "Volerdie will soon reveal his reward to the faithful. We've waited patiently for the day, as our ancestors waited before us. I know some of you question whether the day will ever come. Yet, here we stand on the cusp of salvation. When Giigal falls and darkness descends, Volerdie will return home to the city *you* resurrected. And he will reward each of you with a place in his glorious paradise."

"Praise Volerdie!" yelled the crowd.

"First, we complete the celebration of our victory at Gestade by excising the last traitorous poison from Enthilen. The venom that crippled the minds of those who cowered behind Gestade's walls."

Malphas nodded his head. From the crowd, soldiers dragged two naked, almost comatose prisoners into the centre of the pillars encircling the calendar of life. One prisoner was a short man with a strong jaw and taut muscles, the other a tall woman with strands of greying hair long enough to brush against pendulous breasts sagging with age. Her right arm appeared to be broken. Mirrian expected the woman had carried herself with dignity once, but any semblance of poise had been beaten from her by Malphas' servants.

"Here they are," cried Malphas. "The two most vile traitors in all Enthilen. The treacherous Commander Hartmut, who turned his back on his own people, and the despicable *Lady* Lily LáDown, Dobunni sympathiser and architect of Laodicea's defeat during the barbarian war. It is custom to let the guilty utter a final word before the end, but their deceitful shame is so immense, the Divine Creator has rendered them speechless."

"Kill the traitors!" yelled someone in the crowd.

Malphas waved his hand, and the soldiers bound Lily and Hartmut to two timber uprights, an arms-length apart and facing each other. Another soldier strapped a cage with a solid metal floor between the prisoners, the two open ends pressing against Lily and Hartmut's bare stomachs. The soldier opened the lid of the cage and dropped in four rats.

*   *   *   *

Through the slits of swollen eyes, Lily studied the faded paintings on the floor of the open temple, wishing they'd come alive and carry her away. Grells harvested food from green fields stretching to the horizon. Marvelled at the moons and stars from atop their giant pyramid. Watched painted dancers, twirling feathers and fur, perform inside a crowded amphitheatre.

Lily stood inside the most revered place in grell culture, the calendar of life. Grells in Laodicea had shared stories of this place, whispering words of longing reverence. The calendar was the beating heart of their once beautiful city of Malang Gunya. The new inhabitants had scarred the heart by scratching a pentagram into the flagstones, larger than a wagon wheel. The symbol defaced the grell paintings with a devotion foreign to anything Lily had known.

The rats hadn't bothered her yet. They ran up and down the cage, sniffing her naked stomach but not showing much interest. She lifted a lolling head, surprised to be met with a face she longed to see before the end. Hartmut had found the strength for one last act of love. Slumped against the timber post, his arms and legs bound, his eyes gazed at her with longing, waiting for recognition. He was with her right to the end, as he'd always been these last twelve yarles. Her companion. Her friend. Her lover.

She couldn't rouse Hartmut in the prison cell. Her attempt to overpower the guards when they opened the door earned her another beating and nothing more. It didn't matter now. She welcomed the pain because Hartmut had arrived to make it all better. To mend her broken body with his eyes and fill her soul with a potion matching the skills of any healer.

Dressed in the Master's Shield armour, a soldier approached, holding a firebrand.

"Who goes first?" he asked Lily.

She kept her tongue.

The soldier persisted. "Would you prefer to be eaten alive first or watch the life drain from your lover's face?"

"Me, first," rasped Hartmut. "Take me first."

The soldier faced Lily's lover. "So be it."

No, thought Lily. Take us both at the same time. Hartmut, remember? It's what we always wanted.

But the words didn't come.

The Shield waved the torch over the cage, scaring the rats towards Hartmut, then slid closed a metal panel dividing the cage in two. The panel squealed shut like a guillotine descending to lop off Lily's head.

"You're no protector of the realm," said Hartmut, his gravelly, broken voice challenging the soldier. "The Erstürmen kings of old would be ashamed of you. Nothing more than a finger-puppet for a madman."

The soldier spat in Hartmut's face. Lily wanted to cut the man's throat.

"What would you know of Erstürmen heritage?" said the soldier. "Your treachery ran so deep; you couldn't wait to bed the enemy." He held the firebrand aloft and faced the pyramid shadowing the calendar of life.

Lily's eyes climbed the pyramid steps to a balcony partway up. Standing on the balcony, an old man in white robes looked down on her, swaying on legs that bent from the weight of his malevolence. Although she'd never seen Malphas before, she knew it was him. He raised an arm to the crowd and held it there, smiling.

What are you waiting for? thought Lily. Do you find the anticipation of your evil so gratifying?

Malphas' smile disappeared as he dropped his arm to the side. The crowd cheered as if he conducted a choir. The soldier with the firebrand placed the flame underneath the floor of the metal cage.

It began. Slowly. The agony of the wait so excruciating Lily forgot about her broken arm and bruised body. The metal absorbed the heat, warming Lily's skin with false comfort. The rats reacted to the fire beneath them, skittering across the hot metal floor between Hartmut's stomach and the dead-end guillotine. Eventually, they recognised their only escape. Pushed up against bare flesh, the four terrified creatures gnawed and burrowed, biting and scratching at the skin Lily once kissed. Once caressed. Still loved.

Hartmut's eyes wept with dismay, but he never looked down. He watched only her.

"I remember," he said, "...*urgh*...walking with you across the silken sand of Tolson's Beach. The breeze carried...scents of a better place. The turquoise waves...*argh*...brought treasures from an ocean deeper than our love. Remember...the rainbow shell? We'd never seen so many colours... such...such...beauty...."

At Hartmut's stomach, the rats had excavated their escape and piled inside.

"Keep your eyes on me, Lily," he urged with a mouth twisting in pain. "We're still strong. Remember how the...*urgh*...how the sun rose from the horizon like the breach of a crimson whale? It...*ahhh*...promised a new day. The land will hold the sun to its promise."

Hartmut passed out.

"Take me!" Lily screamed at Malphas. "Save him and take me! Please. Hartmut is a brave warrior. A great leader. He could be vital in coming battles. Don't waste such strategic importance."

Malphas took no notice of her. He'd returned to his throne, sitting on a pile of warped bodies and staring off into the distance, looking bored.

He can't even be bothered gloating, thought Lily. Our lives are of so little consequence to him; he can't find a skerrick of joy in their passing.

"Set Hartmut free!" she screamed, but her voice grew hoarse, and her energy drained. The heat from the wire cage burned her skin, the smell making her nauseous.

On the pyramid balcony, no-one moved. No-one raised a finger to save her. The crowd surrounding the calendar of life, the thousands and thousands of people watching her and Hartmut die, stood still and silent like statues carved by a maniacal despot.

Hartmut's lolling head swayed from side to side.

"I'm here," Lily said to him. "I'm still here. I love you. They can't break our love."

Hartmut's head stopped moving, and his body went limp.

Anger, hotter than the metal cage, coursed through Lily. "Your empire will fall!" she screamed at Malphas. "This is the turning point. This day marks your end." She faced the crowd. "For all of you! Before the next harvest season, all you have built will be gone. Pergamos will be rubble again, and you will be buried beneath it."

The soldier placed another four rats in Lily's side of the cage and waved his firebrand under the floor.

Let them come, thought Lily. Our victory is assured.

~ Chapter 22 ~

Saskia strolled into Portum's kamel yards, planning to say goodbye to her kamel, Nibloo, for the last time. Now a wind-rider, she'd never need to climb into the saddle of one of these cantankerous and uncomfortable beasts ever again. A wall of stink slapped her face, smelling like damp compost mixed with the urine the kamels splashed on their legs to keep cool. Hundreds of beasts lined up along fences in single rows, snouts buried in feeding troughs as they grunted and moaned their way to satiation. An eddy raced across the yard, swirling dust into the air that caught in Saskia's throat. She coughed and walked along the lines of kamels, searching for Nibloo. Since the Eligens fourteen days ago, she'd been overwhelmed by wind-rider training and forging a stronger bond with Namu and had avoided the kamel yards. Now she worried she'd forgotten what Nibloo looked like.

A tuft of black fur in the middle of his forehead, Saskia reminded herself. Resembles a horn.

The kamels raised their heads as she passed, but they all looked the same. A handler brushed past Saskia and tossed another bucket of grass, grains and vegetable scraps into the feed trough. Sometimes, handlers fed the kamels fish bones ground into a paste. Whatever the nutrition, the animals lapped it up with their long, pink, bulbous tongues. Saskia's stomach churned at the spectacle, and she considered abandoning the last goodbye and heading to the griffin barn to feed Namu.

Another outcome undermined her resolve to farewell Nibloo; the chance she might see Heron in the yards. Since becoming a wind-rider, she'd avoided him, letting the flower of a blossoming relationship wither on the stem.

As she turned to leave, a kamel poked its head through the throng, trying to reach the feeding trough.

Saskia smiled to herself. *Nibloo.*

Stepping up to the trough, she pushed another kamel aside to make room for her mount. "Get out," she said to the greedy kamel.

The animal raised its head and battered long lashes over lovable brown eyes.

"I'm not falling for that," said Saskia. "You've had enough. Nibloo needs to eat."

She pushed the kamel's head again. Rising above the moaning calamity of the holding pens, an unmistakable gurgle bubbled in the pit of the kamel's belly. The animal opened its mouth, and a ball of spit and vomit shot out and splashed into Saskia's face.

"Damn it! Yuck."

Someone behind her laughed. She spun around, ready to tear a strip from the insolent handler, and found Heron standing there holding a wet cloth.

"Do you need this?" he asked.

She snatched it from his hand and wiped the mucous off her face.

"I hope you're not going to ask me to kiss you now," said Heron, smiling.

Saskia threw the cloth at him. "I wouldn't ask you, regardless."

He caught the cloth and dropped it into a bucket. "Isn't that why you're here?"

"I came to say goodbye to Nibloo. Now I'm a wind-rider; this will be the last time I ever step inside a kamel yard."

"Not even to visit me?" asked Heron.

Saskia averted her eyes from Heron's yearning face. "We can meet elsewhere," she mumbled.

"Where? When? I haven't seen you in days."

Nibloo pushed his head forward and dropped his snout into the feeding trough. Saskia scratched him between the ears, right on the tuft of black fur.

"Make sure he gets a good rider," she said. "A kind one."

"I'll do my best," said Heron. "You're avoiding my question."

Saskia tilted her head skyward, trying to escape Heron's expectation.

"Since the Eligens, training hasn't stopped. Flying manoeuvres. Weapons training. Everything's different up in the clouds. I've been chosen for my first mission, scouting the outer reaches of Magna Avium. We leave tomorrow and will be gone for many moons."

"Then we should make the most of the time before you leave." Heron wrapped his arm around Saskia's waist and pulled her close.

She stepped away. "Not here. I can't be seen...."

"What? Cavorting with a kamel handler?" Heron's arm dropped to his side.

"It's not that...it's, well...now I'm a wind-rider...."

"You're too good for me?"

"No. It's just...we should be more discreet. Wind-riders have an honoured position among the Germalians. A certain status to uphold."

"I thought...I thought we were...*together.*"

Saskia reached her hand across and grabbed Heron's wrist. "We can be. I need time to sort a few things out."

"Is there someone else?"

Saskia squeezed his wrist. "No. Why do men always think there's someone else? With training and this new mission...well...I've got so much going on. No time for...."

Heron yanked his arm away. "You've decided you're too good for me. Someone better will come along. Like one of those men who find criminals for the vigilum. A kamel handler isn't a fit partner for a Volatal Vexil soldier." He turned and marched off.

Saskia called after him. "Wait. It's not that."

"Missing the kamels already?"

Saskia turned at Thaly's voice. "Arve, Sis."

"Why did Heron leave in such a hurry?" asked Thaly.

"I hurt his feelings."

"How?"

"Should I court a kamel handler now I'm in the Volatal Vexil?"

"Do you care for him?"

"Yes, but...I don't know."

"Let your heart decide, free from the desire to meet society's approval."

"Life here is complicated," said Saskia. "The higher status you gain, the more complicated things become. Female rule doesn't make things simpler or easier."

Thaly laughed. "Don't nominate for the conventus; you'll hate it."

"Portum *is* better than Sardis, though."

"Erstürmen kings were responsible for so much death and trauma. I understand why the conventus limits men's authority and ambitions. But women aren't immune to the lure of unbridled power. Temptations born from evil intent can corrupt any of us. The Dobunni shared power equally among genders. One day, the Germalians might follow their lead."

Saskia smiled. "When you're the Sella, you can draft any rule you want."

Thaly placed her arm around Saskia's shoulder. "It's bad enough being a senator. If I was the Sella, I'd never escape those endless meetings."

"What are they talking about now?"

"The usual. While some senators want to confront Malphas, others fear the Pordillo will attack Portum."

"Don't worry, Sis, I'll sort it out when we find Qaysar Rais. With six griffins on our mission, we'll rout the Pordillo once and for all and return home in time for supper." Saskia beamed.

"Your orders are to scout positions, not wipe the Pordillo from Magna Avium in a single swoop. It's a long mission. I wish I was going with you."

"Why aren't you?"

"The conventus has important things to discuss. Politics comes before everything else. Otherwise, how else would we know who to fight?" Thaly pulled Saskia close. "Do you remember your training?"

Saskia rolled her eyes. "*Yesss.* Does the training ever end?"

"*Nooo.*" Thaly smiled. "Use the clouds for cover when you can, and stay high enough to keep out of reach of arrows."

"What if the enemy has a wind lance or ballista?"

"Pordillo don't use ballistae. Too hard to drag war machines through the sand."

"Well then, you've got nothing to worry about."

"We worry about you because we love you. If anything happened...."

"It won't. I was born to be a wind-rider, like you. We're going to be riding griffins until we're old women."

Thaly reached into her pocket, then pressed something into Saskia's hand. "I want you to take this. It will protect you."

"This is your amulet," said Saskia, running her fingers over the polished silver griffin attached to a chain.

"It belongs to our family," said Thaly.

Jurelle once gave Saskia the amulet for safekeeping, the day he delivered her and Genevea to the Germalians before returning to Enthilen to find Thaly. Only six harvest seasons old, Saskia didn't understand the enormity of the change in her life. A young Erstürmen princess who would become a Germalian wind-rider.

"Jürgen used to wear this," said Saskia. "Then Ma gave it to Pa before he went to war in the Riverlands. Jürgen wanted him to have it. To keep him safe."

"And Pa returned. Now, the silver griffin will protect you." Thaly hugged Saskia, then sniffed at her cheek. "*Errk.* What's that smell?"

"A kamel threw up on me."

Thaly laughed.

"It's not funny," said Saskia. "Do griffins do that?"

"Only if you make them angry. And you can imagine what it's like — all those mashed-up rats' guts."

"You're teasing me."

Thaly smiled, then released the embrace. "I'm off to feed Yagle. You should go home and pack your things."

Saskia hugged her sister again, and they parted. She gave Nibloo's head a final scratch, right on the spot he liked the best, then strode from the yard, part of her hoping to avoid another awkward encounter with Heron, and part of her hoping he would rush to her side and profess his love. He didn't appear, and her thoughts turned to the coming expedition. Her chance to show Thaly and everyone how disciplined and skilful she could be. She wouldn't make any mistakes, not like at the Wonchulus waterhole when Germalian soldiers died because of her stupidity. She had to be smarter than that, and she would be.

*   *   *   *

Dwarfed by the griffin barn, Thaly stood inside Yagle's stable and ran a stiff brush over his flank, combing out the grit and flakes of dried skin. A vaulted ceiling dressed in tangerine tiles, almost as high as the Pallaxium's golden dome, trapped the smell of straw and fresh manure. Handlers roamed the barn, feeding and bedding down Portum's twelve griffins. Each griffin had its own stable, large enough for six horses, and more comforts than any animal Thaly had known.

These were the original twelve griffins, taken from a remote island, three-days sailing off Germalia's west coast. The island's location remained a secret, the Germalians renaming an archipelago in the Occidian Sea 'Griffin Isles' as a misdirection to any seeking the griffins' home. Despite trying, the Germalians couldn't breed griffins. A book in Portum's library claimed newborns hatched from eggs and could live for a hundred yarles. During mating season, Portum's male griffins would court the females with cooing, preening, and courtship dances involving bobbing heads, elaborate wing sweeps, and tail swishes. Copulation occurred soon after, and around twelve days later, female griffins laid eggs, blue-green and as large as a melon, and became broody. However, not a single egg had hatched, despite most being fertile. Lacking the capacity to raise griffin offspring, some senators wanted to sail back to the secret island and capture more adult griffins. Others worried this would diminish the source population and drive the griffins to extinction. Thaly expected the arguments to continue long after she'd grown tired of them.

As Yagle ran the tip of his bill through his chest feathers, Puer walked into the stable carrying a bag of rats. The griffin stopped his preening and fixed his golden eye on the food.

"Do you want to feed him?" Thaly asked Puer.

"If it pleases you, Domina Stansfield," said Puer.

"I'll brush while you feed. Yagle will be the most pampered griffin in all Portum."

Puer smiled. "Yes, Domina. It would be a great honour." He opened the bag of squirming, kicking rodents. Yagle squawked his attention.

Thaly ran a comb through the tuft of black hair at the end of Yagle's tail. "How long have you been a handler?"

"From the first day the griffins arrived in Portum," said Puer, holding a rat out front of Yagle until the griffin snatched it from his fingers. "I served Domina Aventinus on the ship the *Occidian Wind*."

Thaly's eyes widened. "You were there? When they discovered the griffins?"

"Oh, yes. Six yarles ago, we came upon the island. I remember the day as if it were yesterday. The ocean a mirror to the sky, both deep blue and still. Thin wisps of cloud skirted the island's mountains like angels coming home. Then I saw another cloud, moving faster than the rest. But it wasn't a cloud, Domina Stansfield; it was a griffin, porcelain white, resembling a beautiful, delicate sculpture. It led us to a bay where the *Occidian Wind* dropped anchor. Domina Aventinus allowed me to serve the expedition group that went ashore. Such an honour for a simple man. After two moons hiking over mountains and through dense wildness, we came upon the eyrie. Another thirty-six moons and we had tamed our first griffin. It came much easier than I expected, Domina."

"You must know more about griffins than any other handler."

"You are too kind," said Puer, bowing his head.

"Don't be modest. I wager you know more than the rest of us combined. Why can't we breed griffins?"

Puer scratched the stubble of his balding crown. "No-one has asked me that before."

"But you've thought about it."

Puer peered through the barn door and into the bustle of evening Portum as if gathering his thoughts. "When we were on the island, griffins nested on cliff ledges, way up high. I think they were safest there. We saw packs of wild dogs on the island, large enough to prey on griffin nestlings. Male and female griffins took turns sitting on the eggs, and other griffins brought them food. In Portum, we keep the female isolated in her stable, and the nest is built low to the ground."

"Is breeding communal?" asked Thaly.

Puer nodded. "The support of others and nestling safety appear to be paramount, Domina Stansfield."

"There aren't any cliffs in the desert. We should build a tower specialised for nesting and able to accommodate all the griffins. We need a griffin creche."

"That's an excellent idea," said Puer, handing Yagle another squirming rat.

"It's your idea. If it works, I'll make sure everyone knows."

"Thank you, Domina Stansfield. You're much too kind."

"Nonsense."

Puer turned and bowed low as Genevea walked into the stable.

She smiled at Thaly. "You spend more time with Yagle than with Chloe."

"Did Chloe tell you that?" asked Thaly.

"I don't want to get her in trouble."

"It's vital for a wind-rider to maintain her bond with her griffin."

Genevea flinched as if she'd been struck.

"I'm sorry," said Thaly, realising how cruel her statement sounded to someone who'd abandoned their child. "I didn't mean to...Puer, can you leave us, please?"

"Yes, Domina Stansfield. The bag of rats is now empty." Puer bowed to Thaly and Genevea, then walked from the stable.

"You're not wearing your senatorial robes," said Genevea as she stepped closer to Yagle.

He dipped his bill in her direction, still looking for more rats, and she shied away.

"He won't hurt you," said Thaly.

"Not like I've hurt you."

Thaly fell silent before trying to redirect the conversation. "As Legatus,

355

I issued a decree allowing wind-riders that are also senators to forgo wearing those bulky robes when working with griffins. Cotton pants and shirt are much more practical."

"*Hmmm,*" hummed Genevea, pressing her palms down the front of her ankle-length, lacy blue dress with awkward self-consciousness. "We bonded," she said. "I know you don't believe me and think what I did was easy...."

"Ma, I...."

"No." Genevea raised her hand. "Let me finish. We made a connection during the short time we were together. Before I handed you to the Dobunni rebels. When you were born, I never left your side. We slept together in my quarters. I refused to let the handmaidens take care of you. I kept you at my breast. Woke whenever you needed feeding or changing. I cherished every precious moment in Sardis' inner circle when I was your mother and you were my child. Then King Ewald hatched a plan to force Jurelle to pledge allegiance to the Erstürmen. When my brother told me his plan, he tore my heart open. I thought about escaping. Riding from Sardis in the dark of night with you strapped to my chest. But guards watched my door. If only I'd known about the secret passage leading from the Sunrise Keep to freedom. The one Princess Caeli hid behind her mirror."

Tears of guilt welled in Thaly's eyes. "I'm sorry. I've been so selfish and awful."

Genevea reached for her hand. "You're right to be angry."

"No. It's time to let it go. It's past time I forgave you."

"Jurelle's worried."

Thaly wiped the tears from her cheeks. "Does he ever stop worrying?"

Genevea smiled and squeezed Thaly's hand. "No. But he's never forgiven himself for Jürgen's death. If he loses another child...if *we* lose another child...."

"I'm not going anywhere," said Thaly.

"Despite all your time in the conventus, you're still a wind-rider. Legatus of the Volatal Vexil. You and Saskia are soldiers. Always, you will face danger."

"You can't protect us from the world."

"One day, you may have a child. Then you'll understand. Although, with Chloe...."

"We can adopt," interrupted Thaly, pulling her hand away from her mother and fingering the pearl friendship ring gifted by Chloe. "The Germalians allow it. There are plenty of orphans in Portum. Young boys begging on the street."

"Yes, I see them every day. I find it...," Genevea scanned the barn, then lowered her voice, "*unsettling*. There is such wealth in Portum; why do some go without?"

"We can give one of them a better life. Or maybe two?"

"Either way, a man doesn't have much of a life here."

"Pa does alright."

"He has privileges other men are denied. Senators Zenais and Eutropia saw to that." Genevea stepped closer and whispered, "The senators spoke with your father. They want you to command the entire Germalian army. Invade Enthilen. Bring down Malphas, and lead the people to a new future."

Thaly turned away. "I've heard the rumours. The burden of expectation is a harrowing weight."

"Your blood comes from Jurelle and me. Like it or not, your ancestors are Dobunni and Erstürmen. Heine and Stansfield. Two royal lineages bound together in you and Saskia. Zenais and Eutropia believe only my daughters can unite Enthilen's people."

Thaly folded her arms across her chest. "Malphas must be defeated first. The conventus can't even agree on who should be allowed to run a market stall, let alone cast a unanimous vote to march to war."

"The day is coming. Jurelle says the momentum for war builds like the waters behind the dam wall at the bottom of the Rārian Falls. Soon, something will tip the balance, and the torrent of war will be upon us."

Thaly shook her head. "I can't lead an army to war. I don't want to rule Enthilen."

"You don't have to. There are other ways...."

"Fire!" came a yell from inside the barn.

Puer ran past Yagle's stable carrying a bucket of water. Thaly strode into the centre of the barn, a circular arena of sand where handlers exercised the griffins. Genevea followed. A fire had taken hold near the barn's double doors. With clutching fingers, it climbed up old, dry timber, latching onto the beams that supported the rammed earth walls and tiled roof.

"How did the fire grow so large without us realising?" asked Thaly.

Genevea pointed at shards of clay pots scattered across the sand. "Did those broken pots contain serpent oil?"

There's no reason to have serpent oil in the griffin barn, thought Thaly.

Puer threw a bucket of water on the fire. It sizzled and hissed into steam in the blink of an eye. In the far corner of the barn, other handlers drew buckets from a well and raced to help Puer. Smoke billowed up into the vaulted ceiling and pooled underneath the tiles. Embers dropped to the floor and set stacks of hay alight. Griffins harnessed to hitching posts tossed their heads and screeched in panic.

A gasping Puer rushed over to Thaly. "We must get the griffins out, Domina Stansfield. The fire is spreading too fast."

Thaly nodded. "Take Yagle," she said to Genevea.

"I've never led a griffin," said Genevea. "I'm not sure...."

"He'll follow you. He knows you want to lead him to safety."

Thaly took her mother back to the stable and signalled to Yagle. He bowed his head, and she fixed a harness over his bill and around the back of his neck, then handed the reins to Genevea.

"Out the front doors," said Thaly.

"It's right past the fire," said Genevea.

"Go quickly. You'll be safe."

A terrified Genevea stumbled from the stable towards the doors. Handlers tried in vain to douse the fire. Puer led another griffin, Chirité, to safety. Thaly raced to Namu's stable. The griffin thrashed her head, trying to free herself from the rope tying her to a hitching post.

"It's alright, girl," said Thaly. "I'm here."

She untied the rope and calmed Namu before leading her into the sand arena and towards the exit. Genevea walked on ahead, Yagle following her. The barn doors disappeared behind a curtain of thick, choking smoke that dropped from the ceiling. The fire engulfed the rafters, slinking along the wooden beams like a flaming serpent. Thaly covered her mouth with her forearm and pushed ahead, dragging Namu with her. As they approached the barn doors, the raging fire singed every breath Thaly took. For a horrible moment, her legs became paralysed with fear more scolding than the flames.

Crack!

A whoosh of hot air brushed past Thaly's face as a burning beam crashed down between her and the barn doors. It dropped in front of Yagle, right where Genevea would have been standing.

"No!" cried Thaly, pulling Namu behind as she rushed at the fire.

Puer emerged from the smoke, extending his hand. "I'll take her," said Puer.

Thaly nodded, gave him the reins and raced to where she'd last seen Genevea. Yagle had already fled through the central doorway, now ringed with fire. A tide of flame edged across the straw-covered floor, set the entire front wall of the barn alight, and flared above like a burning sun. Thaly yanked the white handkerchief off her wrist, tied it over her nose and mouth, and walked into the inferno.

"Ma!" she yelled.

The smoke stung her eyes. The searing heat burned her throat. She dropped to her knees and crawled until stumbling upon a bundle, curled up like a baby, lying in the straw. The hem of Genevea's blue dress had caught alight.

She always wears these stupid dresses, thought Thaly. *Portum's one and only princess.* She hovered over her mother. Genevea's eyes and mouth were closed. Her face still. Chest motionless.

You're not dying on me, thought Thaly.

She forced her arms under Genevea's body and lifted her into a sitting position. Thaly stood, hooked her hands under Genevea's armpits and dragged her across the straw on her buttocks. Undignified for a princess, but survival came before dignity. If it came at all.

~ Chapter 23 ~

Adalwolf scuffed his boots on ash and black coals, indistinguishable from the shadows lengthening across the Dambay Plains. Ahead of him, Audie led Girac, the horse harnessed to the cart carrying the remaining supplies. Adalwolf walked more now, not wanting to ride in the cart and burden Girac further. They'd been travelling southwest across the plains for five moons and had reached the outskirts of Grōz Forst — the immense south forest. The stone-grells who lived here called it Babir Birramal. Either way, it wasn't a vast forest any longer. It wasn't even a forest. Charred tree trunks surrounded Adalwolf like an ebony army. The standing dead, defoliated and lifeless. Fallen trees littered the ground in a chaotic ramble, roots weakened by the fire long past. It looked as if a giant child had taken a bucket of twigs and tossed them out one by one. Adding to the despair, torrential rain had gouged channels through the barren landscape, carrying eroded soil into turbid streams. Ash and dirt choked the water, ripples of liquid crystal replaced by a treacly sludge creeping along the streambed like a cold serpent. Nothing stirred in the burned forest. No noise other than the crunch of Adalwolf's boots on the charred remains of what once lived.

Audie brushed her hand against a tree trunk as she walked, covering her pale skin in soot. She resembled a dreaming child, ambling through a forest meadow and caressing every flower in adoring wonderment. As if each tree wasn't the same, depressing stack of charcoal, but a bright, colourful blossom she'd never seen before. She sometimes stared at the sky, maybe expecting to spot a bird flying overhead, or navigated the fallen trees with her horse and cart like a girl skipping through a hedged maze planted in a grand garden inside palace grounds.

Would she find a treasure inside the maze? thought Adalwolf. Or the way out?

Audie stopped at a tree and faced him. "Look. A sign of growth." Kneeling, she ran her fingers over a green shoot growing from the base of the trunk. Girac snorted and scratched his hoof across the scorched soil.

Adalwolf hobbled up to them and forced a smile. "You never lose hope, do you?"

She stood from her haunches. "We should make camp soon. It's getting dark." Then walked off, Girac and cart in tow.

Adalwolf braced his wounded body against the tree trunk with his left hand, wondering where they were going and why Audie persisted in caring for him. Worrying Malphas would find him soon and kill him out of spite. He let Audie walk away and considered turning back east. Or heading north to face his demons in Pergamos. It would relieve the burden he placed on her. Yet, he expected she would come looking, and in the empty forest, there was nowhere to hide.

"There's a spring here!" yelled Audie, stopping the cart and loosening the makeshift harness from Girac's neck.

The sun set behind the Scaur Hills, and Adalwolf walked to Audie, entranced by the healer's grace as she moved about the horse, stroking the animal and talking to him the whole time. Though flora failed to grow in the dead forest, Audie had blossomed into the most beautiful flower Adalwolf had ever seen.

He limped up to her. "I'll start a fire."

"We can camp beside the spring."

Adalwolf leaned over a hole in the ground, ringed by a fringe of green grass, where water seeped up through the soil. Blackened twigs and ash floated on the surface; otherwise, the water looked clean.

"If we can filter it...," he said.

"Through my undergarments," said Audie. "I've done it before."

Adalwolf took a fire striker and flint from a satchel on the cart tray. Audie had packed bark shavings soaked in the melted resin of spruce pines and mashed together into what she called 'fire biscuits'.

Without char cloth and suitable kindling, the biscuits offered the best chance of starting a fire. Adalwolf sat among a pile of dead branches, unsheathed his knife and scraped away the outer charr of a branch to expose the unburned wood underneath. Bracing the stem between his legs, he used the knife to whittle feathers of heartwood to heap atop the fire biscuit.

"How long ago did this forest burn?" asked Audie.

Adalwolf dropped the knife and placed his hand on a patch of soil near a blackened log. "Parts of the soil are still warm. A few days ago, I would guess, but I'm no expert in the ways of wildfire." He cleared a patch of soil, piled heartwood feathers atop a fire biscuit, then jammed the flint between his boot and a rock. With his only hand, he tried to get a spark to hold by thrusting the striker across the flint.

"Do you want me to try?" asked Audie. "We might find an ember in a burned log."

"I can do it," said Adalwolf. "I hate feeling useless."

Audie returned to tending Girac, offering the horse a bowl of soaked grain. "There's little pick for horses," she said, "and our food is almost gone."

"We shouldn't waste what we have on the horse."

"I'm not going to let him starve."

Adalwolf frowned. "I'll hunt tomorrow. We have a quiver of arrows and a bow. Lying on my back, I can hold the grip with my bare feet and draw the string with my hand."

"I don't doubt your archery skill, but we haven't seen a single animal in days."

"I'll set a snare close by. The spring offers precious, clean water. If there's anything in this blackened wasteland, it needs to drink."

"We should head further south," said Audie, "where the fire hasn't reached. The weald-grells of Giigal will give us shelter."

"Why would they shelter a failed Erstürmen king and his healer? Anyway, Giigal won't be safe for long. Now Gestade has fallen, Malphas will turn his malice towards the weald-grells."

"I refuse to relinquish hope, and you refuse to embrace it."

"We're together, Audie. That gives me hope."

Adalwolf raised an ember, lay on his chest and blew into the fledgling fire until it took hold. He searched the ground, scraping charred twigs and branches into a pile.

Girac finished the grain, then Audie sat beside Adalwolf, resting against the cart.

"How is your back?" she asked.

Adalwolf reached for Audie's hand. "Much better. Thank you."

Audie brushed her finger over Adalwolf's knuckles. A gentle, almost loving touch setting his pulse and mind racing. But doubt crept in, and he dismissed the contact as inconsequential. He didn't deserve to be loved.

She pulled away as if embarrassed or offended by his thoughts.

"If you want to travel south, Audie, we'll go south. The weald-grells will give us no less a welcome than Malphas. I'd rather try our luck at Giigal than face the fortress of Pergamos or look for refuge in Sardis or Laodicea, where the black grell spreads his poison."

"You knew the tainted grells once, didn't you? Krieg and Hunger."

"I'm not sure anybody truly knows them or what goes on inside their corrupted minds. They follow Malphas like a salivating dog follows a butcher's cart."

"Lady Lily LáDown told me there are four tainted grells."

"There were. Eroberung, the white grell, died in Sardis, killed by Jurelle Stansfield. Eroberung was known as the grell of conquest. Krieg, the red grell, is the grell of war. Gestade learned that only too well. Hunger is the grell of famine. And Ende...." Adalwolf stopped and caught himself as Ende's pale face emerged before his eyes. She'd been his tutor and tormenter during the early days of his reign. The only days. Malphas had tasked Ende with stripping Adalwolf's emotions bare until he became an unfeeling brute. Even now, he broke out in a shivering sweat at the thought of her.

"What about Ende?" asked Audie.

"She is the pale grell. The tainted grell of death. She rarely leaves

Malphas' side and often dispatches those he despises. It's for her I have the most fear. Fear and sorrow."

"You carry scars from those days," said Audie. "I've seen them on your back and chest. Cuts made by a sharp blade."

Ende's sparth, thought Adalwolf, his face vellicating at the memory of the weapon. "You're perceptive. There are other ways, other times I could have received those wounds."

"Your emotional scars from then are obvious. I assumed you had physical ones to match."

Adalwolf faced Audie, trying to discern the colour of her eyes in the light cast by the full and three-quarter moons. Her dark hair and skin of warm ivory glistened from the body oils accumulated during a long journey without bathing. She scrunched her button nose as if to ward off an itch or suppress a sneeze, then smiled at him with thin lips and the hint of dimples past the corner of her mouth.

"Have you ever been in love?" asked Adalwolf.

Audie's eyes, hazel, Adalwolf concluded, hazel eyes, glistened with surprise.

"Why do you ask?" she said.

"Ewald told me love is a weakness your enemies will exploit. Better to love no-one lest it is used against you. Even my mother never said she loved me, though she must have because she sacrificed so much. Unless it was all to satisfy her own desires. To cling to a royal life for as long as possible."

Audie pulled her knees into her chest. "After I was taken from my family, there was never much room in my life for love. Death follows a healer as sure as Bargan follows Seena across the night sky. I grew so accustomed to losing the sick or injured, strangers whose lives clung only to me, I wondered if losing someone I loved would mean anything. I may fall in love, but not care if it ended, my emotions so numbed I would never desire to be with someone forever."

Adalwolf leaned towards Audie. "Enthilen has become a place where people fear to love. Malphas wants to crush all expectation, so the only hope left is the one he offers. The promise of Volerdie's paradise. Audie...I...."

Audie placed her finger to her lips. "*Sssh.*" Then stood, peering into the half-light. "Something's coming."

Adalwolf crawled to the wagon's rear, retrieved a sword and crouched behind the tray, waiting to surprise any predator — animal, person or tainted grell.

Audie called into the twilight draping the black trees. "Who's there?"

"It might be a plainalope come to drink," whispered Adalwolf. "We could kill it. Have meat for days."

The saliva in his mouth evaporated when two people stepped from behind a tree trunk. Adalwolf sprang to his feet and raised the sword.

The man held empty hands up in surrender. "Wait now. Don't kill your own uncle."

Adalwolf squinted. "Who are you?"

A figure beside the man fluttered in the twilight. "Don't you recognise me?"

Adalwolf's tongue lolled outside his bottom lip, and he lowered his sword, the blade dangling in the forest ash. "Princess Caeli?"

"I have brought my father," she said.

"Uncle Widu? Is that you?"

"Yes." Widukind flashed a smile, walked across to Adalwolf and embraced him.

Adalwolf remained stiff and unsure, wondering if Malphas had sent Widukind to find him. "I...I can't believe it," stammered Adalwolf. "I haven't seen you, Uncle, since...."

Widukind grasped Adalwolf by the shoulders, his breath smelling of mint but his clothes of turpitude. "Since Ewald's last visit to Laodicea," said Widukind, still smiling. "You were only a child. I was...I was a different man then."

"And Caeli...." Adalwolf stepped away from Widukind as Caeli drifted closer to him.

From the darkness emerged his nightmare. The soulless, lifeless mannequin he'd created in Pergamos' throne room when he'd captured Caeli's soul using the dark eyes. The frailty of her form taunted his remorse, the stain of death hugging her dress, threadbare and torn like a rag used too many times. Cheeks, once soft and round, now drooped with skin folds resembling a sagging curtain. Once gleaming eyes sat dark and emotionless. Most of Caeli's beautiful auburn hair had fallen out, only a few strands still clinging to a pale scalp.

He loved her once, thought Adalwolf. Yes, *loved*. The young prince of Sardis rejected his father's proclamation of love as weakness and fell for the princess locked in the tower. His cousin. Voluptuous, curvaceous, alluring.

But look at her now, he chided himself. You did this. Turned her into a draughoul.

Caeli placed her hand on Adalwolf's shoulder as if to still the tremors of repentance.

"Please forgive me, Caeli," said Adalwolf. "I'm so sorry. If you've come to enact your revenge, I deserve it."

"Don't blame yourself," said Caeli. "I had to stop you making a terrible mistake."

"All of us have paid a heavy price for Malphas' ambitions," said Widukind. "Now is the time for us to unite and enact our retribution." He faced Audie. "Who is this?"

"I'm Audie. A healer and Adalwolf's friend."

"I'm glad he's found someone he can trust. A healer, you say? My medicine is almost gone. The leaves of a plant the mouldewerps call ha'nuk. You may know it as seraleaf. Do you have some in your cart?"

"I'll look," Audie said, stepping to the cart tray.

"Why are you here, Uncle?" asked Adalwolf.

"We came looking for you. Can we sit for a while? I have a long tale to tell."

Audie found a pouch of dried seraleaf, which she gave to Widukind. Adalwolf and Widukind collected enough wood to keep the fire burning into the night. Caeli drifted away, among the blackened trees and out of sight. Adalwolf wondered if she left to help relieve his guilt, but Widukind told him she rarely stopped wandering and would likely be back in the morning. Or the day after.

Sitting around the fire, the three travellers shared their meagre food portions and caught up on the yarles they'd missed together. Adalwolf told Widukind of his flight from Pergamos, life on Bramble Island, Romilda's death and the fall of Gestade. Widukind told Adalwolf of Bindari and his journeys across the plains and hills. Yet, his uncle kept the details vague, and Adalwolf needed more.

"You still haven't explained why you're here. Or how you found me."

Widukind stared into the fire. "I used the blood compass."

Adalwolf's mind reeled at the memory of the magical pentagram. The recollection of how it worked. "You can only use the compass if...if you have...."

"Tom Anderson's blood. Yes, I have it. He has returned to Enthilen."

"What? Why?" Adalwolf's mind fixated on the revelation. Widukind wasn't here at the bequest of Malphas; he was here because of Tom Anderson. Adalwolf stood and backed away. "Does he have the eyes of lost souls?"

Widukind nodded.

"Then he wishes to kill me. Tom Anderson wants to steal my soul so he can become immortal. You're his lackey."

"No," said Widukind. "You have it all wrong. Sit down."

Adalwolf reached for the handle of a knife poking out above his belt. His sword rested on the ground beside Widukind. If Adalwolf wanted to defend himself against his uncle, better he retrieves the sword than rely on a blunted knife.

"I'm not here to fight you," said Widukind. "Or take you prisoner. Tom Anderson seeks to shatter the throne of the dead, and he needs your help."

Adalwolf hovered his left hand above the knife. "How?"

"A few drops of fresh blood from you and Tom splashed onto the throne and mixed with the dust of crushed bones taken from Tom's grandmother and Caeli."

Audie looked perplexed. "I'm a healer, and I've never heard of such a bizarre potion."

"Blood and bone, destroy the throne," said Widukind. "The passage comes straight from *Da Und Sepcarture*, the First Scripture. The blood of birth twins. Bone dust from relations who've had their souls taken by the dark eyes. We have all the ingredients."

Adalwolf sat on the opposite side of the fire to Widukind, still wary of his uncle's motivations. "Malphas will know this. He would have worked it out."

"I don't believe so," said Widukind. "At least, I hope not."

"Then cut my flesh," said Adalwolf, extending his left hand. "Drain my blood into a vial, mix it with Tom's and be done with it."

"No. The blood dripped onto the throne must be fresh. Straight from an open wound. We must take you and Tom to Volerdie's throne."

"It's in Pergamos!" cried Adalwolf. "We can't reach it. Not with fifty thousand soldiers can we pierce the city's defences. Malphas' army razed Gestade, and scouts reported that it was less than half his force. Your plan is madness."

"It's the only plan we have."

"Where is this Tom Anderson now?" asked Audie.

"Seeking the help of the rebels living in the Desolate Mountains. We hope the weald-grells will also fight."

Adalwolf scoffed. "Your hopes rest with bands of vagabonds and primitive heathens who use sticks for weapons."

"Where are you travelling to?" asked Widukind.

"I hoped the weald-grells may take us in," said Audie.

"Heathens with sticks," said Widukind with a wry smile before leaning towards Adalwolf. "We're clutching at straws because it's all we have. Would you rather a future of aimless wandering or hiding in a dank hole? Believe me, neither is appealing. Help us smash the throne, stop Malphas, and give purpose to your life. Make the end glorious, not pitiful."

"It would be a great thing," said Audie, "to end the plight Malphas has brought on Enthilen. It would be the most wonderous thing I can think of."

"Would it stop him?" asked Adalwolf. "Without the throne, Malphas is still immortal. He can still seek to rule Enthilen."

"One birth twin, immortal no more," said Widukind. "Another passage from the First Scripture. Destroy the throne, and Malphas becomes mortal."

"How certain are you?" asked Adalwolf.

Widukind bunched the front of Adalwolf's tunic into a ball and spat desperate words in his face, "I can't be certain. But does it matter? Malphas is driven by the desire to see Volerdie return to Enthilen, which can happen only if an immortal is sacrificed on the throne of the dead when darkness descends amid the daylight. It is written in the First Scripture. No throne, no Volerdie. The realisation would crush Malphas. He would shrivel into nothingness." Widukind released Adalwolf and leaned back.

Adalwolf relaxed and pressed his tunic against his chest. "You may be right, though it would be ironic, me trying to dismantle a throne I once coveted."

Volerdie's throne will be underground in Pergamos' throne hall, thought Adalwolf as he pictured the mass of contorted bodies mangled together to make a chair, their mouths open and howling. Calves and feet forming the throne's legs. Fingers clutching stone balls at the end of armrests, and the horned wolf crowning the backrest, with empty, crimson sockets waiting to be filled by the eyes of lost souls.

Sitting on the throne for days, Adalwolf had explored every crevice and crack as he travelled from Laodicea after his coronation to a Pergamos waiting for resurrection. Malphas valued the throne more than anything. It would be heavily guarded by Rephaim, Shield, and Ende, the pale grell.

Adalwolf wondered if he could face Ende again. Or Malphas. Or any of it. And yet, if Malphas *shrivelled into nothingness* as Widukind hoped, Enthilen would need a new leader.

Would they embrace an absent king? thought Adalwolf. Is this another opportunity, probably the last, to reclaim the title of King Adalwolf, the Redeemer, and become the glorious monarch his mother always hoped for?

~ Chapter 24 ~

The guard at Laodicea's south gate ignored Tormil and stared at Hanni from underneath his black spangenhelm. Every piece of the guard's armour was black, in honour of Laodicea's master — Hunger, the black grell. Fixed on Hanni, the guard's eyes had such intensity she wondered if he'd begun to count the heartbeats thudding in her chest. She dropped her head, doing her best to maintain the pretence of slavery. Tormil had bound her hands and tied the rope's loose end to his saddle. He'd also shaved Hanni's head and dressed her like a male grell in a bulky, ragged tunic and pants. The Erstürmen targeted female grells, either killing them to stop the wild population from growing or locking them in fertility prisons to breed more slaves.

While Hanni resembled a male slave, the dark ink of her facial tattoo announced to the world her heritage as a wild stone-grell.

I have my own black armour, she thought.

Yet, the pride of wearing gama, the spear fern, as her crest had now become a threat. Overseers scoured the faces of their slaves to dull the tattoos or remove them altogether. Hanni refused to take the disguise that far, hoping it wouldn't sabotage the mission. Hidden inside the backpack, Dwarrow squirmed, jabbing her spine as if to remind her of the peril of selfishness.

Behind Hanni, hundreds of people lined up, waiting to enter the city. Farmers with carts of food to sell in the markets. Merchants dressed in fine cotton and clutching essential documents. Seafarers heading for the Docklands. Crafters looking for work. Travellers from Sardis, Pergamos or one of the towns scattered across the Dambay Plains. Hanni hoped none of them noticed the wriggling pack.

Laodicea's south wall towered above her with thick, unyielding stone and a timber palisade at the base waiting to impale a misguided attacker. Soldiers in black armour paced along the parapets, watching and waiting for a mistake, a reason to shoot an arrow or throw a lance. The wound in Hanni's shoulder ached, setting further worry in her mind. A wild stone-grell stood out among the throng, head and shoulders above the rest of the rabble waiting to enter Laodicea. An easy target for another arrow.

"I'm taking my slave to market," said Tormil to the guard, interrupting Hanni's thoughts.

The guard peered behind Tormil's horse and called at Hanni, "Lift y'head."

This is it, she thought. My facial tattoo will end it.

Hanni lifted her face but averted her eyes.

"Dat a wild grell?" the guard asked Tormil.

"He was," he replied. "Caught him on the plains a few moons ago and tamed him. Ain't seen a wild one for yarles."

The guard nodded. "Yu'll make some pretty coin, sellin' dat beast. *Real* pretty."

He blocked Tormil's path, halberd clutched in one gloved hand, and fell silent, waiting for his inducement.

Tormil will know what to do, thought Hanni. Yarles dealing with Erstürmen guards in Laodicea during King Ewald's reign had attuned him to the whims of soldiers' desires.

Tormil reached into his tunic pocket, withdrew a clenched fist and moved it furtively towards the guard. The guard stepped closer, turned his back to block the view of other soldiers, and held his free hand open by his side, palm facing up. A glint of silver slipped from Tormil's fingers as he dropped coins into the black glove. The guard's fist clamped shut like a bear trap before he stepped aside and nodded to Tormil.

The old warrior led his horse through the gate, Hanni lumbering behind it. She expected the guard to call her back at any moment, but he didn't. They walked into what once would have been the Southern Vale, the Dobunni stronghold in Laodicea. Now, everything belonged to Hunger, and the Dobunni had long been scattered on the winds.

Tormil untied the rope connecting Hanni to the saddle and stabled his horse at the south gate, greasing more palms with coin. He kept her hands bound and led her along a cobbled street lined with two-storey houses of white-washed, rendered walls sectioned by dark timber beams. Every house window was shuttered, and the doors closed as if no-one wanted to let the outside in. A handful of ruined houses stood as monuments to the barbarian attack twelve yarles ago, mortar crumbling from the roofless walls and weeds growing up from dirt floors. A giggle of children with arms and legs covered in dirt chased each other through the ruins, dodging among refuse piles and scaring rats as they went. Those walking the street bowed their heads, rushing to or from whatever business they had. Nobody lingered to talk with a neighbour or play a game of chasey with a child. A corner food store had been gutted, its empty shell a reminder of the poverty inflicted on the Southern Vale after their defeat by the barbarians.

Following Tormil, Hanni bowed her head, avoiding eye contact with passers-by, especially the soldiers in black armour, Hunger's Shield. Tormil had dealt with the guard at the south gate, but she worried their luck would soon abandon them. They turned into a crowded street, people jostling and pushing against each other, fighting for the space to move. Hanni became jammed up against Tormil. Dwarrow moaned from inside the pack, and Hanni bit her tongue, wanting to tell him to be quiet. The crowd's momentum funnelled them through an alley no wider than two people. Even with her head above the mob, the stifling air suffocated Hanni. A beating harvest season sun split the gap between the three-storey buildings that faced each other across the alleyway, stinging Hanni's bald head and joining with the sweat of the crowd to make it hotter.

Respite came when the throng spewed into Laodicea's central market. Rows and rows of canvas pavilions stretched as far as Hanni could see, thoroughfares snaking through them like wrinkles on an old woman's face. Smoke rose from cooking tents, the aroma of roasted meat fighting against the odour of heaving bodies. Fabrics in all the rainbow colours had been draped over trestle tables next to sacks of grain, wire cages with birds and rodents, rusty tools, smoked fish, swords and knives, and baskets of fruit and vegetables. All appeared as a regular, bustling market, but Hanni sensed an unease. The joyful hustle of spruikers had been replaced by a tense murmur. The tables of many stalls were sparsely adorned or sat empty. The market wasn't brimming as Hanni imagined it to be once upon a time. A blackness had descended on Laodicea in more ways than one. A repression quashing the enthusiasm of the most optimistic merchants.

The rebels in the Desolate Mountains had heard of Laodicea's punishing famine that plagued the city for many yarles. Some travellers claimed Hunger kept most of the food for himself and his soldiers. Hanni believed it after seeing the bounty stored in the Master's Hall of the King's Quarter during the rebels' raid.

Tormil led her deeper into the market, searching for the quickest path to the Docklands and the wharves lining Traders Bay, where merchant ships from across the Veiled Occyan and beyond dropped anchor. Hanni hoped to find a boat to take her and Dwarrow to Giigal. After the raid on Rostard's wagon, she expected they had enough coin to convince the greediest of seafarers to give them passage.

Within the market, they came upon a statue of an old man dressed in hooded robes, a rolled parchment in one hand and a sword in the other. On the sculpture's steps sat beggars; men, women and children with desperate eyes, holding wooden cups or empty hats towards passers-by. Hanni stopped at the statue to read the plaque at the bottom — *Malphas, The Worshipful Master.*

The pause quickly became a mistake. Children swamped her and Tormil, pulling at the hem of Hanni's tunic, scratching her bare legs or stamping her toes.

"Spare some food," croaked one.

"Water, please," said another.

Tormil pushed them away. "We've nothing for you. Go home."

"Ain't got no home," said a boy no older than six harvest seasons with the curse of poverty dulling his eyes.

Around the centre square, peasants drew pictures with grey charcoal on scraps of parchment showing bountiful fields, magnificent castles, fleets of ships, or joyful markets. Others sang songs of ancient times or played harps, lutes or crumhorns, stopping only to touch their forehead when a market-goer dropped a coin or portion of food into their upturned hats, then squirrelling it away before the beggar horde arrived. Hanni's mind drifted with the music, almost forgetting Laodicea's destitution until the singers fell silent, the musicians stopped playing, and the beggars disappeared like mist evaporated by the sun. Merchants and their customers stood in awkward silence, stiff and cold like the stone statue of Malphas watching over them.

The clang of metal on rock broke the tension as the sabatons of black soldiers smacked the cobblestones. Hunger's Shield marched into the market, then lined up along a row of stalls, clashing their halberd blades against the red, two-headed snake embossed on their black breastplates.

"Hail, Vater Hunger!" they yelled in unison.

Hanni froze. The black grell approached.

Memories of the rebels' raid on the Master's Hall made her hands quiver. Hunger didn't appear to recognise her then, but she wore a mask. Now, the nakedness of her facial crest threatened to expose her. The black grell would recall trapping Grin and Hanni in Lokan. He'd remember the female grell with gama tattooed on her face. The female grell who escaped his clutches. Hanni expected tainted grells never forgot their failures.

Flanked by six more soldiers, Hunger lumbered down a thoroughfare straight towards her. His bare black chest swallowed the sunlight, and his black eyes blended into his face such that she couldn't tell where he looked.

"We must hide," hissed Hanni to Tormil.

He nodded and pulled her into a stall selling wicker baskets the size of wine barrels. They crouched behind a stack of baskets, the stallholder too transfixed by Hunger's arrival to notice them. The black grell marched past Hanni, then stopped at the next stall.

A Shield stepped forward and addressed the merchant, "Vater Hunger requires all the food you have."

The stallholder nodded. "Of course. Welcome to oblige."

He packed two wooden crates with dried meat, smoked fish, and jars of pickled vegetables, chattering the entire time. "It's not much, I know, but times are hard. I'm pleased I can supply Vater Hunger with this fine fare. You won't get any better in Laodicea. Give me a few days, and I can find more." He loaded the crates onto the front table. "Since it's for the master, I'll do a special deal on the whole lot. Twenty-four coin...."

"Hunger will pay you nothing," said the soldier.

"I got children to feed...," blurted the stallholder before closing his mouth.

Hunger placed his hand on the soldier's pauldron and pulled him back before stepping up to the table, his bald, black head brushing against the underside of the canvas overhang.

"What is your name?" asked Hunger, his raspy voice rebounding off the cobblestones.

The stallholder shrunk away, his face afflicted with the stupidity of his mistake. "Kenelm, Vater Hunger."

"How many children do you have?" asked the black grell, running a thick finger over the tabletop as if wiping dust from the surface.

"T-t-three," said Kenelm. "They beg for coin on the docks."

Hunger sneered. "Beggars and thieves. This city is riddled with them. Where is your home?"

Kenelm's eyes dulled with dread. "In...in the Southern Vale."

"There is no Southern Vale anymore. There is only Laodicea. One city united under my rule. And my Shield know every house on every street."

"Lebbil St, Vater Hunger," said a soldier. "House number seven."

"Seven, Lebbil St. What might await your children when they return home?" Hunger nodded to the soldier who took the crates from the table.

"Please, Vater," said Kenelm. "They're innocent. I can find more supplies for you. Food, clothing, whatever you need."

"And you will," said Hunger. "Now, you should go home and wait for your children. They will welcome your embrace."

"Yes, Vater. Thank you." Kenelm bowed and backed away.

Hunger turned and stepped towards the stall with the wicker baskets where Hanni and Tormil hid. Behind them, the stallholder whimpered like a beaten dog. Hanni yanked the rope's loose end from Tormil's grip, plunged her teeth into the knot and untied her hands. Both of them tensed, preparing to run.

Hunger collected a basket, squeezing it between his hands. The willow strands buckled and cracked until the basket collapsed into a pile of twigs and fell to the ground.

"Poor workmanship," muttered Hunger.

He wavered on unsteady legs, resembling a shard of night sky that had swallowed the stars. For one horrible moment, Hanni thought he looked right at her. She braced her hands on the cobblestones, ready to spring up and sprint to the docks. But the black grell turned away, leading his Shield back along the thoroughfare.

The crowd's relief washed over Hanni with such force she almost burst into tears. The pluck of a harp string drifted on the sea breeze, signalling the danger had passed.

"We need to get to the wharves," said Tormil.

They left the markets and marched to the Docklands, stopping briefly for a drink of water. Hanni leaned against the wall of an old warehouse, leaden smoke billowing from its chimney, and cleaned the soot from a broken window. Inside, dozens of elderly people, naked and shivering, stumbled in a line towards an arched doorway. They passed piles of clothes and shoes, utensils and blankets, stacked until almost touching the warehouse roof. Grell slaves foraged through the pilfered items, sorting and packing them in crates.

Hanni's jaw clenched at the sight of withered bodies so famished even their bones looked thin. Hands covering their genitals, the living skeletons shuffled towards the doorway, urged on by the thrust of halberds from Hunger's Shield. As the door opened, Hanni shaded her eyes from the assault of a roaring fire at the room's far end. A soldier pushed a handful of people through the door, and it slammed shut behind them.

Muffled screams wafted from the chimney pots as they vomited smoke. Hanni dragged her finger across the dirty window and smeared soot on her cheeks, a reminder that she bore witness to this awful calamity, then turned her back and trudged along the street after Tormil.

The wharves bordering Traders Bay were more crowded than the markets. Hundreds of beggars lined the jetties, shaking empty wooden cups in front of merchant seafarers or their passengers. The stench of poverty overpowered the ocean freshness, a fetid smothering of gaunt bodies desperate for sustenance and cleansing. The beggar-children reappeared and had multiplied, crowding around Tormil and Hanni, hands out, pleading for coin.

The din became smothering, weakening Tormil's resolve. He placed a coin in a wooden cup and was swamped by a maul of children desperate for more. They tugged at his clothes and pinched his skin. Wrapped themselves around Hanni's legs until she couldn't move. The travelling companions became stuck, surrounded by a baying crowd.

Inside Hanni's pack, Dwarrow wriggled and blustered, then loosened the drawstring and popped his head from the top.

"*Arrrgh!*" Dwarrow screamed. "I want to eat children! *Delicious, scrumptious* CHILDREN. Chop their bones and suck the marrow. Roast them, boil them, fry them in a pan. Let me at them!"

The children wailed at the sight of a two-headed stone-grell, then scattered across the wharf like rats from a fire.

"My talents are wasted inside this bag," said Dwarrow. "Completely wasted."

"How are we going to find a ship to take us to Giigal?" asked Hanni.

"Haven't you worked that out yet?" asked Dwarrow. "What have you two been doing while I've been cooped up?"

"We'll find a ship," said Tormil. "Just need a captain who's sailing south. I have enough coin to convince any seafarer to take passengers."

Hanni forced Dwarrow back inside the pack as they wandered around the docks. At least two dozen vessels were anchored in the bay, but Tormil had no luck finding a ship's captain willing to travel south. Wandering behind Tormil, Hanni passed a trading table selling bone daggers. She approached the trader, a woman with fiery red hair.

"Where did you get these daggers?" asked Hanni.

"Y'got an eye for quality," said the freckled-faced woman. "These daggers are very rare. Made by the weald-grells of Giigal. Right at the bottom of Enthilen."

Hanni picked up a dagger and turned it over in her hands. "I recognise the design."

"Each one's different. Y'got a gumpy fish there, carved into the blade. I think...yes, I got a spear fern too, like on y'face." The woman handed another dagger to Hanni. "I can sell that one for twelve coin. Or twenty-two coin for both. Don't see many grells 'round here with painted faces anymore. You a wild grell?"

Hanni ignored the question and asked one of her own, "Have you been to Giigal?"

"Went last harvest season. No other merchant ship goes there, only us. Y'won't find these daggers anywhere else. Top quality they are. Since you're a grell, I'll sell y'both for twenty coin."

Tormil stood beside Hanni. "Would you like to make a lot more coin than that?" he asked the woman.

Mischievous eyes set into a plump face inspected Tormil from head to toe. "To be honest, I doubt y'got the twenty coin for the daggers. You ain't spent any money on clothes. No offence or nothin'."

"You shouldn't judge a person by their clothes," said Tormil.

"Yeah, yeah. I know. My Da used to say that. Rest his soul."

"What's the name of your ship?" asked Tormil.

"The *Grimart*. We've got the fastest whales in all the seven oceans and five seas."

"We are seeking passage to Giigal," said Hanni.

"*Hmmm*. Not sure if we're goin' there anytime soon. My Cap'n wants to head home to Nordland."

"Can we speak to your captain?" asked Tormil.

"Sure. He's comin' up the wharf now."

Tormil and Hanni turned as a wiry man with a hunched back scuttled up the salted timbers like a crab over rippled sand. His physical impairment did nothing to slow his speed.

"Y'sold anythin' yet, Melinda?" asked the hunchback. "Them bone daggers ain't gonna sell themselves."

Melinda rolled her eyes. "I'm tryin'. These two were thinkin' about it until...."

"Until what?"

"Are you the *Grimart's* captain?"

"Who's askin'?"

"My name's Tormil."

"You lookin' to sell that slave?"

"He ain't a slave," said Melinda. "Leastways, I don't reckon he is. He ain't actin' like one, and look at the tattoo on his face." She swept her eyes over Hanni's torso. "I don't reckon you're a *he*, neither. You're a female wild stone-grell, ain't ya?"

Tormil scanned the wharf, his face twisted with dread. "Keep your voice down. We don't want to attract unwanted attention."

"Too late for that," said Melinda. "Y'grell friend stands out like the pecker on a horny tufted goliath."

The disguise has been revealed, thought Hanni. *No point pretending any longer.*

She crouched and reached for Melinda, placing the tips of her fingers on Melinda's cheeks. Melinda did the same, obviously familiar with the grell formal greeting.

"I am Hannian stone-grell. First born...." She caught herself. This would be the first time she would say it. *First born.* Tom Anderson told her Grin was dead. She never accepted it before, always introducing herself as second born. Not anymore. "First born of Frennan and Mirrian. Protector of Enthilen."

"I'm Melinda Firebrace. First and only born of Jameus and Lenora Firebrace. Skullard and whale-master to Captain Whibly of the *Grimart*."

Hanni removed her fingers from Melinda's cheeks and faced Whibly.

He waved her away. "Don't need no clammy grell hands messin' up me nice complexion." Whibly rubbed his chin. "A wild stone-grell. A *female* wild stone-grell. That's a rare sight. Most grells I know fight for the Erstürmen. Rephaim, they call 'em."

"Those fighting for the Erstürmen are vermin," said Hanni.

Whibly cast his eyes over his hunched shoulder. "Don't go sayin' that 'round here. 'Round anywhere."

"We wish to travel to Giigal," said Hanni. "Your skullard...."

"And whale-master," interrupted Melinda.

"Your skullard and whale-master told us you trade with the weald-grells."

"Yeah, but I ain't goin' there again in a hurry," said Whibly. "They shafted me; they did. Not worth the effort."

"We can make it worth your effort," said Tormil.

"Ya can't afford passage south. Stop wastin' me time."

Tormil waited for a group of seafarers to walk past, then pulled Whibly close. "What if I offered you six thousand coin? All in silver tausens with King Adalwolf's image. Three thousand now and three thousand when you return to Laodicea after taking my companions to the weald-grell city."

Whibly scoffed. "No way y'got coin like that. People ain't got those kinds of riches anymore."

Tormil placed his hand on Whibly's shoulder and lowered his voice, "You could be missing out on a big opportunity. It doesn't look like you're selling many of your wares. People are poor like you said. They can't afford nice daggers like these. Most Laodiceans spend their days begging on the street."

Whibly's eyes narrowed. "Where'd y'get so much coin? Ya ain't royalty or nothin'. Y'sound like a Dobunni. They're almost as rare as wild stone-grells."

"Never mind where we got it. My final offer is eight thousand coin."

Whibly's narrow eyes sprang open. Wide. Hanni smiled to herself as the workings of Whibly's mind danced across his twitching face. He ran his fingers over a thin, drooping moustache that tangled up into a platted beard on his chin. His eyes flicked across the faces of passers-by, seemingly undecided if this offer was genuine or if he'd stumbled on an elaborate con he'd yet to decipher.

"Twelve thousand," said Whibly. "Not a coin less."

Tormil shook his head. "Nine thousand."

Hanni waited, the tension of the barter setting her nerves on edge.

"Eleven thousand," said Whibly. "If the coins' got Adalwolf's image, then they ain't legal tender. I can only use 'em on the black market, and I need recompense for takin' the risk."

Tormil stood tall and swelled his chest. "Ten thousand coin. That *is* my final offer. Five thousand now, five thousand when you return to Laodicea."

Whibly lingered over the bone daggers, wood carvings, bags of spices and other wares lined in rows across the trading table. It appeared they hadn't sold a single thing.

Ten thousand coin. An enormous amount of wealth for most people, thought Hanni. Thank goodness they ambushed Rostard's wagon.

"Show me," said Whibly.

Tormil looked up and down the wharf. Melinda stepped from behind the table and joined Hanni to form a protective circle around the negotiators. The cunning old soldier took a pouch from his tunic and untied the drawstring. Whibly glanced inside, and his mouth fell open so wide his tongue lolled from the corner.

Tormil withdrew a single coin. "A silver tausen with King Adalwolf's head. Very, very rare. Worth one thousand regular coins. I have ten of them for you."

Whibly reached his crooked fingers towards the tausen, but Tormil snatched it away, plopped it into the pouch, drew the string tight and balanced the bag in the palm of his hand as if measuring the treasure's weight.

Whibly rubbed his hunched shoulder. "It's a big risk, and I'm supposed to be goin' home. Up north...."

A muffled squawk came from Hanni's pack. Dwarrow had become restless again.

"Hey, the bag's talkin'," said Melinda.

Dwarrow groaned and popped his head out. "I can't take one more moment in this infernal bag. I'm suffocating."

Damn bumptious mouldewerp, thought Hanni. She unshouldered her pack and lowered it to the ground. Dwarrow climbed out in a huff.

Melinda's eyes widened. "What in Marduk's name...is that a talkin'...."

"Don't say it," said Dwarrow. "Do *not* say it."

"It's a mouldewerp," said Whibly. "I seen one of them before."

"Y'sure it ain't a puppet?" asked Melinda. "Where are the strings?" She walked around Dwarrow, poking at his fur.

Dwarrow swatted her away.

"If there's three passengers, I'll need more coin," said Whibly.

"Only two," said Tormil. "You'll take Hanni and Dwarrow, the werp, to Giigal."

"Are they comin' back?" asked Whibly.

"Hanni will accompany you on the return journey," said Dwarrow.

"What?" asked Hanni. "We have not discussed this."

"It's the most logical thing to do. After I convince the weald-grells to join our cause, I'll need to travel into the southern Dambay Plains. The fastest route is over land. You return to Laodicea with our seafaring friends to report on my success to the rebels. Whibly and Melinda collect the reaming coin. Deal done."

Hanni wanted to argue with her tiny companion, but words failed her.

Whibly faced Tormil. "How will I find ya again?"

"Being a seafarer, I imagine you spend a good deal of time in the *Whale and Anchor* in the Docklands," said Tormil.

Melinda laughed. "Not half. I gotta drag him from there all the time."

"Keep ya tongue," said Whibly, "or I'm gettin' another skullard."

"Y'won't. I'm the best there is."

"On the last day of the harvest season, I'll be waiting for you in the *Whale and Anchor*," said Tormil. "At sunset. That should give you enough time to travel to Giigal and back. I'll exchange the remaining coin for Hanni, delivered safe and well."

Whibly frowned. "How do I know yu'll keep y'word?"

"How do I know you'll keep yours? You might take the five thousand coin and drop my friends in the ocean."

"Cap'n Whibly's an honest man," said Melinda. "He'll keep his word."

"And I'll keep mine," said Tormil. "I know trust is rarer than a white whale, but I offer it to you now. My trust traded for yours."

Whibly nodded his head. "Alright, y'have a deal. Lucky for you, me ship's all stored up for the trip to Nordland. Enough supplies to get us to Giigal."

Tormil gave Whibly the coin and said goodbye to Hanni and Dwarrow. As the old veteran weaved back through the crowd, Hanni expected Whibly to flee. Take the riches, scuttle down the jetty, and onto his ship, disappearing across the ocean. But he stayed, helping Melinda to pack up the trading table — a length of flat timber resting across two empty crates.

After tossing the bone daggers and other wares into the crates, Whibly faced Hanni. "Can y'carry the timber?"

She nodded and gathered the tabletop, as long as she was tall.

Hanni, Dwarrow, Whibly and Melinda walked along the jetty, approaching a ship with the face of a bearded man carved into the front.

"Marduk," said Whibly, pointing to the carving. "God of the ocean. Took me ten yarles to pay off this ship."

Inching across a plank, trying not to look at the ocean depths below her, Hanni made it onto the *Grimart's* deck, followed closely by Dwarrow. Around them, crew members stopped their chores and stared at the new arrivals.

"Listen up," said Whibly to the crew. "There's been a change of plans. We ain't goin' to Nordland. We got passengers to deliver to Giigal."

The crews' faces turned sour, and their shoulders slumped.

"No point gettin' all sulky 'bout it," said Whibly. "If we get this job done, I'm doublin' everyone's wages. Soon as we get back to Laodicea, yu'll be bathin' in riches."

A few of the sour faces smiled.

"Y'been on a ship before?" Melinda asked Hanni.

She shook her head. "No. Stone-grells are not fond of water."

"Well, y'gonna have to get used to it. A lot of ocean between here and Giigal. We got eight fast whales, though. No other ship'll get y'there quicker. I drive the whales, not hard enough, accordin' to Cap'n Whibly. Whale-masters are usually big, hulkin' men ya wouldn't want to meet on a dark night. I loves me whales like children, guidin' them through the water usin' deft touches with the harness. It's more effective than a yank on a rope from a clumsy brute of a man. We circumnavigate Ostamp each yarle. My Da would never believe how much travellin' we do, rest his soul."

Melinda trotted up to a platform attached to the front of the ship and adjusted a harness. She kept talking, and Hanni wondered if she ever stopped.

"We had a grell called Annian," said Melinda over her shoulder. "Yarles ago. She was a weald-grell. Not a slave or nothin'. Our housekeeper — me and Da."

At the ship's rear, Whibly stepped onto a crate and rubbed a cloth over a spoked wheel Hanni assumed steered the vessel.

Atop the makeshift platform, he yelled across the deck, "Ulver! Untie the ropes."

A young man, Ulver, leapt from the deck's edge across the watery gap, landing like a cat on the jetty's salty timbers. He untied the ropes from around metal cleats securing the *Grimart* to the wharf.

This is it, Hanni thought. I am returning to Giigal.

Dwarrow swayed beside her on the rocking deck, the mouldewerp having fallen unusually quiet.

"Can you swim, Dwarrow?" asked Hanni

"Yes, yes, yes," said Dwarrow. "I swim like an otter. But I'm not fond of all this moving under my feet. I'm feeling quite ill. Quite ill, indeed."

"Fairly certain it will only get worse," said Hanni.

"*Hmph.*"

As the men and women of the crew prepared the *Grimart* for departure, Hanni retreated into her mind, discovering a long-forgotten memory of a story Grin had told her during the garrabari twelve yarles ago. The recollection made her chest burn with a desire for retribution.

She marched up to Whibly. "Were you the skullard of the *Vulking*?"

A pale dread froze Whibly's eyes. "Why'd ya ask?"

"My brother and his friends travelled on that ship. They met a skullard called Whibly. Then bad things, terrible things happened." She stepped closer, looming over the crippled man to cast a threatening shadow across his face.

"Grin," said Whibly with a tremor in his voice. "I remember. Grin, Thaly and Tom."

"Yes," said Hanni. "Grin and Thaly were...."

Whibly shook the dread from his eyes. "Please, I want to forget that voyage."

"Grin could never forget it. The memory imprisoned him until the end."

"Is he...."

"Yes, he passed away in a distant place."

"I'm sorry to hear it. Truly, I am." A sliver of tears pooled at the bottom of Whibly's eyes, and Hanni pulled her threatening shadow away.

"What about Thaly and Tom?" asked Whibly.

"Thaly travelled to Germalia. Tom Anderson goes there now."

"I helped Grin and Thaly in the end. Got them safely to shore after the shipwreck."

"Grin told me you wanted to redeem yourself," said Hanni. "Consider this journey the final part of that redemption."

Whibly nodded. "I'll see ya safely to Giigal. In Grin's memory."

Hanni returned to Dwarrow's side. "Will we succeed, Dwarrow? Will we convince the weald-grells to fight Malphas?"

Dwarrow pulled his walking stick from the side of Hanni's pack and tapped his nose with the tip. "Oh, most definitely. I've planned a surprise for the weald-grells. A secret to sway their judgement in our favour. You wait and see."

~ Chapter 25 ~

Rosalie breathed the dust particles suspended in the hot afternoon sun and shifted her weight in the saddle as she sauntered her mount, Storvil, west along the lower slopes of the Desolate Mountains. Quenan led the group, the pack horse walking beside her, and Raf brought up the rear. Tom rode beside Rosalie, looking ungainly in the saddle. For five days, she'd guided the group from their hideout and through Lokan. Keeping to the foothills to avoid travellers on the road, the horses had staggered among shifting stones, slowing progress. They'd passed the track to Detranté and planned to cross the River Lousse at a ford before reaching The Feign. Then they would head south, crossing the main road between Sardis and Laodicea before attempting to sneak past Sardis without being spotted. Rosalie wanted to keep close to the Scaur Hills during that leg of the journey, the rocky slopes offering cover from unwanted eyes. Then, they'd navigate down the switchbacks cut into the Riverlands Escarpment at Rārian Falls. Erstürmen soldiers guarded the escarpment, top and bottom. The rebels hadn't discussed how to deal with the soldiers.

During the journey, Rosalie's demeanour changed from despondence to hope. From surrender to defiance. From aversion to desire. Only days ago, she'd considered leaving Enthilen and fleeing to Nordland to build a better life in the cold north. But Tom Anderson's arrival changed everything. The rebels had a vital mission: travel to Portum and convince the Germalians to march their army east and attack Malphas. As part of Tom's escort, Rosalie steeled herself to protect him with her life. He carried the eyes of lost souls. The key, it seemed, to destroying the throne of the dead and persuading the Germalians to confront Malphas. Yet, her feelings transcended guard duty. A longing fermented in her heart. A yearning to forge a closer bond with Tom, more than her childish crush on

Harris Snape or the animal lust she shared with Raf. Something deeper called to her.

Rosalie moved Storvil close to Tom's mount, Juniper, a small, dapple-grey mare. She tipped her head at the sword hanging from his belt. The one she'd given him from the rebel armoury. "Do you know how to use that?" she asked.

"I'm out of practice," said Tom, "but a skilled swordsman, swords*person*, trained me. I hope I can remember it."

Rosalie smiled. "I hope you can, too. I'm not much for fighting, and we'll need all our skills to foil the red soldiers atop the escarpment."

"Red soldiers?"

"From Sardis. They wear red armour in honour of their commander, Krieg. Malphas' servants have mastered the colouring of metal. Something I failed to do."

"How long have you worked with metal?"

"Since I could hold a hammer. My father was...*is* a smithy. We made swords, armour, jewellery, utensils. Anything metal. He even made a necklace for Princess Genevea once. She's King Ewald's sister."

"That tattoo on your arm...."

Rosalie held the inside of her right forearm towards Tom. "It's a branding scar. Sword crossed with a hammer."

"Fifth circle of Sardis," said Tom.

Rosalie laughed. "You know your Erstürmen culture."

"Were there many female metalsmiths?"

"As far as I know, I was the only one. When I reached eighteen harvest seasons, my parents told me smithing wasn't for women, and I must find a husband."

"You should be able to do anything you want."

"Erstürmen women never had such a luxury of choice. Now, I do whatever I need to survive. Only the lucky ones get a choice."

"You've chosen to help me."

Rosalie faced Tom. "Help you or turn my back on this world. Not much choice."

Tom went silent.

The hurt on his boyish face made Rosalie calm her voice. "I know this is our best hope. We had none before." She turned back to the western horizon. "You will be missed."

"By who?"

"Your family. Back where you come from."

"There's only my mother."

"What's it like? This faraway homeland of yours."

"The same and different. Swords and armour, and everyone riding horses, we did all that once long ago. But things moved on. Our society evolved."

"For the better?"

"Yes and no. Each generation thinks the time they came of age was the best, but that isn't true. There never was and never will be a perfect time. Some things get better, and other things worse. We'll always face challenges. Always have to fight for what's right."

"I often wonder who decides right and wrong."

"Those in power. When we end Malphas' reign, we can decide what's right."

Rosalie smiled at the idea, never believing she would have the power to decide right from wrong. "Is Enthilen as you remember it?"

Tom shook his head. "Babir Birramal is almost burned to the ground. Wild stone-grells gone. Travelling to Lokan, Dwarrow and I saw many abandoned farms and villages. Fields overgrown with weeds. Where are all the people?"

"Enthilen's lifeblood has been sucked into the vortex of Pergamos."

"Malphas is making the rest of Enthilen such a horrid place; the dream of his paradise becomes even more alluring."

"The Erstürmen have always longed for paradise, unsatisfied with their world. Malphas' power comes from his promise to lead the people to a better place."

"There *is* no better place," said Tom. "Paradise is here and now if you want it to be."

Raf rode his horse up to Rosalie and Tom. As Rosalie's interest in Tom grew, her desire to avoid Raf grew with it. She'd managed to keep him at bay during the trip, but he pressed harder with each passing moon. She didn't want his attention anymore. His lust. But she struggled to find the courage to end it, worrying about how he would respond.

Raf ogled her from head to toe, then smiled his salacious smile. "I been thinkin'," he said. "What if these Germalian women don't want to fight? Whatta we do then?"

Rosalie smirked to herself. "I don't know about you boys, but I'm staying in Portum. Women rule the world over there. It must be better than this place."

"I doubt it," said Raf. "Stupid idea havin' an army full of women."

What would you know? thought Rosalie.

Quenan jogged up to the three riders, the pack horse trotting behind her. "The path ahead is blocked by a landslide. We cannot reach the ford that crosses the River Louse. Instead, we will have to travel south, crossing the main road and then the river. I know a place where the water is shallow. We can wade across there."

"Shallow for a grell or a regular person?" asked Raf.

"A short rebel like you can cross without drowning," said Quenan.

"Aren't grells afraid of water?" asked Tom.

"Stone-grells, yes. Giigal is surrounded by water, and the weald-grell residents have overcome their fear. Some can even swim, though it is not a pastime I indulge in."

"What about the bridge?" asked Raf.

"It'll be guarded," said Rosalie. "We can't risk crossing there."

Quenan pulled on the reins of the pack horse. "Follow me to the road."

She led Rosalie, Tom and Raf down the slopes and into a sparsely wooded landscape with thin grey soil covering fields of rocks. The group walked their horses carefully, trying to avoid an errant hoof fall leading to an injury. By sunset, they reached the main road between Sardis and Laodicea and dashed across, south into the Dambay Plains. Turning west again, they came to the River Lousse.

Clouds drifted in from the north as the group camped on the riverbank, deciding to cross in the morning. They slept together under a canvas tarp, Rosalie lying awake most of the night listening to the *thud, thud, thud* of driving rain.

By dawn, the rain eased, but the river had swollen, lapping at the campsite.

Rosalie stood on the riverbank, hands on hips. "We can't cross now. The current is too strong."

"We have to," said Tom. "We don't have time to waste."

"Should have tried the bridge after all," said Raf. "Quenan and me could have killed the guards easy enough."

"We can't risk Tom getting injured or worse," said Rosalie.

Raf faced Tom. "Why's it only you who can destroy this damn throne? Why can't someone else do it?"

"It's written in the First Scripture," said Tom.

"The what?"

"Volerdie's own words," said Rosalie. "Written in blood."

"Now we're trustin' this stupid Erstürmen God?" snarled Raf. "How'd I get hooked up with a bunch of fools."

Rosalie didn't want to think it, but she did. Raf might drown in the river.

"I can walk across," said Quenan. "The river will not be too deep for a grell."

"What about the rest of us?" asked Rosalie.

"Do we have a rope long enough to span the river?" asked Tom.

"Yes," said Rosalie. "On the pack horse."

"We could tie one end to a tree on this bank, and Quenan could carry the rope across and tie the other end to that tree over there." Tom pointed across the bank to a gnarled old bullom tree dipping its roots into the swell. "Then we pull ourselves across. The last one to leave this side can tie the rope around their waist."

"And the horses?" asked Rosalie.

"I will lead them across," said Quenan. "Tied together."

"Alright. We have to try."

The group decamped. Rosalie gathered the horses and tied them in a train, one following the other. Raf took the rope from a saddle bag and tied one end to a tree. Quenan tied the loose end around her waist so the others could pull her in should she get in trouble. The weald-grell nodded to her companions and stepped into the river, her calves parting the rushing water like stoic trees refusing to yield to the current. She grasped Storvil's reins, the lead horse tossing his head and snorting in protest at what lay before him.

"*Yindyanga yanha*," said Quenan in Grellian, and Storvil calmed.

The grell and horses waded into the river. The current yanked Quenan sideways, and she almost fell. The horses whinnied, wild eyes flashing from heads washed with the churning flow. Debris clattered into Storvil's flank. Quenan flexed her shoulder muscles, trying to keep the horses together and standing upright. A floating log crashed into the rear of the horse train, snapping a rope. The pack horse trumpeted in horror as the current knocked it off its feet. The beast swam against the flow, trying to return to its companions, but the current dragged it underwater.

"Shit," spat Raf. "There goes our food."

Rosalie slapped her thigh, irate and powerless as the current swept the pack horse downriver; food, ropes and spare clothes surrendered to the chop. Raf's idea of tackling the guards at the bridge didn't seem so stupid now.

Quenan held fast to the three remaining horses and pushed towards the opposite bank lest the river claim another victim. Reaching the other side, she dragged herself up to the bullom tree, tied the rope around its trunk, then secured the horses.

"Who's going next?" asked Tom.

"You," said Raf. "I can't swim."

Tom looked at Rosalie.

She nodded, agreeing with Raf. "I'm not confident in water, either. Best you go first, Tom. If the river takes us, you and Quenan can push on to Germalia."

Tom frowned and clutched the taut rope. After a few steps into the rushing water, the river lapped at his waist, then his chest. Tom's vulnerability exposed, panic swamped Rosalie like churning rapids.

Did he secure the dark eyes? she wondered. Can he swim? What if he drowns?

She considered pulling Tom back and finding a safer crossing.

Tom staggered to the middle of the river and stopped there, shivering, his thinning hair drenched. Water lapped at his chin, and he clutched the rope with fearful desperation. Rosalie could almost hear his teeth chattering with cold or dread. She pictured him giving up. Releasing the rope and floating down the river, carrying all her hopes with him. But he steeled himself and pushed forward.

Past the halfway point, Quenan strode back into the water and helped Tom ashore.

Thank Volerdie's mercy, thought Rosalie.

"I'll go next," said Raf, not waiting to discuss the issue with Rosalie.

The thought of Raf drowning in the river came to her again. She tried to convince herself the mission would be better off without the Dobunni rebel. She and Quenan could protect Tom. But Raf was strong and determined. He fought the current like he fought the enemy, wild-eyed and unyielding.

Brushing Quenan's help aside, he stumbled onto the opposite riverbank and faced Rosalie as if to confront her deceit. She turned away, untied the rope from the tree and secured it tightly around her waist. Quenan took up the slack to help pull her across.

Rosalie faced the river. She could swim, but not well. She'd taught herself in the calm pool underneath the bridge crossing the Anchep River at Sardis. However, the River Lousse wasn't still. Its current had already claimed one victim, and the river looked hungry for more.

Rosalie took a deep breath and stepped into the water. It spilled into her boots, soaking woollen socks. Her foot slipped on a rock, and she almost fell before she'd begun crossing. The biting cold water, straight from the peaks of the Desolate Mountains, set an ache in her calves.

Trembling with chill apprehension, she dug her boots into the riverbed and focused on putting one hand in front of the other along the rope as if scaling a cliff. Quenan kept the rope taut, helping Rosalie to navigate the strengthening flow.

In the middle of the river, the current yanked Rosalie's legs out from under her, dragging her below the surface. Surrounded by water, suspended in airless terror, she released the rope and succumbed to the whims of the foaming monster as it swept her downstream. But the rope tensed as someone dragged her towards the opposite bank like a fish on a hook. Rosalie's head bobbed above the surface.

"Pull faster!" yelled Tom.

Rosalie gasped for air a moment before being submerged again. Whitewash bubbled around her, dulling other sounds and sights. Her arms flailed, searching for the rope slipping from her waist. Her feet kicked into the sand, trying to get a foothold to force her head above water and appease lungs screaming for another breath.

As drowning thoughts overwhelmed her, a shaft of sunlight illuminated a path to the surface. Then an arm wrapped around her back and heaved, hoisting her above the wash. Rosalie broke the surface, expecting to see Quenan come to save her. Or even Raf, unwilling to relinquish the opportunity for another lust-filled night. But it was neither. Instead, the thin, balding man with the kind smile, the birraman from a strange world, lifted her to his chest with strength belying his slight frame. Rosalie dug her heels into the riverbed, steadying herself. Tom twisted a loop in the slack rope and thrust a free arm through it before grabbing Rosalie again.

On the riverbank, Quenan and Raf heaved, dragging Tom and Rosalie to shore. Rosalie collapsed on her back, coughing.

Tom rolled her onto her side and brushed wet hair from her face. "Breathe through your nose."

"You saved...my life," she sputtered.

"Don't try to talk. Focus on breathing."

Rosalie's chest heaved as water and mucus dribbled from her mouth and nostrils.

"That...that was a...*cough*...stupid thing to do," she said to Tom.

"Breathe," he said before flashing a beaming smile with sparkling, satin-grey eyes. "If you're worried about people doing stupid things, you're with the wrong person."

Rosalie laughed, coughed and gasped for breath at the same time.

"I will look for the pack horse," said Quenan, running off along the riverbank.

Rosalie sat up, resting her back against the bullom tree. Tom sat beside her while Raf paced up and down the riverbank. She reached for Tom and clasped his hand. She'd underestimated this man's fortitude, and certainty grew inside her. Tom *would* destroy the throne of the dead and defeat Malphas. Once again, Enthilen would be the land she loved.

But, wondered Rosalie, would Tom be there to share it, or would he return home to his own world?

By mid-morning, Quenan returned to the group empty-handed. "The pack horse and our supplies have gone."

Raf spun around and growled, "It makes an impossible journey even harder."

Rosalie stood. "We must keep going."

Tom gathered the remaining three horses and climbed into Juniper's saddle.

Raf approached Tom and tapped him on the leg. "You might be needin' this," he said, holding a pouch aloft.

Rosalie recognised it as the one Tom had tied to his belt. The pouch containing the eyes of lost souls. Raf dangled the pouch in front of Tom, flashing the same lecherous grin he gave Rosalie when he wanted her sex.

"Must've fallen off when you came out the water," said Raf. "Can't be losin' these. Otherwise, there's no point to it all, is there?"

Tom reached down to grasp the pouch.

Raf pulled it away, laughed, then tossed the pouch into Tom's lap.

*   *   *   *

After the river crossing, the group travelled west towards the Scaur Hills, chasing the setting sun. Tom slumped in the saddle as Juniper plodded over grassy plains. It appeared exhaustion had caught up with everyone, including the horses, this part of the journey marked by silence. They camped on the Dambay Plains at sunset, in the open for the first time since leaving the rebel hideout. Quenan and Raf went to hunt game, leaving Tom and Rosalie alone. Rosalie drove pegs into the ground and tethered the horses while Tom unstrapped the bedroll from his saddle, laid it on the ground and unfurled the sodden blankets. He plonked beside the bed, his thoughts wandering where his legs couldn't.

South lay Pergamos. Malphas' stronghold. The city called to Tom like a siren of the sea. *Does Malphas know I'm here? If he discovered I wanted to smash Volerdie's throne, he'd hunt me to the end of the world. To the end of both our worlds.*

Rosalie sat beside Tom. "We have nothing to make a fire. The pack horse carried the flint and charcloth. Thankfully, we still have our weapons."

"I could make a fire," said Tom, remembering what the weald-grell Annian had taught him. "If I had the right type of wood, I should be able to generate enough friction to create an ember."

Rosalie stared off across the darkening plains. "What have you been thinking about?"

"Everything. So much goes through my head. Waves and waves of thoughts. It's almost impossible to turn it off. I can't sleep sometimes."

"My father would say, 'Worry only about what you can control. Let everything else rest.'"

"Do you ever worry about the future?"

Rosalie faced him. "Can *you* predict the future?"

"Well, no. But there are certain outcomes I'd rather avoid."

"Does worrying about them make them less likely?"

"It forces me to plan ahead. To stop bad things from happening."

"Then I guess you're resolving the issue. You should rest easy because you're doing everything possible to avoid an undesirable outcome."

Rosalie reached across and wrapped her hand around the pouch carrying the eyes of lost souls dangling from Tom's belt. "I thought Raf was going to take these."

"They wouldn't be much use to him unless he has a birthmark and a birth twin."

"He has a birthmark," said Rosalie. "On his lower back."

Shit, thought Tom. *Shit.*

She released the pouch. "Have you ever been tempted by immortality?"

"Sometimes. Not for my own desire, but if I gained eternal life, I could kill Malphas. Only an immortal can kill another immortal. Then we wouldn't have to worry about destroying the throne."

"To become immortal, you must kill your birth twin first, right?"

Tom nodded. "Yes. Adalwolf."

"Does King Adalwolf deserve to die?"

Tom wondered about the answer. *It might be for the greater good. Am I willing to take the same path as Malphas? To sacrifice an innocent life to change the future?*

"So many lives have already been lost," said Tom, "would it matter if I took one more?"

"When you're immortal, would you seek to rule over us?"

"I'm not Malphas. I don't want to rule. I only want to...make it better. But I can't help thinking, what if Raf's right? What if the Germalians won't fight?"

"Then we'll find another way," said Rosalie.

Raf and Quenan returned from hunting empty-handed. With the three-quarter moons of Seena and Bargan overhead, Raf and Rosalie laid out their bedrolls, and Quenan settled into the long grass, her bed lost with the pack horse. Tom moved his bed away from the group, trying to limit the annoyance of Raf's snoring, then slumped onto the wet blankets to stare at the moons and stars swimming in the warm night air.

Late in the night, eyelids heavy, he almost didn't notice the soft footfalls approaching through the grass. Dressed in a delicate slip, the moonlight caressed the curves of Rosalie's body as she sat beside him and put her finger to her lips. He tried to sit up, but she rested a hand on his naked chest, then smiled.

"Is that the earth quaking?" she asked.

Tom fought the dryness in his mouth. "It's...it's my heart."

She lay beside him, leaned across and hovered her lips near his. He tilted his head up, and they kissed, Rosalie pushing her tongue into his mouth.

Tom pulled away. "What about Raf?"

Rosalie placed her hand over his mouth. "Forget about him."

She kissed him again, letting the shoulder strap of her undergarment fall down her upper arm to expose the top of her breast.

The ceaseless thoughts circling Tom's mind spiralled into chaos. He'd never been adept at sex. Not at first. He needed to feel comfortable with someone before intercourse. With a new partner, it often took many attempts before he could *perform*.

Rosalie sat up. "What's wrong?"

"It's hard to explain," said Tom.

"Well, at least something's hard."

Tom should have been offended, but Rosalie smiled her beautiful, mischievous smile.

"Explain it to me," she said.

"The first time is difficult for me."

"Are you nervous?"

"Yes."

"Then we'll be patient. It's a long walk to Portum. Plenty of time to practice."

She straddled Tom, unshouldered the other undergarment strap, and pulled it to her waist, letting him drink in her naked torso. Only a blanket draped across his bottom half, the press of Rosalie's taut bum cheeks against his groin stimulated his penis. Rosalie must have felt it too, grinding her backside into his waist, then hopping off and pulling the blanket away simultaneously.

"Something's happening down here," she said.

"It won't last," said Tom.

"Hush. Stop talking and stop worrying. Clear your head, lose yourself in the stars, and let me do the rest."

Focus on the now.

Rosalie leaned over and kissed Tom's chest. On knees and elbows, she moved her mouth slowly, gently across his stomach. Stopping there, she reached down and caressed his penis. Tom went to stroke Rosalie's clitoris, but she pushed his hand away. He tried to let himself go, calm the vortex of his mind and enjoy the moment. Rosalie's breasts hung low, tickling his skin as she continued to kiss him. Every time he thought about what he should be doing, about pleasing her, his penis went limp. One day, he hoped his desire for her would be instinctive. Once he'd grown comfortable with Rosalie, they could make love together rather than one making love *to* the other.

Then something unexpected happened. Rosalie ran her tongue along the shaft of his penis, and it hardened. Before he thought about it going flaccid again, she straddled his waist and guided him inside her. Despite Tom's lack of attention, Rosalie's vagina spread warm and wet, swallowing the head of his penis with ease. She ground her groin into his and moaned. The yearn of her pleasure stimulated Tom further. He focussed on her sensual silhouette framed by the moons and stars. The shudder of her breasts. The way her hair fell across her shoulders. The urgency in her voice.

Rosalie moved up and down. Faster and faster. Tom tilted his hips forward, and she gasped. He worried about Raf hearing, then forced the worry from his mind.

"Keep going," she moaned.

Tom reached for Rosalie's breasts.

"Pinch them," she whispered.

He squeezed a nipple between his thumb and forefinger.

Rosalie arched her back and lifted her face to the endless night. Tom gave himself to her completely, lifting his buttocks from the blanket and pushing deep. He came inside her before he could worry about coming too soon. Rosalie kept going, letting a shriek escape before her body relaxed.

She lifted herself from his waist, fell beside him and laughed. "I thought you said the first time was difficult."

"Normally, it is."

"Well, I'm not your normal woman."

"Next time, I'll do more," said Tom. "If...if that's what you want. If there is a next...."

Rosalie placed a finger on his lips. "One day at a time. Now, I have to rest."

They fell asleep in each other's arms.

The following morning, when Tom woke, Rosalie had already left. He pulled on his pants and tunic, rolled up his bedroll, strapped on his belt and sword, then walked towards the main camp, where Rosalie grazed the horses on fresh grass.

"Did you sleep well?" asked Rosalie.

"Yes," said Tom. "Thank you."

"What are you thanking me for?"

A fiery blush spread across Tom's face before he changed the subject. "Where's Raf and Quenan?"

"Foraging again."

Quenan returned first, carrying yams and a skinned hare. Tom ate a yam while Rosalie and Quenan stripped pieces of raw meat from the hare and washed them down with water. Raf returned with pockets full of gumul berries, purple fruit the size of grapes and full of tiny seeds. They feasted on the sweet berries before packing the horses and heading west.

For another two days, the group trudged towards the Riverlands Escarpment. They filled waterskins from streams flowing into the rivers Lousse and Anchep, and hunted for food on the Dambay Plains and among the rocks of the Scaur Hills. During the journey, Rosalie spoke to Tom as if nothing had changed, and he wondered if he'd dreamt their love-making. He wanted to talk about it. Needed to know if it would happen again. If she *wanted* it to happen again. If she had feelings for him. But he couldn't get Rosalie alone. When Quenan went hunting, Rosalie went with her, leaving Tom to mind the horses. Raf's demeanour didn't change either, Tom hopeful it meant the Dobunni rebel hadn't realised what had happened between him and Rosalie.

On the evening of the ninth day since leaving the ruined monastery, the group passed to the south of Sardis; the city's crumbling outer wall visible in the distance across the once mighty bridge now standing in disrepair. The main road to Sardis was empty, and only a handful of smoke plumes marked the location of Slumstadt. Tom recalled his journey with the Dobunni rebels into the city's heart to assassinate a king who'd already left. He pictured Princess Caeli standing at the Sunrise Keep's barred window, watching the world below her unfold. The vision of the princess morphed into a monstrous red grell, pacing around the turret atop the watchtower, waiting for something unusual to happen. Waiting for someone like Tom Anderson to make a mistake.

Raf wanted to go to the Slumstadt markets to buy food. They had plenty of coin. Rosalie said it would draw too much attention. Silver tausens with Adalwolf's image were better suited to the black market than handing them to a random stallholder who might alert the authorities. Although the rebels had riches, these were riches with strings attached.

That night, they camped in the shadows of one of the massive gouges cut into the Scaur Hills' northern slopes, where Malphas quarried the rock used to rebuild Pergamos. Quenan shot a wallaby with her bow, then started a fire using the method Annian had taught Tom, twirling the tip of a smooth, cylindrical stick in the notch of a flat piece of wood until the friction created a pile of hot dust. When the dust spilled into a tuft of dry grass, Quenan pressed her face to the ground and blew into the grass until an ember caught alight.

They feasted on roast wallaby, tubers, and gumul berries, the first decent meal since losing their supplies to the river. Tom expected the group to be jovial, but everyone sat quiet and tense. One more day of travelling and they'd reach the Riverlands Escarpment. The rebels told Tom the road down the escarpment would be guarded, top and bottom, by Krieg's red soldiers. They'd avoided the enemy so far, but a confrontation at the escarpment appeared inescapable.

After eating, Tom moved his bed away from the group, as he'd been doing since the river crossing, thinking Rosalie may visit him again. But she didn't come, and he thought she never would. One night of passion appeared to be all she desired, and Tom accepted he'd be nothing more to her than someone who needed protecting for the sake of Enthilen's future.

The following day, the group travelled along the northern edge of the Scaur Hills, avoiding the road between Sardis and the Riverlands Escarpment. They left the cover of the hills at sunset and galloped towards the guardhouse at the escarpment edge. Night time would be better to launch an attack or try to slip past the guards.

*   *   *   *

Tom hid behind a clump of trees with Rosalie, Raf and Quenan, watching the Erstürmen guardhouse built atop the Riverlands Escarpment. Eight soldiers, dressed in dull, blood-red armour that absorbed the moonlight, rode up to the building.

"Might be changin' the guard," said Raf. "We should wait 'til the other soldiers leave. Then attack."

"I thought we could sneak past," said Tom.

"Ain't gonna happen," said Raf. "They're watchin' the escarpment road like hawks."

"We could tell them we're Riverlands farmers heading home with our grell slave."

"Farmers don't have slaves. Anyways, Krieg's Shield are suspicious of everyone; that's why we never raid Sardis. We'll have to kill them all before tacklin' the escarpment. We can't risk one of them raisin' the alarm. There's another guardhouse at the bottom."

"Won't the guards below see us on the road?" asked Tom.

"It zig-zags across the cliff face alongside the Rārian Falls," said Rosalie. "Hard to see riders coming down at night, masked by the mist from the falls."

The uncertainty in Rosalie's voice didn't fill Tom with confidence.

She placed a hand on his forearm. "We'd prefer safe passage without death, but I can't see another option." Rosalie gave him a reassuring smile, then faced Raf and Quenan. "You have the only bows. There's cover to the north and south of the guardhouse. Take up positions there and listen for the hoot of a river owl. That will be my signal to start firing."

Quenan and Raf disappeared as the night took hold.

Tom stood alone with Rosalie for the first time since they had sex. This wasn't the moment to talk about it, but the eagerness in Tom's mind wouldn't abate.

"Four moons ago, we...," started Tom.

"We will again," interrupted Rosalie. "When the time's right. If you want to?"

He nodded. "Yes. I've been thinking about it for days."

"Don't think too hard. You know what it does here." She reached down, cupped his genitals, then leaned across and kissed him.

Tom pulled away. "We might die tonight."

"Your motivation for not dying is another night with me." The cheek of Rosalie's smile faded as her face set stern. "We should focus. I'll sneak up from the east, next to the road, and block any escape. As their numbers thin, I expect the remaining guards to flee towards Sardis. I'll intercept them. You stay here. We can't risk your life if what you say about crushing the dead throne is true."

"It *is* true. But I'm not going to let you face the enemy alone." Tom reached into his tunic pocket, broke a seal on the foil packet, then popped a pill into his mouth.

Three tablets left.

Rosalie didn't argue with Tom. They crept along the roadside towards the round guardhouse, its white-washed stone gleaming under bright half-moons. As eight guards departed, relieved by their companions, Tom and Rosalie hid behind a thicket of bushes to watch them pass. Tom tried to remember what Thaly had told him about the vulnerabilities of Erstürmen armour. 'Gap underneath the arm,' she'd said. 'And between the bottom of the spangenhelm and top of the gorget.' Tom had thwarted the armour before when renegade soldiers from Süden Forst attacked him and Annian. He expected Krieg's men wouldn't be so easily defeated.

At the guardhouse, two soldiers stood outside the door, their halberds leaning against the wall, while another guard watered the eight horses tethered to posts.

Five soldiers inside, thought Tom, their laughter and conversation escaping from an open window and drifting away into the night.

Before Tom's worry grew into a beast he couldn't control, Rosalie cleared her throat, then shrieked a high-pitched cry, "*Shoo shoo, shoo shoo, shoo shoo.*"

The guards at the front door faced the bushes where Rosalie and Tom hid, gathering their halberds. Tom waited for Raf and Quenan to start firing. For their arrows to fell the enemy. Nothing happened. The two guards strode towards Tom and Rosalie.

"*Shoo shoo, shoo shoo, shoo shoo,*" shrieked Rosalie.

Keep quiet, thought Tom. *You're attracting the guards. Where are the damn arrows?*

They came with a whistle through the night, and one of the guards approaching Tom collapsed, clutching his neck. The other went to call out when an arrow lodged in his mouth. The soldier watering the horses lifted his head and yelled to his companions inside.

Five soldiers bolted from the guardhouse, halberds and swords at the ready. Two fell as soon as they stepped outside. One pointed north, and another two guards ran towards the cover where Quenan hid.

The soldier tending the horses and the one giving the commands, untethered two mounts, climbed into their saddles and headed along the road towards Sardis, avoiding the arrows fired by Raf.

"Here they come," said Rosalie. "Get ready."

Tom and Rosalie drew their swords as the horses galloped towards them, their riders clutching the reins with grim determination. With the first horse almost upon her, Rosalie stepped into its path and swung her sword, cutting into the beast's shoulder. Its front legs crumbled beneath it, tossing the rider head-first onto the road. The second horse careered over the top of the first, throwing its rider into a tree.

Tom stepped onto the road to face the dazed enemy. The soldier in red armour lumbered to his feet and staggered towards his ambusher, drawing a long, two-handed sword.

Thaly's voice raced through Tom's head. 'Legs shoulder-width apart, feet in an L position. Bend your knees. Keep your head still. Weak point under the arm.'

The red soldier raised his sword above his shoulders, then swung it towards Tom's head. Tom blocked the swing, the clash of steel jolting through his arm and knocking the sword from his hand. The soldier slashed at Tom's chest. Tom ducked under the flashing blade and picked up his own sword in the same motion. Behind him, Rosalie fought the other guard, the clang of metal-on-metal ringing through the night.

Tom shifted his weight onto his front foot, his sword thrust deflected by the soldier's breastplate. The enemy smiled underneath his spangenhelm and swung at Tom again, the blade nicking Tom's chest before lodging in a tree trunk. As the guard yanked on his sword, Tom thrust his blade through the gap in the armour under the soldier's arm. Metal scraped on bone, and the man screamed. He yanked his weapon from the tree and raised it above his head, preparing to smash down on Tom's skull.

The energy drained from Tom as long days of travelling caught up with him. His arms hung limply by his side as if attached to lead weights, and the tip of his blade dragged in the dirt. The red soldier tensed his shoulder muscles. Tom made one final effort to lift his sword to block the coming blow. As the enemy's blade fell towards him, an arrow flew past and pierced the soldier's throat. He died, blood spewing across his red armour breastplate.

Tom spun around to find Rosalie alive, her combatant lying at her feet.

Quenan emerged from the darkness. "That is the last of them. Raf is gathering the horses. Wait...." She tilted her head to the side. "I hear hooves. More soldiers are coming. At least ten."

"What?" said Rosalie. "Where did they come from?"

Quenan shrugged.

"Damn. We must go. Now."

They sprinted along the road, meeting Raf near the guardhouse.

Rosalie grabbed Storvil's reins. "Soldiers on our tail," she said to Raf.

"We can't fight them and the guards at the bottom of the escarpment," said Raf.

"Then we'll ride through the guards and keep riding." She faced Tom and Quenan. "Don't stop until the pursuit ends. Not even if one of us falls."

"We must protect Tom at all costs," said Quenan.

Raf sneered. "Damn this stupid errand."

The clatter of hooves grew louder.

Rosalie, Tom and Raf climbed into their saddles, Quenan able to keep pace with a galloping horse.

"It'll be slow going down the escarpment," said Rosalie. "After that, we ride as if Krieg is in pursuit."

She led the group past the guardhouse and onto a narrow, treacherous track zig-zagging its way down the face of the sheer escarpment. At the rear, Tom clutched Juniper's reins, worried about the soldiers in pursuit, the guards below, and the deathly fall only an arms-length from his left shoulder. He couldn't see the bottom, but something told him that if he fell, he'd keep falling until he passed out, landed on hard ground, and shattered to pieces. His ears strained for warning of the pursuing soldiers, but the roar of the Rārian Falls drowned out every sound, and sheets of mist from the falls washed across the rocks like fog so thick, he couldn't see Rosalie leading the group. One of Krieg's Shield could be poised to thrust a sword into the middle of Tom's back, and he wouldn't know it.

He focussed on the rear of Raf's horse walking ahead, then grimaced when Juniper's front hoof dislodged a stone and sent it toppling over the edge.

A sure way to forewarn the guards of our arrival.

Clothes drenched from the spray, he shivered despite the warm night.

Raf turned in his saddle and pointed above his head where lit torches bounced along the road after them. "Don't worry," he said, "they can't ride any faster than us down this damn path."

With aching slowness, the group came to the last bend in the road. Once around the bend, the moonlight shadows would no longer mask their presence from the guards at the bottom of the escarpment.

Rosalie gathered the group together. "We rush the guards all at once. Ride in the shape of an arrowhead with Quenan running in the middle. The horses will give her some protection. Wait for...." She stopped when a yell came from above them. Krieg's soldiers shrieked and cursed, trying to attract the attention of the men in the guardhouse below.

"Shit," said Rosalie. "Let's go."

She urged Storvil forward. Raf and Tom did their best to keep pace, Quenan running between them. Krieg's men rushed from the guardhouse as the rebels galloped past.

"Get the horses!" yelled a soldier. "Four to pursue."

Four guards mounted their horses and bolted after Tom and his companions. Another twelve appeared at the bottom of the escarpment road and followed suit. Tom urged Juniper up to Storvil's flank, determined to stay with Rosalie whatever happened. The road veered to the left, but they turned right, heading for the top of a dam wall creating a lake at the bottom of the Rārian Falls. The horses slowed as they walked along a stone path atop the wall, then stepped onto a swinging timber suspension bridge. Beneath the bridge, water gushed over the spillway and plummeted into a gorge.

When the rebels reached the other end of the bridge, the horses of the pursuing soldiers began to cross. Tom ducked as an arrow whooshed over his head. He kicked his heels into Juniper's flanks. The mare cantered with the other horses into clumps of giant sludge grass towering over everyone. Thick grey mud sucked at the horses' hooves. Rosalie dismounted, and the others followed her lead, pulling their beasts along the muddy path. A soldier yelled behind them, urging his men into the sludge grass.

"There's nowhere to hide," said Raf. "The half-moons are castin' too much light."

"I will stay behind and delay them," said Quenan. "You three go ahead."

"No," said Rosalie. "We stay together. Keep moving forward until we reach the sand dunes."

"Then what?" asked Raf. "The sand won't offer us any more protection than these useless bunches of grass."

Rosalie ignored Raf and tugged Storvil forward. Tom and Raf followed in silence while Quenan watched the rear.

The remainder of the night dragged on. Tom expected the pursuers to arrive at any moment. Underfoot, the grass thinned, and the mud buckled and cracked. The sun breached the Riverlands Escarpment as the rebels climbed from a dry lakebed and faced the shining red sands of Grōz Wüste.

Quenan rushed up to Rosalie. "Sixteen soldiers. They are nearly upon us."

"We should stand and fight," said Raf. "We're too tired to go on any further." He drew his sword, his quiver empty.

"Alright," said Rosalie. "We'll climb the first dune and take the high ground."

Pulling their horses behind them, the group trudged up the face of a dune no taller than a house and turned towards the rising sun and an approaching enemy.

This is a stupid place to make a stand, thought Tom. *We're exposed and lit up like a Christmas tree.*

In a swale marking the transition between grassland and desert, Krieg's red soldiers trotted forward, urged on by the sight of their quarry. Twelve men dismounted, unshouldered their bows and nocked arrows, forming a line of archers at the bottom of the dune.

Rosalie pulled Tom down behind the ridgeline. "Take cover," she said. "All of you."

Quenan ignored the order and nocked the last arrow in her bow.

Krieg's archers drew their bowstrings taut, their arms quivering with the strain. The commander raised his hand, preparing to give the order to fire, when his horse whinnied. He spun around to where the sand moved under the horse's hooves. Grains of red bubbled like water and started to cascade into the ground. The horse trumpeted in panic as the sand swallowed its legs. The commander fell from his saddle.

Tom squinted into the sun. "What's happening down there?"

The archers dropped their bows as their legs sank into the shifting sands. They flailed groping arms in frenzied swipes, trying to free themselves. A horse disappeared under the surface. The commander screamed as a wave of sand rose up and crashed over his head.

"This is some witchery," said Raf.

Below the rebels' vantage point on the ridge, s-shaped waves of sand flowed down the dune face towards the terrified soldiers. The waves stopped halfway. The soldiers froze. Waiting.

Then a piercing squeal broke the stillness, and something huge exploded from the sand. Tom's eyes almost burst from his face. *Snakes.* Enormous snakes, as thick as a horse and longer than three horses head-to-tail. To Tom, they resembled gigantic death adders. And riding them were creatures with pink skin, patchy white fur, and twitching pug noses that dwarfed their pin-prick eyes and gnashing mouths.

"Dreadwerps," said Tom, remembering what Dwarrow had told him about the mouldewerps' despised relatives. "Dreadwerps riding slider serpents."

Six serpents and their riders descended on the trapped soldiers. With scissor-like claws, each dreadwerp tugged on reins threaded through a metal ring piercing the serpent's nose. Face-to-face with their quarry, the serpents opened their mouths and spat venom, burning holes through the red armour and searing the soldier's skin. The men screamed as one, sending a chill down Tom's spine.

"We should get out of here," urged Raf. "Those serpent-riders ain't here to save us. Once they're done with Krieg's soldiers, they'll be after us."

The rebels mounted their horses and fled through the swales nestled between colossal sand dunes, some higher than the Scaur Hills. By midday, they stumbled across a waterhole surrounded by bushes with silver-grey leaves.

"I gotta rest," said Raf, almost falling from his horse before staggering to the waterhole's edge. He lay on his stomach and lapped the murky liquid like a parched lizard.

Tom, Rosalie and Quenan filled their waterskins and rested in the meagre shade cast by the stumpy bushes. Only Rosalie slept. Tom was too unnerved by recent events and struggled with the smothering heat. Quenan stood the entire time, watching the surroundings. Raf sat opposite Tom and stared with longing and dangerous eyes.

Rosalie woke before sunset. "Did anyone else sleep?"

Tom shook his head.

"We'll rest here until nightfall," said Rosalie. "Then travel when the moons are favourable. The heat of the desert is treacherous."

"And I've been told serpent-riders are less likely to attack at night," said Raf.

"They're dreadwerps," said Tom. "What were they doing to those soldiers?"

"Meat for their serpents," said Raf. "Men and horses. All of them are in snake bellies by now."

"How do you know so much about dreadwerps?" asked Quenan.

"Spent time in the Riverlands, fightin' alongside the farmers. They had plenty of tall tales to tell."

"Let's fill these waterskins and prepare to move," said Rosalie.

"Then what?" asked Raf. "We ain't got no food, and who knows how far the next waterhole is or in what direction."

"We'll find another waterhole," said Rosalie. "Then another until we reach Portum."

"And I will find food," said Quenan. "I have one arrow left, and I can make more from reeds growing around waterholes."

Raf set a cruel grin on his face. "You make it sound so easy. But it ain't goin' to be easy. We'll be in Pordillo territory soon enough. Them nomads won't be askin' any questions before they stick a dagger in your belly. Or toss you in slave chains. Pordillo, serpent-riders, wurloin nests, and this cursed, relentless heat."

"Then go back," said Quenan. "Face the red soldiers crawling all over the escarpment like ants."

Raf locked eyes with Tom and didn't turn away. "I been thinkin' about travellin' somewhere, but not back to them mountains. And not to Portum either."

"What are you talking about?" asked Rosalie.

Raf jumped on Tom before he could react. In the blink of an eye, the Dobunni rebel drew his dagger and sliced the drawstring tied to Tom's belt, grabbing the pouch containing the eyes of lost souls before it fell to the sand.

Raf stood and backed away from the group.

Tom's mind steeled. "Give them back." He climbed to his feet and rested a hand on the hilt of his sword. Rosalie stood beside him.

Raf clutched the pouch close to his chest. "Not so fast. I'd like to know more about these dark eyes, seein' they're so important and all. Seein' you're askin' me to risk my life for them. Seems they must be pretty valuable."

"They're worthless to most people," said Tom.

"But not to everyone," said Raf, opening the pouch and emptying a dark eye into his right hand. "Them Riverland folk told an awful lot of stories. They had this one about a woman who travelled to another world and returned an immortal. She carried glass eyes with her, like these ones. Black with a flamin' pupil." Raf tipped the remaining eye into his left hand. "But see, not everyone can become immortal. You gotta have a naevus, raised and red, like the one I have on me back. And you gotta have a birth twin, livin' in the other world. I won't know that 'til I get there, but seems to me it's worth the risk."

"Don't close your hands," pleaded Tom, his body shuddering a moment before he drew his sword.

Raf raised his eyebrows. "What did you say?"

"Don't wrap your fingers around the eyes. If you do, you'll be taken to a horrible world and never return."

"More horrible than an endless waste? Anyone with a grain of sense knows we ain't gettin' across this desert alive. Were never goin' to."

"Then why agree to come?" asked Rosalie.

"When I seen the eyes of lost souls in the monastery, I couldn't stop thinkin' about them. Every day they called me. Louder and louder, 'til I couldn't ignore them anymore. They told me I had to follow the birraman. Travel from one world to another. Become immortal."

Raf smiled at Tom, a grin that relished fear and mayhem, then drew his fingers into his palms.

~ Chapter 26 ~

The soles of Mirrian's bare feet rubbed against the flagstones as she lumbered down the empty corridor towards Pergamos' storeroom. On her left, she passed the entrance to the throne hall, double oak doors taller than a grell and encased in plate metal. Rephaim would usually guard the door and the dead throne inside, but it appeared they'd been assigned other duties. The entrance to Malphas' private quarters also sat unguarded ahead of her.

Mirrian stopped. The corridors of Pergamos are *always* guarded, she thought.

Only her breathing broke the silence. No-one else walked the flagstones or admired the paintings or busts of Volerdie's disciples perched on black marble pedestals. Paralysed by uncertainty, Mirrian waited, expecting... *hoping* the Worshipful Master would arrive to guide her. Acting without Master's command had become increasingly difficult. Yet, Ende needed care. The pale grell had sprayed a gluggy, garnet-coloured vomit all over the bed linen. Mirrian decided to collect new sheets from the storeroom. Made the decision by herself, without Master's consent, leaving Ende alone in her quarters. Alone and frightfully ill.

Ende needs a healer, thought Mirrian, not a slave. *No. Master made me Ende's carer. Me, and no-one else.*

Mirrian had avoided granting Ende's request for a merciful death, despite promising she would ease the pale grell's suffering. She expected Ende knew more about Grin. The pale grell said he stole the dark eyes and travelled to Tom Anderson's world, but she didn't say *why* he took this journey.

"Ende can tell me why," Mirrian whispered to herself. "But it's a dangerous game."

The pale grell threatened to tell Malphas about Grin if Mirrian refused to complete the mercy killing, and five moons had passed since Ende made her request. The longer Mirrian kept the pale grell alive, the greater the risk of Malphas finding out about Grin.

Nevertheless, she marched forward, down the passageway, around a corner and into a corridor leading to the storeroom. The firebrands lining the walls had been doused, and she stumbled through a cold gloom, cursing the lazy slaves responsible for keeping the torches lit. Nearing the storeroom door, two other grells emerged from the shadows, blocking her path. Mirrian froze. Carian and Julan waited for her. The two slaves who'd once been her friends before Master began to favour her. Before she became Ende's carer.

For many moons, she'd avoided the judgement of her fellow slaves, but Carian and Julan now loomed with a menace that raised Mirrian's neck hairs. She considered calling a guard, then remembered the guards were absent. Contemplated running, but the younger slaves would catch her. Mirrian couldn't escape the consequences of Malphas' affection.

"What is wrong, Slug?" asked Carian, his arm hanging by his side. "Have you forgotten your way to the storeroom because slave chores are beneath you?"

"She is no longer a slave," said Julan. "She does not share our quarters anymore."

"I heard, Slug shares Malphas' bed," said Carian. "His dirty grell whore."

Mirrian cried, "That isn't true!"

Carian faced Julan. "Did you hear? She speaks like an Erstürmen."

Is not true, thought Mirrian. *Is not.*

"I am a prisoner down here," she said. "Master's soldiers watch me day and night. Master forbids me to go above ground unless in his company."

"No-one above ground misses you," said Julan, her face twisted by a gloating smile. "If you step inside the slave quarters again, you will not leave."

Carian and Julan approached. The shadows around their hands melted away, revealing a fireplace poker carried by Carian and metal tongs, as long as her arm, held by Julan.

"Please," whimpered Mirrian, "let me be. I suffer as you do. As every slave in Pergamos suffers. I don't receive special treatment." *Do not,* thought Mirrian.

"But we have seen it," said Julan. "Sitting at Master's table to feast in the throne hall while we taste the food for poison. Caring for the pale grell like a childhood friend. Standing on the pyramid's balcony holding Ende's sparth and bearing witness to the murder of innocents. I expect Malphas consulted you on how to execute the prisoners."

"That isn't...is *not* true!" Mirrian's ribs tightened around her heart like a cave python crushing a dove. She slumped against the corridor wall and rubbed worn fingertips over tear-drenched cheeks to wipe away her culpability.

"Are those tears of guilt, Slug?" asked Carian. "Remorse for the shame you have inflicted on all stone-grells?"

"Y-y-yes," sobbed Mirrian.

But her pain didn't cause Carian and Julan to falter in their task. They towered over her as she dropped to the floor and curled into a ball. The fire-poker came first, jamming into her shoulder and causing her to scream. It retreated and came again, this time smacking into her ribs. The tongs followed, grasping her left hand and pulling it away from her face. Then the poker struck a third time, the sharp, jagged point hitting her mouth and forcing clenched teeth to bite into her cheek until blood flooded her tongue. The tongs attacked again, wrapping curved metal ends around her throat and squeezing. Blood burst from Mirrian's mouth and spewed down her chin as she gasped for air, clutching at the tongs and trying to pull them apart. A flurry of blows pounded her legs, then moved higher to assault the softer parts of her body. Stomach and breasts.

Mirrian pulled the tongs free and screamed, a death-defying, desperate plea she never knew hid inside her. The tongs tried to grasp her again, but she flailed her arms to deflect the metal clamp. She couldn't fight off another thrust from the poker. It cannoned into the small of her back and sent an explosion of pain up her spine.

Mirrian surrendered. Her hands fell to her side, and she rolled onto her face to press it against the merciless stone floor. She'd die here, in this dark corridor in the Worshipful Master's underground kingdom. Another sacrifice to placate her oppressors.

However, amid thoughts of her last breath, the assault stopped.

The fire-poker clattered onto the flagstones, and something, *someone*, thudded to the floor. Then someone else, gurgling as they collapsed beside Mirrian. The passage fell silent for a moment before wheezing breaths above her disturbed the peace. Then a sticky warmth trickled between Mirrian's cheek and the cold stones. She smelled blood, wondering how much of it was hers.

Mirrian uncurled her battered body, wincing with the strain of every muscle that would soon turn black and blue. Blood pooled on the floor beside her, seeping from Julan's decapitated head. Carian's headless torso lay beside someone standing on bare feet, balanced upright using the heel of a staff.

No, not a staff, thought Mirrian. A weapon. A sparth.

Mirrian rolled onto her back and faced Ende, the pale grell free of her bed for the first time in many moons. Dressed in a gossamer nightgown, she clutched the sparth's timber handle with feeble fingers and wheezed breaths that might be her last.

"Did...did they hurt you?" asked Ende.

"Yes," said Mirrian. "But I will recover."

Mirrian tried to sit up, but pain shot through her chest, forcing her back to the floor. Ende offered the heel of the sparth, and Mirrian reached for it, dragging herself into a sitting position with arms that ached from fingertip to shoulder. Ende wavered with Mirrian's tug, bracing her feet on the floor to avoid toppling over.

"I can get up," said Mirrian, releasing the sparth's handle.

Ende nodded. "I must return to bed. The exertion has...has...." She turned but stumbled, thrusting her free hand against the wall to steady herself.

Flesh burning with torment, Mirrian climbed off the floor and staggered to Ende, draping the pale grell's free arm over her shoulder. They hobbled together, the victim and the executioner, back along the passage to Ende's room.

Mirrian lowered Ende to the bed, then leaned the sparth against the wall beside the cedar bedhead. Ende shivered, pulling the quilt, still covered in bloody vomit, up to her chin.

"It is time, Mirrian," said Ende, with failing breaths. "You have waited long enough. Now you must repay the favour."

The sparth's blade glinted from the fire in Ende's hearth, reflecting a swollen, grotesque face Mirrian refused to recognise as her own. Carian and Julan's headless bodies lay inside a corridor of her mind. Even on death's doorstep, Ende had dispatched the grell slaves with an ease born from wielding razor-sharp steel day after day. Mirrian could do the same. She could swing the sparth and end a life in an instant, right now.

She turned her back to the pale grell and curled aching fingers around the weapon's handle, still warm from Ende's touch. The fire crackled, the flames twisting into the faces of those she'd lost. Her husband, Frennan. Her children, Merran, Grin and Hanni. Her friends, Carian and Julan. Only Mirrian remained. Mirrian and Master.

She released the sparth, climbed onto the bed, straddled Ende's hollow chest and wrapped her hands around the pale grell's neck. "Why did Grin leave Enthilen? Tell me."

Ende gasped, "Yes...Mirrian...yes...."

Mirrian squeezed tighter, lifted Ende's head from the pillow, then forced it down again. Up and down. Tighter and tighter. "Tell me. Tell me! TELL ME!"

Ende choked, spittle, vomit and blood dribbling from the corners of her mouth. Breaths came with despairing irregularity. She would die before giving up any more secrets.

Mirrian released her grip and fell on the bed beside Ende. The pale grell's body shuddered and convulsed beneath the bed covers. Mirrian reached under the sheet to grasp Ende's hand as the pale grell's back arched to the ceiling, and pain contorted her face into a misshapen mask of death. A groping mouth sprayed sangria vomit over the pillow as Ende's head thrashed from side to side.

Mirrian sobbed. "I'm...h-h-here. I'm here, Ende."

Ende's mouth opened and closed, over and over, until she uttered a single word, "Liddian." Then her body went limp, and her breaths stopped.

Still clutching Ende's hand, Mirrian nestled her battered frame against the pale grell and lowered her head to the pillow. Sore, broken and grievous, she rested until her tears soaked the pillowcase.

Unable to bear the anguish of the loss, Mirrian climbed from bed and stumbled into the central passageway. The guards hadn't returned. She limped down the passage to the storeroom, where the headless bodies of her friends lay on the floor. Mirrian rolled them off to the side and placed Carian's head on his chest, doing the same for Julan. When the guards returned, at least they would know who was who. She gathered a bucket of water and scrubbing brush from the storeroom and washed the blood from the flagstones.

When she'd finished, she returned to Ende's room, the door now flanked by two Rephaim guards. Malphas sat inside, on the three-legged stool he always used, next to Ende's bed. He chatted away as if his constant companion still accompanied him, seemingly unaware of, or ignoring, the blood and vomit drenching the bed covers.

"...but our mission is not lost," said Malphas. "I'm doubling my efforts to find Widukind, Apollyon to the Divine Creator; such is the irony. My traitor brother is out there, somewhere, and when I capture him, I'll have the immortal to sacrifice on the throne of the dead. And I *will* find him, Ende. Mother has wilted to my demands and agreed to help."

Mirrian staggered to the opposite side of the bed, faced Malphas and stood in silent pain.

"The end of harvest season," said Malphas to a departed Ende. "That's when darkness will descend amid the daylight. I had it all wrong before. I thought the moment would come twelve yarles ago. But I studied the First Scripture again. My initial reading was mistaken. Not now, though. Now I'm sure I've got it right. Now I'll...."

"She is dead," interrupted Mirrian, licking dried blood from the corners of her mouth.

Malphas paused, then continued, "...be ready. I can picture it, Ende. Savour the taste on my tongue. Widukind bound to the dead throne, waiting for my blade to slice his throat. Waiting to become the immortal vessel to house Volerdie's soul when the Divine Creator returns to Enthilen. My brother will be grateful for the honour."

"Ende is dead, Master," said Mirrian.

Malphas fell silent. He didn't look at Mirrian, continuing to cast his gaze over the pale grell's unmoving face as she lay motionless on her back. Then he began to sway, teetering on the tiny, childish stool, hugging his arms across his chest and rocking back and forth with the regularity of a tolling bell.

When the mournful dance ended, Mirrian expected Master to jump from the chair, grab the sparth and lop off her head. Part of her wanted him to do it. Another part accepted her end wouldn't come so easily.

Malphas stopped swaying, released his self-embrace, and brushed stray hairs from Ende's black eyes. The tip of his crooked, trembling finger, the nail stained yellow from the soil of his soul, traced the outline of Ende's lips. Then he closed her eyelids with the gentleness of a mother kissing her newborn on the forehead, the babe's body still warm from the womb.

Malphas reached to his feet and removed his shoes. He pulled back the bloody quilt and climbed into bed, nuzzling up to Ende. Draping his arm across her stomach, he rested his head on her chest as if hoping to catch a faint heartbeat. He lay there, humming softly as a father would hum a lullaby to their child.

"It's cold in here," said Malphas. "We need to keep you warm." He tugged the quilt over Ende and himself, then faced Mirrian. "Stoke the fire, Slug."

She hesitated, every fingerbreadth of her body aching from Carian and Julan's assault.

"Stoke the fire!" cried Malphas.

Mirrian hobbled to the firebox and gathered a brace of logs. Before placing them on the fire, she faced Malphas. "Ende told me her real name before she died," said Mirrian. "Liddian. That was her grell name."

Under the covers, Malphas flinched, then returned to his humming.

Mirrian tossed the logs on the fire, sparks escaping up the chimney to an outside world she'd almost forgotten, then stepped to the bedhead, taking the sparth in her hand. She stood beside her grieving master, silent and still, and waited for his next command.

*   *   *   *

"Hold your sword up, wench," snarled Sergeant Rork.

Nettie recoiled at Rork's anger, unable to fathom how her new sergeant could be more spiteful than Weedle. If she'd known about Rork, she wouldn't have been so pleased with Weedle's death during the battle for Gestade.

She heaved a two-handed longsword, almost as long as she was tall, above her head, trying to convince Rork of her mastery of the weapon. But the sword's weight pulled her arm down, the blade slashing across the training dummy's straw wrist.

"Not there!" yelled Rork. "Cut down onto the shoulder." He lashed her calves with a whip. "Again."

Nettie flicked sweat-drenched hair from her face and sucked in a deep breath. Pergamos' training ground had no shade, and the midday sun stung worse than a nest of fire ants. Resting the sword against her leg, she wiped sweaty palms on her pants, spat grit from her mouth, then wrapped two hands around the leather-bound grip. She lifted the sword above her chest, strained to hold it while taking aim, then swung down, slicing an arm from the dummy.

"Good." Sergeant Rork moved to the next trainee.

Nettie gasped mouthfuls of hot air, her muscles throbbing from the weapon's burden. Erwin trained beside her, thrusting a halberd blade into a wooden post almost as narrow as Nettie's sword. His ruddy face resembled a cake decoration, grey dirt clinging to glistening ringlets of black hair plastered across his forehead.

Across the training ground, hundreds of trainee soldiers clashed swords or halberds, or fired arrows at bullseyes. Nettie wondered how many of the weapons her father, Yonna, had made. How many *she'd* made, working in the smithy beside him. Swords, daggers, halberds, armour, metal arrowheads, all for the Worshipful Master's army so he could conquer the heathens and traitors of Enthilen. Once, she'd asked Yonna if he felt guilty about making things that kill people. He'd shrugged it off. 'The plans of other men are no business of ours,' he said. 'Work hard and worship the creator. Our commitment will be rewarded.'

However, 'the plans of other men' *had* become Nettie's business. War was her business. Rumours spread among the trainees that an attack on Giigal would be launched before the harvest season ended, less than forty moons away. Another battle where Nettie's life would be dangled like raw meat to lure the enemy wolves into a trap.

After glimpsing him at the victory celebrations five moons ago, and with a second life-threatening experience looming over her, Nettie's thoughts focussed on Yonna, her only family. She had to see him before something awful happened. With days disappearing faster than courage during wartime, she planned to sneak from the barracks tonight and race home. Spend at least a few moments with her father. She hadn't told anyone about her plan, not even Erwin. *Especially* not Erwin. She didn't need a blundering fool as an escort.

If Nettie made it home without being caught, she might not return to the army. She and Yonna could escape Pergamos and head north, across the plains and into the Desolate Mountains. Or go south to Grōz Forst, or east to the coast, steal a boat, and travel into the sunrise. Flee like her big sister Rosalie had done twelve yarles ago. It sounded much more appealing than being hacked to death on the battlefield.

The sweat dripping between Nettie's breasts washed the interlocking bronze circlets of the necklace Rosalie gave her when she escaped patriarchal oppression in Sardis.

I could escape, too, thought Nettie.

Lieutenant Berard strode into the training ground, tall and handsome in his silver armour, the eyes of the two-headed snake embossed on his breastplate seeming to wink at Nettie as if they'd discovered her plan.

Berard marched up to Erwin, grabbed him by the shoulder and spun him around. "Show me what you've learned," said the lieutenant.

A bewildered Erwin stumbled, the point of his halberd swinging down to slice the dirt. "I ain't much for fighting," he said. "Being a baker's son and all."

"The employ of your parents matters not," said Berard. "You're a soldier now. Raise your weapon and prepare to defend against my attack."

Berard drew his sword, the scrape of blade on metal locket sounding like the final breath drawn by a dying child stricken with The Ravage. Erwin's arm quivered as he lifted the halberd and pointed it out from the middle of his chest towards the lieutenant's waist. Berard swung his sword and knocked the weapon from Erwin's hand. As the baker's son went to pick it up, Berard whacked him on the back with the flat of his blade.

"Don't take your eyes off the enemy," said the lieutenant. "Prepare again. Brace your legs shoulder-width apart, knees bent. Like you've been trained. Keep your body low so you can thrust upwards. Aim for my throat."

You're too tall, thought Nettie. Erwin can't get enough power behind the thrust.

Erwin raised the halberd towards the lieutenant's throat, squeezing the wooden shaft until his knuckles turned white. Berard swung again, clashing his sword against the halberd's blade and wrenching Erwin's right arm sideways.

"*Arrgh!*" cried Erwin, dropping the weapon and grabbing at his shoulder.

"Leave him alone," snapped Nettie, grinding her teeth so hard her gums ached. "How can a boy fight a man?"

Berard faced her. "He'll have to fight many men. *And* grells. What's your name?"

Lieutenant Berard's question dented Nettie's pride. He should know me, she thought. He's inspected our troop enough times. Am I so invisible? She swelled her chest. "I'm Nettie Barron, daughter of Yonna Barron, the best metalsmith in Pergamos." *Damn.* Stupid thing to do. If they find me missing tonight, they'll go straight to Yonna.

"The smithy furnaces should have hardened your body, but what about your mind?" asked Berard. "Do you know this boy?"

Nettie didn't look at Erwin, thinking the dismay in his eyes would infect her.

"She's my b-b-best friend," said Erwin.

Nettie's entire body went limp. Idiot, she thought. Don't tell him that.

"Good," said Berard. "Lift your sword, Nettie Barron, and finish the task I've begun."

Nettie couldn't avoid it any longer. She faced Erwin. He stood there, rubbing his shoulder, sobbing and trembling, his face paler than the moons.

"Strike at the boy," said Berard.

They're real weapons, thought Nettie. Erwin's my friend, not a straw dummy.

"Did you hear me?" asked Berard. "Rid yourself of pity and train your mind to yearn for the thrill of battle."

The longsword in Nettie's hands weighed heavier than ever. As she counted every notch in the dented blade, her mind screamed for Erwin to run. Sergeant Rork returned, lashing the whip across Nettie's buttocks.

"You heard the lieutenant," said Rork. "Cut the friggin' boy. Put him out of his misery. He ain't gonna make a soldier anyway."

"He must learn to defend himself," said Berard to Nettie. "Strike at him and keep striking until I say stop. If soldiering is his fate, he'll ward off the blows. If not, he'll die."

The sting from Nettie's buttocks seeped through her body, setting a knot in her stomach and a burn in her heart like the fire from a smithy's furnace. The honour of fighting for the Worshipful Master, for Volerdie's army, wilted under the midday sun, replaced by a brimming anger at the tyrants standing before her. Lieutenant Berard. Sergeant Rork.

How would killing Erwin help her defeat Malphas' enemies? wondered Nettie. For she *would* kill him. He couldn't defend himself against a wooden pole.

"If you refuse the order," said Berard, "both of you will be sent to the ditch."

Nettie almost vomited thinking about being thrown into the privy trench, where the battalion deposited its waste, and left to rot there for days.

She lifted her sword and faced Erwin. He removed his left hand from his bulging shoulder and grasped the halberd. She hoped he'd learnt something about defending himself. Enough to deflect her blows until Berard got bored. Locking eyes with Erwin, she tried to communicate her first move to him. Nettie looked towards his left, nodded, paused, then swung her sword at his left arm. Erwin swiped his halberd, knocking the point of her sword away from his arm.

This might work, she thought.

She looked to his right, paused, and swung. Again, Erwin deflected Nettie's sword. She tilted her head towards the ground, planning to attempt a cut below the waist. As she swept the blade in an arc, Erwin thrust down, forcing the tip of Nettie's weapon into the dirt.

Once more, thought Nettie, lifting her eyes to the clouds to indicate a thrust at Erwin's chest. She drew her sword back, past the front of her shoulder and lunged at Erwin's chest. He swung his halberd up. It deflected Nettie's sword, but the blade's edge caught him across the cheek.

"Ow!" cried Erwin, dropping his weapon and rubbing at the cut.

The smeared blood vanished amid skin flushed red from the urgency to stay alive.

"Finish it," said Berard.

He's unarmed, thought Nettie. I can't....

"Finish it, or I'll finish it for you. He's not a soldier. He's a liability."

Erwin faced her, a trail of blood trickling down to his chin. The cut on his cheek wasn't deep, but he sobbed from the pain or fear of what came next.

Yes, he's *not* a soldier, thought Nettie. Better to end it now, by her hand, than by an enemy's cruel blade. She lifted her sword, guessed the location of Erwin's heart, and prepared to plunge the blade into his chest. Rork stood beside her, arm raised, ready to whip her again should she falter. Berard stared with unrelenting eyes.

Nettie jabbed forward. Before the blade reached Erwin, he collapsed in a heap, his legs kicked from under him by Berard. Losing her balance, Nettie toppled onto Erwin. Rork cackled like a curate drunk on the promise of paradise.

"The boy's not a soldier," said Berard, "but we can use him as a decoy. No point wasting good fodder." The lieutenant marched off with Rork in tow.

That night, Nettie lay awake in her dormitory bunk, more determined than ever to see Yonna. In the bed next to her, Erwin snored, his peeling, sunburnt face twitching with dreams baked, most likely, with honey-devil kuchen. The cut on his cheek had stopped bleeding, and the swelling in his shoulder had diminished, but Erwin wouldn't last. When he arrived, Nettie marvelled at his round, rosy face. But meagre rations and hard training had withered Erwin's glow. He wasted away before her eyes, his body and mind falling apart piece by piece. Nettie could save herself with Yonna's help, but she couldn't save Erwin.

As the snorts and wheezes of sleeping soldiers bounced from the dormitory's stone walls, Nettie rehearsed the escape in her mind. Shutters had been nailed tight to the mullions on every window except the one opposite her bed. Bullwork, Lieutenant Berard's lapdog, had reported the loose shutter to Rork, but the sergeant hadn't bothered to fix it. With guards posted at the front door, the defective window offered Nettie the best chance for escape. She'd prise open the shutter, jump through the window, fix the timber back in place, and discreetly stroll away. Maybe she'd return, no-one the wiser to her abscondment, or perhaps she wouldn't. Yonna would guide her.

Nettie lifted the blanket and swung her feet over the edge, slipping them into her boots. She sat up, leaned down, tied the boot laces, then took a roll of clothes from under the bed, laying them lengthways on the mattress. Masked by the blanket, she hoped the clothes resembled a dutiful, sleeping soldier.

After pulling a tunic over her undergarments and cinching it at the waist with a belt, she tucked in the bed covers, gathered her dagger, and crept towards the faulty window. Bullwork slept beside it, his stocky frame lying naked atop the blanket. Nettie thought his eyes were open, staring into the room, waiting for the first run-away to try the loose shutter, but convinced herself the gloominess played tricks. Not wanting uncertainty to scuttle her plan, she prised the dagger between the shutter edge and mullion, braced her waist against the window sill and levered the shutter open. It swung out, a gust of wind catching in the slats until the timber smacked against the outside wall. Bullwork snorted and rolled onto his back. Nettie froze, her eyes drawn to his genitals as if they might hint at an awakening. But Berard's pet stirred only to suck in another snore.

She didn't hesitate further, climbing through the window, closing the shutter and knocking in the corner nails with the heel of her hand. The half-moons of Seena and Bargan lit a warm, starry night. Guards posted outside every dormitory watched the dozens of long, rectangular buildings that comprised Pergamos' sprawling military complex. Nettie pressed herself into the stone wall, thinking about the best path to avoid the guards and escape into the streets of the civilian quarters. Once there, she'd race straight home.

She slunk away, clinging to the barrack walls and hiding among the night shadows, thankful her short, skinny frame would be hard to spot. Leaving the military complex more easily than expected, with no barrier separating it from the rest of Pergamos, she snuck along quiet, dark alleys, past the calendar of life and stepped pyramid, promising herself one day she'd climb to the top.

Away from the pyramid's shadow, her skin tingled a warning. The night hid a pursuer. She trotted ahead, avoiding the handful of citizens still up this late, then ducked into a side street. Hiding under a portico, she unsheathed her dagger and waited for the stalker to arrive, her thumping heart matching the slap of their boots on the flagstones.

Louder. Louder. LOUDER.

The pursuer walked up to the portico. Nettie raised her arm, ready to strike. But he marched past her as if she was invisible.

Damn it, she thought. "Erwin," hissed Nettie.

He spun around and peered into the portico shadows, looking sheepish and sleepy, his cheek wound re-opened with blood glistening in the moonlight.

"What are you doing?" she asked.

He approached her. "I saw you climb out the window. Thought you were escaping without me. Then I thought, Nettie wouldn't do that. But I wasn't sure. So, I followed."

"I'm going to see my father. You should return before they find us missing."

"I don't want to be there alone, in case there's early inspection. If you're not in the dormitory, they'll blame me. They know we're friends."

Friends, thought Nettie. Erwin's loyalty impressed and bothered her in equal measure.

"Friends don't leave friends behind," said Erwin.

Or get them in trouble, thought Nettie. "Go back or go home to your parents. They can hide you from the army."

"Aren't you returning? To the dormitory, I mean. Once you've talked to your Pa."

Nettie pulled Erwin under the portico as someone walked past. "I don't know," she whispered. "Yonna might help me leave Pergamos for good."

"I want to go with you. My parents won't resist the army. Sergeant Rork will come looking, and Ma and Pa will wilt under interrogation. All I am, all my flaws and weaknesses, I inherited from them. They're feeble, so I'm feeble."

Nettie squeezed Erwin's hand. "Don't say that. You're stronger than you think."

"I'm stronger because of you."

The longing in Erwin's eyes set a lump in Nettie's throat. For better or worse, he looked to her as his saviour.

"Alright," she said. "You can keep watch while I talk to Yonna. I'll try to convince him to help both of us."

As Nettie and Erwin approached Nettie's home, a wind gust sent a whirl of dust dancing across the ground, grit adhering to Nettie's sweat-dampened tunic and stinging her eyes. She cursed the harvest season's stifling heat before stopping opposite a stone cottage with a thatched roof sheltering four rooms and three families. Her home.

Attached to the cottage, Yonna's smithy looked bleak and bare, with no finished weapons in the racks and no scrap metal waiting to be melted. Rusty junk lay scattered across the floor, and the forge fire had died.

Yonna *never* lets the fire go out, thought Nettie. She faced Erwin. "Wait in the smithy and watch for soldiers."

"The smithy's open," he said. "Anyone can see inside."

"Hide behind the hearth. To your left is a doorway into the cottage. If soldiers arrive, run inside to warn us."

"Then what?"

"I don't know," snapped Nettie. "Just do what I say."

She ran across the road to the front door, turned the doorknob and stepped inside a dark koken, the cooking area shared by the three families. Nettie and Yonna's bedroom adjoined the koken. She pulled across the curtain that shielded the doorway and walked into the bedroom. Her bed lay empty, but Yonna slept, his back facing the door.

She knelt by the bed and shook his shoulder. "Pa. Pa, it's me."

Yonna stirred and rolled over. Except, it wasn't Yonna.

"What y'want?" asked Kledo, the oldest boy in the Walcham family.

"What are you doing in my father's bed?" said Nettie.

Kledo rubbed his eyes and yawned. "Ain't his bed anymore."

"Why not?"

"He died. Ages ago."

No, thought Nettie. I saw him at the victory parade. "Are you sure?"

"Malphas' Shield beat him to death for being too slow to make weapons. Dropped a fired axe right on his neck. Sliced it open real good. Ma saw it. Said I could have his bed."

As Kledo rolled away, Nettie wanted to pummel him with her fists. She sobbed instead. "Where is he? Where's his body?"

"Soldiers tossed it into the furnace," mumbled Kledo.

Nettie tugged at the woollen blanket covering the imposter in Pa's bed, then twisted the fabric around her wrist as if she was wringing Kledo's neck.

I'll kill them, she thought. I'll kill every last one of Malphas' Shield.

"Let me sleep." Kledo pulled the blanket from Nettie's failing clutch and wrapped it over his shoulder.

She knelt on the floor, wiping away tears and hating everything. The stupid people in her home who didn't save Yonna. The soldiers who beat him to death and dishonoured his body. The army for taking her away from him. The Worshipful Master for building this awful city. The Divine Creator for ignoring her prayers. And she hated her father for being so devoted to a creator who abandoned his people to seek better fortune elsewhere.

Nettie left the cottage by the side door and stepped into the smithy. It had been stripped bare, the floor covered in metal scraps, ash and dust, with only the furnace's stone chimney left standing, flameless black coals piled inside. Wondering if Yonna's bones rested beneath the pile, Nettie walked to the hearth and thrust her hand inside the coals. Her fingers found a metal rod as thick as a halberd shaft and almost as long. As she grasped the rod, someone stepped from behind the chimney. Simultaneously, she clenched her jaw and spun, swinging the metal rod at the threatening shadow that haunted this special place.

Erwin ducked, and the rod smashed into bricks and mortar, showering him with stone fragments.

"It's me," said Erwin, holding his hands over his head like a helmet.

"What?"

"It's me, Erwin. Your friend."

She wavered inside the smithy, unsure of what to do next. Yonna had devoted his life to his craft. In the end, it killed him.

Blind devotion will do that, thought Nettie.

"Where's your Pa?" asked Erwin.

Nettie dropped the rod onto the ash-covered floor. "He's dead. Malphas killed him."

Erwin placed his arm around Nettie's shoulder. "I'm sorry, Nettie. Truly I am."

She fell into his chest and sobbed.

Almost as inseparable as Nettie and Erwin had become, the half-moon of Bargan followed his smaller companion, Seena, past the apex of Pergamos' pyramid.

Nettie hugged Erwin, indifferent to the world around her and the future beyond. "I'm not returning to the army," she said. "They murdered Pa. He could have made weapons faster if I was here to help. But they stole me away to be one of their soldiers, then punished Yonna for my abduction. Damn the stupid army. Damn Malphas. I hope paradise is a lie, and they all rot in misery."

"We'll work something out," said Erwin. "We'll find a way to escape."

Nettie pulled away, walked to the front of the hearth, gathered a handful of ash and let it run through her fingers.

~ Chapter 27 ~

"I'm not on fire now," said Genevea, brushing away the wet cloth wielded by Jurelle before it sloshed her face again.

Thaly smiled at Jurelle's fussing. Her father hadn't left Genevea's side since the fire in the griffin barn six moons ago. She'd recovered from the burns, a Germalian healer dressing the wounds on Genevea's arms and legs with strips of cloth soaked in a blend of cactus milk and seaweed extract. The potion worked wonders, the healer declaring Genevea would have only minor scarring. Trapped in the three-room apartment with Jurelle's worry, Thaly sensed her mother needed to escape.

She walked from the balcony, where Jurelle and Genevea sat at the breakfast table watching Portum's crowds shuffle along the streets below, through the main living area and into the bedroom she shared with Saskia. *Shared* was a misnomer. Thaly rarely slept here anymore, preferring Chloe's apartment or occasionally sleeping in the Volatal Vexil barracks. Saskia had exploited her sister's absence, using Thaly's bed as a vestium, piling an endless array of clothes on the quilt. She'd also stacked books from Portum's library on the dresser and filled the drawers with jewellery, carvings, and a concerning number of knives.

Thaly took a knife from the half-open top drawer and ran her fingers over the alabaster handle, carved from elephai horn into the shape of a scorpion, its stinging tail designed to wrap around the tops of fingers like a cutlass grip.

This is a Pordillo knife, thought Thaly, likely claimed as a battle trophy.

With Saskia flying over the deserts of Magna Avium to scout Pordillo positions, Thaly hoped her sister wouldn't have the need to add another knife to the collection.

She tossed the trophy back in the drawer and picked up a book:

Social Class in Germalian Society. After she'd learned to read Germalian, Zenais gave Thaly this book, telling her every adult in Portum should read it so they knew their place. Thaly opened the volume to the chapter on housing.

A Portum resident is afforded housing in accordance with their status. Conventus Senators qualify for fully furnished apartments with a maximum of five rooms, including private bathing and cooking facilities. Apartments with ocean views near The Hive are reserved for orators...The Sella commands the most generous living arrangements....

Thaly learned quickly that status was a flexible ideal in Germalian society. Jurelle and Genevea's apartment better reflected their daughters' status rather than their own. Should Jurelle become a single man, he'd be forced to live in a commune with other single men, despite Thaly's position as a senator. He could improve his status if he remarried.

Thaly flicked to the chapter on employment.

Senators are paid a modest wage to cover rent and other living expenses... some establishments in Portum offer free meals and/or free entertainment to senators...men are paid a standard minimum wage, less tax, to cover room rent, food and clothing...slavery is outlawed in Germalia...any employer engaging in slavery will be sentenced to life imprisonment in the carcer at the discretion of the conventus....

While Germalians abhorred slavery, senators often employed male servants on inadequate pay to cook, clean, and help raise children. Child-rearing also occurred in creches managed by women, a precursor to school, which children started at four yarles of age.

"What are you thinking about?" asked Genevea.

Thaly closed the book, placed it on the dresser and faced her mother. "Nothing and everything. The life ahead of me."

Jurelle poked his head through the doorway and smiled. "Grandchildren?"

"Chloe and I might adopt," said Thaly. "One day."

Jurelle's smile broadened. "One day soon?"

Genevea leaned on the door jamb and rolled her eyes at her husband. "Are you in such a hurry to have more children to worry about?"

Thaly laughed. "Pa's desperate for another man in the family. To even up the numbers."

"I'm happy with you and Saskia," said Genevea, stepping into the room and taking Thaly's hand. Over the last six moons, they'd grown closer than ever.

Pity, thought Thaly, it took a near-death experience to find the love she'd suppressed for her mother.

"I want to get out of here," said Genevea. "Go for a ride."

"You're not well enough," said Jurelle.

"Nonsense. I've been trapped in this apartment for days. I need fresh air."

"Start with a walk, Ma," said Thaly.

"How about a kamel ride?" said Genevea, turning expectantly to Jurelle.

He frowned. "You know I dislike kamels."

"You might like them more when you get to know them."

"Ma's right," said Thaly. "They're not as bad as Saskia makes out. When I rode in a kamel turma, I adored my mount, Sheba. The trick is to align your expectations with theirs."

The Hive clocktower tolled four lumina.

Thaly rubbed Genevea's hand. "Conventus begins in an hour. I have to go."

"Another session on designing kamels?" asked Jurelle, not bothering to mask his sarcasm. "Or will you spend the entire day debating how to bake a cake?"

"Very funny, Pa," said Thaly. "You're jealous you can't attend the meetings."

"That's one thing I'll never be jealous of."

Genevea squeezed Thaly's hand, then released her grip. "Go, Thaly. You have your report on the fire to present. I feel much better today, and your father won't leave my side."

Thaly nodded, lifted a green senator gown from the hook behind the door, kissed her Ma and Pa on the cheek, then scooted from the apartment and down the stairs.

Portum's main boulevard, Lata Via, bustled with the morning crowds heading to work. Germalians weren't early risers, most starting their employ at five lumina and often working into the night. Carrying the robe in the crux of her arm, Thaly joined a pomposity of senators striding to the Pallaxium, nodding hello to her colleagues as they darted through the pageantry of Portum society. Vendors carried baskets laden with fruit and vegetables. Weavers had cloth slung over their shoulders. The satchels of administrators bulged with parchments. Street sweepers, sailors, teachers, and kamel handlers; all kept in order by the vigilum, directing traffic and enforcing Portum's laws.

The morning sun already burned Thaly's olive cheeks. The hottest season in Portum coincided with Enthilen's harvest season. Thaly missed the changing seasons she grew up with. The long dark's biting chill, where each breath set an ache in your chest, but reminded you air was life. The storm season's rolling black clouds, surging over the Scaur Hills and descending on Bagendon like an army wielding swords of white heat that split the sky, and beating drums so loud as to strike terror into the bravest soldier. The eddies of the wind season flinging dust into spirals that danced across the Dambay Plains like lovers at a ball. The season of blossoms, where even the barren Scaur Hills could be covered in wildflowers. The growing season's promise and the fulfilment of the pledge as harvest began. She missed the harvest season the most. It was Enthilen's reward to those who called the land home. Bounty to share, making up for life's many challenges.

Arriving at the Pallaxium, Thaly took the outside steps two at a time, racing ahead of the other senators and through the main entrance framed by huge metal doors weighing more than a ship's keel, but which could be opened by the slightest of anitors. Chloe stood in the foyer, handing cups of water to passing senators.

"How's your mother?" Chloe asked Thaly.

"She wants to go kamel riding."

Chloe's merlot lips parted to reveal glistening white teeth. "Did the fire impair her ability to make rational decisions?"

Thaly laughed. "Let's go out tonight, after conventus. I could do with a nice meal."

"Senator Stansfield, is that a diplomatic attempt to complain about my cooking?"

"No. It's my turn to cook, and...well, you know the limits of my culinary skills."

"A meal out sounds wonderful."

Thaly wanted to lean across and kiss Chloe, but conventus formality smothered affection and frivolity. Instead, she donned the green senatorial robes and took a cup of water from her lover's hand, caressing Chloe's fingers with a knowing touch.

After strolling into the zōdiakos, Thaly sat among her fellow senators in the Capri faction and pulled a parchment from the pocket inside her robes that detailed the events surrounding the griffin barn fire. Despite gathering evidence for three days, the report was inconclusive. But she'd been there when the fire started, and the conventus ordered her to identify its cause.

The zōdiakos filled to capacity as an anitor blew into a bellum cornu to call the senators to assemble. Using a private access at the lowest level of the room's five tiers, the Sella, Charmion, wheeled her chair into the centre circle, then lifted herself onto the cushioned red seat reserved for the most influential person in Portum. Anitors offered to help, but she brushed them aside and ordered them from the chamber before tapping the malleus on the giant seasnail shell. Straggling senators took their seats, and Charmion waited for the murmurs to subside before returning the malleus to its holding rack.

"Order," she cried, gathering a parchment from the side table and scanning the transcript. "Today's agenda...order, please!" The senators hushed, and Charmion continued, "The first item on today's agenda is the report on the griffin barn fire presented by Senator Athalee Stansfield of Capri. Proceed, Athalee."

Thaly cleared her throat, nodded to the Sella, and stood, wiping nervous sweat from her hand before unfurling the report. "Thank you,

Sella Charmion. Six moons ago, a fire started in the griffin barn on a day when all twelve griffins were stabled. Thanks to the griffin handlers' quick thinking, especially a man named Puer, the griffins were saved, and no-one was killed. However, my mother, Genevea Stansfield, and two handlers suffered minor to moderate burns, and it will take twelve days to repair the barn. After an extensive investigation into the fire's cause, I'm almost certain it was…deliberately lit." Thaly stopped to compose herself as a thrum of concern echoed around the chamber.

"Order," said Charmion before nodding at Thaly to continue.

Thaly's tongue searched her dry mouth for a droplet of spit. She swallowed, then continued, "Deliberately lit because there's no other explanation for the presence of a significant quantity of serpent oil in the barn. No handler or wind-rider knew where the oil came from or why it was there. Among the ashes, I discovered shards of clay pots. These pots must have contained the oil, were thrown against the barn wall, and then the oil set alight. This would explain the fire's rapid spread."

"Sabotage!" a senator yelled, followed by an echo of agreement.

"Order!" cried Charmion.

"I thought…" started Thaly, raising her voice, "…thought about that, gathering all the shards and taking them to a potter. He reconstructed one of the vessels and found a scorpion image stamped on its base. Similar clay pots are used by the Pordillo to carry supplies."

"Insurgents," murmured a senator sitting beside Thaly.

She faced the senator. "If Pordillo insurgents started the fire, why did they strike during the day and not at night when there are no handlers in the barn?"

Melitta, the Sagit faction orator, sprang from her seat. "The Pordillo recognised the opportunity to kill *all* the griffins, and they took it. They're desperate to wound our defences before launching a major assault. We should double the patrols around the barn."

"Pordillo spies have infiltrated Portum," said a senator sitting behind Melitta.

"We must attack the desert rats," called another.

Charmion yanked the malleus from its holder and banged the shell. "Order! If I have to expel senators *and* orators for disruption, I will do so. Athalee, continue."

Thaly nodded. "The potter identified seven clay pots able to contain enough serpent oil to set alight the entire barn. I spoke to vendors who trade with Magna Avium's nomadic tribes. No vendor admitted to buying from the Pordillo, as it's forbidden by the conventus. None knew how the clay pots came to Portum, and those who've traded in serpent oil previously said they hadn't handled such a large amount in recent yarles. I also checked the inventories of merchant ships arriving at The Hive in the last twelve moons, but discovered nothing suspicious. That is the end of my report."

As Thaly resumed her seat, Melitta, still standing, raised her hand.

"The Sella recognises Melitta of Sagit," said Charmion.

"It's obvious, isn't it?" said Melitta. "There's no record of the serpent oil being purchased, no account of it arriving on a ship because Pordillo spies smuggled the oil into Portum. Do we need more evidence? A major attack on our city is imminent, and we must confront the Pordillo before it happens."

Zenais raised her hand.

"The Sella recognises Zenais of Capri."

"If it *was* the Pordillo," said Zenais, "where did they get so much serpent oil? It's no longer common in Germalia, especially the Pordillo lands in Magna Avium, and Portum's streetlamps are fired by slow-burning carborupem. Only the curmudgles of Grauberge mine serpent oil, extracted from fountains of hot lava that spew from the ground like dragon vomit. It's still common in Nordland and Enthilen, and since the Nordmen don't trade with the Pordillo, our enemy could only have obtained a substantial oil supply from the Erstürmen. The real threat Germalia faces is Malphas."

Melitta raised her hand, and Charmion acknowledged her.

"Why must Senators Zenais and Eutropia link everything to the Erstürmen?" asked Melitta. "What is their agenda? Why are they so desperate to begin a war with Malphas?" She faced Thaly with eyes that could burn the feathers from a griffin, stabbing a finger in her direction. "I'll tell you why. Zenais and Eutropia plan to instate Athalee Stansfield, daughter of Dobunni and Erstürmen royalty, as the leader of Enthilen. They yearn to place a new tyrant on Enthilen's throne who will grant their every wish."

The eyes of two hundred and eighty-eight senators turned to Thaly, and she wanted to melt into the floor, seeping into the porous flagstones like water spilled on desert sand. She pulled the cuff of her senatorial robe over the white handkerchief knotted around her wrist, a reminder of her ties to Enthilen.

How did Melitta discover Zenais and Eutropia's plan? wondered Thaly. And she's twisted it into something it's not in front of the entire conventus.

Eutropia raised her hand.

"The Sella recognises Eutropia of Arie," said Charmion.

"Melitta mispresents our motives," said Eutropia. "It's true, Athalee Stansfield is best placed to unite Enthilen when Malphas falls, but she'd lead temporarily until the election of a democratic council."

Loud jeers came from the Sagit faction, egged on by Melitta.

Charmion tapped the malleus on the shell. "We're getting ahead of ourselves. Germalia is not at war with Enthilen. There are no plans to begin a conflict or install a new leader. The meeting must return to the Pordillo threat."

But Thaly's thoughts drifted away, across Magna Avium, up the Riverlands Escarpment and into Enthilen. Zenais and Eutropia wanted her to conquer Malphas. This immortal, seemingly invincible fanatic whose mocking smile defiled her dreams. More than ever, she felt like a doll in a child's hands, being twisted and squeezed to fit a bounded obsession with realising vain ambitions.

Politics is a game, Thaly concluded, and I'm being played. She fixed burning eyes on Zenais and Eutropia, and sat smouldering until the meeting ended.

As she marched into the foyer, Zenais and Eutropia pulled her aside.

"We were going to tell you," said Zenais. "At the right time."

"You expected my father to keep the secret?" said Thaly. "Or for him to sway my decision without me knowing the full extent of your aspiration? You've underestimated Stansfield family loyalty."

"Yes, we desired Jurelle's support," said Eutropia.

Thaly raised her eyebrows. "How strange. A man's opinion is readily dismissed in Germalia, yet you seek the backing of one who's a foreigner."

Beneath her red senatorial gown, Eutropia's shoulders relaxed. "You're right. If Jurelle backed our plan for you to lead Enthilen...."

"It would be easier to mould your figurehead," interrupted Thaly. "I didn't ask for any of this." She turned, trying to push through the crowd until Zenais grabbed her forearm.

"Wait," said Zenais. "If you desired such power, we wouldn't ask you. The best leaders come from the pool of the reluctant. Your hesitancy gives me hope we've made the right choice."

"Since you arrived in Portum eleven yarles ago," said Eutropia, "we've watched you blossom into a respected senator and an accomplished military commander. You hesitated at every step, but with a little affirmation, you took the step with an assured stride. You'll act with the same poise when we march on Enthilen."

"This is a pointless conversation," said Thaly. "We're not declaring war on Malphas."

Zenais pulled Thaly close and whispered, "We almost have the numbers. Soon we'll propose a vote to march on Enthilen and confront Malphas. Only a handful of doubters remain to be convinced. Distractions with the Pordillo aren't helping our cause."

"Is that all the Pordillo are?" asked Thaly. "My sister is in Magna Avium now, scouting Pordillo positions. I hope she isn't risking her life for a *distraction*."

Eutropia rested her hand on Thaly's shoulder. "We appreciate the sacrifices our soldiers make. Please understand us. We don't want war — not with the Pordillo *or* Malphas, but war is coming. You must feel it. You have your father's blood. The intuition of a warrior. The battle will be fought on Portum's doorstep if we don't strike first."

"The mix of Erstürmen and Dobunni blood I've inherited feels like a curse."

"A curse or a blessing," said Zenais. "Depends on your perspective."

"You're presumptuous to think Malphas will fall. His army must exceed a hundred thousand. He commands the elite soldiers of the Erstürmen Shield and the monstrous Rephaim. Tainted grells and draughouls and who knows what else serve him."

"We have griffins," said Eutropia. "No army can defeat them."

"Griffins aren't invincible. The fire in the barn proved that."

"Enthilen needs you, Athalee," said Zenais. "Germalia needs you. Malphas' eternal terror will spread across Ostamp. We have to stop him. We'll call the conventus to vote when we have the numbers."

"The vote must be unanimous," said Thaly. "The Pisce faction is undecided, and the Sagit faction will never support a war with Enthilen."

"Melitta will do what her senators demand," said Eutropia. "Despite her bluster, an orator is only the spokesperson of her faction's will."

"The griffin barn fire," said Zenais. "You raised the question, Thaly. Why did Pordillo insurgents strike during the day? Why use clay pots with the scorpion insignia, linking them to the fire? They did little to mask their involvement."

The crowd of senators thinned from the Pallaxium foyer as Thaly mulled her thoughts like red vinum. She'd considered other possibilities regarding the fire, but she dared not include them in her report.

"Because the fire was a distraction," said Thaly. "A ruse to focus our attention on the Pordillo and not let it drift to other matters."

"Who gains by keeping the Germalian army in Portum?" asked Zenais.

"Malphas," said Thaly.

"If we can connect the fire to the Erstürmen, or better yet, Malphas himself, it will be a vital piece of evidence, helping us secure a unanimous vote."

"A smokescreen masks the real culprit and their motivation," said Eutropia. "I know you will see through it."

She and Zenais turned their backs and marched from the foyer. Chloe farewelled them as they exited through the central doorway and into Portum's streets.

She approached Thaly. "I overheard your conversation with the senators," said Chloe. "I didn't want to say anything before because it could get me into trouble, but I might know where to start looking. For the culprit behind the smokescreen."

* * * *

Thaly stood with Chloe at the bottom of the Pallaxium's steps as Portum's clocktower struck seven nocturna. This late at night, most of the city's residents slept, and the streets around the Pallaxium were empty. But two soldiers guarded the front door, resting their hands on the hilts of cutlasses sheathed to plaited belts encircling the bottom of golden, scaled breastplates.

"Are you sure about this?" asked Thaly, turning her back to the guards.

"There's only one way to find out," said Chloe.

She went to climb the steps, but Thaly grabbed her hand.

"We should go to the vigilum," said Thaly. "Let them deal with it."

"They won't investigate a conventus orator."

Dread fixed Thaly's feet in place, but her mind raced. "They might, if...."

"No," interrupted Chloe, "they won't. Senators make the laws, and the vigilum enforces them. But only the conventus can punish one of its own for treason."

"Why Melitta?" asked Thaly. "I mean, why is she working for Malphas?"

"We don't know she is yet. We need evidence. But she's been acting suspiciously. Holding night-time meetings in her private office behind a locked door. Speaking with unsavoury types in the streets."

Thaly raised her eyebrow. "Have you been following her?"

Chloe smiled. "Watching her like a griffin. When we gather the necessary evidence, we can present it to Zenais. Or better yet, the Sella. Charmion will know what to do."

As Chloe's plan unfurled, Thaly's resolution wavered. If Melitta served

Malphas and was responsible for the griffin barn fire, she'd likely do anything to keep the secret, including killing Thaly and Chloe. And if Thaly made a false accusation against an orator, she'd be banished from the conventus and stripped of her military command.

"We won't approach Charmion until we have solid evidence," said Chloe. "You're beginning to worry more than your father."

Thaly gave Chloe a wry smile. "Alright, where do we start?"

"Melitta's office. I have a front door key and another that opens the cabinet where the duplicate office keys are kept. I'll leave you to sweet-talk the guards."

Thaly frowned and nodded, then followed Chloe up the steps, pulling the hem of her green senator gown up to her shins to avoid the embarrassment of tripping in front of the guards. At the top of the stairs, a soldier stepped in front of her.

"Name?" she said.

"Senator Athalee Stansfield of Capri."

"Why are you here so late?" asked the guard.

"I need to collect a parchment from my office. I'll only be a moment. I've brought an anitor with me to unlock the front door."

The soldier, a young woman with cinnamon-coloured hair, unusual for a Germalian, paused for a moment, then turned to her companion. The older woman nodded, looking bored and tired, and the young guard stepped aside.

Chloe strode to the front door, slotted the key into the lock and turned. The lock clicked open, and Thaly and Chloe pushed the door ajar, squeezed inside, and locked it behind them.

"I can't see a thing," said Thaly.

"Wait."

Chloe disappeared into the darkness, returning a moment later with two lit candles. She gave one to Thaly, then led her to the cabinet containing the duplicate keys. After opening the cabinet and taking the key to Melitta's office, she and Thaly walked along the circular hallway until reaching the orator's door.

"Wait here and call out if you see anything," said Chloe.

"What am I going to see this late?" asked Thaly.

Chloe shrugged. "There might be a diligent senator or two, slaving away in their office for the acclamation of their colleagues."

Chloe unlocked Melitta's door and stepped inside, holding her candle out front.

Should have knocked first, thought Thaly.

She waited in the hallway, unable to see much past the pale amber glow of a lone flame as a jumble of thoughts bounced around her head, trying to arrange themselves logically. Trying to identify the next step should Chloe find a clue.

A window rattled. Thaly spun around, sweeping the candle in an arc to brush away the night.

The wind, she thought. Nothing but the wind.

Then a hand clutched her shoulder, tying a knot in Thaly's chest.

"I've got something," said Chloe.

Thaly relaxed. "I thought you were...it doesn't matter."

Chloe held a piece of torn parchment under the candlelight. "There's an impression in the paper. I rubbed graphite over it. Look."

Faint wording, outlined by the grey rub, emerged.

Gustium. Eight nocturna. First night of half/quarter waning moons.

"Tonight," bubbled Chloe, "is the first night Seena is at half and Bargan at quarter waning moons."

"Gustium is one of Portum's seedier neighbourhoods," said Thaly. "Why would an orator be going there?"

"To meet unsavoury types. Let's catch her in the act."

"A conventus senator can't be seen in Gustium."

"There are spare clothes in the anitors' office vestium. Clothes worn by cleaners and cooks. We can disguise ourselves."

"In a crowd of Germalians, my pale olive skin stands out like Portum's lighthouse."

"Don't worry," said Chloe, "we'll cover it up."

She led Thaly to the anitors' office, a room with a dozen desks and chairs arranged in four rows of three, an area for food preparation, and closets and chests lined along a wall. Chloe opened a closet full of beige shirts, scarves and pants.

"We should change back at your apartment," said Thaly.

"It'll be eight nocturna soon. Barely enough time to go from here to Gustium."

Thaly removed her green gown, lacy blouse and ankle-length skirt of fine silk, a dead giveaway she didn't belong in Gustium, and pulled on a tawny pair of pants and shirt made from rough cotton. Chloe wrapped a headscarf around Thaly's hair, face and neck, exposing only the eyes. Brown eyes, like most other Germalians.

"There are gloves here, too," said Chloe.

"I'm sweating already," said Thaly.

"A libation to the betterment of the illustrious Germalian empire."

Dressed head-to-foot, only the olive-white of her toes poking from her sandals, Thaly waited while Chloe changed into a servant's clothes.

"What will the guards think?" asked Thaly, her voice muffled by the facemask.

"We'll use the emergency exit," said Chloe. "It can only be opened from the inside."

"The guards will come looking for us."

Chloe rubbed her tongue over her lips like she did when thinking deeply, then pulled her anitor robe over the servant clothes.

"I'll report to the guards first," she said. "Tell them you've decided to work until morning, and I'm to assist you. They'll forget about us by then."

Thaly groaned. "It feels like a lot of things can go wrong."

"Worry, worry, worry, Senator Stansfield. Where's your sense of adventure?"

Chloe raced to the front door to speak with the guards.

Thaly pulled the mask from her nose and mouth to suck in uncomforting breaths, worrying what she'd do if they found Melitta.

"They bought it," said Chloe as she trotted from the darkness. "Never underestimate my powers of persuasion."

*   *   *   *

Thaly hadn't been to Gustium at night. Now, she understood why. Gangs of drunken men wandered the streets, lurching from one lamppost to the next, vomiting in gutters or trying to pick fights with passers-by. Young boys sat on the steps of dilapidated buildings, holding tin cups towards the passing crowd and begging to catch a stray coin or two. Washing hung on clotheslines stretched across rambling alleys. Timber, tin and rope held together hovels that looked as if they'd been lifted by a mighty wind, then smashed down to earth before someone made a home in them. Human waste trickled along open sewers before disappearing down drains and being carried to who knew where.

Even disguised, conspicuousness gnawed at Thaly. Women rarely frequented Gustium. She and Chloe stood out like crimson flowers in an otherwise barren field.

So will Melitta, thought Thaly. If Chloe's hunch is correct.

"Where do we start?" asked Thaly.

"Melitta lives in an apartment on The Hive. She'll probably enter Gustium from the northwest, along Meretrix Via. We should wait at the corner of Meretrix Via and Gustium's main thoroughfare."

Thaly and Chloe loitered on the corner opposite a row of brothels. Men caked in make-up and dressed in flowing, diaphanous gowns strutted along the street, soliciting passers-by.

"Are there only male whores?" asked Thaly.

"Mostly. *Domina-homines,* they're called. Lady-men. A few women are prostitutes. The popular ones make more in a yarle than a *conventus* senator."

"How do you know these things?"

Chloe turned away. "My mother was a prostitute. Before someone killed her."

Thaly reached for Chloe's hand. "Oh, Chloe. You never said. I'm so sorry."

"Sorry she was a whore, or sorry she died?"

Both, thought Thaly, but bit her tongue.

"Look," said Chloe, pointing across the street. "Is that Melitta?"

As the faint toll of the clocktower striking eight nocturna drifted into Gustium, a person walked past the brothels, a headscarf masking everything but their eyes and nose.

She moves like a woman, thought Thaly, but so do these lady-men.

"The stranger's the same height as Melitta," said Chloe, "and the headscarf is silk. A fabric a conventus senator could afford, but few others."

The masked stranger entered an establishment called *Lupanar*.

"I'm going after her," said Chloe.

"No." Thaly pulled Chloe back. "I should do it. If I discover anything suspicious, I'll be the one reporting to Charmion. I need to see it firsthand. You wait here. Come find me if anything goes wrong."

"Wait." Chloe dug into her pants pocket and pulled out a handful of coins. "Take these. Everything in Gustium costs something."

Thaly nodded, shoved the coins in a pocket, pulled the cuffs of her shirt over her wrists and adjusted the headscarf, hoping no-one would notice an olive-skinned imposter from the conventus. As soon as she stepped across the road towards *Lupanar*, a domina-homines approached.

"I think you're in the wrong place, Deary," said the lady-man, in a voice sounding both gruff and shrill.

Another lady-man appeared from the crowd. "She might prefer her men in dresses."

"Or have mother fantasies," chuckled the first.

"I don't want sex," said Thaly.

"Then you're definitely in the wrong place," said the second domina-homines.

"Are you from *Lupanar*?" asked Thaly.

"I am," said the first lady-man. "I'm Lucinda." She offered her hand, palm facing downwards as if expecting Thaly to kiss it.

Thaly glanced at Chloe, who stood among the crowd, smiling, then bent over and kissed the back of Lucinda's hand.

"Oh, soft lips," said Lucinda before withdrawing her hand. "And such exotic, yellowy-green skin."

"They call it olive," said the second lady-man. "A delicacy in a world of chocolate."

"Oh, yes," said Lucinda. "I love olives. Especially stuffed with spicy red pepper." She chuckled. "Why are you trying to hide it under all those clothes?"

Thaly ignored the question and asked one of her own, "If I wanted to hold a secret meeting in *Lupanar*, where would I go?"

"All our rooms are private," said Lucinda. "You can explore whatever fantasy lands you desire, and no-one will be the wiser."

"Did you see a short woman enter a moment ago? She had her face covered."

Lucinda nodded. "She's been here before. Not for sex, mind you. She always books room number twelve at the back of the building. Whatever she gets up to in there, I'll never know."

"Is there any way I could...*uhm*...eavesdrop?"

"Now I'm feeling titillated," said the second lady-man.

"Hush, Viola," said Lucinda before leaning in and whispering to Thaly, "Truth is, Deary, the walls are as thin as parchment. If you booked room number ten...."

Thaly fished around in the front pocket of her pants and retrieved the coins. "I don't know how much."

"Twenty-four coin will suffice."

Thaly counted the coin into Lucinda's open palm. Lucinda snapped the hand shut, grabbed Thaly with her free hand and dragged her into *Lupanar*.

"I've booked room ten," said Lucinda to a man sitting behind the reception desk.

She led Thaly down a hallway and stopped outside the open door of number ten, adjacent to the closed door of number twelve.

"You've got until nine nocturna," said Lucinda. "That should be plenty of time to satisfy your desires." She beamed, attempted a pirouette and almost fell over, then laughed her way back down the hall.

Thaly stepped into room ten and shut the door behind her. She sat on the bed, hoping the bed covers and sheets had been washed recently, and pressed her ear to the wall adjoining number twelve.

"You must do more," came a male voice through the wall, drifting in a straining wail that reminded Thaly of a draughoul. And it spoke Erstürmen, not Germalian or Pordillo.

"I've risked so much already," replied a female voice, also in Erstürmen.

Despite speaking another language, the voice sounded familiar, and Thaly convinced herself it was Melitta.

"Master offers more coin," said the draughoul, followed by a jangle of metal clinking against metal.

"The conventus isn't convinced," said Melitta. "The fire got their attention, but we need something more dramatic."

"Fire kill no griffins."

"It was only supposed to send a message. If it had spread further, there would be no evidence linking the attack to the Pordillo. Already, other senators are suspicious."

"Master dislikes mistakes," said the draughoul. "You must convince conventus, Pordillo too dangerous to weaken Portum's defences by sending army to Enthilen."

"I keep arguing the case, but other orators shut me down, and those wanting to confront Malphas, their numbers are building. My faction is on a hairline. If Sagit decides to vote for war, then your master will face the might of the Germalian army."

"Must not happen; otherwise, Volerdie's Wrath will fall on me *and* you."

"What else can I do?" asked Melitta.

Thaly pressed her ear closer, worried she might force a hole in the wall. The voices fell silent, but she heard shuffling, then a gasp.

"What is this?" said Melitta.

"Pordillo dagger," replied the draughoul. "Belongs to the Infada, Qaysar Rais' elite guard. Very rare weapon. Plunge it into your Sella's heart."

The shock yanked Thaly from the wall, her mouth hanging open as if waiting to catch Melitta's reply.

"You...you want me to assassinate the conventus Sella?" cried Melitta, loud enough for Thaly to hear without an ear pressed to the divider.

"Hush," hissed the draughoul.

Thaly resumed her listening post, straining to decipher the conversation above a thumping heart.

"You wish to see husband again?" asked the draughoul. "Escape this place together?"

"Yes," said Melitta.

"Master can arrange it if you please him. He offers bountiful reward or gruesome punishment. The choice is yours. Kill the Sella with the Infada dagger, and the conventus will vote against war with Enthilen. They will fight the Pordillo, not the Worshipful Master."

The voices fell silent. The door to number twelve opened.

Thaly leaned away from the wall and sat on the bed, stunned. After gathering her thoughts and courage, she marched from the room, flinging the door open and crashing into a domina-homines. The open door of number twelve revealed an empty space.

"Did you see anyone leave this room?" Thaly asked the lady-man.

"No-one interesting."

Thaly ran back down the hallway, past the reception desk and outside into a flood of people. Melitta had disappeared. Chloe waited on the other side of the street.

"Did you see her leave?" asked Thaly as she approached her lover.

Chloe raised an eyebrow. "Melitta?"

"Yes. Did you see her leave?"

"No. There *was* one person dressed in a grey, hooded cloak. Almost floated rather than walked. I couldn't tell if it was a man or a woman. Disappeared into the crowd."

"He was a draughoul. Are you sure Melitta wasn't with him?"

"Sure."

"Damn it."

Thaly crossed the street to speak with Lucinda. "Is there another way out of *Lupanar*?"

449

"A few," she said. "Some men are boastful, happy to swagger through the front door. Others desire discretion. We offer them confidential access." Lucinda masked her mouth with her hand and leaned into Thaly. "We sometimes host conventus senators. Women lusting for sex with men dressed as women. It's a funny old world."

Thaly returned to Chloe. "Melitta probably left through a different door."

"What happened in there?" asked Chloe.

"The draughoul gave Melitta a rare Pordillo dagger. A weapon from Qaysar Rais' elite guard."

"The Infada?"

Thaly nodded. "Rumour has it, only a dozen Infada exist. The metal of their daggers is infused with a poison that never loses its potency. A nick is enough to kill a kamel. The draughoul demanded Melitta kill Charmion with the dagger."

"Why?"

"Another ruse to inflate the Pordillo threat and stop the conventus voting for war with Malphas."

"We have to warn Charmion," said Chloe.

"Do you know where she lives?" asked Thaly.

"Yes. Before you became a senator, Charmion hosted a function for the entire conventus, including the anitors. It was a grand affair."

Thaly's eyes widened. "We must go there. Right now. Melitta could strike tonight."

Thaly and Chloe hailed a chariot outside Gustium. Pulled by two hulking men, the cart sped off down Meretrix Via towards Ellumina Beach, north of The Hive, where Charmion had her apartment.

They arrived after nine nocturna, paid the chariot drivers, and stood outside a palatial dwelling, five stories high and surrounded by sprawling, manicured gardens of hedges trimmed into animal shapes, espaliered fruit trees, and a maze of flowers in all the colours of Germalia's factions.

"What floor does she live on?" Thaly asked Chloe.

"Every floor."

"It's *all* hers?"

"As far as I know."

"How does she get up the stairs?" asked Thaly.

"There's a lift," said Chloe as she stepped forward.

Thaly held her back. "Wait. The draughoul said something I didn't understand. He promised Melitta would be reunited with her husband."

"He's been imprisoned for life in the carcer. The vigilum found him guilty of a senator's death. Melitta claimed he was innocent. She's demanded his release ever since."

"Malphas' draughoul promised to free her husband."

Chloe nodded, opened the gate of the iron palisade fence surrounding the gardens, and led Thaly down a path lined with flaming lanterns, swinging from their posts with the gust of a gentle sea breeze and swaying amber light back and forth across the path's flagstones. A dog barked, and a shadow stepped out from a roundhouse, no larger than a closet, at the base of the stairs leading to the porch of Charmion's house.

As Thaly approached, the shadow took the shape of a thick-set woman, almost as tall as a stone-grell with shoulders broader than most men. Strips of black leather, studded at the ends, wrapped around her waist like a skirt, and she wore a black breastplate and open-faced helmet. The armour's colour made it difficult for Thaly to determine where the clothes ended and the guard's bare skin began. The guard held a pike in both hands, diagonally across her chest. Gold inlaid in the silver blade caught the glow from lamps burning carborupem that lined the steps to Charmion's front door.

Resembling a child caught in a monster's shadow, Chloe crept up to the guard. "We need to see the Sella."

The guard sized up Thaly and then faced Chloe. "Need or want? The Sella is busy, and it's late."

"It's a matter of life and death," said Thaly. "I'm Athalee Stansfield, a conventus senator from Capri and Legatus of the Volatal Vexil. We must speak with Charmion."

"Show me your face," demanded the guard

Thaly pulled the headscarf away from her mouth and chin.

The guard's disapproving frown didn't soften. "Where are your senatorial robes?"

"I left them in the Pallaxium. It's a long story."

"Who gave you this address?"

"I did. I'm Chloe Floriana, a Pallaxium anitor. I've been here before as Charmion's guest."

"Listen," said Thaly, getting agitated, "do you want to be responsible for the Sella's death? If you keep delaying us, you will be."

"*Wind*-riders," sneered the guard. "Always putting themselves above everyone else. Wait here."

The guard lumbered up the steps and knocked on a front door taller than her and redder than a sunset over the Occidian Sea. The door opened, and a bald man poked his head out. They exchanged words, and the man disappeared. The guard stood outside the door while Thaly paced back and forth at the bottom of the steps, wondering if Melitta already hid in the garden shadows, clutching a poisoned Infada dagger and waiting for the right moment to break in and stab Charmion.

The streets outside the grand house were quiet, and the usually bustling wharves around The Hive had fallen silent to the darkness. Tied to a jetty, six barges bobbed atop the water, their sides knocking against timber pylons with each wave drifting in from the northwest. In the middle of Slyencia Bay, a classem warship sat at anchor. Thaly hadn't been on a Germalian ship. She wondered if she could ever set foot on a boat again after what happened to her and Grin on the *Vulking*.

The front door of Charmion's mansion opened, the bald man and the guard exchanged words again, then the guard marched back down the steps to Thaly and Chloe.

"Arms out to the side," said the guard. "I need to search you for weapons."

"We can enter?" asked Chloe.

"Don't make a habit of it."

The brawny guard groped every inch of Thaly and Chloe's bodies with huge hands before letting them through. They climbed the steps like mice sneaking below a perching owl. The front door swung open, and the bald man stood there, his bulging chest muscles dressed in a thin sheen of sweat. Naked other than a short skirt around his waist, it appeared the man's entire body had been shaved.

He nodded to Thaly and Chloe, then walked off into a passageway.

"Do we follow him?" asked Thaly.

Chloe shrugged, then walked after the man. Thaly followed, marching through rooms larger than most houses in Portum and full of porcelain vases perched on marble pedestals, paintings that covered entire walls, tapestries hung from the ceiling like curtains, golden sculptures of griffins and kamels, padded couches and chairs, and six-tiered chandeliers, every candle alight, the melting wax caught by silver drip-trays.

They came to a black door with a brass knocker fashioned as a lion's head. The bald man tapped the knocker.

"Yes," said a woman's voice from inside.

The man opened the door, stood aside and waved Thaly and Chloe through.

In the middle of a room no larger than Thaly's Pallaxium office sat Charmion in her wheelchair, a silk robe draped over her shoulders and open at the front such that the areola of one of her nipples peeked out from the fabric's edge. Another man, as tall and muscled as the first and completely naked and shaved, stood behind Charmion, massaging her shoulders as her head lolled forward. A couch lined one wall, a bookcase the other, and a display cabinet the third, with collections of jewellery and crystal rocks displayed on glass shelves.

Charmion opened dreamy eyes, looked straight at Thaly, then placed her hand on the male servant's arm. "Who disturbs us, Augustine?"

"Athalee Stansfield, Senator of Capri," he replied. "Legatus of the Volatal Vexil."

"Ah, yes," said Charmion, offering a condescending smile. "The Erstürmen."

"Dobunni, actually," said Thaly.

"Your mother's Erstürmen, is she not?"

"Well, yes, but my father is Dobunni."

"*Hmmm.* The Traitor General who turned his back on his own people and fought alongside the Erstürmen King Ewald. The same General who murdered brave Germalian soldiers in the Riverlands War."

Thaly's cheeks burned as if they'd been slapped. "My family history isn't...."

Charmion clapped her hands once, cutting Thaly off mid-sentence. The naked man, Augustine, leaned down, kissed Charmion's neck, then left the room.

"You can shut the door, Quintus," Charmion said to the other servant. "I don't believe these two offer me any harm."

Quintus nodded his bald head, then closed the door.

"Who have you brought with you, Athalee Stansfield of Capri?"

"This is Chloe Floriana, a conventus anitor."

"And how did you find me?" asked Charmion.

"You held a function here once," said Chloe. "Inviting all the senators and anitors."

Charmion combed her fingers through long, greying hair, brushing it down to the front of her shoulders. "I didn't invite you this time."

"No...but...," started Chloe.

"We have important news," said Thaly.

"Sit down," Charmion waved her hand at the couch.

Thaly and Chloe sat beside each other, perched on the edge of the plush, paisley cushion like naughty children.

"Vinum?" asked Charmion, using the spoked handwheels on the armrests of her wheelchair to move around to a side table before taking the lid from a crystal decanter.

"No," said Thaly and Chloe together.

Charmion poured herself a white vinum in a glass resembling the shape of her exposed breast, then wheeled the chair to the front of the couch.

"So," she said, taking a sip, "you bring news?"

Thaly gulped. Too late to go back now, she concluded. She would accuse a conventus orator of plotting to murder the Sella.

"Melitta plans to assassinate you," said Thaly.

Charmion coughed up a sup of vinum, spat it back into the pendulous glass, then laughed. "That strumpet," she scoffed. "She's the worst orator in the entire conventus." Charmion stopped, studied the vinum in her glass where spittle floated at the surface, shrugged and took another mouthful. "Capri and Sagit have never been friends. I tire so much of their bickering. Did Zenais put you up to this?"

"This isn't about a dispute between factions," said Thaly. "Melitta was behind the fire in the griffin barn. Tonight, I overheard her planning to assassinate you with a poisoned dagger stolen from Qaysar Rais' Infada and delivered by one of Malphas' draughouls."

"You presented your report about the fire to the conventus yesterday. Why didn't you mention Melitta's involvement then?"

"I didn't know then."

Charmion waved her free hand in Thaly's face. "It's irrelevant. When the fire started, Melitta and I were in a meeting inside the Pallaxium."

"She must have helpers. They started the fire, using clay pots embossed with scorpions to implicate the Pordillo. But the Pordillo aren't the real threat; Malphas is. He's trying to focus our attention on the Pordillo and stop us marching to Enthilen."

Charmion rolled her eyes. "Zenais *did* send you. She and Eutropia have been advocating for war with Enthilen for yarles. They sit in my office and beg for support, thinking I have the power to sway other factions."

Thaly ground her teeth. "Zenais didn't send me." She half-stood, leaning towards Charmion and thinking of shaking sense into her.

Charmion's eyes grew fearful, and Chloe pulled Thaly back onto the couch cushion.

"You will not sway me with intimidation, Athalee Stansfield," said Charmion, almost spitting out Thaly's name. "Should I call for my servants?"

"Men are forbidden to engage in acts of aggression," said Thaly.

"You deign to lecture me on Senatorial Dictum rules? My servants could snap your arm like a twig."

Thaly sank into the couch, trying to still her anger and compose herself. "Melitta met the draughoul in a Gustium brothel. I sat in the next room, listening to their conversation through the wall. Melitta admitted to arranging the fire. The draughoul gave her an Infada dagger to kill you, further enhancing the perceived threat the Pordillo pose to Portum."

Charmion wheeled her chair away and poured more vinum. "Did you see Melitta? Or this *draughoul*?"

"We saw a woman who resembled Melitta enter the brothel," said Chloe. "Her face was covered...but...and something...someone left the brothel. A draughoul, I think."

"Have you seen a draughoul before?"

Chloe shook her head.

"I have," said Thaly. "I know how they talk, and the woman sounded like Melitta."

"But you didn't see her?" asked Charmion.

"No."

"Only overheard a conversation in a whorehouse."

"In Erstürmen," said Thaly.

Charmion sighed. "In Erstürmen. Neither of you saw a face. Cleo saw...."

"Chloe," interrupted Thaly.

Charmion offered a feeble smile. "Quite. *Chloe* saw what she thought was a draughoul, though she's never seen one before, leaving the brothel. Why didn't you see Melitta leave as well?" Charmion asked Chloe.

"She might have left via a secret exit," said Chloe.

"*Mmm.* How convenient. And this magic, poisoned dagger, did you at least see that?"

"No," said Thaly, the weakness of her story crumbling around her.

"Do you even know what one looks like?"

"I've seen drawings. It resembles no other weapon, a blade tapering to a needle tip, like a scorpion's stinger. One scratch, and you're dead. A handle carved from a wurloin exoskeleton. When Melitta, or her servant, take your life, they'll leave the dagger behind to incriminate the Pordillo."

Thaly shuffled to the edge of the couch again, seeking Charmion's devoted attention. "The woman in the room *was* Melitta. I know her voice. I listen to it long enough in those infernal meetings in the zōdiakos."

Charmion wheeled her chair to the front of the couch and sat forward, her silk robe gaping open such that her breast fell free and its nipple almost sipped from the vinum glass.

"Those *infernal meetings* are crucial to Portum's survival," she growled. "If you tire of being a senator, many others would willingly take your place."

"I honour my position," said Thaly. "Believe me, your life is in danger. If Melitta assassinates you, Qaysar Rais will be blamed for your death. This will almost certainly start a war, but with the wrong enemy. Malphas, not Rais, is our gravest threat. Malphas is orchestrating this. He orchestrates everything. He *wants* us to fight the Pordillo. Even if we defeat them and march on Enthilen afterwards, our military strength will be diminished, giving Malphas the upper hand."

Charmion leaned back and tucked her supping breast into the robe. "Such a powerful man, this Malphas. All the way across Magna Avium, from his lair in Pergamos, he manages to hatch a plan to kill the Sella of Portum's conventus. His reach is great indeed."

"You've never lived in his shadow," said Thaly, her voice hardening like the snarl of a boulder lion. "You've not seen what he's done to Enthilen. To the stone-grells. To the Dobunni. You know nothing of Malphas' threat."

"Calm your temper, Senator Stansfield of Capri. The accusation you make is a serious one. If false, you will be expelled from the conventus forever and stripped of your military rank. With my blessing, your family *may* remain in Portum, but I cannot guarantee it. You accuse Melitta, yet you have no evidence other than a whispered conversation between two strangers in a whorehouse. Why is the draughoul not the assassin?"

Thaly narrowed her eyes. "What?"

"Why send Melitta at all? Draughouls can do all sorts of tricks."

"But only Melitta can get close to you without raising suspicion. Your male servants would snap a draughoul in half."

"True. But...*ah*...." Charmion took another sip of vinum. "How did you know Melitta would be in the whorehouse? Senators rarely frequent such places, let alone an orator."

"I searched her private office," said Chloe. "Found a parchment with an impression on it. Time and place of a meeting."

Charmion turned cold brown eyes to Chloe. "You've broken the law. It's an offence for an anitor to enter a senator's chambers without permission."

"She had to do it," said Thaly. "We had to find the evidence you demand."

Chloe jumped to her feet. "Are you such an old fool as not to see what's in front of you? Do you *want* to die?"

Sit down, thought Thaly. Sit down, please. She tugged at Chloe's hand.

"Quintus," Charmion called to her man-servant.

The door opened, and the bald, muscled black man strode into the room.

"Bring a guard. Cleo here is to be taken to the carcer, pending an investigation by the vigilum into burglary and theft from an orator's private chambers."

"No," cried Thaly, standing.

Charmion flashed a glare that could melt ice. "Do you wish to join her?"

Thaly softened her voice. "She didn't mean it. I asked her to do it. I forced her to enter Melitta's office."

"No, she didn't," said Chloe.

Shut up, thought Thaly, tugging at the pearl friendship ring on her finger. I'll fix it.

"You've made grave errors of judgement," Charmion said to Thaly. "I will speak with Zenais about your conduct, and to think she and Eutropia are lobbying for *you* to lead our army. Now, I understand why. You're desperate to command the Germalian military. Desperate to march our forces back to your homeland. Desperate to install yourself as Enthilen's ruler. Erstürmen and Dobunni blood swilled together in a cocktail of megalomania. Drunk on the lust for power. You want the corpses of our brave soldiers to pave your road to autocracy."

"No," pleaded Thaly. "No."

A guard entered the room and dragged Chloe away.

"Get out!" yelled Charmion, throwing her empty vinum glass at the wall.

Thaly followed Chloe and the guard, her future in Portum as fractured as the glass lying on Charmion's floor.

~ Chapter 28 ~

Adalwolf walked behind Princess Caeli as she drifted ahead of the group, her frayed skirt caressing a patch of cropped grass in the Dambay Plains. A stone's throw away, a herd of over six hundred plainalopes grazed the plains. A dominant female, about half the size of a horse, with corkscrew horns covered in tawny velvet, lifted her head and flicked away flies with ears as long as Adalwolf's forearm. Saucerous brown eyes watched the intruders approach, but the female appeared to dismiss any threat Adalwolf, Caeli, Audie and Widukind posed and returned to her grazing. Beside Adalwolf, a spotted quail exploded from a clump of strap grass and flew towards a horizon decked in swirling, dark clouds. He wished his group could travel as fast. Even with Caeli's intimate draughoul knowledge of the landscape, they'd been walking for five moons, leaving a burnt Grōz Forst behind and travelling northwest, trying to find the secret mouldewerp dwell. Adalwolf wondered if the dwell never existed and the mouldewerps had played a cruel trick on Uncle Widukind. It seemed plausible. After sharing his company for five days, Adalwolf had decided Widukind was more than a little unhinged.

Yet, he'd presented Adalwolf with a second and probably last chance at redemption. Gestade hadn't been the glorious resurrection Adalwolf hoped for, the celebration of the absent king's return short-lived. But days of wandering set his mind on another path; dethroning Malphas. He never considered doing it literally by *destroying* the throne of the dead. Widukind claimed this would shatter Malphas' grip on power and could transform the immortal Worshipful Master back to a mortal. Back to someone who couldn't escape the punishment of a returned king. Adalwolf, the Redeemer, indeed.

Adalwolf accepted his plan had weaknesses. The people may punish him for destroying Volerdie's throne and quashing any hope of the Divine Creator returning to Enthilen. They may discover the lie underpinning his claim on the kingdom. Adalwolf wasn't the rightful heir to the Erstürmen throne because he wasn't the departed King Ewald's son. He was Malphas and Romilda's son. With the death of Ewald and his brothers, Hadufuns, Widald and Gerulf, Widald's eldest son, Helmut, would be next in line for the throne should Adalwolf's true parentage be revealed.

Yet, who would reveal it? thought Adalwolf. Romilda is dead, and few would believe Malphas, likely viewing any revelation about Adalwolf's illegitimacy as an attempt by the Worshipful Master to retain power.

One weakness played on Adalwolf's mind the most. Destroying the dead throne relied on the cooperation of Tom Anderson, Adalwolf's birth twin. The man whose soul Adalwolf tried to steal with the dark eyes. The man who could steal Adalwolf's soul and secure immortality. While Adalwolf appreciated his own motivations for wanting to rid Enthilen of Malphas, he struggled to understand Tom Anderson's. He couldn't identify the reward a traveller from another world would garner for foiling Malphas, and he expected Tom's commitment to waver when facing the enormity of the challenge.

As the sun set, Adalwolf limped up to Caeli's shoulder and pointed at the plainalope herd. "We should kill one of those deer. Would make for a good meal tonight."

"There's no need," said Caeli. "We'll arrive at our destination soon."

"Are you certain? We've been searching for five moons. Part of me thinks we're lost. Another part thinks you're taking me to Malphas."

"We go to meet the mouldewerps in their most sacred and secret dwell."

"How do you know where it is?"

Widukind approached Adalwolf. "We don't know, exactly. We're to meet a werp at a place called glor'suk, where six boulders encircle an enormous tree stump. The werp will lead us to the dwell. Then we can prepare our plan to destroy Volerdie's throne."

"What if the plan fails?" asked Adalwolf. "What if Tom Anderson falters?"

"Then I'll kill Malphas myself."

"How will you do that?"

Widukind grasped Adalwolf by the shoulder, pulling him to a stop. "I'm immortal."

Masked by a wiry beard, Widukind's unbalanced face twitched and quivered, Adalwolf searching the spasms for a sign of a lie as if dissecting a page of scripture to find the hidden meaning.

Widukind dug his dirty fingernails into Adalwolf's shoulder. "Do you have a sword?"

"In the cart," said Adalwolf, confused by his uncle's request.

Widukind waited for Audie and Girac to catch up, strode to the cart's tailgate and retrieved a sword from among the dwindling supplies.

"Plunge this into my chest," he said, handing the sword to Adalwolf.

Audie stopped beside the two men. "There's no need for this game. We believe you."

Widukind ignored Audie, fixing his eyes on Adalwolf. "With all of your strength, thrust the blade into my heart. If you believe me, you'll know the sword can do no harm."

Audie's worried face pleaded with Adalwolf to stay his hand. He wanted to please her. Every muscle in his body ached for her affection. But he also wanted to discover the truth of Widukind's pronouncement.

Widukind pulled off his gloves and held up palms marked with circular scars. "Look, I have the scars of a traveller. I've used the dark eyes to journey between worlds and steal my birth twin's soul. You can't hurt me."

Adalwolf collected his thoughts. It seemed Tom Anderson had travelled between worlds *without* becoming immortal, so Widukind may be lying. He braced his legs, grasping the sword in his left hand, then shifted his body weight forward, lunging at his uncle. But he aimed the blade wide of Widukind's shoulder.

"I can't strike you," said Adalwolf. "Immortal or not."

Widukind snarled, his eyes glowing with madness, wrenched the sword from Adalwolf's grasp and thrust it into his own stomach. The blade's tip burst from his spine.

Audie's gasp set Adalwolf's pulse racing. It stilled almost as quickly when Widukind withdrew the blade.

Audie's hazel eyes grew wider than Adalwolf had ever seen. "The blade's clean," she said. "No blood. Nothing." She poked her fingers through the hole in the back of Widukind's tunic. "There's no wound either."

"There never will be," said Widukind. "Blades pass right through me. Sticks and stones bounce off. I can walk through fire and never get burned. Throw myself from the highest cliff and walk back up to the top again. Bury myself under a mound of dirt and still breathe. Believe me, I've tried all these things."

"How is it possible?" asked Audie.

Widukind shrugged. "When you're immortal, anything's possible."

"Do you need to eat?"

"Hunger plagues me occasionally, but I eat for the pleasure of the taste, not because my body needs food. And small rituals are important to ward off the madness."

"Do you feel pain?" asked Adalwolf.

"Physical hurt is but a shadow. There are other pains more de...."

"Then immortality is a gift," interrupted Adalwolf.

"A gift I'd never bestow on anyone, including my worst enemy. Don't be blinded by wicked temptations gorging themselves on reckless ambition. Though my flesh and bones are whole, an agony has wracked my mind for half a generation, worse than the slash of a blade across a mortal heart. My mind is my gaoler, the terrors inside stopping me from facing my brother. Yet, the gaoler carries the keys to my liberation, and when the cage is open, I will confront Malphas once more."

"I know how you became immortal," said Adalwolf, "but *why*?"

"Malphas didn't tell you?"

"He said you betrayed him. He didn't elaborate, and I didn't press."

"I fled Malphas because he wanted me as the immortal sacrifice. My brother lured me with the bait of eternal life as he lured you, Adalwolf. Planned my journey to Tom Anderson's world, where I killed Tom's grandmother. Malphas promised I would rule beside him and Volerdie for eternity. That *you* would be sacrificed on the dead throne to tempt Volerdie home once you'd captured Tom Anderson's soul with the dark eyes.

"But Malphas grew impatient and turned his attention to me, his immortal brother, the perfect vessel to host Volerdie's soul. While he searched for the throne of the dead, Malphas imprisoned me in a dungeon beneath the Desolate Mountains. With the help of my poor, inflicted mother, I escaped and have been running ever since."

Anger stewed in the pit of Adalwolf's stomach. He failed to stop it boiling over. "All this time," he growled. "All this time, you could have thwarted Malphas. One immortal can kill another. You're the only person in Enthilen who could have ended Malphas' tyranny. Why didn't you?"

"If ever I had the courage to face my brother, it stayed buried, deep below the grell tombstones of Bindari."

"You've found your courage now, Papa," said Caeli, who drifted up behind her father like a ghost rising from Bindari's graveyard.

Widukind faced her. "Sweetness, if Malphas falls, will *you* stop me replacing him? Will you stop me claiming to embody Volerdie's will?"

"You're not Uncle Oldaric," said Caeli.

"He ceased to be Oldaric a long time ago. We know what he became. My fate, however, remains elusive."

The herd of plainalopes scattered. Behind Adalwolf, a creature wailed, the rapacious howl ripping away the dusk's stillness.

"What's that?" he asked.

Audie petted the horse. "Girac is sweating and shivering with nerves."

"Something's not right," said Widukind before turning to Caeli. "What is it, Sweetness? You know the ebb and flow of Enthilen better than anyone."

"Evil approaches," she said.

"We have to hurry," urged Widukind.

"How far away is this meeting place?" asked Adalwolf.

"Not far," said Caeli, disappearing into the darkened plains as if fleeing in terror.

Widukind followed her, Adalwolf helping Audie pull Girac and the cart forward.

But the horse stumbled, setting Adalwolf's nerves on edge. "Leave the cart and horse. They're slowing us down."

"I can't leave Girac," said Audie. "He'll die out here."

"And so will we."

"Then help me untie him. At least give him a fighting chance."

The wails grew louder. Adalwolf drew his knife and hacked at the rope harness that attached Girac to the cart.

Audie wrapped her arms around the horse's neck, kissing the side of his head. "Run, boy," she whispered. "Run like the wind."

With the harness free, Adalwolf slapped Girac on the rump. The horse whinnied and bolted off. Behind Adalwolf and Audie, wails became growls. The dusk light fled with Girac, and the growls intensified as if the growing blackness fed the creatures' guttural hunger. Adalwolf grabbed Audie's hand, and they ran together, trying to find Widukind and Caeli.

Seena and Bargan emerged above the eastern horizon. Adalwolf and Audie caught up with Widukind as the growling faded away.

"Where's Caeli?" asked Adalwolf.

"She's disappeared," said Widukind. "I hope whatever killers hunt us haven't captured their first prey."

The three companions ran together, Adalwolf straining his ears for any sound. Up ahead, a shadow with twelve legs snuffled among a clump of long grass. The shadow divided, and three wolf-like beasts, noses pressed to the ground, came towards them.

Not wolves, realised Adalwolf. Weregrims, sent by Malphas.

The loping creatures' coarse fur bristled, and sepia fangs dripping with rancid spit glistened under the shine of the half and quarter moons.

"The weregrims have cut us off," said Adalwolf.

Volerdie's hounds released a triumphant howl, then stopped dead. Adalwolf caught his breath when the snort of a horse sent a sliver of ice down his spine. He spun around to face not a horse, but a dozen undreds, trotting towards him and carrying grell soldiers.

465

"A satch of Rephaim," said Widukind.

The weregrims approached again, snarling across the grassy plain.

"Hold!" a Rephaim shouted. The weregrims dropped to their stomachs and waited.

"We're trapped," said Audie.

"Do you have a weapon?" asked Adalwolf, unsheathing his knife.

"No, but Widukind still carries the sword."

"Do something, Uncle," pleaded Adalwolf. "You're immortal."

Widukind raised a trembling arm and pointed the sword at the weregrims' eyeless faces, their snouts sniffing the air for the scent of weakness.

"I can't protect you," he said. "There's too many of them."

The Rephaim stopped their undreds. A grell soldier dismounted, took a double-headed axe from his saddle, and marched towards Adalwolf, Audie and Widukind. A moment before he reached his quarry, Caeli appeared from the dark and blocked his path. Without a word, the Rephaim swung his axe, smashing the blade into Caeli's forearm.

Bones shattered, and Widukind cried, "Caeli!"

He raced to his daughter's side and thrust the sword at the Rephaim. The grell dodged the blade, brushing past Widukind and striding towards Adalwolf.

"He knows who I am," said Adalwolf, his legs as heavy as boulders. The Rephaim raised his axe, then swung at Adalwolf's torso like he was felling a dead tree. Audie stepped into the arc of the swing, the blade slicing open her stomach. Adalwolf tried to catch her, but she slipped through the grasp of his left hand and fell to the ground.

"Two hands!" he screamed. "I need two hands!" Kneeling beside Audie, he smashed the stump of his right wrist into the dirt, crying, "Useless, useless, useless."

Adalwolf pulled a wounded Audie close. The Rephaim hovered above them like a masked vulture, preparing his axe for the fatal strike. But the soldier's legs buckled as a blade slashed through his hamstrings. Widukind swung his sword again, cutting the grell's back above the straps that fixed the plackart to the soldier's stomach. The Rephaim dropped his axe and fell to his knees. Widukind heaved a mighty swing, decapitating Malphas' servant, the grilled metal helmet clanging against a rock as the unfettered head tumbled to the ground.

The weregrims raised their hackles and bounded towards Widukind. The remaining eleven Rephaim charged their undreds forward. Widukind dropped the sword. Clutching Audie to his chest, Adalwolf waited for death to arrive. It never did.

From among waist-high clumps of wild strangle grass, stunted shapes appeared as if they'd grown there on the spot. More and more rose up; dozens of shrieking, warring, unstoppable mouldewerps. Legend came to life before Adalwolf's eyes. In Laodicea's library, books told of mouldewerps living in the Dambay Plains before Volerdie built Pergamos. Adalwolf never believed it. But his mouldewerp saviours moved atop the plains like ripples across the surface of a lake. As if the soil, grass and stout, furry creatures were a single living being.

A swarm of black and pink descended on the weregrims, undreds and Rephaim, stone-tipped spears finding their mark with a precision born from generations of practice. Malphas' servants fell as one, thwarted by the first creatures to call these plains their home.

Guilt twisted Adalwolf's stomach. The last time he'd seen mouldewerps, he ordered their massacre. Sent Rephaim and Erstürmen Shield to cut them down as they stood side-by-side with wild grell pilgrims in the calendar of life, defending the memory of the stone-grell ancestors who built Malang Gunya. The werps repaid this atrocity by saving his life.

Such is the madness of Enthilen, thought Adalwolf.

The attack ended, the mouldewerps victorious. A handful of the bouncy, jittery creatures fashioned a stretcher from spears, leather straps and saddlecloths taken from the dead undreds, then approached Adalwolf and Audie, babbling in a language Adalwolf thought he'd never decipher. A werp tugged on Audie's limp hand and pointed to the stretcher. Adalwolf held her closer, Audie's stilted, shallow breaths caressing his cheek. *He* wanted to carry her to safety. He wanted to be her saviour. Her prince. Her king.

But he was none of those things, and he let the werps take her away.

Four of the creatures laid Audie on the stretcher and raised it onto their shoulders. Adalwolf stood and placed his left hand on the cut across Audie's stomach to stem the bleeding. One werp barked, swatted Adalwolf's hand away, then carried Audie off into the night with the help of his companions.

Adalwolf sought solace from Uncle Widukind, but he'd returned to Caeli, wrapping a torn cloth around her injured arm. So, he marched after Audie instead, following the werps across the plains.

After walking half the night, the werps stopped at a flat rock, about half the size of a wagon wheel, lying among a ring of grass taller than a horse. To Adalwolf, the location looked insignificant. Something you'd step around during an evening stroll. A female werp mimicked the call of a frog.

"Burrowing plains frog," said Widukind, who'd kept pace with Adalwolf, bringing Caeli along with him.

The flat rock moved aside, pushed from below, exposing a hole barely as wide as a man's shoulders.

"We can't fit down there," said Widukind.

A mouldewerp poked his head from the hole. "You have to," he said in Erstürmen. "More evil grells will come. Only safe place is underground."

"Wirrikow," said Widukind. "Glad to see you again."

"Yes, yes, yes. No time for pleasantries. Down the hole you come."

The werps put the stretcher on the ground and lifted Audie, lowering her through the hole into the clawed hands of others waiting below. Adalwolf followed, tucking his arms against his chest and wiggling into the hole head first. His shoulders jammed into the sides of the entrance, and he stuck fast. The mouldewerps muttered among themselves, then lifted Adalwolf's legs, thrusting him through the hole like a battering ram. Caeli came next, cradling the broken bones in her arm, followed by Widukind and the werp rescuers.

Inside the hole, the new arrivals stood on a rock landing with steps leading down into further darkness. The werp fighters marched off, carrying Audie with them. Adalwolf went to follow them, but Wirrikow tugged on his pants leg, holding him back.

"Treacherous stairs with no light," said Wirrikow. "For those with inferior olfactory senses." He barked an order in his native tongue, and along the stairway, werps lit cressets, pools of light appearing in sequence as if descending the stairs.

The darkness retreated, and Adalwolf gasped, wonderment momentarily replacing his concern for Audie. An enormous cavern stretched before him, its walls lined with limestone and floors crowded with a city of towering stalagmites. From the roof, stalactites hung like an upside-down forest, water drip, drip, dripping from their tips. Where the stalagmites and stalactites joined, columns formed as thick as the trunk of an ancient panalope tree.

"Werps don't need lights," said Wirrikow, "but we made arrangements for our guests. Follow my nose!"

The werp led Adalwolf, Widukind and Caeli down a winding staircase cut into the limestone, its steps worn smooth by generations of werp visitors. The air cooled as they descended, Adalwolf wishing he'd brought his coat and other supplies still lying on the abandoned cart. In alcoves beside the stairway, pools of crystal-clear water sparkled in shallow craters, fed by the trickle of tiny waterfalls. Werps filled wooden buckets from the puddles and carried them down the stairs.

At the bottom of the stairway, Wirrikow led his guests through a narrow path between rows of limestone columns, then into a naturally-formed hall filled with hundreds of werps. The little creatures had gathered food, clothes, bedding, weapons, utensils and other supplies, enough to last a siege spanning all six seasons, and Adalwolf soon forgot about the scant provisions he'd left on the cart.

At the front of the hall, a werp dressed in a grass skirt, with metal rings pierced through her nose and ears, and blue paint smeared on her salmon-coloured face, hovered over Audie, who lay on the ground. The werp peeled back the folds of Audie's tatty dress to expose the gaping wound from the Rephaim axe, mopped up the blood pooling on Audie's stomach with a cloth, then spread a poultice across the broken skin.

Adalwolf knelt by her side. "Audie?" he said in a faltering voice, brushing strands of raven hair from her pale forehead with the stump of his right wrist. Audie responded with breaths weaker than a dying sparrow. He grabbed the werp healer's clawed hand. "Can you help her?"

She pulled away and began an incantation in the chattering, babbly werp language.

Adalwolf faced Wirrikow. "She has to save Audie. Tell her she has to."

"She will try," said Wirrikow before sniffing at Caeli's arm. "Broken bones, Princess."

Caeli offered a ghostly smile. "There's no pain, but my fingers won't work."

"The bones could knit in time," said Widukind.

"No, Papa. My body cannot heal anymore. There is only slow decay."

"I hope we're all still here when Dwarrow and the weald-grells arrive," said Wirrikow. "And the birraman brings his army."

Widukind's eyes narrowed. "Army?"

"Oh, yes, you probably haven't heard. Where's Tilly?" Wirrikow's nose waved like a grass stalk in a gale as he sniffed the air. "*Ah*, here she comes."

A young woman waded through the sea of werps, brushing them aside with her knees. She had dirty blonde hair, broad shoulders and fair skin, and wore a sword on her belt.

"I'm Tilly," said the woman. "I bring a message from Dwarrow for Widukind."

"I'm Widukind."

Tilly looked to Wirrikow, who nodded.

"Tom Anderson is travelling across the Grōz Wüste to Portum," said Tilly, "to convince the Germalian army to march on Pergamos."

Widukind looked puzzled. "The Germalians? What about the weald-grells?"

"Dwarrow and Hannian stone-grell are travelling to Giigal. If Tom and Dwarrow succeed, war will come to Malphas on two fronts."

"Enthilen can't be breached from the west," said Widukind. "There's no safe place to march an army up the Riverlands Escarpment."

"Dwarrow has another plan. Princess Caeli must travel north to lead the Germalians along a secret road under the Desolate Mountains."

"Caeli's injured. She's not going anywhere."

"She must," said Tilly. "It's the safest path into Enthilen."

"How do we know the Germalians will come?" asked Adalwolf.

"We don't. But we have to hope."

Caeli reached down and pulled a stone-headed axe from the belt of a passing werp. She knelt, placed her broken left arm on the hard floor and smashed the axe down onto the crux of her elbow, sheering her forearm clean off. Not a drop of blood spilled.

Caeli stood, leaving a werp to dispose of the severed limb, and approached a wide-eyed Tilly.

"My arm is fixed now," said Caeli. "I'm ready to travel north."

Tilly moved her gaping mouth. "You're to meet the Germalians at the Lost Sisters in Nordland."

"I know the place," said Caeli.

"You could be waiting there for a season," said Widukind. "It will take the Germalians many moons to march from Portum, if they march at all."

Caeli placed her right hand on Widukind's shoulder. "Time is one thing draughouls have in abundance."

The group joined the werps for a meal, but Adalwolf refused to leave Audie's side, eating only a mouthful of food. The werp healer stemmed the bleeding by applying a salve to the wound and covering it with panalope leaves matted together. In quiet moments, Adalwolf spoke to Audie, as much to keep himself awake as try to soothe her hurt with his voice.

"Audie, the Germalians are coming," he said with a surety that belied his doubt. "A mighty army will bear down on Malphas, shattering every stone in the walls of his evil kingdom. The Germalians will take the same road as King Faramund when he led Erstürmen refugees from Nordland to Enthilen. The road under the mountains. Caeli will guide them, and the werps will ask the weald-grells of Giigal to fight. Forces are gathering against Malphas like a storm on the horizon. His hold over Enthilen will soon end, and I can...."

Audie stirred and opened her eyes. "Where am I?"

"Safe," said Adalwolf. "The mouldewerps saved us."

"Mouldewerps?"

Adalwolf caressed Audie's cheek. "How are you feeling?"

"Sore. It hurts to breathe...to move."

"Do you want water or food?"

"Water, please."

Adalwolf fetched a cup of crystalline water from a rock pool, lifted Audie's head, and placed the cup to her lips. She took two sips.

"I'm supposed to be healing you," said Audie.

"Forget about me," said Adalwolf. "I'm my mother's son. I'm a survivor."

Audie lay back and winced, clutching the wound on her stomach. "If Malphas falls, will you...."

Adalwolf placed a finger on her lips. "I don't wish to see Enthilen free of one tyrant, only for the people to be enslaved by another. Whatever the future holds, I want us to face it together."

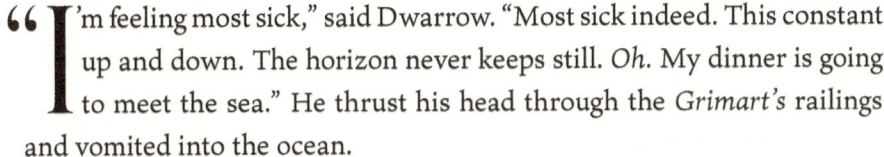

~ Chapter 29 ~

"I'm feeling most sick," said Dwarrow. "Most sick indeed. This constant up and down. The horizon never keeps still. *Oh.* My dinner is going to meet the sea." He thrust his head through the *Grimart's* railings and vomited into the ocean.

Hanni held a hand to her mouth as if she might do the same, then leaned against a crate in the middle of the ship, as far away as possible from the deck's edge and the endless deep surrounding her. Although she'd spent many seasons living with the weald-grells in Giigal, surrounded by the Bay of Marrumin, she retained her stone-grell fear of water.

Melinda unbuckled her whale-driving harness, poured a strange liquid into a cup, then stood and trotted from the bowsprit to Dwarrow.

"Drink this," she said, holding the cup towards him. "It'll help."

Dwarrow took the cup, sniffed the liquid and screwed up his face, thrusting it back at Melinda. "I can't possibly...."

"Drink it."

"It smells like...like...."

"Fermented whale oil," said Melinda. "It'll settle y'stomach."

Hanni stumbled across to Dwarrow, knelt down and yanked the cup from his grasp. After sniffing the yellow, gloopy oil, she pinched her nose and took a gulp.

"It tastes better than it smells," said Hanni. "Try it, Dwarrow."

She returned the cup to the werp. He tugged a handkerchief from his britches pocket and held it over his nose before swallowing the remainder of the oil.

"*Errghh,*" moaned Dwarrow. "I'm not convinced the taste is an improvement on the smell." He tossed the empty cup to Melinda.

She caught it, standing stable as a rock on the lurching ship, as if her boots had been nailed to the deck, and smiled down at Dwarrow. "How many are there like you?"

He squeezed his squinty eyes almost shut. "I don't understand the question."

"How many more mud-werps are there?"

"*Mouldewerps*," huffed Dwarrow. "Enough to cause a fright of bother for our enemies."

"Why ain't I seen any 'til now? We've travelled all 'round Ostamp's coast; Enthilen, Germalia, Nordland, even Pordillo territory. Never seen a mouldewerp before."

"We keep ourselves to ourselves. Most people nowadays have their heads in the clouds. Henceforth, we are easily missed."

"Gestade!" cried Ulver from the eagle's nest, perched at the top of a mast at the ship's stern, his eye pressed to a looking glass. "Gestade's been razed, Uncle Whibly! Can't see a single wall standin'."

Everyone on the ship turned west. Hanni stood and followed their gaze, hoping to catch a glimpse of the Erstürmen outpost's ruins. Since leaving Traders Bay two moons ago, Whibly had kept the *Grimart* close to the shore. 'Easier to hide from barbarian raiders,' he'd said. Shading her keen grell eyes from the late afternoon sun, Hanni couldn't find where Gestade once stood. Still, she trusted Ulver's ability to spot the inconspicuous using the looking glass.

"Malphas must 'ave unleashed his legions on Commander Hartmut," said Whibly from the helm, the stooped captain standing on a crate to reach the highest timber handles of the ship's wheel. "The old Enthilen is dead now."

"Not all of it," said Hanni. "Giigal still stands. I am hopeful the weald-grells will join our cause."

Whibly let a crew member take over the ship's wheel, then hobbled down the helm's steps and towards Hanni, Dwarrow and Melinda.

"Y'haven't exactly told us what y'cause is," said Whibly. "I ain't complainin' 'bout the coin or nothin', but I'd like to know *why* y'willin' to pay so much to get to Giigal."

Hanni looked to Dwarrow. She didn't want to give too much away, and the werp was better at guarding secrets than her.

"Is Enthilen a better place with or without Malphas?" Dwarrow asked Whibly.

"He ain't done me no favours," said Whibly. "Hunger rules Laodicea with a fist wrapped in black iron. A merchant seafarer can't make enough there to feed his crew. Everyone else along Enthilen's coast is terrified of Malphas. Frightened people go into their shell, if y'know what I mean. Don't buy goods. Don't trade. Even in Nordland and Germalia, people are worried Malphas will spread his terror."

"Then, you would not be sorry to see Malphas dethroned."

"Not sorry at all," said Melinda. "His dirty Erstürmen soldiers killed my Da; rest his soul. Enthilen would be better off without any of 'em."

"We will see to it," said Dwarrow. "We will end Malphas' reign."

"How's a knee-high werp and one stone-grell gonna do that?" asked Whibly.

"With an army of weald-grells and Germalians by our side. *And* a secret weapon," said Dwarrow, tapping the black button-tip of his nose with his walking stick.

"I doubt the Germalians will come," said Whibly. "Mighty stubborn them females."

"Watch what y'sayin'." Melinda's eyes fired redder than her hair. They dimmed again as smoke on the western horizon hung like a raincloud over the coast. "The heathlands 'round Gestade have been set alight. I hope the fire don't spread to Dorfisch."

"Is Dorfisch your home?" asked Hanni.

"Da and me had a shack, half-day's walk south of the town. Shared it with Annian."

"The weald-grell?"

Melinda nodded. "Ma died soon after I was born, and Da needed to fish to keep us fed. Lyin' in a boat ain't no place for an infant, so we had to get a housekeeper. Da rescued Annian from the slave markets at Dorfisch. No-one else wanted her since she was so old. I loved Anni, and she loved me."

"What happened to her?" asked Hanni.

"Her time came, and she walked to Bindari to rest with her ancestors. A stupid boy chased after her."

Dwarrow's eyes widened. He leaned forward and ran the tip of his nose over Melinda's bare skin.

She jerked her arm away from his probing snout. "What y'doin'?"

"I thought our paths may have crossed with the same person," said Dwarrow. "His smell doesn't linger on you, but smells fade over time, and the ones on your skin are masked by the distinct pungency of fish guts."

"Hey, I wash."

Dwarrow searched for a sign Melinda had met Tom Anderson. Grin told Hanni the *Vulking* sank in a storm, and he and Thaly were separated from Tom. Whibly helped Grin and Thaly row back to Enthilen while a fisher and his daughter from Bramble Island saved Tom.

One day, thought Hanni, she'd ask Melinda about it. But not yet.

"The wind's carryin' smoke across the ocean," said Whibly. "We're gonna be swamped soon enough."

The bone-coloured fumes drifted low, smothering the waves and clinging to the *Grimart* like an unwelcome fog. The westerly wind dropped, and the sea calmed, the smoke seeming to mask every sound except the splash of six whales as they surfaced for air and dove again, pulling the ship south. Freckles, Melinda's favourite whale, led the pod. Melinda had told Hanni every whale's name and their corresponding personalities. 'A good whale-master knows everything about their pod,' she'd said. Melinda also taught Hanni the special names for each part of the ship.

Although Grin's traumatic journey on the *Vulking* sat restless at the back of Hanni's mind, a clutch of worry sometimes telling her the crew would turn bad at any moment, life on the *Grimart* had been comfortable enough. Whibly kept his crew in order, and Melinda had taken a shine to the passengers, casting steely glares at any crew member who muttered a discourtesy. Being the skullard and the whale-master, only Captain Whibly outranked her authority on the ship.

The smoke enveloped the *Grimart*. In the eagle's nest, Ulver almost disappeared from view as he swept the eastern horizon with his looking glass as if to brush the smoke aside. Hanni followed his line of sight, fixating on an object floating on the water, barely visible through the haze. Before she could raise the alarm, Ulver called from the lookout.

"Barbarians! Uncle Whibly! Barbarians approachin' from the northeast."

"Damn it," cursed Whibly. "I don't need barbarians chasin' me rudder. Melinda, fire up them whales."

Melinda sprinted to the bowsprit, strapped herself to the whale-master's seat and tensioned the harnesses attached to the six whales. Sitting at the helm, the drummer pursed his lips and whistled into the brass tube that ran down the *Grimart's* side and disappeared below the depths. The ship lurched forward, the whales responding to the call for more speed.

Hanni grasped the deck's outer railing, trying not to fall overboard, as the crew rushed about, moving the *Grimart's* only ballista into position along the port side. Others strung longbows and filled quivers with arrows. Hanni helped herself to a bow and full quiver. Dwarrow stood beside her, using his walking stick for balance as the ship's bow smashed through the waves. She wondered what use a stick would be in a fight against barbarians. She'd never faced them before but had heard stories. Veiled whispers of burly men and women, painted torsos dressed in bones, teeth and feathers. Twelve yarles ago, they'd brought Laodicea to its knees in a matter of days, appearing to relish the ravage and chaos. A small merchant ship with a motley crew of less than two dozen, one stone-grell and a werp, had little chance of staving off a barbarian assault.

Despite Melinda's best efforts at pressing more speed from her whales, the barbarian ship gained ground. A vessel with twin hulls joined by a flat deck and pulled by a pod of eight whales bore down on the *Grimart*. The barbarians flew a dark blue flag with a white circle at its centre that encompassed a red bird.

"A tribe from Oder," called Ulver from the eagle's nest. "They're gainin' on us!"

Tribe, thought Hanni, estimating at least two hundred barbarians standing on the deck.

"What's towin' their ship?" said Whibly. "Melinda! We need more speed."

"They're at full speed now, Cap'n," said Melinda. "We've pushed the whales hard since leavin' Laodicea. I can't get no more from 'em."

"We'll be caught soon," said Whibly. "Brace for an attack!"

The crew jumped at Whibly's order, lining up along the ship's port side and nocking arrows in their bowstrings. Hanni did the same. Dwarrow stood behind the ballista as if the war machine might offer him protection.

Ulver climbed down from the eagle's nest and raced to Whibly. "Still gainin' on us, Uncle. There's a name painted on the hull; *Murdark*."

"When they get closer, I'm turnin' the *Grimart* portside," said Whibly. "Try to cut across their bows. Make sure the crew are ready. Tell Melinda to prepare the whales for a sharp turn to port. Somethin' tells me we ain't bribin' our way out of this one."

Ulver scampered about the crew, relaying Whibly's plan, as the *Murdark* loomed.

The arrow notched on Hanni's bowstring slipped through her fingers and clattered to the deck. She bent down to pick it up, fighting against stiff muscles. A wave hit, and the arrow slid along the deck away from her. She slammed a bare foot onto the fletching to hold the arrow in place and rubbed her hand over the stubble on her scalp to improve her grip. Dwarrow wavered behind the ballista crew. Hanni wished she had an armoury of stone-grells as her companions, not a middling little mouldewerp.

Clutching the arrow, she stood to face two massive eyes painted on the outside of the barbarian ship's hulls. Breaching whales filled the air with fountains of sea spray. The smoke from the fires around Gestade cleared. Two hundred barbarians lined the *Murdark's* deck; heavyset men and women brandishing bows, spears and axes, and wearing little more than loin cloths and menacing smiles.

"This is quite inconvenient," muttered Dwarrow. "Don't these savages know we're on a vital mission?"

"Melinda!" yelled Whibly. "Portside!"

Melinda and her whale crew yanked on the ropes to the whales' left, dragging the beasts east in a sharp turn. The *Grimart* cut straight across the *Murdark's* bows, almost colliding with the barbarian ship. The attackers cursed in a language Hanni had never heard, then launched a swarm of spears. A blade lodged in a crew member's chest, the hapless woman toppling overboard into her salty grave.

"Fire!" Whibly yelled to his crew. "Fire, dammit!"

Hanni and the *Grimart's* crew loosed arrows while the ballista launched a lance as thick as a panalope sapling at the *Murdark*. A handful of barbarians fell to the arrows, but the lance missed its mark.

The barbarians drove their whales east, turning the starboard hull to face the *Grimart's* port. A wall of shields sprung up from the *Murdark's* deck, protecting the line of archers. The barbarians dragged two ballistae armed with grappling hooks attached to chains and rope from the quarters built in the middle of the deck.

"They ain't lookin' to kill us," said Whibly. "They want to board."

"Oh, my," said Dwarrow. "I can't live my elder days as a barbarian slave. I simply can't."

Hanni fired arrow after arrow at the barbarians but couldn't pierce the shield wall. The crew around her left their arrows in the quivers, either giving up or waiting for a better opportunity to inflict casualties. The barbarians turned the ballistae to face the *Grimart's* side and launched the two grappling hooks. They flew over the railings and embedded in the front and rear of the *Grimart's* deck, the slap of chains attached to hooks shuddering through the soles of Hanni's feet. The barbarians tensioned the ropes on their side using a winch, the incisive prongs of the hooks ripping the *Grimart's* deck timbers until taking hold.

"Target the ballistae crews," cried Whibly.

"We can't pierce the shield wall," said a crew member.

Whibly fought with the ship's wheel as it spun from his hands. "They've trapped us. I can't manoeuvre me ship."

"This is not good," said Dwarrow. "Not good at all."

Hanni strode to a grappling hook, its chain taut across the deck. Even with an axe of the strongest steel, she couldn't break the chain, a single link almost as thick as her wrist.

Ulver ran up beside her. "I'll cut the ropes," he said, placing a dagger between his teeth and stepping towards the deck's edge.

With the balance of a tree-dwelling wildcat, Ulver climbed over the deck railing, crouched and leaned forward, grasping the chain with his hands and ankles. He pushed himself out above the open water, swinging down underneath the chain, then pulled himself forward, hand over hand, heading towards the halfway point between the *Grimart* and the *Murdark*, where the chain ended, tied to a thick rope.

Abandoning reason, Hanni hoped the barbarians didn't notice the diminutive saboteur. A yell from the barbarian deck shattered her hope, and enemy arrows whizzed past Ulver's ears. The young man kept his nerve and inched forward, dagger clenched between his teeth, his stick-thin frame offering a difficult target for the barbarians. He reached the join between the chain and rope, wrapped one arm and his legs around the chain, freed a hand, took the dagger from his mouth and began hacking at the rope.

The wiry fibres unravelled with agonising slowness, Hanni wishing she could join Ulver and tear the rope free. Then she caught herself, realising once Ulver decoupled the chain and rope, he'd plunge into the ocean below.

An arrow lodged in Ulver's calf. He cried aloud but continued cutting. With a final lash, the rope broke, and Ulver and the chain plummeted into the water.

"Pull him in!" cried Whibly.

Hanni bent down, lifted the chain over her shoulder and used every skerrick of stone-grell strength to heave the chain, and Ulver, onto the deck.

Forearm muscles flaring in agony, Hanni thanked the ancestors when Ulver scrambled over the *Grimart's* deck railing. He smiled at her, then gritted his teeth, broke off the fletching end of the barbarian arrow and pulled the shaft through his leg.

"Wasn't deep," he said. "One more rope to go." Ulver hobbled to the bow, where the other grappling hook attached the *Grimart* to the *Murdark*.

A lance flew from the barbarian ship, striking one of the whales pulling the *Grimart*.

Blood filled the water under the bowsprit, and Melinda shrieked, "They've hit Freckles. Those dirty, stinkin' bastards. I'm cuttin' the whales free."

She unstrapped herself from the whale-master's chair, tied a rope around her waist and dived into the ocean, clutching at the long knife sheathed on her belt. Other crew members fought the web of ropes forming the whale harness, bringing the whales to a stop. A lance from the *Grimart's* ballista punched a hole in the barbarian shield wall. Hanni reached for her longbow, pulling arrows from the quiver slung over her shoulder, nocking them on the bowstring and letting fly with the angry speed of a charging plains buffalo.

Barbarians toppled into the water. Arrows filled the sky, flying from both ships and passing each other across the water like flocks of seabirds hunting schools of fish. Men and women of the *Grimart* collapsed onto the deck with arrows sticking from their flesh, toppled overboard, or gave up the battle with the barbarians altogether, fighting each other to be the first one into the ship's hold.

"Get back 'ere, ya cowards!" yelled Whibly.

Hanni reached for the last arrow in her quiver. Dwarrow cowered behind a crate on the deck. Ulver shinned along the second chain. It yanked the two ships together, and Hanni expected the young man to be crushed between the bows at any moment. Then a baleful scream strangled the chaos of battle. Hanni couldn't tell if it came from the sky or the ocean. The barbarian whales broke free of their harnesses and disappeared beneath the surface. Crew members on both ships lowered their weapons and fixed their eyes on the narrow channel of ocean between the two vessels.

The *Grimart* and the *Murdark* came to a dead stop, bobbing side-by-side atop a deep blue vastness that mocked their pitiful attempt at fear-mongering.

Whibly stood beside Hanni as the water began to bubble. "The sea looks like a pot of boilin' stew," he said. "I seen a lot of things in me travels. Ain't never seen this."

"Help me!" screamed Melinda, flailing in the middle of an enormous churn of white and froth on the ocean's surface.

The whale crew yanked on the loose end of the rope tied around Melinda's waist. Her body bounced and whacked against the *Grimart's* side as her shipmates dragged her onboard. Beneath her, the sea rose up, a mountain of water reaching for Melinda's feet like a grappling, aqueous hand. She flopped onto the deck as the wake parted.

Hanni's mouth dropped open. She tried to form words, but none came. Beside her, Whibly trembled like a sodden mouse caught outside on a dark, cold night. Between the ships appeared the head of a beast. From its flaring nostrils to the frilled skin around its neck, the head matched the *Grimart's* size. Spines as tall as a ship's mast and joined by curtains of translucent ruby skin ran from the top of its skull along the ridge of its neck and backbone. The creature bared rows of serrated teeth, each one the size of a grell, glops of chewed seaweed dripping from its rosewood-coloured tongue.

Grasping the deck's side rail, Whibly's face turned whiter than sea froth. "Marduk's holy beard. It's a le-le-leviathan."

Leaving Laodicea, the *Grimart* had travelled beneath the leviathan statue bridging the headlands to Traders Bay.

A poor imitation, thought Hanni.

The real leviathan wailed a painful squeal, forcing Hanni to cover her ears. It raised itself further from the water, twisted its spine-covered head towards the *Murdark* and smashed a neck of sinew and scales down onto the barbarian ship. The deck splintered, cleaving the twin hulls apart. Hulking men and women, who only moments ago seemed invincible, tumbled into the ocean like pebbles tipped from a cup. The leviathan grasped a hull in its mouth, clamped its jaws shut, then thrashed its head. The *Grimart* flew sideways, still attached to the *Murdark* by the rope, chain and grappling hook.

Ulver, clinging to the chain with desperate hands, dangled above the water.

"Cut the rope!" screamed Whibly. "For Volerdie's mercy, Ulver, cut the rope!"

The young man heaved his legs up, wrapping them around the chain, then pulled himself towards the knot connecting the rope to the chain. He took the knife from his mouth and went to cut the rope when the leviathan thrashed again, snapping the chain and the rope apart and sending Ulver splashing into the water.

Hanni wished she could swim. Wished she could dive into the water and save Ulver.

"We're goners," said Whibly. "We're all goners."

The leviathan crunched the first hull to pieces, then started on the remainder of the *Murdark*, swallowing barbarians, ballistae, crates and whatever else fell into its mouth.

Melinda stood by her captain. "We can't escape. I set all the whales free. Freckles is dead."

"We're goin' down with the ship," said Whibly.

With the *Murdark* sunk and the barbarians drowned or swallowed, the leviathan turned its ravenous appetite to the *Grimart*, hovering its head above the deck and casting a shadow over the entire vessel. The length of a dozen ships away, a tail resembling a nest of writhing snakes broke the surface. What remained of the *Grimart's* crew stared in awe.

Dwarrow crawled from behind the crate where he'd been hiding, heaved himself up with his walking stick and stood on the deck right underneath the leviathan's nose. The werp turned his head skywards and sniffed the air as if to confirm the monster's intent.

Set beneath scaled brows, the leviathan's emerald eyes focussed on the tiny creature before it. Slowly, almost hesitantly, the beast lowered its head towards the deck, stopping with its nostrils poised above Dwarrow. The behemoth inhaled, lifting the werp off his feet. Suspended mid-air, Dwarrow thrust his walking stick into the leviathan's nostril. The beast sneezed, sending Dwarrow crashing to the deck, covered in mucus.

The leviathan raised its head and bayed at the sky before plunging beneath the ocean's surface, a plume of bubbles marking its descent.

Dwarrow pulled sticky arms from the deck and faced Hanni. "If I'd known travelling by sea would be this much trouble," he said, "I would have forced you to carry me to Giigal."

*   *   *   *

Despite losing half its crew, including Ulver and Freckles, the *Grimart* continued its journey south to Giigal. Melinda had repaired the whale harness and called up the remaining five whales to pull the ship. Hanni hardly slept, keeping watch on the ocean, expecting another leviathan to explode from the surface at any moment. The crew sulked around the deck, pining for their missing friends and the promise of a safer life on dry land. The usually boisterous Melinda had fallen silent, spending her days alone in the whale-master's seat on the bowsprit. The whale pod mourned Freckles' death, emitting haunting calls from the depths that made Hanni cry.

Five moons from Laodicea, hugging Enthilen's coastline, the *Grimart* passed sheer cliffs of white stone, their grassy peaks shrouded in mist.

Dwarrow tugged on Hanni's pant leg and pointed his walking stick at the cliffs. "Bindari," he said. "What's left of it."

Never initiated, Hanni had no knowledge of Bindari's location. "Will grells ever be buried there again?" she asked.

"Yes. I'm sure of it."

By late afternoon, the *Grimart* rounded the Bindari peninsula and entered Gadhang, the vast southern ocean. Hanni's ancestors had crossed the same ocean to arrive in Enthilen many generations ago. Babir Birramal dominated the landscape, swathes of dense forest lining the shore above pearl-white sandy beaches.

A forest of memories, thought Hanni, recalling time spent with her mother, Mirrian, gathering berries, yams and sedge grass. Playing *gubarra* with the other children of Giigal, running and hiding among the hollow trunks of panalope trees. The last ever garrabari ceremony in the middle of the forest at Dalman, where Grin had been initiated, and she'd received the facial crest of gama, the spear fern. The garrabari was also the last time Hanni saw her parents before the massacre of grells at Malang Gunya. She always believed Mirrian and her father, Frennan, had died. But Tom Anderson made her think otherwise. Mirrian could still be alive, trapped inside Pergamos as one of Malphas' slaves. Dwarrow said Pergamos' walls had to be breached so Tom could destroy the throne of the dead. But Hanni cared more about saving her mother. Pulling the walls down and setting Mirrian free.

It's what Grin would want, she thought.

Lost in her daydreams, and with no-one else willing to replace Ulver in the eagle's nest, the weald-grell war canoes got closer than they should have before Hanni noticed.

"I smell a mischief of grells," Dwarrow called across the deck.

"I can't see anythin'," said Whibly from behind the ship's wheel, the handles brushing the underside of his chin.

"Four canoes," said Hanni. "Carrying dozens of weald-grells painted for war."

A drummer sat at the front of each canoe, beating a hollow log to keep the rowers in time as they cut through the waves. The oars' white blades flashed in and out of the water, reminding Hanni of the legs of a water-skimming centipede. The canoe resembled a swordfish, with fins on the side to stabilise the vessel and a sharpened metal prong at the front, longer than Hanni's arm and twice as thick as any spear. The prong could easily punch a hole into the side of a ship like the *Grimart* and send it sinking to the depths.

"They're a long way from Giigal," said Whibly. "I don't much like the look of this."

"First, barbarians, then leviathans," muttered Dwarrow. "And now this. You better do something quick smart, Hannian stone-grell. Quick smart indeed!"

Hanni walked to the *Grimart's* bow and climbed onto the bowsprit, standing beside Melinda.

"Hold the whales in place," said Hanni. "We should not travel any closer to Giigal."

"They won't hold for long," said Melinda.

Hanni raised her arms to the approaching canoes, palms pressed together — a sign of submission in weald-grell culture. The lead canoe pulled up alongside the *Grimart* while the other three held back. Hanni kept her arms raised and stepped towards the deck's edge. A male weald-grell, his naked torso painted in white, blue and ochre, stood on the bow beside the canoe's gleaming metal prong. He didn't acknowledge Hanni's gesture, instead bending down to gather a spear from inside the canoe.

"*We mean no harm,*" said Hanni in Grellian.

The weald-grell grasped his spear but didn't respond.

Hanni lowered her arms. "*I am Hannian stone-grell, first born of Frennan and Mirrian, protector of all that is sacred to grells. We come in peace and for counsel.*"

The weald-grell spoke with a crew member before facing Hanni again. "*What is your crest, Hannian stone-grell?*"

"*Gama, bestowed on me at the last garrabari before the end of days. I come on behalf of all remaining stone-grells to honour the truce written on Marradir, and in memory of the stone- and weald-grells who lost their lives during the massacre of Malang Gunya. I come on behalf of my mother, Mirrian, enslaved by Malphas in his lair in Pergamos. And on behalf of my brother, Grinnian, who sacrificed his life to save our land.*"

Whibly and Dwarrow stood beside Hanni.

"We've traded before," Whibly called to the weald-grells. "Why so uppity now?"

Keep quiet, thought Hanni.

"Can we at least speak a language we all understand?" asked Dwarrow.

"Understand this," said the weald-grell, reverting to Erstürmen, "you travel across Gadhang, the ancestral ocean of the weald-grells, during a time of great upheaval. Malphas' spies are everywhere. The clouds of war gather in the north, threatening to bring a deathly storm to our homeland. None shall approach Giigal without challenge."

Dwarrow poked his head through the *Grimart's* side railings. "I'm no spy. I am Gwuendā-hæ Dwinë D'elch, the one who signed the alliance between grells and mouldewerps at Dalman, in the shadow of the truce rock, Marradir."

"That was a different world," said the weald-grell. "Dalman is gone. The truce rock shattered into thousands of pieces. We need no allies to protect our home. Depart these waters, else we ram your ship and send it to the ocean floor."

While the weald-grell spoke, another canoe approached, and Hanni's heart lifted at the sight of a familiar face standing near the bow.

"Wyan!" she called. "Wyan, weald-grell. Third born of Ulan and Wirrian."

Wyan smiled as his canoe sidled up to the *Grimart.* "Hanni. I almost did not recognise you. It has been so long since you lived among us."

"We danced together at the last garrabari," said Hanni.

"I remember. Then I marched with your father, mother and brother to Malang Gunya. Before the Erstürmen slaughtered our kin in the calendar of life."

"It is time to seek revenge," said Hanni.

Wyan nodded.

The other weald-grell snarled at Wyan. "You are not the leader here; I am. These intruders must leave."

"And who might you be?" asked Dwarrow.

He turned to Dwarrow, his facial crest of *bagal*, the tiger snake, seeming to tense, ready to strike. "I am Symian weald-grell, first born of Wendan and Virrian, protector of Giigal and leader of the *murriyan-wargang.*"

Dwarrow muttered, "*War-gang.* An appropriate name if ever there was one."

"The massacre in the calendar of life will fade in memories, replaced by the horrors Malphas' army will inflict on Giigal," said Hanni, her voice booming over the water. "Gestade has been razed to the ground. Smoke from the outpost's ruins mingles with the ash of Babir Birramal, the forest you failed to protect."

Dwarrow tapped her thigh with his walking stick and whispered, "Stay calm. Anger will only make them more stubborn."

"Please, Wyan," said Hanni. "Honour the memory of my father, Frennan, who died in the massacre of Malang Gunya. Escort us to Giigal. We seek an audience with the elders."

Wyan climbed into Symian's canoe, and they spoke to each other in Grellian.

Dwarrow tilted his head to the side. "Oh, they're talking in that infernal language again. Hannian, can you hear what they're saying?"

Hanni shook her head.

Whibly scuttled to the helm, then returned carrying a conch shell. He blew into a hole at the narrow end, and a mournful wail drowned the weald-grell voices. They turned their tattooed faces towards Whibly.

"Ain't no time for debatin'," said Whibly. "A huge army's comin' from the west to fight Malphas. The largest army Enthilen's ever seen. But it can't defeat him alone. If the weald-grells march from the south, Malphas' forces will be stretched to breakin' point, and Pergamos will fall."

"What army do you speak of?" asked Symian.

"The Germalians," said Hanni. "The Germalians come to finish Malphas."

Symian and Wyan returned to their discussion.

Dwarrow leaned on his walking stick. "Important dealings have a habit of going awry when you over-promise and under-deliver. I hope Tom and his friends don't fail us."

Hanni caught only a few words of Symian and Wyan's ongoing debate, hoping the decision would fall in the visitors' favour. The *Grimart's* crew looked beaten. A dozen gaunt, tired faces ready to cut their losses and head home. Whibly limped up and down the deck, constantly rubbing his hunched shoulder as if trying to massage the twist from his spine. Melinda sat quietly in her whale-master's seat, and Hanni remembered the whales would want to move again soon. Dwarrow fidgeted in one of the many pouches strung to his belt, indecision etched on his salmon-coloured face.

Hanni leaned over the *Grimart's* deck railing and called down to the weald-grells in Grellian, *"The elders must decide. A stone-grell has requested an audience, and only the elders can deny her. I know the law of Giigal."*

Symian's shoulders relaxed, and he faced her. "I will let you anchor in the Bay of Marrumin. You will wait there while I speak with the elders, then return with their answer. Follow our canoes to Giigal."

"Finally," said Dwarrow. "Somebody sees sense."

The canoes moved off, and Melinda urged her whales forward.

Hanni's childhood home beckoned to her. She had much to tell the elders. If only they would listen.

~ Chapter 30 ~

As parched as Grōz Wüste, Tom's gaping mouth sucked in a breath with such force he thought it might wrench the eyes of lost souls from Raf's hands. Beside Tom, Rosalie clutched the pommel of her sword, but she'd never reach the Dobunni rebel in time to stop him from using the dark eyes to flee Enthilen. Raf curled his fingers inwards, a fingernail's width away from clenching his fists and completing the compact. His palms began to blister and fume as the eyes melted into his hands, preparing to take him to Earth.

As the last glint of obsidian glass disappeared from view, Tom gave up. Until an arrowhead burst from Raf's cheekbone, and his face froze with pale shock. The rebel's arms went limp, his fingers unclenched, and the dark eyes fell to the sand, followed by Raf's corpse.

Standing behind Raf, Quenan slung her bow over her shoulder. "I had no choice," she said. "All would be lost if he took the dark eyes. I will dig a grave."

Tom reached for an anxiety pill, his instinctive response to calming jangled nerves, then stopped, determined to deal with the trauma without medication.

Still three left.

Rosalie crouched down, plucked the obsidian balls from the sand, stood and returned them to Tom, her fingers caressing the back of his hand. With Raf's death so immediate and sudden, Tom expected more emotion from her. She'd been Raf's lover only days ago. Outwardly, Rosalie showed no sorrow, offering Tom the faintest of smiles.

She turned away and helped Quenan dig the grave, kneeling and knitting her hands together to plough sand away from the growing depression. Tom placed the dark eyes in his front pocket, then knelt to help his companions.

By the time the first star appeared in the sky, they'd excavated a hole large enough to accommodate the short, wiry Dobunni rebel. Quenan rolled Raf's corpse into the grave, and the three of them pushed sand over his body. Rosalie gave the eulogy as they buried her ex-lover, reminiscing about happier times. Raf helped her build the smithy beside the monastery in the Desolate Mountains. After raiding towns and villages, he'd return with scrap metal for Rosalie to forge into weapons or tools. As a young man, he would have welcomed being Rosalie's apprentice, but youth disappeared too quickly for the battle-weary rebel. Recently, he'd grown tired of fighting Malphas, often talking about leaving the rebels behind and making a new life elsewhere. He begged Rosalie to go with him. She refused.

"I wonder if my rejection fed his desperation?" said Rosalie as she thrust Raf's sword into the sand at the head of his finished grave.

A warrior's desert tombstone, thought Tom.

The group gathered their belongings and horses, and trudged across the wasteland, following the stars. Even at night, the sand burned, slinking into Tom's boots and scalding his ankles through worn socks. The horses struggled with the heat, Rosalie deciding not to add to their burden by riding them.

Why bring them at all? Tom thought. Nothing for horses to eat out here. Then he realised the *horses* were food. The only food the group had.

"See in the sky, Tom Anderson," said Quenan, "where five stars form the head of an arrow, and another seven form its shaft?"

Tom nodded.

"The arrow tip points directly west. We follow the western star."

Nobody spoke again for the remainder of the night.

They rested in a barren swale at dawn, trying to avoid the day's heat by hunkering down among the shadows of towering dunes. After pegging the horses, Quenan fell asleep, but Rosalie and Tom sat together, leaning their backs against a wall of sand.

"When death is close, embracing life becomes more urgent," said Rosalie.

Before Tom could protest, she stripped naked and straddled his waist, pressing her mouth against his. He wouldn't resist, of course. He'd been dreaming of this moment since the first time. Despite their exhaustion and the pulsing heat, they made love on the sand. Tom's confidence grew with the comfort of familiarity. Rosalie's eagerness helped, toned muscles tightening underneath pale skin drenched in sweat as she reached her climax. They collapsed and pressed in close to the foot of the eastern dune, providing them with a sliver of shade from the rising sun.

"We should dress," said Tom. "Sunburnt genitals aren't a lot of fun."

Rosalie didn't respond, her eyes already closed. He pulled on his pants and tunic, then laid clothes over her body like blankets to stave off the sun's rays.

As he rested beside her, he tried to embrace the joy of a new affection, unsure where the budding relationship would lead. Sex came easier than he expected, but beyond lust, an emotional connection with Rosalie proved difficult. His mind soon wandered down different paths of worry, scorched by brutal heat and vistas of endless red sand dunes. The ground beneath his feet appeared to shift and swirl. At any moment, he expected slider serpents to burst from the sand and spit venom in his face.

Tom sat up and gathered his waterskin, squeezing the last mouthful of tepid water onto his tongue and wondering how much Rosalie and Quenan had left. Coming from the driest inhabited continent on Earth, he understood heat and deserts and their dangers. Groz Wüste, however, was a terrifying unknown. Sand dunes west, north, south, and east, as far as the eye could see. The first waterhole they found, the one where Raf tried to steal the dark eyes, had signs of life. A few shrubs. Lizards that sprinted across the sand to stop their feet from burning. An occasional bird drinking from the dirty pool. Since then, Tom hadn't seen a single plant or animal other than the horses. *Food.*

During the day, the group chased the shade as it moved from the east to the west, and Tom snatched a few moments of sleep. At sunset, they walked again, taking the horses with them. All the waterskins were empty now.

After a long night of stumbling through ankle-deep sand, they stopped beside a dry waterhole at dawn. Quenan made arrows from reeds and killed three lizards, each no larger than Tom's hand. They couldn't make a fire, so they ate the lizards raw.

"How are we going to find water?" Tom asked.

Quenan pointed to a flock of birds flying north. "The birds will show us."

"We'll have to walk during the day if we want to follow them," said Rosalie. "Risk the punishing sun. Thirst will kill us before the heat, anyway."

"We cannot take the horses," said Quenan. "They are too weak."

Tom waited for someone else to suggest a horse be slaughtered so the group could eat. He was starving, but the thought of consuming raw flesh made his stomach churn. Rosalie stared into space as if her desire to lead had evaporated like the waterhole beside them. And Quenan loved the horses, so either Tom or Rosalie would have to do the butchering.

"We should slaughter one," said Rosalie. "Fill our stomachs. But I can't face it."

"Setting them free is no mercy in this place," said Quenan.

"I'll do it," said Tom.

"Do you know how?" asked Rosalie.

"Show me."

Rosalie led Tom to the horses, tethered to wooden pegs barely holding in the sand. The animals lay on their sides, skin stretched over bulging ribs, legs tucked underneath, and heads drooping listlessly on the ground. From a saddle bag, she took a hatchet, then unsheathed her long knife.

"I've not done it before," said Rosalie. "But I've seen Raf do it. Strike the horse in the centre of the forehead with the axe's blunt end. Hit as hard as you can. It should kill the animal. It might not. When it falls, stick the long knife into the top of its chest, above the collarbone. Go in as deep as the hilt to ensure it's dead."

Rosalie handed Tom the hatchet and long knife and walked away, leaving him alone with the horses. This is mercy, he tried to convince himself. A quick death is better than dying of thirst or starvation. He approached Juniper first. She clambered to her feet as if committed to the burden of carrying Tom to Portum

"Steady girl," he whispered.

Juniper met his eyes and snickered a welcome that flared Tom's guilt. He scratched the white stripe on her forehead, the way she liked, and her mouth tried to find his other hand, hoping it held food.

"Sorry, girl. Nothing to eat."

She lowered her head and pushed her muzzle into his chest.

Tom dropped the knife and clutched the hatchet's handle. Tears streamed down his cheeks, but they couldn't clean the stain already fixed on his conscience. The other two horses stood and tugged at their tethers as if they knew what would happen next.

Juniper remained quiet and still, her trust in Tom unwavering. He'd been kind to her during the journey from the Desolate Mountains. Loving, even. Why would today be any different?

"Sorry, girl," Tom whispered again.

He clenched his jaw, flushed the emotion from his mind and swung the axe, smashing Juniper in the centre of her white stripe. She squealed, a noise Tom never thought he'd hear from a horse, and staggered sideways. The other horses trumpeted, their eyes and nostrils flaring together. They yanked the tether pegs from the sand and bolted off into the desert, using their last energy reserves to escape him. Tom focussed on a wounded Juniper, stepping closer to finish the job. He flailed the axe again and missed as she almost toppled over, his tears continuing their attempt to absolve the sinful guilt.

Hurry up and finish it, he thought.

Another swing. This time, the blunt end of the axe cracked Juniper's skull, and she collapsed onto the sand, her legs in spasms. Tom dropped to his knees, grabbed the long knife and plunged it into the horse's chest, where Rosalie had shown him, up to the hilt. Juniper's blood seeped around the blade. When Tom withdrew the knife, blood sprayed over his pants and boots.

Juniper lay dying, sucking her last breaths through nostrils ringed with red sand.

Anger replaced Tom's guilt; furious at Rosalie for leaving him here to do this himself. He sat with Juniper as she bled out, until her spasms and breathing stopped, then left her to waste in the desert and walked back to Rosalie and Quenan.

They stood waiting for him, empty backpacks already shouldered.

"I can't...I won't butcher Juniper," said Tom. "The others have run off."

"It doesn't matter," said Rosalie. "We have to go. Another bird flock flew over, low in the sky and in the same direction as the first."

"Water is north of us," said Quenan. "Not far. I am certain."

Tom nodded, gathered his bed roll and pack, slung them over his shoulder and followed Rosalie and Quenan further into the desert, the blood on the lower half of his body already crusty and dry. The death of his horse had little consequence when thirst beckoned.

They walked until midday, always north. With keen turquoise eyes, Quenan spotted more birds heading for the same place, the other side of a dune taller than the pyramid at Malang Gunya.

"Too many birds for it to be a coincidence," said Quenan. "On the other side of the dune is water."

Tom, Rosalie and Quenan climbed the dune, the bank of sand too large to walk around. Grains funnelled into Tom's boots as he heaved his legs up and forward; every step an exertion he expected to be his last. Bare-footed, Quenan strode ahead with the power of a grell, unaffected by the scorching sand. Tom tried to channel Grin's strength. Draw on the commitment of his dead friend to propel himself to the summit.

Quenan dropped to her stomach at the dune's crest and lay still. Beside Tom, Rosalie tensed, unsheathing her sword.

"What is it?" asked Tom.

She glared at him, placed a finger to her lips, and then marched ahead. Tom followed. Before reaching Quenan, they got down on their stomachs and slithered to the dune's crest.

In the swale below, Tom wished for a pool of cool, clean water sparkling in the sun. His wish came true, then became a nightmare haunted by the dismay writhing across the garra tree tattooed on Quenan's face.

"Pordillo," she said.

Dozens of bone-coloured tents circled a waterhole, spreading from the centre and filling the swale between three intersecting dunes. A canvas pavilion bigger than four houses sat at the water's edge, its roof shaded by a cluster of palm trees, the first Tom had seen in Groz Wüste. Dressed in black cotton robes and headscarves, or stripped to the waist, men armed with lances patrolled the lanes among the tents or stood guard around the camp's perimeter. Others cooked on open fires or drew water from the oasis. In pens roped off between the trees, white creatures with long necks like camels and heads resembling a horse grazed on fresh hay.

A banner of black cloth with a red scorpion insignia flew above the pavilion.

"Five, maybe six thousand Pordillo," said Rosalie. "Too risky to get water."

"I can go," said Quenan. "Under cover of night. You and Tom should rest, then...." She stopped mid-sentence.

A sharp point dug into Tom's back. He turned to face a Pordillo soldier poking a lance towards him.

"*Coum star el reap*," said the soldier from behind a bind of black cloth wound about his mouth, nose and head.

Tom rolled onto his back and raised his hands in surrender. Another two soldiers trained the blades of their lances on Rosalie and Quenan.

"*Coum star el reap*," spat the soldier again, the brown skin at the corners of his almond-shaped eyes furrowing in anger.

"Get up," said Rosalie, also raising her hands.

Tom, Rosalie and Quenan stood. Tom hoped the weald-grell would fight. Use her height and strength to overpower the Pordillo and save her companions. But it seemed the journey had exhausted her as much as Tom.

"We're no threat," said Rosalie to her captor.

He spun the lance around and butted her in the face with its heel. She screamed, spurring Tom to unsheathe his sword. As he drew the blade, the first soldier nicked the back of Tom's hand, causing him to drop the weapon.

"Do not fight," said Quenan. "We are trapped."

The Pordillo soldiers took the weapons and packs, then marched Tom and his friends down the dune face and into the bustling camp.

Groups of stout, burly men, torsos thick with body hair, paid little attention to the new captives as if taking prisoners happened often. Tom stumbled behind Rosalie and Quenan along a narrow, well-trodden path between two rows of canvas tents with open flaps. Inside each tent, half a dozen bedrolls were laid on the ground between woven cane shelves that held clothes, cushions, multi-coloured boxes, metal and glass pipes, goblets and other belongings. As Tom walked, the dark eyes in the front pocket of his pants pressed into his thigh. Should the Pordillo soldiers decide on a more thorough search, he risked losing his most important possession.

They arrived at a steel cage, taller than Quenan and large enough to house a dozen prisoners. Two captives cowered in the corner underneath a snatch of shade; an old woman with dark skin and frizzy white hair, and a younger man with pale skin hanging from thin bones. The gaoler, a man with braided hair hanging down to the small of his back, and brimming chest muscles, unlocked the door. The soldiers pushed their new captives inside, Tom falling face-first onto the ground. He used the opportunity to pull the eyes of lost souls from his pants and grasp them in his fist. Behind him, an argument erupted among the Pordillo. Tom rolled over. A bald, thickset man wearing nothing but a skirt and sandals, his entire body covered in circlets of bristly hair, pushed a chubby finger into the chest of one of the soldiers who'd captured Tom, Rosalie and Quenan. With the Pordillo distracted, Tom shoved the dark eyes down the front of his pants.

The argument over, *Hairy Man* dismissed the soldiers and marched into the cage.

"*Da huk mun spel?*" he said to Tom.

Tom shrugged.

"*Ello sim allus Germalian?*" asked Hairy Man, getting agitated. "Erstürmen? Speak, Erstürmen?"

"Yes," said Tom.

"Empty pockets. All pockets."

Tom, Rosalie and Quenan turned out their pockets. Hairy Man grabbed Tom's foil packet of anxiety pills, held it to his nose and sniffed, then scrunched the foil in his fist and threw it back at Tom. The man took more interest in Dwarrow's key, plucking it from Tom's palm and dropping it into a pouch at the front of his skirt.

He waved a finger at Tom. "No escape." Then faced Rosalie.

She opened her hand, revealing a pile of silver tausens.

Hairy Man snatched the coin, glanced over his shoulder, then returned his attention to Rosalie. "My treasure now," he said before stepping towards Quenan. With his free hand, he reached up and clutched her chin, turning her face side-to-side. "Grell. Make good slaves."

Hairy Man walked to the cage door, stopped and pointed to his bearish chest. "Um-huk. You belong to Um-huk." He laughed, slapped the gaoler on the shoulder, then left.

"*Shit,*" Tom cursed in English as the gaoler locked the cage door.

"Where are the dark eyes?" whispered Rosalie.

"In my pants," said Tom.

"Find a better hiding place."

"Where?"

She pointed to his backside.

"My...my arse?"

She nodded. "Inside."

"Well, I haven't needed to go for days. I guess I could."

Quenan herded Tom and Rosalie into the corner opposite the other two prisoners and as far from the gaoler as possible. "We must plan an escape," she said.

The old woman, her dark skin vandalised with suppurating wounds, overheard. "No escape," she said. "Try to escape. Die."

The three travelling companions crowded into the corner. Rosalie and

Quenan shielded Tom from the gaoler's view as he tried to insert the dark eyes into his anus. With his hand down the back of his pants, he pressed a glass eye in place, winching and squirming at the uncomfortable awkwardness of it all.

This is stupid, Tom thought. They won't stay there. Or they'll never appear again.

But he had no choice. He forced the second eye up against the first and pushed them as far inside as he could with his index finger.

The treasure buried, Rosalie and Quenan slumped to the sandy floor.

"Sit," Rosalie said to Tom. "Save your energy."

Tom frowned. "I'm not sure I can sit."

He stood for a while, then slunk down the cage bars and perched on his bottom's left cheek. The sun dipped below the western dune, providing respite from the scornful heat. Flocks of small birds with stunted bills and plumage resembling striped pyjamas of green and purple, flittered among the umbrella-like canopies of the trees surrounding the waterhole or flocked to the water's edge to drink. They reminded Tom of zebra finches.

Black monitor lizards, as long as Tom's forearm, rested in the boughs or propelled themselves through the water using their tail, snapping at bugs floating on the surface. An animal resembling a grey cat with pointed ears as large as a grell's hand snuck up to the shoreline and lapped at the water until a Pordillo soldier passed by. Spooked by the disruption, the cat disappeared into a thicket of shrubs.

At dusk, the gaoler threw two waterskins into the cage. Rosalie grabbed one while the bony young man snatched the other. Tom, Rosalie and Quenan emptied their waterskin, sharing three gulps each, not enough to quench Tom's thirst. He considered wrestling the second waterskin from the other prisoners until realising they'd already emptied it.

"Will they feed us?" asked Tom.

Rosalie shrugged.

He faced the old woman, gagging at the smell of her threadbare clothes stained with faeces and urine.

"Food," said Tom, poking his fingers into his mouth.

"Sun up," she replied, rolling onto her side and pulling her knees to her chest.

"If I can overpower the guard..." started Quenan, then stopped when Rosalie grasped her wrist.

From a gap between the three dunes surrounding the camp rode a column of soldiers dressed head-to-toe in silver armour.

Stupidly impractical for the desert, thought Tom.

And the soldiers rode horses, not the strange creatures favoured by the Pordillo. The lead bannerman raised a flag of white cloth and waved it across his body, announcing the visitors' arrival to the camp. Tom had seen the banner's sigil many times. A two-headed red serpent, curled face-to-face. The Erstürmen symbol. But a new design had been added to the flag, equally familiar to Tom — obsidian black eyes with flaming pupils sitting on either side of a golden sun and touched by the sun's rays. He'd seen the picture for the first time twenty-three years ago when he opened the front cover of the blue book.

"Malphas' Shield," whispered Rosalie into Tom's ear. "From Pergamos."

Among the dozens of soldiers on horseback, and coffles of grell slaves with crates or wicker baskets strapped to their backs, four slaves carried a dark timber palanquin with closed red curtains. The soldiers stopped at the pavilion's entrance, and Pordillo fighters milled around the new arrivals as the Erstürmen dismounted. The palanquin's curtains opened, and a short man wearing sangria robes stepped out.

"Only the highest-ranked curate in Enthilen is permitted to wear sangria red," said Rosalie. "That man is the Hoch-Vater. High-Father of Enthilen."

Tom had seen another man wear those robes; Lothar, who he first met in Süden Forst, then again in Pergamos' throne room before it collapsed. This short, fussy man with bowed legs and a pursed face wasn't Lothar.

"Do you know who he is?" Tom asked Rosalie.

"Anselm is the Hoch-Vater of Enthilen and Malphas' curate in Pergamos."

"Malphas must consider this meeting important," said Quenan, "to send such a man."

Um-huk, the squat, hairy man who'd fleeced Tom and Rosalie of their treasures, unlocked the cage door, marched inside and pointed a stubby finger covered in gold rings at Rosalie. "Speak Erstürmen, good?"

She nodded.

Um-huk reached down and yanked her to her feet.

"Where are you taking her?" said Tom, standing.

The gaoler pushed past Um-huk and poked the point of a lance into Tom's chest. Tom raised his hands in deference.

"I'll be alright," said Rosalie. But the terror in her eyes betrayed her.

With his bejewelled hand wrapped around Rosalie's wrist like a manacle, Um-huk led her from the cage and towards the pavilion.

Tom sagged to the ground, and the gaoler locked the cage door. The journey to Portum presented another challenge. One he didn't know how to overcome.

"No escape," said the old woman in the corner.

* * * *

Um-huk dragged Rosalie to the pavilion, a white canvas tent painted with images of scorpions, slider serpents, and creatures with claws large enough to crush a horse. After passing the entrance guards, everything but their sandaled feet and almond-shaped eyes wrapped in black cotton, Rosalie followed Um-huk down a passageway lined with dozens of Pordillo soldiers on either side. The fighters drew and raised their cutlasses, pointing the weapons forward so the blade tips met in the middle to form a steel archway. At the end of the passage, she entered a room blurred by a smoky haze that smelled of lavender. Rosalie expected to see Anselm and his Erstürmen escort in the pavilion, but it seemed they'd been taken elsewhere.

Um-huk pushed Rosalie forward, and the haze parted to reveal the room's far end. On a scatter of cushions, each one larger than a dining table, lounged an apparently naked man, the sagging rolls of fat from his waist hanging low over his genitals such that Rosalie couldn't tell if he *was* naked or, indeed, a man. A female servant, dressed only in a grass skirt, held the man's left arm while another half-naked woman washed the puffy curtains of flesh and skin dangling towards the floor. A third attendant appeared from behind the cushions carrying a copper bowl. She placed the bowl on a pedestal next to the man, dipped her fingers inside, then began to massage the bald head of her master with oil. He smiled at the pleasure; the point of his chin drowned in the scarf of corpulence strangling his neck.

As Rosalie stepped forward, the man's smile broadened. He licked his lips until webs of saliva formed at the corners of his mouth. She shivered, despite the cloying heat inside the pavilion. The man burst into laughter. His breasts, larger than any Rosalie had seen on a man *or* a woman, didn't jiggle; they shuddered — quakes of body fat rippling out from the nipple epicentres and brushing against the top of his stomach.

Um-huk kicked the back of Rosalie's knees, and she fell to a floor covered in rugs of every colour and design she could imagine.

"Crawl to Qaysar Rais," said Um-huk.

On hands and knees, Rosalie crawled to the edge of the cushioned platform where Qaysar Rais held his court.

"Head to ground," said Um-huk.

Rosalie dropped her forehead onto a plush woollen rug, her bottom pointing to the pavilion's roof. Qaysar Rais groaned, and she sensed a shadow move over her. Then she smelled a mix of wine and perfume, like crushed grapes soaked in rosewater. A bulbous drape of skin brushed against her hair as Rais sniffed, then cooed like a dove.

"*Hmmm*," he said before sinking back into his cushions.

"Stand," said Um-huk to Rosalie.

She stood and met Qaysar Rais eye-to-eye. He appeared to have paler skin than other Pordillo until she noticed his face had been dusted with white powder streaked by the sweat that beaded on his forehead, the only part of his body not succumbing to obesity. Rais clapped his hands once. One of the half-naked servants dropped her washcloth in a bucket, then gathered a fan, broader than her own body and made from the plucked tail feathers of sand-runner cocks. She wrapped both hands around the fan's shaft, as long as a spear, then swirled the air above Rais' head.

Um-huk leaned into Rosalie's ear. "Kiss."

She faced him, thoughts and stomach churning.

"Kiss Qaysar Rais," said Um-huk, pointing a jewelled finger at his cheeks.

A servant took Rosalie's hand and pulled her closer to Rais. The Qaysar lifted his drowned chin and poked his head forward. Rosalie leaned in, held her breath, and pecked Rais on each powdered cheek.

Rosalie and Rais pulled away simultaneously, and he laughed.

"Speak Erstürmen, *hmmm*?" asked Rais in a sickly-sweet voice, dripping like honey from shattered comb.

Rosalie imagined that if she swallowed the honey, there'd be a sting waiting for her.

"Yes, I do," said Rosalie. "But I don't speak Pordillo."

Rais laughed until his stomach quavered. With a wave, he beckoned her closer. She leaned in, and he whispered, "*Hmmm. Does Hoch-Vater know you don't speak Pordillo?*"

Rosalie pulled away and shook her head.

Rais smiled. "You keep Hoch-Vater honest, *hmmm*. Ears open like desert fox. Listen every word. When I call, whisper to me. *Hmmm*?"

A servant thrust a clay pitcher into Rosalie's hand. Qaysar Rais held out a silver goblet and smiled at her. She tipped red wine into the goblet, then he waved her away. Um-huk pushed Rosalie to the side, where she stood like a statue, cradling the wine pitcher.

The night wore on, and Qaysar Rais continued to drink, keeping his Erstürmen guests waiting. Rosalie pondered her new role, suspecting Rais had a limited grasp of the Erstürmen language. She couldn't translate Erstürmen to Pordillo, but if Anselm *thought* she could, he would be less likely to try to deceive Rais. She assumed Rais' believed the same.

Late in the evening, Rosalie's legs aching from standing in one place, a troop of twelve fighters marched into the pavilion. Unlike any soldiers Rosalie had seen so far, their faces were covered by masks of impassive silver, and they wore tangerine robes cinched at the waist by indigo belts. A wide strap of black leather had been buckled across a left or right shoulder, with daggers sheathed at the front, near their chest.

Not an ordinary dagger, thought Rosalie, admiring the blades of wavy steel and red handles carved from bone or another material, each with a unique design.

A masked soldier stepped up to Um-huk and whispered in his ear.

Um-huk nodded, then strode to Qaysar Rais, bowed his head, and proclaimed, "*El em Erstürmen.*"

Rais offered a drunken acknowledgement, his powdered face almost eroded back to brown by rivulets of sweat.

The soldiers in black garb lining the passage formed their cutlass archway again as Anselm, Enthilen's Hoch-Vater, tottered along the carpeted runway, clutching a fistful of sangria robe at the waist to lift the hem from the ground. He headed straight for Rais' platform and stood in front of the Qaysar, hands resting over his groin. Anselm didn't glance at Rosalie, and she wondered if he'd seen her. They stood out, being the only ones in the canvas room with pale skin.

Rais pursed his mouth as if kissing the air, then beamed a smile, red wine dribbling down his breasts like watery blood. "Welcome! Anus… ah…An-*selm*, Pro-*belch*-Proclaiment of…of…." He waved at Rosalie.

She stepped towards him and leaned forward, tasting the reek of alcohol, then whispered in his ear, "Proclaiment of Pergamos."

Rais laughed and pushed her away. "Proclaiment of Pergamos, *hmmm*. Hock-*burp*-Vata of…of Enthilen." His face turned sour. "Footstool for Malphas."

Anselm glared at Rosalie. He'd noticed her now, his pious stare burrowing into her chest to find the deception hiding inside. Holding the pitcher of wine, her bare forearms exposed, she realised her stupidity too late.

"You're from Sardis," Anselm said to Rosalie.

She couldn't deny it. He'd seen the branding scar on her right forearm, a hammer crossed with a sword. The symbol forever marking her as a one-time resident of Sardis' fifth circle.

Rais grumbled, then snapped at Anselm, "To me. Only to me, *hmmm*."

Anselm shifted his piety to his host. "Thank you, Qaysar Rais. I welcome the opportunity to finally speak with you."

"Why not, *hmmm*? We are...*belch*...new friends, soon old friends."

Anselm bowed his head. "I have a gift from the Worshipful Master. To celebrate and honour the alliance we have forged."

Rais beckoned Rosalie, then yanked her close.

She whispered in his ear, repeating what Anselm had said.

"Gift?" asked Rais. "I worthy, *hmmm*?"

He pushed down against the cushions with his hands until his face burned red under the white powder, and his bottom lifted slightly. Then the Pordillo leader farted.

The soldiers lining the passageway chuckled. Anselm brushed at his sangria robes as if trying to deflect Rais' stench, the thick wool and linen apparel unsuited to the Groz Wüste heat. Sweat streamed down Anselm's face like the Rārian Falls, and he cast a jittery glance at Rosalie, then back to his host. Rais tapped the bottom of his silver goblet on the table beside his cushions, and Rosalie filled the cup with wine.

The Qaysar held the goblet up to the lantern hanging above his head. "Not silver, *hmmm*. White gold from Thyatira. Very rare." He turned to a half-naked female servant and barked in Pordillo, "*Uck um drak el.*"

She poured wine into a wooden cup and took it to Anselm.

The Hoch-Vater waved her away. "Curates have taken a vow of sobriety."

"*Hmmm*?" said Rais, turning a perplexed face to Rosalie.

She spoke in his ear, "No drink."

Rais lurched around to Anselm and bellowed, "No drink!? No drink!?" He thrust his white gold goblet at the curate. "Drink, *hmmm*. Drink!"

Anselm took a sip, screwed up his face, then held the wooden cup at his waist.

Rais heaved his body up and tugged a cushion further under his bottom. "Why great Malphas...*hiccup*...great, wonderful...*ah*...."

"Worshipful Master," whispered Rosalie.

Rais sneered. "Yes. *Worshipful Master, hmmm.* Why offer gifts?"

"The Erstürmen and Pordillo have formed a strong alliance," said Anselm. "Malphas sends more supplies to aid in your efforts against the Germalians. To help you reclaim the land they stole from you. But the

Worshipful Master is concerned. The Germalians threaten Enthilen with talk of war."

Rais drew a bubbling, gurgling sound from the pit of his throat, hacked up something into his mouth and spat a slimy glob of bile on the floor at Rosalie's feet. She thrust her hand to her mouth to hold a vomit.

"*Hmmm*," said Rais. "Germalia." He wiped the spit from his lips and rubbed it on his naked breasts. "Cesspit of femality. *Al morun dun ek-hand, enk Almahud et enk Almunash elum!*" yelled Rais in the Pordillo language. "Us," he reverted to Erstürmen and pointed to his chest. "Land given to us, the *Almahud*, by the mighty *Almunash* himself! Then women steal." He spat on the floor again.

"The Worshipful Master is willing to offer generous terms to bolster our alliance," said Anselm.

Rais beckoned to Rosalie, who whispered in his ear, repeating Anselm's sentence.

The Qaysar looked at her but pointed to Anselm. "You continue."

"I don't understand," said Rosalie.

"You continue," Rais said again.

Um-huk stepped towards her. "The Qaysar orders you to continue the negotiation."

Me? she wondered.

Rosalie faced Anselm. He didn't acknowledge her. After all, she was an Erstürmen traitor, and he was Enthilen's Hoch-Vater. She thought back on her days in the Slumstadt markets, haggling on the best price for scrap metal for her father, Yonna, to turn into something much more valuable.

I can do this, thought Rosalie, steadying her nerves.

"What are these terms?" she asked Anselm.

Anselm rose onto his toes but still refused to look at her, keeping his eyes on Rais.

"Malphas offers soldiers to fight with the Pordillo against the Germalians," said Anselm. "*But...the Pordillo must attack Portum. Soon.*"

Rais choked on a mouthful of wine, spitting red down his waggling breasts. "Attack? Attack? *Hmmm*. Too dangerous."

Anselm shuffled his bowed legs, wiping his pontifical white shoes on the Qaysar's beautiful carpets.

Um-huk poked Rosalie in the back. "Continue."

She gathered her thoughts, unsure where to take the negotiation. Anselm offered the Pordillo military support for a price. An attack on Portum may stop the Germalians declaring war on Malphas. Yet, if Rosalie could persuade Anselm to commit substantial forces to the Pordillo, it would mean fewer fighters to defend Pergamos, strengthening the chances of a Germalian victory in Enthilen.

Do, and be damned, she thought. *Don't*, and be no better.

"The Germalian army numbers in the tens of thousands," said Rosalie to Anselm. "They are skilled fighters. Portum is a fortress with huge walls and powerful war engines." She didn't know any of this but wagered Anselm knew as little as her. "An attack on Portum by Qaysar Rais requires forces much greater than he currently commands."

"Griffins, *hmmm*," said Rais. "Women have griffins."

Rosalie caught her breath. She'd never seen a griffin. They'd been lost to Enthilen generations ago. Now she *really* wanted to reach Portum.

"Malphas offers a thousand Rephaim and five thousand soldiers," said Anselm.

Rosalie faced Rais, who waved his hand at a servant. She dabbed a damp cloth across his chest, mopping up the wine. The Qaysar tapped his empty goblet on the table again, and another servant scuttled forward to fill it. Two more servants brought in a silver platter, carrying the roasted head of a horse surrounded by palmberries. They placed the platter on the table beside Rais. His eyes bulged as he leaned across, stripped the blackened skin off the horse's nose, popped it in his mouth and licked his fingers.

The Qaysar locked eyes with Rosalie and shook his head. She guessed the game. She'd played it before with scrap-metal merchants in the Slumstadt markets.

"Not enough," Rosalie said to Anselm. "Qaysar Rais requires five thousand Rephaim and twenty thousand soldiers. The elite ones, too. The Master's Shield. Not the rabble."

Anselm's face blushed red, matching his sangria robes. Negotiating with a woman was as unfamiliar to most Erstürmen men as speaking Pordillo.

"One thousand Rephaim and six thousand Shield," Anselm blustered.

Rosalie smiled. "You've hardly budged, Hoch-Vater. This must be a negotiation, not a robbery. Try again."

"The Worshipful Master will not risk the defence of Pergamos for this gambit."

But he must, thought Rosalie. If I can trick you, he will.

"It seems Malphas refuses to risk anything and demands the Qaysar risk everything," said Rosalie. "The Germalians have dozens of griffins. Do you remember the stories about them, Anselm? The tales of brutality and terror. Griffins take to war as a boulder lion devours a wounded hare. A single griffin carried a strong, fully armoured King Giltbert to his death. Plucked him from the midst of a barbarian horde, the creature unscathed by the assault. A mighty force is needed to confront the griffins of Portum."

Anselm sighed. "One thousand Rephaim and eight thousand Shield."

"Where *are* these fighters?" asked Rosalie. "You've arrived with barely two dozen."

"In Sardis," said Anselm.

Rosalie's rebel companions had snuck into Sardis occasionally, but they never reported seeing that many soldiers and Malphas wouldn't empty the city of all its fighters. She needed to push Anselm for more soldiers so the numbers could only be filled by taking defenders from Pergamos. And marching from Pergamos to Portum would take many moons, leaving more time for her, Tom and Quenan to reach Portum and convince the Germalians to fight Malphas.

Have to escape the Pordillo first, Rosalie reminded herself.

"Two thousand Rephaim and ten thousand Shield," said Rosalie. "The Qaysar's final offer. Reject it, and our negotiation ends. You can return to Malphas and report your failure."

Rais beckoned Rosalie over. She whispered in his ear, trying to explain how many two and ten thousand were. He pushed her away, then gestured to two male servants with swelling muscles dressed in tan skin. The servants stood on either side of Rais, placed their hands underneath his armpits and heaved, lifting the Qaysar from his cushions. Rais wavered for a moment, his toes clutching at a rug to gain purchase, then stood, awkward and unsteady, like a tufted goliath balanced on its hind legs. Drapes of body fat descended past his waist as he tottered to the front edge of the royal platform and placed his hands out, one palm facing up and one facing down.

He locked eyes with Anselm. "Deal, *hmmm?*"

The Hoch-Vater of Enthilen brushed his fingertips across his lips, glancing at Rosalie, then back to Rais. He stepped forward and rested his palms above and below Rais'. "Deal."

The Qaysar beamed. "A feast!"

He lurched towards Rosalie and pulled her into a hug of smothering obesity.

She gasped for air, wondering if she'd made a terrible mistake.

~ Chapter 31 ~

Mirrian embraced the scorching sun, celebrating another rare occasion above ground in Pergamos. In the calendar of life, Rephaim had built a funeral pyre as ordered by the Worshipful Master. Logs hewn from panalope trees and soaked in serpent oil, crisscrossed each other to tower above Mirrian's head. Atop the pyre lay Ende's body, wrapped in a cerement of pale yellow. The old Mirrian would have been insulted by this desecration of the most sacred place in stone-grell culture, but she'd died along with Ende. The new Mirrian looked on with a sense of rejuvenation. When the pale grell burned, another would rise from the ashes. Master promised as much. Mirrian would honour the promise.

Sweat from the palm of her right hand soaked into the sparth's handle as if the sap of her body would renew the wood's lifeblood. The weapon gave Mirrian comfort.

More than comfort, she thought. *Power.* Master said he would teach her how to swing the blade in the same exacting way as her predecessor. He'd also given her a new, flaxen dress. It no longer fit a shrunken Ende, but the diaphanous, delicate silk clung to Mirrian's naked body like lichen draped over a tree branch.

Malphas stood beside her, forsaking his usual white robes for black, spun from the wool of mountain sheep found in The Feign. Krieg, Mirrian's tainted brother, flanked Malphas, the colossal grell gleaming in resplendent blood-red armour.

The Master's Shield and Rephaim encircled the stone columns of the calendar of life, forming a guard to honour the pale grell's passing. One of Pergamos' many curates strolled around the base of the funeral pyre, seeking Volerdie's blessing for Ende's last journey. Master told Mirrian that Anselm, Enthilen's Hoch-Vater, would typically conduct a service of such importance, but he'd been dispatched to Grōz Wüste to win favour from the Pordillo.

It's strange, thought Mirrian, for a curate's prayers to honour Ende since grells are not permitted to enter Volerdie's paradise.

Mirrian accepted this fate would also be hers. Her ascent ended here. Service to the Worshipful Master *was* her paradise.

Malphas nodded to Krieg. The red grell removed his spiked, grilled helmet, handing it to a Rephaim, who exchanged it for a lit torch. Grasping the firebrand, Krieg walked up to the tower of glistening wood, the soles of his metal sabatons scraping against the open temple's painted flagstones. As the curate scuttled away, the red grell touched the torch to the pyre, and it exploded in flames and black smoke.

Mirrian recoiled from the heat, shielding her eyes. Sweat streamed down her chest and stomach, soaking her dress until the translucent silk of pale flaxen melded with her skin.

Ende is dead, thought Mirrian. Long live Ende.

The smoke caught in her throat, but she didn't cough. She wouldn't show any weakness in front of Master. Weakness would be banished forever after completing her transformation to the new pale grell.

Mirrian turned away from the fire to face Pergamos' citizens, who'd stopped to gawk at the spectacle. Stepping closer to Malphas, she held the sparth across her chest. She would protect him. She would behead anyone who threatened Master.

The flames died at sunset, and grell slaves swept up the ash. Malphas had commissioned a painted vase to hold Ende's remains. It would sit on a pedestal beside the dead throne in Pergamos' grand hall. Mirrian followed Malphas to the hall, down the stairs and into the city's depths. Walking past the corridor to the storeroom, where Carian and Julan had almost killed Mirrian, a razored tinge of dread sliced across her chest. But she quashed it the same way the old Ende had thwarted Carian and Julan's attack — with impassive and brutal efficiency.

Malphas led Mirrian through the throne hall's double oak doors. In the centre of the cavernous room, large enough to accommodate a gathering of several thousand, a table had been set for dinner with two places. Grell slaves brought in silver trays of food; roasted meats and vegetables, freshly baked bread, and pitchers of groomberry sauce. The slaves would have heard of Julan and Carian's death, but Mirrian didn't fear retribution. Her feebleness had burned in the pyre.

Master beckoned Mirrian to sit opposite him. She leaned her sparth against one of the fluted stone columns supporting the roof, the column's base cast as four cloven hooves pointing north, south, east and west. The pentagram at the column's capital spread into a ceiling painted with scenes of Pergamos during Volerdie's rule. As Mirrian sat, a slave placed an empty plate in front of her, then filled a goblet with meduz. Malphas draped his black robe over the back of a chair, his shirt stained with sweat under his arms. Another slave offered to fill his plate, but he waved her away.

"Leave us," said Malphas. "All of you."

The slaves bowed their heads and walked out. The Rephaim guards followed, closing the oak doors, the strap hinges squealing with the weight of the metal-encased wood.

Malphas sat in silence, picking meat from the ribs of a plains goat and laying it on his plate. Mirrian took a sip of meduz, the cloudy alcohol stinging her tongue with its bitterness. As she weighed her hunger against the offerings on the table, the door to the throne hall creaked open. Mirrian sprang from her seat. By the time she'd grabbed her sparth, a draughoul had already floated past her and knelt beside Master.

Malphas spat gristle onto his plate and wiped the back of his arm across his mouth. "What news do you bring?"

"Your quarry will soon be captured, Worshipful Master," said the draughoul.

Malphas pointed a chewed rib bone at the ghostly creature. "Are you sure it's him?"

"Yes, the immortal one. He was with a woman — one of us. And two others."

"The draughoul is Princess Caeli, still pining for her father's love. Others?"

"Another woman and a younger man with no right hand."

Malphas stopped chewing, and his eyes narrowed, the solemnity replaced by a pinpoint curiosity. "Did the man have curly black hair?"

"Yes, Master. He resembled the absent king."

Malphas nodded. "Widukind has found Adalwolf. My brother is plotting something." He turned his fork upside down and dug the prongs into the table.

"The Rephaim failed, Master. Mouldewerps helped the quarry escape. The draughouls will not fail."

"Did my mother go with them?"

"Yes."

Malphas smiled. "She'll lure him here. When Widukind sees what I did to Mother, his anger will march him all the way to Pergamos." He dismissed the draughoul and faced Mirrian. "It seems the massacre in the calendar of life twelve yarles ago didn't rid Enthilen of all those annoying werps. Why are they helping Widukind and Adalwolf?"

Mirrian sat, pondering an answer. But she had nothing to ease Master's burden.

He continued without her condolence, "I've searched for my brother for half a generation. Always he evaded me. We were close in Bindari. Capturing Fullō has turned into an unexpected blessing. I should have known she would finally lead us to Widukind."

"It will be a momentous day," said Mirrian, "when your brother arrives in Pergamos, and you can offer him to Volerdie as the immortal sacrifice."

"Yes, it will be a great day. But it must be the *right* day. When darkness descends amid the daylight. Ancient Erstürmen legend says it happened once before, during King Managold's reign, six hundred and sixty-six yarles ago. The First Scripture, Volerdie's words written in his own blood, hint at the next occurrence." Malphas leaned forward in his chair and held Mirrian's gaze. "The last day of this harvest season. Seena and Bargan will steal the sunlight, and the world will grow dim."

Behind Mirrian, the door to the throne hall opened again. Malphas looked over her shoulder and nodded to someone at the door. She turned as a naked Krieg walked into the room, pushing a flat, four-wheeled cart carrying a copper bathtub large enough for a grell. Wisps of steam rose from the bath and disappeared into the tiered chandeliers like vaporous ghosts. Malphas had used the same bath to taint Grin's skin white.

Krieg stopped the cart beside Mirrian. Inside the bath, a viscous, sepia-coloured liquid bubbled and spat.

"I brewed the mixture last eve," said Malphas. "Extracted fresh ölblut from the throne of the dead and boiled it with strips of skin from the fallen pale grell. The colour is perfect. Do you agree, *Ende?*"

Mirrian stood, hovered above the mixture and inhaled vapour that smelled like rotten eggs. Krieg balanced a scrubbing brush on the lip of the bath and stepped back, the wound on his chest, the one she'd inflicted as his punishment for the misstep at Gestade, still wept.

"Remove your dress," said Malphas.

Mirrian undid the ties across her shoulders and let the delicate fabric slip down to her bare feet. The underside of her breasts brushed against her stomach as she circled the bathtub, tracing a finger along its edge, not flinching at the copper's heat.

"Once I've tainted your skin, we'll remove the rest of your facial tattoo."

"Yes, Master," said Mirrian.

Except, it wasn't Mirrian who replied. It never would be again.

"Into the tub," said Malphas.

She stepped onto the cart, then climbed into the bath. As she immersed her naked body in the pond of scalding liquid, she gritted dogged teeth and clamped her mouth shut lest it betray any frailty. The taint soaked every part of her body. Flooded the pores of her skin. Channelled through the wrinkles on her hands. Seeped beneath her fingernails. Penetrated her vagina and anus like a salacious lover.

Malphas knelt beside the tub, took the scrubbing brush, and ground the taint further into her skin. Her arms. Her legs. Her stomach, breasts and face.

Krieg lifted a pitcher from the table, emptied the meduz onto the floor and handed the jug to Malphas. Master filled it with tainted liquid, then tipped it over her thinning hair.

"Tilt your head back, Ende," he whispered.

She complied, closing her eyes as the taint washed over her face. When she opened them again, the throne hall began to transform. Tapestries and paintings hanging on the walls became more beautiful than she'd ever imagined. Shimmering halos crowned the sculptures of Volerdie. Perched on its royal platform, the dead throne shone like a beacon lighting the way to paradise.

Malphas pushed her beneath the surface and held her there. When he removed his hand, she stayed submersed, surrounded by the nourishing liquid like a baby in the womb.

But her lungs ached for air, and she rose from the depths.

Then Mirrian — no — *Ende* took the first breath of a new life.

*   *   *   *

Nettie pulled rags over her aching body. Despite the balmy night, she shivered with a cold sweat, her mind retching from the thought of her most recent meal, a dead rat Erwin found on the road. They skinned, gutted, and cooked it over a tiny fire, eating bones and all, washed down with dirty water. Hunger made for desperate choices. Nettie had never been more desperate. Since discovering her father, Yonna, had died, she'd been living with Erwin in a place called the ossuary. Nettie had nowhere else to go other than back to the army, and Erwin refused to return to his parents lest it put them in danger. Lieutenant Berard had told his recruits the military executed deserters. Erwin hoped the punishment didn't extend to the deserter's family. Nettie expected it did but wouldn't burden her friend with the suspicion.

Built beneath Pergamos' streets by the original stone-grell inhabitants, the ossuary spread like twisting, turning ant tunnels into dark corners full of bones. Before King Alaric stole the city from the grells, when they called this place Malang Gunya, the original inhabitants buried their dead children here, in a labyrinth of holes. So many children had died, the once solid stone walls now resembled honeycomb. A dozen or so graves had been looted, but the ossuary's living residents mostly kept their distance, fearing the wrath of stone-grell ghosts would descend on them for any desecration.

The ghosts are already here, thought Nettie. They wailed at night when the wind whistled through rifts in the ceiling, threatening to extinguish the campfires and plunge the ossuary into darkness before the spectres launched their assault.

She sat up and rested her back against a rock wall, concerned the rat would make another appearance by scampering up her throat and bursting from her mouth. Littering the ossuary tunnels, the dachlos, people without homes, huddled around dwindling fires despite the stifling air. Most of the dachlos were older than Nettie's father. Younger residents had been conscripted into Malphas' army.

And this is no place for children, thought Nettie. Except dead ones.

The dozens of dachlos coughed and groaned their way through night after night of painful hunger. Some told Nettie and Erwin stories of lost times in an Enthilen full of beauty and wonder. Others rued past mistakes and treated the future with disdain. None knew how to escape Pergamos. Nettie kept asking, but the old people replied with careless vacancy.

'Dreams rest with the bones of grell children in the catacomb's graves,' one woman had said. 'The chamber of the dead offers only nightmares.'

As the nights passed, Erwin grew increasingly restless, and Nettie feared he'd return to the army, thinking a plea for clemency would lessen the punishment. She refused to accept that fate or becoming one of the dachlos embracing a slow death. An escape from the labyrinth existed for those who believed. Faith would reveal the path.

Inside the home of the dead or dying, Nettie still prayed to Volerdie, asking the Divine Creator for mercy and guidance. Begging him to lead her to a new life outside the walls of the city he once called his own. Yonna couldn't help her now, but Volerdie, the holiest of fathers, would answer her prayers.

Lying beside Nettie, Erwin rolled onto his back, moaning and clutching his stomach.

"I don't feel too good," he grumbled.

"We can't eat any more rats," said Nettie. "We'll have to steal proper food."

"Our bakery would be full of bread and cakes. My parents could sneak us a loaf of sourdough. They wouldn't tell anyone."

They're already dead, thought Nettie.

"I can't stay here another night," said Erwin.

Nettie turned away. She had no answer for him, wishing he'd stop asking.

Through the mullings of dachlos, a man strode towards her dressed in a crisp white shirt, polished leather pants and boots, and a spotless horsehair coat reaching down to his shins. Although a cowl hid the man's face, Nettie guessed he didn't belong here. The soles of pulsing boots blew the dust from his path with intent. His straight, rigid posture hadn't been crippled with misery or infirmity. This man had a purpose. Carried a surety about the future and the will to see it happen.

He stopped at Nettie's feet.

As firelight burned the shadows from the man's face, she gasped. Erwin jolted upright, throwing the rags off his legs lest they tangle his feet during the escape. For fleeing was the only thing on Nettie's mind because an ossuary ghost had finally found them.

The man appeared to smile, but Nettie couldn't tell, his expression garrotted by a wiry mesh of red scars contorting across his face and neck and disappearing down into the top of his shirt. He had no eyebrows, slitty eyes masked by drapes of scar tissue hanging from his forehead, and drew breath through the stump of a nose, two tiny nostrils besieged by mutilations whose assault extended down past thin, pale lips.

The lips relaxed, and the ghost began his haunting. "Not seen you in the ossuary before," he said.

"W-w-w-we w-w-won't be here long," said Erwin.

"Young people don't last. Soldiers come and raid this place all the time." With a gloved hand, the man pointed to the rodent skull on the ground that had escaped Nettie and Erwin's hunger. "You eatin' rat?"

"It's all we can find," said Erwin.

"Want a proper meal? Won't cost nothin'."

"We're doing alright here," said Nettie, trying to escape the pry of a blistered face.

"Lyin' won't help you. The truth catches up with those who sleep with the dead, one way or another. Me name's Snick. I can show you the way out."

Volerdie hadn't come to save Nettie despite her prayers, and she doubted Snick delivered the Divine Creator's blessings. Averting her eyes from a face that spoke of hurt beyond her comprehension, she hoped silence would make Snick disappear. Fade into the night like the ghost she thought he was.

Yet, Nettie's aversion couldn't compete with Erwin's attachment. He'd engage with Snick. He'd be led astray, and she would have to follow him.

"I'm Erwin," chirped Nettie's companion, like a canary perched on her shoulder. "The baker's son. Then they forced me to be a soldier."

"You deserters?" asked Snick. "That's a dangerous game, right there. If they find y'down here, they won't bother takin' y'back. They'll shove you into one of them empty graves and brick up the hole while you're still breathin'. Dain't need to be like that."

"Will you help us?" asked Erwin.

No, thought Nettie. Don't engage. Don't fall under his spell.

"First things first," said Snick. "How 'bout a proper meal? Then we can talk more."

Erwin licked his lips, and Nettie's resistance washed away with the flick of a tongue.

"What kind of meal?" asked Erwin.

"Fresh stew with taters, pigs' trotters and barley. Sourdough bread. Cream cakes."

As Erwin jumped to his feet, Nettie reached for his pants leg to drag him back to safety. But his naïve hunger slipped her grasping hand.

He looked down at her. "I'm starving, Nettie. It's rude to reject an offer of food."

"How much will it cost?" asked Nettie.

"Nothin'," said Snick. "Not a single coin."

"Why help us?"

"When I first came to Pergamos, I ended up here. I know what it's like bein' at the bottom of the barrel. Someone has to help y'get out."

Nettie stood, fingering the metal locket at the top of her empty scabbard. The dagger it used to house had been stolen on their first night in the ossuary. While she slept.

Despite not having a weapon, she persisted with a bluff. "Don't try anything. We're trained soldiers."

Snick nodded. "I'll watch meself, don't worry. The food's close. Follow me."

Erwin scurried after Snick as if the scarred man had adopted an ossuary rat. Nettie lagged behind, expecting a trap to be sprung from every dark corner. They walked up a ramp and into Pergamos' busy streets. It appeared to be early evening; the moons partially obscured by low clouds blanketing the city.

Snick led Nettie and Erwin away from the ossuary's decrepit pauperism and into a neighbourhood with respectable, detached houses, stone-built with thatched roofs and glass windows, and courtyards with thriving plants bordered by picket fences. As they walked the footpaths along the housefronts, the crowds disappeared, and Nettie's apprehension grew, expecting Lieutenant Berard to be waiting for her behind one of the painted doors.

At least the end would be quick, she thought.

Snick opened a wrought iron gate, leading them into a garden of trimmed hedges surrounding a water fountain. They skirted around the fountain, Nettie leaning in to let the spray cool her face, then climbed seven stairs to a porch with a mahogany red front door. Snick used the silver knocker, shaped like a barking jackal's head, to tap three times, pause, then tap three times again.

The door opened, and a bald man with a grey beard, his toneless, hairy chest barely covered by a velvet peach robe, frowned.

"What is it, Snick?" asked the man, cinching the robe at his waist. "I'm in the middle of something."

"Got a couple of hungry young people with me."

The bald man looked Nettie and Erwin up and down with arresting green eyes.

"Found 'em in the ossuary," continued Snick. "Livin' with the dachlos. Broke me heart, it did, to see such young'uns homeless. They're scared and hungry." He pulled the cowl from his head, then leaned towards the man's ear. "*Deserters.*"

Snick didn't bother to whisper. Nettie believed she and Erwin were meant to know the bald man understood their predicament and the risk he took in granting them this favour.

The man stepped onto the porch, glanced up and down the street, then ushered them inside. A runner woven with a picture of naked pixies dancing across flowering fields covered the hallway floor below a chandelier with at least a dozen lit candles. They followed the man into a reception room with a bookcase, a side table, padded wooden chairs and a strange-looking device hanging from the ceiling that resembled a cart wheel with broad, flat spokes but no rim.

Snick stopped at the doorway and turned a crank handle around. The rimless cartwheel spun, and cool air breezed across the room.

"Thank you, Snick," said the bald man before facing Nettie. "I can't suffer this heat. Once upon a time, I could jump into the Anchep River on nights like these. Those were good days. Please, sit. I'll return in a moment."

Nettie and Erwin perched on the edge of padded chairs, their hands resting on their knees, while the bald man disappeared down the hallway. A muffled conversation drifted in above the pulsing air from Snick's cooling apparatus, followed by shrieks of laughter. A woman wearing a chiffon nightdress appeared at the doorway to the room, pecked Snick on the cheek, smiled at Nettie and Erwin, then scampered out the front door.

The bald man returned, his cheeks flushed like ruddy wine, and slouched into the only couch chair in the room.

"*Relax*," he said, the leather chair squeaking as he leaned back until his peach robe almost betrayed his modesty. "Sorry, this *is* rather awkward. Trust is a rare commodity these days, so I have to be especially careful. I'm Elmbray."

"A mage," said Snick.

Elmbray shook his head. "Now, now, don't go filling their enquiring young minds with all that nonsense. Anyone can conjure up magic; it's all in the art of the illusion."

He danced his hands, one around the other in a theatrical flourish, making Nettie's eyes giddy, until stopping with both fists closed.

"Who wants to choose?" he asked, holding the fists towards Nettie and Erwin.

"Me," said Erwin, almost jumping from his chair.

He stumbled against the table leg in his eagerness to reach Elmbray, tapping a finger on the mage's left hand.

Elmbray locked eyes with Erwin, then unpeeled his fingers to reveal a glossy blue chickaney berry sitting in the middle of his palm. "Take it," he said. "There's plenty more where this comes from."

Erwin nodded, popped the berry in his mouth, then sat back down. "Snick said you had cream cakes."

Elmbray laughed. "Did he? Well, my young lad, I'm sure we'll find a cake in the pantry. You're welcome to share our food and company until your fortunes shine brighter. But first, your names."

"I'm Erwin Brotmacher, son of Wilfred and Adelina Brotmacher."

Nettie wanted to slap Erwin for giving so much away to strangers.

Elmbray's green eyes lit up like magic mushrooms at night. "Not the bakers on Bunder Strabe?"

Erwin nodded with such eagerness Nettie thought his head might fall off.

"They make the best honey-devil kuchen in Pergamos," said Elmbray.

"I know," said Erwin. "It's my favourite. Have you seen them recently?"

Elmbray looked to Snick, who still cranked the handle to swish the air. "When did you visit the baker last, Snick?"

"Have to be half a dozen moons ago," said Snick. "Real busy it was. Had to push me way to the counter."

"It's always busy," said Erwin.

Elmbray faced Nettie. "And you are?"

"Nettie." That's all she would say. He didn't need to know more.

Elmbray pulled his robe together and smiled at her. "Of course. Nettie and Erwin. Well, let's get you some food. Snick, you can retire for the evening. I'll entertain our guests."

Snick nodded, released the crank handle and disappeared down the hallway.

"I can do it," said Erwin, springing from his chair and grasping the handle. He turned furiously, and the rimless cartwheel whooshed air above Nettie's head.

"Not too eager," chuckled Elmbray. "You'll set us airborne, and we'll land at the top of that colossal pyramid." He leaned towards Nettie and placed his hand on her knee. "Now, wouldn't *that* make Malphas furious?" He winked, stood and left the room.

Erwin cranked as Nettie pushed herself off the padded chair and took six steps to the other side of the room to examine the trinkets lined along a mantle above an empty hearth. She picked up a cylindrical brass lantern, shapes cut from the metal to resemble stars, moons, trees and birds. The quality of the workmanship stirred a familiarity in the depths of Nettie's hungering belly. After turning the lantern upside down, she nearly dropped it into the fireplace. Etched on the underside were the initials YB. Her father's mark.

"You have exquisite taste," said Elmbray as he strolled into the room carrying a tray with two bowls of stew and a plate of crusty bread. "That lantern was made by the finest metalsmith in all of Sardis. For the life of me, I can't recall his name."

"Yonna Barron," said Erwin.

Nettie stabbed him in the face with her glare, hoping it would clamp his mouth shut.

"You're right, Erwin," said Elmbray, placing the tray on the side table and slumping back into his leather chair. "What a joy it is to have young people in my house again to help an old man with a failing memory. Snick is losing his touch. His faculties are almost as deficient as mine."

Nettie placed the lantern on the mantle and pulled her tunic sleeve down to her wrist to cover the branding scar. Elmbray didn't need to know she came from Sardis' fifth circle. He didn't need to know she was Yonna Barron's daughter.

"You can stop the cranking," Elmbray said to Erwin. "I'm cool enough now, thank you."

Erwin released the handle and resumed his seat, scooting it so close to the side table he almost fell into a bowl of stew.

"Don't wait on ceremony," said Elmbray. "Slide that stew into your bellies. Pork and barley broth with new season taters. I made it myself from a recipe handed down by my dear departed mother. If anyone deserves a place in Volerdie's paradise, it's her. Never offended a soul in her entire life."

After resuming her seat, Nettie took a silver spoon, dipped it into the stew, brought it to her mouth, blew the heat off and tipped the broth onto her tongue.

"Delicious," said Erwin, vocalising Nettie's own thoughts.

"You're very gracious, young man," said Elmbray. "How in Volerdie's name did such well-mannered citizens end up in that awful ossuary?"

"We don't have anywhere else to go," said Erwin. "Nettie's father died. I can't go home to my parents because soldiers will execute them for harbouring a deserter. We want to leave Pergamos but don't know how to get past the gates."

Stop talking, thought Nettie. Fill your stupid face full of stew and shut up.

Elmbray shuddered. "*Ugh*. War. Can't stand the thought of it. Sends shivers seeping into the marrow of my bones. What a brave thing both of you have done; fleeing the military. I'll never understand why men have to forge their egos into the blade of a sword or halberd, then thrust it into another man's chest. Some sort of sexual repression, I imagine, if you'll excuse the crudity of the thought. Well, good on you for escaping. Very admirable."

Erwin reached for a chunk of sourdough bread.

"Country boy?" asked Elmbray. "Or Laodicea, perhaps? You weren't born in Sardis."

"You mean, I don't have a branding scar like Nettie."

Nettie almost choked on her stew.

Elmbray cast different eyes at her now. Ones shining like sunlight through jade.

"I was born in Breadelbane," said Erwin, apparently not noticing how the looseness of his tongue had changed the atmosphere in the room. "It's a village on the western edge of the Dambay Plains. Well, it *was* a village. We were the last family to leave. Came straight to Pergamos. Must have been ten yarles ago."

Elmbray had stopped listening to Erwin. Nettie sensed it. The bald man with the beckoning smile and bewitching hands noticed only her.

"I lived in Slumstadt," said Elmbray, "before it all burned down. The original neighbourhood, mind you. Not those awful slums. Poor Snick barely escaped the inferno. The hideous scars carved into his skin remind me every day of that horrid event. Before the fire, citizens of Sardis enjoyed the hospitality of my home on many occasions. I know every branding scar by heart. Shall I try and guess, Nettie?"

"It was a long time ago," said Nettie, pressing her branded forearm into her lap.

"*Hmmm*," said Elmbray, twirling hairs from his grey beard around his little finger. "Let — me — ponder. Let — me — ponder." He tilted his head backwards, and his eyes rolled back even further.

Erwin stopped chewing, his half-open mouth threatening to drop a clump of mashed bread into his lap.

Elmbray sat up straight and exclaimed, "Fifth circle! Sword crossed with hammer."

"You *are* a mage," said Erwin, spitting the bread out in excitement before catching it in his hand and shoving it back into his mouth.

Elmbray laughed, then clapped his hands together once. "The fifth circle, home of the crafters. Am I right?"

Nettie couldn't hide any longer. She nodded, then tipped another spoonful of stew into her mouth.

If this ends badly, she thought, I might as well get my fill first.

"Do you do anything else other than magic?" Erwin asked Elmbray.

"Yes, indeed. My most important and rewarding mission is to ensure the less fortunate of Pergamos aren't forgotten. You could call it penance for a sometimes-wayward life. I import precious supplies into the city. Clothing, food, utensils, animal hides, furniture, and many other necessary items. Everything's so expensive here. How are poor people supposed to afford to live? I offer my wares at greatly reduced prices. The profit margins are slim, and Snick and I often go without meals, but someone has to look after the needy. Malphas is so obsessed with sitting around waiting for Volerdie's return, he's probably glued his backside to that ghastly throne. Some say he's drilled a hole through the seat so his lackeys can pull decrees from his arsehole." Elmbray scoffed and shook his head. "There I go again with my crude thoughts. I apologise. My passion for protecting the less fortunate occasionally gets the better of me."

Nettie and Erwin finished eating, then Elmbray cleared away the dishes. Nettie wanted to leave. The food wouldn't be free, despite what Snick said. She and Erwin would pay a price. Before she could stand, Elmbray returned with three glasses of scarlet liquid.

"Sweet berry liqueur," Elmbray said. "To finish off the meal." He handed a crystal glass to Nettie and then Erwin.

Erwin took a sip. "*Yummm.*"

Nettie sniffed the liquid, then drank, a honeyed, spicy tang persuading her to try more.

"After this, we should go back," said Nettie.

"Nonsense," replied Elmbray. "I have a spare room. You can sleep there. Soldiers will raid the ossuary soon enough and take anyone able to fight. You can't hide among the old people forever."

"We can't hide anywhere," said Erwin, downing the rest of the berry liqueur in a single gulp.

"It's safe here," said Elmbray.

"You want something," said Nettie. "In return for this hospitality."

Elmbray flashed a calculating smile. "The fifth circle tutors taught you well. You're smart and strong, too, I wager, despite your size. Quick and agile on your feet and as cunning as a snow fox. You're right, Nettie; I *do* have a business proposal for you and Erwin. But it can wait until morning. Then we'll discuss how you might return this favour."

~ Chapter 32 ~

Adalwolf dreamt he was bound to the throne of the dead, perched high above Pergamos on top of the stepped pyramid. The same monument he'd climbed as a young man, all three hundred steps, when he reigned over an Enthilen now barely recognisable. Needles of panic jabbed at Adalwolf's face as the throne moved and writhed around him. Grasping hands clutched his wrists. Legs entwined with his own. Faces once set in stone now leaned into his ear and breathed words. *Volerdie comes for you. Your body will be the vessel for his soul. You and he will be one.*

Above him, the eyes of lost souls had been placed in the eye sockets of the horned wolf crowning the throne's backrest. The burning eyes singed the curls of Adalwolf's black hair, and the wolf snarled as if announcing the arrival of his master, Volerdie.

Tom Anderson lay prostrate beside the throne on the flagstone floor of the roofed platform atop the pyramid. Somehow, Adalwolf had killed his birth twin. Stolen his soul with the dark eyes. He flexed the fingers of his aching right hand. *Right hand*. The dream had reattached the hand severed twelve yarles ago. Adalwolf could now fulfil his destiny.

Malphas and Widukind stood side-by-side before the throne, their smugness mocking the naïve Adalwolf. This had been their plan all along, to sacrifice Adalwolf on the dead throne to bring forth Volerdie, then rule with the Divine Creator in an immortal triumvirate over the famed paradise kingdom of the Erstürmen.

Behind the brothers, the city of Pergamos sprawled, roads and buildings stretching to horizons lit by a scorching sun. Citizens gathered in their thousands, lining the streets or clambering onto rooftops to witness the return of their Divine Creator. An enormous shadow passed across the sun's face, and day turned to night. Malphas cried joyfully, raising his arms skyward as darkness descended amid the daylight. Widukind approached Adalwolf and placed a knife against his throat.

"*Ahhh!*" Adalwolf jolted awake.

Inside the cathedral-like dwell under the Dambay Plains, clatterings of mouldewerps stopped their work and stared at him.

"I'm alright," he said, sitting up and sluicing sweat from his brow.

The werps continued on with their essential dealings.

Beside Adalwolf lay Audie on a hammock of animal furs stretched between stalagmites. He'd stayed by her side, sleeping on the floor, holding her frail hand or counting the rise and fall of her chest since the attack by the weregrims and Rephaim. He didn't know how long they'd been here, unable to tell night from day in the werps' underground hide-out, where only amber light from burning cressets wavered among the shadows.

Audie had drifted in and out of sleep, the werp shaman attending to her every need. Adalwolf treasured the moments when Audie woke and they could talk, exorcising past regrets and sculpting future dreams. He sometimes wondered how many lives Audie had saved during her time as a healer. How much the people of Enthilen owed her. Adalwolf would have died without Audie, and he longed to repay the debt.

He tensed when Widukind ambled towards him, the dream still fresh in his mind and feeding a distrust of this dishevelled immortal.

Widukind hovered over Adalwolf. "How is she faring?" he asked, tilting his head towards Audie.

"It's been a long while since she last opened her eyes. The werp comes to drip primitive concoctions onto her tongue. The poultices appear to be healing her wound." Adalwolf brushed Audie's hair from her forehead and rested his hand there. "But she still has a fever. I'm worried...."

Widukind sat on the ground beside Adalwolf. "At least you have the hope to love again. My wife died soon after Caeli's birth, leaving me with a tiny princess. I raised Caeli with the help of a wet nurse. Neglected my duties as Master of the King's Quarter and my allegiance to my brother, King Oldaric. Despite fussing over my daughter, I managed to fail her again and again. Before she'd seen twenty harvest seasons, I left Enthilen for Tom Anderson's world. Ewald had already imprisoned Caeli in the Sunrise Keep. Instead of rescuing her, I ran away, further than you can imagine, and set in motion events that would steal her love from me forever."

"We all have guilt to bear," said Adalwolf.

Widukind faced him with anguish watering his eyes. "Mine will last an eternity."

"An immortal life is like any other. It offers joy or misery depending on how you use the time given to you."

Tilly, the rebel from the Desolate Mountains, approached. "Wirrikow told me that big, flightless bird is yours," she said to Widukind.

Widukind nodded.

"Can I eat it?"

"No. Of course not. Mr Prickles is my faithful companion."

"He looks mighty plump underneath all them feathers." Tilly scanned the dwell. "Has Princess Caeli left already?"

Widukind shrugged. "I'm not her keeper."

"Even for a draughoul, it will take days to reach the northern side of the Desolate Mountains," said Adalwolf.

"Caeli will wander as Caeli does," said Widukind.

"As long as she escorts the Germalians under the mountain," said Tilly before fixing a steely glare on Adalwolf. "We've met before. Many yarles ago."

Adalwolf couldn't recall meeting the dirty-blonde, boyish young woman standing before him. She wasn't Erstürmen nobility, and he doubted their paths had ever crossed.

Tilly continued, "You were a prince back then. Little more than a child. Sitting on your fancy chair high on the balcony of Sardis' inner circle. Did you enjoy it?"

"Enjoy what?" asked Adalwolf.

"The execution of my mother and father. Ella and Darius Roebolt. Your filthy, bloated father killed them."

"King Ewald wasn't my father."

"How did it make you feel, watching innocent people murdered?"

"They weren't innocent," said Adalwolf. "They wouldn't have been executed if they were blameless."

"My father's only crime was stopping the King's Shield from beating a young boy to death. My mother did nothing but love my father. For some reason, your king considered both acts of treachery."

Adalwolf bowed his head. "Let it go. Much has happened since then."

"I will never let it go. I joined the rebels and swore to end the life of every last Erstürmen." Tilly drew her sword. "And now I have the one-handed absent king trapped underground with only a knife for protection." She stepped towards Adalwolf.

Wirrikow burst from the crowd of werps and grabbed onto the hem of Tilly's tunic, pulling her back. "Now, now," he said. "This is completely unnecessary. We all want the same thing. To end Malphas' tyranny."

"Put your sword away," Widukind said to Tilly. "If you kill Adalwolf, our mission ends here and now. Tom Anderson will also die, and there will be no-one left to destroy the throne of the dead."

Tilly sighed. "Waiting in this damn, stanky hole is torturing my mind."

"It's a dwell," said Wirrikow. "A comfortable one at that."

"Why don't you return to the mountains?" Widukind asked Tilly.

"If what you say about Volerdie's throne is true," she said, pointing her sword at Adalwolf, "I'm not letting *him* out of my sight. I'll make sure he honours his pledge."

"The waiting will be over soon," said Wirrikow. "In the meantime, we have everything here you could ever need."

"As soon as Tom Anderson shows the Germalians the dark eyes and tells them of our plan, they will march," said Widukind. "They've never been friends of the Erstürmen. When my ancestors lived in what is now Nordland, they took the city of Ephesus from the Germalians. Held the Afonwee River and launched raids as far south as Portum. The Germalians will not let a chance at revenge escape them."

"I hope you're right," said Tilly, sheathing her sword. "Otherwise, I *will* have to execute the absent king."

She walked off, Wirrikow scuttling after her.

"At least we'll know if Tom Anderson falls," said Adalwolf. "The end of my life will signal his failure. Can we check on his progress?"

Widukind pulled the blood compass from his coat pocket and dug two points of the gold pentagram between his thumb and index finger, holding it beneath a cresset's glow. "It doesn't work underground. We'll have to go outside."

"Wirrikow has forbidden us to leave the dwell."

Widukind scooted his bottom closer to Adalwolf and whispered, "If we work together, we can sneak past the guards. I need fresh air. I feel like I'm trapped again at the bottom of that gorge in Bindari."

"How did you escape Bindari?"

"When the Rephaim arrived to devastate the grell graveyard, a draughoul called Fullō led me down a secret path to safety. Once, she was Queen Sigilind, your grandmother. My...my mother." Widukind buried his troubled face in gloved hands. "She's still my mother, draughoul or not, as Caeli is still my daughter. Malphas captured Sigilind's soul with the dark eyes, as you captured Caeli's. Like father, like son, it seems."

Widukind lifted his eyes to Adalwolf, their bristling anger unsheathing a threat more dangerous than Tilly's sword. Wrinkles of torment gave way to furrows of hate, ploughed and seeded by yarles of living alone, pondering the wrong Malphas and Adalwolf had done to Widukind Heine. Malphas was safe from Widukind's ire behind Pergamos' walls, leaving Adalwolf to face his uncle's damnation.

The abhorrence lasted only a moment before Widukind's eyes turned sorrowful again. "I've not seen Fullō since Dwarrow sent her to Pergamos with a message for the white grell," he said. "The same grell who convinced Tom Anderson to return to Enthilen. I fear Malphas has buried her in the city's catacombs."

Adalwolf clutched Audie's hand, using their friendship to foil his dread, as he'd done since the fall of Gestade. He tried to smile, but age and the sun had dried his skin, splitting the corners of his mouth such that it hurt when he parted his lips.

"She looks so peaceful lying here," said Adalwolf.

Widukind placed the blood compass back in his coat pocket, stood and dusted himself off. "She won't think less of you if you're not here when she wakes again."

Adalwolf nodded. If he went aboveground, it would be the first time he'd left Audie's side since arriving in the dwell, other than finding a place to deposit his waste.

He stood and brushed the dirt from his pants. "How will we get past the guards at the entrance hole?"

"Tilly can distract them," said Widukind.

"She hates me. You heard her. Why would she help?"

Widukind walked off without answering, and Adalwolf followed. They found Tilly sitting beside a campfire, sharpening her sword with a whetstone. She'd made a straw and animal fur bed that reeked like a Slumstadt hovel, and at her feet sat a bowl of half-eaten stew with chunks of meat drowning in a pale broth. Adalwolf expected she'd slaughtered the animal herself.

"You've settled in," said Widukind.

"Might as well make myself comfortable," said Tilly.

"Would you like to relieve the boredom for a moment?"

Tilly stopped sharpening her sword and fixed her eyes on Adalwolf. "How?"

"We want to go above ground," said Widukind. "Relieve ourselves from the smother of this hole. But the werps refuse our requests, and their guards watch the entrance hole."

Tilly tilted her chin towards Adalwolf. "He's not running away, is he?"

"I'm not going anywhere," said Adalwolf. "I won't leave Audie behind."

"She's a lucky girl," said Tilly, not bothering to hide her sarcasm.

Adalwolf faced Widukind. "Show her the blood compass."

"It's not a toy to be passed around among children."

"Show me anyway," said Tilly.

Widukind frowned, withdrew the compass from his coat and balanced it on his palm.

"That's a fancy star," said Tilly.

"We can use it to check on Tom Anderson's progress," said Adalwolf. "It will point in the direction of his location and give us an idea of how far away he is."

Tilly chewed the inside of her lip. "Doesn't sound very precise."

"It's all we have," said Widukind.

"What do you want me to do?"

"Distract the guards. Long enough for us to sneak outside. Tell them you need help with something."

"Pretty sure only Wirrikow speaks Erstürmen."

"Use that to your advantage. Lead the werps away from the entrance by pretending you want to show them something you're frightened of."

"This sounds stupid."

"Please," said Widukind. "I can't take it down here a moment longer."

"Leave any weapons you have," said Tilly. "You're less likely to run off unarmed."

Widukind and Adalwolf nodded together, both unsheathing long knives and placing them on Tilly's animal-fur bed.

"That's everything," said Widukind.

"Alright," said Tilly, standing and sheathing her sword. "You might need this." She picked up an unlit firebrand from the ground and handed it to Adalwolf. "The werps let me soak the cloth in serpent oil. Will burn for a while yet. Light it on a cresset before you leave."

Adalwolf and Widukind followed her up the steep path to the entrance hole. On the path's edges slept mouldewerps in swales lined with feathers, fur and grass, reminding Adalwolf of birds' nests. But the two guards weren't resting, standing to attention at the entrance hole with their noses primed and clawed hands clutching stone-tipped spears.

Adalwolf and Widukind shrank into a cleft in the wall as Tilly marched on. She stopped and waited, seemingly gathering her thoughts, then sprinted forward, flailing her arms and pointing back down the path and into the cavern. When she reached the guards, she thrust a hand around her throat and acted-out choking. Adalwolf almost laughed aloud.

Tilly resembled a terrible actor in a peasant theatre. Nevertheless, the melodrama worked, and the guards followed Tilly back down the path, running straight past Adalwolf and Widukind's hiding place.

Widukind led Adalwolf up the stone stairs to the flat rock covering the dwell's entrance. He heaved the rock aside and squeezed through the hole. Adalwolf went to follow, but Widukind pressed on his shoulder to stop him.

"We'll need that torch," said Widukind. "It's dark out here."

Adalwolf touched the firebrand against a burning cresset. The torch ignited, and he handed it to Widukind before clambering from the pressing hole and onto the Dambay Plains. Even at night, the sky appeared grey, the air polluted with smoke from the fires burning Grōz Forst to ash.

Widukind pushed the rock back over the entrance hole, reached into his pocket, withdrew the compass and tossed it to Adalwolf.

"Stab yourself with a point," he said. "You know how to use it."

Adalwolf nodded, then rubbed his fingers over the goat's head etched on the surface of the pentagram, wondering how best to stain a point with his blood and not cause himself too much pain.

Delaying will only make it worse, he thought.

He lifted the hem of his tunic, grasped the pentagram and stabbed it into his stomach.

"*Aaah!* Damn."

Blood seeped onto the compass, bubbling and hissing as it bonded with the gold. Adalwolf pulled it away from his body, knelt down and placed the conical underside of the magic star on the rock covering the entrance to the werp dwell. The compass balanced in place for a moment, then spun as fast as a spinning top released by an excitable child. But it slowed and stopped too soon for Adalwolf's liking, pointing northwest.

"Sardis?" said Adalwolf. "Tom can't be far away. The compass slowed abruptly."

"Sardis is too close," said Widukind. "Based on the compass' speed, I estimate he's already in Grōz Wüste."

Adalwolf hoped so, picturing Tom journeying far into the vast wasteland with less than a handful of moons to travel before reaching Portum.

The rock lurched to one side, and Adalwolf scooped up the compass as Tilly popped her head from the entrance hole.

"The guards are returning," she said. "Oh, and Audie's asking for Adalwolf."

"We're coming," said Adalwolf to Tilly.

"I need more time," said Widukind. "Leave me be for a while longer."

"It's dangerous out here," said Adalwolf.

"I've been running from danger for half a generation. It hasn't caught me yet."

Adalwolf shook his head, then followed Tilly back into the werp dwell, leaving Widukind alone on the plains.

* * * *

Widukind covered the dwell entrance once more, then turned and walked off into the Dambay Plains, holding the firebrand to light his way and breathing in night air tinged with smoke.

Better than the claustrophobic nausea of the werps' limestone cave, he thought.

Outside, a weight lifted from his mind, the grass and flowers surrounding him as welcome as a visit to the garden he'd cultivated in Bindari, on a ledge overlooking the Veiled Occyan. If he stayed out long enough, he might stumble across Caeli. While he hoped she wandered close by, part of him accepted she'd already left for the Desolate Mountains. The love he nursed for his daughter vacillated between comfort and distress. Underneath the crumbling façade of the draughoul mantle, he still saw the young woman he'd abandoned so long ago. If he'd interpreted the First Scripture correctly, Caeli would be free of her torment once Adalwolf and Tom destroyed the throne of the dead. All of the black magic imbued in the eyes of lost souls and the blood compass stemmed from the throne. When the throne melted, the spell would be broken, and every draughoul in Ostamp would reunite with their soul in a better place.

Widukind hoped for this truth more than anything else. Even more than regaining his own mortality. He'd not spoken of the wish to anyone, lest they think his plan to destroy the throne was driven only by his desire to free Caeli from her soulless torment and had nothing to do with ridding Enthilen of Malphas.

Using the firebrand to navigate in the darkness, Widukind roamed further from the dwell entrance. Filtering through the smoky haze, Seena's quarter moon offered little light, and the flower petals of Dambay poppies had folded in on themselves, tucking up for another night of rest. Widukind tried not to step on a single orange flower as he walked through the poppy field. A chill wind, unusual for the harvest season, swept the grass to and fro until it batted against Widukind's shins. A burrowing owl hooted in the distance, and a wild dog bayed at the crescent moon.

With his mind wandering more than his feet, dark, decrepit shadows bore down on Widukind before he could react. Six draughouls encircled him, their wasting skin and brittle bones leaving no path in the grass as if they floated above the surface like the coming of a frost. When Widukind stopped, the draughouls closed in and blocked his escape. Two of the six carried a stretcher with a backrest, allowing the passenger to sit upright.

Widukind peeled back the night with the firebrand. "What do you want?"

The stretcher-bearers lowered their passenger to the ground and stepped away.

"I have nothing for you," said Widukind. "Go back to your master or the dank cave from which you sprang."

The creature strapped to the stretcher moaned a word resembling his name. He stepped closer. The torso of a female draughoul had been propped upright and tied to the backrest. Her bottom half was missing, the base of her spine trailing along the taut canvas. It appeared she couldn't speak, but Widukind didn't need to hear any words to feel his mother's agony. Malphas had taken Queen Sigilind, Fullō the draughoul, and torn her asunder.

Anger burned like the torch in his right hand. "Mother, what has he done to you?"

She moaned a wailful lament, parting thin lips to reveal the stump of a severed tongue. And tears, glistening in the torchlight, streamed down her limpid cheeks. *Tears*. Widukind had never seen a draughoul cry or show any emotion. But here was Fullō, his mother, weeping. She clutched at the ropes binding her to the backrest with bony hands as if trying to free herself so she could embrace him.

Widukind dropped the firebrand, fell to his knees and crawled to his mother. "I thought you were dead. When Dwarrow sent you into Pergamos, I thought you'd never return."

The torch's flame flickered, then died. In the growing black, Widukind dug his fingernails into the stretcher's canvas. "I'll kill him. I'll kill Malphas for doing this to you."

A male draughoul decked in King's Shield armour placed a hand on Widukind's shoulder. "You must come with us."

"How did you find me?" asked Widukind.

"There is a secret place nearby," said the male. "We felt a void in the earth one moon past and have been searching for it ever since. Then someone used the blood compass, drawing us near and revealing the quarry we sought. We've come to take you to Pergamos and prepare for Volerdie's return."

"There'll be no return," said Widukind. "No *resurrection*. It's all a lie."

"You're wrong. The Worshipful Master will bring Volerdie back to Enthilen. Then our bodies and souls will be reunited, and the true believers will be taken to paradise."

"Only one thing can free you from this suffering," growled Widukind. "The destruction of Volerdie's throne. *Every lost soul, again made whole.* Your master is lying."

Fullō combed her fingers through Widukind's knotted hair. He pulled her hand away and kissed the back of it, not flinching at the cold, lifeless skin.

The other five draughouls stepped closer. Widukind grasped the extinguished firebrand and sprang to his feet.

"I'm taking my mother with me," he said. "Leave us alone. Return to your master."

"No," said the male draughoul.

Widukind swung the flameless torch, batting away groping hands. But there were too many. A draughoul grabbed him from behind and pinned his left arm behind his back. Another gripped the wrist of his right arm and squeezed until the firebrand fell to the ground. The draughouls pulled Widukind down into the long grass and smothered him with their deadly decay.

All the time, his mother cried.

~ Chapter 33 ~

"How long is this going to take?" huffed Dwarrow, crossing his arms and leaning against the *Grimart's* deck railing.

"The elders will not be rushed," said Hanni. "It will take as long as it takes."

Dwarrow shook his furry head. "I should have known. It would have been quicker racing snails from here to Sardis. I'm going to have a nap."

He stormed off to his werp nest, crawling into woollen blankets shoved inside a barrel lying on its side and jammed between two crates to stop it from rolling into the ocean. He and Hanni had been awake all night, waiting for a war canoe to return, carrying the answer from the weald-grell elders. The *Grimart* had anchored in the Bay of Marrumin last evening after following the weald-grell canoes for five moons. According to Whibly, the journey from Bindari to the bay wouldn't usually take that long, but the weald-grells often went ashore to scout for possible incursions by Malphas' forces. The delays made Dwarrow furious. Hanni learned long ago that patience was a necessary virtue when it came to weald-grells.

The sun peaked above the tops of panalope trees lining the Bay of Marrumin's eastern shore, casting its morning glow across Giigal. Built on an island of sheer rock, the city loomed from the ocean like an immense finger. A lush, dense forest covered the fingertip, tree trunks Hanni could barely squeeze between forming a perimeter around the island like a massive timber wall. The weald-grells had planted the trees this way to protect Giigal from attack. Scaling the cliffs of the rocky finger was nigh impossible, and an ocean-based assault would require a substantial barrage from ranged weapons to penetrate the botanical fortifications. The only way to reach the island on foot was across a narrow suspension bridge made of vines and tree roots spanning farther than an arrow could fly.

In the still morning, across water as smooth as ice, Giigal's astonishing centrepiece snatched a breath from Hanni's throat. In the middle of the city stood the largest panalope tree ever recorded in grell culture, the trunk so thick, it took forty-eight grells standing arms out, fingertip touching fingertip, to encircle it. The tree's canopy reached into the clouds, and no grell had climbed to the top since they settled Giigal generations ago.

The weald-grells named the tree *yurrubang* and claimed it was older than the mountains. A relic of an ancient forest now lost. Many of Giigal's residents lived inside the tree where a massive hollow stretched up through the trunk's centre like a chimney for giants. The grells had built platforms and walkways spiralling towards the crown, leading to shelters carved into the heartwood. The elders lived at the highest accessible point inside the tree and rarely descended. Hanni had never spoken with them or been that high inside *yurrubang*. But Mirrian had taught her all the weald-grell laws. She knew the elders must consider a stone-grell's request for an audience. The law had been written on Marradir, the truce rock.

Consider, thought Hanni. There is no guarantee the request will be granted.

As the sun warmed the glassy bay, Melinda stepped from her quarters, stretched her arms and yawned. She'd set the whales free last evening to roam and forage. 'They won't go far,' Melinda had said. 'The bond between a pod of whales and their ship can last lifetimes.'

She walked towards Hanni and smiled. "This place is so beautiful. Y'must have loved livin' here."

"I did," said Hanni. "But Malang Gunya is where a stone-grell belongs."

"Can't say I've ever been. Looks like I missed my opportunity, what with Malphas turnin' it into Pergamos and all."

"When we defeat Malphas, it will be Malang Gunya again, and you will be welcome to visit."

Melinda pointed to a snoring Dwarrow. "How can he be comfortable in that barrel?"

"It reminds him of his burrow back home," said Hanni. "They call it a dwell."

"Canoe starboard!" yelled Whibly from the stern.

Hanni knocked on the side of Dwarrow's barrel bed. "The weald-grells are returning."

"*Snore...snort...what...oh, it's about time,*" said Dwarrow. "I've been trapped on this infernal ship much longer than necessary. If I have to eat one more fillet of salted fish, I'll turn into a wave lion. What I wouldn't give for a lovely meal of pusclegrubs, pickled lizard and slitherweed."

"You will not get such food in Giigal," said Hanni.

"I expected as much."

Hanni, Dwarrow, Melinda and Whibly stood together on the *Grimart's* deck, waiting for the weald-grells to arrive. The canoe paddles shattered the aqueous glass as the drummer kept everyone in time by beating her stick against a hollow log. The weald-grells had removed the war paint from their naked torsos, the dozen paddlers dressed in skirts made of animal skins stitched together.

"They ain't in a hurry," said Whibly.

"As long as they come with an invitation from the elders," said Hanni, "I am happy if they take all morning."

"More than likely, they will," mumbled Dwarrow. "Take all morning, I mean."

For once, Dwarrow was wrong. The weald-grells headed straight for the *Grimart*, Wyan standing on the canoe's bow and greeting the ship with a wave. As the canoe pulled alongside, the drumming ceased, and the rowers lifted their oars from the water, pointing the blades to the cloudless sky, the tips almost as high as the *Grimart's* deck.

Wyan rubbed his hand across the merchant ship's timber, then smiled at Hanni. "The elders have granted you an audience."

"When you say *you*," began Dwarrow, "do you mean the collective you, as in all of us?"

Wyan paused, looking confused, then replied, "No. Only Hannian stone-grell is permitted to speak with the elders."

"That's ridiculous," said Dwarrow. "If only one of us goes, it should be me."

"The weald-grell law is clear," said Hanni. "The elders will always speak with other weald-grells or consider a request for an audience from a stone-grell. The laws say nothing about mouldewerps."

"Laws *shmores*," said Dwarrow, tapping the heel of his walking stick on the deck with annoyed monotony.

"While only one of you may speak with the elders," said Wyan, "three may enter Giigal."

"Well," said Dwarrow, "that most certainly must include me."

"I should be the third," said Whibly. "Bein' the ship's captain and all."

"Why can't I go?" asked Melinda. "I've never been inside the city."

"Yur me skullard," said Whibly. "I need ya to keep the crew in order. None of 'em are goin' to be happy there's no shore leave."

Melinda frowned and crossed her arms.

"It is an honour to be permitted to enter Giigal," said Hanni.

"I prefer to think of it as an obligation rather than an honour," said Dwarrow.

Melinda flung a rope ladder down the *Grimart's* side. Hanni raised Dwarrow onto her shoulders, then climbed down the ladder, Whibly scampering after her with the agility of a howling gaffe. After boarding the canoe, Hanni placed Dwarrow on a seat, then greeted Wyan in the formal way, each cradling the other's cheeks with their fingers. Hanni considered Wyan's crest, the fire ant, gunhama, to be the most impressive facial tattoo she'd ever seen.

"It has been a long time since I have engaged in such a greeting with another grell," said Hanni. "Except for Quenan weald-grell."

Wyan removed his fingertips from Hanni's cheeks. "Quenan? She is with you?"

"She is part of the resistance, fighting Malphas."

"I begged her not to leave Giigal, but she did not listen. I have missed her company for many seasons. The elders forbid her to return. I do not support such a decree, but I do not make the rules. What of your brother, Grinnian? I remember him from the garrabari."

Hanni shook her head, casting her eyes towards the bottom of the canoe. Wyan placed his hand on her shoulder.

"We have all lost loved ones to Malphas' ambitions," he said.

Hanni, Dwarrow and Whibly squashed into the canoe between the weald-grell paddlers, whose stern faces focussed on empty horizons. None had facial crests Hanni recognised. She hoped to reunite with her guardian family in Giigal, the ones who sheltered her and Mirrian before the massacre of Malang Gunya, and to reclaim her mother's remembrance totem. Yet, the canoe's atmosphere suggested much had changed in the city since Hanni left. Embracing life's joys appeared to have been replaced with an acceptance of impending disaster.

"*Dayangun!*" yelled Wyan in Grellian to the canoe's drummer.

She smacked her stick against the hollow log. Oars descended from the sky and kissed the calm waters, pushing the war canoe home.

By mid-morning, the paddlers beached their craft on a sandy shore at the base of a limestone cliff. Flight upon flight of timber stairs towered above Hanni, leading to a guard post at the clifftop.

"Do we have to climb all those stairs?" asked Dwarrow.

"I will carry you again," said Hanni.

"No. It's not appropriate given current company. Did you see the judgemental glares we received when we disembarked from the *Grimart*? They weren't impressed with me using you like a horse."

Wyan led his rowers up the stairs, followed by Hanni, Whibly and Dwarrow, the werp using his walking stick to lever himself onto each step, made for the giant strides of grells.

"I could help ya," said Whibly to Dwarrow.

"I'll manage," said Dwarrow. "Though, you seem very agile for a…a…."

Whibly glanced over his hunched shoulder. "A what? Cripple?"

"Well, I mean, it can't be easy. All twisted and lop-sided."

"I've learned to live with it. Ain't slowed me down none."

"I can see that. Age is *my* biggest handicap. I'm not getting any younger. Being an elder means additional privileges, but also extra aches and pains."

At the top of the stairs, Wyan led the group along a path hugging the cliff edge, weaving its way through ferns taller than Hanni and creepers twisting their way around tree trunks and into the canopy. The creeper's lilac flowers nodded their heads to the whoosh of a morning breeze, reminding Hanni she'd not seen the lilac eyes of another stone-grell since her last time with Grin.

Along the path to Giigal, weald-grell guards skulked among the dense vegetation shadows, silently keeping watch on the new arrivals. Hanni wondered if Dwarrow or Whibly noticed them. Whibly kept his eyes to the ground, picking his footfalls carefully, while Dwarrow's nose pointed directly at Giigal as if sending a signal to the elders to grant him an audience.

Before reaching the footbridge, the group passed through a grove of gunyi trees, the lower half of their trunks covered in spines large enough to skewer a werp. The barbed maze formed an almost impenetrable barrier protecting the landward side of Giigal and its only access. The war canoe's crew dispersed, using the base of the tree spines like rungs in a ladder, climbing up into timber turrets and lookout platforms built among the canopies and connected by rope swings.

Wyan navigated the spine maze easily, Hanni following in stern concentration, disadvantaged by her long absence from Giigal. Dwarrow and Whibly barked an *ow* or an *argh* with almost every step as the spines inflicted their welcome. Hanni had to cover her mouth to mask a smile more than once.

As the group reached the bridge's mainland end, the wind picked up, and living tree roots that had been knitted together to form the narrow passage to the island lurched with the gusts, threatening to unravel under Hanni's feet. She shuddered at the gaping maw separating Giigal from the rest of Enthilen. Far below her, waves crashed onto cragged rocks, sending plumes of saltwater smacking onto the cliff face. She'd crossed the bridge many times, but the thought of plummeting into the churning whitewash always made her nervous.

"Ain't fond of heights," Whibly said to Hanni. "Always hated it when Cap'n Adcock sent me up the eagle's nest."

They would have to cross in single file, the bridge too narrow to walk side-by-side, even for someone as small as Dwarrow or Whibly. Wyan went first, trotting across the tree roots as if traversing a meadow. Hanni stepped onto the bridge and grasped the vines on either side that had been twisted together and glued with resin to form handrails. The wind swirled, pushing the bridge one way then the other as Hanni walked above the ocean, trying to cross as quickly as possible.

"I thought the rocking on that dreadful ship was bad," said Dwarrow, sticking close behind Hanni. "Trust the grells to invent something even more nauseous. I can't wait to get my feet on solid ground for good. Even better, solid *underground*. This journey has put me off travel once and for all."

Lurching from side to side, Hanni quickened her step, ignoring the creak and crack of the roots underneath her feet and Dwarrow's anxious nattering. The bridge had held her weight before. She convinced herself it would hold again. Wyan reached the island, turned and beckoned his guests to keep moving forward. A pod of dolphins swam under the bridge, leaping from the water and diving back down again. The familiar sight calmed Hanni's nerves. She'd almost reached her second home. Memories flooded back, punctuated by an image of Mirrian's smiling face, white teeth shining through the fringed panalope flowers tattooed on her chin and cheeks.

Hanni joined Wyan at the entrance gate to Giigal, followed by Dwarrow and Whibly. Embedded in the middle of a single tree trunk wider than two wagons side-by-side, the main gate was the only fortification made of metal. It came from an abandoned castle on the plains between Laodicea and Malang Gunya. Guards stood on either side of the gate, holding spears and dressed in grass skirts with bare torsos painted in alternating vertical stripes of white, blue and ochre. The guards glared at the new arrivals as Hanni and her companions followed Wyan through the gate.

"Friendly lot, aren't they?" whispered Dwarrow to Hanni.

"It is not the welcome I expected," said Hanni. "Suspicion has replaced courtesy."

Inside the main gate, weald-grells wandered streets winding around and through enormous tree trunks. Above Hanni, platforms and bridges of timber and rope linked boughs to create thoroughfares across the canopy, leading to shelters built into the trunks. She smiled at everyone she passed, hoping to spot a familiar face. Yet no-one reciprocated her friendly gaze, averting their eyes and quickening their pace away from the visitors.

They walked into yurrubang, assaulted by the chatter of hundreds of weald-grells bouncing around inside the colossal, hollow tree trunk. Wyan grasped Hanni's hand and led her into a side room carved from the majestic tree's heartwood. Mats woven from dried sedges lay on the dirt floor, surrounding a table with a water pitcher and three cups.

"You may rest here until the elders are ready," said Wyan. "They will send someone to collect Hanni."

"What about the rest of us?" asked Dwarrow.

"You must stay here until Hanni returns. A guard will be posted on the doorway to ensure you do not wander."

"This is preposterous," blurted Dwarrow. "I'm a mouldewerp ambassador. A mouldewerp *elder*. I demand your elders reconsider my request for an audience. I signed the treaty at Dalman with the weald- and stone-grells. It was me that...."

"Yes, I know," said Wyan. "Such history means little to us now. The elders will only speak with another grell."

Whibly cast a look of disdain at the water pitcher. "Is that all we're gettin'? What about food? Meduz?"

"I will see what can be arranged. Please, do not leave this room. If you do so, you will be expelled from Giigal and never permitted to return."

Wyan marched from the room as a guard took her place outside the doorway.

Whibly grabbed Hanni's wrist. "Where do we...y'know...deposit our... stinky things. After that bridge crossin'...."

Hanni tugged on a knot in the wood. A door opened, revealing a room no larger than a closet built into the tree trunk. "Do it there," she said, pointing to a hole in the ground.

Whibly disappeared into the room while Dwarrow paced around in circles. "I can't believe I'm being restrained. Me! Gwuendā-hæ Dwinë

D'elch. They must know who I am. Is this island populated entirely by fools?"

"It is fortunate they have agreed to speak with any of us," said Hanni. "I did not hope for any more and expected much less."

"Do the elders understand the situation's gravity? Shutting themselves away from the world has dulled their minds."

"It is unwise to say such things."

Whibly returned, tucking his shirt into his trousers as he hobbled back into the room. "I won't be in a hurry to return," he said. "Y'get better hospitality from barbarians."

The three companions rested their backs against the inside of the tree trunk and waited. A female weald-grell arrived with a tray of food; gamalang fruits collected from the forest and yirany tubers grown inside the city.

The female smiled at Hanni and nodded.

"*Mandaang guwu*," said Hanni, thanking her for the food and the welcome.

The weald-grell placed the tray on the table, nodded again then left.

Dwarrow inhaled. "The air here is so clean, even inside this claustrophobic monstrosity of a tree. I haven't smelled such fresh air for a long time. In one or two days, my olfactory senses would be completely cleansed. I wish I could explore more."

"They will not let us stay a few days," said Hanni. "After my audience, I suspect they will demand we leave."

"Then your audience must be successful, Hannian stone-grell. The fate of Enthilen rests on your shoulders. If you fail...well...I may have to resort to violence. A few sharp jabs of my walking stick into weald-grell shins should shake them up a bit."

"I want to see my guardian family, but it seems that will not be allowed either."

"None of us are getting what we want. If this poor excuse for food is all they're offering, I see no reason to do anything other than sleep."

Dwarrow lay on a sedge mat and began snoring before his head hit the ground. Whibly ate while Hanni rested, responsibility quelling her hunger. She tried to construct an argument to convince the weald-grell elders to send their warriors to Pergamos.

Will they risk thousands of weald-grell lives on the promise of Tom Anderson and Adalwolf Heine destroying the throne of the dead? she wondered. Will they believe the throne's destruction will end Malphas' tyranny or that the Germalians will march their army to Enthilen?

Hanni had nothing other than the truth, so that would have to do. Gestade had fallen, and Malphas would send his soldiers to attack Giigal. She had to convince the elders the best way to dull this attack was by launching one of their own on Malphas' doorstep.

With Dwarrow and Whibly snoring beside her, Hanni opened her eyes when Symian walked into the room.

"The time has come," he said. "I am to escort you to the elders."

Hanni nodded, stood and followed Symian to a spiral path, a construction marvel of polished timber flooring winding its way up the centre of yurrubang and supported by braces driven into the botanical behemoth's trunk. They climbed the path to the first level, more than a stone-grell's height above ground, where it branched left and right, the left leading to homes built into the wood. When Hanni and Mirrian lived in Giigal, they had a residence on this level. Symian led Hanni on the right path, climbing towards yurrubang's canopy and the waiting elders. As they passed levels two, three, four and beyond, Hanni wished for handrails to stop her from taking a misstep and plummeting down the centre of the tree. Symian didn't attempt to alleviate her worry, fixing a severe, unapproachable gaze for the entire journey.

After level twenty, Hanni stopped counting, happier to remain ignorant of how high she'd climbed. A handful of levels beyond that, they reached a platform decorated with dozens of forest creatures carved from the heartwood and lit inside by glowing stones, their light reflected in the burnished timber's glossy surface.

Hanni's mouth dropped open. "Gibas," she said in Grellian. "I have never seen so many sacred stones. I thought they were rare."

"This is the Cathedral of the Elders," said Symian. "Every giba in Giigal is stored here. Sit and wait. The elders will arrive shortly."

Symian directed Hanni to a spot on the floor covered with the striped hide of a wolf-tiger. She sat cross-legged, and he disappeared into the shadows. In the hallowed cathedral, the living wood surrounding Hanni creaked and groaned as it melded together in an unbreakable embrace. Branches that had turned inwards, wove among the heartwood like sinews connecting muscle to bone. A peaked ceiling opened to the sky, revealing boughs supporting a rooftop of sage-green leaves. In the silent anticipation, Hanni swore she heard sap pulsing through the xylem.

The botanical illusion evaporated when four ancient weald-grells, two males and two females, ambled from behind a sedge screen woven into an image of yurrubang. Their bodies hunched and frail, the elders stood no taller than an average Erstürmen and much shorter than an adult stone-grell. Shaved heads crowned naked bodies painted in ochre, noses, earlobes and lips pierced with bone, fingers decorated with pearl rings, and ankles dressed in feather bracelets. The elders shuffled over to Hanni and sat in a circle, each on their own animal-skin floor rug. Hanni prepared for a formal greeting, but none came, the elders not even meeting her gaze. One of the females hummed a haunting lament, caressing the floor with the palm of her hand where the polish had been rubbed back to raw timber. The gathering sat quiet and still until the humming ended.

The other female stared past Hanni and spoke in Grellian, "We are magu. The space between the things that do. The space where thought must thrive before action. You are Hannian stone-grell, first daughter of Frennan and Mirrian, sister to Merran and Grinnian. You and your mother sought shelter here before the massacre of Malang Gunya. After the pilgrim march, your mother did not return. You, Hannian stone-grell, continued as our guest until abandoning Giigal for a life elsewhere. I am Ayran, third daughter of Ayan and Pirrian. One of the four magu who guide weald-grell culture."

"I am now Hannian first born," said Hanni, wondering if she had permission to speak.

Ayran faced her with eyes of glistening turquoise, like the waters of Marrumin. "We are saddened by your loss."

"I am honoured you have granted me this audience," said Hanni.

"It was not an easy decision," said Ayran. "Some do not welcome your return. We fear your words will be the first step toward destruction."

"Many already travel that path. My words cannot divert them, but your actions might. Destruction will soon be upon you. Malphas has crushed the souls of all stone-grells. He prepares now to crush yours."

"You have undertaken a lonely quest, Hannian stone-grell. Why did you leave Giigal?"

"I long to honour the memory of my ancestors. My father and brothers gave their lives to protect Enthilen. My mother is Malphas' slave. I will not hide here and do nothing."

Ayran waved her bony hand around the cathedral. "Look around you. We have much to protect and cherish. The ancestors wish for us to guard this place, nothing more."

Impatience and anger burned inside Hanni, but the elders wouldn't be swayed by pleading or begging. By threats or demands.

"What you cherish is at risk," said Hanni. "As we speak, Malphas prepares his army to march on Giigal."

"We see him coming," said Ayran. "He has burned Babir Birramal to clear a path, hastening his arrival at our gate. The weald-grells are ready. Our defences are strong."

"They will not hold against his legions. You should confront Malphas now. Attack when and where he least expects it. At Pergamos' front gate."

"We are strongest here, in this place."

"You cannot stand against the Rephaim. Against the Erstürmen Shield and their war machines."

Hatred smouldered in Ayran's eyes. "Yes, the Rephaim. The traitorous grells and their tainted masters. Once, they were stone-grells. Slaves who became soldiers. Was it not enough for *your kind* to succumb to slavery? Did you also desire to fight for our enemy?"

The questions punched Hanni in the chest like a swinging log. She wanted to protest. Weald-grells had also become slaves and Rephaim. But the words stuck in her throat.

"You see, Hannian stone-grell," continued Ayran, "we trust no-one except ourselves. Those not weald-grells living in Giigal wish to see our end. We accepted great risk, allowing strangers to enter our city. We did so to honour the truce signed at Dalman."

"A birraman has arrived in Enthilen," said Hanni, desperation cracking her voice. "He will destroy the throne of the dead. When he does, Malphas will fall. But the birraman cannot enter Pergamos without your help."

"Our numbers are too few. We cannot help your birraman."

"Another army is coming to fight Malphas. They will march from the west, across gali-ngin-banga."

"We have no alliance with the dark-skinned women. There is nothing you can offer, Hannian stone-grell, to sway our mind."

"Then why did you agree to see me?"

"We hoped to persuade you to stay and help defend Giigal."

Hanni stood, clenching and unclenching her fists. "No. I will not stay."

"Then you must leave," said Ayran, "and never return."

Hanni had failed. The long journey to Giigal had been for nothing. Everything she hoped for dissolved with Ayran's callous dismissal. Without the weald-grells' help, Tom Anderson may never reach the throne inside Pergamos.

As she turned on her heel, preparing to march back down the spiral path, Dwarrow stepped from the shadows and cleared his throat.

"*Ahem.* Excuse me," he said in Erstürmen.

"*Ngandhi ngidhi?*" responded a male elder in Grellian.

"Who dares to approach the magu without permission?" asked Ayran in Erstürmen.

"Well," said Dwarrow, tottering into the circle of sunlight streaming through a hole in the ceiling, "I believe there's been a *misunderstanding*. Language difficulties and all that. I should have been invited to this gathering, but my invitation must have been misplaced."

An elder called out, and Symian marched into the cathedral.

"They are going to expel us," said Hanni to Dwarrow.

"Don't be so hasty, Hannian stone-grell," said Dwarrow, fumbling around inside one of the dozen pouches dangling from the belt holding up his britches. "I have something that could change the outcome." He pulled a giba from the pouch and held it aloft.

"Where did you get that?" asked Ayran, raising her hand to stop Symian's advance.

"A stone-grell friend gave it to me. You see, I've been friends with grells for countless seasons."

"You hold a sacred object. Return it to us immediately."

Dwarrow pirouetted on the spot, sniffing at the scores of giba stones shining from inside the wood carvings. "You already have plenty. I will keep this one. It was a gift after all and illustrates the kind of respect I'm *normally* granted in the company of grells."

Beside Hanni, Symian tensed, reaching a clutching hand towards her arm.

"Hold steady," said Dwarrow to Symian. "This audience is not yet complete." He placed the giba on the floor. "I have something else of interest." He patted his pockets, then every pouch in turn as he searched for his next surprise. "Where did I put it? Ah yes, here it is." He undid a pouch drawstring and withdrew another rock, placing it beside the giba.

"This is gulba," said Dwarrow, "the peace stone given to me by the Mulugan, the stone- and weald-grell leaders of the last garrabari in Dalman. Maybe you've heard of them? Anyway, this shard comes from Marradir and has a symbol scratched on its surface, confirming the alliance forged between mouldewerps and grells on that day. Stone- *and* weald-grells promised to fight beside the werps in any conflict. Indeed, the mouldewerps stood with the grell pilgrims in the calendar of life as King Adalwolf slaughtered your kin. Without our help, many more lives would have been lost."

"Such alliances mean nothing now," said Ayran.

"Must you be so difficult?" asked Dwarrow. "So be it; I have one more surprise." He pulled another object from his pouch, cradled it in the palm of his clawed hand and tilted it towards the sunlight stream until it glowed amber.

The wrinkles at the corners of Ayran's eyes stretched open as she glared at Dwarrow. The other elders gasped and whispered among themselves as Hanni tried to understand the significance of Dwarrow's reveal. Inside the amber crystal floated a black speck the size of a pinhead. Sunlight refracting through the crystal sent bolts of glowing orange into all the dark corners of the Cathedral of Elders. The treasure looked both magical and insignificant.

Ayran struggled to her feet and pointed a trembling finger at Dwarrow. "What do you hold?"

"You don't know?" asked Dwarrow. "That *is* surprising. Surprising indeed." He closed and opened his hand, pulsing light across the elders' stunned faces. "It's only a small thing. A little thing, like a mouldewerp. Renowned grells such as yourselves probably consider it immaterial. But once, your kin cherished this treasure beyond everything else."

"The magu tire of your games," said Ayran.

Dwarrow kept his hand open, flashing the werp equivalent of a smile, before fixing his squinty eyes on the elders. "I hold a seed. The only one known to exist. Encased in a prison of solid amber."

"A seed?"

"Yes. One that grows into a scared tree. The most sacred tree in grell history. The tree you call *ngayirr biyal*. Do you remember? It was famed because of the blessings it bestowed on grells. Your ancestors worshipped *ngayirr biyal*, as the Erstürmen worship Volerdie. Even with your age-addled minds, you must remember the sacredness of this tree."

The other elders climbed to their feet.

Ayran stepped towards Dwarrow, her hand out as if she expected him to gift her the blessed seed. "Where," she started. "Where did you find it?"

"Beneath Malang Gunya's stepped pyramid, there is a tomb. Deep, deep underground. I doubt a grell or anyone else has visited the tomb for generations. But anything underground cannot remain secret from a mouldewerp for long. Inside the tomb, I found the last seed of *ngayirr biyal*, perched on a stone pedestal carved from turquoise."

"*Garrama!*" shouted Ayran. "You are nothing more than a thief. You entered the tomb of the first ancestors to steal the most revered object in grell culture."

Ayran whispered to the other magu, and they became agitated. Symian disappeared into the shadows, then returned carrying a spear. Hanni expected the weald-grell to skewer Dwarrow on the spot. She blocked Symian's path, prepared to die for her friend.

"You weren't looking after it," continued Dwarrow. "Malphas would have found your precious seed soon enough. I saved it from his clutches. You should thank me."

Ayran nodded to Symian. He raised the spear and lunged at Dwarrow. Hanni lashed out, wrapping her fingers around the spear's stone blade and wrenching it towards the floor. Symian tried to pull the spear up, but Hanni smashed her bare foot down on the shaft, snapping the wood in two. She kicked the pieces away and pushed a bloodied hand into Symian's chest, forcing him against a wall.

Dwarrow continued, "This seed, the *last* seed, is of no value unless it's planted in a special type of soil. The exact soil found *only* beneath Malang Gunya. Beneath Pergamos. Why do you think your ancestors settled there in the first place? They discovered the perfect soil in the Dambay Plains to grow *ngayirr biyal*, and there, they planted the seeds carried from your homeland far across the ocean. There, they built your precious city."

"*Ngayirr biyal* has not grown in Malang Gunya for many generations," said Ayran.

Dwarrow leaned on his walking stick. "Indeed. A disease in the soil killed all the adult trees and any seedlings the grells planted. I have the last seed that was saved."

"Any tree that grows from it will die," said Ayran. "Your seed is worthless. The soil under Malang Gunya is cursed."

"Not anymore. This seed will germinate, and your sacred tree will grow tall and strong. I guarantee it."

Ayran squinted. "How do you know this?"

"Because my ancestors poisoned your soil as retribution for destroying our homes and murdering our families."

"*You?* You desecrated our most scared...."

Ayran barked at the remaining elders, who circled Dwarrow and closed in.

The werp raised the amber-encased seed above his head. "*Mandura wirigiya*," he said in Grellian. "Stay back. If I drop this, the amber might crack, and the seed will be lost."

The elders froze.

Dwarrow lowered his hand, trapping the amber in a cage of claws. "My dear elders, it is time for you to listen. The soil under Malang Gunya is pure again. My nose can attest to that. Your tree will grow, but first, you must break the seed's dormancy."

"How?" asked Ayran.

"You don't remember? *Tsk, tsk.* That is unfortunate. Unfortunate, indeed. Thankfully, I haven't been idle these past seasons. In Laodicea's library, I found a parchment entitled *Murrugay Giilang* — the first story of the stone-grells. It included instructions for breaking the dormancy of this seed. I memorised the instructions, then burned the parchment."

"No!" shouted Ayran. "This is an act most grievous."

"*Hmmm.* Well. We live in grievous times. One of the pitfalls of relying on oral history is the fading memory of elders. If only your ancestors had taken more care to write things down. Nevertheless, a werp has come to the rescue once again. I desire nothing more than to plant this seed with you in Malang Gunya. But someone stands in our way. If you wish to be blessed by *ngayirr biyal* again, you must help remove Malphas from his throne."

"This is bribery," said Ayran.

Dwarrow shrugged. "I do what I must, so common sense prevails. Your days of cowardice have come to an end, my dear elders. Either wait here for Malphas to arrive and burn your home to the ground or join the force that will breach Pergamos' walls and help the birraman destroy the dead throne, plunging a dagger into Malphas' heart. Then we will tend a patch of soil in Malang Gunya, plant this seed, and nourish it with the milk of our victory."

As one, the elders slumped back to the floor.

"We will consider what you say," said Ayran, "before delivering our decision."

Dwarrow popped the precious seed back into his pouch, tugged the drawstring closed and turned on his heel.

"Come along, Hannian stone-grell," he said. "Let's leave the elders to their deliberations."

Hanni crouched down and whispered into Dwarrow's ear, "What have you done, Dwarrow?"

The werp swelled his chest. "I'm a fixer. I fixed it."

~ Chapter 34 ~

As Thaly laboured towards the griffin barn, the most hated wind in Portum, the easterly howler, blew hot and dry across the city, carrying sand grains that stung her face as if the barbs had been sent by Malphas himself. Her enemy seemed to be winning at every turn. Even here in Portum, he taunted Thaly like he'd done when she was imprisoned in Pergamos' dungeon twelve yarles ago. When she'd promised to take her revenge on him. It appeared such a feeble threat now. Charmion didn't believe anything Thaly told her about Malphas' ploys to keep the Germalian army in Portum. The vigilum had imprisoned Chloe in the carcer. The Sella laid her charge, and Chloe admitted breaking into Melitta's office, stealing confidential information and stalking the senator. If Charmion dropped the charge, Chloe would be freed. Thaly needed more evidence of Melitta's plot to kill the Sella, believing the orator would convince an accomplice to commit the assassination, just as she'd used someone else to start the griffin barn fire.

Who *is* Melitta's collaborator? wondered Thaly, rubbing the pearl friendship ring gifted to her by Chloe as if it had been imbued with revelatory powers.

Incomplete details about the fire plagued her. The griffin handlers on duty when the fire started offered vague recollections. Puer, Yagle's handler, had been unusually evasive. At the time, Thaly let it be, assuming the elderly handler suffered from the memory failings typical of old age. However, gut instinct told her that Puer had been deceptive. She respected his deep knowledge of griffins and grown fond of him, but expected this fondness had clouded her judgement. The threat of a long stint in the carcer for Chloe forced Thaly's hand.

Walking past the blackened barn doors, she stepped into the dormitory housing the private rooms of twelve griffin handlers, one for each griffin. The crowded, cramped space smelled as if the timber walls were cobbed with a mix of griffin dung, handler sweat and straw. Washing hung from lines stretched across the hallway, Thaly brushing aside male undergarments in her search for Puer's room. She stumbled into the meal area, half a dozen handlers sitting at a table, eating the morning meal of dry bread and kamel cheese, washed down with uva juice. The men stood as one and bowed their heads.

"Domina Stansfield," they announced in unison.

"Please, sit," said Thaly. "I didn't mean to interrupt your meal. I'm looking for Puer."

One of the men lifted his eyes. "Room number six, Domina Stansfield. Far end of the hall, beside the washroom."

"Thank you," said Thaly, continuing down a hall lined with rooms on either side.

The further she walked into the dormitory, the stuffier it became, the stewing claustrophobia drawing sweat from every pore of her skin. She stopped outside the closed door to room number six, pausing to gather her thoughts on how to approach Puer, expecting the wily old man to keep his secrets close. Another handler stepped from the washroom carrying a bundle of wet clothes. He nodded and scurried past her.

Thaly knocked on Puer's door.

"Yes," came his voice through the flimsy wood panelling.

"It's Domina Stans...it's Thaly. May I come in?"

The door swung open, a wide-eyed Puer silhouetted in the sunlight beaming through the only window. "Domina Stansfield. I wasn't expecting you. If I'd known, I would have...."

Thaly raised her hand. "I apologise for the unannounced visit. May we speak?"

"Of course."

Puer placed a cane chair in the middle of a room large enough for a single bed, clothes rack and bookcase, then brushed the creases from a grey blanket covering the straw mattress and moved an open book onto his pillow.

"You may sit on the chair or bed," said Puer. "Sorry, those are the only options."

"Chair is fine," said Thaly, settling her backside into the mesh of woven cane.

"Water?" asked Puer, pointing to a clay pitcher and cup sitting atop the bookcase.

"Yes, thank you."

Puer stepped around Thaly and poured her a cup of water.

"How do you stand the heat in here?" she asked as he handed her the cup.

"We get used to it, Domina Stansfield. Today is quite mild."

Thaly downed the tepid water in a single gulp, then scanned the spines of three dozen books lined up from tallest to shortest along wooden shelves. "Have you read all these?"

Puer smiled. "More than once, Domina Stansfield."

She faced the bed and pointed to the open book on Puer's pillow. "What are you reading now?"

"The Annals of Thyatira."

"You're interested in Erstürmen cities?"

"Thyatira's history goes back long before it was colonised by the Erstürmen." Puer closed the book and ran a gnarled finger over the cover embossed with a man playing a panpipe. "This book claims one of Volerdie's disciples, Beleth, built Thyatira long before the Erstürmen or Germalians existed. Beleth was a mighty king with many legions at his command, and a lover of music."

"What about that sketch?" asked Thaly, pointing to a portrait of a young woman pinned to the wall above Puer's bed. "Did you draw it?"

Puer nodded. "It is my wife."

"You never told me you were married."

Puer shuffled his bare feet across the dirt floor. "Once. A long time ago."

Thaly wanted to ask what happened, but the anguish in Puer's eyes sealed her lips. The woman in the carbon sketch looked no older than Saskia, and the parchment had yellowed and frayed with age.

She tugged the sleeve of her green senatorial robes up to her elbow, leaned forward and placed a hand on Puer's knee. "When we're together like this, just the two of us, I'd like you to call me Thaly."

"You are too kind," said Puer, keeping his eyes fixed on the sketch of his wife.

Thaly leaned back. "I need to speak with you about the fire in the griffin barn."

Puer faced her and shook his head. "I'm so sorry, Th-Thaly. I should have asked sooner; how is Princess Genevea?"

"She's doing well. Went for a kamel ride."

"The fire was a terrible thing. I'm so relieved your mother has recovered. It's a miracle no-one was badly hurt, and the griffins were rescued. All down to your quick thinking, Domina Stans...Thaly." Puer trapped her with gleaming eyes — a look of awe, thankfulness and wonder swirled through his caramel irises.

Hesitation flooded her brow with sweat as she returned the empty cup to the bookcase. She couldn't accuse Puer of any wrongdoing, knowing where it would lead in a place like Portum. Knowing how much Puer would be punished — a lowly man accused by a conventus senator of covering up a major crime. Even if innocent, Thaly expected Puer to admit guilt simply out of acquiescence. She needed to tread carefully.

"I presented my report on the fire to the conventus. Evidence suggests Pordillo insurgents lit the fire, but I've discovered someone else may have been behind it. A Germalian orator, no less. However, a Pallaxium anitor, Chloe, has been imprisoned because she helped me identify the orator."

"How awful," said Puer, staring through the gaps in the shutters covering the glassless window. "The easterly wind is bad today. I will tend to the griffins after our meeting. Heat and wind cause them stress. Yagle especially dislikes the sandstorms." Puer faced Thaly. "Of course, you understand that better than I ever could."

"You're too modest," said Thaly. "We both know Yagle equally well, and he adores you. I would choose no other handler."

The glisten in Puer's eyes dried, and they set on her with piercing sternness. "Why are you here, Thaly? A conventus senator, Legatus of the Volatal Vexil, does not call on a humble griffin handler for a social visit. You speak of plots involving Portum nobles. How might a lowborn such as myself help in these matters?"

The question's tone took Thaly aback. Puer had begun to close his shutters to ward off her prying.

"I need to ask you again...." started Thaly

"About the fire," interrupted Puer.

"Yes. During my initial questioning, you were evasive. Holding something back. That's not like you. You've always been honest with me."

"Perception dictates truth," said Puer. "The truth I see through my eyes may not be the one seen through yours. Your report on the griffin barn fire was the truth as you saw it."

"But I asked for *your* truth."

"No-one was hurt in the fire. What is done is done. The handlers will learn and make sure it never happens again. Some risked their lives to save the griffins."

"Yes, but Chloe is imprisoned, and Melitta plans...." Thaly stopped. At the mention of Melitta, Puer flinched. Sitting this close to him, she couldn't miss it. He couldn't hide it.

"You know Orator Melitta," said Thaly.

Puer sat motionless for a moment, then picked up the book on Thyatira, turning to the last page. He pulled out another sketch on a piece of parchment no larger than a playing card.

"This is a picture of me with Yagle," he said, "before you became his rider. Before he chose you at the first Eligens, I was the only one who could ride Yagle."

"Men are forbidden to ride the griffins."

"*Now.* But not during the first seasons of training, when trying to ride a griffin could mean death. And I was old, even back then. No harm to the Germalian Empire should Yagle toss an old man from his saddle while swooping through the clouds." Puer placed the drawing back inside the book and sighed. "Soon, my time will end, and you will appoint another handler for Yagle. Do you know what happens to old men in Portum, Thaly? Those who can no longer fulfil their duties."

She had never considered it. Most men she knew worked. Some begged on the streets, but these were primarily children or adolescents. She shook her head.

"They are taken to the desert and never return," said Puer. "Given to the eternal mother, Magna Avium, for her to suck the last, frail breaths from weakening lungs."

"I didn't know," said Thaly, bowing her head. "It's never spoken of in the conventus."

"Perception dictates truth," repeated Puer. "Likely, my truth is foreign to the conventus senators."

"I won't let it happen to you," said Thaly, raising her eyes but knowing she didn't have the power to honour the promise.

Puer smiled at her.

"Please help me," said Thaly. "Melitta is planning to murder the conventus Sella using a dagger stolen from the Pordillo Infada."

Puer shuddered. "Very dangerous. The metal is infused with poison. One scratch...."

"She wants to blame the Pordillo for the crime, the same as they were implicated in the griffin barn fire. But they're not behind this; Malphas is. He wants to start a war between Germalia and the Pordillo to stop our army from marching to Enthilen. Melitta is helping him. I overheard her speaking with one of Malphas' draughouls." Thaly left her seat and sat on the mattress beside Puer. "How do you know Melitta?"

"Her husband, Flane, was one of the first griffin handlers," he said. "Before the vigilum threw him in the carcer."

"What happened?"

"In the early days, the griffin Chirité was wilder than the others. Unpredictable. Flane was her handler. One night, a drunken senator tried to ride Chirité. The griffin tore her apart with its talons. The vigilum claimed Flane didn't warn the senator of the danger. He did his best, Thaly, but she wouldn't listen. She died, and Flane was sentenced to life imprisonment for dereliction of duty."

"That doesn't sound fair," said Thaly.

Puer picked at the sketch of his wife pinned to the wall, crumbling a corner of the dry parchment and watching flecks of yellow dust his bed.

"There is no greater sadness than a broken family," he said.

"Malphas' draughoul promised to free Melitta's husband and help them escape Portum as reward for murdering Charmion."

"The Sella's death will not be the only price paid," said Puer.

"Tell me what you saw on the day of the barn fire."

"If I do, I worry another innocent will be punished."

"I'll make sure it doesn't happen."

"You cannot make such assurances, Domina Stansfield. You are a foreigner here. You will always be a foreigner. Whatever influence you have, has been granted to you by others, and they will take it away if they see a better path to achieve their ends."

Thaly faced the world outside Puer's window, more aware of her naiveté in Germalian politics than ever.

Puer sighed with a heaving relax of his shoulders. "But you wish to save your lover. That is something I understand. What will you do, Thaly, with the information I give you?"

Thaly turned to him. "Honestly, I'm not sure. I will do my best to avoid innocent people being punished."

Puer nodded. "On the day of the fire, an unexpected visitor was in the barn."

"Who?" asked Thaly.

"A kamel handler named Heron."

Heron, thought Thaly. Saskia's love interest.

"Do you know why he was there?" she asked.

"There *may* be an innocent explanation, but I fear there is not. Heron is Melitta and Flane's son."

The revelation hit Thaly like a slap. She'd discovered Melitta's accomplice.

Puer grasped Thaly's hand — something he shouldn't have done. Men were forbidden to touch a woman without her permission.

"Heron's a good boy," said Puer. "He's been lost since his father was imprisoned. His mother spends all her time in the conventus. I've tried to guide him. Keep him from trouble. But the promise of seeing his father again would be hard to resist."

Thaly placed her hand over Puer's and squeezed. Damn the Senatorial Dictum's decrees, she thought. Puer wants nothing more than reassurance.

"Melitta is devious," said Thaly. "If Heron is caught committing these crimes, he will be punished, and she will likely remain free by claiming he acted alone."

"Heron is not perfect, but I cannot believe he would assassinate the conventus Sella."

"He may have no choice."

Thaly removed her comforting hand, and Puer half-stood, pulling another book from the shelves. He sat back on the bed and opened the book to the first page, showing Thaly an image of two black eyes with flaming pupils.

"Do you know about the eyes of lost souls?" asked Puer.

Thaly's mind reeled back to Hansen's Bluff overlooking Laodicea when she stole the dark eyes from a stumbling Prince Adalwolf who'd used them to try to capture Tom Anderson's soul. Then her memories sprang forward to the *Vulking* when she showed the eyes to Tom, and he shoved her into the railings to steal them back. Jumped ahead again to the chaos in Pergamos' throne hall when Tom placed the eyes in the sockets of the horned wolf crowning the dead throne.

"I've held them," whispered Thaly.

Puer's brown eyes glowed. "Is it true? Can they be used to steal someone's soul?"

"Yes."

"This is what turns people into draughouls. The book says so. It also claims draughouls may be truthful, despite being soulless." Puer closed the book.

"What are you thinking?" asked Thaly.

"I'm wondering if the draughoul would confess. Tell the conventus it gave Melitta the Infada dagger and demanded she assassinate the Sella as Malphas ordered."

"I'd have to find the draughoul first," said Thaly. "If I did, I don't know how to make it confess."

"The creature will be here in Portum, waiting for evidence of the Sella's death before reporting back to its master."

Thaly chewed the inside of her lip. The draughoul confession could be the evidence she needed to free Chloe, charge Melitta, and avoid the worst outcome for Heron.

"Be kind to Heron," said Puer. "His heart is pure. He's only done wrong because of his mother's deception."

Thaly nodded, leaned across and kissed Puer on the cheek, the rub of his grey stubble tickling her lips. "I'm honoured to have you as my griffin handler. I will do whatever I can to help Heron, but I have to set Chloe free."

Thaly left Puer to his books and walked into the Volatal Vexil mounting yards beside the dormitory. The wind had dropped, and the yards sat quiet, six griffins resting in the barn, with the other six, including Saskia on Namu, on patrol. She recalled Saskia's most recent encounter with Heron, where her sister had rejected his advances.

A man with an injured heart is likelier to do something rash, thought Thaly.

"I expected to find you here."

She spun around to face the joy of Jurelle's beaming smile.

"Pa." She hugged him tightly.

"Steady on," he said, hugging back. "Don't squeeze the rest of the life out of me. There's not much left."

Thaly released her embrace. "Nonsense. There are yarles left. You'll be a doddery old man sitting on the porch of your apartment, bouncing grandchildren on your knee."

"That day is coming sooner rather than later. I've been dismissed from advisory duties. It appears my military expertise is now redundant."

"What? Why?"

Jurelle shrugged.

Anger simmered in Thaly's gut. "I wager it's Charmion's doing. She's sending a message to me about the consequences of flimsy accusations."

"Don't upset the Sella. She's the most powerful person in Germalia and can ruin your future with the stroke of a quill."

"I have to expose Melitta. It's my only chance of freeing Chloe."

Jurelle placed his arm around her. "Genevea and I hoped you'd visit tonight. Our apartment block is having a feast with flame-grilled fish and flatbreads. You've been so preoccupied with Melitta and Chloe and conventus politics we haven't spent much time together."

"I need to do something first, but I'm worried about the outcome."

Jurelle raised an eyebrow, the way he did when puzzled.

Thaly leaned into her father's chest. "Puer, Yagle's handler, told me Heron is Melitta's son. And Heron almost certainly started the fire in the griffin barn."

"Aren't Saskia and Heron together?"

"Yes and no. She dismissed him the last time they spoke, but I know she likes him. I don't want to get Heron in trouble and risk hurting both of them. Puer says he's a good man, only doing Melitta's bidding to free his father from the carcer. I'm worried Melitta has convinced Heron to murder Charmion with the poisoned Pordillo dagger. I have to stop him. Then I have to find Malphas' draughoul and make him confess to his relations with Melitta." Thaly pulled away, searching for wisdom in her father's face. "Pa, I'm floundering."

Jurelle's aging legs wavered before he replied, "A leader will always be faced with difficult decisions."

Thaly turned her back. "I never asked to be a leader. I never wanted any of this."

"When a group seeks a leader, the first people to dismiss are those eager for the role. Experience suggests most will struggle with the responsibility, focussing more on their own glory. The best leaders consider others first, empowering those around them and embracing the wisdom of their companions."

"My heritage has placed me in this position. My Erstürmen and Dobunni bloodline."

"Part of that's true, but don't let it undermine your resolve. Eutropia and Zenais have tested you at every turn, raising the stakes with each passing yarle. If the Germalians march on Malphas, they'll nominate you as Legatus of the invading army. When Malphas falls, and I'm convinced he will, you'll be asked to guide Enthilen in the aftermath. Then you'll have the chance to empower others to lead."

"My fate is tied to Enthilen, no matter how hard I try to break the bond."

"Your broad shoulders will carry the responsibility," said Jurelle.

"I have to deal with Heron and this draughoul first," said Thaly. "Then Melitta."

"Gather the evidence you need. Build the case against Melitta until it's irrefutable. Don't expose your hand too early. Otherwise, she may wriggle from the trap."

Thaly smiled. "What will you do now you're not working?"

Jurelle smiled back. "Sit on the balcony and wait for my grandchildren."

They laughed together, and she embraced him again.

"Come see us tonight," he whispered in her ear. "We love you, Thaly. Share our love before you leave us."

Thaly hugged her father closer and squeezed tears from her eyes. He pulled away, kissed her on the cheek, then strode from the mounting yards, not looking back. Fear and regret hit her. If she led the Germalian army into Enthilen, she might never return to Portum. She may never see her parents again. Rekindled twelve yarles ago, their love could be lost to her forever.

*　*　*　*

At midday, the sun's heat baking Thaly's dark hair, she walked into the kamel yards to find Heron. He stood alone, a feed bucket at his feet, scratching a kamel's forehead. Thaly hadn't spoken with Heron before, other than a brief greeting when she'd visited Saskia in the kamel yards. She knew him only through Saskia's eyes.

Be kind to Heron, came Puer's words inside her head. *His heart is pure.*

However, Thaly's ambitions took precedence over everything else. As she approached, Heron turned from the kamel and bowed to her.

"Domina Stansfield," he said.

"You know who I am?"

Heron raised his eyes. "Senator of Capri, and Legatus of the Volatal Vexil. It's an honour to meet you."

"You're working alone today?" asked Thaly.

"One of the other handlers is ill. I've taken his place."

"Do you enjoy being a kamel handler?"

"Yes, Domina Stansfield. Although...." He averted his eyes.

"Although what?" prodded Thaly.

He faced her again, boyish excitement gleaming in his eyes. "I would give anything to be a griffin handler. I've memorised the names of all the griffins and their riders. Domina Athalee Stansfield, that's you, rides Yagle. Domina Saskia Stansfield rides Namu. Domina Berenice Atallum rides Nia. Domina...."

Thaly chuckled and raised her hand to cut Heron off. "I believe you."

The conversation died, and they waited together in awkward silence, Thaly gathering her courage and Heron tapping the empty feed bucket with the toe of his sandal.

"You must miss Saskia," said Thaly.

"It did not go well when last we spoke. Now she's a wind-rider; I'm not a suitable match. She needs someone of higher status. If I was a griffin handler...."

"I know Saskia still cares for you. Don't give up on her. She's struggling with Germalian society's expectations. Hierarchy can be a horrible thing sometimes. Saskia will see beyond the confines of cultural dictums one day."

"You are wise, Domina Stansfield. I expect that is why you are here." Heron's voice faded to a resigned whisper, almost as if he anticipated this moment.

Thaly breathed deep, tasting the aroma of sun-baked kamels, and distressed by the trepidation soiling Heron's face.

"The fire in the griffin barn...." she started but stopped when Heron raised a hand.

"I won't do what my mother asks," he said. "I won't take another life, no matter who it is. The fire was only supposed to send a message. I would never hurt the griffins, but I spread too much serpent oil. Things got out of control, and I panicked and fled like the coward I am. Now, she wants me to kill the Sella. But I can't. I won't. Mother says I'm weak and submissive like my father. I should be stronger. If I do this one thing, Father will be freed, and we can escape Portum. But where is the bravery in taking an innocent life? That is weakness, not strength. Cowardice, not valour." Heron slumped to the ground and buried his head between his knees. "Sometimes, Domina Stansfield, I feel I've been born into the wrong world. There is so much death and betrayal. Life is not valued as it should be. Soldiers, those who kill, are lauded, while peasants are shunned. I want to live in a world where peace is so highly valued, the idea of war becomes unthinkable."

Thaly squatted beside Heron and placed her hand on his shoulder. "I would like to live in such a world, too. But we're going to have to fight to get there. I can't see another way. First, let me help you. I know Melitta is behind everything. She's used you. Her guilt is obvious; yours is not."

"The vigilum won't believe you," said Heron. "I deserve to be punished."

"Let me worry about that. Do you have the Infada dagger?"

Heron nodded. "It's hidden. Mother won't find it. The Sella is safe. But I worry my mother is growing more desperate with each passing moon."

"I'll need to show the dagger to the conventus. If necessary, will you confess to receiving it from Melitta? Will you confess to her plans?"

"Yes."

"I won't mention your part in the barn fire."

"Mother will blame me."

"We'll deal with that later. I expect Puer would testify to your innocence."

"He's been like a father to me."

Thaly squeezed Heron's shoulder. "Has Melitta ever mentioned a draughoul?"

He looked up at her. "Malphas' servant. He promised to free my father and lead us to a better life in Pergamos. Do you believe it, Domina Stansfield?"

"I don't believe a single word that escapes Malphas' lips."

"Have you seen him? Mother says he's a god. As revered as Volerdie himself."

Thaly shook her head. "He's nothing more than an evil man besotted by power. An obsession that could last generations." She sat in the dirt next to Heron. "Do you know where to find the draughoul?"

"After the Sella is dead, Mother told me to meet her in an abandoned house in the Portum neighbourhood of Putri. I believe the draughoul is hiding there."

"We need to capture it. I must make the draughoul confess to Malphas' plans in front of the conventus."

"I have an idea, Domina Stansfield."

~ Chapter 35 ~

A wild wind churned the red sand into a massive vortex, swirling around the Pordillo campsite and threatening to rip tents from the ground and fling them over the towering dunes. Tom, Rosalie and Quenan huddled together in a corner of the prison cage, backs to the wind, trying to stop the sand from blasting their sunburnt skin. The calm night had morphed into a rusty morning sky, howling gusts rushing through the oasis like a pack of desert wolves biting Tom's neck and arms. He longed for shelter. Or better clothes. Anything to ward off the sun and wind.

Quenan wiped gritted sweat from her face, the chain locked around her wrists clinking against a prison bar. The Pordillo considered a weald-grell more of a threat than Tom or Rosalie, chaining Quenan to the cage each night. Quenan's plans for an escape dried up amid the exhaustion of forced labour and dutiful imprisonment by the Pordillo guards. Tom wished he'd managed to hide Dwarrow's key from Um-huk like he'd hidden the eyes of lost souls. Then he might be able to open the locks and free his friends.

The man and woman who occupied the cage when Tom first arrived had disappeared three moons ago. He doubted they'd escaped. More likely, the Pordillo had worked them to death. Tom expected to soon follow, his last five days spent shovelling khorsal shit from the corrals and bucketing it into a hole in the ground. Quenan dug the holes for everyone's excrement, including the Pordillo soldiers. Rosalie collected the soldiers' waste buckets, brimming with urine and faeces.

With the other two prisoners gone, Tom buried the dark eyes in a depression he'd dug between the metal bars at the bottom of the cage. Despite consuming only a few mouthfuls of fermented grain each day, he couldn't withhold a bowel movement forever. One night, when the gaoler turned his back, Tom squeezed the dark eyes from his own anus and plonked them into the hole. He hadn't thought much beyond hiding the eyes from the Pordillo, instead focussing on one moment at a time.

As the sun crested the eastern dune, a soldier marched into the cage and jabbed Tom's thigh with his spear.

"*Och ere el hosh!*" barked the soldier through the gusting howls of wind.

Tom stumbled to his feet, shielding his face from the swirling sand.

"*Och ere el hosh!*" repeated the guard, turning his attention to Rosalie.

She stood and pointed to Quenan. "What about her? You can't leave her chained in this sandstorm."

The soldier sneered, swung his spear and nicked Rosalie's calf. Her leg buckled. Tom grabbed her arm to stop her from falling.

Two more guards strode into the cage and pushed Tom and Rosalie out. Tom steeled himself for another day of shovelling khorsal waste, but the two guards shepherded him and Rosalie away from the corrals and through the camp. They passed the pavilion where Qaysar Rais had entertained Anselm and the Erstürmen entourage five moons ago. In late-night, whispered conversations, Rosalie told Tom and Quenan what happened during the meeting between Rais and Anselm. The news played on Tom's mind. He'd find it much harder to convince the Germalians to march their army to Enthilen if the Pordillo and Erstürmen attacked Portum. Tom, Rosalie and Quenan had agreed that if they escaped the Pordillo, they'd keep the attack plan secret. Rosalie believed it would take many days for Malphas' forces to march from Pergamos to Portum. Tom wasn't convinced, expecting Malphas' preparations to be well advanced. While he despised everything Malphas represented, Tom understood the old man's cunning.

At the camp's fringe, the guards untethered two khorsals, bound Tom's wrists and tied the rope's free end to a saddle. They did the same to Rosalie before mounting the khorsals and walking them into the desert. Dragged behind the animals, Tom struggled to keep pace, his boots churning through the sand chopped up by the khorsals' splayed feet. He worried Rosalie would fall, the wind buffeting every footstep and blood dripping from the cut on her leg.

They rounded the base of a dune, hugging the western face to gain respite from the easterly wind. Whirling sand and low cloud shielded Tom and Rosalie from the baking sun, but sweat trickled down Tom's ribs, squeezed from under his arms by the weight of the humid air. Without the wind to swat them away, flies swamped Tom's face, crawling up into his nostrils and across the corners of his mouth. He snorted, spat and cursed, trying to dislodge the swarm, but the insects clung to him like the starved skin hanging from his bones.

Following the khorsals' swishing tails, Tom and Rosalie staggered into a swale covered in bushes with furred, silver leaves and orange berries. The guards reined in their beasts, dismounted and untied the prisoners. One of the soldiers gathered two cotton sacks from a saddle bag, shoving one each into Tom and Rosalie's hands.

The guard pointed to the orange berries. "*Qata. Qata.*"

"Water," said Tom, his split lips stinging with the plea. "Water. Please."

The soldier shook his head and pushed Tom towards the bushes.

Rosalie and Tom dropped to their knees and began picking the berries. The fruit had rough, hard skin reminding him of quandongs.

"Go slow," he whispered to Rosalie. "Let the bastards wait."

His mood lifted with her smile. Despite their trauma, she still had a smile for him.

The sandstorm abated, and the Pordillo guards erected a canvas shelter. One soldier fell asleep in the shade while the other watched the prisoners. From the south, stratus clouds drifted in.

"It might rain," whispered Tom.

"What?" asked Rosalie, her fingers stained tangerine from the berries she'd squashed in her fist before dropping them in the bag.

"It might rain by the look of those clouds."

Rosalie lifted her face skyward as dark clouds gathered and sank lower, touching the dune peaks. A single raindrop landed on Tom's cheek. He poked out his tongue, trying to catch the precious driblet of water before it fell to the sand, then willed the clouds to shed more of their cargo. Across a single patch of blue sky, a shape flashed, flying from one cloud and disappearing into another.

Tom grasped Rosalie's hand. "Did you see that?"

She nodded, crawling further into the bushes and dragging Tom away from the guard. "I saw something flying through the clouds."

"An eagle?"

Rosalie shrugged. "Vulture more likely."

The patch of blue shrank as the clouds closed in again. Light rain fell, washing the berry stain from Tom's hands. He dropped his sack and faced the clouds, catching raindrops in his mouth. Rosalie did the same. They knelt together in the sand, heads skyward as if praying to the rain gods for a deluge.

"*Um-ulk dahim,*" said the guard, ending Tom's moment of worship by grabbing his arm and yanking him to his feet.

Rosalie and Tom gathered their bags of berries and returned to the khorsals, followed by the guard. He took the full sacks and handed them two more empty ones. His companion still slept, snoring beneath a canvas roof pattered by the rain.

As the guard stashed the berries inside the saddlebag, a gust of wind swirled wisps of cloud directly above him. The wisps parted when a medallion-yellow talon the size of a horse's head descended from the sky like an angel. Unaware of the divine intervention, the soldier continued to organise the saddle bag. The talon hovered above his bowed head, suspended in silence, then, with lethal speed, four claws drove down and in.

The Pordillo soldier screamed. Tom retched at the squelch of brains mashed with skull fragments.

"G...g...griffin," stammered Rosalie.

The sleeping guard woke. He grabbed his spear at the exact moment an arrow flew from the clouds and pierced his chest.

The griffin shook the flesh off its talon, then landed beside Tom.

I'm dead, he thought. *This beast will kill me.*

A steeled golden eye fixed itself on Tom, the griffin's eagle-like head rigid and unyielding. The flick of a tufted tail drew Tom's attention to the beast's body, where a female rider with dark skin and dressed in furred leather sat in a saddle.

"*Aut no gu mus*," said the griffin rider.

Tom shook his head. "I don't understand your language."

"Ah, you speak Erstürmen," she said. "Are you from Enthilen?"

"We've travelled from there, but we're not Erstürmen."

"You've come a long way to end your journey in a nest of vipers."

"We're slaves," said Rosalie. "The Pordillo have imprisoned us. Are you Germalian?"

"Yes. I am Demetria. And you are?"

"Rosalie and Tom. Friends of those who oppose Malphas."

Beneath the metal skullcap, Demetria raised her eyebrows. "Then *we* could be friends if you help us find the Pordillo camp."

"It's not far," said Tom. "We can take you there."

Another griffin and its rider descended from the clouds, landing beside the khorsals. The Pordillo animals moaned and snorted, brown eyes glistening with fear as a creature four times their size turned its bill towards them and cawed.

"How many Pordillo in the camp?" asked Demetria.

"Thousands," said Tom.

"That many? Are you sure?"

"Qaysar Rais is there," said Rosalie.

The whites of Demetria's eyes signalled her disbelief. "You saw him?"

Rosalie nodded.

"We've been seeking his whereabouts for many seasons."

Demetria whispered into her griffin's ear. It dropped the front of its body and pressed its head sideways against the sand. "One of you will fly with me," said Demetria. "Show me the camp's location."

"Our friend is there," said Tom. "Quenan weald-grell. We have to rescue her."

"We've been ordered to scout Pordillo positions, not launch rescue missions."

"Is your army here?" blurted Tom, his voice almost muted by panic as he wondered whether to begin arguing his case for war against Malphas.

"The strength of our force is none of your concern," said Demetria. "Rosalie will show me the camp."

Tom pulled Rosalie away from the Germalians and leaned into her ear. "We can't leave Quenan. And the dark eyes are buried under the sand inside the prison cage. Without them, there's no point going to Portum."

"Do we tell Demetria?" asked Rosalie.

Tom would have to tell the Germalians everything, but now wasn't the right time.

"There's something else I have to retrieve from the camp," he said to Demetria.

"We scout the position and enemy numbers first," said Demetria. "Then we consider our options. If Rais is indeed in the camp, word must be sent to our commanders immediately. Rosalie comes with me. Tom flies with Berenice."

Rosalie whispered to Tom, "Go with Berenice. We'll find a way to save Quenan and regain the dark eyes."

Tom clutched Rosalie's hand. "Remember, don't tell them about the Erstürmen."

She nodded, pulled away from Tom and approached Demetria.

The second griffin lowered its body, and the rider, Berenice, spoke to Tom in Erstürmen, "You come with me."

Tom stepped around the griffin's head, locking eyes with an animal who watched him with an intensity that made his legs shake.

"Grasp the wing's shoulder and pull yourself up," said Berenice.

Tom climbed onto the wing as Demetria and Rosalie took to the sky, disappearing into the clouds. Berenice pointed to a padded section at the rear of her raised leather saddle. Tom flung his right leg across the griffin's back and lowered himself onto the saddle, sitting astride the creature and behind Berenice.

"Is there a harness?" asked Tom, checking either side of the saddle for something to strap himself in place.

"Not for passengers," said Berenice. "But do not fret; Nia is a skilful flier.

He won't let you fall. If it makes you feel safer, place your arm around my waist. I will ask Nia not to make any sudden dives."

Sudden dives? Tom shoved a hand into his pants pocket to finger the foil packet of anxiety pills.

Three left. How stupid. Still got my pills but not Dwarrow's key or the dark eyes.

Tom dismissed the false assurance of the drugs, wrapping his arm around Berenice and grabbing at the cords that cinched her leather breastplate together.

"We will stay low," she said. "You are not dressed for higher altitudes."

Nia raised his head and screeched before lunging a few steps and taking flight. The ball of knotted nerves tightening in Tom's chest dropped to his stomach as the ground disappeared, replaced by misty grey. Among the clouds, fine droplets of moisture clung to his beard as Nia raced forward. With no landmarks to gauge the griffin's speed, Tom relaxed. But the clouds soon parted, revealing the desert of Grōz Wüste speeding past, far below him, like the rush of a churning red torrent.

Euphoria overtook him.

"I'm flying!" he cried into the horizon, gripping Berenice's breastplate tighter.

The air blasted through his ragged clothes. The ground sped by. Nia's wings flapped, a slow *thworp, thworp, thworp,* then the griffin glided with the air currents. The bi-animal mash of eagle and lion looked ungainly on the ground, but airborne, the creature soared as majestic as any bird of prey, its wingspan greater than four wagons side-by-side.

The desert heat faded as Nia climbed higher.

Tom shivered, leaned forward and yelled in Berenice's ear, "It's freezing up here."

She nodded and tugged on Nia's reins. The griffin spiralled down gradually until his lion feet and tufted tail skimmed the dune crests. Tom beamed as warmth returned to his body, and the thrilling flight swept the worries from his mind. Cresting dunes. Diving down through swales. Red sand flashed past in a blur. Tumbleweeds bounced like balloons as the griffin created its own whirlwind. Every moment became weightless. Effortless. An exhilarating thrust up a dune face. The stomach-turning plunge down the other side. A pair of hawks descended from the clouds and wheeled around the tips of the griffin's wings. On the ground, lizards scuttled across the hot sand, spooked by the swooping shadows.

Tom's head lightened with the buffeting wind. "*Yee-hah!*" he screamed with unbridled joy. It had been so long since he felt it.

Berenice turned and smiled at him before guiding Nia down to a waterhole surrounded by a shrub thicket. Another Germalian appeared from the thicket and waved.

The ride of Tom's life ended too soon as Nia alighted beside the waterhole.

"*Wow,*" he said in English. "*That was unbelievable.*"

"What language do you speak?" asked Berenice.

"Oh. Sorry. I forgot myself for a moment. Do all Germalians speak Erstürmen?"

"We are expected to learn many languages. I will tend to Nia. Ask one of my companions for food and water."

Nia lay on his stomach, and Tom climbed from the saddle and back onto the burning sand. He wandered through a gap in the shrubs, most of them taller than him, stepping into a clearing where another four griffins rested with their lion-like tails curled up towards their bills. A griffin lifted its head as Tom passed and whistled a call of welcome or warning. He stepped away and quickened his pace, almost walking straight into a muddy pool surrounded by rocks. Four females dressed in thin, billowing pants and shirts of cream and tan, sat around the pool talking among themselves. Furred leather armour and metal skullcaps, etched with scenes of temples, ships, oceans and fields, rested across the top of the rocks. Three females had dark skin, like Berenice, but one had pale skin, like Tom. He assumed all of them were Germalian. They stood as he approached, one resting a hand on the hilt of a cutlass tucked between her belt and shirt.

Tom raised his palm in deference. "H-h-hello. I'm Tom. Berenice and Demetria saved us from the Pordillo. We were their slaves."

Three of the women sat down and resumed their conversation without acknowledging him. The youngest one, with fair skin, walked towards Tom and smiled.

"Welcome," she said. "Are you thirsty?"

"Thirsty and hungry," said Tom. "Thank you."

"I'll see what we have," said the woman, crouching down and searching through a pack lying on the sand.

Her accent sounded familiar. Not the same as Berenice or Demetria. More like people Tom had met in Enthilen.

"Cold meat and water," said the woman, holding a cloth package and waterskin towards Tom. "It's all we can spare."

He placed his hands together, palm against palm. "Thank you." Then took the waterskin, popped the cork and gulped down a mouthful of gritty liquid.

"The water isn't very clean here," said the woman.

Tom took another mouthful, then reached for the package, unwrapping the cloth to reveal strips of cooked meat.

"Slider serpent," said the woman as Tom popped a strip into his mouth.

He coughed and choked. She laughed.

"Kidding. It's desert hare."

"I didn't catch your name," said Tom, still chewing the stringy meat.

"If you caught it, what would you do with it?"

"Well, if it's a good name, I might use it myself."

The fair-skinned Germalian beamed. "I'm Saskia. You said Demetria saved *us*. Where are the rest of you?"

"My companion, Rosalie, went with Demetria to show her the location of the Pordillo camp. Our other friend, Quenan, is still there. Held prisoner."

"How did the Pordillo find you?"

"We're travelling from Enthilen to Portum."

"You're not Erstürmen," said Saskia. "Your accent's all wrong. You're not Dobunni either."

"We're...resistance fighters. Against Malphas."

She nodded. "I was born in Sardis. Left when I was six yarles old."

"Then you're Erstürmen."

"Yes and no. My mother is an Erstürmen princess. My father, Dobunni."

Tom pulled open his ripped tunic to expose the pledge scars on his chest. "A long time ago, I pledged allegiance to the Dobunni."

Saskia's eyes grew wide. "My sister has scars like those."

"Your sister?"

"Athalee Stansfield."

Tom staggered backwards. Images of Thaly flashed through his mind. Duelling with swords on the Riverlands Escarpment as she taught him how to fight. Celebrating the Dobunni Pledge Feste in Bagendon. Riding to war in Laodicea. Hunched together on the *Vulking* as leering crew stalked the deck. Thaly bound to a column in Pergamos' throne hall.

Her last words filled Tom's head, as clear as if she stood in front of him now. 'Do what you came here to do. I trust you. I trust you're doing what you believe is right.'

The exhaustion of enslavement. The giddiness of the rescue flight. The guilt of Grin's death. Bearing the responsibility for destroying Volerdie's throne. All of it had been stacked one on top of the other like a rickety, tottering wall, and now it crashed around him. Tom fell to his knees and wept.

Saskia sat beside him. "Are you alright?" She rested her hand on his shoulder as he sobbed, his aching body trembling with the lurch of emotions.

They sat in silence for a moment before Tom composed himself, rubbing the tears from his face. "The...the last time I saw Thaly, I was trapped on the dead throne, and Malphas plunged a knife into her side. I couldn't save her. I abandoned her instead."

"You're Tom Anderson," said Saskia, the shrillness of her voice attracting the attention of her companions. "The traveller who disappeared from Enthilen. Thaly told me about you."

"I've returned."

"What for? Why are you here?"

The time's come to reveal my plan. No point delaying any longer.

"We're travelling to Portum to convince the Germalians to fight Malphas. March their army into Enthilen and defeat him."

"Then your battle has only begun," said Saskia. "The conventus won't be swayed by the argument of a stranger, especially a man. Other senators, including Thaly, have argued for a confrontation with Malphas for seasons."

"I have information to persuade them."

"What sort of information?"

"I can destroy the throne of the dead and return Malphas to a mortal life."

"How?"

Tom didn't offer an explanation, keeping his most important secret, the eyes of lost souls, close.

Saskia pressed no further, instead introducing Tom to the other griffin riders, who seemed disinterested in anything about him, including his plan to topple Malphas. So, he and Saskia talked about Enthilen and Thaly. She told him how they'd escaped Sardis and how Jurelle rescued Thaly from Pergamos' collapsed throne room and brought her to Portum. She told him about Thaly's leadership roles in Germalian society, and he began to worry that someone of Thaly's standing would have no interest in reuniting with a foolish boy returned from a faraway land with a ridiculous plot to topple a tyrant.

That evening, Demetria and Rosalie landed in the Germalian camp without Quenan. Demetria wouldn't save the weald-grell, and Rosalie couldn't convince the Germalian otherwise. After Rosalie wolfed down food and drink, Demetria called the group together.

"We must get word to Portum immediately," said Demetria in Erstürmen. "The conventus may wish to launch an attack on Qaysar Rais' camp."

"The Pordillo will move on long before the conventus make a decision," said Saskia. "We should attack now."

"No. The Pordillo number at least five thousand. Too many for six wind-riders."

"We have to rescue Quenan," said Tom. *And retrieve the dark eyes; otherwise, the plan will fail.*

Demetria clenched her jaw and turned a cold face to him. "You have no authority here. Be thankful we saved you from the Pordillo. With the death of the two guards, the enemy will be on edge. Ready for another attack. I won't risk my fighters on a rescue mission. At sunrise, we fly to Portum and report the location of Qaysar Rais' camp."

Tom stood and stormed off into the moonless night, using the dark to mask his frustration. Rosalie followed him.

"There's nothing we can do," she said.

Tom stopped and faced her. "We have to go back. The eyes of lost souls are still buried under the prison cage."

She grabbed his hand and held it to her chest. "We can't do it ourselves. It would take us days to walk there. And then...."

"I could help."

Tom and Rosalie spun around at the sound of Saskia's voice.

"How much...." started Tom.

"...did I overhear?" finished Saskia. "If you are indeed Tom Anderson, then I know you're a traveller, and you've carried the eyes of lost souls." She grabbed Tom's hand and prised open his fingers. "Scars on your palms confirm it. Do you have the eyes with you?"

"I had them. They're back at the Pordillo camp. Buried in the sand. Without them, there's no point in us going to Portum."

Saskia fidgeted with her ponytail, twirling it around her hand. "I shouldn't get into any more trouble. I've already made mistakes, and I'm the newest wind-rider. If I do something *really* stupid, I could be expelled from the Volatal Vexil."

"Please, Saskia," said Rosalie. "We have to save Quenan, and without the dark eyes, Tom can't destroy Volerdie's throne."

Saskia tapped her lips with her index finger, her pale blue eyes drifting away with pressing thoughts.

"Thaly would help," blurted Tom, not sure she would. But Saskia was his only hope, and he was prepared to convince her using guilt or sibling rivalry. "Thaly would recognise the importance of this moment. I'm the only person in Ostamp who can stop Malphas. We need the Germalian army to breach Pergamos' walls. Then I will march into the city and thrust a dagger into Malphas' heart by shattering the throne. I know Thaly would help me."

Saskia's mouth curled and contorted in a battle of indecision before she sighed. "I'm on watch tonight," she said. "We could sneak away then."

"What if the other riders notice your absence?" asked Rosalie.

Saskia grabbed Rosalie's arm. "I'll dress you in my spare clothes. You can pretend to be me. Tom and I will fly to the Pordillo camp, save your friend and retrieve the eyes."

"Can a griffin carry a weald-grell?" asked Tom.

Saskia nodded. "Namu can carry the grell in her talons. She won't injure her. Where is the camp?"

"Around a waterhole bigger than any we've seen so far in the desert."

"I know where it is. We leave when everyone else is asleep. If you see anything suspicious, Rosalie, you'll have to sound the alarm. I'll deal with the consequences later. I'm good at that."

* * * *

Under cover of night, Tom and Saskia snuck down the face of a sand dune, past the Pordillo guards, to the rear of the prison cage. The gaoler stood at the cage door, back turned. Quenan lay naked in the corner, unshackled and holding her knees to her chest, a mesh of bloody slashes littering her pale skin.

She looks so small. Tom dropped to his stomach, crawled to Quenan, and whispered in her ear, "We've come to rescue you."

She didn't move, but a catch in her breath offered an acknowledgement.

Tom poked his finger through the bars, jabbing Quenan in the side. She lifted her head, squinting at him with bruised, swollen eyes.

"Can you move?" he asked.

She nodded.

"Underneath you are the eyes of lost souls."

Quenan pulled an arm away from her knees and scraped at the sand.

Saskia drew a dagger from her belt. "I'll kill the guard and open the door."

She crept towards the prison cage's door.

With a feeble hand, Quenan dug deeper. Tom clutched the prison bars as if he might pull them apart. Saskia loomed up behind the gaoler and slit his throat. Quenan froze when the Pordillo soldier gasped his final breath. Tom reached through the bars, pawing at the sand. The jingle of keys spurred Quenan on. Saskia pulled the keyring from the gaoler's belt and unlocked the cage door. The flaming pupils of the eyes of lost souls glimmered in the moonlight as Quenan swept away the last grains of sand. She reached in, grabbed the eyes, and handed them to Tom.

"*Um-urk al behaji!*" yelled another Pordillo soldier before racing towards the cage.

"Hurry," said Saskia, reaching down and grabbing Quenan's hand.

The weald-grell dug her other hand into the sand and heaved herself onto battered feet.

"We need to run," said Saskia.

Following Saskia, Quenan staggered to the cage door. But she stopped there and picked up the fallen gaoler's spear as more soldiers appeared.

"We have to go," urged Saskia. "Now!"

Quenan shook her head.

Tom squeezed the dark eyes in his fist. "Quenan. Please. We can outrun them. We have a griffin."

An arrow whizzed past Saskia's head. The enemy would swamp all of them in a heartbeat. Quenan faced the coming tide and raised the spear.

No.

"Damn it," said Saskia. She raced to the back of the cage and grabbed Tom's arm. "Quenan won't make it. We have to leave her."

No.

Saskia dragged Tom up the dune face. He could have resisted. He *should* have resisted, but he knew Saskia was right.

As they escaped into the night, Pordillo soldiers swarmed over Quenan. She fell to her knees, metal blades slashing at the branches of her garra tree facial crest as the last sparkle of life died in turquoise eyes.

~ Chapter 36 ~

Widukind jolted awake to the squeak of a pulley wheel. Grell slaves yanked on a rope, tugging a gilded cage towards a ceiling painted with the image of an effeminate-looking man with long hair, soft eyes and a knowing smile, standing over a crowd of people prostrated before him. Trapped inside the cage, knees crushing his chest, Widukind ascended into the embrace of his creator.

All hail Volerdie, he thought.

He tried to stretch his legs out, his bottom pressing into the mesh of the cage's floor. But the heaviness of his bones and the paucity of space defeated him. He curled up again, leaning his shoulder against the steel bars. Beneath the cage, the slaves tied the rope around a cleat bolted to the wall, and Widukind's ascension ended.

He couldn't recall how he'd arrived at this place. The draughouls who'd captured him on the Dambay Plains, near the mouldewerp dwell, must have administered a sleeping potion. He remembered his mother, Fullō, reduced to a legless, distressed torso, trying to speak his name with her tongueless mouth, then everything went black.

The slaves marched from the hall, closing metal-encased doors behind them. Around Widukind, stone columns as thick as tree trunks supported a ceiling decorated with paintings and a frieze honouring the same promise: the blessed gifts to be bestowed on the faithful by Volerdie. The slightest breeze wafted up from the floor, setting a shiver in Widukind's naked body that threatened to start his teeth chattering. On a platform below him sat the throne of the dead. The cathedra's description written in the First Scripture didn't convey the brutal hideousness of the conglomeration of petrified bodies, each with a mouth frozen open, appearing to call for mercy, or praise Volerdie for this honour. The wolf's head atop the backrest guarded the hall, snarling its desire for another sacrifice. Its empty eye sockets pulsed a faint, bloody glow. Beside the throne stood another grell.

Not a slave, thought Widukind.

She had pale yellow skin, almost as if she suffered from a disease, and wore a diaphanous dress, the hem brushing the bottom of her shins. The grell carried a weapon, its silver blade glinting under the candlelight of a dozen chandeliers hanging from the ceiling. Fresh, bloodied scars blighted her chin and cheeks, where a wild grell's facial tattoo would normally be, but she had lilac eyes, the same colour as most stone-grells. Widukind surmised this poor mortal had been recently tainted by Malphas.

He leaned forward and pressed his face to the cage bars, trying to catch the pale grell's attention. "Your eyes," he said.

She looked up at him, then stepped forward, using the weapon's shaft like a walking stick, the wooden *tap, tap, tap* echoing through the chamber.

"Your eyes are lilac," said Widukind. "Tainted grells have black eyes."

"Master says they will grow a little darker each time I dispatch one of Volerdie's enemies."

"Have you come to dispatch me?"

The pale grell almost smiled. "We both know that is not possible. You are one of the few my sparth cannot slay, and you are not Volerdie's enemy. Master says you will be the vessel for the Divine Creator's soul."

Widukind slumped down in the cage. Since becoming immortal, every day of his life had been poisoned by the fear of this moment. The sacrifice of his immortality on the dead throne. Yet, now the moment had arrived, the fear dissolved, replaced by an emotion that some would call relief. The running had ended. The torment of watching his beautiful Caeli crumble away bone by bone would soon be over. The emotions warring inside his head would finally be silenced.

"It is written on your face," said the pale grell. "You recognise the sublimity of what awaits you."

"What is your name?" asked Widukind.

"Master has named me Ende."

"Yes, but what is *your* name?"

The grell tilted her head to the side, confusion dulling her lilac eyes.

"Ende," she repeated. "My name has always been Ende."

"You could cut the rope with that keen blade of yours. Lower the cage and let me out. I won't flee. I only want to see my brother. Where is he? Where's Malphas?"

"Master says little birds must stay caged, lest they fly away."

The door behind Widukind creaked open. Ende's eyes beamed in worship. Widukind turned to face Malphas, marching into the throne hall. No, not marching — strutting and whistling as he moved. He looked the same as Widukind remembered from twenty yarles ago. He *looked* like his older brother, Oldaric. He may have taken the name Malphas, but to Widukind, he would always be Oldaric. And despite the victory trot as he marched down the hall, Malphas' body stooped as his bones struggled with the peril of eternal existence.

Rephaim, the abomination of grell soldiers, followed their master into the hall and lined up along the walls. Malphas strode beneath Widukind's cage, not bothering to look up, then bounded up the stairs two at a time. On reaching the throne of the dead, he swivelled his bottom around and sat. A slave pulled a cart up to the throne platform, its only passenger the dismembered draughoul Widukind once called his mother.

Malphas clapped his hands twice, and the slave left the hall.

"Come closer, Ende," he said in a raspy voice, sounding like stone rubbed against glass.

The pale grell shuffled across the platform to stand beside her master. Together, they peered into Widukind's cage.

"We've finally caught our little bird," said Malphas. "For many yarles, he's flittered away his meaningless life. But I've trapped him now, and his pathetic existence will soon fulfil a glorious purpose."

"He says he's your brother, Master."

Malphas avoided looking Widukind in the eye, keeping his face half-turned towards Ende. "Yes. My younger brother." He waved a finger at the cart. "That creature spawned both of us. Mother and her two sons reunited. We should have a feast. To celebrate."

"Your plan will fail," said Widukind. "Volerdie will forsake you."

"Do you hear, Ende? The little bird squawks. The pitiful cry of a scorn-crow."

Widukind leaned forward and wrapped his fingers around the steel bars. "Look at me, Oldaric. At least dare to face your depravity eye-to-eye."

Malphas ignored him, instead focussing on Ende. "The moment is very close. Darkness will descend amid the daylight, signalling Volerdie's readiness to return to Enthilen. Then our scorn-crow will transform into a phoenix, the Divine Creator rising again to guide his followers into paradise."

"What will happen to you and me?" asked Ende.

Malphas reached across and took her free hand. "My dear, sweet Ende. I'm afraid your reign as the pale grell will be short. When I ascend to paradise...."

"You'll be left behind," interrupted Widukind. "To burn in the torturous fires ravaging Enthilen. That's the future Malphas offers you, Ende."

The pale grell glanced at him before returning loving eyes to her master.

Malphas stood, ambled down the stairs, and approached Fullō, who'd been strapped upright to a backboard fixed on the cart's tray. She groaned, opening her mouth to poke out the stump of a tongue. Malphas twirled his fingers in the last strands of hair clinging to her decaying scalp.

"Mother always favoured her younger son, even when his anaemic constitution took her away from her beloved twins. Even when *Widukind* was responsible for the twin's demise. Now our little bird is trapped; there's no need to keep his treacherous mother alive. She's served her purpose."

"Leave her alone," growled Widukind. "You've done enough to her already."

Malphas paused as if he'd heard Widukind, but he didn't face him, keeping his eyes fixed on Fullō.

"Don't do it, Oldaric," Widukind begged. "Grief cursed our mother. Alfwin and Colobert's death wasn't your fault. She's always regretted punishing you for the loss."

"Yes," said Malphas, "she *did* punish me. Ende, come here."

The pale grell descended the platform, carrying her sparth. The *clack, clack, clack* of the timber handle knocking against the steps pulsed through Widukind's head. As Ende stood beside Malphas, Fullō looked at her and wailed, the most bone-chilling howl Widukind had ever heard.

"You *can* kill draughouls," said Malphas, tracing his finger across Fullō's cheek. "It isn't easy, mind you. Decapitation will do it."

Malphas placed his finger inside Fullō's mouth, and she snapped her lips shut like a rat trap. He laughed, pushing his hand in further until she gagged.

"Leave her," cried Widukind. "Please, leave her."

"Are you ready, Ende," asked Malphas, "to further darken those savage lilac eyes?"

"Yes, Master." Ende raised her sparth.

Malphas pulled an unmarked hand from Fullō's mouth, then wrapped her hair around his fingers, yanking her head down to expose the back of her neck.

"You'll need all your strength," said Malphas to Ende.

Rage throbbed through Widukind's body, squashed together in the tiny cage. He smashed his fists against the bars. "NO! Don't fall into the abyss, Ende. It's not too late to turn back. Become a stone-grell again. Malphas' time is over. We have a plan...."

Widukind stopped, cursing his stupidity.

Malphas stared at him for the first time. "A plan? Might it involve the coward Adalwolf? I know he was at Gestade. I expect you were with him before being captured. The draughouls spoke of a void under the Dambay Plains. A secret place. Underground lairs are the habitat of mouldewerps. Are *they* mixed up in your plan?"

Widukind clenched his jaw. Say nothing, he thought. Give nothing more away.

Malphas turned back to Fullō. "Now, Ende, where were we? Cut down on the back of the neck. Pick your spot and thrust with every fibre of strength you have."

Widukind wrapped his arms around his shins and cried like a child who'd grazed his knee, begging mummy to kiss it better. Fullō fell silent as if resigned to her fate. Ende tensed. The sparth's blade wavered, candlelight from the chandeliers flickering across its keenness.

"Kill me," pleaded Widukind. "Kill me, Oldaric. End my misery with your mercy."

"Oh, I *will* kill you, dear brother, when day turns to night." Malphas rested a hand on the small of Ende's back. "Now, Ende. It's time."

She hesitated for a moment. Then the sparth flashed through the air, and a stone-grell's strength severed Fullō's head from her neck like a fire-iron slicing through an icicle.

* * * *

Nettie sat beside Snick on the driver's seat of the empty wagon inside Pergamos' south gate. Since Yonna's death, she'd wanted to escape the city. As the line of people leaving Pergamos inched closer to the exit, her dream had almost become reality. Yet, the escape wasn't as planned, and her freedom would be brief. Elmbray kept Erwin in his house, an implied prisoner, though Elmbray never said it outright. Surety, at the very least. An almost rock-solid guarantee Nettie would return to Pergamos after completing the trading mission with Snick. She expected her new, fire-blighted companion wouldn't let her out of his sight. It didn't matter. She'd go back for Erwin's sake. Only Volerdie knew what Elmbray might do to Nettie's friend if she didn't return.

Snick smacked the reins, and the two draft horses lumbered forward, only a handful of dutiful citizens between the wagon and the guards at the gate. Nettie worried about what would happen if Snick carried illegitimate merchant papers. Or one of the guards recognised her as a fugitive soldier from Malphas' army. *Or* they discovered the secret of Snick's wagon. Granted, it resembled an ordinary wagon: flat tray, timber sides with metal braces, spoked wheels with metal rims. Yet, the wagon had a false floor. Timber slats beneath the tray slid out to reveal a hidden compartment, large enough to fit six people lying flat, side-by-side and head to toe.

Nettie and Snick would present themselves to the guards as merchants. In truth, they were smugglers, hoping to sneak weapons, clothes, food, meduz or other supplies into Pergamos. The military controlled the flow of goods to and from the city, keeping the most prized items for themselves and on-selling the remainder to the citizenship at inflated prices. To counter the military's exploitation, a thriving black market had spread through Pergamos. Yonna had sometimes bought scrap metal from black marketeers, though he never admitted it to Nettie.

A savvy entrepreneur could make a lot of coin from the black market. After spending the last six moons with Elmbray, Nettie concluded few entrepreneurs would exhibit the same guile as her new employer.

"Papers," snapped a guard, decked in the silver armour of the Master's Shield. Armour Nettie once coveted.

Another guard grabbed the bridle of one of the horses to hold them in place.

Snick reached into his horsehair coat, withdrew a parchment with a wax seal, and handed it to the guard. The soldier broke the seal, read the parchment, then skewered it on a spike protruding from the middle of a table beside the gatehouse. He strolled around the wagon, tapping the sides with his halberd blade.

Don't inspect the cart tray, thought Nettie. Please, don't check the tray.

If the guard found the secret compartment, Nettie would run. She could outpace Snick, and the scars of melted skin on his face made him stand out in a crowd. Snick would take the fall for breaking the law while she'd run to Erwin, tear him from Elmbray's grasp and escape back into the ossuary labyrinth.

The guard stopped at the wagon's tailgate, and Nettie tensed.

"What'll be your cargo?" he asked.

Snick called over his shoulder, "Bales of hay from Beitrag. Need to feed them cavalry horses and undreds before the long march to Giigal."

The guard checked the opposite side of the wagon, then stopped beside

Nettie. "You're too pretty to be stuck with the likes of him," he said, pointing a gloved finger at Snick. "I'm on duty tomorrow. We'll go for a drink in the tavern when you return."

Nettie nodded and tried to smile.

The soldier reached inside a satchel slung over his shoulder, withdrew a piece of folded paper, and handed it to Snick. "Your re-entry permit is good until sunset tomorrow." He turned and yelled to the gatekeeper, "Let 'em pass!"

A stout man, hair tied in a ponytail and a beard down to his waist, slapped the calves of two grell slaves with his whip. The slaves yanked open the south gate, the hinges creaking with the weight of timber doors thicker than Nettie's arm.

"See ya tomorrow," said Snick to the guard as he shoved the re-entry permit into his coat pocket and urged the horses through the gate.

Nettie and Snick entered a stone tunnel twice as long as the wagon and horses.

Snick leaned into her ear. "They call this the *murder chamber*."

More than a dozen arrow slits lined the tunnel's walls, archers' faces lurking behind the gaps in the stone, waiting for the order to let loose their carnage.

At the other end of the tunnel, the wagon passed beneath the portcullis, Nettie hoping a grell slave didn't slip on a winch and send a metal spike hurtling down through her skull.

The slaves did their duty, and Nettie escaped onto the main road connecting Pergamos to the rest of Enthilen. She'd been here once before when she marched to Gestade, a proud soldier in Malphas' army. But she didn't want to be a soldier anymore. She wanted to flee, and her chance would come soon if she kept her wits. Elmbray had told her, 'One day, you'll drive the wagon without Snick.' She could hide Erwin in the secret compartment. They'd disappear into the long grass of the Dambay Plains and never look back.

Out of earshot of other travellers, Nettie faced Snick. "Are we really getting hay?"

"Sure," he said. "Wouldn't pay to lie to a Master's Shield." He leaned across and fashioned the red-raw scars on his face into something resembling a smile. "One of the bales will have treasures buried inside. Y'know, a few gifts for the guards, so they don't bother to look any further."

The road branched in three directions; east to the coast, west to the Scaur Hills, and south to Süden Forst. Snick took the wagon south, heading for the trading outpost of Beitrag, about half-a-days travel from Pergamos. Nettie had never been to Beitrag, but she didn't expect the visit to be pleasurable. Elmbray told her it was a den of lawlessness. 'A pit full of vipers with deceitful eyes and words that bite like fangs to poison your mind,' he'd said. The Master's Shield knew about Beitrag, but they let it be. Soldiers' families also benefitted from a healthy black market.

Clouds taller than Pergamos' walls drifted across the sun's face and cooled the harvest season air. The monotony of the Dambay Plains, clusters of grassy knolls, followed by sweeping meadows, followed by more mounds, made Nettie's eyelids heavy, and she almost drifted away.

Don't fall asleep, she thought. Keep your wits.

"How long have you worked for Elmbray?" she asked Snick.

"Most of me life," he said. "Elmbray rescued me from Slumstadt's filthy streets. When Ma and Pa died, I had to beg for food with the other orphans. We lived in a hole in the riverbank. Too poor for a snatch of canvas to throw over a bundle of sticks for shelter."

"Is Snick your real name?"

He flinched, smacking the reins against his leg before geeing the horses into a trot.

"Yes," he whispered before falling silent.

Nettie didn't press, the battle among Snick's emotions revealed by the duelling twitches of fire-born scars defiling his face.

He found his courage, nonetheless. "Pa named me. When I was a babe, he would cut me with his knife. Little slits, mind you. Not deep, but enough to draw blood. *Snicks*."

"That's awful," said Nettie.

"S'pose it is."

"Why didn't your mother stop it?"

Snick shook his head. "Too mixed up with embruisia. Y'heard of it?"

"Yes. It's poison. Messes with your mind."

"Near enough. Embruisia killed Ma, and Slumstadt killed Pa soon after. Reckon that's why Elmbray found me. When Ma died, he lost one of his loyal customers. Came lookin' for what he was owed. Guess he considered me suitable payment. I never discovered how she could afford the embruisia."

"Will Elmbray hurt Erwin?" asked Nettie, fearful of the answer.

"He might. Do what he says, and you'll be fine. Ya friend'll be fine, too." Snick sucked on the inside of his cheek like he often did, pursued his lips, then launched a spit-ball onto the plains.

Nettie took a swig from a waterskin, then held it towards Snick.

He waved it away. "We ain't so different, you and I. Neither of us got any family."

"I have a sister," said Nettie, hopeful she still lived. "Her name's Rosalie. Left Sardis twelve yarles ago."

Snick faced her with eyes marred by droops of burnt skin. "What's y'family name?"

"Barron."

"I thought y'looked familiar. 'Cept, I ain't seen you before, but I've met ya sister."

Nettie jolted upright. "Where? When?"

"Don't get too excited. Was a long time ago. Last I saw her, Slumstadt burned, and she ran right into the middle of the flames. Best y'can hope; she died quickly and isn't sufferin' like some of us."

As he turned away, the nausea of disappointment singed Nettie's throat. Snick's recollection explained why Rosalie had never come to Pergamos to find her family. Nettie fingered the necklace of bronze circlets inside her tunic, considering whether to wrench it off and throw it into the long grass. The present from Rosalie only reminded her of a sister's love long gone and never coming back.

At midday, Beitrag appeared over the crest of a hill. A pieosphere of trails radiated out from the trading hub like wagon-wheel spokes. Merchants on horseback or driving carts headed to or from the rectangular, three-storied timber building towering above a cluster of ramshackle shelters made from clay, straw and canvas.

Snick urged the draft horses on, dust choking the air as the grassy plain ceded to bare dirt. The main building, longer than twenty wagons lined end-to-end, had three doorways, each larger than Pergamos' south gate. Near the centre door, a dome-shaped cage had been built, bigger than a house, made from saplings bound with twine. Inside the cage, two men, their bare chests covered in dirty sweat, fought a grell slave. One man brandished a net with metal spikes embedded in the rope mesh while the other fought with a trident. The grell slave had his bare hands, his body naked, but for a slip of loin cloth covering his genitals.

Around the cage, a crowd yelled encouragement and exchanged coin. The net-wielder smacked his weapon into the grell's stomach, and blood splattered onto the face of a female spectator. The woman beside her licked the blood from her companion's cheek. Then they kissed.

Nettie fought a spew of breakfast back down her throat and turned away. She didn't need to witness the murder of a defenceless grell.

Through the centre doorway, people carrying wicker baskets, or driving empty carts, bustled their way into the belly of the building. Out from the doorway to Nettie's left came a wagon laden with supplies, escorted by dirty men with swords and spears who snarled and lashed their weapons at anyone getting too close.

The belly holds all the goodies, thought Nettie.

Snick drove the wagon through the centre doorway and into a cavernous void. While the building appeared to have three stories from the outside, inside was a single space with a tall ceiling, its rafters supported by the hewn trunks of panalope trees. Raucous music and laughter came from one corner, where patrons soothed dusty throats with tankards of meduz.

"*The Cutters Tavern,*" said Snick to Nettie. "We ain't goin' nowhere near that."

He drove the wagon to the centre of the building, entering a cage almost as large as the kirika in Pergamos, with metal bars as thick as Nettie's wrist. Men stood around the perimeter, glaives and spears at the ready, waiting for a misstep from the desperate or foolish. Inside the cage, rows of shelves full of provisions reached towards the thatched roof. To Nettie's right, slaves unloaded laden wagons bringing supplies into Beitrag. To her left, more slaves packed empty wagons. The circle of commerce swirled around her in a dusty, stuffy, noisome vortex.

Snick pulled the wagon up to a countertop and reined in the horses. A circular dais resembling a cart wheel, fixed to the end of a pole longer than six spears, swivelled around a centrepin driven into the countertop. As the platform circled towards Nettie, a creature with black fur and a pinkish face jumped from a shelf and landed on the moving podium.

Snick whispered in Nettie's ear, "That's Chitti Coin-tail. She's a werp."

A woman standing at the pole's opposite end stopped the rotation when the platform reached the driver's seat of the wagon.

"Snicky is back," said Chitti, looking up from a pile of parchments scrunched between clawed hands, eyeglasses set in a wooden frame saddling a long, swaying nose.

"How are ya, Chitti?" asked Snick. "Business good?"

Chitti laughed, squashing her squinty eyes closed. "Always good business in Beitrag. Always good. Better now I smell you, Tricky Snicky."

"You're a sweet talker."

Chitti leaned towards Nettie and inhaled. "Who this?"

"Me new assistant," said Snick. "Remember her smell. She'll be comin' on her own soon enough. Elmbray got more important things for me to do."

"Oh, yes," said Chitti, "Snicky important man. *Very* important. Too important to come visit his friend Chitti Coin-tail more often."

The werp put down her parchments and stepped from the dais onto the driver's seat. She brushed her wet, black nose all over Nettie's face and bare arms.

"Alright," said Chitti, "I remember her smell. Once inside a werp's nostrils, it never escapes. Name?"

"Nettie," said Nettie.

"Nettie Tenderfoot. I remember."

"No, it's Barron. Nettie Barron."

"Hush! Not here. Nettie Tenderfoot."

"Chitti gives everyone a new name," said Snick. "I'm Snick Smartburn."

"Yes, yes, yes," said Chitti. "Or sometimes, Tricky Snicky. My favourite customer." She nestled her bottom back onto the platform.

"Any payin' customer is *your* favourite," said Snick.

Chitti narrowed her slitty eyes. "What you want?"

"A woman called Murtril should have delivered twenty-four bales of hay."

Chitti took a quill from an inkwell built into the platform's floor and ran the tip over a parchment. "Hay, hay, *hay*. Here it is. Twenty bales of hay."

"Twenty-four," said Snick.

Chitti looked up at him. If her eyes opened any further, Nettie swore the werp would be glaring.

"*No*," said Chitti. "Twenty. Murtril Yellowtooth couldn't pay our holding fee. We took four bales."

"What about the other provisions?" asked Snick, glancing over his shoulder at the rider behind him.

"All here. You do business direct with Chitti Coin-tail; I look after you. Third parties get involved, always trouble for everyone. This way."

The woman controlling the platform's arm swung Chitti around, stopping her outside a padlocked gate to another cage. Chitti unclipped a key ring from the belt holding up her pants. The jangle of dozens of keys sang a hopeful song of prosperity as Chitti sniffed each one until locating the right key. She unlocked the padlock, and a grell slave opened the gate.

"Holding bay twelve," said Chitti. "All yours. Two hundred and forty coin." She held out a clawed hand with a pink palm.

Snick pulled the cowl from his face and scratched his bald, fire-warped scalp. "Geez. Prices are goin' through the roof."

Chitti pointed to the ceiling with the feather of her quill. "Go through roof, end up with head in the clouds. No supplies up there."

Snick leaned forward and felt underneath the driver's seat. A latch clicked, and he withdrew a locked metal box. After pulling a key at the end of a neck-chain out from the top of his shirt, he unlocked the box, lifted the lid and began counting to himself.

"Each pouch has fifty coin," said Snick as he handed a pouch to Chitti.

She opened the drawstring, withdrew ten coin and shoved it into her pants pocket, then cinched the drawstring and sent the pouch down a tube that disappeared under the ground beside the gate.

Chitti leaned towards Nettie and whispered, "Treasury," before pointing towards the ground. "Right under our feet." She faced Snick. "Four more pouches."

He handed over the coin. Chitti opened and checked each pouch, sent them all down the tube, then scribbled on a parchment before rolling it tightly and slipping it into the cylinder. The paper tally slid its way underground.

"We double-check every coin, Nettie Tenderfoot. Nobody cheats Chitti Coin-tail. Snick Smartburn learnt the hard way. Now I trust him."

"Does the price include an escort?" asked Snick. "When we leave in the mornin'."

"Yes, yes, yes. Four strong men to protect your wagon until out of sight of Beitrag. You be safe. Very safe, indeed. Holding bay twelve." Chitti handed Snick a piece of paper.

Her dais swung around to meet the next customer as Snick urged the horses into the cage inside a cage.

Metal and timber scaffolding towered above Nettie, fixing in place shelves as wide as a wagon tray stacked with provisions. Children with wicker baskets strapped to their backs climbed the scaffolding with the deftness and confidence of squirrels harvesting acorns. They filled the baskets with supplies, then returned to the ground, handing the bounty to paying customers. Nettie counted at least a dozen empty wagons, people on horseback filling saddlebags, and walkers loading baskets full of food, weapons, tools or medicines.

Snick pulled the wagon up to holding bay twelve in front of twenty hay bales.

"Load the hay onto the wagon," he said to Nettie.

"Can't we get a slave to do it?" she asked.

"Slave labour costs us coin. You're free. See the bale with the blue twine? Leave that 'til last. We'll put it at the back so the guards can find their treats nice and easy."

"What are you going to do while I load the hay?"

He waved the piece of paper in front of her. "This'll get us supplies to hide in the secret compartment. Food, utensils, meduz, armour, you name it. See these little boxes...." Snick ran his finger over lines of boxes drawn across the paper. "When I take somethin', the controller puts a stamp in one of the boxes. When the boxes are filled, that's our lot. Elmbray's given me a list." Snick pulled another piece of paper from his coat pocket and started reading. "A dozen swords, four sacks of grain or flour, three crates of salted meat, a box of bunbili weed...."

"I get the picture," said Nettie.

"No pictures on the list," said Snick. "Anyways, it all costs somethin' different, but the controller will work it out. We get what we get. Chitti won't short me."

Snick climbed from the driver's seat and disappeared into the maze of scaffolding and shelves. Nettie jumped off the wagon, walked to the hay pile, heaved the first bale up to her waist and staggered to the wagon tray. After throwing the bale onto the tray, she turned and leaned against the wagon.

No point knocking yourself out, she thought.

Around her, merchants, children, slaves and their masters were intent on keeping the wheels of commerce moving. No-one appeared to notice an undersized, unimportant peasant from Pergamos. Nettie could slip out of Beitrag before Snick returned with the first of his contraband. Walk into the plains and down to the south forest.

Even grells can escape notice down there, she thought, surrounded by all those trees. Then I'd find someone with a boat and travel across the ocean to lands I've never heard of. But what about Erwin? When Snick returns to Pergamos without me, Erwin will suffer Elmbray's wrath. I can't escape without Erwin. For better or worse, we're bound together.

~ Chapter 37 ~

"This is one of my more foolish errands," said Jurelle. "Are you sure it's the right house?"

Heron nodded. "I've been on the porch already, General Stansfield. There's a symbol scratched into the timber of the front door — a two-headed serpent, curled up, face-to-face."

"I know the symbol."

"After killing the Sella, I was told to meet the draughoul here. Mother said he would free father and help us escape Portum."

"Charmion still lives. Let's hope the draughoul doesn't know."

Crouching behind a rubble pile, Heron fixed his youthful eyes on the rundown house across the street while Jurelle scanned the abandoned neighbourhood. Most buildings in Portum were made of stone, rammed earth or mudbricks, but here, dozens of timber houses lined the streets, each with boarded-up windows. Some residences had holes in the tiled roofs large enough to fly a griffin through. Others had doors hanging from hinges, or partially collapsed walls. Plants growing in the courtyards had spread like weeds, choking rusted picket fences or breaking apart stone paths as they climbed onto front porches as if to knock on the door. No-one walked the streets. Even the beggars of Portum shunned this place.

"Why is it so quiet here?" asked Jurelle.

Heron shrugged. "I heard disease cursed the neighbourhood. A long time ago, a fever killed most of the children. Families abandoned their homes and never returned."

"Only children?"

Heron nodded.

"We should be safe then. Will you and Saskia...."

Heron faced Jurelle with creases worrying his forehead. "With all due respect, General Stansfield, your daughter is too zealous for a simple kamel handler like me."

Jurelle laughed aloud, then slapped a hand over his mouth to mask the merriment. "She's headstrong," he said through parted fingers, then removed his hand. "She has to be, in a place of ambition this like. Fathers know little about the romantic desires of their daughters, but she seems to like you. If you're hopeful of a closer bond with Saskia, don't give up yet."

They returned to their vigil, Jurelle wondering how long they should wait until convincing themselves no-one watched the two-storey, timber-shingled house. Every window had timber boards nailed across, so he couldn't see in. With only Bargan's quarter moon illuminating the night sky, they'd need a torch inside the house, Jurelle hoping Heron carried a candle or firebrand in his backpack. Of greater concern was their lack of real weapons. Jurelle had removed an old table leg and carved a comfortable handle so he could use it like a hammer. It would hardly damage a draughoul, but he might knock the creature unconscious for a while. Heron had a chain and padlock to bind the draughoul when they caught it. The young man refused to go against the Senatorial Dictum and wield any weapon. Jurelle found the reluctance puzzling, given Heron had almost razed the griffin barn.

Melitta's hold on the boy must be strong, he thought. This entire plan could be a trap.

Yet, Jurelle trusted Thaly's acumen. She'd become a much better judge of character than he ever was.

"If we find the draughoul, how long will it take to reach the storehouse?" he asked.

"One hour," said Heron.

"You're certain no-one uses it anymore?"

"Yes. Hasn't been used in yarles. We'll chain the draughoul to a metal beam."

"It'll have to be restrained properly. These things can walk through stone walls."

"I'll watch it day and night. Mother will come looking for me. I need somewhere to hide."

"With any luck, you won't have to hide for long. Once we convince the draughoul to admit he's Malphas' servant and has been working with Melitta, you can resurface."

"If you don't mind me asking, General Stansfield, how are we going to get the draughoul to confess?"

"Thaly will arrange something." *I hope*, thought Jurelle. *At least, imprisoning the draughoul means Melitta's pathway out of Portum is closed. With Charmion still alive and Heron missing, Melitta will become desperate, and desperate people make mistakes.*

"We won't catch the draughoul hiding here," said Jurelle. "Let's go."

He squeezed the handle of his makeshift weapon, rose up from a crouch, and stepped from behind the rubble pile. Heron trailed him, the chain in his hand tinkling in the calm night such that Jurelle winced. It sounded like a warning bell for any draughoul who didn't want to be trapped.

"Hold the chain tight," he said. "Keep the noise to a minimum."

They crept across the empty street, through the front gate and along a path overgrown with waist-high weedy burs that attached to the hem of Jurelle's tunic like flies on a carcass. He placed his foot on the first porch step, and the timber gave way, cracking beneath him.

"Damn," he hissed.

Heron put a hand on his shoulder.

Jurelle nodded, then eased his weight onto the second step. It held. Two more steps, and he was on the porch. Heron followed, with the chain wrapped securely around his fist. Jurelle twisted the front door handle and leaned his shoulder against the timber panels. The door didn't budge. He tried again, bracing his sandals against the porch to get more leverage and thudding his shoulder into the door. No movement.

"I'll try a window," whispered Heron.

He approached a front window covered in slats nailed across the jambs and fed a loose end of the chain through a gap between the middle boards until it appeared at another hole above the windowsill. After threading the chain around the back of three nailed boards, Heron grabbed the two loose ends in his hands. He paused, glanced at Jurelle with pale dread, then yanked. The boards worked loose. Heron tugged again, and they came free, creating a hole large enough to crawl through.

They clambered over the windowsill and into a dark room. Heron unshouldered his backpack, uncinched the top and withdrew flint, oilcloth and two candles melted inside a metal holder. He clicked the flint until sparks landed on the oilcloth. It started a flame, which he used to light a candle, before placing the oilcloth on the floor and stamping it out with the heel of his sandal.

"You take this one," whispered Heron as he lit the second candle and handed it to Jurelle. "We'll stick together."

He returned the flint to his backpack and shouldered it. With the chain in his right hand, he used his left to wave the candle across the dark room. Empty, other than a layer of dust on the mantle, black coals in the hearth, and vermin excrement littering the floorboards.

Jurelle stepped to a doorway, flinching with every creak of a floorboard beneath his sandals, then cast candlelight into a dark passage. A breeze wafted down the hallway, almost extinguishing the flame.

Breeze from where? thought Jurelle.

Heron pushed past and turned left, creeping down the passage. Jurelle followed, passing another empty room on the right before they both stumbled onto the staircase to the first floor. Behind the stairs, at the far end of the passage, was a shut door.

"Wait here," whispered Jurelle.

"What?" asked Heron.

"Wait here in case the draughoul comes down the stairs. I'm going to see what's behind the door at the end of the passage."

"If it wants to escape, won't it simply walk through a wall like you told me?"

"They can't walk through every wall. There has to be a path, hidden from regular people like us."

Jurelle went to leave, but Heron clutched at his wrist, the tremble of his hand setting the candle flames aflicker. The young man's face conveyed his dismay. He didn't want to be left alone, weaponless, at the whim of a ghastly draughoul who might float down the stairs and strangle him. But they had no choice. Jurelle gave Heron a reassuring smile, then tugged his arm free, turned and tiptoed down the passageway to the shut door.

Arriving at the door, Jurelle pressed down on the cold metal latch, and it clicked open. The door swung inwards, rusted hinges offering a rasping complaint at being disturbed. Behind the door, a stone staircase led down into a cellar.

Perfect hiding place, Jurelle thought.

He stood on the first step and almost rolled his ankle on a loose stone. Kicking the rock out of the way, he descended the stairs, swatting cobwebs from his face using the table leg. Despite a warm night, cool, musty air wafted up from below, raising goosebumps on Jurelle's bare arms and legs.

The stairs continued down, deeper than any cellar Jurelle had visited. As he neared the bottom, the stone lip of the last step broke away, and he fell forward. Turning sideways, he thudded into the flagstone floor with his right shoulder, dropping the table leg. It skidded off into the darkness. The candle still burned, held steady in his left hand. Jurelle cursed his stupidity, then stood, dusted himself off and used the candlelight to push back the darkness. He found the table leg resting against a wall with mortar crumbling from rising damp. A *drip, drip, drip* echoed in the cellar, and tiny feet skittered and scattered across the flagstones.

After gathering his makeshift weapon, he turned down a passageway as black as pitch, stumbling into a room no larger than two wardrobes on his left. The candle revealed nothing. He snuck, as quiet as an owl hunting a fieldmouse, down the passage, discovering another empty room on his right. Further into the darkness. Room on his left. Empty. Another on his right. Empty. Then he came to the back wall and stopped.

Drip, drip, drip.

Skitter, scatter.

Drip, drip, drip.

Skitter scatter.

Drip, drip, hiss.

It's here, thought Jurelle.

In the furthest, darkest corner of the cellar, a shape cowered from view.

"Show yourself," said Jurelle, holding the candle at arms-length in one hand and raising the table leg above his head with the other.

"Is it you?" hissed the draughoul.

"Yes...yes, it's me, Heron. Melitta's son."

The draughoul stepped from the corner. "Where is the Sella's multicolour robe?"

What? thought Jurelle. Why does he want to see it? Think, dammit. "Ah, it's in my pack upstairs. Follow me, and I'll show it to you."

"No. Bring it down here."

Jurelle couldn't turn his back on the draughoul. If he yelled for Heron, it would expose his falsehood. He needed to trap the creature himself, then call for help.

"The light is better upstairs," said Jurelle. "You can see it is indeed the Sella's robe."

"Why do you delay? Bring it now."

"Melitta is waiting with the robe," said Jurelle, becoming desperate.

The draughoul emerged from the shadows and tilted his head to the side. "She is not supposed to be here yet. Not until a new Sella is appointed."

Dammit. Charade over. Jurelle shifted his feet shoulder-width apart and braced his body. The draughoul glanced at the table leg in Jurelle's hand, then back at his face.

"You're lying," said the draughoul. "You're much too old to be Melitta's son."

He sprang at Jurelle, who swayed back, letting the creature fall forward before belting him on the neck with the table leg.

"Heron!" yelled Jurelle. "Down here."

The draughoul lashed out a hand with fingernails like claws, cutting through Jurelle's tunic and slicing the skin on his chest. Jurelle dropped the candle, then spun around in the blackness, swinging the table leg again and again. It smacked into the draughoul, the snap of a bone echoing through the cellar. The draughoul lunged forward, digging his teeth into Jurelle's shoulder.

"*Arrgh!*" cried Jurelle, smashing the table leg down onto the draughouls skull.

Don't kill it, his mind pleaded. We need it alive.

"Heron!" Jurelle screamed.

The draughoul released its bite, then clawed at Jurelle's face. The candle lying on the floor went out. As darkness enveloped the combatants, Jurelle jabbed the table leg into the creature's chest to push it away. It gasped and stepped back. Jurelle thought it might flee. Instead, it jumped at him, landing a bite on his nose. They tumbled to the ground wrapped together, embracing the furious desire for survival. Jurelle rolled his body on top, pinning the draughoul to the floor. It flailed and screamed, scratching, biting and kicking to free itself. Heron appeared with his candle and chain. A dangle of metal hit Jurelle's shoulder. He reached across, grabbed the chain and searched for the creature's wrists.

"I have the legs," said Heron, kneeling on the draughoul's shins.

Jurelle found one wrist, then the other, yanking them together before wrapping the chain tightly.

"Padlock," he said.

Heron yanked the lock from his pocket and snapped it through the chain links.

"We have it," said Jurelle.

*   *   *   *

Six griffins wheeled over Portum's tangerine roofs, and Tom, riding pillion behind Saskia on Namu, caught his breath at the city's immensity. The Germalian metropolis dwarfed Sardis, Laodicea, and Malang Gunya combined. Thousands and thousands of people hurried along cobblestone thoroughfares, like ants following well-worn trails, moving between neighbourhoods of multi-storey townhouses, shops, market squares, and manicured public gardens. A circular building with stone archways climbing to five stories dominated Portum's skyline. Saskia had told Tom to watch for the Pallaxium, its architecture reminding him of the colosseum in Rome, except the Germalians had crowned their monolith with a golden cupola. And inside, politicians, not gladiators, fought with words and subterfuge, not tridents, nets and swords.

Where the city's western fringe met the coast, a wharf with a dozen jetties reached into a crystal ocean. Ships with towering masts bobbed in calm waters while seafarers and labourers loaded or unloaded barges, moving cargo to and from merchant vessels. On the wharf, a clocktower, the first timepiece Tom had seen in Ostamp, kept the workers honest by tracking the duration of their labour.

Saskia banked Namu left, turning into the city centre. Demetria brought her griffin, Eluji, up to Namu's wingtip, Rosalie clinging to the rear of Demetria's saddle, looking more comfortable with the flight than Tom felt. They'd been travelling day and night since the rescue from the Pordillo, Demetria adamant the conventus must be told about the location of Qaysar Rais as soon as possible. Tom and Saskia's failed mission to rescue Quenan had gone unnoticed, except by Rosalie, who cried in Tom's arms when he delivered the news of Quenan's death.

As soon as Tom regained the eyes of lost souls, he showed them to Demetria, explaining the plan to destroy the throne of the dead. He had to. The Germalian commander wanted to leave him and Rosalie in the desert to fend for themselves. Tom's revelations fuelled Demetria's urgency to return to Portum and report her discoveries to the conventus. Yet, she showed little interest in the dark eyes beyond what they might do in the fight to topple Malphas, and she dismissed Tom's requests to speak to the conventus himself. He needed to find another way past the Pallaxium's front door. He needed to find Thaly.

Saskia guided Namu down into a yard where dark-skinned men dressed in simple clothes carried ropes slung over their shoulders or clambered up stairs to the top of timber platforms. Namu alighted beside a platform, and a young man hitched a rope to the harness around the griffin's head.

Saskia glanced over her shoulder to Tom. "You can climb down now."

He stumbled from the saddle, his thighs and lower back aching from the rigorous journey on the winged eagle-lion. The young man, looking bemused, offered his hand to help Tom climb onto the timber platform.

As Saskia dismounted Namu, the man bowed to her.

"*Arve, Domina Stansfield*," he said in the language Tom recognised as Germalian.

Saskia handed the man Namu's reins, then trotted down the stairs. Tom followed her as Rosalie dismounted Eluji on another platform.

The three companions walked across the courtyard, brimming now with dark-skinned people welcoming home the wind-riders. Most welcomers wore thin, cream robes and sandals. Some donned broad-brimmed straw hats to ward off the beating sun. Tom longed to remove the flight leathers borrowed from Saskia and find a hat to protect the already peeling skin on his balding scalp.

At least the sunburn gives my skin colour, he thought, worrying how a pale-skinned stranger might be received in a place like Portum.

Saskia pushed through the crowd, Tom and Rosalie trying to keep up with her.

"They're here," she said in Erstürmen. "I knew they would be."

Saskia waved at an older man and woman with fair skin standing on the fringe of the crowd. As she reached them, the woman, stately and beautiful, with long tawny hair and high cheekbones, held her arms wide.

"*Arve, Sas,*" said the woman in Germalian.

Saskia broke from the woman's embrace and hugged the man, a tall, solid, chiselled male with grey hair and solemn brown eyes. He had cuts and scratches on his face and a ring of small, red gouges on his beakish nose that resembled a bite mark. Tom and Rosalie held back, waiting for an introduction.

"*Et to ex um lumono,*" said the man to Saskia.

She pulled away from him. "We have to speak Erstürmen, Pa. What happened to your face?"

The man waved her away. "Nothing. A few scratches."

"Your father still thinks he's eighteen harvest seasons old," said the woman. "Needing to go on stupid adventures to prove his manhood."

The man smirked and rolled his eyes.

Saskia giggled, then faced Tom and Rosalie. "This is my stubborn father, Jurelle Stansfield, and my patient mother, Genevea."

The stifling heat beaded sweat on Tom's forehead as Jurelle Stansfield turned his inquisitive gaze on him.

"Ma, Pa," continued Saskia, "this is Rosalie Barron from Sardis."

"My goodness," said Genevea, eyes wide. "That's a long way to travel. Are you related to Yonna Barron, the metalsmith?"

"Yes," said Rosalie. "I'm his eldest child."

Genevea parted the frilly lace on the neck of her gown. "Your father made this necklace. It's my favourite."

Rosalie smiled and nodded.

"And who's this?" asked Jurelle, pointing his finger at Tom.

"Tom Anderson," said Saskia. "The traveller."

The brown eyes of inquisition made their judgement in a heartbeat. A hand flew from Jurelle's side and slapped Tom's cheek so hard the smack shocked the crowd into silence. Tom careered into Rosalie before crashing to the cobblestones. Jurelle loomed over him, his chest heaving with vitriol. He swung his leg back as if preparing to bury his foot in Tom's stomach before Saskia pulled him away.

"Pa!" she cried. "Stop it. Not here. Not this."

Jurelle fumed, his face redder than the sands of Groz Wüste. Gasping breaths formed words, but Tom couldn't hear them, pulling his knees to his chest and covering his head with his hands. Rosalie knelt beside him, begging Jurelle to end the assault.

"Stupid old fool," said Genevea to Jurelle. "You'll be in the carcer with Chloe if you keep this up. Control your temper."

Saskia turned to the milling crowd. "*Et lou mon esta spurrum. Inus spa mortus.*"

The onlookers ambled away. Rosalie pulled Tom's hands from his face.

"Get up," she said. "Stand up to him."

Tom pushed his tongue into his cheek, tasting blood, then stretched his jaw open.

Not broken. Could have been worse.

Rosalie helped him to his feet. Saskia and Genevea stepped between Tom and Jurelle, Tom wondering who they were trying to protect.

"I don't even know you," mumbled Tom.

"I know *you*," snapped Jurelle, stabbing his finger at Tom and trying to push between his wife and daughter's shoulders like a raging bull bashing against the gate of his pen.

Saskia's hand went to the hilt of her cutlass, but she fixed her eyes on Tom. He almost laughed at the thought of him being a threat to the legendary General Jurelle Stansfield.

"I know you," repeated Jurelle. "You're the craven who left my daughter to die in Pergamos. You're the coward who fled into Princess Caeli's arms while my son...while *my son*...." A whimper caught in Jurelle's throat, and he stilled. A single tear rolled down his cheek, evaporating in the heat before reaching his chin. "While Jürgen was cut to pieces by murderers," he continued, "outside Caeli's locked door. Tell me, *Anderson*, what did you do? Did you try to help Jürgen? Or was it you who locked the door, leaving my son no escape?"

"It wasn't like that," said Tom.

"Did you hear his dying breaths? Did you hear him plead for mercy?"

"No," said Tom. "No. It didn't...it wasn't...Jürgen wanted to protect Caeli from the soldiers. I didn't ask for his help. I'd never met him before he dragged me from the needle in Sardis up the stairs to Caeli's room. I...."

"What did you do behind the locked door?"

"Talked, then...then...." *Then I ran again. Crawled into the space behind Caeli's wall mirror and slinked away down the secret passage like the coward I am.*

He shoved his hand into the front pocket of his leather pants, popped two chambers in the foil packet of anxiety medication, and tossed the pills into his mouth. He needed another escape, and this was his only option.

One left.

"Why have you returned now?" Genevea asked Tom in a soft voice that sounded like his mother's.

"He's come to defeat Malphas," said Rosalie, setting a glare of defiance on Jurelle.

Jurelle scoffed. "Even the Germalian army will struggle to defeat Malphas if they can get off their backsides. How will a weakling like this Anderson boy stop an immortal?"

Tom lifted his head, fighting against the guilt flamed by Jurelle's judgement. "I'm sorry Jürgen fell. If there was anything I could have done to help him, I would have. I'm sorry I left Thaly wounded and alone in Pergamos' throne hall. I'm sorry for a lot of things. But I've returned to right these wrongs. I've returned to destroy Volerdie's throne."

Jurelle laughed aloud, pacing back and forth. "You're delusional." He tapped his temple with a finger. "The sun has scrambled your mind. That's it. Madness is your cloak."

"Malphas' greatest desire still eludes him," said Rosalie. "All his will is focused on sacrificing an immortal on the dead throne to lure Volerdie back to Enthilen. If Tom demolishes the throne...."

"*If*," interrupted Jurelle. "If, if, if!" He stopped pacing and glared at Tom. "Maybe this *boy* wants to be the sacrifice. Maybe *he* longs to be the body welcoming Volerdie's soul."

"That isn't true," snapped Tom. "We've all made poor choices, *Traitor General*, and we must live with them. Now I have a chance at redemption."

Jurelle bristled, clutching at his waist. "If only I had a sword. Damn women!"

Genevea grabbed his wrist and held it firm.

"We have to help Tom," said Rosalie.

"Thaly almost died helping him," said Jurelle. "I won't let that happen again." He yanked his wrist free and stormed off.

Genevea stayed, offering Tom a feeble smile. "He'll calm down," she said. "Losing Jürgen was a terrible blow for both of us. Jurelle refuses to move on. You would have helped our son if you could. Wouldn't you?"

Tom sighed. "It all happened so fast. I was only sixteen yarles old. Still a child in many ways. Princess Caeli dragged me into her room, and my whole life changed. Jürgen refused to follow me, determined to stay outside Caeli's door to protect her from an attack. I doubt...I doubt anyone could have saved him."

With Jurelle gone, the atmosphere calmed. Saskia relaxed her hand, letting it fall from her cutlass, but Rosalie pressed her shoulder against Tom's as if making a point to everyone around them.

"Tom wants to speak with Thaly," Saskia said to Genevea.

"She's in conventus," said Genevea.

"Again?" Saskia faced Tom and Rosalie. "I'll find lighter clothes for you. Then I'll take you to the Pallaxium. We can wait for Thaly there."

Genevea said goodbye, and Saskia led Tom and Rosalie from the mounting yard.

Does Thaly hate me as much as her father does? wondered Tom, stewing over his confrontation with Jurelle. He'd anticipated a fond reunion with Thaly, but now he didn't know what to expect. The anxiety meds did nothing to alleviate Tom's growing concern. Portum became a bottomless lake, and he was barely keeping his head above water. If he couldn't convince Jurelle of the importance of his mission, how would he ever convince a gathering of Germalian senators? Unable to control all the cogs in the machinery of his plan, a depressive vortex threatened to pull Tom under. He couldn't control the conventus. Or the outcome of a war. Or what Adalwolf did. Or Widukind. Tom couldn't control any of it.

Walking beside him, Rosalie held his hand. "We're doing this together," she said. "I'm not leaving you to face the challenge alone."

He wanted to hug her then. Fall into comforting, loving arms. But love still eluded Tom and Rosalie. Snatches of lustful sex hadn't blossomed into anything more. Their life, days of exhausting travel, fighting for survival, and escaping fiends, didn't leave much space for romance. Tom wanted it. Couldn't stop thinking about it, despite everything else. But he had no idea if Rosalie wanted it too.

* * * *

The conniving press of the conventus threatened to suffocate Thaly's hopes. Jurelle and Heron had captured the draughoul, but the creature refused to utter a single word about his relations with Malphas or Melitta.

Thaly should have realised the plan's futility from the start. A clever senator, a *scheming* senator, would have devised a much better strategy. Heron still had the Infada dagger and would testify to its origin.

Maybe that's enough? thought Thaly. Malphas' draughoul will never talk.

Chloe remained imprisoned in the carcer; inmates were forbidden to see visitors even before a trial. Thaly needed the most robust evidence she could gather to free her lover. Pressure grew from elsewhere. The bellum cornu of war wailed louder than ever. Zenais and Eutropia pushed harder for a confrontation with Malphas, but new information threatened to unravel their plans. The scouting party of wind-riders had returned, rumour filtering through the conventus that they'd discovered Qaysar Rais' camp. The appetite for an attack on the Pordillo would be almost impossible to satiate, practically guaranteeing the Germalians wouldn't march to Enthilen.

Resisting Malphas' ambitions seemed futile. His lackey in Portum, Melitta, sat in the zōdiakos, back turned to Thaly, fidgeting nervously with the sleeve of her yellow robe. Thaly hoped the treasonous orator's thoughts pulsated with unease. Heron hadn't murdered Charmion, and now he'd disappeared along with the draughoul.

Melitta must be worried, thought Thaly. Fear will unveil the duplicitous orator.

On this morning, for the first time in her life, Thaly felt more like a politician than a warrior, beholden to a world of lies, half-truths and deception. A weaver of cunning words to push an agenda. She hated the feeling and longed for a simpler life.

Resign, thought Thaly. Leave the conventus and the Volatal Vexil, and find a different path.

A yell came from behind her. An anitor opened the zōdiakos door, and in burst Photina, Pisce faction's orator, her indigo robes blotched with sweat.

"Demetria demands an immediate audience," called Photina from the top of the stairs.

This is it, thought Thaly. The rumours about Rais' camp are true.

Charmion looked up from a parchment, its text outlining amendments to the privileges afforded retired senators, a debate Thaly had long since grown tired of.

The Sella frowned, then wheezed an exaggerated sigh. "Alright. If it can't possibly wait."

Photina called into the foyer, and Demetria appeared at the doorway, still dressed in her Volatal Vexil flight clothes, covered in red dust and looking exhausted. Thaly welcomed the wind-rider's return because it meant Saskia had also returned, unless Thaly's sister had gotten herself into more trouble. Photina led Demetria to a lectern in the centre of a staircase where conventus guests could present reports. Demetria stood there, hands clasped at the front of her waist, while Photina returned to her orator seat in the zōdiakos' inner circle.

Charmion tapped her malleus on the pony-sized shell beside her plush red chair. "Order. *Or-der*. The Sella recognises Demetria of...of...what faction are you, Dear?"

"Pisce," said Demetria.

"Pisce, of course, I should have guessed. Let's have your report."

Demetria nodded and took a deep breath. "We've discovered Qaysar Rais' camp."

A handful of senators gasped, the rumour evidently not reaching them yet.

"Where?!" cried a senator.

Charmion winched her chair around to face the disruptor. "Order, please. I will not tolerate any more interruptions to these reports. The next senator to speak out of turn will be expelled." She turned her seat to face Demetria again. "Please continue, Demetria of Pisce."

"Thank you, Sella. We located Rais' camp in the eastern region of Magna Avium at Morchulus Waterhole. He's gathered a formidable force of thousands of fighters."

"He's going to attack!" yelled a senator from the Leo faction.

"Senator Arianus," said Charmion, "you are expelled from the conventus for seven days." The Sella nodded to an anitor who trotted down the steps and waited for the expelled senator to join her before being led from the zōdiakos.

"Continue, Demetria," said Charmion.

"We mapped a further twenty-four Pordillo positions, many closer to Portum than previously recorded. It appears the Pordillo are indeed preparing to attack Portum. I can offer no other explanation for it."

Melitta spun in her chair and smiled at Demetria with a smugness that made Thaly's skin crawl. The orator didn't need to assassinate Charmion to fulfil Malphas' ambition. The threat of Qaysar Rais was enough for the Germalians to keep their army in Portum. Melitta would escape prosecution, Chloe would be convicted at the trial, spending yarles in the carcer, and Senator Athalee Stansfield would fade into insignificance, nothing more than a memory shared by the few who cared for her.

But, at the point when Thaly's despair had almost overwhelmed her, Demetria asked permission to present further information, and Charmion granted her request.

"There's something else," said Demetria. "We rescued prisoners from Rais' camp and have brought them to Portum. One is a traveller. He carries the eyes of lost souls."

Thaly's mouth dropped open. She hadn't seen the dark eyes since Tom placed them into the eye sockets of the horned wolf crowning the dead throne, releasing a torrent of chaos. She wondered who in Portum understood their power or danger.

"Did he show you the eyes?" asked Charmion.

Demetria nodded. "Yes. But there's something else...."

The usually combative chamber stilled to deathly silence as Demetria paused to collect her thoughts.

"Proceed," said Charmion.

"The traveller claims he can destroy the throne of the dead and annul Malphas' immortality. He seeks our help."

The question bubbled inside Thaly like a pool of hot lava, threatening to burst from her open mouth. She had to ask. She couldn't wait for permission. Damn the expulsion.

"What is his name?" asked Thaly.

"Order!" yelled Charmion. "Senator Stansfield, you are expelled...."

Thaly stood and screamed at Demetria, "What is his name!?"

"Tom Anderson," said Demetria. "His name is Tom Anderson."

Thaly didn't wait for the anitor to arrive to escort her from the zōdiakos, pushing her way past other seated senators until she reached the staircase. She sprinted up the stairs, through the doorway and into the foyer.

Saskia stood there, smiling. "That didn't take long."

"Where is he?" asked Thaly.

"Lovely to see you, too, Sis. I'm fine, thanks. Yes, we had a successful mission...."

"Yes, yes." Thaly hugged her sister. "I'm glad you're back safe. Is it really him?"

"Seems to be."

"Where is he? Why did he return?"

"You better ask him yourself. He's outside, waiting on the steps."

Thaly followed Saskia through the Pallaxium's front doors and into the burning sun. At the bottom of the steps, under the shade of a zylium tree, sat a slight, unassuming man with pale, sunburnt skin and a balding crown. Thaly wrapped her hand around the handkerchief tied to her wrist, the tatty white fabric given to her by Tom yarles ago to bandage a wound.

The man stood and faced her, and she caught her breath. He was older, of course. More *worn out*. But it was Tom Anderson. Without a doubt, it was Tom. He'd returned to Ostamp, and Thaly knew her world would never be the same again.

*   *   *   *

Thaly? wondered Tom.

Dressed in emerald robes that draped along her arms like curtains and swept down to brush her sandalled feet, a woman stood at the top of the stairs leading to the imposing building with the golden dome. She had olive skin and dark hair, like the young warrior Tom remembered, but this older woman carried herself with a stately elegance he didn't associate with Thaly. Then he noticed the strip of white cotton tied to her wrist. His handkerchief. She'd kept it after all these yarles.

Tom wept as he stumbled up the steps while she walked down. They met halfway. He mumbled her name, "Thaly," then averted his gaze, culpability dragging his eyes to the ground. Culpability, fear, sadness, relief, joy. His heart couldn't cope with all the emotions pulsing through his body. Thaly placed a finger under his chin and lifted his face. Then she smiled and pulled him into a hug.

Tom stammered and blubbered, "I'm so sorry. I'm so sorry I abandoned you. I'm so...." His legs buckled under him.

Thaly held him up. Stopped him from falling over. Gave him the strength to stand on his own two feet.

"Now you've returned," she said.

Tom whispered into Thaly's ear, "I came back to finish it. To finish Malphas."

She held him at arms-length, her hands resting on his shoulders. "Still full of surprises, Tom Anderson. You have to tell me everything."

Saskia joined Thaly and Tom, and they returned to the shade where Rosalie sat waiting. Tom introduced Thaly to Rosalie, then recounted the tale of their adventures and his plan to topple Malphas.

While he spoke, another woman with dark skin, dressed in the same green robes as Thaly, approached them.

"*Et alto es ummus?*" said the woman.

"He only speaks Erstürmen," said Thaly.

The woman nodded and smiled at Tom. "I am Zenais Orelus, orator for the Capri faction and Praefecti of the Germalian Classem. Please, show me your hands."

Tom looked to Thaly for guidance.

"We don't have much time," said Zenais.

Tom unfurled his fingers to expose the scars on his palms.

"And the eyes of lost souls," said Zenais.

Thaly nodded at Tom. Rosalie stood beside him, her body tense and face set in grim defence. He retrieved the dark eyes from the pocket of the cotton trousers Saskia had found him, then offered them to Zenais.

"I don't wish to hold them," she said. "I seek only confirmation you are who you claim to be. Apparently, you have a plan to shatter Volerdie's throne?"

"Yes," said Tom. "But I need the Germalian army to breach Pergamos' walls. We can't reach the throne without your help."

"I'll do everything in my power to ensure you have it," said Zenais before turning to Thaly. "The moons have aligned, Athalee. We must act quickly."

"What are you talking about?" asked Thaly.

"Charmion has adjourned the conventus, but she's called a meeting of orators in her chamber at twelve lumina. At the meeting, we must confront Melitta and reveal how far Malphas has infiltrated Portum. Where is the draughoul?"

"Wait," said Thaly. "How do you know...."

Zenais grabbed Thaly's wrist, smothering Tom's handkerchief. "I watch my senators closely." She faced Tom. "Draughouls are slaves to the dark eyes, true? They'll do anything to be close to them. *Hold* them."

"Well...yes," said Tom. "But...what's going on?"

"Where is Heron?" asked Zenais.

"Hiding," said Thaly.

Zenais released her grip. "Where?"

"In an abandoned storehouse near The Hive. He's guarding the draughoul."

"Does he still have the Infada dagger?"

Thaly nodded.

"I need the dagger and draughoul brought here. We might be able to keep Heron out of trouble."

"What are you planning?" Thaly asked Zenais.

"At twelve lumina, I'll ask an anitor to let you into the Pallaxium via the emergency exit. You, Tom, the draughoul, and the Infada dagger. Bring them all to the meeting in Charmion's chambers."

"I've been expelled from the conventus," said Thaly.

"The conventus, not the Pallaxium itself. You can still enter the foyer, access your chambers, and attend meetings. Your presence won't raise suspicion. But Tom and the draughoul must be disguised. You have less than five hours to arrange everything. At twelve lumina, we reveal all. Do you understand?"

Thaly nodded, but her face paled with confusion or terror. Zenais turned on her heel and marched back up the stairs.

"What's happening, Thaly?" asked Tom.

"Melitta, a conventus orator, is helping Malphas. I've been trying to expose her treachery. This might be our last chance to convince the conventus of Malphas' power." Thaly pulled Tom away and whispered to him, "Do you trust Rosalie?"

"Yes," said Tom. "She's a rebel fighting against Malphas in Enthilen."

Thaly fished inside her robes and withdrew coin. "Take this. Buy women's clothes, enough for you and the draughoul. Long dresses, face scarves, headwear, anything to mask your appearance. Saskia and Rosalie can buy them for you. When the clocktower chimes eleven lumina, come to the north side of the Pallaxium, ground floor. There's a door painted red. Wait for me there."

"Clocktower? What's a *lumina*?"

"Saskia can explain. At eleven chimes, come to the Pallaxium."

Tom reached for Thaly's hand. "This is all happening so fast. I feel like a twig rushing down a stream."

"I trust you," said Thaly. She hugged Tom again, then left, racing down the street and into the crowd.

Tom returned to Rosalie and Saskia.

"What's going on?" asked Rosalie.

"We have to buy women's clothes. I need a disguise."

"Easy," said Saskia. "I know all the best merchants."

Tom didn't absorb any of Saskia's confidence. He'd been swept up in something he didn't completely understand. He wanted to speak with the conventus, but not like this.

* * * *

The Hive clocktower rang eleven lumina as Thaly climbed the stairs to the Pallaxium's red door marking the location of the emergency exit. Jurelle followed her, leading the draughoul, its wrists bound and connected to the end of a chain. At the top of the stairs, Tom waited with Saskia and his friend, Rosalie. He'd dressed as a woman in a long-sleeved gown with a hem down to his knees. A straw hat covered his balding crown, the lower half of his face wrapped in a headscarf, but he still resembled a man. Men couldn't enter the Pallaxium without conventus approval. Thaly had to get Tom and the draughoul into Charmion's office without raising the suspicion of the guards inside the foyer. Otherwise, they'd all be expelled or incarcerated. Once inside the Sella's chambers, she only had to worry about the consequences of disrupting a private meeting by exposing all the conventus orators to the pleadings of a strange man and the menace of a draughoul.

What might the Senatorial Dictum say about senators who threaten orators with draughouls? wondered Thaly. At least I'll see Chloe again when I'm imprisoned in the carcer.

As she reached Tom at the top of the stairs, the draughoul wailed behind her.

"The eyes. He carries my lost soul. Show me the eyes. *Pleeeassse.*"

"Quiet," hissed Jurelle, yanking on the chain. "You'll get your wish if you do what we say." He reached into his pocket, bunched a piece of cloth in his fist and shoved it into the draughoul's mouth, stifling the moans.

"You make a handsome Germalian woman," Thaly said to Tom, smirking.

"We both know that isn't true," said Tom.

"We only have to fool them for a short time."

Tom glanced at Jurelle, then stepped back. Rosalie stood between Tom and Thaly's father, her steely amber eyes set inside a stern face.

"What's going on?" asked Thaly.

"Didn't Pa tell you?" said Saskia. "He clobbered Tom in the griffin mounting yards. Slapped him to the ground."

Thaly glared at her father. "Why did you do that?"

Jurelle turned an abashed face away. "Lost my temper. Genevea's been harassing me about it all day."

"He blamed me for Jürgen's death," said Tom, "and for leaving you to face Malphas alone. He's right to do so. I deserve the punishment."

"No," said Thaly. "No, you don't. I can't have you feeling sorry for yourself. None of us can predict where our choices might lead."

"If Tom hadn't returned home," said Rosalie, "he wouldn't be able to destroy the dead throne now. That's right, isn't it Tom?"

He nodded. "I needed my grandmother's bone, though I didn't know it at the time."

"Maybe others *wanted* you to return to your world," said Thaly. "Those that seek the throne's destruction."

Tom retreated into silence. Thaly began to guess his thoughts until Saskia interrupted.

"What happens now?" she asked.

"We wait until twelve lumina," said Thaly. "An anitor should open the door from the inside. Then Tom, the draughoul and I will head straight for the Sella's chambers."

"Heron has been asking about you," Jurelle said to Saskia.

"I should go to him," she said. "Talk things through."

"He's in the abandoned storehouse in The Hive, near the sea falcon statue."

"I know the one." Saskia hugged Thaly. "Good luck, Sis. This'll work out. I have a feeling." She turned and trotted back down the stairs.

"What do I do?" asked Rosalie.

"Wait outside for us," said Thaly. "You can keep my cantankerous father company."

Rosalie rolled her eyes. "Great."

The group tied a gag over the draughoul's mouth, then wrapped throws of fabric around his body, fashioning makeshift robes to disguise his appearance. Thaly thought it looked ridiculous, but there was no time to find a better costume.

When the clocktower chimed twelve lumina, the red door opened. An anitor poked her head outside, looked at Thaly, then held the door open. Thaly took the chained draughoul from her father.

"Be careful," he said. "Let Zenais do the talking."

She dragged the draughoul inside.

Tom hesitated.

Rosalie pulled the cloth away from his cheek and kissed him. "Good luck," she said. "You have a compelling story to tell the conventus. They'll have to listen."

She's more than a friend, thought Thaly.

Tom followed her inside, and the anitor closed the red door behind them.

Thaly led Tom and the draughoul into the Pallaxium foyer. Every footstep on the ceramic tiled floor echoed into the vaulted ceilings, and the draughoul's moaning lament threatened to expose the infiltrators. Guards armed with cutlasses stood statuesque at the zōdiakos entrance or wandered the foyer, mingling with senators moving to or from their offices. As Thaly approached the door to Charmion's office, a guard left her post and marched towards them, resting a hand on the hilt of her cutlass. Tom tugged at Thaly's robe. She brushed him away and fixed her eyes forward. Almost upon them, the guard swished past, striding back down the corridor.

Thaly calmed her breaths as she stopped outside the frosted glass diamond embedded in the centre of the door to Charmion's chambers. She stood there, paralysed with uncertainty. The murmur of harried senators in the foyer died down. Voices from the meeting inside the chambers filtered through the glass. Thaly raised her fist to knock but held back. From behind her, Tom reached around and tapped on the glass. She glowered at him. He shrugged. The draughoul wailed louder.

The door opened, and Zenais stood there.

Thaly faced Tom, handing him the end of the chain binding the draughoul. "Wait here until I call you," she said.

Zenais led Thaly inside the chambers. Eleven orators sat on plush leather seats around an oval-shaped table, all eyes turning to Thaly as she walked through the door. Charmion wheeled her chair back away from a bookcase and glared.

"What is this?" she asked. "Senator Stansfield, you're expelled from the conventus."

"She's still able to attend private meetings," said Zenais.

"But she wasn't invited to this one," said Charmion as she wheeled to the head of the table. "Lead her out, Zenais, or I'll call the guards."

"Wait," said Thaly, stepping forward. "I have the evidence you asked for, Sella Charmion. Proof Melitta conspired with Malphas to assassinate you."

"Nonsense," snapped Melitta, flailing her arm and knocking over a goblet of vinum.

Garnet stains seeped into the fibre of parchments spread across the table, like an invading army driven to unwrite every law of their conquered land.

"Senator Stansfield must be heard," said Zenais, returning to her seat.

Murmurs filled the room as the orators turned to each other for an explanation.

Melitta stood, clutching her yellow Sagit robes at her waist. "This is preposterous. Our meeting is for orators only. You've had your chance, Athalee Stansfield, to prove your false accusations, and you failed."

Thaly withdrew the poisoned Pordillo dagger from her robes.

"She's armed," cried Photina.

"Erstürmen can't be trusted," said Sophia.

"Let her speak," said Eutropia.

"This dagger comes from Qaysar Rais' personal guard," said Thaly. "The Infada. Only twelve daggers are known to exist, the metal infused with slider serpent poison. One nick from the blade is enough to kill an elephai, let alone a frail, chair-bound Sella."

"You stole the knife during one of your missions into Magna Avium," said Melitta before facing Charmion. "Please, Sella, expel this traitor before she kills all of us."

The room fell silent as Charmion tugged rainbow-coloured robes over her lap. The Sella sipped vinum from her goblet, placed the cup back on the table and folded her hands together. "There appears to be an interesting story here," she said. "You may continue, Senator Stansfield, but make it quick."

Melitta's face flushed redder than the vinum stains on the parchments.

Thaly put the dagger on the table. Orators close to the weapon leaned away as if the poison might spring from the metal like spit from a slider serpent's mouth.

"As far as we know," said Thaly, "the Infada never leave Qaysar Rais' side, and no Germalian fighter has breached Rais' inner circle. We haven't had the opportunity to steal such a rare weapon. However, others have been welcomed into the Qaysar's inner circle. Allies from Enthilen. Servants of Malphas. One would have had the chance to steal this dagger and arrange for the most horrendous deed; assassinate the Sella of the Germalian Conventus." She pointed the dagger tip at Melitta. "This weapon was given to Melitta by a draughoul who serves Malphas. The orator is too cowardly to complete the murder herself, so she arranged for her son, Heron, to do it. He will attest to this fact."

Melitta's body shuddered, her face spasming with contortions of anger or dread. "These lies can't continue," she said. "This mutinous Dobunni rebel must be imprisoned in the carcer. She hungers for war with Malphas and will do anything to inflate his threat to Germalia. She pleads for war because she wants to rule Enthilen in Malphas' stead."

"You'll need more than a dagger to prove your story," Charmion said to Thaly.

"Tom!" called Thaly.

The door behind her opened. Tom led the chained draughoul inside. The creature yowled and gnashed, chomping the gag away from his mouth. Then he released the most hideous wail.

626

Photina jumped from her seat. "What's this? You've brought a draughoul into the Pallaxium? Into the Sella's private chambers."

"A draughoul and a *man*," said Charmion. "His disguise fools no-one. Men are forbidden to enter the halls of power. Men and these...creatures." She pointed a trembling finger at the draughoul.

"Guards!" yelled Photina.

"This is an abomination," said Melitta.

Thaly faced the draughoul. "Tell us who you are," she said in Erstürmen.

Guards arrived at the door. Zenais and Eutropia stood together, pulled cutlasses from under their robes, then marched to the door, blocking the guards' path.

"Is this a coup?" asked Charmion, her aging face wrinkled with panic.

"Order the guards to stand down," said Zenais. "There's more to the story, and it must be heard."

Charmion waited, her eyes flitting between Tom, the draughoul, and the Infada dagger. Then she mumbled at the guards, "Stand down."

The draughoul pawed at Tom, pleading in Erstürmen, "Keep your promise."

Tom reached inside his dress, withdrew a dark eye, then held it in his palm to show the orators. The draughoul whimpered.

"What black magic is this?" asked Melitta.

"It's one of the eyes of lost souls," said Zenais. "From the throne of the dead."

"I have both of them," said Tom in Erstürmen, handing the eye to the draughoul.

The creature cradled it in his hands, confined by the chain binding his wrists together, and rubbed a finger over the smooth obsidian like a child would pet a kitten.

"My soul," said the draughoul. "My soul dances among the flame."

"Tell them what you know," said Thaly. "All here understand Erstürmen."

"Both eyes," said the draughoul. "I want to hold both."

"I'll grant your wish," said Tom, "after you've confessed."

"Now," snarled the draughoul, turning a gruesome face on Tom. "I want them *now*."

"Confession first," said Tom.

The draughoul screamed. He dropped the eye, yanked the end of the chain from Tom's hand and rushed at Charmion, thrusting his arms over her head and bringing his bound hands down to the front of her neck. It all happened so fast; Thaly had time only to reach for her waist before realising she should have grabbed the Infada dagger. The draughoul snapped his arms back, and Charmion choked, her bulging eyes pleading for deliverance.

Zenais rushed from the door and swung her cutlass down, severing the draughoul's arm at the shoulder. He retreated into the corner as Charmion fought to regain her breath.

The draughoul scowled at Melitta. "You should have killed the woman in the wheeled chair. Master demanded it. Now we have failed, Master will punish us."

"Who is your master?" asked Zenais, pinning the draughoul with the tip of her cutlass.

"*Mal-phas*," he cried. "Malphas is everyone's master."

Thaly picked up the Pordillo weapon. "You wanted Melitta to kill the Sella with this dagger, didn't you?"

"Yes," said the draughoul. "Yes, yes, *YESSSSS!* Kill and keep the army here. Away from Master."

"No!" cried Melitta. "I've never seen that dagger before. I've never met this creature."

"Lies," said Eutropia. "All lies."

Charmion regained her composure, wiping blood from her neck where Zenais' cutlass had nicked her skin. "Orator Melitta Mendax of Sagit, I charge you with conspiracy to murder. You are to be incarcerated until being tried in front of your peers." She called to the guards still standing in the doorway. "Take her away."

The guards entered the room and pulled Melitta from her seat.

"This is a Dobunni plot," shrieked Melitta. "An Erstürmen plot.

Stansfield wants to rule Enthilen. Remember, it was Athalee's father, Jurelle Stansfield, who fought against us in the Riverlands War. Unhand me! Heron was going to kill Charmion. I had nothing to do with it. Heron lit...."

But her voice faded as the guards dragged her into the Pallaxium foyer.

Tom gathered the dark eye from the floor, and Thaly took the Infada dagger from the table lest someone poison themselves with it.

"This man is Tom Anderson," she said. "A traveller from another world who comes to Portum with a plan to finish Malphas. But he needs our help."

"What is this plan?" asked Charmion.

"Let him speak tomorrow," said Zenais, still keeping the draughoul trapped in the corner. "Let him speak in front of the entire conventus."

"It has been many yarles since a man presented to the conventus," said Charmion. "Only in extreme circumstances can...."

"Tomorrow," said Zenais. "Tom Anderson speaks tomorrow, or the Capri, Arie and Gemi factions will demand a vote for a new Sella."

Charmion's mouth twisted in confused anger, but she said nothing. Thaly expected Zenais would get her way. Capri's orator made a habit of it. Tom would speak tomorrow, and Thaly would have to school him, so his only chance at swaying the conventus wasn't lost in a jumble of confused ideas.

* * * *

"More vinum, Tom?"

"No, thank you, Genevea."

"How's your face? It doesn't look bruised."

"It's fine."

"My husband isn't as strong as he used to be. More cantankerous, but not as strong."

"Rosalie?" asked Genevea, holding a clay jug towards her.

"A little more," said Rosalie.

"I can't believe Saskia rescued you," said Genevea.

"It was Demetria and Berenice," said Saskia. "They saved Tom and Rosalie from the Pordillo, then Tom and I went back for...." Saskia looked at Tom.

"Quenan," he said. "Quenan weald-grell. We couldn't save her."

Hunger trumped Tom's guilt over Quenan's death. He plucked a flatbread from the dining table in the Stansfield apartment and spooned on a dollop of yellow mash, sniffing the food before placing it in his mouth.

"Sweetuba," said Genevea.

"Sorry?" said Tom.

"What you're eating. It's sweetuba from an island off the Germalian coast."

"Have you seen Grin, Tom?" asked Thaly.

He stopped chewing, thinking about the best way to announce bad news.

"Grin's dead," said Rosalie, with a bluntness that hurt Tom as much as he knew it would hurt Thaly. "It wasn't Tom's fault," continued Rosalie. "Grin died when he travelled to...to Tom's world." She faced Tom.

"Yes," mumbled Tom. "I buried him there."

"Oh," said Thaly.

Her eyes glistened without tears, and Tom wondered what thoughts she battled. Thaly and Grin had grown close when they'd been shipwrecked together, and something happened on the *Vulking* to both of them that neither would talk about. Something awful and frightful, forging a bond of suffering.

"Why did he travel to Earth?" asked Thaly.

"He brought the dark eyes and Dwarrow's message," said Tom, "and begged me to return to Enthilen."

"*Hmph*," said Jurelle. "Another sacrifice made for the mysterious Tom Anderson." He grasped the clay jug and poured himself a goblet of red vinum.

Genevea frowned at her husband. "Hush." She smiled at Tom. "Ignore him."

"There's nothing mysterious about Tom," said Rosalie. "He's trying to save our homeland." She glared at Jurelle. "The one *you* abandoned."

"I don't want to fight you, General Jurelle," said Tom. "I'm sorry for what I said."

"What did you say?" asked Thaly.

"Tom called Pa the Traitor General," said Saskia.

"Oh, is that all," said Thaly. "I used to call him that all the time. Remember, Tom, when we saw him leading those Erstürmen soldiers to fight the poor farmers in the Riverlands War? I vowed to strike him down then and there. Ironically, the fabled General's army was defeated by the women he now pledges allegiance to."

"I'm sitting right here," said Jurelle.

Thaly placed her hand on her father's wrist. "And you've atoned for your mistakes."

"I want to do the same," said Tom.

"You will," said Thaly. "Don't blame yourself for Grin's death. You can't carry another burden of injustice. Grin wouldn't have sacrificed his life if he didn't believe in you."

"We all believe in Tom," said Rosalie, her body stiffening as if she perceived a threat.

"When will they release Chloe?" asked Genevea.

"Tomorrow morning," said Thaly, "once they complete the paperwork. Now we have proof Melitta plotted to murder the Sella, Chloe is free to go."

"It will be so wonderful to see her again. What about young Heron?"

"He's co-operating with the vigilum," said Saskia.

"Don't worry, Sis," said Thaly. "I'll do my best to keep him out of the carcer."

"One thing I know for certain," said Genevea, "is that Thaly is as stubborn as her father. If she wants to fix something, she won't let it go until it's fixed."

"I hope she can convince the conventus to vote for war with Malphas," said Tom.

"Once you've told them your plan," said Thaly, "they won't have another choice."

"How will you destroy the dead throne?" asked Jurelle.

"My blood mixed with King Adalwolf's," said Tom. "And bone dust from our draughoul kin, all have to be splashed onto the throne together."

Jurelle scoffed. "Adalwolf's long dead."

Thaly rolled her eyes. "He can't be. If Tom's alive, so is Adalwolf. I've explained all this to you before, Pa. Don't you listen?"

"*Yes*, but Malphas is immortal. Breaking the throne won't change that."

"Widukind thinks it will," said Tom. "He believes all immortals will become mortal again once Volerdie's seat of power is crushed."

Jurelle raised his eyebrows. "Widukind? Oldaric's brother still lives?"

"He's also an immortal."

"So, he'll become mortal when the throne is destroyed?"

Tom nodded.

"Then he also has a stake in what happens to Volerdie's throne," said Jurelle.

Tom didn't reveal his thoughts about Widukind's motivations. After dinner, he escaped to the balcony to quell a growing anxiety. Never understanding why, socialising in small groups inflamed his vulnerability. With everyone's eyes on him, he worried about saying or doing something stupid. A worry that had plagued him for most of his adult life.

In the warm, clear night, Portum shone, a glowing oasis wedged between the desert and the ocean. Flickering lights stretched along the coast as houses elbowed each other for a sea view and an unobstructed coastal breeze. Lanterns hung from the front door of every building and sat atop pedestals lining the paved streets so residents could navigate through the darkness. The city bustled more at night than the day, a legacy, it seemed, of the constant heat. Residents wandered along pavements, shopped at open-air markets, sat outside eateries or milled around street performers.

"It's a beautiful city." Jurelle stood beside Tom and leaned on the balcony railing.

Tom tensed. "I'm not fond of cities, but this one *is* pretty."

"After yarles trapped in Sardis' inner circle, I'll take any view."

"Where are...." Tom started.

"Women's business," said Jurelle. "Happens a lot in this place. You know, I don't have a single male friend. Most men resent me because I get privileges they don't."

"Do you miss Enthilen?"

"I miss what it was. We had a coastal farm at Sand Bēċe, south of Laodicea. Ma, Pa, four girls and four boys."

"That's a big family."

"Our neighbours had twelve children. Some died, of course. Famine, disease, war."

"Where are your brothers and sisters now?"

"Two died from disease before seeing six harvest seasons. My eldest sister, two remaining brothers, and I joined the Dobunni rebels after celebrating my eighteenth harvest season. All three were killed by the Erstürmen. Two sisters remained on the farm until my parents died. I don't know what happened to them."

"Is it true your ancestors were Dobunni royalty?"

Jurelle nodded. "The Germalians reminded me of a heritage my parents never talked about. Dobunni kings and queens reigned a long time ago. We grew out of that." He clutched the railing. "Look...*ah*...I apologise for my temper. I shouldn't have hit you. Thaly said you had no choice but to leave Enthilen. And Jürgen died protecting his princess, not you."

"Guilt punishes me more than you ever could," said Tom.

"My daughters have atoned for my mistakes. I'm proud of what they've become."

"I sometimes wonder if my father was ever proud of me."

"Why wouldn't he be?"

"He never said, and I did nothing to warrant it."

"I refuse to believe it. From what Thaly has told me, you've done many things to make a father proud, and you hold the key to free those trapped under Malphas' spell. If you succeed, all of Enthilen will be in your debt."

"And if I fail?"

"Don't think about it. Focus only on what you can control."

Focus on the now, thought Tom.

"Here you are," said Thaly as she stepped onto the balcony.

Jurelle pushed away from the railing and yawned. "It's time for me to retire. I'll see you both in the morning. Good eve." He excused himself, leaving Tom and Thaly alone.

"Where's Rosalie?" asked Tom.

"She, Genevea and Saskia are reminiscing about Sardis," said Thaly, craning her face to the night sky. "It's so warm and clear tonight. Look at all those stars."

Tom took Thaly's lead, losing himself in the infinity of the cosmos. "Somewhere out there is Earth. A long way away."

Thaly untied the white handkerchief from around her wrist and held it towards him. He remembered his grandmother stitching his initials into the fabric's corner. His mother handing it to him when he left Earth for the first time. Him giving it to Thaly on the *Vulking's* deck to bandage her wound.

Tom took the handkerchief and rubbed his fingers over the frayed cotton. "It's falling apart, but I want you to keep it," he said, handing it back.

She nodded and re-tied the fabric around her wrist.

"This is strange, Thaly. Us, here like this. So much has changed since I met you in Süden Forst. Now you're a Senator. Leader of the wind-riders. Jacob would be proud."

Thaly smiled. "I'm not made for politics, but they let me fly griffins, so I don't complain too loudly." She faced him. "What was Grin like? At the end?"

"Malphas almost turned him into the next white grell. But the old Grin was still there. Still in love with nature."

"I can't imagine the courage it took to resist Malphas. What about Dwarrow and Caeli?"

"Dwarrow is travelling to Giigal with Grin's sister, Hanni, to beg the weald-grells to fight Malphas. Caeli is a draughoul. If the Germalians march east, she will lead the army under the Desolate Mountains." Tom grasped Thaly's hand. "Will they march?"

"They might not even hold a vote. It depends on how convincing you are."

"I'm terrified of speaking in front of hundreds of senators."

Thaly laughed. "I know how you feel. I'd rather face a ravaging horde of barbarians."

"Will you go with the army?"

"Zenais and Eutropia want me to lead it."

"You're the perfect choice."

"When I came here, I thought I left Enthilen and my old life behind. Part of me doesn't want to go back."

"It's your home." Tom lifted the hem of his shirt to expose the pledge scars on his chest. "We pledged allegiance to the Dobunni rebels, you and I. We pledged to honour the companionship and fight the Erstürmen. To fight anyone who threatens peace in Enthilen. I'm going to honour that pledge. Jacob would have honoured the pledge."

"Bagendon is gone," said Thaly. "The wind carried its ash away. My old family disappeared with it."

"No," said Tom. "Emelin is alive. She's with the rebels in the Desolate Mountains."

Thaly staggered, clutching the balcony rail for support. "She's *alive*? Dayna?"

Tom placed a comforting hand in the middle of Thaly's back. "Dayna didn't make it. Few did. Yet, the mouldewerps saved Emelin. She longs for your return."

"Even after she told me about my birth parents, I wanted Emelin as a mother. Emelin, Thane and Dayna were the only family I knew. The only family I loved. Then Jurelle came for me, and everything changed. But the thing I ran away from, confronting the pillage of my homeland, has followed me here. It seems I can't escape the past until Malphas is defeated."

"Then we will defeat him," said Tom, trying to gain strength from his convictions. The worry of failure began to fade like a star at dawn.

After arriving in Portum, the momentum of his journey turned. Now, it had become a raging fire, sweeping across the plains, bearing down on Pergamos' walls. Yet, a hesitation threatened to douse the flames.

Thaly leaned across and pecked him on the cheek before bidding him goodnight. She left the balcony, crossing paths with Rosalie.

"Oh, that meal," said Rosalie to Tom. "Best I've had in yarles. Almost makes walking across the desert worth it." She wrapped her arm around his waist, but he pulled away.

"What's wrong?" she asked.

"We should tell Thaly about the Pordillo and Erstürmen plan to attack Portum."

Rosalie closed the balcony door and whispered, "Don't be a fool. If the conventus finds out, there's no chance they'll send their army to Enthilen."

"Thaly would keep the secret."

"Would she? Wouldn't her duty as a senator demand she raise the alarm? And her family are here. Her lover. What point would there be in telling her, only to ask that she tells no-one else?"

Tom turned from Rosalie and sought comfort and certainty in the stars.

She put her arm around his waist again and pulled him close. "Think of the greater good. The Pordillo and Erstürmen might raze Portum; they might not. The Germalians won't leave the city undefended, and if we don't defeat Malphas, he'll come for them anyway, with a much larger army."

She's right. Tom knew it. He smiled for her. "This is the first time we've been alone since the Dambay Plains."

She smiled back. "Do you want sex?"

"No. Well, yes, but...*ah*...I'm not sure what this is. You and me."

"What do you want it to be?"

"More than sex, if that's what you want. I don't know how things work in Ostamp."

"Yours worked alright," said Rosalie, grabbing Tom's groin. "After a bit of practice."

Tom squirmed from her grip. "I mean, *relationships*. How do they work here?"

Rosalie leaned on the balcony railing. "I've had only two. The one with Raf was a relationship of circumstance and convenience. I thought I loved Harris Snape, but I'm not sure now. There was nothing worth mentioning in between."

"I've had two failed relationships," said Tom. "In the first, I was young and inexperienced. She was older. I didn't know what I wanted from life and decided it wasn't fair that I couldn't offer her a stable future. So, I ended it."

"And the second?"

"A mirror image of the first. She ended it. Strange, it took me much longer to get over the first relationship than the second, even though I thought I was still in love."

"What are you looking for now?"

"It's hard to find time to fall in love when every day is about fighting for survival."

"These are the days when love is needed more than ever."

Tom held Rosalie's eyes, not letting them drift away as they sometimes did. She smiled, leaned forward and kissed him on the lips. Tom kissed back.

She pulled away. "I'm learning to trust you, Tom, but it will take time. Harris kept secrets from me. Had pledge scars on his chest like yours but didn't tell me he was a Dobunni rebel. And he asked me to make keys that were used in a Dobunni plot."

"Those keys saved my life," said Tom. "The rebels used them to unlock their chains before entering Sardis' inner circle. Harris and Ryder fought off the Erstürmen guards while I escaped from the needle."

"Then this friendship of ours must be fate." Rosalie leaned in and kissed Tom again, locking his lips in a gentle, longing embrace.

Tom leaned back. "I don't know what the future holds. If we destroy the throne, Adalwolf and I might die alongside it."

"Hush," whispered Rosalie. "You worry too much. Has anybody told you that before?"

Tom laughed. "Just about everyone."

*   *   *   *

The clocktower rang three lumina. Tom and Rosalie stood at the bottom of the steps outside the Pallaxium's front doors, the entrance arch tall enough for a stone-grell to walk through without ducking. Soldiers wearing golden armour that reminded Tom of fish scales guarded the doors as senators strode into the building, a hot wind dishevelling robes of red, blue, yellow, green or another colour Tom failed to name easily. Nothing had been finalised, but he hoped to speak with the senators today, convincing them to start a war.

Thaly had schooled Tom on what to expect, but it didn't still the nerves churning his insides so much he expected to vomit on the Pallaxium steps at any moment.

End of presentation, thought Tom. '*Thank you, Mr Anderson, but we can't have someone spewing globs of sweetuba and oats all over our nice clean steps. Scuttle back to Enthilen. Give Malphas our regards.*'

The Pallaxium's towering golden dome cast a shadow over Tom, accentuating his insignificance. A drifter from a faraway land come to tell a story in a hall of unimaginable power. It had been a long time since a male presented to the conventus. Yarles, apparently. And a man from another world? Well, likely never.

But the story isn't insignificant, and it's all I've got.

"I'm so nervous," he said.

Rosalie clutched his hand. "You'll be fine."

"Everything rests on this moment. Everything."

"I know you'll do your best. It's all anyone can ask." She kissed him on the cheek.

"I think I'm falling...." started Tom, but Rosalie placed a finger on his lips.

"Not now. This is your moment, and whatever happens, the future will be ours."

The Pallaxium doors opened. Thaly appeared and trotted down the stairs.

"They're ready for you," she said. "I can take you into the foyer, but I can't enter the zōdiakos. That's the room where you'll present to the senators."

"I'll have to do it alone?" asked Tom.

"I'm still expelled from the conventus, but Zenais will guide you."

Rosalie squeezed Tom's hand. "When you're done, come find me in the griffin barn. I promised Saskia I'd help groom Namu."

Rosalie walked away, and Tom followed Thaly up the stairs. With each step, he recalled a moment that brought him here. He thought of all those who'd given their life to change Enthilen's future for the better. His grandmother, Jean Anderson. His loyal friend, Grin. The Dobunni warrior, Jacob Seamaster. Grin's father, Frennan. The grells and mouldewerps killed in the massacre of Malang Gunya. Harris, Ryder, Dayna and the rebels of Bagendon. The Dobunni slaughtered in the barbarian invasion of Laodicea. Princess Caeli forfeiting her soul. Many sacrifices had been made, and so far, all for nothing. But now, Tom Anderson could change that. If he seized this moment, he could change everything.

Thaly led him through the colossal doors and into the Pallaxium foyer. During his visit to Charmion's chambers, he'd been too frightened to appreciate the majesty of this place. The granite flagstones on the floor, each one larger than a dining table. The gold-flecked cornices decorating the ceiling. Gemstones of every colour embedded in the capitals of towering, fluted columns, sunlight streaming through skylights casting rainbows across marble statues of women dressed in flowing robes. Dozens of tapestries and paintings masking sandstone walls. Clear glass windows forming atriums planted with emerald green vines and cooled with water fountains. Walnut, hickory, tawny and caramel timber, carved into shapes of exotic animals and perched on pedestals.

Amid the opulence, the foyer was empty other than a woman with dark skin, long black hair and round cheeks holding open a door to another room.

Thaly approached the woman, kissed her lips, and then faced Tom.

"This is my lufu, Chloe," said Thaly in Erstürmen. "This is Tom."

"*Ah,*" smiled Chloe. "You're the owner of the famous white handkerchief Thaly refuses to take from her wrist."

"Yes," said Tom.

"You've caused a stir by all accounts. I've never seen the conventus so abuzz with anticipation. Everyone's inside waiting."

"You should be home, resting," said Thaly.

"And miss the most important day I can ever remember?" said Chloe. "Not likely. I had plenty of sleep in the carcer. Nothing else to do." She laughed with a light-heartedness that calmed Tom's nerves.

"I hope I don't make a fool of myself," he said.

"Put aside your self-doubt," said Thaly.

Zenais stepped from the zōdiakos. "Tom. It's time."

The few drops of saliva in Tom's mouth dried up, and a swollen tongue pressed against the back of his front teeth. Thaly embraced him. His moment had come. He hugged her back, then marched towards Zenais' reassuring smile, following her into the zōdiakos. The room went silent as he entered, hundreds of faces turning on him as one. His heart dropped to his stomach like a block of ice and froze him in place. Zenais tugged on the sleeve of the clean, crisp, ballooning white shirt he'd borrowed from Jurelle, guiding him to a lectern within a timber-panelled chamber resembling a witness box in a courtroom. Tom stepped into the box and stood at the lectern.

"Wait until the Sella recognises you," said Zenais before walking down a flight of stairs and taking her seat at the front of a wedge of senators all dressed in green.

Tom counted twelve wedges of colour comprising the circular meeting room of the zōdiakos, each wedge with twenty-four female senators dressed in the robes of their faction. At the centre of it all, at the bottom of the steps, sat the shrunken figure of Charmion, the Sella, on a plush red chair with golden studs. She used a handle at the side of the chair to spin it around, checking the reflection of senators in the convex mirror suspended above her head.

A panic of conspicuousness overcame Tom as Charmion swivelled her chair around to face him before tapping a wooden hammer on a giant shell beside the chair.

"Order," she called in Erstürmen. "The time has come to hear from our *invited* guest." She glanced at Zenais, failing to mask her annoyance, then returned her gaze to Tom. "A man, not from this world. Never before has someone claiming to be from another world been granted an audience with the Germalian Conventus. I presume you've been familiarised with the protocol of these meetings?"

Tom nodded.

"Good. Then, the Sella recognises Tom Anderson."

Tom reached into the pocket of his navy-blue pants, another donation from Jurelle's wardrobe, and withdrew the foil packet of anxiety medication. He rubbed the last sealed section between the tips of his index finger and thumb.

One tablet left.

With a deep sigh, he crushed the foil and tossed it on the seat behind him.

"I'm sorry, I don't know Germalian," muttered Tom.

"Speak up," said Charmion.

Tom swallowed the last drop of saliva in a mouth drier than Groz Wüste, then started to count each senator in the chamber.

Stop it, he thought, digging fingernails into his thigh. *Don't let your friends down.*

"Well?" said Charmion.

"I am a naevus," said Tom. "One who has been marked by the Divine Creator himself, if you believe that sort of thing. My birth twin is King Adalwolf Heine. Well, he *was* king before Malphas claimed Enthilen's throne. At Malphas' command, Adalwolf tried to steal my soul with these." Tom pulled the dark eyes from his pocket and held them aloft in his left hand. The senators sitting nearby gasped.

Charmion interrupted, "For those senators seated further away, let it be known that Tom Anderson carries the eyes of lost souls. One of the seven treasures belonging to Volerdie's throne. Some may consider the eyes a curse, not a treasure."

Yes, a curse. Nevertheless, Tom pictured birth-marked senators salivating at the chance to wrench the dark eyes from his grasp and disappear from this world to begin their journey to immortality.

He returned the obsidian baubles to his pocket and continued, "The dark eyes transported me from my home, a world called *Earth*, to Ostamp. I was tricked the first time. Deceived into travelling to Ostamp after being accosted by a draughoul. Eventually, I realised someone wanted me here. Had planned for my arrival over many seasons. That person was Malphas. He brought me to Ostamp so Adalwolf could steal my soul with the dark eyes and become immortal, like Malphas. However, he lied to Adalwolf. They were never going to rule together for eternity. Malphas wanted to sacrifice an immortal Adalwolf on the throne of the dead to entice the Divine Creator back to Enthilen. Volerdie would inhabit Adalwolf's body, and through him, the Divine Creator and Malphas would rule forever.

"That threat remains while the dead throne still exists. Though Malphas failed with Adalwolf, he has another option. His brother, Widukind, is also immortal. Malphas has long sought the whereabouts of his brother, destroying the grell burial ground of Bindari to find him. But Widukind is safe for now and seeks the absent King Adalwolf."

"Why does Widukind search for the king?" asked Charmion.

"We need his blood to destroy Volerdie's throne."

Murmurs rippled through the assembly.

Tom pushed on, "Blood and bone, destroy the throne. My blood, Adalwolf's blood, and the dust of bones from two draughouls. Our kin. Widukind studied the First Scripture, written by Volerdie himself, uncovering the secret to destroying the throne, buried deep within the scripture's passages. Should we succeed, it will thwart Malphas' life-long ambition of Volerdie's return. It will crush an ancient seat of malevolent power and, I hope, open Erstürmen eyes to the false promise of a fabled paradise, setting all of Enthilen free."

A senator raised her hand.

"The Sella recognises Elowen of Leo," said Charmion.

"Will Malphas die?" Elowen asked Tom.

"I don't know," he said. "Widukind believes all immortals will become mortal again when the throne perishes."

"What is it you want from us?"

"We have what we need to shatter the throne, but it's well protected behind Pergamos' walls. Those who resist Malphas in Enthilen can't bring down the walls alone or breach his defences. We need you to do that. We need your army to march to Enthilen and open the gates of hell."

Murmurs boiled over. Tom's ears recoiled at a calamity of jumbled shouts coming from across the room. Charmion tapped the shell with her wooden hammer and called for order, but the words disappeared in the rumblings of discontent or demand. Tom's face flushed with determined anger.

"He'll come for you!" yelled Tom. "You aren't safe here, strolling through your beguiling city and filling your heads with romantic ideals. He'll infect your dreams until they decay into nightmares."

The din subsided. Tom held the room's attention again.

"I don't believe in Volerdie," he said. "Or any god. But my beliefs don't matter. What do you think will happen if the one desire that's consumed Malphas' life turns out to be a vain hope? What if he sacrifices an immortal on the dead throne, and Volerdie doesn't return? Will Malphas try again? Construct another false dream to pursue at any expense? I fear he will, further enslaving Enthilen's people until his ambition is realised. But he won't stop there. He'll chase his desire to the ends of this world. It's only a matter of time before Malphas turns his attention west to Germalia. Already he forges an alliance with the Pordillo. Already you are deep within his thoughts.

"If Giigal falls, it will be the end of wild grells forever. Imagine Ostamp, bereft of those beautiful, gracious souls. Free spirits crushed by slavery or twisted to follow a vicious leader. How can you sit back and watch that happen? Even the mouldewerps, small in stature and number but with the courage of giants, prepare to face Malphas. Will you let them do it alone? Will you sit under your golden dome, waiting until Malphas arrives on your doorstep before you face his evil? I've already waited too long. My best friend, Grinnian stone-grell, died because he believed Enthilen could be saved. Because he believed in me. I was a coward once. I ran away. Turned a blind eye. But now I'm ready to stand and fight. Now I'm ready to do whatever it takes to stop Malphas. You can help me or not. I will enter Pergamos one way or the other and smash the vile ambition of a crooked man. Only you have the power to make my path easier. To make certain we change the future."

Exhausted, Tom slumped onto the seat behind the lectern.

The conventus fell silent until Zenais raised her hand.

"The Sella recognises Zenais of Capri," said Charmion.

"Tom Anderson is right," said Zenais. "We must breach Pergamos' defences so he can destroy Volerdie's throne. The time for debate is over. The time to act is now. We must march east, with haste, and bring the might of the Germalian army down on Malphas' head."

Charmion tapped the shell with her hammer. "To declare war requires a unanimous vote of the conventus. Such a decision can't be taken lightly. We'll rise now to consider the implications of what's been revealed at this meeting. The conventus will reconvene at twelve lumina. Then, every faction must be prepared to cast their vote."

The senators disbanded. Tom stood, shuffled to the aisle, up the stairs and through the doorway into the foyer.

Thaly waited for him, wrapping her arms around his gaunt body and whispering in his ear, "I'm so proud of you."

* * * *

Dark clouds drifted in from Slyencia Bay like merchant ships carrying a cargo of doom. The afternoon light in the Pallaxium foyer turned grey, enhancing Thaly's apprehension. Zenais and Eutropia pressed in around her, using their words to poke and prod at her conscience. To remodel her desire to align with theirs.

"We need this," said Zenais. "Otherwise, the vote may fail."

"I'm not ready," said Thaly.

"Two factions want the entire army to remain in Portum," said Eutropia. "To defend against the Pordillo."

"We can do both."

"They don't see it that way," said Zenais. "If the vote fails, there can't be another for sixty days."

"Our plan will sway them," said Eutropia. "Before the vote, we'll propose that you lead our army into Enthilen to defeat Malphas."

After Genevea's warning about the senators' plan, Thaly had tried to prepare for this moment. With Tom Anderson's return, Enthilen consumed her thoughts. The tug of her chest scars recalled her pledge to the Dobunni rebels long ago. The promise to forever fight against Erstürmen tyranny. Here in Portum, she'd dismissed that commitment.

Jacob would be ashamed, thought Thaly. But she could make him proud with a single word. Yes.

"You're ready, Athalee," said Eutropia. "You command the Volatal Vexil with bravery and honour. You're a valued conventus senator and know our enemy and his dominion better than any native Germalian. You're an ally to Tom Anderson, the man who plans to destroy Volerdie's throne. You can be the lightning rod to tip the vote our way."

"If you lead us," said Zenais, "the others will follow."

Thaly bowed her head at the realisation of a dreaded ambition; to march to war.

Eutropia placed her arm around Thaly and lowered her voice, "You're our strongest hope, Athalee. Tom might have the power to crush the dead throne, but only you can bring down the walls of Pergamos."

"We need your decision before the vote at twelve lumina," said Zenais, "so we have time to secure the commitment of the undecided factions. You have less than two hours."

Zenais and Eutropia walked off, and the foyer sat empty. Chloe worked in the anitors' office, preparing the paperwork to tally the vote. Tom and Rosalie had gone to the griffin barn to help Saskia. Thaly didn't know the whereabouts of Jurelle, but she could use his counsel. She left the Pallaxium and ambled down the steps to Lata Via, the boulevard splitting the centre of Portum.

Genevea emerged from the crowd. "I've seen that worried look before, Thaly. But only on your father's face."

"Zenais and Eutropia have revealed their hand," said Thaly. "Before the conventus votes on war with Malphas, they will recommend that I lead the Germalian army."

"Will you agree?"

"I'm terrified, Ma. Why have they put their faith in me? I worry if I march to Enthilen, I'll never return. I'll never see Chloe again. Or you and Pa. Saskia."

Genevea clutched Thaly's arm, and they walked side-by-side down Lata Via.

"When your father went to battle, I would sit at the window of our quarters every day, staring into the courtyard of Sardis' inner circle, wishing I could see beyond the walls. Imagining I could watch his every move as if that would keep him safe. I often wondered what I would do if he never returned. But I kept my worry to myself. I didn't want to burden him further or infect Jürgen or Saskia with my fear. Jurelle made a pledge, and I knew he would honour it. The Dobunni called him a traitor, but he's a noble man. When he pledged fealty to King Ewald, he did it to protect his family. He did it to protect you.

"There's so much of your father in you, Athalee. You have an innate understanding of what's right, even when others can't see it. I know you want to protect what you cherish. The time has come for you to decide how. Whatever decision you make, your father and I will always respect it. We will always love you."

At twelve lumina, Thaly sat in the zōdiakos with the other Capri senators after meeting with Zenais and Eutropia to deliver her decision. On such a momentous occasion, Charmion had ordered expelled senators to return to the conventus to cast their vote. Despite brimming with nearly three hundred senators, a quiet foreboding hung in the room. Six anitors stood in the aisles, waiting to coordinate the vote. The usual blooming smile had disappeared from Chloe's face, her eyes fixed on Charmion.

Thaly wondered what thoughts drifted through her lover's head. How Chloe responded to Thaly's decision mattered more than anything.

Charmion tapped the shell, her rainbow robes bunching at the crux of her elbow.

Photina's hand shot up.

"The Sella recognises Photina of Pisce," said Charmion.

"*If* we vote for war, how will we enter Enthilen? We can't risk our army marching across Magna Avium. Attacks from Pordillo insurgents could decimate our forces before we reach the Riverlands Escarpment. And then, *then* we have to snake our way up that infernal zigzag road, single file. We'll be picked off by Krieg's soldiers one at a time. It's madness."

Thaly stood and raised her hand.

"The Sella recognises Athalee of Capri," said Charmion.

"Our ships can't carry all the troops and supplies we need to attack Malphas," said Thaly, "so we must march. But Photina is right; we can't travel across Magna Avium. Instead, we should march north, through the border town of Ephesus and into Nordland."

"Then what?" asked Photina.

"Order," snapped Charmion. "Continue, Athalee."

"Our relationship with the Nordmen is solid. They'll let us pass without trouble."

"How will the army cross the Desolate Mountains?" asked Charmion.

"Detranté is a death trap!" yelled a senator.

"Order! Please. Continue, Athalee."

"We won't march through Detranté," said Thaly. "We'll enter Enthilen via a passage *underneath* the Desolate Mountains. A path wide enough for any army. And we'll have a guide to lead us."

"Who told you this?" asked Charmion.

"A mouldewerp called Dwarrow assured Tom Anderson. The werp is an old acquaintance of mine. A friend. Our guide will be Princess Caeli Heine of Sardis."

Photina stood and glared at Thaly. "Can we trust an Erstürmen Princess? It seems the entire success of this mission relies on a ball of fur, a stranger from another world and our enemy. This is preposterous." She slumped back in her seat.

The conventus threatened to descend into disorder.

Thaly tried to stem the tide of discontent. "Caeli is now a draughoul," she said. "The soulless know all the secret paths under and above ground, and she despises Malphas. I was there when Adalwolf trapped her soul. I feel it's my duty to release her from the most awful torment. To release all souls trapped within Malphas' tempest."

She resumed her seat, the words in her head now spent.

Charmion took the malleus, preparing to tap the shell to announce the vote. "The time has come. We must cast...."

Zenais raised her hand.

Charmion sighed. "Zenais, this will be the last statement before the vote."

Zenais nodded her head in acknowledgement. "I propose that, if we vote for war, Athalee Stansfield should be appointed Legatus of the army marching to Enthilen."

Eutropia raised her hand. "I second that proposal."

Charmion sat in silent contemplation for a moment before responding. "Since Athalee's role as Legatus depends on an affirmative vote for war, I see no reason to hold two votes. Is there any faction who objects to Athalee Stansfield being appointed commander of the air *and* ground forces?"

The room fell silent. Photina looked behind her, checking the faces of her faction's senators. None raised their hand.

Charmion fixed her eyes on Thaly. "Athalee Stansfield, senator of Capri and Legatus of the Volatal Vexil, are you willing to accept this leadership responsibility?"

Thaly stood again. "Yes, I am."

"Good," said Charmion. "Then it's time to cast our vote. A simple question with momentous consequences requires serious consideration. Do we declare war on Malphas and invade Enthilen? We have debated this issue for many days. I know all of you will treat the question with the gravitas it deserves. Only through unanimous agreement from every faction can we declare war on another culture. Each orator should consult their senators, and the anitors will tally the votes. Begin."

The anitors moved about the zōdiakos, handing out strips of parchment for senators to vote. Orators consulted with their faction members. Chloe walked towards Thaly, who sat beside the aisle, and handed her a parchment. Thaly almost burst into tears, her mind stung by the thought of leaving Chloe behind. But Chloe remained impassive and professional.

"Write your vote on the parchment," she said. "Do we declare war? Yes or no."

Chloe moved to the next senator. Thaly wanted to spring from her chair and hug her lover. Promise to never leave. Instead, she took a quill from the inkwell built into the seat and scrawled a vote on the parchment.

The orators returned to their seats encircling Charmion. The anitors collected the votes, and the count began. The usual bubbling murmur of politics characteristic of the conventus failed to rise above the muted unease.

The anitors completed their task, then whispered the factional result to each orator.

Charmion tapped the seasnail shell. "I, Charmion, Sella of the Germalian Conventus, call for a vote. Do we declare war on Malphas and his followers? Yes or no? Faction Arie, what is your vote?"

Eutropia stood. "Yes."

"Faction Capri."

Zenais stood. "Yes."

"Faction Leo."

"Yes."

Charmion addressed each faction in turn. Eleven voted for war, including the Sagit faction once led by Melitta. Only one faction remained.

"Faction Pisce," said Charmion.

Photina stood. "All here know I consider this action a mistake. A folly. *Stultitia*. Yet, I must accept the will of my faction. Our vote is *Yes*."

Photina sat, the shuffle of her indigo robes the only sound to breach the hush of the meeting. There was no applause. No celebration by those who'd advocated for war. Sadness descended on the senators. A collective realisation, they were the architects of a dismal outcome. A tragedy.

Charmion cleared her throat. "Stand, Athalee Stansfield. You've been handed an immense responsibility to lead our forces in war. I can think of no heavier burden. But I believe there's no better choice for such a grave task. Tomorrow, you will prepare our army."

~ Chapter 38 ~

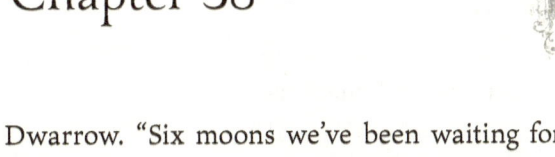

"Six moons!" cried Dwarrow. "Six moons we've been waiting for those infernal, incorrigible, confounding, stubborn, dilly-dallying weald-grell elders to come to their senses. When are they going to give us their answer? I can't wait here forever. If I have to fight Malphas myself, I will."

Hanni sat in the forest of Babir Birramal while Dwarrow paced up and down the camp they'd made outside Giigal. The weald-grells had granted Whibly, Melinda and the *Grimart* crew permission to come ashore, build lean-tos and hunt in the forest for fresh game. Only Hanni could enter Giigal, but she preferred to stay with Dwarrow and the seafarers, embracing the new friendships. Despite Dwarrow's raging temper, a coastal breeze cooled the dawn air. Gawimarra, the harvest season, waned, and guma would soon batter Enthilen with violent storms. Yet, the forest still brimmed with a bountiful harvest, and Hanni welcomed the opportunity to reconnect with her home. Long, bleak days in the Desolate Mountains had worn her down like metal grinding against stone. The tranquil, familiar landscape surrounding Giigal had renewed her determination to see this journey to its end.

"If they ain't made a decision by tomorrow," said Whibly, "I'm headin' back to Laodicea."

"Then you will not receive the remainder of your coin," said Hanni. "For I am not leaving until the elders have agreed to face Malphas."

"Ya can't do that. We had a deal. Five thousand coin now, and five thousand when I return ya to Laodicea."

"We should wait," said Melinda. "I also want t'know what them elders are gonna do."

"Someone's coming," said Dwarrow. "This might be it. Oh, I hope it is.

If it's not it...then, well...I'll be whacking some weald-grell noggin with my walking stick."

Symian, the weald-grell leader, strode into camp as Hanni climbed to her feet.

"The elders have made their decision," Symian said to Hanni. "You must come with me. I have something to show you."

"Can we all go?" asked Melinda.

"You are not grell," said Symian.

"Please. We've been waitin' so long."

"Yeah," said Whibly. "Let us come. I'm goin' stir-crazy in this forest."

"I should definitely be going," said Dwarrow. "Being a mouldewerp elder, ambassador, and pillar of this entire undertaking."

Symian rolled his turquoise eyes. "Alright. If you cease your babbling. But you must be blindfolded. Only Hanni can know the location of this place."

"Streams babble," muttered Dwarrow. "Werps utter profound enlightenment."

Symian tied strips of cloth around Dwarrow, Whibly and Melinda's eyes, either forgetting or not appreciating the navigational prowess of a werp nose. Dwarrow could find the secret location again if he wanted to, blindfolded or not.

Hanni tied a rope around her waist, handing the free end to her three blind companions. She followed Symian into the forest, Dwarrow, Whibly and Melinda stumbling behind her. They took a path unfamiliar to Hanni, despite her living here for all her childhood, weaving through a dense grove of bilawi trees, crammed together like fish in a drying lake. She slowed, trying to stop her friends from colliding with tree trunks or tripping over roots.

Shafts of mid-morning sunlight streamed through the forest canopy as Hanni climbed a wooded ridge and came to a line of saplings resembling a picket fence. The fence ran north and south, further than she could see. Symian tapped on a sapling, and a hidden gate opened. Wyan stood inside. He smiled at Hanni, then ushered them through the entrance.

"We've passed through a door," chirped Dwarrow. "I can smell it. Or a gate. Turnstile perhaps. Or another portal. My nose is seldom wrong."

They walked together until reaching a clearing, but it wasn't clear. Weald-grells stood on every blade of grass. Weald-grells painted for war.

Hanni drew a deep breath.

"What is it?" asked Dwarrow. "Something's here. I've inhaled the most paralysing confluence of grell stench ever imagined." He ripped the blindfold from his face, squinted into the sun, then opened his eyes and nostrils wider than his gaping mouth.

"Can we see?" asked Melinda.

"Yes," replied Wyan.

Melinda and Whibly removed their blindfolds.

"By Marduk's beard, Volerdie's mercy, and all the leviathans in the Veiled Occyan," said Whibly. "I never would have believed it."

A sea of weald-grell faces turned to Hanni, some younger than her, others older than her parents. The black ink of facial tattoos, countless plant and animal totems, glistened in the sunlight. Naked torsos had been painted in swirls of blue and white, reminding Hanni of the unfurling fronds of her facial crest, gama. Males and females wore skirts made from animal hide. They carried stone-tipped spears, or supple bows and ironwood arrows, with fletching made from the feathers of bibidya, the fish-hawk. But they had no war machines or armour. No horses to ride. No battering rams to break down Pergamos' gate.

While Hanni's heart first lifted at the spectacle, it now tightened in her chest at the thought of what Malphas would do to her kin.

"We have not been idle," said Wyan. "The elders have decreed for us to march on Pergamos."

"When was this decided?" asked Dwarrow.

"Four moons ago."

"Why weren't we told? We've been waiting and waiting, and all along, you've been busying yourselves...."

"Now, you know," interrupted Wyan. "This occasion is momentous and troubling. Grells have vowed never to attack, only defend. Yet, you ask us to attack Malphas. The elders' decision goes against generations of peaceful existence. It is a sad day. But I am proud we will face the evil infecting our homeland."

"I will march with you," said Hanni.

"Hang on," said Whibly. "Y'have to return to Laodicea with me."

"These are my kin. I will not forsake them."

"A deal's a deal," said Whibly, crossing his arms and scuffing his boot in the dirt.

"Wait," said Dwarrow. He fished inside a pouch, then withdrew a gold coin.

Whibly's eyes grew as wide as the moons.

Dwarrow held the coin between the claws of his thumb and forefinger. "Very, *very* rare. A gold coin with King Giltbert's image. This is the only one I've ever owned, and I will likely never own another. But for all you've done, I offer it as payment." He handed the coin to Whibly.

The captain's trembling fingers grasped the treasure, his eyes salivating at the thought of what he might purchase. "I could buy a castle with this. Two castles. Three!"

He turned it over and over in his fingers. Held it up to the sun. Showed Melinda. Then did something Hanni never expected. He gave the coin back to Dwarrow.

"I can't take it," said Whibly. "Use it to buy weapons to defeat Malphas."

"What about our deal?" asked Hanni.

"Forget it. I have enough coin. Y'should march with the weald-grells."

"You are an honourable man," Wyan said to Whibly.

"First time he's been called that," said Melinda.

"Shut it," said Whibly.

Symian stepped closer. "The elders request a favour from you, Captain Whib...."

"Captain Whibly Horsars of the *Grimart*, at your service."

Melinda burst into laughter. "Horse arse? Y'never told me...."

Whibly's face turned scarlet. "Not horse arse. *Horsars*. Hor–sars." He looked up at Symian. "Apologies for me simple-minded skullard. She's not as cosmopolitan as me."

"Captain Whibly Horsars," announced Symian, "the elders have asked if you would carry weald-grell scouts to Sand Bēċe. We wish to keep watch on Hunger's soldiers. They may flock to Pergamos once Malphas is at war. We would like forewarning of their arrival."

"Yes," said Whibly. "Happy to oblige."

At midday, the elders came down from their chamber, high in the colossal panalope tree, yurrubang. They sat in the middle of the secret clearing and offered a formal grell goodbye to every warrior by placing the tips of ancient fingers on tattooed cheeks. Then they called Hanni and her companions to an audience. Hanni was gifted a new bow, hewn from supple marrung wood, and a spear with an ancient stone blade carried by the first ancestors across Gadhang. The elders gifted Dwarrow a wooden trowel, so he may dig the hole to plant the sacred *ngayirr biyal* seed, and to Whibly and Melinda, they gave a whistle fashioned from an oyster shell that would call up another whale to replace Freckles.

The weald-grell warriors marched from the clearing, filing one by one through the narrow gate. They would travel north, through Babir Birramal and onto the Dambay Plains. Hanni and Dwarrow would march with them.

With the clearing almost empty, Hanni faced Melinda, bent down and placed the tips of her fingers on the young woman's cheeks. Melinda reciprocated.

"I remembered his name," she said.

"Who?" asked Hanni.

"The boy who followed Anni to Bindari. His name was Tom Anderson. I found him floatin' on a piece of driftwood, shipwrecked and starvin'. I saved him from the ocean."

Hanni pulled her fingers away. "Then you have saved all of us. Tom holds the key to defeating Malphas. Farewell, Melinda. May your whales forever ride the ocean waves."

Hanni faced Whibly, preparing for another formal farewell, but he brushed her aside.

"I don't need any of that," he said, shyness shrinking his twisted body away from her.

"Captain Whibly, you have redeemed yourself for what happened on the *Vulking*. Grin would tell you to hold your head high."

Whibly nodded, then reached for Hanni, wrapping his arms around her waist and pressing his head into her stomach. She hugged him back.

Whibly and Melinda left, taking with them twenty-four weald-grell scouts who would travel on the *Grimart* to Sand Bēċe and watch for Hunger and his black soldiers.

As the last weald-grell warrior disappeared into the forest, Wyan approached Hanni. "Your guardian family passed away after you left," he said. "This was among their belongings." He handed her a remembrance totem, many words etched across the green-white softstone.

Hanni cradled it in her palm as tears welled in her eyes. "This is my mother's totem."

"Then we will return it to her when Malphas has fallen."

"Come on, Hannian stone-grell," said Dwarrow. "Enough tears. You have to carry me to the Dambay Plains."

Despite the melancholy, Hanni smiled. "It is alright to carry you now? Before, you worried the weald-grells would consider it an insult."

"Well, yes, that was before. Now I've convinced them to help us; there's no turning back. I knew that precious seed would do the trick."

"You are a terrible schemer, Dwarrow."

"Oh no, I'm actually very good at it. Excellent, in fact!"

Dwarrow slung his satchel across his shoulder and grasped his walking stick. Hanni reached down and picked him up, balancing the little werp behind her neck.

"Giddy u...." started Dwarrow.

"Do not say it, Dwarrow mouldewerp," interrupted Hanni. "Do not even think it."

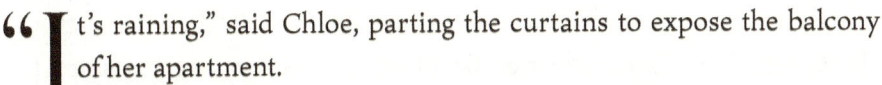

~ Chapter 39 ~

"It's raining," said Chloe, parting the curtains to expose the balcony of her apartment.

In bed, Thaly rolled onto her back. "One of Portum's famously rare rainstorms."

"Hardly a storm," said Chloe, jumping back into bed. "But a good excuse for us to stay in." She leaned over and kissed Thaly on the breast.

"You know what day it is," said Thaly.

"I know, but I don't want to know."

"After Malphas surrenders, I'm coming straight home. To you."

Chloe traced her finger across the knife scar on Thaly's side, marking the bottom edge of her ribcage. "This is from Malphas, isn't it? When he stabbed you in the throne room before Tom Anderson disappeared."

Thaly nodded and pulled the sheet over her torso.

"What if you don't return?" asked Chloe. "What if you decide Enthilen is your home after all? Or Malphas...."

"We've talked about this," interrupted Thaly, wrapping an arm around her lover.

Chloe rested her head on Thaly's chest. "The talk won't stop me from worrying."

Thaly kissed Chloe's hair, tasting a hint of lye soap perfumed with lavender. "It's no different to any other mission."

"I worry then, too. And it *is* different. Enthilen is far away, and Malphas is a much more formidable enemy than the Pordillo."

"There's nothing I can say to stop your fretting. Ma told me about all the times she pined for Pa when he went into battle. Such is the life of a soldier's lover. I'll forgo a warrior's charge one day, and we can live the rest of our days carefree."

"I can't believe it's all happened so quickly. Only three days since the vote."

Thaly also struggled to believe it, but Zenais and Eutropia hadn't been idle while the conventus argued about confronting Malphas these past seasons. The two senators had ordered military personnel to stockpile supplies, arms and materials to build war machines in preparation for a long march to Enthilen. Zenais had used her position as Praefecti of the Germalian Classem to significant effect, readying twelve ships to sail north and meet the marching army in Ephesus, Germalia's northern city. While the ground forces marched from Ephesus to the Desolate Mountains, the classem would sail across the top of Nordland, through the Nordargen Sea, around the Grauberge peninsula, and down the east coast of Enthilen, landing near Gestade.

"Why can't the ships carry all the army?" asked Chloe, as if reading Thaly's thoughts.

"Not enough space for seventy thousand soldiers and their supplies. Zenais will lead a ground force of twelve thousand. When they land, they'll march west to Pergamos."

"What about wind-riders?"

"Three will fly with the classem. Three with the army; me, Saskia and Berenice."

"Can't you take them all? Malphas won't defeat a dozen griffins."

"Half will remain here in case the Pordillo attack."

Thaly hoped eighty thousand fighters and six griffins would be enough to defeat Malphas. Charmion had demanded at least twenty thousand professional soldiers stay behind to defend Portum, in addition to five thousand reservists. The Sella refused to compromise the city's safety further.

"Enthilen's resistance fighters will help," said Chloe. "Dobunni rebels. Grells."

"There are few rebels left," said Thaly. "But yes, if the weald-grells join us, we'll have a much better chance of victory." However, if our forces splinter or fracture, she worried, Malphas could win. Division is death. "I have to get ready." She slunk away from Chloe's embrace, climbed out of bed and walked to the vestium.

After opening the door, she removed the thin woollen pants and shirt she wore under her flying leathers. They provided warmth at higher altitudes and wicked sweat from her body when flying closer to the ground. Over her underpants, she pulled on fur-lined leather trousers with clasped pockets and cinched a belt around her waist with sheaths for a cutlass and a dagger. Over her undershirt, she laced a fur-lined leather coat before slipping into knee-high leather boots. Finally, she placed the pearl friendship ring gifted by Chloe on her forefinger. Thaly's lover would be with her in spirit, in victory or defeat, until the end.

Chloe climbed from bed, opened the window and leaned outside. "The rain's stopped, and it's humid. You'll be sweating buckets walking to the mounting yards in that garb."

"They should call us perspiration wells, not wind-riders."

Thaly embraced Chloe's naked body. They stood at the window, kissing, not caring who in Portum might see them. Not, in this last moment together, having a care in the world.

* * * *

The grey clouds parted, and steam rose from the crowded Volatal Vexil mounting yards. Family and friends of the six wind-riders packed in, shoulder-to-shoulder, to farewell their loved ones. Thaly stood with Jurelle, Genevea and Chloe. Saskia and Heron, the young man having avoided incarceration for now, checked Namu's harness and saddle. Tom and Rosalie helped Puer brush Yagle's fur. The old handler would travel with the army to provide the care Yagle had grown accustomed to.

"Watch your sister," Jurelle said to Thaly. "She's not as experienced as you. Not an accomplished fighter."

"Saskia can hold her own," said Thaly.

"But you *will* keep an eye on her?"

"Yes, Pa."

Jurelle sluiced the sweat from his brow. "Damn humidity. Wish I could escape to the clouds on one of those winged lions."

"When I get back, I'll take you up," said Thaly.

"Your father is afraid of heights," said Genevea.

"I can ride a griffin," said Jurelle.

Genevea raised her eyebrows. "Can you?"

Saskia and Heron hugged, then Heron pushed his way through the crowd and out of the mounting yard.

"How is Heron?" asked Genevea as Saskia approached.

"Worried about me," said Saskia.

"I know how he feels," said Genevea and Chloe simultaneously before smiling at each other.

"The vigilum want to see him today. To discuss his role in the griffin barn fire."

"I hope things work out," said Genevea. "He seems like a nice boy."

"Are we ready, Sis?" said Saskia, turning to Thaly with expectant eyes.

"Almost," said Thaly. "Waiting on two more riders to finish their preparation." She was apprehensive about Saskia's keenness for battle. Heroism had its downside, and overconfidence could get you killed. *Watch your sister.*

"Rosalie will ride with you," Thaly said to Saskia, "and Tom with me."

"Will he survive the journey?" asked Jurelle. "He's quite sickly looking."

Of all those under her command, Thaly was most concerned about Tom. The thin, weathered man faded before her eyes. While his disposition suggested an unyielding determination to succeed, his body withered. Thaly worried about him failing. Worried Malphas would get the upper hand at a critical moment.

How can such a delicate man overcome the challenge of destroying the dead throne? she wondered. But destroy it, he must.

"The last two riders are ready," said Jurelle.

"Time to go," said Saskia, smiling.

Jurelle hugged Saskia. "Do what Thaly says. Obey every order."

Saskia leaned back and rolled her eyes. "*Paaaa.* I'll be a model soldier.

We'll return before the storm season ends. It won't take long to crush Malphas the worm."

"Don't underestimate him. Winning this war won't be easy."

Saskia kissed tears from Jurelle's cheeks.

"Farewell, Ma," said Thaly, embracing Genevea.

Genevea went to speak but choked on the words and wept on Thaly's shoulder. Thaly held her mother tighter than she ever had.

"It...it...." sobbed Genevea. "It feels like I'm...I'm giving you up, all over again."

"You never gave me up," whispered Thaly. "I understand that now. You were always my mother. You always loved me, and I love you."

They hugged and cried together as if they were the only two people in Portum.

Thaly pulled away to let Saskia say goodbye to Genevea, then faced Jurelle. He held Thaly's hand and caught her with deep brown eyes that mirrored her own.

"I always feared your destiny would be to follow my footsteps," said Jurelle.

Thaly hugged her father, clutching at his back. "I'll avenge Jürgen's death. Then Saskia and I will return home, and we can be a family again."

Genevea and Jurelle stepped back into the crowd, and Thaly faced Chloe.

"Ma said she'll look after you," said Thaly. "She knows how to handle the worry."

"I'll be fine," said Chloe. "The endless conventus meetings will keep me busy."

They rested their foreheads together.

"Come back to me," said Chloe.

"I will."

"I remembered an old Germalian saying. 'When he falls, she will rise.' I'm convinced *he* is Malphas."

"And she?"

Chloe smiled, kissed Thaly on the lips and turned away.

Saskia tugged on Thaly's sleeve. "Here, you'll be needing this." She held the Stansfield family amulet towards Thaly — the silver griffin dangling from a neck chain.

Thaly pushed it away. "Why don't you hold onto it?"

"No," said Saskia. "The eldest child should carry it, and we must ensure our commander is well protected."

Thaly sighed, took the amulet, and looped the chain over her head, tucking the silver griffin into the front of her coat. Fighting the anguish of separation, she didn't linger, turning on her heel and marching towards Yagle. She twisted the pearl ring on her forefinger, wondering how she'd keep it safe when the battle began. Also dressed in Volatal Vexil flight clothes, Tom Anderson wandered around the mounting yard, kicking clumps of griffin droppings the size of his head across the dirt.

"Are you ready?" she asked him.

He nodded. "Victory or death."

They trotted up the mounting platform stairs. Puer handed Thaly Yagle's reins, and she climbed into the saddle, cinching the flight harness across the top of her thighs. Tom sat behind her, wrapping his arm around her waist. Yagle crowed, eager for flight.

"Good flying, Domina Stansfield," said Puer. "The wind is at your back. I will see you again at first camp."

"Arve, Puer," said Thaly. "I hope the march is not too arduous."

Puer smiled. "Heron found me a comfortable kamel to ride."

A trumpeter blew a bellum cornu. Six griffins, armed for war, shrieked as one. Thaly yanked on Yagle's reins, and he trotted forward before spreading his wings and launching into the sky above Portum. The wind-riders wheeled over the harbour, where twelve classem ships floated in Slyencia Bay. Zenais' vessel, with a green mainsail bearing the Capri faction totem of the dune goat, raised a red flag to the top of the foremast. Almost as one, the other eleven ships opened their mainsails, the twelve insignias of the Germalian factions facing west, preparing to sail from the bay, then north to Ephesus.

The six wind-riders flew low along Lata Via, Thaly leading the formation. Below her, seventy thousand Germalian fighters waited for the order to march. Foot soldiers arranged in legions of five thousand each. Kamel riders in a cavalry of twenty thousand strong. Each soldier or kamel carried enough supplies to cover the march to Ephesus. There, they'd meet the classem ships to replenish their supplies and buy horses and elephai for the journey through Nordland and into Enthilen.

The golden scaled armour strapped to the soldiers' torsos and legs sparkled under the morning sunlight. Heavier than their regular garb, the armour would hold the fighters in better stead against Malphas' legions. While they donned it for the parade, it would be removed before the march to Ephesus began.

Lining Lata Via, tens of thousands of Portum's citizens sprinkled salt water and red sand at soldiers' feet. Children handed the women pale pink flowers, the *Flosrosea*, Portum's floral symbol. Thaly flew over the golden Pallaxium dome, descending to hover above the steps to its entrance. Charmion and the remaining senators waited there, dressed in silk robes embroidered with faction emblems and gossamer stitching. Charmion wheeled her chair to the front and held Thaly's gaze, communicating without words the seriousness of the coming mission. Then, the Sella raised both arms above her head, palms facing out.

Thaly thrust her fist skyward, and Yagle shrieked as he ascended. Tom clutched Thaly's waist tighter than ever. Saskia and Berenice followed Thaly, while the other three wind-riders flew to meet the classem.

The army on Lata Via raised cutlasses, javelins and shields. "VICTUM!" they yelled as one, loud enough even for a wind-rider to hear, then turned and marched towards the city outskirts.

*   *   *   *

The sight of seventy thousand soldiers marching into the desert north of Portum terrified and thrilled Tom in equal measure. Sitting astride Yagle, he flew with Thaly over the army, keeping watch on the eastern flank, inland from the coast. Relinquishing their heavy armour for the march, the Germalian soldiers were now more vulnerable to enemy attacks. Tom expected Malphas had planned for this moment. Imagined Erstürmen and Pordillo fighters swarming from the dunes and descending on the Germalians at their most vulnerable. Or hordes of dreadwerps exploding from the sand, riding ghastly slider serpents to spit venom into the soldiers' faces. The responsibility of sending tens of thousands of innocents to war burdened his thoughts. Thaly had told him many in the conventus wanted to confront Malphas long before Tom arrived. And yet, his presentation had been the tipping point. He'd been the catalyst to start a war. While it had always been the plan, the realisation of the ambition felt like a python's squeezing crush.

The army travelled north, between long, flat beaches on their left, stretching to the horizon, and the red sand mountains of Magna Avium, the Germalian name for Groz Wüste, on their right. Kamels carried most of the supplies, packed into cane panniers hanging from harnesses strapped across the beasts' hump. Teams of khorsals, the white horse-kamel hybrids favoured by the Pordillo, pulled wagons with slick, waxed-timber runners that skimmed easily across the sand. The march to Ephesus would take six days, then another six to travel from the border city to the Lost Sisters, where, hopefully, Caeli would be waiting.

Atop Yagle, Thaly scouted north, ahead of the marching column, or west, further into Magna Avium. She sometimes flew the griffin across the ocean to check on the classem, Tom holding on with grim determination lest he plummet into the depths. With the wind whipping past his ears, talking was difficult, so he kept company with his thoughts, though they weren't always the best companions. Some told him this crusade would be his last. That he and Adalwolf would die inside Pergamos, and their deaths were the only way to defeat Malphas. Others reminded him of the growing affection he felt for Rosalie. That he had something to live for beyond the destruction of Volerdie's throne.

At the end of the first day, the army encamped on a flat, featureless beach. Dark clouds closed in again, and drizzle threatened to dampen spirits but evaporated in the heat as soon as it hit the sand. The classem had sailed ahead and would wait for the army in Ephesus on the banks of the Afonwee River.

With flawless precision, the Germalians raised tents, shelters and corrals, and set guard posts north, south and west. Rosalie helped Saskia prepare Namu for the night while Tom sat with Thaly inside the command tent. Old friends forging new bonds.

Thaly ran her finger over a map of Germalia and Nordland. "When we reach Ephesus, we'll exchange the kamels and khorsals for horses and elephai, replace wagon runners with wheels, and purchase timber and steel to build war machines."

"Elephai?" asked Tom.

"The Nordmen and Erstürmen call them tufted goliaths. Beasts three times larger than undreds, with horns and tusks, thick, woolly hides, and broad feet better suited to traversing Nordland's muddy bogs. I only hope they can fit inside the mountain pass."

"And Caeli's there to meet us."

"You doubt she will be?"

Tom shrugged. "I don't fully understand the motivations of draughouls, but Widukind said something to me before we parted. *Every lost soul, trapped in glass. Again, made whole, free to pass.* When the throne is crushed, Caeli's soul will be released from the dark eyes and reunited with her body. Then body and soul will pass together into the world beyond life. I hope that's enough motivation for her to remain our ally."

Thaly unrolled a map of Enthilen across the table, studying it with grim sternness.

"You never told me what happened to you and Grin on the *Vulking,*" said Tom, deciding to broach a subject that had plagued his curiosity for yarles. "I know something happened before the storm hit. Something awful. Grin wouldn't talk about it."

Thaly looked up from the map, glaring at Tom with a bitter hatred that shrank him in his seat. "Why raise painful memories? What good will it do either of us?"

"I only want to understand your hurt."

"Can you understand an innocence stolen by the vilest of assaults? The *Vulking's* crew abused something precious. They abused our intimacy. They raped us."

"Oh, Thaly," said Tom. "I'm so sorry...."

"Stop," snapped Thaly. "I know you mean well, but I don't want to relive it. Ever."

She returned to her map, and Tom fell silent, picking at the woven cane chair with dirty fingernails. He shouldn't be in the Germalian command tent. A man, a stranger, shouldn't be afforded such a privilege. But Thaly treated him as an equal, and he respected her for that.

Breaking the tension, Rosalie limped into the tent rubbing her backside.

"Flying on a griffin is great and all," she said, "but this saddle rash is going to...did I interrupt something?"

Tom half-smiled.

"You're fortunate you don't have to ride a kamel all day," said Thaly, not looking up from the map.

"Should I leave?" asked Rosalie.

No, thought Tom. *Please don't.*

"The guards let me through. I wasn't sure if I needed permission or...."

Thaly waved her hand at a chair. "Sit, Rosalie. The guards have orders to let you and Tom enter at will, and you're not interrupting anything. In fact, your insights might be valuable. When we reach the Desolate Mountains' southern slopes, do you expect any threat from Laodicea?"

Rosalie placed a chair beside Tom, on the opposite side of the table from Thaly.

"Hunger's force is efficient and brutal," said Rosalie, the strips of woven cane creaking as she slumped into the chair, "though small in number. If the black grell knows we're coming, I expect he'll attack."

Tom shook his head. "No. Malphas will make his stand in Pergamos. He'll bring Hunger, Krieg and all his forces into the city. He only cares about protecting the dead throne until completing the immortal sacrifice."

Thaly raised her eyes to Tom. "Are you sure?"

"I've been a victim of Malphas' motivations for yarles."

"Then you understand him better than any of us. I trust your judgement."

Ten Prime Lieutenants arrived at the command tent for a briefing. Tom and Rosalie left Thaly and her soldiers to strategize while they strolled around the Germalian camp.

"I wish there was more I could do," said Tom.

Rosalie took his hand. "The time will come when only you can do what needs to be done."

"Why did you leave your family?"

"I couldn't watch blind faith destroy my father. Yonna looked to Volerdie for answers and found none. Yet, he kept asking."

"It's a madness that traps the wariest."

"I never believed in the promise of Volerdie. The words of the scripture verses remained hidden, interpreted only through the eyes of curates. We were fed what they wanted us to consume. Knowledge held by the few, who demanded unquestioning trust from their followers. I always wondered what lay behind the mask, and now I know."

"I could be wearing a mask," said Tom.

"Are you?"

He smiled. "Not now. Not with you. But the face I offer others changes like the colour of leaves before they fall from the tree. A mask protects me from the naked uncertainty of my own convictions."

"A mask offers no protection," said Rosalie. "Only a false belief that others will think less of you should you remove it. Promise me you'll never wear a mask when we're together. I want to see the real you."

"I promise."

Rosalie wrapped her arm around Tom's waist and squeezed. "I've made us a bed."

They walked to a tent, not bothering to look for food or drink. Collapsing onto the bedroll, a lustful urgency overcame both of them as if tomorrow may never arrive. Rosalie pulled off Tom's clothes, then removed her own. They kissed each other's skin. Bit each other's nipples. Tasted each other's sex. Then Rosalie straddled Tom and guided him inside her. He thrust. She ground her buttocks into his thighs. He arched his back. She screamed. He exploded inside her, unable to control his lust. Then he lifted her off, rolled her onto her back, and buried his head between her legs. He flicked his tongue across her clitoris. With every moan from Rosalie, he pushed his mouth harder against her desire. Not drawing breath, he pressed and plunged and licked until she came, the juices of sex smeared across his face.

Rosalie fell asleep in Tom's arms while he lay there thinking about falling in love and placing that love in the gravest of dangers.

*   *   *   *

On the afternoon of the sixth day since leaving Portum, the Germalians arrived on the outskirts of Ephesus. Saskia flew Namu along the army's eastern flank, scouting for danger. The Pordillo wouldn't encroach this far north, but unruly Nordmen tribes sometimes roamed the Afonwee River's western bank. She didn't expect trouble, the Germalians and Nordmen living in peace for many yarles, but her companions had told her stories about Ephesus. While Portum was civilised and tranquil, Ephesus was wild and untamed. After a long, tedious march, Saskia yearned for some frontier excitement.

With Rosalie clinging to her waist, Saskia took Namu over the Germalian Classem anchored at Ephesus' docks, the river mouth large enough to accommodate twelve warships. Thaly had ordered the soldiers not to enter Ephesus until she'd arranged permits to cross the Afonwee Bridge, the longest, river-spanning structure in Ostamp, and secured a commitment from the Nordmen Chieftains for free passage through Nordland. Because Thaly issued the command, Saskia considered it her sibling duty to ignore it, planning a night of feasting and drinking before facing Nordland's frozen wastes and squelching mud.

Saskia and Rosalie alighted on a grassy plain adjacent to the western edge of Ephesus. Male handlers ran to Namu, taking the reins from Saskia and preparing to feed and preen the griffin. Saskia uncinched her saddle harness and commanded Namu to lower her chest to the ground so she and Rosalie could dismount.

As they climbed off the griffin's wing, Saskia's plan for a wild celebration formed. Tom jogged to meet them, kissing Rosalie when he arrived.

"Where's Thaly?" asked Saskia.

"Already left for Ephesus to meet with the Nordmen," said Tom.

"Good. Tonight, we're going into the city."

"Thaly ordered us not to."

"When Prince Adalwolf thrust the eyes of lost souls against your chest, did he drain all the fun from you as well?"

"*No.* I can have fun."

"Really?" said Rosalie. "Since when?"

Saskia laughed. Tom looked annoyed.

"Listen," said Saskia, pulling her new friends close, "there's a tavern nearby called the *Elephas Tusk*. I've been told it has the best meduz in all of Ostamp. We'll get a group together for one final drink before the long journey to Enthilen."

Rosalie looked at Tom.

He frowned. "We're supposed to remain in camp."

"The tavern is on the Germalian side of the river," said Saskia. "All the Nordmen are on the other side. There's no danger. You're the golden boy, Tom. If you come with us, we won't get in trouble should Thaly find out."

"I want to go," said Rosalie. "It'd be nice to have a night on the town and forget our worries for a while."

Tom's shoulders slumped in defeat. "Alright. One drink can't hurt."

Yes, thought Saskia. *The golden boy has delivered a golden mug of meduz.*

At sunset, she, Tom, Rosalie and six others snuck past the guards surrounding the Germalian campsite and walked into town.

Ephesus wasn't Portum. The border city straddling the banks of the Afonwee River suffered from long neglect. Crumbling mortar that had escaped stone walls formed sandy piles with flakes of rotted timber along dark, narrow streets lined with buildings of two and three stories. The structures leaned towards each other such that Saskia expected the rusty tin roofs to clash with the next wind gust. Behind leadlight windows embedded in white-washed walls, candles shone, casting a dull amber hue across the cobbled footpath and compensating for the unlit streetlamps. Beggars missing limbs or stricken with scarred faces sat on street corners surrounded by waste smelling like rotten animal carcasses.

Saskia shivered, donning her Volatal Vexil coat and leading the group into a market square, empty besides a handful of dark-skinned residents walking the streets. Germalian soldiers guarded a town hall with a marble portico and iron gate protecting the front door. They wore woollen hats and canvas pants and tunics underneath copper breastplates, nothing like the thin cotton of Portum's desert soldiers or the scaled, golden armour of the advancing army. And the guards bore hand axes tucked into their belts, not cutlasses.

They tensed as Saskia and her group passed. She smiled at a soldier and nodded but received a blank, cold-eyed response.

"Not very friendly," whispered Rosalie.

"Where's this tavern?" asked Tom.

"Through the market square and down Munboggle Lane," said Saskia.

As they entered the lane, four male Nordmen approached. They were tall, about a head shorter than an adult stone-grell, and thickset with broad shoulders and barrel chests. Curly brown hair down to their shoulders framed gnarled faces with ruddy skin, not as dark as a Germalian but not pale like Saskia's. The men wore black leather coats, the hems brushing the tops of boots laced up to their knees, with swords, daggers and axes strapped to their waists and across their backs. Other than the Pordillo, Saskia couldn't remember the last time she'd seen a man bearing a weapon.

Tom grabbed her arm. "Are these Nordmen?"

"Yes," said Saskia.

"I thought there weren't any this side of the river?"

She smiled and shrugged at the same time. But as the Nordmen got closer, her hand went to the hilt of her cutlass.

The men of the north ignored the new arrivals, grunting as they pushed past Saskia and her companions.

At the end of Munboggle Lane, the *Elephas Tusk* overlooked a slovenly

Afonwee River, its creeping flow choked with woody debris. Despite being on the Germalian side of the river, male and female Nordmen milled around firepits outside the tavern, drinking meduz from leather mugs.

"There's more," spat Tom into Saskia's ear.

She stopped the group. "We're here now. No point going all the way back without a drink. The Germalians and Nordmen signed a truce yarles ago. We'll be fine. Who wants the best meduz in Ostamp?"

Everyone in the group, except Tom, nodded their agreement.

Saskia turned on her heel and led them into the *Elephas Tusk*. As she walked through the front door, a pungent concoction of body odour and meduz assaulted her nostrils, followed by the whiff of smoke from clay pipes stuffed with a leaf smelling like burnt kamel hide. Tall, broad men and women crammed into the tavern, shoulder-to-shoulder, dressed in dark coats and knee-high, mud-caked boots. Most men had thick beards, while the women had woven their straggly hair into plats reaching down to their waists. They talked and laughed in a guttural language that reminded Saskia of a primitive form of Erstürmen.

A dozen or so Germalians sat at tables scattered around the tavern, but there were no Germalian soldiers. Saskia sucked a breath from the smothering, smoky air and pushed her way to an empty table with ten chairs.

"I'll order the drinks," she said. "You wait here."

Squeezing between two Nordmen, Saskia leaned on the bar and waved to the bartender to get his attention. He looked Germalian, a short, wiry man with dark skin and an oiled moustache curled at the ends.

"Nine tankards of meduz," she said in Germalian. "How much?"

"Germalian coin or Nordmen trinkets?" asked the bartender.

"Germalian."

"Ten silvers."

Saskia unlaced her wind-rider coat and pulled the coin from an inside pocket.

"We're sitting over there," she said, pointing to the table with her friends.

The bartender nodded as he took the coin. "Won't be long."

Saskia re-joined her companions, who sat quietly, shrunken into their chairs and resembling nervous children compared to the Nordmen.

"Meduz is coming," said Saskia as she sat.

"Better be as good as you say," said Berenice, the wind-rider who'd been scouting Pordillo camps with Saskia when they found Tom and Rosalie.

"Secret recipe," said Saskia. "From the Grauberge mountains."

"Where are they?" asked Tom.

"Far east of Nordland. You'll see them when we arrive at the Lost Sisters."

The stringy bartender weaved through the crowd, carrying a tray of nine tankards to Saskia's table. He placed the tray in the middle of the table, bowed his head and disappeared back into the throng.

Saskia raised a tankard. "Here's to our army."

"Our army," replied her companions, taking a tankard each.

"The strongest to ever set foot in Enthilen. Malphas doesn't stand a chance against eighty thousand ferocious Germalians and a traveller from a far-away land."

Rosalie glared at Saskia. "*Sssh.* Don't give away our entire plan."

"Doubt any of these Nordmen care. They'll know soon enough where we're going once Thaly gets permission to cross Nordland."

"Then Malphas will find out," said Tom.

"Likely, he already knows. Won't change anything. Either way, he'll cower inside Pergamos until we arrive." Saskia downed the rest of her meduz in a single gulp. "*Burp. Ahhh.* It's as good as they said. Another one?"

"I'll wait," said Tom, echoing the sentiment of the other fighters.

Saskia ordered another drink, carrying the tankard from the bar back to the table.

"I don't usually drink this much," she said, returning to her seat, "but, well...who knows what awaits us?"

"How long before we hear from Thaly?" asked Rosalie.

Saskia shrugged. "Shouldn't be long. The Nordmen won't deny passage and risk upsetting the leader of an army numbering in the tens of thousands. Their population is spread thinly across the boglands, in villages of a few hundred each. They'd struggle to amass a thousand fighters if they sort to block us."

Rosalie placed her hand over her mouth and stood. "Is there a privy here?"

"There," said Saskia, pointing to a door adorned with a picture of a hole in the ground. "Are you sick?"

"I'll be alright. Feeling a bit nauseous." Rosalie rushed off to the privy.

The crowd thinned as the night wore on. Five of Saskia's companions returned to camp, leaving her, Tom, Rosalie and Berenice alone at the table.

"We should get back," said Tom.

"One...one final drink, Tommy Boy," said Saskia, her muddled head threatening to tip right off the end of her neck. "The last before we win the war." She stood, stumbled, then fell back onto her chair.

Three Nordmen lurched over to the table and hovered above Saskia.

"You ladies want another drink?" asked one of the men in Erstürmen, a scar blighting his clean-shaven chin.

"We'll get it ourselves," said Saskia, a meduz-soaked bile bubbling up into her throat.

"It's custom to accept a drink when offered," said a second man with a red beard almost the colour of his skin.

"Especially since you're marching through our homeland," said scar-face.

"*Ssshure*," said Saskia. "Why not? We'll all have another meduz."

"Why drink Erstürmen swill?" asked red-beard. "We got she-bear juice here. What you women call it? *Ur-sa*. That'll put hairs on your tits."

"She's losing her hair," said the shortest of the three Nordmen, pointing at Tom. "I don't want the bald one."

"I'm not a woman," said Tom.

"You sound like one," said short-man.

"If you had hair, you'd look like one too," said scar-face. "A right pretty little maid."

Saskia pulled her coat off the chair. "We should go. We'll be marching tomorrow."

Red-beard towered over her. "You ain't going anywhere 'til we say so."

Saskia stood, fumbling for the dagger sheathed on her belt.

Scar-face pulled open his coat, revealing the hilt of a broadsword. "Don't be thinking of drawing weapons. You might get lucky and stick one of us, but they're twenty more Nordmen in the tavern. You reckon you can take us all?"

"Let us leave in peace," said Tom. "Any trouble won't go well for you."

Red-beard glowered. "Says who?" He grabbed Saskia's arm. "Let's start with this one. I'll take her out back. You two watch the others."

"Let me go!" Saskia yanked her arm free.

Berenice stood, brandishing her cutlass. The three Nordmen drew swords, attracting the attention of the tavern's other patrons.

Shit, thought Saskia. *How are we getting out of this?*

Red-beard wrapped his arm around her waist, hoisting her off the floor. She screamed and punched him in the chest.

He laughed. "You're a feisty one, that's for sure. It'll be fun cutting you down to size."

Saskia kicked and screamed, trying to free herself. Tom picked up a chair and threw it at short-man. Berenice lunged at scar-face, but he dodged the blade and smacked the cutlass from her hand with his sword. Red-beard laughed the whole time. Saskia thought about biting off his ear. Then his laughing ended, drowned in a bloody gargle as the tip of a blade burst from his throat.

Saskia found her feet as Thaly appeared from behind the dying Nordman.

"Be thankful your life ends quickly," Thaly said to red-beard.

Saskia pulled away from her assailant before his body slumped to the floor.

Two dozen Germalian soldiers crowded into the *Elephas Tusk,* and the remaining Nordmen slinked away into the shadows.

Mouth ajar, Tom gawked at Thaly. "How did you know?" he asked.

Thaly sheathed her cutlass. "I urged Saskia not to go into Ephesus. But I know my sister well. When she wasn't in her tent, I guessed she'd probably defied me. And there's only one establishment on the Germalian side of the river open this late at night that serves Saskia's favourite beverage." She faced Saskia. "This encounter could jeopardise our plans to march through Nordland."

"I'm *shorry*, Sis," said Saskia. "Wasn't meant to end like this."

"We need to leave before things get worse."

Saskia stumbled after Thaly, and her drinking friends followed. The headache due tomorrow morning had already started.

~ Chapter 40 ~

Strolling beside Audie on the Dambay Plains, the hairs on Adalwolf's bare arms bristled with the cold dusk air. The harvest season in Enthilen faded. The sun set sooner, and the nights cooled faster. The storm season would soon arrive, lashing the plains with swirling wind and pummelling rain, adding to the tumult Malphas had already conjured. Since Widukind's disappearance fourteen moons ago, the mouldewerps had pleaded with Adalwolf to remain below ground. But he resisted their pleas, threatening to reject any plan to destroy the throne of the dead and run away into the mountains.

It's all hopeless now, anyway, he thought. Malphas has Widukind.

The werps had discovered evidence of a scuffle, grass and soil churned up on the plains near the secret dwell. Widukind's scent had been mixed with draughouls', no doubt Malphas' servants like the ones the old man sent to Gestade. Adalwolf was convinced they'd taken Widukind to Pergamos. After yarles of searching, Malphas had finally captured his brother and could enact the immortal sacrifice on the dead throne at any moment. The quest to shatter the throne had become a race with an urgency that pressed more with each passing moon. If Tom Anderson didn't arrive in Enthilen soon, Malphas would win. Adalwolf *expected* Malphas to win. The Worshipful Master always won. Yes, he experienced setbacks, but in the end, the will of Malphas prevailed.

Adalwolf's thoughts focussed on Volerdie's return, wondering if he would recognise the moment. Would Enthilen look or feel any different? Would paradise be revealed straight away? *When darkness descends amid the daylight.* To Adalwolf's knowledge, this event hadn't taken place, Volerdie still absent from his homeland. Yet, Adalwolf had been stuck underground with the werps for so long that he could have missed it.

He and Audie turned for the werp dwell as the sun dipped below the Scaur Hills, far on the horizon. She stumbled and grabbed his handless wrist, a cough rattling her chest.

"Are you alright?" he asked.

Audie gathered her breath, lifted her head and smiled. "Yes. Probably indigestion from werp food."

Adalwolf smiled back but knew Audie's discomfort stemmed from more than pickled lizard. She hadn't recovered entirely from the Rephaim attack, struggling with the lingering effects of having an axe blade slice open her stomach. The werp shamans did their best, rubbing poultices on the wound and tipping potions down Audie's throat, but she spent most of her time asleep and rarely ate. Tonight's walk was the first she'd been on since the attack. Before they'd taken one step, Adalwolf worried it would be too much.

"We should sit for a while," he said. "It's not far to the dwell, and with Seena and Bargan at three-quarters, we can find our way there easy enough when night falls."

They found a patch of short-cropped grass. Adalwolf removed his coat, laid it on the ground, and helped Audie sit on it. He sat beside her.

"Is it strange," said Audie, "for Widukind to be gone so long?"

Adalwolf shrugged. "I don't know him well enough."

He didn't need to say more, not wanting to burden Audie with his belief that Malphas had Widukind and all might be lost. And the werps hadn't given up. They continued their busyness inside the dwell under the Dambay Plains, preparing as if they'd storm Pergamos all by themselves. Sharpening stone-tipped spears and bone daggers. Devising battle plans on maps scratched into the soil or painted on cave walls. Adalwolf found their enthusiasm surreal, almost theatrical. Furry puppets planning to topple the evil sorcerer in his impenetrable tower.

Adalwolf's reality centred entirely around Audie. She *was* real. Sitting beside him, as she'd done since Gestade's demise. Yet, the healer's strength he'd encountered outside the infirmary many moons ago had withered to an unexpected fragility. A vulnerability he'd not experienced since Romilda's last days. He dismissed the chance of Audie's death by dreaming of a life together far away from Enthilen's tumult. Fantasising about a journey across the Veiled Occyan to Audie's homeland. *He needed to be the healer now.*

Adalwolf cradled Audie's hand in his, and she didn't pull away. He leaned in, and she didn't lean back. Then he kissed her, and she returned the kiss, soft and delicately sweet, like rosewater. Other than a peck on his mother's cheek, Adalwolf had never kissed anyone he truly loved until now. The kiss lingered, and they pulled each other close. Worries of Malphas and Widukind vanished from Adalwolf's mind. He didn't care about Enthilen's future or destroying Volerdie's throne. He cared about Audie. Only Audie.

"Ow!" cried Adalwolf.

He pulled away from Audie's lips and spun around on his buttocks. Behind him, a mouldewerp wielding a walking stick whacked him in the back again.

"Ouch! What was that for?" Adalwolf asked the werp.

"The wits of the smitten, as weak as a kitten," said the werp in fluent Erstürmen. "What wasn't it for? I should give you a few more wallops to knock sense into you. Usurping the throne from a murdered King Ewald, trying to steal Tom Anderson's soul with the dark eyes, fulfilling every one of Malphas' wishes."

"Who are you?" asked Audie.

"Well, I'm not Volerdie, am I? Thank goodness I'm here; that's all I can say."

Over the crest of a hill, a female stone-grell marched through the long grass carrying a spear and a bow and quiver slung over her shoulder.

"Who have you found, Dwarrow?" asked the grell.

"The royal buffoon, Adalwolf, and one of his servants."

"I'm not his servant," said Audie. "I'm a healer from Laodicea and Gestade."

"No more Gestade," said Dwarrow. "No more Laodicea either if we don't get a wriggle on."

Adalwolf stood and helped Audie to her feet. The grell lifted the spear and pointed the stone tip at his chest.

He raised his hands in deference. "I'm no threat."

"You are an Erstürmen king," said the grell.

"A failed king," said Dwarrow.

"How do you know Adalwolf?" asked Audie.

"Never spoken with him," said Dwarrow. "But I remember his smell from Malang Gunya. The smell of an imbecile."

"He's not a fool," said Audie. "He's going to defeat Malphas."

"About time," said Dwarrow.

"I've seen you before," said Adalwolf. "In Pergamos' throne hall with Tom Anderson and that grell. Before Volerdie's Wrath descended on us."

"*That grell* was my brother," said the stone-grell, pressing the spear tip into Adalwolf's ribs.

"I'm sorry," said Adalwolf. "About everything that's happened. I didn't know your brother. I don't know you."

"I am Hannian stone-grell. First born of Frennan and Mirrian. Protector of Enthilen."

Dwarrow waved his walking stick in Adalwolf's face. "I hold you responsible for most of this mess. You could have stood up to Malphas. Made it your business to thwart his plans. And you turned Princess Caeli into a draughoul."

"Adalwolf will atone for his mistakes," said Audie.

Will I? thought Adalwolf. "Did you reach Giigal?" he asked.

"Yes, yes, yes," said Dwarrow. "Despite the awful boat ride and being attacked by barbarians. *And* a leviathan. Hanni carried me home, thank goodness. Never setting foot on another ship again. Ever."

"Where are the weald-grells?" asked Audie. "Will they fight?"

"I made sure they had no choice."

"My weald-grell kin are setting up camp over that ridge." Hanni lowered her spear and pointed east.

Dwarrow relaxed, resting the heel of his walking stick on the ground. "Everything is falling into place. Now we wait for the arrival of Tom Anderson and the Germalians."

Adalwolf reached down, picked up his coat and pulled it over his tunic as the night air chilled. "There *is* one problem," he said. "Widukind's missing."

"What?!" Dwarrow thumped his walking stick into a rock. "Love has clearly addled your brain. Now I know where you got your name from. When did this happen?"

"He went for a walk fourteen moons ago and never returned."

"Went for a walk? This isn't the time to be strolling in the meadow. Malphas has him as sure as the storm season follows the harvest season. This puts us in a right pickle. A right pickle, indeed. How could you let this happen?"

"Adalwolf is not Widukind's keeper," said Audie. "The werps didn't stop him."

"Well," said Adalwolf, "we kind of snuck out."

"Escaped," said Dwarrow. "You left the safest place in Enthilen to go wandering. Why must you people jeopardise my arrangements? Do you at least have the blood compass, or did you lose that as well?"

Adalwolf reached into his coat pocket, withdrew the compass and handed it to Dwarrow. The werp leaned towards him, then jammed a star point into his thigh.

"Damn it!" cried Adalwolf. "Not again. Why don't you just kill me?" He rubbed his blood-stained pants.

"That would be too easy." Dwarrow balanced the underside point of the gold pentagram on a flat rock. The compass spun rapidly, then slowed, stopping with the blood-stained tip pointing northward. "*Hmmm*," he said.

"It pointed in a more westerly direction when last we used it," said Adalwolf.

"How fast did it spin? And for how long?"

"Not as fast as this time, and it slowed sooner."

"This is very imprecise," said Hanni.

"Nobody likes the messenger who delivers the obvious, Hannian stone-grell," said Dwarrow. "My guess is that Tom's further away but not in Portum."

"Could he be in Nordland already?" asked Adalwolf.

"Possibly. Or Ephesus. And if he's in either of those places, it means the Germalians are marching to Enthilen. Or he's gotten lost." Dwarrow snatched up the blood compass, uncinched a pouch and dropped the treasure inside. "I'm off to the dwell."

"Is Tilly still here?" asked Hanni. "We have been apart for so long."

"Yes," said Audie. "Underground with the mouldewerps."

"Grells won't fit through the entrance," said Dwarrow.

"Take me there, anyway," said Hanni. "You can go and fetch her."

"Alright," said Dwarrow. "I must speak with Wirrikow and the elders who've travelled here. And Tilly should return to the Desolate Mountains, taking news of the weald-grells' arrival. And I must begin preparing for the assault on Pergamos. Jobs, jobs, jobs. So many jobs." He faced Adalwolf. "Don't go wandering off like your uncle. Or get captured by our enemy. Or anything else remotely stupid." Then turned his back. "Come on, Hannian stone-grell. We need to get going, quickerty quock. Follow my nose!"

Dwarrow marched off, and Hanni trotted after him.

Audie clasped Adalwolf's hand. "I want to see the weald-grells."

He smiled at her, and together they walked, hand-in-hand, into the long grass and over a ridge. In a swale, lit by the three-quarter moons as if candle chandeliers hung above the Dambay Plains, the weald-grell camp sprawled across flowered meadows. Hundreds of shelters, animal skins stretched over wooden frames, had sprung up like mushrooms after rain. Tall, lithe creatures walked among the shelters or sat around fires cooking meals, flickering shadows tracing black fingers across naked torsos painted in blue and white.

Two thousand weald-grells? wondered Adalwolf. Three thousand?

Not enough to defeat Malphas, but the sight of the grell army lifted his spirits. They'd come to fight for Enthilen. The werps underground also prepared for battle, and Tom Anderson marched across Nordland with countless Germalians in tow. Momentum had swung, yanking Adalwolf forward like a train of oxen.

Audie squeezed his hand and kissed him on the cheek. "It's breathtaking, isn't it. I've never seen so many wild and free grells."

"I hope they don't gather for their slaughter. If Malphas finds out they're here...."

"We can't let him. We can't let him have what he wants." She stood before Adalwolf, trapping his eyes with her stoic beauty. "What kind of world do you want to live in? One divided by fear or united by the promise of something better? There's no future for us should Malphas continue to rule. You can stop him. At least try."

Yes, thought Adalwolf. *At least try.* If only for Audie's sake.

~ Chapter 41 ~

The incident at the *Elephas Tusk* didn't jeopardise Thaly in securing safe passage for the Germalian army across Nordland. Apparently, brawls in Ephesus taverns happened most nights, often with a death or two. The Nordmen Chieftains of the border city gave Thaly a parchment inked with a bear pawprint and a flourish of scribbles she didn't understand. The parchment was her ticket across the north, which she exchanged for food and gifts.

Thaly made Saskia and her Germalian drinking companions scrub fifty kamels as punishment for disobeying an order. The kamels and khorsals would return to Portum, the beasts of burden replaced by horses and gigantic elephai. The thick, matted hair on elephai hides could repel the coldest Nordland day, and the curled tusks growing either side of their mouth and the javelin-like horns protruding sideways from the top of their skull meant few predators, including boulder lions, would dare confront an elephai. Yet, Thaly found the animals placid in nature, perfect for carrying heavy loads lashed to oversized saddles that supported three riders at a time.

On the afternoon of the seventh day since leaving Portum, the Germalian army marched from Ephesus, parting ways with the classem who would sail through the Nordargen Sea, around the Grauberge peninsula and down Enthilen's east coast to Gestade. While much of the sea ice had thawed, icebergs drifting across Nordargen waited to destroy the hulls of timber ships. Zenais' navigational ability as Praefecti of the Germalian Classem would be tested to the limit in the treacherous waters.

Riding Yagle, Thaly flew along the endless rows of marching soldiers as they crossed the Afonwee Bridge and through the eastern half of Ephesus ruled by the Nordmen. While the Germalian side of the border city could be generously described as unrefined, the Nordmen half made the shantytown of Slumstadt in Enthilen look respectable. It reflected primitive, nomadic people who preferred to live in round tents or lean-tos that could be pulled down in a day and packed on elephai to move to the next encampment. A handful of more elaborate structures, rendered in mud or clay, stood among the ramshackle scattering of tents strewn across the landscape. But they also appeared to be temporary. During her studies in Portum, Thaly learned the Nordmen of Ephesus and the southern boglands differed from their kin living on Nordland's north coast. Kogot, the stone city, remained isolated from the rest of Ostamp, the residents rarely trading with others. The Erstürmen once occupied the city, but it had been built by a people called the Uralt long before the rise of Erstürmen kings. The Nordmen also manned the frozen outpost of Morskoy, near Grauberge. Here, they traded with the curmudgles, mysterious creatures from the settlement of Karlik, hidden in Grauberge's icy mountains. Thaly had never seen a curmudgle or met anyone who had.

She wouldn't lead her army near any of these places. They'd travel the south road, following the Afonwee River before traversing the boglands that dominated Nordland's southern half. Always frozen during the long dark, the boglands began thawing during the growing season and now, with the harvest season almost over, would be a sucking mess of mud and sludgegrass. The army would pass close to Thyatira, a ruined city, and then onto the town of Revelé at the foot of the Desolate Mountains.

As the Germalians left Ephesus, the main road became a track and then a path, nothing more than a faint line among the clumps of fawn sedges and blackwater bogs. The marshes arrived more quickly than Thaly anticipated. She flew low over her soldiers as they engaged in their first battle, fighting off midges that swarmed about their faces, trying to find patches of bare skin. In Ephesus, the marchers had exchanged the light cotton garb better suited to the desert for woollen tunics, fur-lined coats, leather pants and furred hats. Yet the midges persisted, turning on the cavalry horses if they failed to make a meal of a soldier. Only the elephai seemed immune, not bothering to swish their tufted tails to rid themselves of the pest.

A wagon carrying armour became bogged. Thaly urged Yagle to land so she could help, but before he alighted, Eutropia rode up on her horse, issuing orders to free the carriage. While Thaly commanded the ground forces, Eutropia was a conventus orator; of higher standing than a senator. Such seniority played on Thaly's mind, causing her to second-guess her orders or defer to Eutropia when undecided. Once the war commenced, confusion about authority could cost many lives. Thaly needed to reaffirm her place as Legatus, lest the battle for Pergamos be lost in the command tent before they reached the battlefield.

At sunset, after a slow march, the army camped near a village on the edge of a vast bog. Thaly walked into the settlement to meet the chieftain, a stern, hulking woman with a flat nose, gnarled cheeks and wisps of facial hair hanging across her lips. But she smiled when Thaly showed her the bear-print parchment and offered gifts of food and vinum.

Returning to the command tent, Thaly stumbled on a troop of soldiers sitting around a campfire, trying to heat a pot of water. She held back in the shadows as the soldiers talked among themselves, seemingly unaware of her presence.

"How long is this march going to take?" asked one.

"Even with these new clothes, I'm still freezing," said another.

"And the midges!" cried a third. "They'll kill all of us before we set foot in Enthilen."

"I bet the wind-princesses aren't bothered by midges," said the first. "Swooshing high above us on their mighty steeds."

"Don't worry," said the second, "Queen Athalee will find a warm place for you in her sky castle."

"Only if you get past the guard," said the first. "Her traitor father."

"Not much of a guard without a weapon," said the third, smirking. "Thank goodness the conventus disarmed the men."

The soldiers laughed. Thaly turned away and marched off, brimming with a maddening embarrassment. While she'd gained respect as Legatus of the wind-riders, more than half the Germalian army was another matter. Portum's foot soldiers barely knew her, and now she'd led them into a bleak wilderness, unprepared. For the first time, she worried some of her fighters wouldn't make it across Nordland, succumbing to the cold, mud or relentless midges.

Thaly stepped through the flaps of the command tent. Inside, Eutropia sat alone, drinking vinum and warming her body with a heater run on serpent oil, a commodity too precious to waste on foot soldiers.

"We should build larger fires," said Thaly, removing her coat and hanging it over the back of a canvas chair. "The soldiers are freezing out there."

"Not enough wood in the boglands," said Eutropia.

"We should have brought more from Ephesus."

"And sacrifice what to make space? Armour, weapons, food?"

"Another five days of this will sap the army's strength." Thaly slumped into the chair.

"You knew what we'd face. As Legatus, you should have been better prepared."

Thaly sat forward, resting clenched fists on her knees. "You and Zenais threw me into this. Begged me to take charge. Since then, you've offered little support. I see you issuing orders and undermining my authority."

Eutropia placed her goblet on the map table. "You are mistaken, Athalee. I would never do such a thing."

Thaly gritted her teeth. "We're not ready to face Malphas. Jurelle could have trained the lieutenants to fight wars on open plains if he hadn't been dismissed. We could have lobbied Charmion for more wagons or ships. Your yarles of scheming did little to place us at an advantage."

A snarl flashed across Eutropia's usually impassive face. "Zenais and I could not foresee all events. Tom Anderson's arrival bolstered our cause with an urgency we had to exploit, and much of what we did had to be in secret, known only to a handful."

"Furtive and deceptive," said Thaly. "The two most important traits of a senator."

Eutropia leaned forward and placed her hand over Thaly's fist. "If you're worried about your soldiers, Athalee, find a solution to their woes. Take charge. *Lead.*"

*   *   *   *

On the second day out of Ephesus, Tom walked beside Rosalie, following a Germalian wagon pulled by a team of horses. He wore the Volatal Vexil leathers, with a woollen hat and scarf wrapped around his face, leaving only a slit for his eyes, yet the cold wind still chilled his bones. They marched to try to warm their blood, and Rosalie had grown tired of riding a griffin, a recurrent illness plaguing her day and night. She'd become quiet, too. Withdrawn. Tom worried about the thoughts rattling inside her head, concerned she might not survive the journey back to Enthilen. He worried about losing her.

Though beautiful in its own way, Nordland's flat, austere landscape depressed him. He couldn't remember the last time he'd seen a tree. Only grass, rocks, squelching mud and more mud. The track from the first village traversed a seemingly endless bog the Nordmen called Medlemire, filled with sepia-toned water surrounding clumps of sludgegrass. While rough and rutted, the track had been raised above the waterline using a foundation of rocks and gravel and was wide enough to accommodate the elephai. Tom hoped the marsh would end soon; otherwise, they'd be camping on the track.

While seventy thousand Germalians marched to defeat Malphas, the midges of Nordland did their best to bring down the Germalians. Clouds of tiny insects swarmed around Tom, wriggling through the slit in his face scarf and smacking into his eyes or crawling up his nose. He swatted, coughed and spat, but the attack never relented.

Rosalie slapped her face. "These bugs are more trying than Magna Avium's dunes."

Tom shoved a hand into a coat pocket and withdrew a clay pot with a corked top. After removing the cork, he held the pot towards Rosalie.

"Smear this on your clothes. It's an ointment Thaly found in the last village. Supposed to repel the midges. She ended up trading a dozen crates of vinum for as much ointment as the villagers could spare."

Rosalie dipped her finger in the ointment, then smeared it over her cheeks. Tom did the same.

"It's working," she said.

"You should ride in a wagon," said Tom. "Given your nausea."

"I'm fine. It comes and goes. Too cold sitting in a wagon."

"Will you return to the rebel monastery when we arrive in Enthilen?"

Rosalie faced him, her amber eyes smiling. "I'm not letting *you* take all the glory, Tom Anderson."

He laughed aloud. "You've caught me out. I so wanted them to build a statue of me in the centre of Pergamos. A *huge* statue to rival the giant grell pyramid."

"It would fall over. Top heavy because of that ginormous head of yours."

He tickled her ribs through the thick leather. She laughed, then pulled away, placing a hand over her mouth and dry-retching.

"You're not going to be sick again?" he asked.

"Not used to this foreign food. Upset my stomach."

Tom guessed the illness had nothing to do with food, but its cause eluded him. Despite the cold, they'd made love last night. *Love*. A blissful feeling beyond the carnal, sometimes awkward sexual encounters at the beginning of their relationship. Last night had been gentle. Thoughtful. Connected. Lust became love, and they made it together.

Medlemire bog didn't end, and the army camped on the track at nightfall. Some raised tents, but most slept in or under wagons or hunkered around the horses and elephai, drawing warmth from the animals. The Germalians had been marching for eight days with only a short break in Ephesus. They aimed to cross Medlemire as quickly as possible, planning to rest again in the town of Revelé.

Tom and Rosalie huddled around a campfire with Saskia and Berenice. Thaly walked among the troops, stopping and talking to anyone who acknowledged her, handing out more of the midge ointment and sharing a drink or a morsel of food. For the first time since leaving Portum, she'd let Yagle fly alone while she spent her day marching with the ground forces.

Saskia made a lukewarm stew of yams and rich, tender kamel meat from the animal's shoulder. Half the kamels from Portum had been butchered in Ephesus, the fresh meat likely to keep for a few days in Nordland's cold temperatures, while salted strips had been prepared for the journey under the Desolate Mountains and into Enthilen. Saskia and Berenice drank meduz, while Tom and Rosalie favoured a fermented juice made from jabklo fruit. It tasted sweet and slightly alcoholic but not as strong as meduz.

After the meal, Tom and Rosalie squeezed onto a wagon tray with a handful of soldiers and tried to sleep. But Tom's mind wandered ahead to Revelé, recalling the town's name written in a margin of the blue book on page four hundred and sixty-two, next to a lemniscate. The book written by Malphas and delivered to Earth by Widukind before he stole Jean Anderson's soul and turned her into a draughoul twenty-three years ago. The book Tom used to teach himself Erstürmen and learn about Enthilen. Widukind claimed not to know about the margin inscription, but the handwriting didn't match the rest of the book.

Who, then, wrote Revelé in the blue book? wondered Tom in a half-sleep. *Did they want me to visit the town? Have they drawn me here? How? Why?*

The next morning, he and Rosalie marched with the army, following the road through Medlemire bog. Thaly joined them for a short while, letting Yagle fly riderless with Saskia on Namu and Berenice on Nia. The presence of their commander lifted the soldiers' spirits, the atmosphere becoming more cheerful, and the pace of the march quickening as word arrived from the head of the column that the boglands would soon end.

After midday, the promise arrived. Medlemire disappeared, replaced by streams of babbling, crystalline water flowing down from the northwest slopes of the Desolate Mountains. Lush, undulating meadows bordered the roadside, as far as Tom could see, thick with white, red and violet flowers. Farms and villages dotted the landscape, the first since the settlement on the bogland's western edge.

The road improved; flat, hard ground replacing the aggravation of muddy potholes. The wind calmed, and the sun burst through the clouds, enough for Tom and Rosalie to remove their face scarves to enjoy the warmth. Thaly pushed her soldiers a little harder, taking advantage of the longer days. At sunset, they reached their next campsite, adjacent to the crumbling foundations of a ruined city.

"Is this Thyatira?" asked Tom.

"Yes," said Rosalie. "Home of the Erstürmen, before being exiled from Nordland."

"Wonder why the Nordmen don't live here."

Rosalie shrugged. "Must prefer their yurts and mud huts."

"Thiemo, the youngest Erstürmen king, was crowned in Thyatira."

Rosalie faced him, eyes wide. "You know your Erstürmen history."

"Legend has it, Thiemo was an immortal, sacrificed to entice Volerdie to return."

"*Hmmm.* Sounds like a fairy tale. How did Thiemo become immortal? Who had the power to sacrifice him?"

"He must have killed his birth twin on Earth, then returned here. Only another immortal could have sacrificed him."

"Where *are* all these immortals?" asked Rosalie. "If they can never die, why do we not see more of them? Malphas is the only one I've heard of."

"Malphas and Widukind," said Tom. "I've seen proof both are immortal. I don't know why there aren't more."

Rosalie chuckled. "Likely, they've been so busy killing each other to bask in the glory of Volerdie's resurrection that they're all dead."

"That *would* be ironic," said Tom, smiling.

"What about on Earth? How many immortals live there?"

"None that I know of. I mean, people worship gods that I guess could be considered immortal. But there's no physical proof of such things."

"It seems immortality is rare."

"Maybe that's good," said Tom.

"No maybe about it," said Rosalie.

As the army made camp, Tom and Rosalie strolled through Thyatira's ruins. Nature ruled the city now. Strangling vines choked decaying stone walls as if trying to pull bricks and mortar back into the soil. Moss and lichen traversed the flagstone streets, leading to a town square populated with shrubs and grass. Around the square, statues that once celebrated famous Erstürmen had fallen and shattered. Every roof of every house had caved in, the occasional residence occupied by creatures resembling rabbits, with floppy ears and pouched young, living in rock crevices. Wells, once filled with water, were choked with debris. Thyatira's ruins were nothing like Malang Gunya. The grell city still offered hope of rejuvenation. Thyatira was a monument only to despair.

Back in camp, after the evening meal, Thaly sat with Tom, Rosalie and Saskia.

"Saskia and I will fly to Revelé tomorrow," said Thaly, "to make arrangements for our visit. I'll seek permission for the army to camp outside town and rest for a day."

"I want to come," blurted Tom. The memory of the scrawl in the blue book taunted him. Dared him to face an unknown destiny.

"And me," said Rosalie.

Thaly nodded. "We'll fly together. Eutropia can lead the army to Revelé."

On the afternoon of the fourth day since leaving Ephesus, the tenth out of Portum, Yagle carried Thaly and Tom up a valley nestled between two rolling green hills topped with jagged boulders. In the valley's centre, overshadowed by the Desolate Mountains' snow-capped peaks, sat Revelé, the largest town in the east of Nordland. According to Thaly, nearly three thousand people lived here in houses similar to those in Enthilen. Saskia and Rosalie on Namu glided up to Yagle's wing, and the wind-riders skirted the town's perimeter. Nordmen gathered on the dirt streets, huddling together and pointing skyward. Others ran inside, dragging children with them. Then arrows flew, whizzing past Tom.

"Damn it," said Thaly.

She signalled to Saskia. They wheeled away from the town, returning down the valley to alight on a rock ledge.

"We'll leave Yagle and Namu here," said Thaly, "and walk in. Few outside of Germalia would have seen griffins before, and there are too many people in Revelé for us to avoid trouble."

Tom, Rosalie, Thaly and Saskia hiked up the valley, following a well-worn path until reaching the first houses on the township's edge. Revelé had no boundary walls or guards watching the road, and the sight of four hikers in Germalian leather armour roused little interest among the townsfolk.

Thaly faced Tom and Rosalie. "Are you hungry?"

They nodded as one.

She reached into a pocket, withdrew a handful of coin and gave it to Tom. "Find some food while Saskia and I locate the chieftain. Afterwards, we'll meet in the market square."

They parted ways, Tom and Rosalie heading for the town centre, following a quaint street lined with cottages. Every window had a flowerbox, flashes of crimson, indigo and shamrock contrasting against white-washed walls shimmering from the afternoon sun.

In the town square, a bustling market drew a crowd, the threat of griffins not enough to hobble the march of commerce. As soon as Tom and Rosalie entered the market, vendors swamped them, crowding in to spruik an array of wares. They spoke in broken Erstürmen, guessing, correctly, the new arrivals weren't Germalian or Nordmen.

"Ground goliath tusk," said a vendor, shoving a handful of powder under Rosalie's nose. "Make good babies."

"Pickled sand eel," said another, holding a jar in front of Tom.

"New boots," said a girl, tugging at Rosalie's pant leg. "New boots for long march."

Rosalie crouched beside the girl to examine the boots.

Tom waved the vendors away as the crush of people sucked the air from his lungs. The crowd parted, and a bald, pale-skinned man approached, dressed in blue robes. His amber, almost red eyes fixed on Tom, and the man raised a wooden cup.

"Meadow juice," he said, in a voice dripping with nectar. "Squeezed from lemnis flower petals."

"What flower?" asked Tom, the question catching in his throat.

The young man beamed. "Rosettes of cerulean blue. Found high in the mountains."

"Did you say *lemnis*?"

The man broadened his smile.

Rosalie stood beside Tom and glanced into the cup. "It looks refreshing," she said.

"Sustenance for a weary traveller," said the man, holding the cup closer to Tom. "First sip, free. No coin."

"Try it, Tom," said Rosalie. "Then he'll leave us alone."

Tom took the cup, then sniffed the clear, blue liquid. It smelled like eucalyptus.

That's strange.

"One sip," said the man.

One sip. What harm will it do?

Tom lifted the cup to his lips and sipped. The drink tasted like lemon cordial. "It's lovely," he said. "But I don't want any more."

He handed the cup back. The young man stood in front of him, smiling and waiting.

"That's enough," said Tom, his mind drifting into a blurred reality.

The crowd swelled again, smothering the sky. Tom's knees threatened to buckle. He reached for Rosalie, but she'd disappeared into a sea of strange faces.

"Where's Rosalie," said Tom, his tongue lolling over the words.

"We are waiting for you, birraman," came a voice. "We have been waiting for a generation."

Tom pushed against the crowd. Urged his gaping mouth to cry for help. Prayed for Rosalie to save him.

But his legs failed, and Tom fell into the arms of the young man in blue robes.

~ Chapter 42 ~

As the sun rose above mountainous red dunes, turning the mahogany sand cherry-red, Jurelle stood atop the northeast turret of the wall surrounding Portum. The one where he always waited for his daughters to come home. But there'd be no homecoming anytime soon. Thaly and Saskia would be in Nordland by now, marching across the northern wilderness before sneaking into Enthilen. He'd been restless ever since they departed ten moons ago. Waiting for news didn't appeal, and Genevea's efforts to distract his worry proved fruitless, so Jurelle had appointed himself one of Portum's sentinels.

He paced in circles behind the turret's battlements, enjoying the cool morning air and the chance to escape the bustling city streets. At the foot of a dune, something caught a glint of sunlight and threw it across the fields outside Portum's east wall and between the turret's merlons. Jurelle reached for the spyglass attached to a metal stand in the middle of the tower and swivelled it towards the dunes. Pressing up to the eyepiece, he searched the endless sandscape until lurching to a halt. In a swale between two dunes marched hundreds of soldiers decked in silver armour. The bannerman carried a white banner emblazoned with the Erstürmen sigil of the two-headed serpent encircling a sun and two black spheres. Malphas' attack on Portum, long feared, had arrived.

Why has no-one raised the alarm? wondered Jurelle.

He released the spyglass and bolted down the turret steps. The wheeze of his gasping breaths drowned out every other sound as he sprinted through Portum's streets, then bounded up the Pallaxium stairs. Two guards tried to block his path, but he pushed them aside and burst through the front doors into the foyer.

Chloe sprang from her chair. "Do you have permission to be here? The conventus meets today."

"Let me through," said Jurelle. "The enemy is on our doorstep."

He brushed past Chloe and opened the door to the zōdiakos. As he burst into the famed room where men rarely trod, the eyes of hundreds of senators turned on him. Sitting in the centre of the colourful circle, Charmion's withering frame stiffened.

"What are you doing?" she asked.

Jurelle stopped and bent over, resting his hands on his knees and catching his breath. Then he stood tall and yelled, "An attack has begun! Erstürmen from the east. Pordillo won't be far behind."

"Erstürmen?" asked Charmion. "We've had no warning from our lookouts."

"I saw the enemy with the spyglass. They've probably reached the fields by now."

"Men are forbidden inside the conventus, Jurelle. You know the rules. Without a formal notification from a lookout, I can't...."

"They're coming!" screamed Jurelle. "Notification or not."

Charmion frowned. "I'll send a scouting party to the fields to verify your statement."

"No time for that. Secure the gates. Get soldiers onto the walls. Now!"

Jurelle strode from the zōdiakos, snapping at Chloe as he passed, "Arm yourself and find shelter."

"W-w-what?" she stammered. "Who?"

He didn't have time to explain, racing through the Pallaxium doors and down the steps. He headed home to find Genevea. Portum needed defending, and he needed her help.

* * * *

Jurelle marched into his apartment. Genevea sat at the table eating her morning meal.

"The Erstürmen and Pordillo are attacking from the east," he said. "Help me break into an armoury. Find me a damn weapon."

"We should wait it out here," said Genevea. "I'm sure the Germalian army has things well in hand."

"There was no warning. The enemy must have killed the lookouts." He crouched in front of Genevea and clasped her hands. "They're almost upon us, and I *want* to fight. The warrior's call won't relent. It demands I defend my home."

Genevea shook her head. "You're too old for this. Let it be."

"I know Erstürmen soldiers better than anyone in Portum. I know how they've been trained. I know their weaknesses."

She squeezed his fingers, tears welling in her eyes. "Promise me you'll stay out of harm's way. Don't go rushing into any battles."

"I promise."

Her shoulders slumped in resignation. "What do you need me to do?"

"We head for the armoury."

*   *   *   *

Jurelle held back in the shadows of a portico while Genevea stood outside the armoury door, trying not to look suspicious. But the shuffle of her feet across the pavers broadcast a nervous energy that caused Jurelle's palms to sweat. A guard with a stern face blocked the armoury entrance, her hand gripping the pommel of a cutlass.

"I need a weapon," said Genevea.

"Purpose?" asked the guard.

"We're under attack or soon will be. The Pordillo are coming."

The guard opened her stance and tensed. "I've not been notified of an attack. Without a pronouncement from the conventus, I can't hand out weapons like honey-cakes."

"We saw the enemy. Marching from the northeast."

"We?"

Genevea's face turned crimson, and she fussed with the sleeves of her dress. "It doesn't matter. *I* saw them. Erstürmen soldiers armed for war."

"A moment ago, you said it was the Pordillo."

"Pordillo *and* Erstürmen. They've formed an alliance."

"I wasn't aware of such an alliance."

"Oh, for goodness' sake," cried Genevea. "We're all going to die if you don't start issuing weapons now."

"Without a formal pronouncement of an attack, I can't *humph....*"

The guard collapsed backwards into Jurelle's arms. Genevea glared at him.

He shrugged. "Diplomacy wasn't working."

"Did you hurt her?"

"She'll wake up with a headache, that's all. Get the keys from her belt. We'll unlock the door, leave it open, and take the keys with us. Carry as many weapons as you can hold."

Jurelle and Genevea raided the armoury, taking cutlasses, javelins and knives.

"Give weapons to whoever you come across, man or woman," said Jurelle. "Send others here and have them spread the alarm."

"I'll go to the clocktower," said Genevea. "Demand they ring the bell."

"Good idea. I'll return to the northeast turret to survey the enemies' positions."

Jurelle and Genevea kissed, then she headed for The Hive.

He called after her, "If things go bad, wait in our apartment. I'll come for you."

Jurelle carried an armload of weapons into the street and handed them to men and women, all staring at him in stunned silence. A few men dropped their weapons onto the flagstones as if they'd picked up a burning coal from a fire.

"We all need to fight," said Jurelle. "The Pordillo and Erstürmen are here."

He tucked a cutlass and dagger under his belt, then raced to the east wall.

* * * *

Jurelle stood atop the northeast turret, using the spyglass to map enemy movements as they marched through the crop fields separating Portum from Magna Avium. Smoke billowed into the sky, clouding his view, as Erstürmen soldiers burned Portum's breadbasket. Farmers fled from the fires only to be felled by Pordillo arrows. A dozen Germalian soldiers guarding the perimeter confronted the enemy, but they were cut down in a heartbeat.

Jurelle caught his breath as thousands of Erstürmen marched from the smoke and down the main road towards Portum. He muttered to himself, "Erstürmen Shield from the north...five, maybe ten thousand. Pordillo south of us...ten...twenty thousand at least. No war machines... wait, a battering ram. Armoured. They'll focus their effort on the main gate."

He raced down the turret's staircase and grabbed the first soldier he found. "Place archers atop the wall. As many as you have."

"You're armed," said the soldier. "Men aren't supposed to be...."

"Get it done!" snapped Jurelle. "Where's your commander?"

"In the gate guardhouse, waiting for orders from Prime Lieutenant Eudokia."

Jurelle ran to the guardhouse.

He passed an open east gate, then burst through the guardhouse door. "Who's in command?"

A young woman stepped forward. "I am. Centure Isidora."

"Close and bar the gate, *now*. Reinforce it with whatever you can find. Send your troops to the top of the wall, prepared to rain terror down onto our attackers."

"Who are you, exactly?" asked Isidora. "What authority do you have to issue orders?"

"General Jurelle Stansfield of the King's Shield of Sardis. Once the leader of the Dobunni rebellion. Germalians choose not to recognise my authority, but I've fought many battles. More than the yarles you've lived, I'll wager." As Jurelle spoke, the clocktower bell rang, a manic, furious toll that set a quivering dismay in Isidora's brown eyes.

"That's the alarm," said Jurelle. "War is upon us."

Isidora sluiced sweat from her brow and barked orders to the soldiers nearby, "Bar the gate. Everyone onto the wall. Bring arrows and javelins. Arm the ballistae."

*   *   *   *

Six griffins shrieked overhead as Jurelle and Isidora stood on the east wall, directing the defence of the main gate. They ducked as a volley of Erstürmen arrows swooped past.

"Take cover and hold your fire," ordered Jurelle to the two dozen Germalian archers beside him. "Wait until the enemy is closer. Erstürmen armour has gaps under the armpits and between the spangenhelm and gorget. That's where you should aim. Remember, they want to breach this gate, so we know where they'll focus their attack."

Prime Lieutenant Eudokia, a Germalian commander Jurelle had trained yarles ago, arrived atop the wall wearing the impractical golden armour that made her look like a warring fish.

"Jurelle Stansfield," said Eudokia. "I'm in charge here. You must stand down and relinquish your weapons."

"No," said Jurelle. "I have a right to defend my life, the woman I love, and my home."

"The General has been instrumental in organising our defence," said Isidora.

"Rules are rules," said Eudokia. "We can't abandon our culture because...."

A volley of arrows clattered into the merlons, cutting Eudokia off mid-sentence.

Jurelle clutched her shoulder and pulled her below the parapet. "How many soldiers stayed in Portum?"

"Twenty thousand," said Eudokia. "Five thousand reserves."

"I estimate at least thirty thousand enemy soldiers," said Jurelle.

"Thirty thousand!"

"You're outnumbered. Everyone that can fight must be armed, including the men."

Underneath the chinstrap of her plumed helmet, Eudokia scratched her cheek, then peered through the embrasures towards the smoke billowing from the crop fields.

Jurelle's eyes demanded her attention, then he lowered his voice, "Arm your men. It's our only chance."

Eudokia faced Isidora. "Spread the order. Open all the armouries. Arm every woman, man and child old enough to fight. We prepare for an assault on the main gate."

*   *   *   *

Too obvious, thought Jurelle. The attack's too obvious. He'd left Eudokia and Isidora to direct the east gate defence and returned to the spyglass atop the northeast turret. His instincts nagged an unrelenting doubt. The enemy had more surprises to reveal.

Swivelling the spyglass north, he scanned Concha Beach, where Portum residents scampered among the rocks harvesting mussels or sat on the sand to bask in the sun.

"Can't they hear the bell?" he muttered. "Don't they know we're under attack?"

A boy and girl played on the beach, digging a moat to capture the frothy edge of an invading wave before it washed away their sandcastle. The boy ran up the beach to a man lounging against a wooden crate and tugged on his hand. The man tried to stand, but as he pushed into the sand to get leverage, his forearms disappeared beneath the surface.

What madness is this? wondered Jurelle.

The beach sand shifted like water, swirling as if flowing down a drain, and sucked the man and boy into the depths. The girl dropped a handful of shells and abandoned her castle, running towards the empty churn. But she stopped, dead, staring into the dunes lining Concha Beach. There, lumbering over the sand, came hundreds and hundreds of giants. Malphas' grell army. The Rephaim.

They poured onto the beach, striding past the little girl. Other beachgoers fled, running towards the gateway in the north wall where the stone battlement entered the ocean. At high tide, seawater blocked the opening, rising above the apex of an archway no wider than a house door. But it was low tide now. Anyone could wade through the shallows and stroll into Portum.

*   *   *   *

"Block the water gate!" yelled Jurelle as he sprinted to the beachward point of the north wall. "The enemy approaches."

"I heard the enemy is on the east gate," said a man fishing on the beach. "We got no problems here."

Jurelle yanked the fishing pole from the man's hands and clutched his shoulders. "Rephaim. Grell soldiers marching on Concha Beach. We need to block the gateway."

"Can't block the gateway," said a woman sitting nearby. "My daughter is on Concha Beach collecting mussels. Other people out there, too."

A soldier trotted down the north wall staircase and approached Jurelle. "What's all the fuss here?" she asked.

"You must have seen them by now," said Jurelle. "Rephaim marching up the beach."

"Beach is empty."

"What about my daughter?" asked the woman.

Slaughtered, thought Jurelle. They've all been slaughtered.

"They came from the dunes...." started Jurelle, then stopped.

At the north wall's base, the sand buckled in waves of convulsion as large as a row of houses. In an act of ill-advised curiosity, the soldier walked towards the edge of the churning sand and poked the tip of her javelin into the ground. She held it there for a moment until something yanked the weapon downwards. The soldier tugged back. Then the sand rose like a gaping, grainy mouth and swallowed her.

"What the?" said the fisher.

The writhing sand stilled. The clocktower bell stopped tolling, and silence descended over Portum. Jurelle expected Rephaim to wade through the water gate at any moment. He was wrong. At the bottom of the north wall, the sand collapsed, falling into a chasm as large as the Pallaxium. Jurelle jumped backwards to avoid being devoured, pulling the fisher and the woman with him. As he tumbled onto his buttocks, a slither of enormous serpents crawled from the hole. Poisonous slider serpents ridden by dreadwerps. A snake came straight towards him, spitting venom. He rolled aside. The venom splashed onto the fisher's face, and he screamed, his skin blistering and melting into a hideous gloop of blood and ebony.

Six serpents slid off into Portum's streets, following the screams of the heedless. But the hole in the sand wasn't empty. Out climbed the Rephaim. One. A dozen. A hundred. Rising up from the earth like colossal undead soldiers. They sliced a path through the panicked crowd with notched broadswords, swivelling faces covered in grilled helmets left and right to search for victims.

Jurelle reached for his cutlass. But every muscle in his body screamed for him to run. A griffin shrieked overhead, swooping down across the Rephaim. One of the grells hoisted a lance and launched it at the griffin. It punctured the creature's chest and burst through the other side. The animal spiralled out of control. Its wind-rider slipped from her harnessed saddle and plummeted onto a roof, smashing through the terracotta tiles. The griffin regained its bearings for a moment, then flew into the north wall, shattering the parchment-thin bones of its skull. The Rephaim turned his attention to Jurelle.

Run! thought Jurelle. For Volerdie's sake, run.

* * * *

Portum fell into chaos. Dreadwerps riding slider serpents writhed across the wharves of The Hive, showering panicked crowds with caustic venom.

The clocktower was on fire, flames burning hours from the clock face. People clambered onto boats, trying to escape the bedlam.

Genevea, thought Jurelle. Is she among them?

He hadn't seen his wife since they parted at the armoury, but he recalled his last words to her — *wait in our apartment. I'll come for you.* That's where he had to go.

Two dozen Germalian archers arrived on the wharves and fired arrows at the slider serpents. Most of the projectiles bounced harmlessly off the scaly skin.

"Aim for the dreadwerps!" yelled Jurelle as he ran past the archers, heading for Lata Via. I need a damn horse, he thought.

He trotted along Portum's main boulevard, fighting against a calamity of men, women and children who ran in all directions. Legions of soldiers marched east, carrying their rectangular shields out front, cutlasses unsheathed. Two more griffins flew overhead, swooshing through the smoke haze that had settled over the city.

Jurelle turned from the boulevard into the laneway to his home.

Arriving at the apartment building, he climbed the steps, opened the door and walked into his quarters.

"Genevea," he said. No answer. "Genevea!" Not here.

He stepped onto the balcony. In the distance, smoke plumes billowed above the east wall battlements. West, Rephaim lumbered through The Hive's streets, cutting down innocent after innocent with the slash of a broadsword. At the end of Lata Via, near the Pallaxium steps, Germalian soldiers fought off a troop of Erstürmen Shield.

They've breached the gate, thought Jurelle. *Wait in our apartment.* No. I can't.

He ran down the stairs, along the laneway and onto the boulevard. A driverless cart pulled by a frenzied, wild-eyed khorsal clattered past. Jurelle flung himself onto the cart tray, gasping when the timber punched the air from his lungs.

The cart careered along Lata Via, the khorsal bursting through crowds of bewildered citizens as it galloped towards the Pallaxium. Jurelle clutched the side of the tray, trying to stop himself from being thrown off. The animal smashed through a stall selling earthen jugs, pottery shards pummelling Jurelle like serrated hail. The beast continued east, parting the fearful crowd as a ship's bow parts the waves. Then it whinnied in terror.

Thwack! The khorsal turned sharply, and the cart jack-knifed, flipping onto its side. Jurelle tumbled onto the pavers, ripping skin from his knees and elbows. He lay there, dazed, the sky above him turning black.

Then a hand reached down and pulled him up.

"Are you alright?" asked a female voice.

Jurelle shook the daze from his eyes and focussed. Prime Lieutenant Eudokia, her face cut and bruised, grasped his forearm.

"The...the east gate?" asked Jurelle.

"Breached," she said. "The enemy has invaded Portum."

"Reph...Repha...."

"Rephaim to the north and west. Slider serpents at The Hive."

"We're surrounded."

"We need a plan. Otherwise, the city will fall. General Jurelle, can you help us?"

Jurelle nodded.

"Follow me," said Eudokia. "Into the Pallaxium vault."

* * * *

Inside the zōdiakos, Eudokia prised open the headrest of Charmion's oversized red leather chair, exposing a lever. She lifted the lever, and a trapdoor, built into the floor beside the chair, flung open.

"What is this?" asked Jurelle.

"Entrance to the vault," said Eudokia. "A room built beneath the floor."

"How do you know about it?"

"I'm also a senator. In an emergency, this is where we are supposed to gather."

"Thaly never told me about this."

"We're sworn to secrecy."

Eudokia replaced the chair's headrest, then dropped down through the trapdoor and into a metal chamber. Jurelle followed. Chloe stood inside the chamber, large enough for six people, her hand resting on a winch.

"You knew about this as well?" said Jurelle.

Chloe smiled. "Secrets and lies. The conventus motto."

She shut the trapdoor and turned the winch clockwise. The chamber lurched to the side, then descended. Jurelle pressed his hands into the wall to steady himself.

"It's safe," said Chloe. "The cogs and cables are fashioned from the hardest metals."

After countless turns of the winch, Chloe brought the chamber to a halt somewhere beneath the Pallaxium.

"Charmion won't be happy," she said to Eudokia.

"We need all the help we can muster," replied Eudokia. "It's a disaster up there."

Chloe pulled on another lever, and a door, built into the metal wall so seamlessly Jurelle didn't notice it, opened. He followed Eudokia into a room with hewn granite walls, candle chandeliers, tables, chairs, beds, and enough food and crates of vinum to satiate a couple of hundred senators for a whole season.

In the middle of a babble of thirty to forty senators, Charmion spun her wheeled chair around and glared at Jurelle. "Jurelle Stansfield, you can't...."

"We don't have time," interrupted Eudokia. "We need the General's help."

Charmion pushed through the crowd of senators, wheeling her chair up to the Prime Lieutenant. "You've broken the vow of secrecy, Senator Eudokia, *and* brought a man into the vault. This will be your last day as a member of the conventus."

"It'll be everyone's last day if we don't turn the tide of this battle," said Jurelle. "Hundreds of Rephaim are dismantling what's left of The Hive after slider serpents rained poison on your citizens. Pordillo and Erstürmen have breached the east gate."

"We should never have marched on Enthilen," said Charmion. "Your daughter...."

"Shut up!" shrieked Chloe. "Stop with the politics and the hypocrisy. Show some damn leadership."

The room fell silent. Jurelle almost chuckled. *Almost.*

"Do you have a city map down here?" he asked.

Charmion nodded, wheeling her chair to a table strewn with parchments.

Eudokia pulled a map of Portum to the top.

Jurelle traced his index finger along the streets. "We know this city better than any invader. There must be a way to use the layout to our advantage."

"Some of the streets are dead ends — *finem mortuorum*," said Eudokia. "We could use them...."

Charmion interrupted, "Do you have a plan, Prime Lieutenant?"

Eudokia looked to Jurelle.

"We need to split the enemy forces," he said. "How many *finem* streets in Portum, Charmion?"

"There are six off Lata Via," she replied.

"If we can funnel the Pordillo and Erstürmen down the boulevard, then lure smaller groups of soldiers into the dead-ends...."

"And cut off their escape," said Eudokia. "Block the open end of the street."

"How?" asked Charmion.

"All the *finem* streets have two and three-storey buildings on either side. We could empty the buildings. Throw everything onto the street."

"And place archers at every window," said Jurelle. "If we can isolate the enemy fighters, we might have a chance."

"What about the Rephaim?" asked Charmion.

"Send all your griffins to The Hive. Attack from above and push the grells towards the wharves. Then have your remaining warships ready to fire their ballistae into the enemy."

"Slider serpents hate water," said Eudokia.

"And they can't fly," said Jurelle. "An attack from the air and sea is the best chance of defeating the Rephaim and the dreadwerps."

"How will we entice the Erstürmen and Pordillo into our traps?" asked Charmion.

"Bait. Germalian soldiers feigning a retreat, leading the enemy into the dead ends."

"Surely, General, that would be suicide?"

"I will do it," said Jurelle. "I will lead a group."

"As will I," said Eudokia.

"Then spread the word among the lieutenants and Centures," said Charmion. "Concentrate our archers in the buildings lining the *finem* streets. Others should be ready to empty the buildings and block the exit once the enemy has fallen for the trap. And we need more volunteers to act as bait." Charmion grabbed Eudokia's hand. "Make certain they know what they're volunteering for. Likely, most will not survive."

"I'll lead my group here," said Jurelle, placing his finger on the map. "To the street called Postremus Stabit." He faced Eudokia. "Prepare to risk everything to save Portum."

*　*　*　*

"With me!" screamed Jurelle. "Into the street."

Jurelle Stansfield led a hundred Germalian soldiers and a handful of armed civilians past a cornerstone with the name Postremus Stabit carved into its surface. The Germalians had managed to funnel the Erstürmen and Pordillo down Lata Via, and now, five Prime Lieutenants and Jurelle prepared to split the enemy forces, trapping them in Portum's dead-end streets.

He strode down to the end of Postremus Stabit, a line of two-storey townhouses blocking further progress. After gathering his fighters, they turned to face Lata Via, waiting to see if the enemy had taken the bait. Around him, nervous Germalians clutched their weapons with quaking hands.

Jurelle raised his cutlass, sunlight catching the edge of the polished blade. "Let them come to us. We are not alone here."

Brandishing swords and halberds, Erstürmen Shield streamed into the street.

Two or three thousand, thought Jurelle.

A young man standing beside him, digging the pommel of his cutlass into his thigh, began to sob. "We're going to be slaughtered," he said.

"Hold steady, brave Germalians," said Jurelle. "One day, our city may fall, but it will not be today. Today, our hearts are strong. Today, our courage burns like a raging fire. Today...we refuse to yield."

The Erstürmen slowed to a walk, the clink of their cuisses echoing down the closed street. Beneath the rim of spangenhelms, mocking smiles betrayed the enemy's thoughts. Trapped prey made for easy slaughter.

The first wave of Erstürmen lunged at the Germalian defenders. Blade clashed against blade, the clang of thrashing weapons bouncing from the walls. Above the din, a yell came from a second-storey window near the open end of the street. Furniture flew from houses, raining down onto the cobblestones. Chairs, tables, crates, statues, bowls — anything the Germalians could find to block the street and thwart an escape. With the barrier in place, hundreds of archers leaned from the townhouse windows, showering the enemy with arrows.

Jurelle forced himself into the middle of the battle, slashing at an Erstürmen soldier with his cutlass, trying to direct tired muscles to the armour's weak spots under the arm and above the gorget. The archer attack didn't thin the enemy numbers as quickly as Jurelle hoped. The well-trained Erstürmen soldiers pushed him and the other defenders back against the townhouse walls at the dead end of Postremus Stabit.

Jurelle turned from the battle and tried to open a door. Locked.

He thumped on the timber. "Let us in!"

A terrified face peered out from a townhouse window, then pulled the curtains closed as if they were a shield.

Jurelle tried another door. Also locked. Germalian women and men fell at his feet, defenders who didn't waver when he demanded they follow him. He needed to give the survivors a chance to escape. He pushed his way to a window and smashed the glass with the pommel of his cutlass.

"Through here!" he yelled. "Through...."

The last word never came. An enemy soldier plunged a halberd into Jurelle's spine, and he collapsed to his knees. The Erstürmen Shield, a young man the same as many Jurelle had trained back in Sardis, steadied his hand as he thrust his weapon a second time, slicing the blade through Jurelle's ribs.

He remembered his tuition, thought Jurelle. He'll make a fine soldier.

Jurelle slumped to the pavement, and the world went black. A world trapped between life and death. A calm and quiet place. Genevea came to him, placing her fingers on his cheek as gently as a florist handling a dried flower petal. Then Thaly and Saskia arrived, resting their heads on his bloodied chest and listening for an elusive heartbeat. Finally, Jürgen stood over him, dressed in the King's Shield armour, and thumped his fist against his breastplate.

* * * *

The sun's warmth coaxed Jurelle's eyes open. The enemy had fled Postremus Stabit, leaving behind a mountain of corpses. He went to sit up, but his arms and legs wouldn't work. So, he lay there on his back, staring at a sky filled with ashen clouds and shattered blue. A griffin wheeled overhead, and the wind-rider threw her lance to stem the invader assault.

At the street's far end, a blurred shape pushed aside a broken table and weaved its way through the litter of bodies.

A looter seeking treasure? wondered Jurelle. Or an enemy soldier come to finish off the wounded?

Halfway down the street, the blur sharpened into a familiar form. A woman, checking every corpse, inspecting every injured fighter. A woman with pale skin and loving green eyes the colour of jade. Genevea's eyes.

Jurelle tried to call her, but when he opened his mouth, the words drowned in blood bubbling up from his chest. One body at a time, Genevea came closer. The slow, painful search for her loved one.

I'm here, thought Jurelle. Right at the end, slumped against the locked door.

Genevea stepped over a corpse and looked to the dead end. Her furrowed face lightened with recognition, then darkened with understanding. She raced to Jurelle and dropped to her knees.

"You're alive," she said, clutching his limp hand. But her jaded eyes said something different as they recognised the extent of his wounds. Then she sobbed. "Stupid old fool. Why would you make a stand in a place with no escape? Your daughters are going to be so angry with you. Stupid old fo...." She slumped beside him, her body bent over with heaving anguish.

He knew then he would die. Genevea's face, the one he'd loved for more than thirty yarles, confirmed what he already expected. Death would come soon.

She wiped the tears from her cheeks, those beautiful, silken cheeks, and tried to smile. "The battle is turning in our favour," she said. "Your plan worked. A divided enemy is failing, and the griffins have almost thwarted the Rephaim. Portum is saved."

She squeezed her hands under his back and lifted his torso, hugging him to her chest. Tears came again. Not from Genevea. From Jurelle as he strained with every skerrick of energy to say his final words.

"Thank...you. My light, my life, my hope."

The cradle of his lover's arms stilled his heartbeat, and he could think of no better place to be at the end of it all.

~ Chapter 43 ~

Sitting cross-legged on a hard floor, Tom sucked air through a cloth bag covering his head. He'd woken a moment before when footsteps shuffled nearby, and a smell resembling cinnamon incense wafted into his nostrils. Like the lemnis drink from the Revelé market, the aroma reminded him of home. He flinched as someone pulled the bag away, then raised his arms to ward off an attack. But none came. Instead, a male draughoul dressed in hickory-coloured robes floated past, carrying a wooden cup towards a small person propped upright on a white cushion atop a marble pedestal.

Small? wondered Tom. *Person? No arms or legs.*

The draughoul stopped beside the limbless torso on the pedestal, then lifted the cup to pale lips, tilting the liquid into the person's mouth.

"Thank you, Pida," it said, in a comforting, melodious voice, like the dawn chorus on a warm spring morning heralding the promise of new life.

Female. I think. Not sure.

The draughoul stepped aside and waited. The woman, only a cotton sheet wrapped around her limbless body, smiled at Tom, the wrinkles on her face and bald head tracing an existence that could have stretched back generations.

"Would you prefer we speak Erstürmen or *English?*" she asked.

Tom wriggled his toes, wondering if his legs would carry him to safety. Except, he didn't know where to run.

"To your left," said the woman. "Through the middle arch, down four hundred and sixty-two steps, along a narrow path that, by the end of the day, will return you to Revelé. But, Tom Anderson, we have much to discuss before you leave."

"*Who taught you English?*" asked Tom in his native tongue.

"*I've learned many things. You may learn them, too, if you are worthy.*"

Tom reverted back to Erstürmen. "Who are you?"

"It appears you are comfortable with a language of Enthilen," said the woman. "My name is Hál. It means *whole*. Complete."

"Where's Rosalie? The woman I was with in the market." Tom clambered to his feet, clasping and unclasping his fingers to get the blood flowing.

"She's with the Germalians. They search for you now."

"I want to return to my friends."

"Wait," said Hál. "You cannot walk away from this responsibility."

"I don't need another burden. I'm going back to help my friends."

Tom turned left. *Middle arch. Four hundred and sixty-two steps....*

Also dressed in hickory robes, six more draughouls appeared, each standing in the centre of an open archway to block his escape. Silhouetting sunlight framed their crooked bodies like halos.

"You *will* help your friends," said Hál. "After you've been tested."

Tom faced her. "Tested?"

"We're all students. From the day we are born to the day we die. Some forget the lesson the moment it ends. Others hold the knowledge for a lifetime and always hunger for more. Relishing the opportunity for another test."

Tom patted the pockets of his pants. *Empty.*

Then a glint of sunlight through obsidian emerged from a folded black cloth at the base of Hál's pedestal. The first draughoul, Pida, approached the fabric, crouched and peeled it open, revealing the eyes of lost souls.

"You have the dark eyes," said Tom.

"Do you desire their power?" asked Hál. "The chance for immortality."

"No. The eyes are simply a means to an end."

"Others thought the same, yet succumbed to the lure of eternal life. Why should I consider you any different?"

"I could have killed Adalwolf if I wanted. In Pergamos' throne room. Stolen his soul and returned to Earth."

"But you did not. The absent king still lives, and you took another path home."

712

"Thanks to Widukind."

Hál smiled. "*Ah* yes, our dear Widukind. Pida, may I have another drink?"

The draughoul stood, took the wooden cup from a table beside the pedestal, tipped more refreshment into Hál's open mouth then stepped away.

"Please sit, Tom," said Hál. "Are you thirsty or hungry?"

Tom shook his head and returned to the cold floor, crossing his legs again as if they might shield him from an uncertain threat.

"It's been such a long time since Widukind graced this hall," said Hál. "He failed the test, and it has cursed him ever since."

What test? "Malphas' brother seeks to redeem himself."

"I hope you're right. Widukind's constitution is frail. I worry for his future and the future of us all should Widukind falter."

A female draughoul appeared from the shadows carrying a cup and a plate of food. She approached Tom and placed the items at his feet, then returned to the half-light.

"You lied to me," said Hál. "Please, don't do it again. I know you desire sustenance."

Tom lifted the cup to his nose and sniffed.

"If I were to poison you," said Hál, "I would use one with no scent or taste, and you would die instantly."

"What did that man give me in the market?" asked Tom. "It smelled like *eucalyptus.*"

"Your memories create the smells."

Tom sniffed at the cup again.

"It is water only," said Hál.

Mouth parched, Tom drank the cool, bubbling water, then placed the cup on the floor beside plated food resembling toasted, unleavened bread and a puréed mash of green beans.

"What is this place?" he asked, dipping a strip of bread into the purée and placing it in his mouth. It tasted like ful medames. *Another memory?*

"A chamber of learning, should you desire it." Hál nodded to Pida, and the draughoul reached down into the top of the cotton sheet stretched across Hál's chest and withdrew a jewel of polished white gold with embedded gemstones.

Tom stopped chewing, bread crumbs tumbling from his gaping mouth.

"My heart stopped, too," said Hál. "When first I saw the jewel, I would bear for generations."

Simultaneously, the six draughouls stepped away from the arches, letting shafts of morning sun stream into the hall, joining at a single point of light to enter the jewel and burst out again in a rainbow of colour.

"The gems are jasper, sapphire, chalcedony, emerald, sardonyx, sardius, chrysolite, beryl, topaz, chrysoprasus, jacinth and amethyst," said Hál.

"The...the shape...." stammered Tom.

"A lemniscate. The symbol for infinity."

Revelé. A lemniscate. Drawn in the margin of page four hundred and sixty-two in the blue book. Four hundred and sixty-two steps lead to this hall. Widukind was here. Widukind left the blue book for me.

"Your mind opens, Tom Anderson," said Hál. "I see it in your eyes."

"Did you write in the blue book?"

Hál smiled, glancing down at her armless torso. "I cannot write a single letter, but maybe our message was not wasted on Widukind after all."

"Did you send Widukind to Earth?" asked Tom, his mind racing with possibilities.

"We didn't stop him. We are not gaolers. Here, only your thoughts can imprison you."

Tom's face burned with rising anger. "My life in Enthilen isn't my own. Dwarrow, Widukind, Malphas, all want something from me. You're no different."

"You wish to be the master of your own destiny."

"Yes!"

"Good. Your time is close. When Volerdie made the throne of the dead, he embedded in it seven treasures; the eyes of lost souls, the First Scripture, four blood compasses and this jewel — the *Infinitas.*"

Pida unclasped the jewel from the chain around Hál's neck and laid the Infinitas across his bony hands, holding it towards Tom.

"When Volerdie fled to Earth," said Hál, "out of all the throne's treasures, he took with him only the Infinitas."

"Fled to...*Earth?*"

"Do you not know who Volerdie is?"

"The Divine Creator," said Tom. "An imaginary God worshipped by the Erstürmen."

"A deity who fled this land aeons ago and established a new kingdom to fight over the dominion of Earth. To begin the eternal struggle between evil and good in your world."

"Do you mean Satan? Is Volerdie the Devil?"

"Lucifer, Satan, Volerdie, Beelzebub, *Malphas*. Evil has many names and many faces but only one purpose. To crush weak and innocent souls and spread chaos wherever it roams. Malphas seeks to return a greater evil to Enthilen in the form of the Divine Creator."

Tom shook his head. "Lucifer doesn't exist. He's imagined. Used to scare the gullible into following rules devised by self-proclaimed luminaries."

"Does evil exist?" asked Hál.

"Of course, but...."

"And do those who are evil crave power?"

"Yes, sometimes."

"Then evil has a name, a face and an ambition. Many names. Many faces. But only one purpose. To hold dominion over others through misery and death. Volerdie is the embodiment of evil that Malphas longs to resurrect. Yet, even I do not know what the Worshipful Master will bring forth if he sacrifices an immortal on the throne of the dead. One thing I am certain of, though, is he will not rest until his desire is fulfilled."

"We're going to end it," said Tom. "We're going to destroy Volerdie's throne."

"That fate is yet to be determined," said Hál. "As is your own, Tom Anderson. If you break the throne, your actions will halt the arrival of one future and mark the beginning of another. I cannot say if the new world will be better than the old. None of us can. The future will be dictated by those who imagine it and live it. You will have a say in that future if you survive your quest."

A female draughoul stepped from the shadows and offered Tom a piece of fruit.

"Thank you, Wynok," said Hál. "Take the tarnello, Tom. You need your strength."

Tom grasped the tangerine-coloured fruit, shaped like a banana, and bit into it. Juice like watery honey dribbled down his chin. In three mouthfuls, the fruit was gone, and he wanted more.

Still cradling the Infinitas in his hands, Pida stood beside Tom. The kaleidoscope of colour from the embedded gemstones bathed Tom's mind with a wash of unlimited promise. His heavy arms lightened as if gravity had disappeared, reaching up to take the jewel.

But Tom stopped himself and faced Hál. "Have *you* travelled to Earth? Are you immortal?"

"I am a descendant of Lycious," said Hál. "She who found the First Scripture but searched in vain for the eyes of lost souls. During her journey through Ostamp, she gave birth to a child in this monastery. The child continued her mother's legacy, studying a copy of the First Scripture for many seasons. Then, Lycious' daughter began her search for the dark eyes. But unlike Lycious, she found them."

"Did Lycious' daughter travel to Earth?" asked Tom.

"Yes. Her name was Maray. In your world, she was called Mary. But she did not go to find immortality. Instead, she sought knowledge. Using the amber light cast from the flaming pupils of the eyes of lost souls, she travelled through the underworld you call *Hell*, searching for the most valuable treasure from Volerdie's throne, the Infinitas. Only she and Volerdie understood the power unleashed when the eyes are reunited with the jewel. In a foul place full of desperation, Mary found the Infinitas. She was about to escape when Volerdie, *Lucifer*, appeared. A battle of wills ensued, raging for many days and nights. Through light and darkness. Down into bottomless pits, then climbing boundless pinnacles.

Fear wrestled hope until hope prevailed. Mary fled with the treasures, returning to Ostamp. In Revelé, she gave birth to a son, then bestowed on him all the knowledge of past lives. On the first day of his twelfth harvest season, Mary urged her son to travel to Earth to share this knowledge."

Wynok gathered the dark eyes from the black cloth. Tom expected the female draughoul to wail and moan, searching the flickering, flaming pupils for her lost soul. But she made no sound, drifting across to stand beside Pida.

Hál smiled. "We've been waiting for this moment for a long time, Tom Anderson. To re-unite the dark eyes with the Infinitas. To create the bond that will offer the knowledge of the ancestors to an open mind."

"What's this got to do with me?" asked Tom.

"For generations, we have patiently waited for someone to continue Mary's work. She saw through Volerdie's deception, confronting his evil on Earth, as you have seen through Malphas' lies, and seek to destroy the dead throne. Your actions speak of someone who will carry the legacy of generations into a better world. The time has come for you to be tested. To see if you are a worthy custodian of the wisdom of ancestors."

"How will I...." started Tom.

"Place the eyes of lost souls into the Infinitas and grasp it in your hands."

"Wait," said a voice from outside.

Tom turned. Through an archway, materialising from the sunlight like an angel descended from heaven, floated Caeli, bearing no resemblance to the draughoul she'd become, but looking every bit like the princess he'd first met in Sardis' Sunrise Keep.

"It's almost done," said Caeli to Tom. "I never doubted your resolve."

"Princess Caeli," mumbled Tom as she knelt before him. "How did... where...?"

"Our worlds have many mysteries. Soon, you will be able to solve all of them." She reached a steady hand to her neck and pulled over her head a necklace with a silver pendant in the shape of a lemniscate. "My father gave this to me before he disappeared from my life. I want you to have it as a reminder of this moment." Caeli leaned forward and let the necklace drop down over Tom's head.

He grasped the pendant, pressing it against a thumping heart.

Caeli stood.

Tom reached for her, but she dissolved in the sunlight like morning dew.

"A valued life is not one in which you live for an eternity," said Hál. "It is one in which you make such a contribution to your world that others remember it forever. Seek an *immortalised* life, Tom Anderson. Not an immortal one."

Pida knelt before Tom, holding the Infinitas towards him. Wynok did the same with the eyes of lost souls.

"The dark eyes and the Infinitas are more ancient than Volerdie himself," said Hál. "He did not create them. He *stole* them. Twisted their purpose to suit his ambition. Used the knowledge trapped inside to meet his own ends. But you will reclaim them. The eyes of lost souls will be known again by their true name. *The Eyes of Relevation.*"

"Relevation," whispered Tom. "Reveal?"

"No," said Hál. "More than reveal. To uplift all of those around you." She leaned forward. "Take the eyes from Wynok and place them, one at a time, in the bosom of the Infinitas. Then grasp the renewed jewel in your own hands."

Tom's hand moved as if he had no choice. As if he didn't control the muscles in his arm. With quavering fingers, he plucked an eye from Wynok's palm and placed it into one of the silvery loops of the Infinitas. A click like a tumbler turning in a lock echoed through the chamber. The black of the obsidian glass vanished, the eye's flaming pupil replaced by a circle of incandescent light.

Tom did the same with the other eye. *Click, vanish, shine.*

Wynok stood and stepped away.

"Take the Eyes of Relevation from Pida," said Hál.

Tom followed her instructions, resting the jewel across his open palms. Pida stood, returning to Hál's side.

"Now," said Hál, "close your hands around the Infinitas."

Tom inhaled one deep breath after another. Hál's voice hummed inside his head. *Do not jeopardise the moment with hesitancy.* Tom closed his hands, encasing the Eyes of Relevation. A whirlwind of visions flashed through his mind. Events tracing back to the beginning of everything. Images of mouldewerps dancing and feasting on the grassy Dambay Plains. Stone-grells landing on the southern shore of Babir Birramal, then marching into the plains to build Malang Gunya. Kings crowned in Thyatira and flying to Hurst on white griffins. Germalians building the Pallaxium in Portum. The Dobunni travelling across the Veiled Occyan and settling in Bethesda. Erstürmen refugees fleeing Nordland. The transformation of Iglund to Sardis.

Then Tom's mind lurched home to Earth, travelling back through millennia of civilizations wracked by war, famine, poverty and disease. But also the celebration of remarkable achievements. Exploration and invention. *Homo sapiens* huddling together in caves overlooking savannah plains in Africa. Dark-skinned people arriving on the northern shores of the land he called Australia. Settlers building Mesopotamia. The rise and fall of ancient Egypt, the Aztecs and Mayans. The expansion of the English and Spanish empires. Nazis in Europe. The cold war. Americanisation of modern life. The rise of China.

As each vision emerged, Tom did more than simply witness significant moments in the history of two worlds. He absorbed every detail about those moments. Gained knowledge from the people who were there. Strangers' thoughts and feelings became his own. He lived their dreams and nightmares. His mind assimilated everything.

A final vision emerged before it all ended; the ancient civilization of Pergamos, a glimmering city in the middle of a plain. Proud, prosperous citizens wandered manicured paths in the shadows of towering spires. Abundant fields brimmed with food. Clear waters trickled along expertly crafted aqueducts.

Is this the paradise Malphas seeks? wondered Tom.

In Pergamos' grandest hall, a man sat on a throne. Tom's mind hovered beside the man, listening to him speak to a crowd of people. Then the man stopped and turned face on. He smiled as if he knew Tom's mind watched over him.

Tom collapsed to the floor in front of Hál.

"I saw him," he gasped. "I saw Volerdie. It wasn't what I expected."

"No-one is born evil," said Hál. "Ambition and power corrupted Volerdie. Weakened his soul until not a shred of goodness remained. Of course you know that now. You know more than anyone alive."

Tom pushed himself off the floor and stood, clutching the Infinitas in one hand and brushing the dust from his leather coat with the other. "I don't feel any different. I thought I'd feel *wise*. All-knowing."

"The knowledge is inside your mind. You must learn to access it. I cannot help."

Pida took the Infinitas and removed the Eyes of Relevation, giving them to Tom.

"The jewel must remain here," said Hál. "It will be waiting for your return."

"Return?" said Tom.

"When Volerdie's throne is broken, you will begin the rest of your mission, guarding the Infinitas until you die."

"I can't do that," snapped Tom. "I have other plans. I might go ho...."

"You will never return to Earth," interrupted Hál. "This is your home now. The draughouls will be gone. The destruction of the throne will release their souls from the dark eyes, freeing their bodies from this purgatorial decay. *Every lost soul, trapped in glass. Again, made whole, free to pass.*"

"What if I falter?" asked Tom.

"Then we remain the jewel's custodians until the next worthy birraman graces these shores. But my time in this body is coming to an end. You must do one more thing before leaving us — capture my soul with the dark eyes. Only as a draughoul can I continue my guardianship of the Infinitas."

Tom didn't want to steal anyone's soul, and by making her request, Hál admitted that Tom's plan may fail.

"You will *not* fail," said Hál. "I must prepare for any outcome, but my heart tells me you will destroy the throne, and I will ascend with the other lost souls to paradise. The wisdom of ancestors is locked inside your mind, Tom Anderson. With this knowledge, anything is possible. I know you will find the key."

* * * *

Rosalie braced herself against a boulder, leaned forward and vomited up the morning meal, a waste of oats mixed with fermented kamel's milk. The sight of the sludgy mess sprayed across the dirt made her want to vomit again.

"Are you alright?" asked Saskia, placing a reassuring hand on Rosalie's shoulder.

Rosalie nodded. "I'll be fine. We should get airborne."

"Not today. Thaly ordered me to stay with the army. And Namu needs a rest."

Rosalie pushed herself back from the boulder and brushed Saskia's hand away. "What about Tom? He's been missing for two moons."

"Thaly and Berenice have already begun a new search. They'll find him."

"I should have gone with Thaly."

"Yagle will cover more ground with only one rider."

Rosalie stumbled to the campfire and slumped to the ground as scattered raindrops sizzled onto hot coals. A blustery, north-easterly wind brought cold air from Grauberge, threatening to turn the rain into hail or snow. In the valley below Rosalie, the Germalian army camped on Revelé's western fringe. The town where she'd lost Tom. One moment, they were together in the market, and the next, he was gone, swallowed up by the paralysing crowd. She'd spent the day searching Revelé's streets, then flying with Saskia in ever-increasing circles around the town. Tom had disappeared, and Rosalie blamed herself. She'd lost the one person who could stop Malphas. She'd lost the only person she cared about.

Namu cawed as Saskia sat beside the campfire. "I'll get you something to eat in a moment," she called to her griffin.

"What do we have?" asked Rosalie.

"One marsh-hare. Won't be enough. I'll ask the griffin handlers to trap more." Saskia poked at the coals with the tip of her boot. "Do you think...." she started, then paused, her eyes drifting away with the smoke. "Do you think Tom could have run away?"

"No," snapped Rosalie. "He wouldn't do that."

"I mean, the responsibility might have gotten all too much. No shame in...."

"Stop it. He didn't run. He'll face Malphas in Pergamos."

"Are you certain?"

A simple question opened a floodgate. Rosalie cried. No, *bawled*. Let out a cataract of emotions held fast by her desire to appear resilient, able to tackle anything this world threw at her with a wink and a smile. But Tom's disappearance had been the final crack in the dam wall before it broke.

Saskia shuffled closer to Rosalie, placing her arm around her shoulder. "I'm an idiot. I didn't mean to say that about Tom."

"It's...it's not...." sobbed Rosalie before sucking in a handful of breaths to steady herself. "Honestly, it is, and it isn't about Tom. It's everything. Returning to Enthilen's misery. Pretending I'm a soldier when I can't even fight a cold. Falling in love with a man from another world. A man I barely know. And now...now...."

"You're with child," said Saskia.

"Is it so obvious?"

"The regular puking kind of gives it away, considering you're well otherwise."

"My Ma was the same. She had bad sickness with the twins, Allum and Nettie."

Saskia's eyes grew wide. "You could be having twins."

Rosalie wiped the tears from her cheeks and chuckled. "Don't wish that on me. One will be enough of a handful." She turned away from Saskia. "I don't know if I want to bring a child into a world of misery. I don't...." she whispered, "I don't know if I want it at all."

"Have you told Tom?" asked Saskia.

"I can't be certain it's his. There was another before Tom, but the timing seems wrong. I've missed only one bleeding. A part of me is scared to admit it's Tom's. Now he's disappeared; the child could be without a father. And have a mother with little to offer."

"If you don't want the child, I can arrange it," said Saskia. "In Germalia, the woman alone makes the decisions about pregnancy and childbirth. Our healers have a procedure to flush the womb. It must be done soon; otherwise, it will not work. I can ask for you."

"No. I want to tell Tom. I want to talk to him about it. If I ever see him again."

Saskia pulled Rosalie close. "If anyone's going to find him, it'll be Thaly. She has a knack for these things. She's saved me enough times."

Rosalie shivered as sleety rain snuck through the defences of her furred leather coat.

There could be nothing to find, she thought.

Malphas' spies would be on watch. Likely, the Worshipful Master already knew the Germalian army marched across Nordland. Draughouls, lured close by the eyes of lost souls, could have captured Tom. Or killed him. She wondered if the Germalians would still fight if they knew the one person who could shatter Volerdie's throne had gone missing. Seventy-thousand soldiers covered the valley floor below her, their round tents resembling giant mushrooms. Tufted goliaths, Rosalie preferred the Erstürmen name for elephai, browsed on a scattering of stunted trees while horses grazed inside corrals formed by wagons and driftwood fences. Male servants scurried about the tents, tensioning ropes and hammering in stakes, or prepared meals around a massive fire in the middle of the camp. Others groomed pack animals or checked supplies. The march would have taken much longer without the servants, and the fighters would have been much wearier.

Groups of soldiers wandered off towards Revelé, chatting and laughing, clearly looking forward to a day of rest in the town. Every action by the Germalians exuded a surety unfamiliar to Rosalie. A certainty this fight was good and decent and the only path forward. She had believed it. For most of her life, she'd fought against the Erstürmen patriarchal monarchy that had morphed into a maniacal dictatorship. Hiding with the rebels in the Desolate Mountains, she had nothing to lose by resisting Malphas. No care if death found her or not. But things had changed. She'd lost Tom, which hurt as much as the day she abandoned her family in Sardis. And, a new life grew inside her, one hoping to be born into a world full of love.

Now, Rosalie had a lot to lose, and returning to Enthilen could see it all vanish.

* * * *

Arms outstretched, Tom ran his fingertips over the smooth rock walls rising up either side of him as he ambled through a narrow mountain pass.

"Detranté," he called, the pronouncement bouncing from the stone. *I'm in Detranté.*

He'd been walking all day, down the four hundred and sixty-two steps from Hál's mountain hideaway, along the winding path that should have led back to Revelé. But the path branched, left and right, on multiple occasions, and he'd become lost.

So much for the wisdom of the ancestors.

Pebbles shifted under his feet as he stumbled almost every step through Detranté. The sun disappeared behind dark clouds, and rain threatened. He hoped he headed north, desperate to return to Nordland and find the Germalian army. To find Rosalie. The skin on his right hand burned, and his arm still ached from when he....

Did I really do that? Take Hál's soul?

Detranté narrowed further. Tom turned sideways to squeeze through a gap, then walked into a gorge wider than Lata Via in Portum. The clouds parted, and the sun peeled back the ravine shadows. Tom sat on a boulder to rest, slipping his hand inside the front pocket of his pants to check on the Eyes of Relevation. They nestled, one beside the other, but something else shared the fabric pouch. He removed the unexpected object, a luminous sapphire of transparent blue, one of the gemstones from the Infinitas. A parting gift from Hál, reminding him it wasn't a dream. He *had* taken her soul. He *did* hold the wisdom of the ancestors, and if he survived this journey, he'd return to the mountains to replace the gemstone and guard the Infinitas until the end of his days.

Tom held the sapphire sunwards and rolled it between his fingers, filtered blue light from the faceted prism dancing across his skin. His mind drifted for what seemed an eternity. It focussed when a rope dropped from the sky and landed at his feet.

A woman's voice called from above, "Tom!"

He placed the sapphire back in his pocket, then shielded his eyes from the sun as Thaly and Yagle alighted on a ledge above his head.

"Tie the rope around your chest," called Thaly. "Under your arms. We'll pull you up."

Tom followed Thaly's instructions.

Yagle took off, flying along the ravine's length, gradually increasing his altitude to keep Tom from crashing into the rock walls. Tom emerged above the lip of Detranté, Yagle easing his passenger onto a rock shelf. The griffin landed and pressed the front of his body to the ground, allowing Thaly to dismount. She trotted towards Tom.

"Are you alright?" asked Thaly. "What happened?"

"Where's Rosalie?" said Tom.

"She's waiting back at camp. Worried sick. You've been missing for two moons."

"Two? I lost track. Where's the army?"

"Outside Revelé."

"We must go there."

"Where have you been?"

"I'll tell you what I can during the journey. Let's fly."

At sunset, Yagle returned Tom and Thaly to the Germalian army. Amid a rocky outcrop overlooking the valley leading to Revelé, the Germalians had fashioned a makeshift dismount area. Two griffins waited there — Namu and Nia, Berenice's mount. Yagle alighted beside them, handlers pushing a wheeled platform next to his flank to allow an easy dismount for the wind-riders. Tom climbed from the saddle, trotted down the platform steps and sprinted off to find Rosalie.

He skirted through the rocks, past tethered elephai, around the command tent and towards the valley. At the edge of the encampment, on a grassy knoll, Rosalie stood beside a waning fire, her arms wrapped around her chest and her body buffeted by the cold wind pressing from the north. Tom tried to call out, but the words stuck in his throat.

Nevertheless, Rosalie turned to him. Her arms unfolded and dropped to her sides. She stepped towards him. He stumbled, over grass and stone, eager for her embrace. She held her arms wide and ran to him. He toppled backwards as she flung herself into his chest.

They collapsed in a laughing, crying, wailing mess of entangled limbs and lips.

Rosalie straddled Tom's waist as he lay on his back. "I didn't see you...." she started. "Where? Did Thaly? What happened?"

"You're crying," said Tom, wiping a tear from her chin.

She smacked him in the chest. "What did you expect? Where have you been?"

"I'll explain it all later." Tom clasped her hands. "Rosalie, I love you."

Rosalie's tears came again, falling from her eyes like raindrops.

"That wasn't the response I imagined," he said.

She caressed his face. "Tom, I'm so scared."

She climbed off his chest, and he sat up beside her.

"Does love scare you?" he asked.

"No...and yes. When you disappeared, everything I hoped for vanished as well. Conjuring dreams that could be shattered at any moment...I'm not sure I can face it."

Tom rubbed Rosalie's back. "People do it every day. They climb out of bed each morning and plan for a brighter future. And every time they try to realise that future, every time they attempt to turn dreams into reality, they risk it all crumbling down around them. But they still get up the next day and try again. If you're worried about loss, then you have something worth losing. Already, your dreams are coming true."

Rosalie leaned across and kissed him on the lips. "I love you, too. Tom, I'm...I'm with child. Your child."

He pulled her into an embrace. "Then I have reason to love you even more."

"The baby's future could be over before it starts," whispered Rosalie. "That's what I fear the most."

"Then we fight for our future with every scrap of courage inside us."

* * * *

Two days from Revelé, Thaly marched with her army into the rock formation known as the Lost Sisters. Pillars of stone, narrow like tree trunks, but five or six times taller than most trees, towered above the Germalians as they weaved their animals and wagons among the craggy forest. Nordmen legend claimed the pillars were once the legs of giants; a dozen sisters from the same family hunting for game, who'd become stuck in a vast bog up to their waists. To save her cubs, a snow bear turned the mud encasing the giants' legs to stone, so the sisters could never escape. Over generations, the bog dried up, and the sisters' bodies crumbled to dust, leaving only the stone-sheathed legs behind.

On the other side of the Lost Sisters loomed the sheer north face of the Desolate Mountains. Thaly knew of no-one who'd scaled the mountains into Enthilen, and no army could pass through Detranté. So, she had to lead her soldiers under the mountains, and she needed a guide.

At sunset, Thaly let her army rest, lit a firebrand, and walked on, skirting an outcrop of boulders at the base of a colossal, snow-capped mountain. Yagle flew above her, riderless, keeping watch over the soldiers. Saskia on Namu, and Berenice on Nia, scouted the northern flank in case of trouble from Grauberge.

As she stepped between two boulders, Thaly stopped. Ahead, at the mouth of a cave, stood a frail, faint figure wavering in the dusk like a lone candle barely holding its flame.

"Caeli," Thaly whispered to herself, pained at the sight of the Erstürmen princess.

The woman who'd offered her heart and friendship to Thaly at the stone-grell ceremony, who began the healing after Thaly's rape on the *Vulking*, had become no more than a shadow. Enthilen had taken so much from Caeli. What more did she have to give?

"Athalee," said Caeli as she drifted closer. "Did you bring the birraman?"

"Yes," said Thaly. "Your arm...."

Caeli glanced at the stump of her left elbow as if noticing a bug on her sleeve. "I refuse to let my condition become my wallow," she said. "Since escaping Sardis, I've seen more than I ever imagined, and now I'm here, ready to lead an army under the mountains."

"We owe you an enormous debt."

"When Volerdie's throne is gone, the debt will be paid. My final freedom granted."

Thaly walked with Caeli to a towering wall of stone where windows and doorways had been built into the rock. Most of the entrances had crumbled into disrepair. Others were dead ends. Only a handful appeared to lead further into the mountain depths.

"Was this a settlement?" asked Thaly.

"Yes," said Caeli. "Curmudgles once lived here."

"Which is the way in?"

Caeli drifted to an opening no larger than herself, surrounded by fallen rock. "There are many ways into the mountain, but only this path leads to the other side. Two days march to Enthilen."

"The entrance is too small for our mounts and wagons."

"You have mammoth beasts of burden. Tufted goliaths. Use them to clear the boulders. The cave soon opens to a mighty chasm, and the road to Enthilen is flat and broad. Your army will have no trouble navigating the depths."

"What waits for us on the other side?"

"Malphas knows you are coming. He gathers all his forces in Pergamos. Krieg and his red soldiers have abandoned Sardis. Hunger will soon

follow from Laodicea. Malphas' army won't meet you on the Dambay
Plains. They'll stay behind the walls to defend their master's city."

"We should leave tomorrow," said Thaly. "Will you be ready then?"

"I've been ready for many seasons."

Caeli disappeared into the stone forest. Thaly wanted to call her back. To
hug and cradle her as the princess did to Thaly at the stone-grell ceremony.
Instead, she gripped the firebrand's handle and squeezed through the cave
entrance. Once inside, the mountain opened into a darkness the torch
flames couldn't melt. The click of Thaly's boots on cobblestone echoed
in the vastness. Someone had built a road into the mountain's underbelly.
The stumps of broken pillars marked the road's beginning, surrounded
by hewn stones that may have once formed an archway. As Thaly walked
further along the road, the air grew heavy and still. Bats whirled overhead,
chattering a warning to the intruder below. Bones littered the roadside,
skeletons of creatures that called the cave home or came here to die.

Thaly wondered how many bones her army would leave behind if they
became trapped under the mountain. She knew what awaited them on the
other side but not at the mountain's roots. The unknown secrets hidden
in its darkest depths.

Behind her, stones shifted in the gloom. She used her torch to cast away
the shadows.

"Who's there?" asked Thaly.

A man, no taller than Thaly's chest, stepped into the circle of amber
light. He was naked, but for a pleated skirt, his entire body covered in
long hair, some platted into braids and wrapped around his chest and
shoulders like the straps of a backpack. Two hatchets hung from the belt
around his waist. Thaly clutched the grip of her cutlass with her free hand.

"Sven won't harm you," said the man in Erstürmen, but with a thick
accent unfamiliar to Thaly. "If you don't harm him."

"Who is Sven?" asked Thaly in the language she'd been taught as a child.

"He is curious as to why you march an army towards Grauberge."

Thaly stepped closer. The man pulled an axe from his belt quicker than
lightning, then ran his hairy finger nonchalantly along the blade.

"Are you from Grauberge?" asked Thaly.

"Sven is from Karlik."

"Let me speak to this Sven."

The man rolled his eyes. "Are you a nuncehead? Sven *is* speaking to you."

Ah, thought Thaly. "You're a curmudgle," she said.

"The lady from the west isn't such an ignarse after all."

"Why are you following me? Are there more of you here?"

"Sven guards the road under the mountain. Only Sven. No-one else wants to do it."

"We're not marching to Grauberge. We offer no threat to your home."

"You're the commander. Sven has watched you."

"Yes. Senator Athalee Stansfield of the Germalian Conventus in Portum, Legatus of the Germalian army."

Sven twirled his axe around his hand like a baton, then slipped it back into his belt, handle first. "Nope. Complexion wrong. Voice wrong. You're no Germalian."

"I'm from Enthilen," said Thaly.

"Sven guessed it. You're leading the army under the mountain. Following the draughoul."

"Have you travelled the road?"

Sven looked to where the cobblestones disappeared into the darkness. "Very long road. Long and lonely. Sometimes, Karlik forgets Sven is here."

"Is it dangerous?"

Sven stepped up to Thaly, lifted his chin and glared with piercing blue eyes, almost lost amid a face covered in tawny hair, tangling seamlessly with the locks flowing from his scalp. "Yes," he said. "But no more dangerous than where it leads." He stepped back into the shadows. "Sven has decided you shall pass and wishes you good fortune."

At that, the curmudgle disappeared into the shadows, leaving Thaly to face the darkness alone.

She returned to the encampment, ordering servants to attach harnesses to the elephai so they could drag the boulders away from the cave entrance.

They might have to work all night, but she was determined to begin the march under the mountain in the morning. She found Tom, Rosalie and Saskia with the griffins, feeding and grooming Namu. Puer tended Yagle as the old man had done for yarles. Thaly missed the company of her griffin handler. The simpler life they shared back in Portum. But he offered no quarrel to the tasks she gave him or bemoaned the lack of care she showed Yagle as her thoughts turned elsewhere.

"Did you meet with Caeli?" asked Tom.

Thaly nodded. "She has shown me the pass under the mountain. We leave in the morning."

Tom pulled on a chain around his neck and withdrew a pendant from the top of his tunic. "During my encounter with Hál, Caeli gave me this necklace. A lemniscate. I wanted to thank her."

"She disappeared, but you may see her in the morning."

"What exactly happened to you in those mountains?" Saskia asked Tom.

"It's hard to explain," he replied.

Rosalie chuckled. "All I can get out of him is a babble about an armless, legless torso, a bunch of draughouls, a rainbow-coloured jewel, and now knowing everything anyone could possibly ever know."

"Will you march under the mountain?" Saskia asked Thaly.

"Yes. It's my duty."

"What about Yagle?" asked Tom.

"Saskia and Berenice will fly their griffins over the mountains. Yagle will follow."

"I could ride him," said Tom.

Thaly raised an eyebrow. "You don't know how, and Yagle must accept you first."

"I do know. Ancestral wisdom rests inside my mind, waiting to be awakened."

"I didn't think it was possible, Tom Anderson, but you've become even stranger."

"You can't be a wind-rider just like that," said Saskia. "You have to complete the Eligens. There are tests and challenges, and then...."

"Without a bond between rider and beast," interrupted Thaly, "the griffin will toss you into the clouds and watch as you plummet to your death. But if you wish to try, and Yagle accepts you, then he's yours to ride."

Tom walked up to Yagle. Puer looked to Thaly, and she nodded her approval. The handler stepped aside as Tom ran his fingers through the feathers on Yagle's chest. The griffin squawked, bowed his head and rubbed his bill on Tom's back.

Tom spoke into the griffin's ear, "*Gmarra bun-gurang,*" in a language reminiscent of Grellian. "*Yarra mun-borong curra.*"

Yagle cooed, and Tom stepped away. The griffin knelt on its front knees and dropped its head to the ground, inviting Tom to ride.

Tom stepped onto Yagle's wing and climbed into the saddle. "Easy," he said.

"Oh, for goodness' sake," cried Saskia. "After everything I went through, and this, this know-it-all, wisdom-of-the-ancestors guru strolls up and *ta-dah!* The next wind-rider. Men are forbidden to ride griffins. Thaly, tell him."

"Do I need these reins?" asked Tom.

"How else are you going to guide him?" said Thaly.

"Words will be enough."

Rosalie laughed. "You speak griffin now?"

"It's possible. I might be able to talk to all the animals."

Saskia leaned into Rosalie. "Maybe forget about the marriage thing."

"It's settled," said Thaly. "Tom joins Saskia and Berenice as the third wind-rider. You'll fly over the Desolate Mountains and meet us on the other side, in the foothills above Lokan. Caeli estimates it will take the army two days to travel the underground road."

"If Tom's flying," said Rosalie. "So am I."

"Yes," said Tom. "Yagle will carry both of us."

"We'll camp at our old monastery," said Rosalie. "It's well hidden, and we have supplies there."

"Stay above the clouds," said Thaly. "Avoid being spotted. Malphas won't let us stroll into Enthilen. He'll have set traps."

~ Chapter 44 ~

Widukind's bones ached. His muscles had a cold brittleness, like icicles clinging to a cliff edge. Malphas had kept him squeezed into a foetal ball inside the tiny cage, dangling naked above Pergamos' throne hall for days.

That's the point, thought Widukind. He wants me to feel as helpless as a baby.

Widukind hadn't eaten or been given water or any modicum of comfort. On the few occasions he had to defecate or urinate, he did it through the bars and onto the floor. Grell slaves mopped up the septic mess.

Immortality didn't allay pain, so the torture of an immortal could be ruthless with no risk of premature death. Brutal and satisfying for the torturer. Widukind doubted he could take much more. After gaining eternal life twenty-four yarles ago, he'd entered a never-ending prison, trapped by his own failings as Caeli's father. Trapped by Malphas' desires. Trapped at the bottom of the gorge in Bindari. Trapped in this cage. Death seemed the one path to freedom, and only Malphas could lead him there. Yet, Widukind's death threatened more hurt. If his body became the vessel for Volerdie's soul, he feared part of his own soul would remain, sharing a new, everlasting anguish with the Divine Creator. Nevertheless, as each day passed, Widukind's longing for release intensified. He'd even considered pleading with Malphas to enact the immortal sacrifice. But Malphas waited, until Seena and Bargan blocked the sunlight, and darkness descended amid the day. The wait could last for yarles. Widukind dreaded the thought.

From the shadows of the cavernous hall, Malphas appeared with Ende, the pale grell. They walked to the throne platform and climbed the six stairs to the top. Malphas took his seat on Volerdie's throne, and Ende stood beside him as she always did, clutching her sparth with a deathly grimness. Behind Widukind, the doors to the throne hall creaked open. He turned as the humungous red grell, Krieg, lumbered into the room, dragging a shrunken man with bowed legs dressed in the sangria robes of Enthilen's Hoch-Vater.

Krieg tossed the man at the foot of the platform steps like a farmer throwing an animal carcass into a pit. The Hoch-Vater lay there, hunched and motionless, shallow, vacillating breaths smothered by the threat of impending fatality. Krieg stepped back, dropped to both knees and bowed his head to his master.

A sigh from Malphas echoed around the hall. "Sit up, Anselm."

Enthilen's Hoch-Vater, Anselm, pushed his chest from the floor and knelt in front of the throne platform, raising his chin to face the conductor of his fate.

"For those who rule," continued Malphas, "the failings of their trusted servants can be the most painful of slights. My draughoul spies tell me the Germalian army marches through Nordland. Your meeting with Qaysar Rais was supposed to quell this threat. I gave those desert rodents thousands of my best fighters in exchange for an attack on Portum *before* any likelihood of the Germalians marching east. To keep those blasted women at home. And yet, they are coming. How do you explain this, Anselm?"

Legs tucked beneath his buttocks, clasped hands cradled in his waist, Anselm's body shook in deferential spasms. "I made it clear, Worshipful Master. Rais was to attack as soon as our forces arrived in Groz Wüste. He must have betrayed us."

Malphas scowled. "Betrayal. I'm forever plagued by traitors."

"It's not too late," spluttered Anselm. "If we send our forces to Detranté...."

Malphas jumped to his feet. "They won't come through Detranté, fool! There's a path *under* the mountains. The same road King Faramund travelled when the Erstürmen reclaimed Enthilen." Malphas stepped to the platform's edge, narrowed his eyes and pointed a bony finger at

Widukind. "My brother's seed will lead the Germalians to Pergamos. Princess Caeli. Another treacherous infection."

"She doesn't know the path under the mountain," said Widukind, the words cutting his dry throat like razors.

Malphas scoffed. "A feeble lie. Nothing can stop the wandering of draughouls. Nothing but death."

Widukind pulled an arm from his chest and unfurled his fingers, convinced the bones cracked with the effort, then clutched at the air. "Leave Caeli alone."

"Your daughter died long ago, by Adalwolf's hand. The same man whose company you shared until recently. It seems you forgave him for stealing Caeli's soul. Maybe you came to realise what I accepted long ago? Offspring are either encumbrances or opportunities. Nothing more." Malphas returned to the throne. "Lift your head, Krieg."

The red grell raised his chin, staring at his master from behind a grilled helmet.

"Has Sardis been purged?" asked Malphas.

"Yes, Worshipful Master," said Krieg. "All those who would fight for you, march to Pergamos."

"Good. Double the patrols around the city's borders. Send word to Hunger in Laodicea. He must lead every man, woman and child who can hold a sword to Pergamos. We make our stand here."

Krieg stood, bowed, then ground the heels of his sabatons into the flagstones and marched from the room.

"On your feet, Anselm," said Malphas. "What is it you desire most?"

Anselm's bowed legs wobbled as he lifted himself from the floor. "To enter paradise beside Volerdie and yourself, Worshipful Master."

"Yes, obviously. But you're the Hoch-Vater. The highest theological authority in Enthilen. What sacrifice would you make to read the First Scripture? Volerdie's own words, written in blood."

"Such a relic was lost when Volerdie fled Ostamp. Only the scripture verses give voice to Volerdie's will."

"I found the First Scripture."

"What?" Anselm staggered backwards as if he'd been punched in the chest.

Cruel, thought Widukind. Malphas taunts the Hoch-Vater. Offers him the most treasured prize before snatching it from his grasp.

"Can you be certain it's the famed parchment?" asked Anselm.

"Ask him," said Malphas, pointing at Widukind. "Our mother stole a copy."

Anselm looked up at Widukind, bewilderment twitching at the corners of his eyes. Widukind considered lying, proclaiming the First Scripture didn't exist. It would be the merciful thing to do. Malphas wouldn't let Anselm near the parchment. Widukind expected his brother only mentioned the document to inflict more torment before the Hoch-Vater's death.

"It is true," rasped Widukind. "Because of the scripture, I'm trapped in this cage."

Anselm faced Malphas, his hunched body unfurling with defiance. "This treasure must be protected inside the kirika, and its words should be read only by curates."

"I have more piety than any curate," said Malphas.

"No," said Anselm, slapping a polished white shoe on the first step of the throne platform.

Ende shuffled closer to her master and tensed.

"You dare challenge me?" asked Malphas.

"Erstürmen lore is clear," said Anselm. "Only curates are permitted to read Volerdie's words. *You* are not a curate." He took two more steps towards the top of the platform.

An image of a younger Anselm drifted into Widukind's memory. The Hoch-Vater had been a curate in Sardis when Widukind was a child. Anselm injected such a pious energy into his sermons that the kirika walls virtually shuddered with reverence. While the body had withered with age, Anselm's spirit appeared not to have dimmed. But the curate's devotion to Volerdie's teachings would be his undoing.

"The First Scripture holds many secrets," said Malphas. "It marks the day when my immortal brother, Widukind, will be sacrificed on the throne of the dead. The day when Volerdie returns to his flock. But you will not see that day, Anselm. You will not revel in the Divine Creator's joyous return. You will not pass through the door to paradise."

Anselm's chest swelled. He took another step closer to the throne, leaned forward and heaved a scream of vicious anger at Malphas.

For an aging, sickly grell, Ende moved with devastating speed. She sprang in front of her master and swung the sparth in the same motion. Anselm's head, mouth still open, fell from his neck and tumbled back down the stairs. His body collapsed forward, prostrate one last time in front of the Worshipful Master.

Malphas stood. "Bravo, Ende. Another enemy of Volerdie dispatched. Soon those primitive lilac eyes will be as black as pitch." He stepped to the platform's edge and sought Widukind's attention. "You can feel it, can't you, little brother? The moment of your sacrifice is imminent."

Widukind wanted to taunt Malphas. To announce the throne would be crushed before darkness descended. But he wondered if it would. He wondered if Tom and Adalwolf would ever complete their task.

Malphas ordered Ende from the room. She returned with Rephaim soldiers and grell slaves in tow. The slaves unhitched the rope holding Widukind's cage in mid-air, then lowered him to the floor. Ende unlocked the cage door.

Widukind unfurled his naked body, wincing at the stretch and tear of frigid muscles, then crawled from the cage.

Standing beside Ende, he whispered in her ear, "Hand me your weapon. I can free you from Malphas."

She turned to him with eyes of painfully dark violet. "The Worshipful Master is my only salvation."

Widukind's heart sank as Ende led him to the top of the throne platform.

Malphas stepped to the side and waved his hand at the throne. "Sit, little brother. What an honour this is for you."

Ende pushed Widukind onto the throne and bound his hands to the armrests.

"Volerdie is always testing us, Widu," said Malphas. "Always assessing our worth. While I learned from the First Scripture *how* the immortal sacrifice must occur, I failed to understand *when*. Until now." His cackle echoed through the throne room like a mocking ghost. "I could have wasted Adalwolf's life for nothing. Thankfully, Volerdie foresaw this foolishness and brought his wrath down on Pergamos to avoid my embarrassment. But now, I have deciphered the final piece of the puzzle. After twelve yarles of study." Malphas leaned towards Widukind and whispered, "Six hundred and sixty-six."

As Ende bound his legs, Widukind's spine pressed into the throne's backrest, rubbing against the open mouth of a face contorted into a frozen scream. "What are you talking about, Oldaric?"

Malphas flashed a bitter smile. "I thought you would have already uncovered the answer. An accomplished scholar such as yourself. Darkness descends amid the daylight on the last day of every six hundredth and sixty-sixth harvest season. According to Erstürmen history, written on a parchment brought by Faramund from Thyatira, the most recent day of darkness occurred during King Ermenrich's reign. In the year of his coronation, no less. By my reckoning, that was six hundred and sixty-six yarles ago. At the end of *this* harvest season is when it will happen again. Seena and Bargan will block the sunlight, preparing Enthilen for Volerdie's return. We have only days to wait, Widu."

"Your time is running out," said Widukind. "Armies come to tear down your walls."

"Let them come!" cried Malphas. "They'll never breach our defences. The chaos surrounding us matters none. Volerdie will return. Nothing can stop him. He'll inhabit your body and reclaim the throne of the dead. And for all those deemed worthy, he will open the door to paradise." Malphas turned to the grell slaves. "You're to carry the throne to the pyramid summit, as close to the moons as possible. There, the immortal sacrifice will await his destiny." He faced Widukind. "Volerdie will soon be home, little brother."

* * * *

Nettie sat at Elmbray's breakfast table, holding the pendant of Rosalie's bronze necklace between her thumb and forefinger while Erwin wolfed down porridge. Yonna had made the necklace for Rosalie's sixteenth harvest season, setting rose-coloured glass resembling ruby gemstone in the pendant's centre. Nettie doubted it was a genuine gemstone, her parents not wealthy enough to afford such riches, but she treasured the last tangible reminder of her family above everything else, even her friendship with Erwin. Yet, some days, the necklace reminded Nettie of how Rosalie abandoned everyone. Left Yonna and Nettie feeling helpless as the rest of the family withered and died from The Ravage. Allum first, followed by Petas, then Nettie's mother, Heady. Part of Nettie hated Rosalie for not staying to treat the sick. They might have survived with her help. Another part longed to see Rosalie's smile again. Nettie had convinced herself that would only happen if she escaped Pergamos.

She and Erwin had been with Elmbray and Snick for twenty-four moons. Nettie had taken three wagon trips with Snick to get supplies from Chitti Coin-tail at Beitrag. Nettie had behaved herself each time, and Erwin continued to serve Elmbray dutifully. Nettie hadn't told her friend about the escape plan, worried he might expose her to Elmbray. Erwin was happy here. He'd put on weight. Hung on every word from Elmbray's lips. And the mage promised big, wonderful things for both of them. But Nettie needed to steal her friend away before he became wholly trapped under Elmbray's spell. She would make her move today because she'd been permitted to take the wagon to Beitrag alone. Snick had already left to complete another task, and Elmbray believed he could trust Nettie.

It will be his downfall, she thought. If I can trick him into taking one sip.

"You're not eating," said Erwin to Nettie, tipping a porcelain bowl to his mouth and slurping up the last skerrick of porridge.

"Not hungry," said Nettie, opening the collar of her tunic to let the necklace fall between her breasts.

"Smugglers need a full belly."

Nettie nodded, willing Elmbray to enter the koken, take his seat and pour himself a cup of herbal tea like he did every morning.

"Where's Elmbray?" she asked.

"Don't know. Probably still asleep." Erwin leaned across the table and whispered, "He goes out at night after he's locked us in our room. Sometimes, he brings women back. You must have heard them." Erwin pulled away when Elmbray strolled into the koken.

"What a lovely morning," he said, pulling a chair out, then swishing his silk robe away from his bottom before sitting. "I'm famished." Elmbray peered into the copper pot of porridge sitting in the middle of the table, screwed up his nose, then plucked grapes from the fruit bowl, tossing them onto his plate. "Where's the cheese, Erwin?"

"In the pantry. I'll get it." Erwin sprang from his chair and scooted off to the storeroom.

"Good boy," said Elmbray after him before grinning at Nettie. "Snick let you out of your room this morning?"

She nodded.

"And here you both are, innocently eating breakfast and preparing for a big day. So wonderful we can trust each other. Are you ready for your journey?"

"Yes," Nettie said.

"I know you won't let me down. All the paperwork is in order. It's underneath the driver's seat. Remember, don't make idle chit-chat with the guard at the gate. Or look sideways at him. Anything that might raise suspicion. Keep your eyes dead ahead."

"What if they find the secret compartment?"

"They haven't found it yet. Most soldiers in Pergamos are lazy or corrupt. We don't have to worry about the first; we can buy off the second. Being ex-military, you should know what I mean."

Despite Elmbray's reassurances, Nettie still fretted about being discovered driving a smuggler's wagon all by herself. No doubt, the paperwork implicated only her.

Erwin returned with the cheese, carried on a wooden board, and placed it on the table beside Elmbray. The mage cut a slice of pale yellow that crumbled like a dry wall, then popped the cheese in his mouth, followed by a grape. Nettie fought the urge to ask him if he wanted tea lest it appeared suspicious. Staring at the teapot, she willed Erwin to ask. Elmbray wouldn't suspect his loyal house boy, and Erwin knew nothing about the potion.

But as the morning meal faded to scraps, the herbal tea grew cold.

Elmbray faced Erwin. "With Nettie gone for two days, it's time for you to learn about some of my other business dealings. Just between us, Snick's health is deteriorating. I can't be certain how much longer he'll last."

"It sounds exciting," said Erwin, pawing at the mage.

Elmbray chuckled. "The business dealings or Snick's imminent demise?"

"Yes...no...I mean, I'll do whatever you want."

Elmbray reached across the table and clasped Erwin's wrist like a manacle. "I'm sure you will, dear boy. I'm sure you will." He released Erwin, then grasped the teapot handle.

This is it, thought Nettie. Pour the damn tea.

Elmbray lifted the pot and tipped tea into his porcelain cup. He held the pot towards Erwin. "Would you like some?"

No, thought Nettie. She kicked Erwin in the shins. He flinched and glared at her.

"Yes, please," said Erwin.

"Excellent. Let's celebrate our blossoming business ventures with a morning brew." The mage poured Erwin a cup of tea, then faced Nettie. "Tea?"

"No, thank you," she said.

"Suit yourself." Elmbray placed the pot back on the table.

Erwin lifted the cup to his lips.

"Erwin," said Nettie, pushing down on his forearm to move the cup away from his mouth. "I've changed my mind about porridge. Can you get more milk?"

Erwin pulled away from Nettie and hesitated, holding the cup beside his chin.

"Please," she said. "Before the porridge gets too cold."

Erwin's shoulders slumped as he placed the cup on the table. "Alright." He stood and disappeared into the pantry.

Elmbray chortled. "He's so eager to please."

Drink the tea, thought Nettie. *Please.*

Elmbray lifted the cup, blew a breath across the surface, parted his lips, then tilted the beverage into his mouth.

Chitti Coin-tail's words filled Nettie's head. 'Why you want this potion, Nettie Tenderfoot? You becoming like Tricky Snicky. Careful! Works straight away. Victim will be knocked out for long time.'

"This tea tastes...*unusual*," said Elmbray. "What is the brew?"

"Slitherweed and dandelion," said Nettie.

"*Hmmm.* Normally my favourite but...." Elmbray took another sip. "No, something's not right." He banged the cup on the table. "Erwin's got the blend wrong."

He didn't make the tea, thought Nettie, waiting for Elmbray to fall asleep. Nothing happened. Did Chitti Coin-tail lie to me? she wondered. Take my coin for a dud potion?

Erwin ambled back into the koken. "This is the last of the milk."

As he sat down, Elmbray began to sway in his chair.

"Mage Elmbray," said Erwin. "You look pale."

"I *am* feeling off-colour," said Elmbray. "Maybe the cheese was mouldy."

Elmbray's eyes rolled back into his head, and he slumped, face first, onto the table.

Erwin jumped from his chair, rushed to his master's side and shook his shoulder. "Are you alright? Wake up?"

Nettie stood. "Leave him. We need to go. Now."

Erwin glared at her. "Go where?"

"We're leaving Pergamos. I've packed supplies."

"What have you done to Elmbray?"

"He's asleep. This is our chance. Where are the front door keys?"

Erwin stiffened with stubbornness, his hand clutching Elmbray's shoulder. "I'm not going anywhere. I like it here."

Nettie stepped across the room and peeled Erwin's hand from the mage. "This might be our only opportunity. I'll go alone if I have to, but I want you to come with me."

"Why?" asked Erwin.

She grabbed him by the shoulders. "Because you're my friend. I'm not leaving you here to become Elmbray's pet. He'll do horrible things to you when he learns I've escaped."

"We're going to be business partners," said Erwin. "You heard him."

"It's a lie. We're not his partners; we're his prisoners. He keeps us locked up day and night."

"That's for our own safety."

Nettie's face flushed with anger. "Don't be a fool. Where are the damn keys?"

Erwin sighed. "I think they're in his room."

"Under my bed is a pack full of food. You get the pack, and I'll find the keys."

Nettie raced from the koken down the hall to the door of Elmbray's room. She turned the handle, and the door opened. Inside, every wall had been covered in black silk curtains, like the stomach lining of a fabric beast. A colossal, four-poster bed filled the middle of the room, with lace hanging from the tester and a dozen pillows strewn across a dishevelled quilt. On top of a chest of drawers, among a clutter of perfume bottles, pots of coloured powder, combs and handkerchiefs, Nettie found a keyring. She grabbed the keys and ran back into the passage. Erwin stood there, the backpack dangling from his hand.

"Come on," said Nettie.

Erwin stayed put. "I don't understand. Where are we going? It's warm and comfortable here. There's plenty of food, and we have a future."

Nettie snatched the pack from Erwin. "When we're of no more use to Elmbray, he'll discard us like a dirty rag." She jumped at a groan coming from the koken.

"I asked you a question, Nettie," snarled Erwin, his pudgy cheeks blushing scarlet. "Where are we going?"

"Away from here. Away from Pergamos. We'll use the wagon to escape."

Erwin leaned against the wall and crossed his arms. "No. I don't want to."

"Don't be stupid. We have to go."

"No."

"Then I'm going without you. When Elmbray wakes up, you can explain what happened."

Nettie marched into the koken. A snoring Elmbray hadn't moved, his cheek pressed against the tabletop. She took a kitchen knife, slid it into the backpack, and then made for the front door. Fumbling through the ring of keys, she found one that unlocked the door. Nettie turned to Erwin a final time. He stood in the passageway, shoulders slumped, tears trickling down his cheeks. Back to the wall, he slid onto the floor and buried his face in his hands.

With every fibre of Nettie's heart aching, she stepped out the front door, shut it behind her, shouldered the pack and ran down the street to the stables.

Elmbray had his own private barn where he housed the wagon, horses, and items he sold on the black market. Nettie expected the barn doors to be locked. A padlock bigger than her hand usually fixed a metal bar across the doors. Elmbray always unlocked it for Snick and Nettie before their trips to Beitrag, using one of the keys from the keyring she grasped in her hand. But as Nettie arrived at the barn, she found the padlock open and hanging loose on its shank, and the metal bar lifted from its braces.

Poking her fingers between the gap in the doors, she pulled one open and stepped inside.

"Hello?" she called into the shadows.

The snicker of a horse replied.

"Anyone here?" said Nettie.

Blood pulsing, she pushed the doors open to let in the sunlight. The two draft horses stood, tethered to a post but already harnessed to the wagon.

Snick must have done it, thought Nettie, before he started his new job.

She stood beside the wagon, unshouldered and uncinched her pack, and dropped the keyring inside.

"What y'got there," said a voice from behind her.

Nettie spun around as Snick walked from the darkness at the rear of the barn.

"Er...ah...food and drink," stammered Nettie. "For the trip."

"Sounded like keys," said Snick, placing himself between Nettie and the door to freedom. "Where's Elmbray?"

"He's feeling ill. Gave me the keys to unlock the padlock. I will drop them back home on my way to the gate."

"Must have been some kinda sickness to trust you with all the keys."

"You opened the barn door," said Nettie, trying to redirect Snick's focus.

"Yeah. Elmbray gave me a key so I could get supplies. Part of me new duties. Only *one* key, though. Not a whole bunch."

"I only have them for a moment. Erwin and Elmbray are working together today."

"Thought y'said Elmbray was sick?"

"He is. He is...but...ah...Erwin's tending to him. Thinks he'll get better soon."

Snick stepped closer to Nettie. "I better look inside y'pack. Guards might search it. Don't want ya carryin' anythin' that could raise their suspicion."

Damn, thought Nettie. Snick will notice the food. Too much for a two-day return trip to Beitrag. Then there's the kitchen knife.

"Elmbray already checked it," lied Nettie. "Said everything's fine."

"Seems the mage is feelin' healthier by the moment."

Snick straightened his back, dull eyes staring at Nettie from a face ravaged by fire scars. The brutal network of blistered skin made it impossible to read Snick's emotions. To pick the moment he might lunge for her.

Nettie reached inside her backpack, withdrew the kitchen knife and pointed it at Snick. "I don't want to hurt you," she said. "I only want to escape Pergamos."

Snick smiled a cruel grimace that mocked his wounds. "Now the truth comes out. If I let y'take the wagon, Elmbray's gonna hurt me more than you can imagine."

"He's dead," said Nettie, the lies becoming desperate as freedom slipped from her grasp.

"I'm bettin' that ain't true," said Snick, reaching inside his horsehair coat.

"Hands out," snapped Nettie, poking the knife at his chest. "Where I can see them."

Snick withdrew his hand and raised it in deference.

"Come with me," said Nettie, not meaning it but hoping Snick might see her as a friend.

He shook his head. "Only got a permit to let one person through the gate. A young woman called Nettie Armbuckle. Guards see me, and it's all over."

"Then walk away."

"Y'know I can't do that."

The draft horses stamped and whinnied, distracting Nettie's attention. Despite his hindrances, an enflamed body covered in an inescapable maze of scars, Snick engulfed her like fire on serpent oil. In a single movement, he clutched her wrist and bent it backwards. She screamed in agony and dropped the knife. He swooped down, snatched it from the dirt, and jabbed the tip into her breast.

"Elmbray ain't gonna be happy about this," said Snick. He stood from a crouch, still holding the knife on Nettie. "Not happy at all. He trusted you and the boy...*urgh*...."

Snick didn't finish his sentence. He crumpled in a heap at Nettie's feet with a paring knife jammed into the back of his neck. Erwin stood beside the horses, shaking.

"Did I...." stumbled Erwin. "Did I kill him?"

Nettie dropped to her knees, placed a finger on Snick's neck and felt for a pulse as blood spewed across her hand. "He's still alive, but he won't last." She gathered the kitchen knife, dropped it in her backpack, cinched the straps, stood and threw the pack onto the driver's seat of the wagon.

"Why did you change your mind?" asked Nettie.

"You called me your friend," said Erwin. "I've never had a friend before, and I don't want to lose you already."

She leaned across and pecked him on the cheek. He pulled her into a hug that almost cracked her spine.

Nettie laughed and pulled away. "Careful. Don't break the wagon driver."

"Where's this secret compartment?" asked Erwin.

Nettie took his hand and led him to the tailgate. She squatted and slid open a hidden door underneath the tray.

"Crawl under the wagon and climb into the compartment," said Nettie. "I'll shut the door. When we get to the south gate, don't move a muscle or make a noise."

* * * *

"Nettie Armbuckle," said the guard at Pergamos' south gate, casting his eyes across the parchment.

Perched on the edge of the wagon's driver seat, reins held so tight her knuckles ached, Nettie nodded and fixed her eyes dead ahead. 'Don't make idle chit-chat,' came Elmbray's words. 'Or look sideways at him.'

Storm clouds blocked the sun as the guard folded the permit and tucked it inside the armhole of his breastplate. He strolled around the wagon, tapping the sides with the blade of his halberd.

"Twenty-four sacks of flour from Beitrag," said the soldier.

"That's right," said Nettie.

"Only flour?" asked the soldier as he stopped at the tailgate.

If Erwin moves, thought Nettie, if he coughs, sneezes or shuffles, it's all over.

"Bakers are all out," said Nettie.

"That so," said the guard, rattling the tailgate.

"Special trip, so there's plenty of honey devil-kuchen for end of harvest season celebrations." *No chit-chat!*

747

"Only twelve moons to go," said the guard, walking along the other side of the wagon and stopping beside the driver's seat. "Where's Snick?"

Shit, thought Nettie, he knows Snick.

"Got other business to attend to," she said. "I'm doing these trips from now on."

The guard stared at her from under his spangenhelm. His companions milled outside the guardhouse with their backs turned. The young soldier, about Nettie's age, removed a gloved hand from the handle of his weapon and rested an open palm on the wagon step. Nettie nodded to him, reached inside a pants pocket and withdrew four coin. She tipped the coin into his palm. He dropped the bribe into his shoulder satchel, removed a re-entry permit and handed it to Nettie.

"Back by sunset tomorrow," he said, then shouted to the gatekeeper, "Open the gate!"

The timber doors creaked on their hinges as grell slaves yanked the south gate open.

Sweat poured into Nettie's eyes. The reins almost slipped from her hands. Blood pulsed along her neck.

We're almost free, she thought.

As Nettie went to gee the horses, someone yelled from behind, "Stop her! She's stolen my wagon."

Nettie spun on her bottom. Elmbray staggered down the street.

"Stop her!" he screamed.

The young soldier raised his halberd. The slaves began to close the gate.

Nettie slapped the reins against her legs and screamed, "Yah! Yah! YAH!"

The horses bolted. Through the gate. Into the stone murder chamber where archers fumbled to nock arrows. Underneath the portcullis and out onto the road to freedom.

Nettie didn't look back.

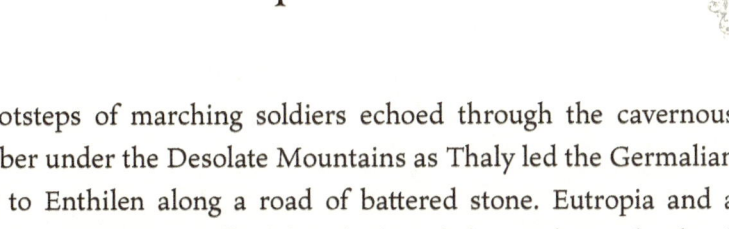

~ Chapter 45 ~

The footsteps of marching soldiers echoed through the cavernous chamber under the Desolate Mountains as Thaly led the Germalian army to Enthilen along a road of battered stone. Eutropia and a handful of torchbearers walked beside her, lighting the path ahead. Behind them, the cavalry had dismounted, their skittish horses refusing to accept riders in this bleak, murky place. Further back, dozens of elephai lumbered forwards, pulling wagons full of armour, supplies and materials to build war machines. A quiet chatter drifted among the soldiers. A soft, collective whisper, as if no-one wished to speak too loudly lest they awaken a nefarious beast dwelling among the roots of the mountains.

As the army approached Enthilen, the air became warm and cloying. Nothing stirred inside the endless cavern. No bats or rodents. Not even a bug or worm. Sometimes, an unnerving silence descended on the seventy-thousand fighters. In those moments, an unease chilled Thaly's bones that she struggled to shake off. She'd marched her soldiers almost non-stop since Nordland, allowing only short breaks when they tired. She feared spending too long under the mountain, but she accepted they would have to make camp soon; otherwise, the army would be exhausted when they arrived at Malphas' doorstep.

As always, Princess Caeli drifted ahead, almost invisible in the darkness, never wavering in the certainty of her navigation when the path forked left or right. The Germalians would be hopelessly lost without her.

Thaly jogged up to the princess. "Caeli, we'll camp here."

"This is not a good place," said Caeli. "There are many caves near the road. Too many places to hide. I can't search them all."

"I'll put guards on the perimeter," said Thaly. "Do you expect trouble?"

"Cold air wafts from some of the caves. Air that's travelled from the snow-capped peaks, down through unknown passages and into this junction."

"How much longer to Enthilen?"

"Another day of travel, at least."

Thaly shook her head, the journey taking longer than she anticipated. "We have to rest. I can't push the soldiers any further."

Caeli took Thaly's hand. "You are our commander. I will follow your orders."

Thaly tried not to flinch at the numbing, lifeless cold of Caeli's touch, instead forcing a smile. "You knew my brother in Sardis."

Caeli released her grip and bowed her head. "Yes. Jürgen. He died outside my door."

"What was he like? I never met him."

Caeli lifted her gaze. "Brave, strong and true. Like his sister." She turned and drifted away, disappearing into a grotto beside the road.

Thaly waited for Eutropia and the torchbearers to arrive, then issued the order to make camp. Soldiers and servants unloaded food and bedding from the wagons and tethered horses and elephai to metal pins hammered into the rock. Only four barrels of serpent oil, purchased in Revelé, remained; enough to light a dozen lanterns hung among the boulders lining the road, leaving the rest to feed the torches during the journey's final leg. If the march dragged on, Thaly feared they would run out of oil altogether and become lost in the dark forever.

No-one lit a fire; wood was too precious to waste on cooking food. Most of the fighters ate stale bread, cold mash and salted meat, then went straight to bed. Thaly walked among them, offering words of assurance and comfort. She assigned healers to tend foot blisters and other ailments, checked on the horses and elephai, and ensured the male servants rostered their duties so all would have time to rest. Then she climbed on top of a tall boulder, sat down and set her watch over the army. Eyes heavy, feet and back sore and tired, she fought to stay awake amid the murky light. The murmurs of the camp subsided as soldiers retired to their bedrolls. In the stillness, General Jurelle Stansfield's legacy pressed down on

Thaly harder than ever. The Dobunni leader turned traitor to his people. Loyalty and treachery wrapped up in the same man. She wondered what weaknesses she'd inherited from her father. Feared how she might falter when faced with Malphas' hordes.

Malphas has no hold over me, thought Thaly, like King Ewald did over Jurelle.

Then her worry turned to her impulsive sister, Saskia, and what might be waiting for her, Tom and Rosalie when they landed the griffins on the southern slopes of the Desolate Mountains. With a clenched fist, she pressed the griffin amulet hanging around her neck into her sternum, wishing she'd given the family heirloom to Saskia before they parted.

A broken sleep pulled Thaly from her thoughts. She drifted off, woke, slept, then woke again. Beside a cave entrance illuminated by a single lantern, two guards had slumped against the rock wall, their heads lolling on their chests, javelins lying on the ground. Thaly considered waking them, but her eyelids grew heavier than her legs. As she forced her eyes open, a mist drifted out from the cave near the sleeping guards and seeped into the chasm. Bone-coloured tendrils inched up the rock wall like a ghostly spider and wrapped themselves around the guard's faces.

Only a dream, thought Thaly.

But a guard snorted, then choked, her mist-shrouded body convulsing for a moment before going rigid.

Only a dream. Thaly's chin dropped to her chest. *Only a...no. They're here.*

A snarl came from inside the cave. Thaly jerked her head up. The wisp of mist had billowed, creeping through the gloom and fogging the glow from the scattered lanterns. Grasping strands of white swirled around Thaly's ankles, dangling over the side of the boulder. She pulled her legs from the mist and stood above a lake of white, lantern halos marking its shores. And skulking beneath the lake's surface....

"Weregrims!" Thaly screamed. "Weregrims!"

She expected her soldiers to spring from their beds, ready to fight, but those surrounded by mist didn't move. And all the guards watching the caves had collapsed onto the chasm floor. Only where the fog hadn't reached did the Germalians gather their weapons and prepare for the assault.

"Keep out of the mist!" yelled Thaly. "Climb onto the rocks. Into wagons. On horses and elephai. Don't breathe the mist."

She drew her cutlass and waited for the enemy to come. The heads and shoulders of draughouls emerged from beneath the surface of the fog. Three to four dozen draughouls riding weregrims. Thaly guessed the mist affected only living people. Weregrims and draughouls were neither.

The gruesome riders and their mounts descended on the paralysed soldiers trapped in the fog. Gnashing teeth ripped limp bodies apart, the weregrims feeding on their prey like a dog devours lumps of chopped meat. No soldier raised a hand in defence. They didn't even scream, the silent slaughter punctured only by the clap of weregrim jaws shutting tight.

Safe under the blanket of fog, the draughouls unshouldered bows and fired arrows at the retreating Germalians. Thaly stood a helpless witness to the horrid spectacle as her fighters ran back down the road and into the darkness. Malphas was winning their first battle.

"Archers and javelin-throwers onto boulders and wagons!" she ordered. "Target the weregrims! Stay out of the mist."

Germalian soldiers scrambled onto the largest rocks they could find and searched the mist, trying to pick out the enemy from their paralysed companions. Archers fired arrows into the thickening white pouring from the cave mouth. A handful of projectiles hit their mark, weregrims snarling at the annoyance, or a draughoul rider toppling into the mist. But many arrows didn't, and some pierced limp bodies still lying in their beds.

"Hold your fire!" yelled Eutropia, standing between two archers perched on a rock. She called to Thaly, "We can't see what we're shooting at."

Thaly shifted her weight from foot to tired foot. "Damn it! Shit, shit, shit!" Unable to do more to protect her fighters, she flung her cutlass at a draughoul in frustration. The weapon flew past the soulless body, clattering harmlessly onto the chasm floor.

A swirl of fog encircled Eutropia's rock. A weregrim sprang from beneath the cover, burying its saliva-drenched canines into the orator's thigh and pulling her into the depths.

"No!" cried Thaly, her agony drowned out by Eutropia's screams.

Thaly planned to jump into the fog and hold her breath until she reached her companions. But something stopped her. An elephai lumbered through the chasm, the top half of its body protruding from the mist like a mountain peak ringed with cloud. And riding the huge beast was Princess Caeli. She led her mount to the cave spewing the deadly fog. The elephai lowered its head and used its tusks to push a boulder as big as a horse across the cave entrance. Caeli guided the beast's head down again to push another boulder into the cave. As the entrance filled with rocks, the flow of mist stemmed, and the air began to clear.

Germalian archers resumed their attack. Other soldiers rode elephai through the thinning mist, sitting above the threat and flinging javelins at weregrim shadows. The dissolving enemy cover exposed the draughouls and weregrims, and tens of thousands of Germalian soldiers hungered for revenge, squashing the threat like a bug under a boot heel.

Thaly jumped from her boulder and ran towards Eutropia, who lay on the chasm floor, chest ripped open and heart still beating.

Thaly dropped to her knees and clasped Eutropia's hand.

"Stay the path," whispered Eutropia.

With those last words, the orator died, Thaly cradling her head in her lap until Eutropia's heart beat no more.

*   *   *   *

"It's a nice day for flying," said Tom, slinking down to his buttocks and rubbing his shoulder blades against the stone wall of the rebel monastery hidden in the valley above Lokan.

"Clear blue and not a breath of wind," said Rosalie sitting beside him. "Saskia and Berenice would be enjoying themselves."

He faced her. "But no cloud cover to mask their presence."

She poked him in the ribs. "Don't spoil the moment with worry. Enjoy the sunshine."

He turned away and smiled to himself. The Germalian army should arrive in Enthilen soon. Saskia, Berenice and a riderless Yagle searched for them now in the foothills between Lokan and the Desolate Mountains. When Thaly and her soldiers emerged from under the mountain, the wind-riders would spot them. Then the journey to Pergamos could begin, Tom more prepared than ever for the quest's final leg.

Tilly had returned to the monastery with news from the south. The weald-grells camped on the Dambay Plains, waiting to launch their attack. Inside the secret dwell, hundreds of werps prepared for battle, and Adalwolf waited there, ready to help Tom destroy the throne of the dead. Those who would oppose Malphas had assembled an irresistible force. Yet, Widukind's disappearance gave Tom pause.

At the entrance to the hidden valley, Emelin stood on the lookout rock where Tom had spoken with Hanni. Ignoring the hindrance of a wooden leg, the old rebel fighter had hobbled her way along the narrow, rocky track to the lookout, determined to be among the first to hear of Thaly's arrival. When Tom told Emelin her adopted daughter would return to Enthilen, a frail tremor set in the old woman's fingers, and a yearning sparkled in her left eye to counter the blinding scar across her right. She spoke of little else but her desire to see Thaly one more time. So consuming was Emelin's longing, Tom worried about what would happen if the reunion faltered.

"How much longer do we wait?" asked Tilly as she sat beside Tom and Rosalie.

"They will emerge today," said Tom.

"How can you be certain?" asked Tilly.

Rosalie smiled at Tilly, then tapped her finger against her temple.

"It's not my fault I *know* things," said Tom. "I didn't ask for this burden of knowledge to be bestowed on me. Anyway, I trust Caeli. They'll be here soon enough."

"When they arrive, then what?" asked Tilly.

"The Germalians will set up camp north of Pergamos," said Tom. "I'll fly south."

"Tom and Adalwolf must seek the throne together," said Rosalie.

Tom held Rosalie's hand. Although he needed to be with Adalwolf, he *wanted* to be with her.

Vlostak, the Nordman rebel, called from the top of the valley and pointed skyward. Three griffins swooped over the western ridgeline, where water from a melting glacier trickled into a bottomless pool: Saskia on Namu, Berenice on Nia, *and....*

"Thaly!" yelled Tom, jumping to his feet. "Thaly's here." He waved his arms at the griffins, then ran to get Emelin.

The griffins landed beside the monastery and lowered themselves to the ground to let the wind-riders dismount. Tom helped Emelin along the path from the lookout to the griffins. Leaning on her crutch, the old woman shuddered and sobbed, her breaths gasping with joyful exertion.

As they approached the wind-riders, Tom held back, letting Emelin walk ahead to reunite with her adopted daughter. Dressed in the Volatal Vexil leathers, Thaly looked regal and statuesque, like the leader Enthilen's people had longed for. But the mirage faded when Emelin arrived. The little girl abandoned by her birth parents reappeared, pining for the mother who'd raised her.

"Welcome home, Athalee," said Emelin through a stream of tears.

"I thought you'd died," said Thaly, embracing the first mother she ever knew and weeping on her shoulder. "In Bagendon. I thought you'd died... with Dayna."

"The mouldewerps put me back together again."

"There is less of you than before," said Thaly, lifting her head and tracing her finger along the scar blighting Emelin's face.

"I still have my gumption," said Emelin, smiling. "It's brought me to this day when I see my eldest daughter as the leader of a great army."

"I've been so fortunate to have two mothers. Without you, I wouldn't be who I am."

"Don't forget Jacob. He's watching over you, proud a Dobunni will finally rid Enthilen of the Erstürmen."

"I haven't come to rout the Erstürmen," said Thaly, her body stiffening. "They will be offered sanctuary when Malphas falls."

Emelin pulled back. "Then we will have another tyrant to overthrow soon enough. The Erstürmen will not change their ways."

She turned to walk away, but Thaly grabbed her shoulder. "The new world cannot be like the old. We must put aside past grievances and forge a future together."

"*Grievances,*" snarled Emelin, digging the heel of her crutch into the rocky soil. "Is that what you call the murder of innocent Dobunni? The fall of Bagendon and Laodicea? The slaughter of grells and werps in Malang Gunya? Grievances?"

"Malphas did all those things."

"Malphas was once an Erstürmen king. King Oldaric. Now he has absolute power. See what calamity this has brought on Enthilen. Mount your griffin and fly across your homeland. See if you can recognise it beneath the refuse piles of shattered lives."

"There will be no more Erstürmen kings in Enthilen," said Thaly. "I promise you that."

"There should be no more Erstürmen!" cried Emelin.

She shook her head and hobbled off.

Thaly tried to go after her, but Tom held her back.

"Eventually, she will see the path you're taking is the right one," he said.

That evening, the visitors shared a meal with the rebels inside the monastery and made plans to march into the Dambay Plains.

"I must leave in the morning," said Tom, "to unite with Adalwolf. Tilly has marked the location of the weald-grell camp on a map."

"Namu is the fastest griffin we have," said Saskia. "I can fly south with Tom."

Emelin scowled, her wrinkled face pursed in the firelight. "*Erstürmen* can't be trusted. Adalwolf will betray us."

"I used to be Erstürmen," said Rosalie. "In some ways, I still am."

Thaly glared at Emelin. "And Princess Caeli has shown honour many times. Without her, we would have died beneath the Desolate Mountains. Pergamos' citizens may call themselves Erstürmen, but they're nothing more than puppets in a madman's pantomime."

"Adalwolf is ready," said Tilly. "He won't falter."

Thaly ran her finger over a map of Enthilen spread across the floor. "Berenice will fly with you, Sas. The Dambay Plains are dangerous, and Malphas' scouts will be on watch. After the attack under the mountain, we should be prepared for anything. I'll lead the army south and camp here, near the village of Rasstym." She pointed to a spot on the map less than half-a-days march from Pergamos' north wall.

Tom muttered to himself, "Six hundred and sixty-six."

"What?" said Thaly.

"Six hundred and sixty-six," said Tom, louder.

"You're not counting again, are you?" asked Rosalie.

"No. That number has been churning around inside my head since Revelé. In my world, it has a particular meaning. Here, it means something else."

"I knew he was a strange boy the moment he arrived in Bagendon," said Emelin. "He's getting stranger by the day."

"It has something to do with the moons and the sun," said Tilly. "Ompa told me a story about it once."

"When the moons block the sun," said Tom, "darkness will descend amid the daylight, and Enthilen will be ready for Volerdie's return."

"But *when* is when?" asked Tilly.

"We don't have time for philosophical musings," said Thaly. "Seena and Bargan are waning. Our plan is to attack when both are absent from the sky. Under cover of darkness. Zenais will hold off her assault until then."

Rosalie sprang to her feet and rushed outside, holding a hand over her mouth.

Tom went after her, finding his lover leaning against a wall and vomiting.

"The sickness is getting worse," said Tom.

"It passes," said Rosalie. "This baby is certainly making its presence felt."

"You should stay here in the mountains. Let us fight Malphas."

"Don't presume to tell me what to do, Tom Anderson."

"You would risk the baby's life as well as your own?"

Rosalie pushed herself from the wall, wiped the corners of her mouth and glared at Tom. "Are you happy about the child? You don't seem happy."

He tried to hug her, but she leaned away. "How do *you* feel?" he asked.

"Confused and scared. I never considered becoming a mother. Not sure I'd make a good one. It's all happening so fast. I feel like the future is being ripped from my hands. Saskia said...."

Tom placed his arm around Rosalie's waist. "What?"

"The Germalian healers can remove the baby."

A confusing mix of sadness, relief and anger welled up inside Tom. "Abort it?"

"But it must happen soon," said Rosalie.

"Is that what you want?"

"The decision should be ours, together. This child is as much yours as it is mine."

"While my father and I shared a house, we shared little else. He had no interest in my life or upbringing. I sometimes worry that I've inherited his character. That I would also make a terrible father."

Rosalie smiled. "This poor child. Its parents stumble even before it's born."

"Maybe," said Tom, holding Rosalie's hand, "maybe alone we are each defective, but together we'll make wonderful parents."

Rosalie kissed Tom on the lips. "If our child inherits stubbornness from both of us, we'll have no hope."

"There's always hope. New life is a testament to that."

"Then I can't extinguish hope, whatever challenges we face."

"Neither can I."

Early next morning, Tom, Saskia, Rosalie and Berenice prepared Namu and Nia for the long flight south while Thaly fed Yagle before returning to the army.

"Don't fly close to Pergamos," said Thaly. "No matter what."

Saskia rolled her eyes. "We won't. You know me."

"Yes, that's why I'm emphasising the point. Tell the weald-grells and werps we'll attack on the night of Seena and Bargan's absence. They shouldn't approach Pergamos before then. Zenais will advance from the east. Malphas will face an assault on three sides."

Thaly faced Tom. "When the city's defences are weakened, griffins could fly you and Adalwolf into Pergamos."

"Dwarrow has his own plans," said Tom. "You can be certain of that. And he carries the bone dust to sprinkle onto the throne."

"Nevertheless, if you need us, we are here."

Thaly pulled him into an embrace, and he squeezed her tight.

"You will succeed," whispered Thaly in Tom's ear. "For all our sakes, you must."

She pulled away as Emelin limped towards the group, helped by Tilly.

"Are we ready?" asked Emelin.

Thaly nodded.

"Ready for what?" asked Tom.

"I'm going flying," said Emelin, standing tall with a sparkle in her good eye. "Thaly is taking me to see this colossal army of hers. I'm too old to fight, but I can help in camp." Emelin brushed her arthritic fingers across Tom's cheek. "Farewell, Tom Anderson. Your journey has been a long one, but it's coming to an end. I hope for the betterment of all of us."

Emelin turned away. Thaly hugged Saskia, Berenice and Rosalie goodbye.

"What about you?" Tom asked Tilly.

"I'm not missing the biggest battle in Enthilen's history," she said. "I'm taking a rebel group into the plains to meet the Germalians. Then we'll rain serpent fire down on the old bastard." She slapped Tom on the back and kissed Rosalie on the cheek.

Dressed in the fur-lined leathers of the Volatal Vexil, Saskia and Tom mounted Namu while Berenice and Rosalie climbed into Nia's saddle. They waved farewell to the rebels and took off, flying the griffins into thinning stratus clouds that drifted over the Desolate Mountains' rocky slopes, then banking south on their way to meet their destiny.

~ Chapter 46 ~

Adalwolf and Audie walked beside Dwarrow, the querulous werp, and Hanni stone-grell towards the weald-grell camp. Dwarrow had grown impatient, and Adalwolf feared the mouldewerps and weald-grells would make a hasty and regretful decision by attacking Pergamos without help. Malphas almost certainly held Widukind prisoner. The Worshipful Master waited for his moment to complete the immortal sacrifice. Dwarrow was convinced a fateful darkness would descend within days. Volerdie would return to Enthilen, and all would be lost.

Arriving at the perimeter of the weald-grell camp, Hanni greeted a guard. "*Marang ngarin,*" she said.

"*Ngandhi nganha?*" replied the guard.

"Not Grellian," huffed Dwarrow. "Speak the common tongue, please."

The guard glared down at the mouldewerp.

Hanni pressed on, "This is Dwarrow, Adalwolf and Audie."

"Your leaders should be expecting me," said Dwarrow. "I come with a plan to enter Perg...*ah*...Malang Gunya." He tapped his walking stick on the guard's shin. "Hurry along and fetch them."

The weald-grell looked to Hanni, who rolled her eyes and nodded, then he turned on his heels and led the new arrivals into the camp, followed by hundreds of werps who'd emptied the secret dwell of all their supplies and weapons.

In the hazy light of late afternoon, the sight of thousands of wild grells appeared to Adalwolf like a dream. As he walked among the animal-skin tents, the grells watched him pass, their black facial tattoos seeming to melt into pale skin, swirling and dancing in his mind. He'd ordered the massacre of grell pilgrims at Malang Gunya twelve yarles ago. The thought of shedding the blood of hundreds of innocents twisted his dream into a nightmare. Some in the weald-grell camp may have survived the massacre and would remember his face. No doubt, they'd heard stories of the murderous King Adalwolf.

The sun shone in keen turquoise eyes, deflecting shards of light into Adalwolf's soul like daggers. It would take no more than an innocuous sweep of a weald-grell spear to slice open his chest, the giants rejoicing at his stilled heart.

Should have stayed inside the dwell, thought Adalwolf. It was safe down there.

Near the camp centre, the guard stopped and introduced the guests to a handful of weald-grells roasting plainalopes on spits above a crackling fire. A male weald-grell, almost as tall as Hanni, stood and welcomed her in the formal way, a greeting Adalwolf had only recently learned. Dwarrow tugged on the hem of Adalwolf's tunic as they waited to be acknowledged.

"That's Symian," whispered Dwarrow, "one of their leaders. The *grumpy* one."

Symian broke from Hanni's embrace and looked at Dwarrow with an unyielding sternness. "Dwarrow mouldewerp. You again seek our hospitality."

Dwarrow pointed his walking stick towards the fire. "Werps used to ride plainalopes. Before your ancestors hunted both to near extinction."

Hanni scowled at Dwarrow.

"But past is past," spluttered Dwarrow. "Now we seek mutual purpose. To join forces and plan the assault on Malphas."

"The elders are extremely displeased at your extortion involving the last seed of the sacred tree *ngayirr biyal*," said Symian.

"Extortion? That's a harsh description. I considered our meeting quite amicable. Tell the elders that the seed is safe. No need for their old bones to fret away to nothing."

"Any news from the scouts?" Hanni asked Symian.

"Hunger marches from Laodicea with scores of Rephaim and Erstürmen soldiers in black armour."

"He comes to bolster Malphas' forces," said Dwarrow.

"You should intercept him," said Adalwolf. "Don't let him into the city."

As soon as Adalwolf spoke, he regretted it. Symian fixed burning eyes on him, turquoise turning white hot.

"My brother and sister joined the last pilgrimage to Malang Gunya," said Symian. "I never saw them again. You might remember their faces, *King* Adalwolf. My brother, Karian, with the crest of *waagan*, the raven, and my sister, Winonian, with the crest of *gulumba*, the box tree. When you strolled among the grell corpses in the calendar of life, moments before you burned them to ash, do you recall seeing these tattoos?"

Around the fire, four other weald-grells stood. One brandished a dagger she'd used to cut chucks of meat from the plainalope carcass. Audie shuffled closer to Adalwolf and grabbed his hand. He wanted to pull away from her so he didn't appear weak. But he *was* weak. He was a coward. A monster. He didn't deserve Audie's affection. There should be no salvation for a murderer.

The grells around Adalwolf fell silent. No talking or singing. No rubbing of stone against stone to sharpen spears. No laughter. The silence demanded his response.

"I don't deserve it," said Adalwolf, "but I beg your forgiveness. Fate has delivered me an opportunity for redemption. I promise to destroy the dead throne and end Malphas' tyranny. I promise to see Pergamos returned to the grells, reclaimed as Malang Gunya. I offer my life to achieve these ends."

Audie squeezed his hand.

"We will keep you to your promises, King Adalwolf," said Symian.

"Good," said Dwarrow, "that's all sorted. Now, let's get down to business. Are you ready to march on Pergamos?"

"The Mulugan leaders meet in the morning to discuss our next action."

Dwarrow sighed. "Not *another* grell meeting. Time is of the...of the... fragrance?" The werp shook his head. "No. Essence. Time is of the essence. Tom Anderson taught me that one. If you must have a meeting, I should be there. Along with the other werp elders."

"You are not permitted. I will advise you of the outcome." Symian returned to his companions, all sitting back down around the campfire.

Dwarrow turned to Hanni, Adalwolf and Audie and screwed up his face. "*Hmph.* This alliance is not getting off to a good start. They won't even talk to me. But we must press on, regardless." He uncinched a pouch hanging from his twine belt and withdrew the blood compass, holding it towards Adalwolf. "Do you want me to do it, or will you?"

Adalwolf frowned. "I'll do it." He took the gold pentagram and dug a point into the stump of his right wrist until blood dripped onto the metal, sizzling and steaming as it bonded with the archaic treasure. Adalwolf handed the compass back to Dwarrow, who crouched down and balanced it on the blade of a grell spear.

The compass turned once, then stopped dead.

"*Hmmm,*" said Dwarrow. He picked up the treasure, shook it, then returned it to the spear. "Might be broken. Let's see." Dwarrow released the compass again. It didn't spin at all. "Yes, definitely broken. Otherwise, Tom Anderson would be standing right...."

"Griffins!" yelled Hanni, pointing skyward.

Two griffins swooped over the weald-grell camp. Every werp except Dwarrow scattered, disappearing into the grass of the Dambay Plains. Dozens of grell giants dropped to their knees and wailed into the sunset. Others ran for cover, diving beneath their shelters. A few raised spears, ready to throw.

"No!" screamed Adalwolf. "They are our allies."

He stood, hand-in-hand with Audie, facing the sky with a soul lifted by the sight of such magnificent creatures. His Erstürmen kin told him he would never see a griffin in Enthilen again. Now, he saw two. And one of them carried a man. Even before the griffins landed, Adalwolf recognised the man's face. As birth twins, their fate was forever entwined.

Tom Anderson had arrived.

*   *   *   *

As the griffins alighted on the Dambay Plains, weald-grells rushed at them, brandishing spears.

Tom jumped from Namu's saddle and raised his arms in deference. "*Gulbalanha*," he said in Grellian. *Be at peace.*

The spear-wielders stopped. Other grells pushed in around them. Then a familiar face burst from the crowd, waving his walking stick.

"Tom Anderson!" cried Dwarrow.

The little werp cannoned into Tom and wrapped his clawed hands around Tom's thigh. "You've returned," gasped Dwarrow. "I never lost faith."

Tom laughed at Dwarrow's excitement, knelt down and embraced his friend.

Dwarrow pulled away. "Did they come? The Germalians?"

Tom smiled. A broad, joyful smile. "Yes, they came."

Dwarrow hugged him again, and together they toppled onto the grass, chuckling.

"Of course they came," said Dwarrow. "Stupid question. You've arrived on griffins."

Standing and brushing himself off, Tom introduced his companions to Dwarrow. "This is Saskia, Thaly's sister. Berenice, a wind-rider in the Volatal Vexil. And my lufu, Rosalie."

"Wait, you have...a lover?"

Rosalie blushed.

"Is it so hard to believe?" asked Tom.

"As long as you keep your mind on the job," said Dwarrow, tapping his furry head. "And not in your pants."

Hanni strode from the crowd and engaged Tom in a formal grell greeting. Then she did the same with Rosalie.

"You made it across the vast desert," said Hanni. "Where is Quenan?"

"She fell," said Rosalie. "Raf and Quenan gave their lives for our cause."

Hanni's chest heaved a great sigh. "They will not be the last."

Saskia and Berenice tended to Namu and Nia, and the anxiety among the weald-grells turned to curiosity as they encircled the griffins.

Dwarrow was particularly captivated by the creatures, trotting around them in circles, then peppering Saskia with questions.

"The griffins need food and water," said Tom.

"We have plainalope," said Hanni.

"That will do."

Hanni disappeared back into the crowd of weald-grells.

Standing beside Tom, Rosalie wavered, clutching his shoulder to steady herself.

"Are you ill again?" he asked.

"We've been flying all day," said Rosalie, struggling to keep her feet. "It's caught up with me."

A woman with short, dark hair and a fair complexion strode from the crowd and grabbed Rosalie's hand.

"I'm a healer," said the woman.

"Erstürmen or Dobunni?" asked Tom.

"Neither."

"Audie's loyalty rests only with the unwell," said a voice behind Tom.

He turned to face a man with curly dark hair, matted in parts, a wiry beard sprouting across his face, and brooding, solemn eyes. While the man had aged and dressed in a peasant's pants and tunic, a missing right hand confirmed Tom's guess.

King Adalwolf stumbled towards Tom, offering his left hand. "Is this correct?" he asked. "Widukind told me about the preferred greeting among men in your world."

Tom nodded and shook Adalwolf's hand. "Yes, this is right."

Audie led Rosalie away. Tom went to follow, but Adalwolf held him back.

"She's the best healer I know," said Adalwolf. "Let her care for your friend."

Tom and Adalwolf stood together in awkward silence, forever connected by the bond joining birth twins in Earth and Ostamp. Should one die, so would the other. If one captured the other's soul with the dark eyes, the one would become immortal while the other would be turned into a draughoul.

"Your birthmark," said Tom. "Let me see it."

Adalwolf nodded and turned his back. "Stretch the tunic down past my shoulder and...well, you know where it is."

Tom pulled the neck of Adalwolf's tunic down and across, exposing his shoulder blade. And there, raised and reddened, was a naevus shaped like a crescent moon, exactly the same as Tom's.

"Were you injured?" asked Tom, pulling Adalwolf's tunic back over his shoulder. "Near the start of harvest season."

"Yes," said Adalwolf, facing Tom with wide eyes. "During the attack on Gestade. How did you know?"

"I felt it. Like someone stabbed me in the back. I fell off a giant lizard."

"A giant...*lizard?*"

"One of Dwarrow's friends."

"The grells have a campfire," said Adalwolf. "Will you join me? I'm sure we can find food and water. Or another beverage."

Tom nodded, and the birth twins walked side-by-side into the weald-grell camp.

"Any news about Widukind?" asked Tom.

"No," said Adalwolf. "I fear Widukind's life will end one way or another. My only hope is that it's not as the vessel for Volerdie's soul."

"Don't you want the Divine Creator to return to Enthilen?"

"The curates always told me to rejoice in the promise of Volerdie's return because that is when paradise will be revealed. But paradise is a lie. Your arrival in Enthilen planted the seed in my mind, and Widukind's interpretation of the First Scripture confirmed my suspicion. I suspect the world you come from is where Volerdie fled. I wouldn't have believed such a world existed if I hadn't met you. I began to wonder if paradise existed, why didn't Volerdie seek solace there? Why flee to another world?" Adalwolf stopped and faced Tom. "Paradise will not be found with Volerdie's return. Instead, we'll have *two* tyrants looking to rule for eternity, and their lust for power won't stop at Enthilen's borders. All of Ostamp will suffer. Our only hope is to shatter Volerdie's throne before darkness falls amid the daylight."

"It could happen soon," said Tom. "Seena and Bargan could block the sunlight. That will be Malphas' signal. We call it a solar eclipse in my world. It happens during the new moon."

"That is seven days away. The last day of harvest season. Both moons will be absent from the night sky."

"We can't be sure it will happen then. Only that it *might* happen."

Adalwolf grasped Tom's arm. "The attack could come too late."

"The Germalians are marching from the Desolate Mountains to Pergamos. They'll need days to build their war machines and prepare their forces."

"Without the Germalians, our numbers are too few, but time is running out."

"The walls will be breached," said Tom. "We won't fail."

Adalwolf pulled Tom close. "Do you carry the eyes of lost souls?"

Tom yanked his arm free and stepped back. "They're safe with me."

Adalwolf held up the stump of his right wrist. "You've nothing to fear. I can't leave Ostamp or capture your soul. I need a right hand for both. Indeed, I should be frightened of you. The dark eyes have a habit of twisting desires."

"I don't want to be immortal," said Tom.

"We should each carry an eye. Share the responsibility of crushing the dead throne."

Tom stood in silent contemplation. *Is this a trick?*

Adalwolf softened his gaze. "I'm sorry for what I did to you on Hansen's Bluff."

"You pulled your hand away. You couldn't go through with it."

"Do you think I'm a coward?"

"No. You were braver than me. If Malphas demanded I steal your soul with the dark eyes, I'm not sure I could have resisted."

"All I did was fool Malphas for a while, like I fooled myself, believing I'd be king forever. The second time, in Pergamos' throne hall, I would have taken your soul if Princess Caeli hadn't intervened. Not to appease Malphas but because my mother, Romilda, begged it of me. As an immortal,

I could have rid Enthilen of its Worshipful Master. Now, Romilda is dead, and I'm no longer king. But I can still deliver justice to Malphas."

Tom unlaced the top of his leather coat and reached into an inside pocket before removing the dark eyes. The radiant light from when they were joined with the Infinitas had dimmed, replaced again by the flaming pupils. He balanced them on the palm of his right hand as a shadow of dread fell across Adalwolf's eyes. If Tom closed his fist and thrust it into Adalwolf's chest, that would be the end of the failed king.

"Are you tempted?" whispered Adalwolf. "As an immortal, you could stroll into Pergamos, kill Malphas and take the throne for yourself."

"No," said Tom. He plucked an obsidian ball from his palm with his left hand and held it towards Adalwolf.

Adalwolf nodded, took the glass eye, and dropped it into his pants pocket.

That evening, the weald-grell leaders, the Mulugan, and the mouldewerp elders entertained their guests around the campfire, feasting on roasted plainalope, plains hare, daisy yams, and the occasional jar of pickled lizard at Dwarrow's insistence. Saskia and Berenice outlined the Germalian's plans for the attack on Pergamos, urging the weald-grells and werps not to advance until the night of the new moons. Zenais and the soldiers from the Germalian Classem would attack from the east. Thaly would attack the north wall, and the grells and werps would try to breach the south gate.

Thanks to one of Audie's potions, Rosalie recovered from her illness. The women joined Tom and Adalwolf, sitting and talking long into the night. Tom marvelled at the normalcy of four people enjoying shared company while the fate of Ostamp hung in the balance.

The following day, Saskia and Berenice bid farewell, keen to return north.

"When I see you again, Tom Anderson," said Saskia, "the deed will be done. Malphas will be defeated, and you will have destroyed the throne of the dead."

Tom nodded and hugged Saskia. "Fly safe."

She embraced Rosalie, then weald-grells lifted the wind-rider into Namu's saddle.

Saskia faced Symian and Dwarrow, who stood together. "Soon, your homeland will be returned."

"Malphas' end will herald a new beginning for stone- and weald-grells," said Symian.

"And mouldewerps," chimed in Dwarrow.

Symian nodded. "Yes, a future together. *Yanhanhadhu* griffin riders. May the winds of Enthilen ensure a swift and safe journey."

Namu and Nia cawed as Saskia and Berenice took flight, circling the camp to the delight of every werp and grell who turned their eyes to the clear blue sky.

Dwarrow trotted over to Tom. "Marvellous creatures, those griffins. Imagine how many important dealings I could complete if I had one of those to fly me around Enthilen."

"What about poor Xaviary?" asked Tom.

"Disappeared," said Dwarrow. "Can't find the blasted lizard anywhere. Haven't seen her since Lokan."

"The cursed wood strikes again."

"It seems that way. But we don't have time to lament wayward reptiles. The weald-grells meet this morning. I believe they'll move their camp closer to Pergamos in preparation for an attack. Hanni is determined to run off and confront Hunger before he reaches Pergamos, and some of her weald-grell friends have pledged to go with her." Dwarrow shook his head. "The foolishness of grells always amazes me."

"Do you have the bone dust?"

"Yes, yes, yes. Safe and sound in my favourite pouch. When the moment comes, you, Adalwolf and my dear self will enter Pergamos together and seek the throne."

"How will we know the right moment?"

Dwarrow tapped the end of his long nose with a clawed finger. "Trust me. I've been waiting for a generation to strike this blow. I won't miss the opportunity."

~ Chapter 47 ~

The morning dawned glorious across Enthilen's Dambay Plains, and Saskia had an eagle's view as Namu carried her north. During her first six yarles of life, she'd only left Sardis' inner circle to escape with her Ma and Pa down the Riverlands Escarpment. Until now, that had been her one experience of Enthilen beyond the royal city's walls. Yet, Dambay's sweeping grass and the snow-capped rise of the Desolate Mountains felt like home, much more than the Germalian desert.

Riding Nia, Berenice flew beside Namu's left wing. Further west, the spires of Pergamos appeared over a rolling hill as needles on the horizon. To Saskia's right, a thin line of sand marked Enthilen's east coast, and below her, a river flowed, emptying into a vast bog that reminded her of Nordland. The morning clouds thinned, leaving the day canopied by blue sky.

Fly high, came Thaly's voice inside Saskia's head. *Out of reach of enemy arrows.*

But we're far enough from Pergamos to avoid patrols, thought Saskia.

She guided Namu lower, and Berenice followed. As they glided over farmland, people stood in their fields and craned their necks skyward.

Don't worry, thought Saskia, we've come to liberate you.

Despite wearing the furred leathers of the Volatal Vexil, she shivered from Enthilen's cold morning air. Saskia waved her hand towards the ground, palm facing down, indicating to Berenice she wanted to descend even lower into warmer air. Berenice nodded and leaned into Nia's ear. Together, the griffins swooped closer to the plains.

They came upon a village with a crowd of people standing on the main street waving. Saskia flew Namu towards the rooftops, following the line of the road. Beneath her, little children scurried from the houses, laughing, clapping and reaching their arms skyward as if they might catch a flying griffin. Saskia smiled at their excitement.

Berenice flew close to Namu's wing. "We're too low!" she yelled into the wind and pointed her finger up, the signal to ascend.

Saskia nodded and pulled on the reins to guide Namu higher. Berenice dropped from Namu's tail as Saskia banked to the left to get a clear view of her fellow wind-rider. As Berenice and Nia ascended, an arrow flew from the ground. Berenice flinched, then slumped forward in her saddle.

Shit, thought Saskia. It's hit her.

She urged Namu closer. Nia threw his head back and crowed, the griffin panicking, then spiralled down. Saskia followed, chasing after Berenice. But she never reached her. Something much bigger than an arrow exploded from the shadows of a barn and lodged in Namu's right wing. Namu screamed a horrifying wail, turning Saskia's blood cold. The griffin plummeted towards the ground. Saskia clutched the saddle, her legs slipping from the harness cinched across her thighs. Namu twisted her head sideways and wrapped her bill around the shaft of a lance, wrenching it from the shoulder of her wing. But the damage had been done. The wing hung limp, and the griffin spiralled towards the plains, Saskia clinging to the saddle. Namu banked, rolled and tumbled. Saskia slipped from the harness, and the ground rushed at her with terrifying speed. She climbed onto Namu's side, hoping to cushion the fall. A moment before impact, Namu pulled up, throwing Saskia into the grass. Then Enthilen's blue skies disappeared.

*   *   *   *

"It's a bird-dragon!" cried Erwin, pointing to the northern sky.

"What are you talking about?" asked Nettie, focussing on the road as she drove the horse-drawn wagon east.

"Flying. Coming this way. Big...thing...eagle, but with a tail like a boulder lion."

Part eagle, part lion, thought Nettie. "Griffin?" she said, turning north.

From the sky, a creature spiralled towards the ground, flailing its right wing.

"It is a griffin!" cried Nettie.

"*Woah*," said Erwin. "Somebody fell off." He grabbed the reins. "Stop the wagon. Whoever was riding the griffin crashed to the ground."

"We can't stop. We need to get further from Pergamos. Soldiers patrol this area."

"The griffin-rider could be injured." Erwin yanked on the reins, slowing the draft horses to a walk. "They might need our help."

Damn it, thought Nettie, as she stopped the horses.

After escaping Pergamos, they'd travelled for less than a day before hitting a rut in the road and splintering a wagon wheel. They nursed the hobbled wagon to an abandoned farm and hid there while Nettie fixed the wheel, scrounging parts from the farm and drawing on what she'd learned as Yonna's apprentice. But it took her days, and she grew fearful of being discovered by one of Malphas' patrols. She had considered leaving the wagon and riding the horses east, but she'd never ridden a horse, and Erwin was terrified of trying. And the wagon gave her legitimacy as a trader on their way to pick up supplies. Tired and hungry, Nettie didn't need another person to babysit, griffin-rider or not.

"Could be an Erstürmen soldier," said Nettie.

"Malphas doesn't have griffins, does he?" asked Erwin.

Nettie shrugged. "Who knows? Griffins haven't been seen in Enthilen for generations. I thought they only existed in stories."

"Well, I saw a griffin, and I'm going to find the rider." He jumped off the wagon and ran into the long grass.

Nettie growled to herself, climbed from the driver's seat, gathered the tie weight from the side of the wagon and tethered the horses to it.

"Where are you?" she called after Erwin.

"Here," he called back, his faint voice drifting on the morning breeze.

She pushed through the long grass, cursing Erwin's stupid kindness with every step.

The grass thinned, trampled and grazed by plains animals. A deer track led to a dry marsh surrounded by cotton-topped reeds as tall as Nettie. Erwin crouched beside a reed clump on the other side of a hollow.

She walked across the marsh, baked mud cracking under her boots, and stood beside Erwin. He pointed into the reeds where a woman, dressed in leathers and a metal skullcap, lay crumpled in a heap, eyes closed. Nettie knelt beside her, brushed the blonde hair from the stranger's face, then hovered her ear above the woman's mouth.

"Still breathing," said Nettie.

The woman moaned, and Nettie jumped up, pulling the knife stolen from Elmbray's koken from her belt.

"She ain't going to attack us," said Erwin.

"How do you know?" said Nettie. "She has a cutlass sheathed on her belt."

"What kind of soldier uses a cutlass?"

"None I've met."

Erwin crawled to the woman and shook her shoulder.

"Stay away from her," said Nettie. "We should go back to the wagon."

The woman opened her eyes.

"Can you hear me?" asked Erwin. "Does it hurt anywhere?"

"Help," whispered the woman in Erstürmen.

Erwin nodded. "Sure. We can help."

"No, we can't," said Nettie.

"My legs," said the woman. "Griffin...wounded...."

"We have to help," said Erwin to Nettie. "We can't leave her like this."

"Whoever shot her griffin down will come looking for it," said Nettie. "And her."

"Who are you?" Erwin asked the injured woman.

"Germalian," said the woman, trying to sit up.

"Germalians have got dark skin," said Nettie. "I ain't stupid."

"Born in Sardis," said the woman.

Erwin placed his arm under the Germalian's shoulders and lifted her into a sitting position. "Nettie was born in Sardis, too," he said. "Was that really a griffin?"

The woman nodded. "Namu. I have to find her."

"It flew off that way," said Erwin, pointing west towards Pergamos.

"Then it crashed. What's your name?"

"Saskia."

"I'm Erwin. This is Nettie."

Saskia tried to stand, pain writhing across her face. Erwin got to his feet and helped her up, letting her lean against his shoulder.

"We can't help you find your griffin," said Nettie, shoving the knife back under her belt. "We're in a hurry."

"What's a Germalian doing in the Dambay Plains, anyway?" asked Erwin.

Saskia didn't reply, looking west where Erwin had last seen the griffin. She tried to walk but stumbled, Erwin grabbing her arm to hold her upright.

"You could ride in our wagon while we look for the griffin," he said.

For goodness' sake, thought Nettie, don't be so foolishly generous.

But he didn't heed her glare, guiding a limping Saskia back towards the wagon.

They reached the wagon around midday, Erwin helping Saskia sit and rest her back against a wheel. Then he gathered a waterskin.

"We found a farm well," he said, handing the waterskin to Saskia. "Otherwise, we'd be out."

"Don't drink it all," said Nettie to Saskia before checking on the horses.

The animals stood with their heads bowed, lacking the energy to do much else. They hadn't been fed properly since Pergamos, the abandoned farm having little hay stored. Nettie worried they wouldn't make it to the east coast, another two days travelling with strong, healthy horses. She wanted to reach Dorfisch, planning to exchange the wagon for a place on a ship, taking her and Erwin to another land far away from Enthilen. But they couldn't walk to Dorfisch. They'd die of hunger or thirst, or at the end of an Erstürmen halberd, before then.

As Nettie untethered the horses, voices drifted on the easterly wind. Further up the road, silhouetted giants shimmered in the midday haze. She spun around to Erwin and Saskia.

"*Rephaim*," she hissed. "Coming up the road."

"We can't outrun grells," said Erwin. "The horses are too weak."

Give Saskia up, thought Nettie. If we give her up, they'll leave us alone.

But Erwin's fearful eyes pleaded for bravery and conviction from his friend.

"If we abandon the wagon, they'll take it," said Nettie. "We'll lose everything." She marched over to Erwin and Saskia. "Hide in the secret compartment. Both of you."

"What will you do?" asked Erwin.

"I've got the re-entry permit. I'll convince the Rephaim I'm a merchant."

"It's not valid anymore."

"I'll say the wagon broke down, and we were delayed. It's half true. Hide. Hurry!"

Erwin helped Saskia to the wagon's tailgate. Nettie slid the hidden panels out from underneath, exposing the compartment. Saskia and Erwin crawled between the wagon wheels and pulled themselves into the secret space, then Nettie closed the panels.

"Don't make a sound," she said. "No matter what happens."

She walked to the horses and held the reins lest the grell soldiers spook the animals. A breath lodged in her throat as the Rephaim approached. Krieg led them, striding forward like a red behemoth painted with his victim's blood. At the rear of the satch, a soldier led a griffin, a hessian bag tied over its head and the tips of its wing feathers trailing in the dirt.

"Hail Malphas," said Nettie, placing her right fist against her heart.

Krieg stopped and lifted the face of his grilled helmet, rivulets of sweat trickling along the scars on his cheeks and chin. His black eyes set a knot in Nettie's stomach as he looked down at her.

"Why are you here?" he asked, the guttural boom of his voice causing the horses to stamp and whinny.

Nettie patted the flank of the animal closest to her. "Resting my horses, Vater Krieg. I'm a merchant, taking the wagon to Dorfisch to get supplies for our brave soldiers."

"You are young to be a merchant," said Krieg. "Where are your papers?"

Nettie dropped the reins and reached inside her pants pocket, pulling out the re-entry permit and handing it to Krieg.

He stared at it with his black eyes, and she wondered if he could read. A dozen Rephaim gathered behind their leader, waiting for his next order. From under the hessian bag, the griffin squawked, and Nettie flinched. Blood dripped from its right wing, pattering the dirt road like scarlet rain.

"This permit is expired," said Krieg.

"I had an accident with the wagon," said Nettie. "A wheel shattered, and it took days to fix. Should be right to go now."

"Rules are rules."

"Is that a griffin?" asked Nettie, trying to deflect Krieg's attention.

"It is not of your concern," said Krieg, returning the permit to Nettie. "We are taking your wagon to Pergamos."

"No...." started Nettie, then winced at the stupidity of defying the red grell.

His giant hand reached down to the mace hanging from his belt, the weapon's spikes tapping against his cuisse as if counting down Nettie's last moments of life.

"Vater Krieg...please," she sputtered. "I can drive the wagon. I know the horses best. I'm a loyal servant of Malphas. Let me return to Pergamos."

Krieg relaxed his hand and faced the Rephaim. "Tie the beast to the wagon."

"What of the griffin rider?" asked a soldier.

"Dead from the fall. The griffin is our treasure. The Worshipful Master will welcome such a prize." He scowled at Nettie. "Drive the wagon, and consider your good fortune."

She nodded, thumped her fist against her chest, and climbed onto the driver's seat.

It had taken Nettie nearly twelve yarles to escape Pergamos. She'd been free for no more than five days, and now she had to return. And she carried a precious cargo. A Germalian soldier, and Erwin, her best friend. If Krieg discovered them, Nettie's good fortune would disappear like a griffin flying into the sunset.

~ Chapter 48 ~

Seena's half-moon disappeared behind a cloud, darkening the night sky and making Thaly's task more difficult as she awaited the returning wind-riders. Saskia and Berenice should have returned from the weald-grell camp by now, griffins easily able to traverse the span of the Dambay Plains in a day. Around Thaly, the Germalian army pitched tents, making camp for the night. They'd been marching out of Lokan and into the northern plains for a day. Another two days of marching, and they'd be close enough to Pergamos to launch an attack.

The cloud drifted on, and a speck appeared in the southern sky silhouetted against the moon. It flew closer, dropping towards the ground until griffin wings swished the long grass.

Why only one griffin? thought Thaly, striding to the temporary dismount area.

But the griffin never reached the platform, crashing into a ridge overlooking the camp. Thaly pulled a cresset from the ground and ran past the sentries guarding the perimeter and into the darkness. As she climbed the rise, the wind-rider slumped forward in the saddle and tumbled to the ground.

Saskia? thought Thaly. No, the griffin is Nia.

She raced up to Berenice, who lay prostrate in the grass, an Erstürmen arrow with red and black fletching protruding from her chest. Berenice groaned and opened her eyes. Thaly thrust the cresset pole into the ground and knelt, clutching at Berenice's coat.

"What happened?" she asked. "Where's Saskia?"

"Shot...down," whispered Berenice.

"Where?" asked Thaly, but the wind-rider closed her eyes again.

Guards came, leading a healer. The healer crouched beside Berenice and placed a hand on her neck. She waited, then faced Thaly with solemn eyes. "She's dead."

Nia cawed, climbing onto unsteady legs before ruffling his feathers.

Thaly stood and walked away. She had to prepare Yagle for flight. Search for Saskia.

Inside the command tent, Thaly donned the Volatal Vexil leathers.

Emelin pushed through the tent flap. "What are you doing?" she asked.

"Saskia's missing," said Thaly. "I'm going to look for her."

"Too dangerous at night. You won't see any ground threats."

"She could be injured. I won't leave her to die on the plains."

"One of your griffins is missing, the other is bereft a rider, and you would risk a third? The griffins give you an advantage over Malphas. Without them, you may not win this war."

"Zenais has another three. My sister is more important...."

"Than what?" interrupted Emelin. "Enthilen's freedom? The safety of your army? If you fall, who will lead them? A leaderless army may well turn for home."

"I'll leave orders with the Prime Lieutenants."

"What would Jacob do?"

At Emelin's question, Thaly stopped dressing and faced the only mother she'd known for the first eighteen harvest seasons of her life. "That isn't fair."

"Jacob was your trainer, mentor and friend. What would he do?"

Thaly sat on the edge of her bed. "Put aside personal desires and stay with his fighters. Lead them in battle."

"That is what *you* must do. The Germalians chose you as their leader because you know Enthilen better than any of them, and you know the enemy they face." Emelin sat on the bed beside Thaly. "The greatest leaders rise to whatever challenge confronts them. Your loyalties are torn between your love for Saskia and your pledge to free Enthilen from a tyrant. You're being tested, Thaly, like your father was tested all those yarles ago when he turned his back on his people to save your life."

"Yes," said Thaly. "And I must save Saskia's life."

Emelin traced her finger diagonally across the front of Thaly's coat. "At the Pledge Feste in Bagendon, I wielded the knife that scarred your chest. Remember? I was so proud of you that night. So proud my adopted daughter would always be a Dobunni rebel, pledging to fight the Erstürmen until her dying day. Will you dismiss the promise like your father did?"

Tears welled in Thaly's eyes, but she wiped them away with a determined hand. "The decision is mine to make."

"I will go," came a voice from outside the tent.

Princess Caeli appeared at the entrance, her thinning body resembling a frail stem of dying long grass. "I can travel the plains faster than most," said Caeli, "and I can enter Pergamos. If Saskia has been taken prisoner by Malphas, I will find her."

"How can you breach the walls?" asked Thaly.

"There is one path through the stone. Only draughouls can travel it, and it is protected by Malphas' most evil servants. I've met draughouls who planned to try the path."

"Did they succeed?"

"I never saw them again."

"Then you can't go," said Thaly. "It is too dangerous."

Caeli picked up a looking glass from the dressing table beside Thaly's bed and held it in front of her face. "I was beautiful once. Your brother, Jürgen, thought so. He never said as much, but I could tell by how he looked at me. How he touched me. Eyes that see me now are filled only with terror. My own father recoils when he touches me. Lingering death is a prison worse than any castle keep."

"Widukind is also missing," said Emelin. "Almost certainly trapped inside Pergamos. Is your desire to enter the city more about rescuing your father than finding Saskia?"

Caeli placed the mirror back on the table and faced Emelin. "It is possible. But familial love has little effect on the decisions of draughouls. The trappings of Volerdie's power draw me near, but otherwise, my wanderings are aimless."

"But you helped us," said Thaly. "There is still a common decency to your actions."

"I want the dead throne broken more than anyone. Only then will I be free of this torment." Caeli leaned towards Thaly and kissed her on the cheek with lips as white and cold as snow. "I will save Saskia if I can."

Then she turned away and disappeared into the night.

The next morning, Thaly donned the Volatal Vexil armour and mounted Yagle. She rose above her troops, preparing to lead them closer to Pergamos. A riderless Nia flew beside Yagle, still struggling with the ordeal of the long flight from the weald-grell camp and his rider's death. Griffins mourned as people mourned, Nia's wingbeats slow and leaden with grief. Below Thaly, seventy thousand Germalians formed their battalions and advanced towards the north wall of Malphas' stronghold. Foot soldiers rested javelins on their shoulders beside shields strapped to their backs. Horses stamped across the plains, carrying riders clad in cotton robes and armed only with a cutlass. Elephai bellowed and lumbered ahead, pulling wagons full of armour, supplies and enough materials to build more than a dozen war machines; trebuchets, battering rams, ballistae and siege towers. Male servants shouldered wicker baskets full of bedding and clothes. Puer, Yagle's handler, was among them, the old man committed to serving Germalia in whatever way he could.

Sitting in Yagle's saddle, Thaly's body tensed at the expectation of the coming battle and the frustration of knowing she couldn't save her sister.

Leaders must make hard decisions, came Jurelle's voice inside her head. *Decisions that can cost lives.* Thaly never thought one of her decisions could cost the life of her own sister.

~ Chapter 49 ~

Hanni dug the ancient stone blade of her spear into the sapwood of a bilawi tree. Trickles of raisin-coloured sap slid down the tawny bark as the tree cried for a life long gone. Beside her, Wyan collected the sap on his bone dagger, then smeared the tree-blood on his cheek. Hanni did the same. If this was her last stand, she'd make it paying homage to her beloved nature.

The late afternoon sun cast lengthening shadows among a grove of trees, a day's march northeast of the weald-grell camp. A track cut through the trees, connecting Enthilen's coast road with the centre of the Dambay Plains. According to weald-grell scouts, Hunger, the black grell, would soon appear on the track, riding a black stallion as large as an undred and leading dozens of Rephaim and thousands of Erstürmen soldiers to Pergamos. The forest remnant was an obvious place for an ambush, but Hanni hoped Hunger wouldn't expect it. She waited with twelve hundred weald-grells, their faces and naked torsos painted in dappled green, yellow and brown hues, and waists covered in grass skirts or animal hides. Even the legendary keenness of stone-grell eyes couldn't spot the weald-grells hiding among the trees. Surprise would be their only advantage over Hunger and his armoured soldiers.

Standing at Hanni's feet, Wirrikow, the mouldewerp, tilted his nose eastwards. "I can smell a tainted grell. A most awful stench."

He barked an order to the werps who'd joined the grells in the ambush. Two dozen furry heads popped up from grass clumps, waved noses in the air like worms poking from a hole, then squealed and scurried into position.

Hanni and Wyan crouched behind the bilawi tree as the hooves of undreds and horses thumped against the pebbles of the dirt track.

They will enter the forest soon, thought Hanni, straight into our ambush.

She handed her spear to Wyan and nocked an arrow in her bowstring. Wirrikow drew a dagger from his belt.

As if anticipating trouble, the galloping hooves of the enemy slowed, then stopped.

Do they know? thought Hanni, her naked chest, painted in forest colours, shuddering with apprehension.

Wyan's glimmering turquoise eyes tried to pull back the shadows. Wirrikow sniffed, sniffed, sniffed the air as if he might suck the danger into his lungs and trap it there forever.

A huge black horse appeared on the track, carrying memories that stabbed at Hanni's mind like needles. Sonya's death in the Master's Hall of the King's Quarter. Terror on stallholder faces in Laodicea's market. The last moment Hanni spent with Grin in Lokan's cursed wood. One scarring image connected all the memories — Hunger's gloating face. And here it was again, straddling the horse less than a stone's throw away. A clear shot for Hanni's arrow. But she stayed her hand with the memory of her mother's voice. *Grells do not attack; we only defend. It is written on the truce rock, Marradir. Aggression led to the tribal war in Malang Gunya, forever cleaving the weald-grells from the stone-grells.*

Hanni lowered her bow and stepped from behind the tree to face the black demon.

"You return to Malang Gunya," she said. "The ancestral home of all grells. Yet it has been defiled by the horror of Malphas, as you have been defiled. Hunger, once you were a wild grell. A *free* grell. You may have this freedom again. Lay down your weapons and re-join your grell brothers and sisters in the fight against our oppressor."

Hunger dismounted, the sheen of sweat on his black skin glistening in the mottled light. "I admire your bravery in confronting me alone. Female fighters are welcome in my ranks. Would you not prefer the life of a Rephaim to one of slavery and miserable death?"

Where are his soldiers? wondered Hanni.

Behind Hunger, the forest track appeared empty.

The black grell stepped towards her. She raised her bow.

"We have met before," said Hunger. "You raided my hall and let your friend die so you may escape. Does your conscience remind you of your cowardice, or are you so bereft of dignity that you are happy to let others die for your so-called *freedom?*"

"I am not the coward here," said Hanni, squeezing the longbow grip. "You allowed an old man to taint your skin and corrupt your soul in exchange for fleeting power."

"To converse with those who refuse to listen is akin to eating a poisoned *guraban*," said Hunger. "Your mouth stings, and your mind swirls."

"I am surprised you remember a single word of your own language."

"I have many surprises." Hunger clapped his hands together, sending a thunderous boom through the trees.

A weald-grell screamed in agony. Then another. And another.

"They surround us!" yelled Wyan from behind Hanni.

From the forest shadows, Rephaim advanced on foot. Weald-grells sprang from their hiding places, brandishing spears and daggers, and firing arrows.

"More enemy to the north and south!" yelled Wirrikow.

"What?" said Hanni, spinning on the spot like the strange blood compass.

Forest greens and browns blurred to black. Panicked, Hanni fired her arrow, without aiming, without thinking. More Rephaim came, scything their way through unarmoured weald-grells like a farmer harvesting wheat. Then Erstürmen soldiers, dressed head-to-toe in black metal. The enemy crushed the weald-grells as a vice would crush an egg.

Hanni nocked another arrow and fired at Hunger. The projectile skimmed his shoulder and thudded into a tree. He stood in place, a mocking, unafraid statue. She fired again. The arrow hit his bare chest, right at the heart. It should have wounded him. It should have lodged in his flesh, but it bounced from Hunger's skin and clattered to the ground.

Hanni tossed her longbow away, bent down and gathered a spear from a dead weald-grell. Hunger moved, pushing Rephaim and Erstürmen out of his way and marching straight for Hanni. She braced herself, waiting for the monster to arrive. He unsheathed a battle-axe and raised it to strike. As the blade fell towards Hanni's skull, she thrust the spear handle skyward with both hands, blocking Hunger's swing. He struck again, with an unsettling, malevolent composure, chopping down into the spear handle and cleaving it in two. Splinters slapped Hanni's face, a punishment for foolishness.

The black grell raised his battle-axe in line with Hanni's neck. An arrow flew from the forest, piercing the back of Hunger's hand. He yelped and dropped his weapon.

He has weaknesses, thought Hanni.

She seized the moment, drawing her dagger and thrusting at Hunger's stomach. Metal hit metal, and the knife shuddered in Hanni's hand. She pulled away, confused. A reflection of sunlight winked out of the darkness of Hunger's skin from the hole made by the knife tip.

The tainted grell crouched and collected his battle-axe as if picking a meadow flower, showing utter contempt for his opponent. As he stood, Hanni slashed her knife across his chest. The skin tore open, revealing a plate of steel underneath. Blood and polished metal glinted in the sun, and Hunger smiled at Hanni.

He swung his axe and nicked her hand. She gritted her teeth and held the knife firm, stepping back to give herself room. Hunger blocked her escape. Hanni poked at his torso with the knife point, but each time, the metal plates beneath his skin foiled her attack. She thrust again. He sliced his axe blade across her forearm. She shrieked in pain and anger, backing herself into the trunk of the bilawi tree where she'd been hiding with Wyan.

Hunger's axe swept across her midriff, cutting open her skin. She dropped the knife, reached back and braced herself against the tree, her fingers dipping into sticky sap. As Hunger raised his weapon for the final blow, Hanni brought her hand forward and rubbed sap-covered fingers across her bare stomach. The tree's blood and her blood fused as one.

The muscles of Hunger's shoulders and arms tensed. His face scars formed a mask of deviant jubilation.

My end has arrived, thought Hanni.

Then a twig cracked in the tree canopy above her. Dropping from the foliage like a cat pouncing on a mouse, a furry ball of black and salmon landed on Hunger's head. Wirrikow thrust a bone dagger into the black grell's neck. Hunger wailed.

No steel plates there, thought Hanni.

The black grell dropped his axe, wrapped his hands around Wirrikow and threw the werp into the forest. Hanni pushed away from the tree trunk, swooped on the axe, and lashed it across Hunger's neck. A gaping wound opened, blood spewing down his chest and splashing onto Hanni's face. She licked the side of her mouth and swallowed the tainted sap. It tasted like hatred and ruin.

Hanni swung again. Hunger's soulless black eyes showed no shock, hinted no remorse. But the last thing they saw was Hanni's facial crest, the spear fern, gama.

As Hunger's headless torso collapsed to the forest floor, Hanni raced to where Wirrikow lay.

"Wirrikow?" she said, kneeling beside him. "Can you hear me?"

Wirrikow opened his eyes. "Of course I can."

"You saved my life."

A hint of a smile appeared on Wirrikow's salmon-coloured face. "I'll wager you didn't know werps can climb trees."

Hanni picked up the diminutive little bundle and hugged him to her chest. Around her, the battle raged on. Dozens of weald-grells lay dead in the forest. Her friend, Wyan, had been pinned, lifeless, to a tree trunk by a halberd driven into his chest. Even without a leader, the Rephaim and Erstürmen soldiers did their duty with lethal precision. Hanni accepted the lost lives would be the price of ending Hunger's malice. But this day had another surprise.

Something extraordinary trundled down the road; a wheeled machine larger than a house and covered in shields that fitted together flawlessly like the plates of *gandhalwurr*, the river turtle. The four wheels moved of their own accord. Nothing pulled the plated wagon along or pushed it from behind. It stopped in the middle of the battle. Weald-grells, Rephaim and Erstürmen lowered their weapons, gawking at the strangeness before them. A horn blew. Gaps opened between the shields, and out poked steel blades like *ganyi* spines.

The Rephaim were the first brave enough to move, creeping towards the plated wagon. The horn blew again. As one, the spines exploded, flying from between the shields and into the forest.

Not spines, thought Hanni. *Lances.*

Every lance found a mark, plunging into a Rephaim chest. The grell soldiers fell like leaves from panalope trees during *ngurung-ginya.*

More lances flew from between the shields, targeting the Erstürmen. Hanni's mouth dropped open as blades sliced through the metal Erstürmen breastplates, usually capable of deflecting any weapon found in Enthilen. The soldiers screamed in surprised terror before joining their Rephaim companions in death.

Another trumpeting from the hidden horn and the shields fell away, revealing dozens of female soldiers with dark skin dressed in golden armour resembling fish scales. The Germalians had arrived.

Brandishing cutlasses, the women fighters sprang from their wagon and rushed at the enemy like a squalling tempest. The Erstürmen standing their ground didn't draw breath for long. Others fled, following a trickle of Rephaim as they retreated to the plains. But they never made it. More Germalians waited there, hiding at the forest fringe like the death adder, *dumiiny*, hides its body beneath leaves and twigs, waiting to surprise unwary prey.

An ambush, of an ambush, of an ambush, thought Hanni, almost smiling to herself.

"You can put me down now," said Wirrikow, his voice muffled against Hanni's breasts. "The smell of victory is in the air."

The sounds of battle subsided. Holding her stomach to stem the bleeding, Hanni stumbled around the plated wagon, marvelling at the cogs and winches, pullies and ropes of a machine she could never have imagined.

"*Gaang-ga gulbir ngidhi*," came a voice from behind her, speaking Grellian.

She turned, expecting to see one of her weald-grell companions. Instead, a Germalian woman stood, holding a cup towards Hanni.

"Drink this," said the woman, this time in Erstürmen. "It will numb the pain. Then I can take you to a healer to mend your wound."

Hanni took the cup, swishing a viscous ginger liquid around the rim before sipping. The medicine stung her lips and fired her tongue.

"I promise you, it works," said the woman. "I am Zenais Orelus, Praefecti of the Germalian Classem. You understand Erstürmen? My command of your language is limited."

Hanni nodded and took another drink.

"I have already met two of your fighters," said Hanni. "The ones who ride griffins."

The whites of Zenais' eyes gleamed from her dark-skinned face. "The army has arrived in Enthilen?"

"They march from the Desolate Mountains and will camp near Pergamos' north wall."

"Then everything is as planned," said Zenais. "You bear excellent news."

"How did you know about this battle?" asked Hanni, returning the cup to Zenais.

"When our ships landed at Dorfisch, we sent scouting parties west into the plains. One of them spotted the black grell and his soldiers, moving with haste. We tracked them, waiting for an opportunity to strike. Your ambush, as it were, forced our hand. But the victory is complete nonetheless."

"How many more...." started Hanni, but didn't finish her sentence.

She doubled over in distress, clutching at her wound.

Zenais grasped Hanni's arm to steady her. "Let me take you to a healer. They will clean and stitch the wound. Then we can speak about what other help the Germalians may offer Enthilen's defenders."

~ Chapter 50 ~

Rain pattered the wagon tray and seeped between a gap in the timbers, dripping into Saskia's eye. She wiped away the annoyance and rolled onto her stomach, wriggling around the secret compartment's tight space. Beside her, Erwin groaned. She wanted to glare at him. Kick him. Anything to keep him quiet lest the grell soldiers marching beside the wagon heard. Saskia worried Erwin might give up. Slide the floor panels, drop from the wagon and let the grell soldiers hack him to pieces. But he hadn't given up yet.

Neither of them had slept for two moons, Saskia waking Erwin whenever he snored. Pain from the fall off Namu writhed through her leg muscles, and she'd soiled her pants more than once, worried the stench might attract the Rephaim. A tiring Namu lumbered behind the wagon, the primary feathers of her injured wing trailing in the dirt. Saskia thought the griffin might die before they reached Pergamos. Then she'd have the unenviable mantle of being the first wind-rider to outlive her griffin, though, without food or water, she expected the crown to be short-lived.

As night closed in, Krieg yelled into the darkness, "Open the gate," in a voice etched into Saskia's nightmares.

The wagon wheel creaked in time with the plod of the wretched draft horses still labouring with their burden. Sitting in the driver's seat, Nettie geed the animals up, and they began a trot, eager to be finally home.

Inside the gate, people crowded around Namu, ignoring the Rephaim orders to stand back. Some onlookers gasped and muttered. Children ran beside the griffin, poking her with sticks and laughing as she tried to fend off the blows. Others threw stones. Saskia wanted to kick the timbers from the wagon tray and batter the children over the head with one.

Then Krieg roared, and the pests scattered like terrified kittens.

At least he's good for something, thought Saskia.

She slid to the wagon's side and pressed an eye to a keyhole. Burning cressets lined the street, their poles fixed into footpaths crowded with people. Saskia wanted to ask Erwin if he knew where in Pergamos they were or where they might be going, but she couldn't risk it. They turned a corner and stopped inside a timber and stone corral. Krieg marched to the tailgate and untied Namu, hitching her to a metal loop embedded in a marble column. The griffin collapsed, tucking her head under her uninjured wing.

"The wagon is yours," said Krieg as he marched off.

Nettie geed the horses again, and they sauntered off, around another corner and down another street. Erwin fidgeted beside Saskia.

"We can get out soon," he said.

"*Sssh*," hissed Saskia.

"Grell soldiers are gone," said Erwin. "Least I think they have."

The wagon stopped. A lock clicked, and doors creaked on hinges. Then the wagon moved again, entering a dark place before coming to another stop. Doors closed, making the dark place even darker. Then the panels of the secret compartment slid open, and Saskia and Erwin tumbled onto a blanket of hay.

"We're in Elmbray's barn," whispered Nettie. "I didn't know where else to go."

"Is Snick here?" asked Erwin, crawling from under the wagon.

"I can't see him."

"Who's Snick?" asked Saskia as she pulled herself into the open.

"Elmbray's servant," said Erwin. "I think I killed him."

Saskia wanted to ask if they should worry about Elmbray, but her thoughts turned to Namu. "I have to rescue my griffin."

"You won't get past the guards," said Nettie. "They've surrounded it inside a corral near the pyramid, and it can't fly."

"*She*," said Saskia. "Namu is a she. And I'm a wind-rider of Germalia's Volatal Vexil. We swear never to abandon our griffins unless they're dead."

"She'll be dead soon enough," said Nettie.

"I won't give up. We can save her if we're patient and wait for the right moment."

"What do you mean, *we?*"

Nettie walked to the barn door and pushed it open, letting in a sliver of moonlight. Erwin crawled onto a pile of hay, pulled down his pants, squatted and defecated.

"I couldn't wait any longer," he said.

"I need a change of clothes," said Saskia. "Volatal Vexil flight leathers will stand out like a sore thumb in Pergamos. And they stink."

"It's safe to leave," called Nettie from the doorway. "Come on, Erwin."

He pulled up his pants, tied the lace at the front and stumbled over to his friend. Saskia tried to stand, but her legs failed, and she fell back into the hay.

"Please," said Saskia, reaching her hand towards Erwin and Nettie. "Please help me. I've travelled for days across deserts and bogs to fight Malphas. To liberate you."

"We didn't ask for liberation," said Nettie.

Saskia dragged herself to her feet, staggered to Nettie and grabbed her tunic. The young woman pulled a knife from her belt and slashed it across Saskia's knuckles.

"*Ahhh,*" said Saskia. "Damn you." She pulled away, then lunged at Nettie, smashing her into the barn door.

"Stop it," cried Erwin.

Saskia unsheathed her cutlass and waved it at Nettie and Erwin. "Help me, or I'll consider you the enemy. Erstürmen loyal to Malphas. Ones I'm here to kill."

"What do *you* know about being Erstürmen?" asked Nettie.

"I lived in the inner circle for six yarles."

Nettie spat on the ground. "The inner circle. Always think you're better than the rest of us. No circles in Pergamos; we're all the same here."

"That isn't true," said Erwin. "Why are you being so difficult?"

"Because," shrieked Nettie, spittle exploding from her mouth, "because if it wasn't for this stupid Germalian, we'd be free now. Travelling on a ship across the Veiled Occyan to a land Malphas doesn't care about. Instead, here I am, back in this damn shithole. Back where I started. I'm never escaping Pergamos, and it's all her fault."

Erwin faced Saskia. "Inner circle. Are you royalty?"

"Yes, and no," said Saskia. "My mother is Princess Genevea, King Ewald's sister. My father was one of his generals, but he was born Dobunni, and now we're Germalian despite our pale skin."

"Royals no use here," said Nettie. "Only Malphas rules."

"Your father made a necklace for Princess Genevea," Erwin said to Nettie. "You told me he was so proud to be asked, remember?"

Saskia lowered her cutlass. "Who is your father?"

"*Was*," said Nettie. "Soldiers worked him to death."

"Yonna Barron," said Erwin. "Best metalsmith in Pergamos *and* Sardis."

"You're Nettie Barron," said Saskia, sheathing her weapon.

Nettie nodded; dreads of matted hair silhouetted against the shine of two quarter-moons.

"And you have a sister named Rosalie."

Nettie's legs wavered, and her face grew pale. "What do you know of Rosalie?"

"She's fighting with us. I carried her from Portum on Namu."

"You're lying," said Nettie. "This is a trick."

"It's no trick. Rosalie is with the weald-grells south of Pergamos, preparing to attack the city. I was returning from the grell camp when I was shot down."

Nettie collapsed, and Erwin caught her, clutching his friend to his chest.

"I...I thought Rosalie was dead," said Nettie.

"She's alive," said Saskia, "and she carries another new life inside her."

Nettie pushed away from Erwin. "She's pregnant?"

Saskia nodded.

Erwin grasped Nettie's shoulders. "It's wonderful news. When Pergamos is liberated, you can be a family again."

"First," said Saskia, "we must rescue Namu."

"Not now," said Nettie. "We have to gather our strength, make a plan, and keep away from Elmbray, the mage."

"The ossuary," said Erwin. "It's the best place in Pergamos to hide."

Nettie nodded. "You two wait here. I'll steal clothes for Saskia, then we make for the ossuary."

*   *   *   *

At least, thought Widukind, it's a beautiful place to die.

On these dark nights, the stars shone brighter, fighting only with Seena's quarter moon for attention. The celestial marquee spread over Pergamos and the Dambay Plains, resembling a vast black blanket with countless pinprick holes allowing light to shine through from an unseen, candescent nirvana.

Volerdie's paradise? wondered Widukind. He'd know soon enough. Bargan had disappeared from the sky. Two more nights, and Seena would follow. Then, all Malphas believed, and Widukind increasingly feared, would be tested. The two moons would block the sun, and darkness would descend amid the daylight. And Widukind's body would become the vessel for Volerdie's soul. Two — more — nights.

Bound to the dead throne, sitting on the pinnacle of Pergamos' great pyramid, Widukind pushed a swollen tongue between his teeth, his naked skin bracing against the cold night air. He'd been trapped here for days without sustenance. Hunger and thirst plagued his immortal body. He considered it part of the penance of eternal life. Another needle stabbed into the cushion of pain Malphas wanted to inflict on his delinquent brother.

The self-proclaimed Worshipful Master came and went, possibly concerned about a miscalculation. That the moment he hoped would arrive might come sooner. Malphas and his serf, Ende, with the violet-black eyes, would climb through a trapdoor opening onto the podium at the pyramid summit. Beneath the trapdoor, winding, anfractuous passages like stone intestines led deeper into the bowels of the pyramid. Grell slaves had carried Widukind through the corridors, climbing past empty rooms once filled with the memories of stone-grell ancestors.

Sarcophagi of eminent, long-dead grells had been entombed in the passage walls, and ghosts haunted the chambers. Lots of ghosts.

Better facing them than the Rephaim, thought Widukind.

Malphas had placed his faithful grell soldiers on every one of the three hundred steps to the pyramid's summit. No-one would dare climb the steps. The only safe way to the summit was through the secret corridors inside.

A cloud drifted across Seena's crescent, and a drizzle enveloped Pergamos, watering the six fluted columns marking the edge of the pyramid's podium. The feathery raindrops continued their journey down, washing the sins from the Rephaim guards and falling onto the lit streets of Pergamos that spread from the pyramid base like fiery tentacles. Widukind poked out his tongue and licked a water droplet from his top lip. The pitiful action only accentuated his desolation.

The trapdoor opened, and Malphas appeared from the pyramid's underbelly, dressed all in white. A ghost risen from a sarcophagus. Ende followed, attached to her master by the umbilical cord of subjugation.

"Wonderful news, little brother," crowed Malphas. "Krieg has captured a Germalian griffin. The first enemy fighter has fallen, and the battle yet to begin. Once we've tamed the creature, we can use it against the invaders to defend the path to paradise."

Widukind faced Malphas. "You don't have the eyes of lost souls. Volerdie won't return to an incomplete throne."

Malphas leaned forward and spat in Widukind's face. "*Liar.* The dark eyes are not needed for the resurrection of the Divine Creator. *Ah...*you taunt me, little brother. You've read the First Scripture. You know the dark eyes have no power in this matter."

Yes, thought Widukind, taunts are all I have left. "What will you do if it doesn't work?" he asked.

"Only an unbeliever would consider such a thing. You've spent too much time among the pagans, abandoning your faith for folly. But fear not; your redemption is nigh."

"The opportunity for the immortal sacrifice has already passed."

Malphas laughed. "Do you take me for a fool? We both know the time is at hand. Seena is waning, and Bargan is gone. Two more nights and your fate will be sealed."

"Armies gather outside your walls," said Widukind, his taunts becoming more desperate. "They will defeat you before...."

"Is that what you're pinning your hopes on?" interrupted Malphas. "The Germalians, exhausted from the trek across Nordland, and the weald-grells, armed with no more than stones and sticks, will miraculously breach Pergamos' walls and rescue you? The city's defences will stand for generations. No-one can defeat Volerdie. He *wants* to return home." Malphas stepped away. "I'll leave Ende here to keep you company, so you can familiarise yourself with the face of death."

Malphas disappeared back into the pyramid, pulling the trapdoor closed behind him. Ende shuffled up to Widukind and stood, holding her sparth and staring into the darkness. Death's servant couldn't use her weapon to end Widukind's misery. She could, however, cut his bonds and set him free. If he could convince her to defy her master.

~ Chapter 51 ~

The foreboding south wall of Pergamos loomed ahead, rising above the Dambay Plains like a tidal wave of mortar and stone. It stood taller than most trees and looked stronger than a mountain. Stretching east and west, the wall disappeared from sight, Tom wondering how anyone could break the defence and how many fighters waited inside Pergamos to slaughter those who tried. Out of range of arrows, lances fired from ballistae or boulders flung from catapults, the weald-grells and mouldewerps encamped, waiting for the moment to strike. During the march north, they'd encountered a handful of enemy patrols but little resistance. The road to Pergamos' south gate was quiet. No travellers, traders, peasants or farmers. Nothing but an uneasy desolation.

Hanni had returned from the ambush on Hunger, bringing with her news of victory, misery and surprise.

Such are the emotions of war, thought Tom

Hunger had been defeated, but hundreds of weald-grell warriors died, their corpses left to nourish the soil of a Babir Birramal remnant. The Germalians' arrival lessened the painful loss. A battalion of one thousand had joined the weald-grell camp, led by Demetria and her griffin Eluji. And they'd brought a strange war machine that could move of its own accord, using a wound-up spring. It reminded Tom of one of his favourite childhood toys; a tank from the first world war.

As dark clouds drifted in from the east, Tom pulled on his furred leather coat and joined old friends and new acquaintances, standing around a cooking fire watching weald-grells skinning plains hares for the evening meal. Rosalie, Dwarrow, Hanni, Adalwolf and Audie gathered in silence, mesmerised by the flickering tangerine flames. Tom tried to guess what each of them thought. What each hoped for. Rosalie — release of her kin from Malphas' sorcery. Hanni — the restoration of Malang Gunya and the reunification of stone- and weald-grells. Audie — the end of wars forever. Dwarrow — a jar of pickled lizard and mouldewerps returning to the Dambay Plains. And Adalwolf?

What did the absent king hope for? wondered Tom. Another chance at the throne?

When the fighting ended, Tom wished for peace and for his friends to survive the battle, though he accepted he may not. Destroying Volerdie's throne would come at a price, but he was prepared to pay it. Only he hoped the chance would not arrive too late. His new-found intuition, drawn from the wisdom of the ancestors, told him time was running out.

"Well," huffed Dwarrow, "aren't we a joyous lot?" He leaned forward and waved smoke into his face.

"Smoking ceremony?" asked Tom.

"What?" said Dwarrow.

"Are you conducting a smoking ceremony?"

"No. Just clearing the grell stench from my nostrils."

The weald-grells crouching near the campfire glared at Dwarrow.

He shrugged, then muttered, "Didn't know they could speak Erstürmen."

"Who will come with us?" asked Adalwolf. "When we seek the throne."

"I like the idea of flying into Pergamos on a griffin," said Dwarrow. "But it seems I'll have to walk."

"I'm going," said Rosalie, flashing defiant eyes at Tom.

"And I will travel with you," said Hanni. "I have arranged for a dozen weald-grells to escort the throne wreckers into the city."

"I'll stay behind," said Audie. "To help the other healers mend the wounded."

"Then it's all settled," said Dwarrow. "Once those Germalians breach the wall, into Pergamos we trot."

"Malang Gunya had no walls," said Hanni. "If it did, my ancestors might have stopped the Erstürmen invasion."

"Walls provide nothing more than an illusion of safety," said Tom. "Peace of mind comes from inclusion and diversity. Segregation and separation breed unease and intolerance."

Hanni smiled. "Then the diversity around us should bring us peace. Weald- and stone-grell, mouldewerp, Dobunni, Erstürmen, Germalian, even a birraman from another world. Malphas has created the very thing he should fear the most: an alliance of unbelievers."

"Before the peace, much blood will flow," said Audie.

"Like a red river," said Hanni. "What is important is where the river leads."

"I'm going to give it another try," said Dwarrow. "See if I can't lighten the mood."

He reached inside his shoulder satchel and withdrew the bullroarer. "She might have sensed our presence. The plains are her home, after all." Dwarrow dropped his satchel to the ground, stepped away from the fire and unwound the string from the thin strip of wood.

"Is this a type of dance?" asked Adalwolf.

"Hush," said Dwarrow. "Otherwise, I'll whack this roarer into your thick skull."

The little werp began his spin, twirling the bullroarer above his head until the wood vibrated and hummed, sending a call into the darkening plains. Weald-grells nearby stopped their chores and gawked at the spectacle. Rosalie and Audie leaned into each other and chuckled. Dwarrow kept whirring, determined to make a last exhaustive effort. Tom hoped the werp didn't expend all his energy and leave nothing for the assault on Pergamos.

In a huffing, puffing splutter of exhaustion, Dwarrow brought the bullroarer to a stop and stood in silence, waiting, sniffing the night with his searching nose.

"The roasted yams are ready," said Hanni.

"Wait!" snapped Dwarrow, holding up a clawed finger. "*Waaaait.*" He sniffed again, then shrieked, "She's here! I knew it. I knew she'd come."

The crowd of weald-grells parted, and Xaviary, the horse-sized lizard, sauntered into the campsite as if she was coming home.

"Move that griffin out of the way," called Dwarrow. "A *real* steed has arrived. Here, Xaviary, I have slitherweed for you. A treat before we stomp on the ruins of Malphas' kingdom." The werp turned to his companions. "The rest of you are still walking."

~ Chapter 52 ~

There had been no word about Saskia or Namu, but Thaly couldn't succumb to the indulgence of despair. She had to keep her army motivated. The Germalians had reached the ridge from which they'd launch their attack on Pergamos' north wall. They'd built their war machines, erected the infirmary tents, armed and briefed every soldier, and filled their stomachs with the finest food available. Now, the soldiers would rest, saving their strength for the coming battle. But Thaly couldn't relax, pacing around the command tent alone with her maps and battleplans. Leading the army from Portum to Enthilen had been easy compared to what faced her. A gateless wall of stone thicker than an elephai, with thousands of enemy soldiers lined along the top, safe behind the battlements. She couldn't launch a surprise attack on the open plain. Malphas would see precisely what confronted him and make his plans to defend the city. Conversely, Thaly knew nothing of what lay beyond the wall. What surprises may rear their demonic heads from above the merlons?

A guard pushed through the tent flap. "Legatus Stansfield, two women, Emelin and Tilly, wish to speak with you."

Thaly nodded, and the guard stepped outside.

Tilly helped a hobbling Emelin through the entrance and straight to a chair.

"I overestimated my abilities," said Emelin. "This journey has been more burdensome than I hoped."

"It's over now," said Thaly.

"I can still help," said Emelin. "Sharpen swords, tend the wounded, feed the hungry."

"Vinum?" asked Thaly, tapping a cask balanced on the table's edge.

Tilly screwed up her nose. "Do you have any meduz?"

"All out. Your rebel friends drank the last of it."

"It gives them courage."

"They'll need it. From what I've seen, your armour and weapons are poor."

Thaly poured herself a goblet of red vinum and beckoned for Tilly to sit beside Emelin. Thaly sat opposite, on her favourite canvas chair, and sipped the liquor.

"The rebels came because of you," said Emelin to Thaly. "Most of those living in the Desolate Mountains were once Dobunni. They heard the daughter of Jurelle Stansfield leads the Germalian army."

"The rebels don't care about my father's treachery?"

"They believe the daughter is here to pay for the father's sins."

Only if I honour the Dobunni pledge and rid Enthilen of the Erstürmen, thought Thaly.

"Have you made your plans?" asked Tilly.

Thaly nodded. "I've scouted positions with Yagle. Berenice's griffin, Nia, will not let anyone else ride him. With Saskia missing...." Thaly stopped. She sipped on the vinum, but it caught in her throat, and she coughed it back up, a splatter of red dribbling down her chin.

"Put your grief aside," said Emelin.

"It's not grief," snapped Thaly. "It's the anguish of not knowing. The frustration of not being able to do anything."

The discipline etched into Emelin's wrinkles melted away, and the old woman let a mother's concern peak from the grimness. "Saskia is alive. I can feel it. Caeli will return at any moment with welcome news."

Thaly dared not give in to a futile hope, refocussing her thoughts on the battle. "We lack aerial support."

"But your forces are sufficient to draw Malphas' attention away from the south gate. He will see the weald-grells and mouldewerps, but he will pay them no mind."

"I hope you're right. I hope he knows nothing of Tom Anderson's plan."

"Widukind must keep his tongue," said Tilly. "Lest he ruin everything."

Emelin and Tilly bid goodbye and left Thaly to her worries. The quiet moment of contemplation revealed a potential solution to one of her most pressing problems. She burst from the tent and strode to the griffin holding pens, where Yagle and Nia rested for the night. Puer kept watch, as he always did, attending to the griffins' every need.

"Arve, Puer," said Thaly as she approached.

He bowed. "Arve, Domina Stansfield."

"How is your spirit?" asked Thaly.

Puer smiled. "Strong. The journey from Portum didn't tire me. I'm ready to serve in whatever way I can."

Thaly took a deep breath. "I've come to ask a favour on behalf of the Germalian Empire."

Puer straightened his elderly spine and looked Thaly in the eye without a hint of fear or apprehension.

"I need you to ride Nia," said Thaly.

"It is forbidden for men to become wind-riders, Domina Stansfield. The Senatorial Dictum is clear."

"We're at war. Battle plans supersede conventus rules, and I've already allowed Tom Anderson to ride Yagle. You know the griffins better than anyone in Germalia. Likely better than anyone in Ostamp. To win this war, we need two griffins in the air, armed and ready to attack." Thaly grasped Puer by the shoulders. "Will you at least try?"

Puer looked to Yagle and Nia, then faced Thaly with glistening eyes. "I ride griffins in my dreams every night, Thaly. I never imagined those dreams would come true."

"It'll be dangerous, and you'll need to use weapons. Bow and arrows. A lance."

"If we're rejecting the Senatorial Dictum, there's no point doing it in half measure."

"I will show you how to use a bow."

"No need," said Puer. "I've used one before. The conventus doesn't know everything that happens in Portum."

Thaly smiled. "Prepare Nia's harness. Let's see if he accepts you as a rider."

"I don't need a harness," said Puer. "I've memorised every movement a griffin makes in the air and on land. Nia will not let me fall, and I will not fail him."

Puer stroked Nia's neck feathers. The creature leaned down towards him, nuzzling his bill into Puer's chest. The old man laughed and whispered in Nia's ear. The griffin dropped his chest to the ground and flattened his wing. Puer climbed aboard and faced Thaly.

"Victum!" he yelled, raising his fist skyward.

Nia crowed, lifting his head and fanning his wings in salute.

Victum, thought Thaly.

~ Chapter 53 ~

The morning mist cleared to the brightest Enthilen day Widukind could ever remember. At the bottom of the pyramid steps, twenty-four curates dressed in white robes cinched with black belts, their heads crowned with a circlet of twigs, filed into the calendar of life, holding the scripture verses at their waists. Widukind imagined them chanting *Volerdie, Volerdie, Volerdie*, pleading for the resurrection of their Divine Creator.

Malphas' Rephaim stood on every pyramid step, and Widukind wondered if the grell soldiers understood the significance of this place to their ancestors. The calendar of life, the definitive pictorial record of stone-grell culture. The monolithic pyramid, where grells of old would stand beneath the imbricated slate roof of the open temple at the pyramid's summit to marvel at the sun, moons and stars, and keep watch over their homeland.

Not anymore, thought Widukind. The zenith of the stone colossus has been repurposed into nothing but a platform waiting for an arrival.

The platform's trapdoor opened, and out climbed Malphas. He'd dispensed with his usual white robes, replacing them with a regality Widukind hadn't seen from his brother since the reign of King Oldaric. Malphas dressed in a sangria robe with gold stitching, draped over a silk shirt of cobalt blue with silver pentagrams. Knee-high, polished black boots that clacked on the flagstones as he approached. White linen gloves. A trimmed beard.

The faithful Ende had been conscripted into the pageantry, wearing a full-length, pale-sepia gown of gossamer lace, almost matching the colour of her skin. Her once lilac eyes had become as dark as raisins, announcing to the world that she teetered on the edge of an abyss.

Malphas will lead the pale grell of death to her own demise, thought Widukind, shedding a tear at the realisation.

Ende's master stood before the throne of the dead, lifting Widukind's sullen chin with his finger. "This is the day," he said. "Our destiny has arrived." Malphas let his finger drop.

The curates inside the calendar of life raised their arms. "Volerdie!" they screamed, so loud the summons reached the pyramid's apex. "Volerdie, Volerdie, Volerdie!"

Widukind shook his head. A feeble attempt to deflect the chants. He focussed on Enthilen's sun. A welcome friend who arrived each morning to warm his aching body. To infuse life into this pitiful existence, tied to a dead throne, wallowing in his own filth. But then, something truly awful happened. His last friend in Ostamp abandoned him. The sunlight bathing Pergamos dimmed. Citizens and soldiers stood statuesque, gaping at the sky with open mouths. The Rephaim guards fell to their knees and bowed their heads.

Malphas beamed a joyous, hideous smile, and Widukind's soul filled with terror as the day faded to black.

This *is* the day, he thought. Darkness descends amid the daylight.

Malphas stepped to the platform edge and reached towards the waning sun. "Volerdie is ready!" His invocation spurred on the curates, their chanting voices congealing into a deafening crescendo.

Malphas returned to Widukind and pulled a dagger from his belt. "Darkness has descended, little brother, on the final day of harvest season, six hundred and sixty-six yarles since last it happened. Let the invading armies break my walls; it matters not. The Divine Creator prepares to return. Then he and I will lead the faithful into paradise."

Malphas drew his hand back and thrust the dagger into Widukind's chest.

*   *   *   *

In the weald-grell camp, Dwarrow turned his nose to the darkening morning and inhaled.

"Oh my," he said. "This is not good. Not good at all."

804

Seena began her journey across the sun's face, with the larger Bargan close behind.

"Volerdie is returning home," said Adalwolf.

"Don't look at it," said Tom to the grells and werps standing beside him, their faces frozen in horror. "Don't look at the eclipse."

Hanni placed her hand on Symian's shoulder. "This is a sign. We must attack now. Before it is too late."

"The Germalians north and east will not attack until tonight," said Symian.

"We cannot wait for them." Hanni faced Dwarrow. "Assemble the mouldewerps. We are launching an assault on the gate now."

"But...oh...yes," said Dwarrow. "I think you're right."

"My orders are to attack after dark," said Demetria.

"Will you stand idle," asked Adalwolf, "while grells and werps are slaughtered?"

"Help us," said Tom to Demetria. "That's what you came for."

Demetria cast skittish eyes at the blackening sun. "Alright. We will fight with you."

She returned to her soldiers. Symian sprinted through the camp, rousing the weald-grell warriors. Dwarrow ordered Wirrikow to do the same with the werps. Every fighter armed themselves with a spear, dagger or bow and lined up along the road to Pergamos' southern gate.

Little more than two thousand grells, estimated Tom, *and six hundred werps. But what will they do? Run at the wall until all are dead?*

"Where are the Germalians?" asked Dwarrow, sniffing the air impatiently.

"There," said Rosalie, pointing to the east.

Demetria flew Eluji at the head of a thousand-strong battalion. Unlike the grells and werps, the marching Germalians looked like soldiers. Scaled armour covered every part of their bodies except their face. They carried octagonal shields of solid metal, javelins and cutlasses. And brought their war wagon, the framework resembling empty honeycomb.

"What will they use the war machine for?" asked Tom.

"Do you think we've been idle these past days and nights?" asked Dwarrow. "While you've been sleeping or gossiping, the werp, grell and Germalian leaders have devised a cunning plan."

"What plan?"

"Never you mind. Can't have clumsy oafs getting in the way of a masterstroke. We'll wait here while others forge a path to glory."

The Germalians unhitched the dozen horses pulling the war wagon and pointed it at the south gate portcullis. A battering ram with metal spikes thicker than panalope saplings had been bolted to the front of the wheeled machine. Four Germalian soldiers jumped onto the wagon tray and turned cranks to wind up two springs.

"Will it break the Portcullis?" asked Adalwolf.

"No," said Dwarrow, "but it *will* smash open the timber gate inside."

Rosalie shook her head. "Then how will you get past the...."

"Questions, questions, questions," interrupted Dwarrow. "Patience, patience, patience."

The Germalians wound the springs so tight Tom doubted water or air would pass through the coiled steel. The soldiers inserted a metal pin to hold the springs in place before waving to Demetria.

She hovered Eluji above Tom, Adalwolf, Rosalie and Dwarrow. "Are you ready, Dwarrow?" she called.

"Yes," he said, lifting his walking stick.

She nodded, raised a clenched fist to her battalion, and flew off.

Forty-eight Germalian soldiers climbed onto the wagon tray and fitted their octagonal shields into the empty honeycomb frame until they disappeared behind a house of metal. A dozen weald-grells lined up behind the wagon, lidded wicker baskets strapped to their backs.

"Patience," said Dwarrow, pre-empting Tom's question.

Eluji shrieked and swooped along the south wall. Enemy soldiers atop the battlements were taken by surprise, most of them mesmerized by the descent of darkness. Seena had drifted to the middle of the sun, but a bright corona encircled her. The larger Bargan would soon mask them both, blocking the light completely.

Demetria threw a lance, felling a guard above the south gate. Erstürmen arrows exploded from the wall, and she pulled Eluji higher. A weald-grell tapped on the back of the war machine with the tip of her spear. Metal scraped on metal.

SNAP!

The machine took off, hurtling towards the portcullis. The weald-grells carrying the wicker baskets raced after it faster than a galloping horse. Demetria swooped Eluji along the top of the wall again, firing arrows at the city defenders. The war wagon rumbled on to Pergamos, Tom hoping the spring's wound energy didn't expire before striking its target.

The running grells caught up with the machine as it slowed. But it struck the portcullis with enough force to send a *clang* echoing back to the weald-grell camp.

"Didn't even make a dent," said Adalwolf, peering into the half-light.

The Germalians detached their shields from the honeycomb framework and jumped off the wagon tray. They used the shields to form a roof as arrows and boulders rained down from atop the wall. The grells stopped beside the roof. The lids of the wicker baskets popped open, and out clambered werps. They hit the ground and ran for cover, hiding beneath the Germalian shields. The grells went to retreat when a wave of serpent oil splashed onto them from above. Then one of Malphas' soldiers dropped a flaming torch.

Grells screamed. Flapped hands and arms over their half-naked bodies to quell the flames. Rolled onto the ground, setting the grassland beside the gate alight. The Germalians closed their shields, creating a dome around them and the werps.

"Dig, dammit," muttered Dwarrow.

"Dwarrow?" said Tom, his confidence reeling from seeing a dozen grells burnt alive.

"To honour the weald-grell sacrifice," said Dwarrow, "the mouldewerps are doing what we have done for generations. We are digging. Malphas buried his walls so deep we can't go under them. But we can dig under his blasted gate."

* * * *

"This is the darkness Tom spoke of," said Thaly.

"Attack now," said Emelin. "Don't wait for nightfall."

Thaly wanted to argue with her adoptive mother, but her instinct agreed with Emelin. She faced one of her Prime Lieutenants, a conventus senator.

"Are we ready, Elowen?" asked Thaly.

"Yes, Legatus Stansfield."

"Then prepare for the attack."

Thaly hugged Emelin, then raced to the griffin mounting platform. Puer stood ready. He'd dressed in the Volatal Vexil leathers at dawn and had been tending Yagle and Nia ever since.

"You're eager for battle," said Thaly.

"Ready to defend Germalia, Domina Stansfield," said Puer. "It's a rare honour to be given the opportunity."

"Did Elowen explain the codes?"

"Yes. Flags with the same twelve colours as the Germalian factions. A single colour or a combination — each means a different battle formation. I've memorised them all."

"Watch the Prime Lieutenants from each battalion. Elowen will make the call first, then raise her flags."

I should be doing it, thought Thaly, *but with so few griffins, I have to focus on fighting the enemy.*

She donned her metal skullcap, jogged up the platform steps and climbed into Yagle's saddle. "Ready, boy?" she said in his ear.

He whistled, the high-pitched wail he always emitted when sensing Thaly's nervous energy. She tucked the silver griffin amulet into the top of her coat, wishing Saskia had taken it after all, re-tied Tom's tattered white handkerchief around her wrist, and squeezed Chloe's pearl friendship ring through the leather of her gloves. Then she checked the two lances in scabbards strapped to Yagle's flanks, the bow slipped into its sheath, and the quivers of arrows hanging on the saddle's left side.

After cinching the flight harness across her thighs, Thaly looked to Puer, who sat whispering in Nia's ear. She caught his attention, and the old man straightened his crooked back, pulled the reins tight and nodded at her. She returned the silent acknowledgement, and together they took to the sky.

Seven blocks of ten thousand soldiers each formed on the plains like ants swarming square pieces of cake. Teams of elephai lugged four siege towers to the front of the formations, and the first rows of soldiers filed inside, filling the six levels to the top. Horses pulled wagons armoured with mobile shields the size of a house towards Pergamos, or dragged ballistae, the firing teams trotting close behind.

Thaly flew along the lines of soldiers, pulling a lance from its scabbard and shaking it at the sky. The soldiers raised their javelins and cutlasses and cheered. She hovered low before the formations, Yagle's dangling talons almost touching the soldiers' helmets.

"Malphas quakes in his boots!" Thaly yelled. "The invincible Germalian army is here to defeat him. Onward, brave soldiers! Onward to victory!" She clenched her jaw and tugged on Yagle's reigns until he reared up mid-air like a phoenix, with his wings spread, the tips pointing to the blackening sun. The front line of fighters raised their cutlasses.

"*VICTUM!*" they screamed.

Yagle crowed. Thaly pulled a green flag from her saddle bag, the only signal code she'd kept for herself, unfolded it and let it fall from Yagle.

Attack, valiant warriors, she thought. Freedom is in your hands.

* * * *

"How is it almost night already?" asked Erwin. "Ain't seen midday yet."

"It's the moment the Erstürmen have long waited for," said Saskia.

"I wish my father was alive to see it," said Nettie.

Together, they hid behind a stack of crates as Krieg, the red grell, lumbered down the flagstone street to the corral holding Namu captive. Disguised as a peasant, Saskia had waited here every day for three days, hoping to rescue her griffin. The descent of darkness might be her opportunity.

"I don't like this," said Erwin. "We should return to the ossuary. Shelter there for another night."

Saskia glared at him. "Then what? Namu is weakening by the day. If we don't save her now, she'll die."

Namu squawked and lifted herself onto unsteady legs as Krieg approached.

He removed a gauntlet and held his dark red hand towards her. "Settle now. Settle. You know I am your master. I can see it in your eyes."

Namu swung her head down, nicking Krieg's wrist with the tip of her bill.

The red grell snatched his hand back to his chest, then turned to a Rephaim guard. "Give me your sword."

Krieg took the weapon, pointing it at Namu. "Do not test my patience, beast. Submit to my will or suffer the consequences."

Namu swung her head again, and Krieg lashed the blade across her cheek. She squealed and stepped back.

Saskia punched a crate and splintered the wood. "Leave her alone."

"*Sssh*," said Nettie. "They'll spot us."

"I don't care," growled Saskia. "I'm not letting that arsehole hurt Namu anymore."

Beside the corral, watching the spectacle, a young woman clutched a newborn child to her breast. Krieg marched towards her and wrenched the baby from her hands. The woman screamed, grasping for the infant, but Rephaim soldiers held her back.

Krieg returned to Namu and held the baby aloft by its leg. It squirmed and squealed, Namu's ears pricking at the sounds of distress.

The red grell smiled. "Now I have your attention. You must be famished; you have not eaten since we arrived." Krieg stretched his right arm, moving the baby closer to Namu, and balanced the broadsword in his left hand, keeping the tip pointed towards the griffin. "Make your choice. Reward or punishment."

"What's he doing?" asked Erwin.

Namu lowered her head. Krieg stepped towards her, holding the baby higher. The griffin opened her bill. Then the half-light turned as black as night.

Krieg spun around to face the pinnacle of the colossal pyramid. At the same time, Namu thrashed her head violently, slicing the tip of her bill across the red grell's bare neck. He dropped the baby and his weapon, thrusting his hands over the gaping wound. Staggering from the effort, Namu lifted her front end using the shoulders of her wings. Balanced on her rear legs and tail, she lashed at her captor with a razor-sharp talon, piercing his chest and back in a single clench.

Krieg gasped for air, rivers of ebony blood gurgling inside his throat. The tainted grell's body shuddered and went limp, hanging suspended on the end of Namu's claw.

"She's killed him." Saskia jumped to her feet. "Now's the moment."

"Wait," said a voice.

A cold hand grabbed Saskia's shoulder.

She turned to face Princess Caeli, the draughoul who led Thaly under the mountain.

"Wait," repeated Caeli. "I can help you."

*　*　*　*

Widukind flinched, the first time he'd felt real pain in half a generation. From the wound in his chest pulsed blood. Thick — red — blood.

Malphas cheered. "It's happening! Did you ever think you'd see your own blood again, Widu? Your life force departs, soon to be replaced by Volerdie's soul."

Ende's voice floated through the darkness. "Divine Creator, we are ready to receive you. The vessel is prepared. Come to us."

The curates in the calendar of life dropped to their knees. Widukind screamed; agony and terror melded as one.

Malphas yanked the dagger from Widukind's chest and turned to his subjects with arms raised. "He's here! Volerdie has returned. Rejoice! Rejoice!"

Widukind squeezed his eyes shut, but it couldn't dim the nightmares pillaging his thoughts. Towers of fire burned higher than the tallest trees and hot enough to melt the swords in soldiers' hands. Walking skeletons piled thousands and thousands of corpses onto mountains of the dead, crammed together along a boundless horizon. A monstrous beast with twisted horns and a stomach full of serpents stood among the chaos. It opened its gaping maw, revealing an infinite blackness filled with screams. With long, bony arms, the beast plucked corpses from the gruesome mountains, throwing one after the other into its bleak orifice. Then it stopped and turned its crimson eyes on an intruder. Black smoke poured from the beast's mouth, slithering along the ground and wrapping itself around Widukind's chest. The vaporous serpent squeezed, crushing ribs protecting a heart that thumped like a battle hammer inside Widukind's chest. A slowing *thud, thud, thud.*

Widukind raised his hand, freed from the throne's armrest, and dipped his fingertips into the blood seeping from his chest. Then he dug his fingers into the dagger wound and pulled. Skin ripped. Bones crunched. Widukind tore a hole in his chest, exposing his beating heart to the darkness.

The organ slowed, then stopped, and he opened his eyes.

Malphas knelt before the throne. "Divine Creator, I bow before your eminence. I offer myself as your servant, Lord Volerdie, ready to do your bidding for an eternity."

Widukind closed his eyes again, and his body went limp.

*   *   *   *

A boulder larger than a wagon dropped from the top of Pergamos' south wall and flattened the Germalian shield-dome. Standing beside Tom, Rosalie gasped.

"It's failed," said Adalwolf.

"Maybe not," said Dwarrow. "The werps could already be underground."

"The boulder must be cleared before the wagon can move forward again," said Hanni.

She ran off, gathering a handful of weald-grells to follow her.

"This wasn't part of the plan," said Dwarrow.

Riding on Eluji, Demetria continued peppering Pergamos' defenders atop the wall with arrows. At the base of the wall, the corpses of burning grells littered the roadside. Hanni and her weald-grell companions sprinted through the gruesome field to the front of the war wagon, where Germalian soldiers lay dead or dying beneath the boulder. Dodging arrows, the grells shoved their hands under the sides of the enormous rock. An enemy lance shattered the spine of a grell, and the giant collapsed.

Hanni? thought Tom. *Was it Hanni?*

The remaining grells heaved, lifting the boulder onto its edge and rolling it away from the entrance. Then they dived underneath the wagon to avoid another enemy barrage.

"Come on," said Dwarrow, "where are those blasted diggers?"

A lone Germalian waited, crouching on the exposed wagon's tray-bed, her hand resting on the pin of the second spring, ready to remove it. The shields fixed to a frame above her head had been battered by the projectiles launched from the wall. The protection held for now. But a direct hit from another boulder would see the shields broken.

As Seena and Bargan continued their journey across the sun's face, the light grew brighter, like a second dawn. A clunk came from the south gate, and the portcullis lifted open.

"They've done it!" cried Dwarrow, dancing from one clawed foot to the other. "Never any doubt, of course."

Up the portcullis climbed, disappearing into the archway, the metal mesh squealing in protest at the affront of being breached by invaders. A werp scooted beneath the portcullis spikes and waved a white flag.

"That's the signal," said Dwarrow. "That's the signal!" he called to the weald-grells and Germalians.

Symian nodded, and Enthilen's liberators moved into position.

As the portcullis disappeared completely, the Germalian soldier on the war wagon pulled her pin and sprang from the tray-bed. The wagon lurched forward, racing into the tunnel.

Now exposed, four grells jumped up from the road, peered into the entrance tunnel, then ran back towards Tom and his companions. One grell was taller than the others.

"Hanni's still alive," he said, grasping Rosalie's hand.

A Germalian commander yelled, "Shields up! Protect our flanks."

The thousand-strong battalion marched forward.

Symian shook his spear at the sky. "*Balubunirra!*"

The weald-grells followed the Germalians.

Hanni jogged up to Tom, gasping. "The inside gate is breached. The war machine shattered it to pieces."

"Now we wait for the Germalians to clear away the riffraff," said Dwarrow, "then sneak into the city like the cleverest of thieves."

"You'll have to get past them first," said Adalwolf, pointing to the wall.

Along the outside of the wall, from east and west, snaked hundreds of Rephaim soldiers. The sun, returned to its former glory, reflected off the metal studs of the pauldrons strapped across one shoulder, then was swallowed by the black plackarts protecting grell stomachs.

The Rephaim turned from the wall and ran in two straight lines, bearing down on the south road like huge hands preparing to clap. They ignored the Germalians and rushed the weald-grells. Giants clashed in the shadow of their ancestral home, Malang Gunya. Spears, swords and axes smashed together in a deafening calamity. Generations of distrust and simmering anger fuelled the weald-grells in their fight against the stone-grell traitors. Despite the truce etched on Marradir, despite the seasons of shared ceremony at Dalman, a deep-seated hatred of stone-grells rose to the surface. Weald-grell bone daggers, whittled to needle sharpness, pierced airways in Rephaim throats. Stone-tipped spears thrown with unmatched balance and precision found gaps in Rephaim armour to puncture vital organs.

Unbroken shield lines protecting their flanks, the Germalians marched into the tunnel leading to Pergamos as their weald-grell allies slaughtered the Rephaim.

"Well," said Dwarrow, "this is a good start."

"Those Rephaim are a fraction of Malphas' forces," said Adalwolf.

"Did you inherit your optimism from your mother or father?" asked Dwarrow.

"The Rephaim were sent to split the invading force," said Tom, "and it's worked. The Germalians have entered Pergamos alone."

"Don't underestimate the desert fighters," said Dwarrow. "I wouldn't want to face a battalion of ferocious females."

"All we can do is wait for the Germalians to give their signal," said Hanni.

A squeal, sounding like the wail of a grieving mother who'd lost her firstborn, shattered the blue sky. The griffin, Eluji, reared up mid-air, a lance jutting from her chest. Demetria clung to the saddle, wrapping the reins around her hands. Eluji flew in erratic arcs, shunting left and right, one wing flapping, the other motionless. The griffin spiralled towards the ground, then rolled on her side. Demetria fell from the saddle, dangling from the reins attached to the griffin's halter. Eluji righted herself but flew straight into the battlements.

Tom had seen birds crash into windows and break their neck. Smack, fall, nerves twitching the last motions of life, then a limp body with a lolling head.

Erstürmen defenders swamped the lifeless griffin slumped over the wall's merlons, hacking it to pieces. Demetria released the reins and fell, five, maybe six stories, thudding into the plains below.

"Oh, bother," said Dwarrow.

*   *   *   *

Thaly hovered Yagle behind the front line of her army as Germalian engine crews released the hooks holding back the counterweights of four trebuchets. Jagged boulders flew towards Pergamos like a flock of suicidal birds, smashing into the parapets or flying over the north wall and landing among the roofs of houses and barracks. Lances fired from ballistae followed, sending deadly spears into enemy soldiers naïvely standing exposed in the crenels between the merlons. Under cover of the aerial assault, elephai butted their heads against the back of wheeled siege towers, pushing hundreds of soldiers towards Pergamos.

The darkness waned as the flight of Seena and Bargan left the sun behind.

A nagging doubt tugged at Thaly's mind. Is it already too late? she wondered. Has Volerdie returned? Is Malphas or the Divine Creator our foe?

It mattered little. The battle must be won, and Thaly had to find Saskia. She signalled to Puer, and the two wind-riders guided their mounts above the aerial assault and towards the north wall.

While Puer and Nia watched Thaly's south flank, she flew Yagle along the wall, scouting for the location of enemy pit trenches. At the wall's base, woven mats of fawn grass contrasted with Dambay's green meadows, marking the location of each trap. Thaly dropped a red flag tied to a stone, signalling a trench's location to the siege crews below. The lead crew halted near the lip of a channel and carried forward telescopic bridges, extending railings, planks and supports using ropes, cogs and pullies.

Puer flew up to Yagle's left wing. "Danger!" he yelled, pointing to the north wall.

An Erstürmen commander waved his arm, and catapults atop the wall sent barrels of flaming serpent oil towards the advancing army. Some crashed into the timber siege towers and set them aflame, while others landed among marching soldiers or cannoned into elephai, lighting their woolly hides on fire.

Puer took off, flying Nia towards the catapults. The old handler leaned into the griffin's ear and swooped down onto a catapult. Nia extended his talons, grasping the top of the throwing arm mid-swing. The war machine tossed Puer and the griffin skyward, but their intervention unbalanced the catapult and sent it toppling over the wall.

Germalian ballistae launched grappling hooks fixed to the end of chains onto the top of the parapets. Soldiers turned winches, tightening the chains. Puer and Nia thwarted another catapult. Thaly banked Yagle left to join Puer. A lance exploded from atop the wall, hurtling straight for her. She pulled Yagle up, but the lance had been fired with deadly aim.

* * * *

"The darkness is fading," said the draughoul.

"We can't trust her," said Nettie to Saskia. "Malphas uses draughouls as spies and servants."

"This is Princess Caeli," said Saskia. "From Sardis."

"Really?" asked Erwin. "She doesn't look like a princess."

"King Adalwolf stole her soul," said Nettie. "I've heard the tragic tale of Princess Caeli, imprisoned in the inner circle's Sunrise Keep for yarles. Abandoned by her father. Abused by King Ewald."

"We don't have time for her life story," said Saskia.

Nettie flinched as a boulder flew into the city and crashed through a roof. Then another chunk of rock smashed into the side of the pyramid. Daylight came with a rush, and Pergamos descended into chaos. Citizens ran from their homes, yelling and screaming. With the death of their commander, Krieg, the Rephaim crumbled into a disorganised rabble. They fled Namu's corral. Streamed off the pyramid steps like a waterfall and rushed along the streets with no purpose but to escape danger.

However, the Erstürmen Shield held firm. They'd trained all their lives for war, and now it had arrived. Half a dozen Shield guarded Namu, swords drawn, ready for battle. Caeli hurried towards the soldiers, picking up a notched broadsword dropped by a fleeing Rephaim with her right hand. She confronted the first Shield, cutting and slashing at the soldier's gorget. He backed away as if faced with a monster.

Nettie exploited the distraction, grabbing Saskia's hand and leading her and Erwin through the maddened crowd. They skirted the Erstürmen Shield, sprang over Krieg's corpse and raced up to Namu. The griffin cooed as Saskia untied the rope binding her to the marble column.

"I'm here," said Saskia, running her hands through Namu's feathers.

"Where to now?" asked Nettie, panicked she may have rushed into a trap.

"Her wing's badly injured," said Saskia. "We need to find shelter from this assault."

"The east wall is under attack!" yelled a soldier.

The Shield fighting Caeli abandoned their battle and ran eastwards. The princess dropped her sword, looked at Nettie, Saskia and Erwin, then disappeared into the chaos.

"The kirika," said Erwin. "It's big enough to hide a griffin."

"Where is it?" asked Saskia.

"Follow me," said Nettie.

She led them again, Erwin at her side and a limping Saskia pulling Namu along at the end of a rope. They pushed through the crowd, no-one seeming to care about a griffin. Most were simply trying to stay alive. On a street corner, Lieutenant Berard, in his polished silver armour, marshalled troops for a defence of the east wall. Nettie and Erwin should have been among the defenders. Should be devouring every word from their commander. But they'd abandoned Malphas and his stupid dream of paradise.

The sandstone spires at the kirika entrance loomed ahead. Nettie ran beneath the sculpted stalactites hanging from the top of the entrance archway and pulled on the front door's metal ring.

"It's locked," she said.

"Is there anywhere else?" asked Saskia.

"Not that I know of," said Erwin.

Nettie scampered into the street and peeled a battle-axe from a dead soldier's hand. Returning to the kirika, she chopped at the timber door until the metal ring broke off and the door swung open.

"Inside," said Nettie, holding the door ajar.

Saskia went first, taking Namu into the chapel's cavernous narthex. Erwin tried to follow when a hand grabbed his shoulder. Nettie gasped.

Covered in blood from head to toe, Elmbray stood behind Erwin, smiling.

"I've been looking for you two," he said. "You killed Snick and stole my wagon. Such acts can't go unpunished."

* * * *

The sun appeared again, and Ende expected paradise to be revealed at any moment. Her Worshipful Master knelt before the throne of the dead, waiting for his anointment from the Divine Creator. Once Volerdie recognised Master and accepted him as his faithful servant, both would lead the believers into paradise. Ende longed to go with them, despite Master's refusal. She would pledge her servitude to Volerdie directly, hoping to secure a place in the world beyond her dreams.

Yet, despite Master's submission, the chance to demonstrate enduring devotion to Volerdie remained elusive. The body on the dead throne that had been Master's brother didn't stir. The corpse remained inanimate. Widukind's soul had departed, but it seemed Volerdie's had not arrived. The lifeless shell was yet to be filled with faith, glory and piety.

Ende raised her head and lifted the pale dress, tugging the hem across her knees, then stepped towards the throne.

Keeping his head bowed, Malphas turned to her and hissed, "What are you doing?"

"There is no sign, Worshipful Master," said Ende. "No sign of *life*."

"You're not worthy to approach the Divine Creator. Move back."

Furrows creased Ende's forehead. "I do not...I do not believe it worked. Your brother is dead, but no-one has taken his place."

"Heathen!" Malphas sprang to his feet, grabbed Ende's sparth and swung it at her. She swayed back as the blade tip caressed her throat. He dropped the weapon, and it clattered onto the cross section of stone at the pyramid's summit. Looking frightened, confused and desperate, the Worshipful Master wavered in place, then faced the throne.

"Is this a test, Divine Creator?" he asked. "Do you wish to identify those true of faith? *I* believe in you. I've always believed in you. Please, offer your most devoted servant the first sign of your resurrection."

Malphas waited. Then he collected the sparth, stepped to the throne and cut the ropes binding Widukind's corpse to the sacred chair. The torso slumped forward. Malphas handed the sparth to Ende, then lifted his dead brother and laid him prostrate on the ground.

"Volerdie," whispered Malphas. "You have returned home. Your subjects wait to enter paradise."

No sign of life resurrected the corpse. The immortal sacrifice had failed.

Ende placed a gentle hand on Malphas' shoulder. "Worshipful Master, it seems our creator has forsaken us."

Malphas stood, mouth agape, spittle dribbling from yellowed teeth. His lips formed words, but his throat refused to utter them. He pressed his eyes closed, and a single tear squeezed from the duct and trickled down his cragged cheek. Then Malphas' legs buckled, and he collapsed.

Ende rested the sparth against the dead throne, bent down and picked up her master, cradling him in the crux of her elbows. Then she descended the stairs beneath the trapdoor and carried Master into the pyramid.

* * * *

A Germalian soldier ran from the tunnel leading into Pergamos, waving a green flag.

"That's it," said Dwarrow. "They've secured a path for us. Follow my nose!"

"Wait," said Adalwolf. "I have to do one thing first."

Before entering Pergamos, he thought. Before confronting whatever fiends wait inside the city. Do it, or live my remaining days in regret.

After sprinting to the infirmary, he found Audie rubbing a salve across the charred, garnet-black skin of a weald-grell who'd survived the attack on the portcullis.

"Audie," he said.

"I don't have time," she replied. "Already, we are overrun."

He grabbed her hand, his fingers slipping on the salve. "We're going in now. To find the throne. I wanted...I wanted to say...."

She stopped healing and faced him, her hazel eyes glistening with urgent beauty.

"I love you," said Adalwolf. "Like no-one ever before."

She caressed his cheek and smiled. "Come back to me. Then we'll discover together what real love is."

Audie kissed him. It tasted sweeter than victory. Sweeter than any revenge he might inflict on Malphas. Adalwolf turned and marched off to face his demons.

Dwarrow had mounted Xaviary, perched behind the frill encircling the lizard's neck. Hanni stood with the dozen weald-grells who'd act as an escort. Tom Anderson held his lover's hand but released it when Adalwolf arrived.

Tom faced him. "Are you ready?"

Adalwolf wanted to reply with certainty and strength, but the words didn't come, and he simply nodded his agreement.

Hanni and the weald-grells leading the way, the group who hoped to shatter a madman's dreams marched down the south road towards the gate into Pergamos. The defenders atop the wall paid them little attention, focussing on the battle inside the city. Adalwolf strolled under the raised portcullis as if Malphas welcomed everyone with open arms. The murder chamber, the tunnel between the portcullis and the internal gate, had earned its name. Dozens of bodies, grells, werps, Germalians and Erstürmen lay slumped against the walls or writhing on the road. The throne destroyers couldn't stop to help. They had to push on. No side-tracking. No diversions. Find the damn throne and smash it.

They stepped through the shattered gate and into the city. Adalwolf returned to his kingdom, but no-one hailed Adalwolf the Redeemer. Pergamos' citizens were too preoccupied with fighting or fleeing to welcome back an absent king. He unsheathed his sword, a weapon he'd learned to use with his non-preferred left hand, but no enemy soldiers rushed at him. The weald-grells and Germalians kept the battle away from the main thoroughfare leading to the underground halls where Malphas housed Volerdie's throne.

Adalwolf followed Hanni along the street, trying to reconcile his memories of the ruined Malang Gunya with the sprawling city Pergamos had become. A few original buildings remained, including the amphitheatre and the colossal stepped pyramid marking the city centre. Summiting the pyramid was Adalwolf's only fond memory of his time in Malang Gunya when he cast his eyes over Enthilen's horizons and pretended he ruled it all.

"The enemy attacks the north wall, and the south gate is breached!" yelled an old man, holding his frail body upright by bracing his hand against a statue of the Worshipful Master. "Pergamos is doomed!"

If the resurrection *was* successful, thought Adalwolf, it appears Volerdie is doing nothing to save his home.

Hanni led the group past an empty calendar of life and into the pyramid's shadow.

"The throne hall is underground," said Adalwolf, pointing to the entrance near the bottom step of the pyramid.

"But the throne is not there," said Hanni. "Look." She pointed skyward.

Perched on the edge of the platform at the pyramid's apex stood a chair. Not any chair. One with a horned wolf glowering and snarling from the backrest.

"It'll take too long to climb those steps," said Adalwolf, "and we'll be exposed."

"There are secret passages inside the pyramid," said Dwarrow.

As the mouldewerp dismounted from his reptilian steed, a Rephaim burst from the entrance to the underground rooms. The grell soldier brandished his notched broadsword at Dwarrow, but Xaviary intervened, smacking her tail, thicker than a ship's anchor rope, into the Rephaim's skull. He collapsed to the ground in a lifeless heap.

"I knew she'd come in handy," said Dwarrow. "But I can't take her underground. We continue on foot."

The werp led the way, scuttling around the pyramid base to its northern side. A colossal building stood nearby with sandstone spires, a belltower, and an entrance resembling a mouth full of spiny teeth.

Malphas' kirika, thought Adalwolf. Grander than any ever built.

Three people loitered outside the front door. Rosalie stopped in front of Adalwolf, staring at the kirika entrance.

"That was Namu," she said. "Saskia's griffin went into that building."

"We don't have time for this," huffed Dwarrow.

"Wait," said Rosalie. "Someone's in trouble over there. It might be Saskia. I'm going to help." She walked off.

"What are you doing?" asked Tom, grabbing at thin air.

"Leave her," said Adalwolf, pulling Tom back. "We must get to the throne as soon as possible. Even if Volerdie has returned, destroying the throne might limit his power or end it altogether."

Dwarrow sniffed the flagstones at the pyramid base. "Where is it? Where is it? Why do grell doors always have to be so hard to find?"

"It is here," said Hanni. She pressed on a hand-sized rock, and two flagstones slid across to reveal an opening on the bottom step.

Tom, Hanni and Dwarrow stepped inside, leaving Adalwolf by himself. He could have turned and run then. The weald-grell escort was busy defending against Erstürmen soldiers. Nothing would stop him from fleeing. Hiding. Waiting for the war to end. And when it ended, he could reveal himself and proclaim his right to the kingdom.

But Audie's last words pulled him back from a coward's path, and he stepped inside the pyramid.

*   *   *   *

Yagle snapped at the lance with his bill, but it flew past the side of his head and grazed Thaly's left shoulder, the blade slicing open her leather armour. She gritted her teeth as pain spread through her muscles like runnels of boiling water. But Thaly didn't drop the reins or fall, or turn back to the Germalian camp to find a healer. She hadn't come all this way to give up so easily.

Puer continued his suicidal missions, flying Nia into the gathering clouds, then plunging the griffin down towards the top of the north wall, targeting the Erstürmen war machines. The griffin grabbed a ballista with its talons, pulled the contraption above the parapets, then threw it inside the wall.

Thaly wanted to help Puer, but her shoulder wound worsened. As blood wept down her side, the four Germalian siege towers butted into Pergamos' wall. Drawbridges flung open, and fighters poured out, screaming a war cry that swamped the chaotic din of battle. Parts of the wall crumbled as grappling hooks dug into stone, their chains pulled tight by teams of elephai lumbering across the plains.

The battle for the north wall turned. Erstürmen soldiers fled or surrendered, dropping to their knees atop the wall as if witnessing the arrival of their beloved Divine Creator. Thaly could do little more here, and her worries returned to Saskia. She flew Yagle over the wall and into the city, skimming across slate or thatched roofs towards Pergamos' pointed heart, the summit of the giant stepped pyramid.

As she wheeled around the temple at the top of the colossus, its slated roof smashed apart, Princess Caeli appeared from a trapdoor and drifted towards a man lying prostrate beside an empty throne.

The throne of the dead, thought Thaly. Still intact.

Tom Anderson and Adalwolf Heine had yet to complete their mission. She went to land Yagle on the pyramid's apex when a boulder fired from a Germalian catapult whooshed past and crashed into the roof of a neighbouring building. A rupture of splinter and stone exploded skyward, followed by a billowing plume of dust.

As the dust cleared, Yagle shrieked, flying Thaly over the hole in the roof. Below them, through a gap no larger than a wagon wheel, the face of another griffin looked skyward.

Namu, thought Thaly. And if Namu's here....

The boulder strike attracted Rephaim soldiers. They launched halberds at Thaly, flinging the heavy weapons like arrows shot from a bow.

She leaned into Yagle's ear. "Fly!"

They escaped the attack, Thaly guiding Yagle above a ruined street full of death and debris. She hovered him there, tying a rope to the horn of his saddle.

"When I reach the ground, find somewhere safe to perch."

She tossed the rope's loose end over Yagle's flank. It dangled to the ground. Yagle cawed. Thaly uncinched her saddle harness and grasped the rope, climbing down into Pergamos. Her wounded left shoulder screamed with the effort. When she dropped to the flagstones, Yagle took off.

Thaly ran back to find Namu, hoping the griffin would lead her to Saskia.

* * * *

Nettie swung the battle-axe, trying to chop Elmbray's arm away from Erwin's shoulder. The mage released his grip and swayed back from the path of the swing.

"Still not a competent soldier," said Elmbray. "Should have stayed a smuggler."

"Leave us alone!" screamed Nettie.

"You know I can't," said Elmbray. "The world is ending. If I am to die here, I will do it with a final act of revenge."

From inside his blood-drenched robe, he pulled a dagger, the blade curved and twisted like a meandering stream. Erwin faced the mage, stepping between him and Nettie. Then Elmbray thrust forward, plunging the dagger into Erwin's stomach and pushing up, almost lifting the young man, the *boy*, off his feet as the blade searched for Erwin's kind heart.

Erwin turned to Nettie and smiled. Faint, weakening, acquiescent.

Smiled? thought Nettie.

Anger tried to gush from her fatigued emotions, but they offered only a dribble of tears. Her arm surrendered, the axe's weight pulling it towards the ground. Erwin slumped in front of Elmbray as if bowing before the wizardry of the mage. His young body folded over itself into a lifeless ball that thudded against the kirika door before sliding onto its deathbed.

Elmbray wiped the dagger blade on his robes, lacing Erwin's blood into the fabric to join the gruesome decoration of murder. The mage stepped towards Nettie, who stood wanting now. Thankful to be soon joining her friend.

Erwin smiled.

But Elmbray never delivered his final revenge.

A halberd blade burst from his chest. As he buckled over, a woman's face appeared behind him, her weathered hand clutching the weapon's handle as a smithy might hold a sledgehammer.

"Smithy," whispered Nettie. *Rosalie?*

Elmbray tried to twist his body around to face the woman, but she yanked him sideways, pushing him against the kirika wall. He smacked into the stone, clawing at the mortar with deceitful fingers. Nettie found a scrap of energy, lifting her axe and chopping it into Elmbray's side. A clutch of air burst from his lungs, followed by a spew of blood. The woman released her grip on the halberd. Then the illusion of the mage evaporated like a morning fog, and he fell dead outside the front door of the Erstürmen house of salvation.

The woman stared at the top of Nettie's tunic, where the ruby pendant dangled at the end of its bronze chain. Nettie's hope turned into reality.

"Rosalie," she said.

Rosalie nodded, then hugged her. And the sisters cried in each other's arms.

Rosalie pulled away. "Are you hurt?"

Nettie shook her head. "But Erwin...." She knelt beside her friend.

"I'm sorry," said Rosalie.

Nettie rolled Erwin over to gaze upon his face, letting her tears fall on his cheeks. Then she kissed his forehead.

"We need to go," said Rosalie. "Before the enemy comes."

Nettie shivered. "How...where did...you...."

"Is Saskia with Namu? Inside the kirika?"

Nettie faced her sister and nodded.

"Come on." Rosalie pulled Nettie up by the arm and dragged her into the chapel.

Saskia waited with her griffin, pressed against the altar stage.

"Saskia," called Rosalie.

"You're here," said Saskia.

"What's happening?" asked Nettie, smacking the tears from her face.

"We're fighting Malphas," said Rosalie. "Together."

The three women sat, resting their backs against the stage and facing the chapel door.

"How goes the battle?" Saskia asked Rosalie.

"Germalians helped the weald-grells and werps breach the south gate," said Rosalie. "Tom and Adalwolf are on their way to the throne."

"You saved my life," Nettie said to Rosalie.

Rosalie wrapped her arm around Nettie's shoulder. "I'm your big sister. Where are Ma and Pa? Petas? Allum?"

"Allum died in Sardis. Ma and Petas died on the journey here. The Ravage killed all of them. Pa was murdered by the Erstürmen."

Rosalie pulled Nettie close, but Nettie had no more tears left.

"We should barricade the door," said Saskia. "Carry some of the pews across."

As she stood, the hinges of the chapel's oak door creaked and in shuffled an old man, hunched over and moving as if every bone in his body had been shattered. In his right hand, he clutched a scroll of yellowed and decaying parchment.

Nausea bubbled in Nettie's throat. She stood, preparing for another fight.

* * * *

Dwarrow led Tom, Adalwolf and Hanni through the bleak, serpentine passages inside the bowels of the pyramid using light from his giba stone. The soles of Hanni's bare feet slapped the pavers, and Tom wanted to tell her to be quiet lest she awakened an immortal evil. They walked ever upwards, climbing a sloping path that branched and twisted like the boughs of a tree. Tom worried Dwarrow may get lost but expected the werp could smell the throne of the dead, his waving proboscis acting as a compass. A desire inside Tom urged him to return to Rosalie. She'd gone off, alone, to find Namu. Any murderous thing could happen to her.

Dwarrow turned a corner and stopped. Firelight flickered from the darkness of a side passage. "Come on," he said, scuttling past clutching amber fingers.

Tom and Adalwolf followed, Hanni guarding the rear. As she passed the firelight, a hissing breath lurched from the side passage. Simultaneously, Tom and Adalwolf stopped and spun around. The firelight grew brighter, casting Hanni's giant shadow against a wall of the pathway carved with scenes of grells burying their dead. Hanni raised her spear.

"Take my sword," said Adalwolf, tossing the weapon back down the passage.

She kicked it away. "I need only my grell spear. I will fight as my ancestors did."

Hanni stepped back against the wall as a creature appeared from the side passage carrying a firebrand in one hand and a sparth in the other.

"It's Ende," cried Adalwolf, his voice trembling with dread. "The pale grell."

"Keep going," urged Hanni. "I will face this tainted monster."

Dwarrow tugged on Tom's pant leg. "Do as she says. We must reach the throne."

Tom faltered.

"For Grin," said Hanni. "Do it for Grin."

Yes, thought Tom. *For Grin.*

He followed Adalwolf and the persistent werp up the path.

* * * *

The glow of Dwarrow's giba faded, the muted sepia of flames the only light licking away the darkness. Ende blocked the path to the pyramid summit as Hanni backed away, keeping two hands wrapped around the shaft of her stone-tipped spear.

"Why have you come?" asked the pale grell.

"To end your master's tyranny," said Hanni.

"Master is not here. He has forsaken me."

"Join us," said Hanni, stepping forward. "It is not too late."

The pale grell shook her head. "No. I have given myself to Master."

"But he left you here. Alone. Weald-grells are reclaiming Malang Gunya. You would be welcomed into the resurrected city."

Ende tilted her head to the side. "Mal...Mal-ang...Gun-ya?"

"The grell city that stood before the Erstürmen invaders routed our ancestors."

"Malphas said this was always Pergamos. From the dawn of Ostamp."

"He lied to you."

The pale grell sighed, letting the heel of her sparth rest against the pavers. "Volerdie did not return as Master hoped. I fear for our future."

"Volerdie is not your creator," said Hanni. "We come from the soil and trees. From the grass and worms and beetles. From the birds in the sky and the fish in the stream. From the forest tiger and the cave python." She relaxed her grip on the spear and took another step towards Ende. "Hold the firebrand close to your face."

"You will see only the face of death."

"No. There are flecks of lilac shining amid the black of your eyes. And beneath the scars on your face is the faint outline of a crest...." Hanni caught herself. "What...what was your grell name?"

"I don't remember it. It seems so long ago."

Hanni took one hand from the spear and reached across, tracing her finger over the shape of a fringed petal still visible on Ende's cheek. The pale grell shivered at Hanni's touch, a teardrop welling in her eye.

"You can see my facial crest," said Hanni. "Gama."

Ende nodded.

"You remember it, do you not?"

"A cave python fang dipped into panalope sap and mixed with...with...."

"A black dye from the guruyangan fruit."

The pale grell dropped her sparth, and it clattered to the floor. She gripped Hanni's fingers. "I tattooed gama onto your face."

"Yes," said Hanni, her voice breaking.

"Because I am your mother."

Ende laid the torch on the ground. But when she stood, the firelight revealed Mirrian stone-grell. Then mother and daughter embraced, Hanni's sobs filling the darkness.

* * * *

"It's Malphas," whispered Nettie, raising her battle-axe.

Rosalie tensed, her hand groping for some sort of weapon, wishing she'd pulled the halberd from Elmbray's pathetic corpse.

As the old man strolled down the aisle, Saskia drew her cutlass.

Malphas stopped halfway and raised his head. "Lower your weapons."

"Don't come any closer," said Rosalie, climbing to her feet. "We know who you are."

"If you know who I am, then you know your blades can't harm me."

Saskia stepped between Malphas and Namu.

"Pergamos will fall, Worshipful Master," said Nettie. "Escape while you can."

A faint smile drifted across Malphas craggy face. "You're probably right, child. Sadly, I have nowhere else to go. All my dreams have turned to dust." He sat on the edge of a pew beside the aisle. "I've come to beg for Volerdie's guidance one last time." Namu cawed, and Malphas flinched as if noticing the griffin for the first time. "You've brought this animal into the holy chapel?"

Saskia waved her cutlass at the old man. "Keep away from the altar. Immortal or not, I won't let you harm us."

Malphas sighed, tucked his robes between his legs, and untied a ribbon wrapped around the rolled parchment. "Do any of you know what this is?" he asked, holding the scroll aloft. "What am I saying? Of course you don't. It's the First Scripture. *Da Und Sepcarture*. Volerdie's words written in his own blood. I've studied it for yarles. Thought I understood all the Divine Creator's desires. All his secrets and commands are hidden on the pages. But I've missed something. I must have." He lowered the scripture and bowed his shaking head.

Nettie and Saskia glanced at each other, wavering on wary feet.

Rosalie stepped towards Malphas, thinking she would confront him.

"No," said Nettie. "Stay back."

Rosalie froze as Malphas lifted his head again.

"Why don't we come to an agreement?" he asked. "I'll sit here in peace, studying the scripture, and leave you and your creature alone."

"How can we trust you?" asked Rosalie.

Malphas shrugged. "What choice do you have?"

None, thought Rosalie, wondering if they could escape through a side door.

She stood beside her younger sister as a clearly injured Saskia staggered closer to Namu. Blood dripped from the griffin's limp right wing; Rosalie certain the three women had no hope of climbing onboard and urging Namu to burst through the roof and fly to safety.

The Worshipful Master pored over the parchment pages, mumbling and cursing to himself. Sometimes, he read passages aloud, then looked to Rosalie, Nettie and Saskia in puzzlement as if they might be able to interpret what he couldn't. Eventually, the muttering stopped, and Malphas fell silent, drilling his eyes into the paper as if to set it on fire.

Rosalie took a candle stick from beside the altar, hoping the weighty brass might do some damage, then cursed her stupidity. *Malphas is immortal*, she reminded herself. *We're helpless here.*

"What do you make of this passage?" asked Malphas. "*A beast came from the sky; a creature once two now one, cloven like a hoof, joined in sacrilege. Feather and fur, beak and tufted tail. The beast had immense power and authority, and was worshipped by the people. And the worshippers forsook all deities before the beast. And the divine refused an audience in the presence of the beast.*" Malphas repeated the last sentence, "*And the divine refused an audience in the presence of the beast.*"

He rolled up the First Scripture, tied it with the ribbon, and placed the scroll on the pew with gentle reverence.

"That griffin," said Malphas, waving a crooked finger at Namu. "The beast you've brought into Volerdie's sacred house. Feather and fur. Bird and lion now one. The beast is an abomination. An affront to Volerdie's greatness. Its presence has thwarted his resurrection. While the beast lives, the Divine Creator will never return." Malphas stood and pulled a dagger from his robe.

Rosalie raised the candle stick above her head.

Namu squawked.

Saskia pointed her cutlass at Malphas. "Leave her alone," she said.

Malphas strode forward, his old body filled with renewed purpose. Rosalie bounded down the aisle and swung the candle stick at his head. It bounced off his skull, leaving no mark. Rosalie swung again but tripped and crashed into a row of pews. The Worshipful Master stood over her, holding the dagger. Nettie dropped her axe and rushed forward, pushing Malphas to the ground. He rolled onto his back. Nettie kicked at him, but her feet bounced from his chest. As she stumbled away, he rose up like a corpse from the grave. Holding the dagger above Rosalie's neck, his shoulder tensed, ready to plunge. Nettie flung her body at him, and he slashed the blade across the small of her back. She screamed and fell to the floor beside Rosalie, writhing in agony.

Rosalie tried to stand, but Malphas kicked her in the face, almost knocking her out.

Saskia left Namu, clambering onto a pew and flailing her cutlass. It knocked the dagger from Malphas' hand. He picked up Nettie's battle-axe and advanced on Saskia, pushing her back towards Namu.

Malphas thrust, Saskia parried. He dropped his guard for a moment, and she rushed at him, slamming her body into his chest and smashing him into the altar.

He regained his balance. "You're going to tire before I do," said Malphas. "Or I'll kill you first. Then I will sacrifice your griffin."

Saskia backed up against the altar stage with nowhere else to go.

As blood filled Rosalie's mouth and a throbbing ache set in her cheek, Malphas loomed over Saskia.

*   *   *   *

Tom, Adalwolf and Dwarrow climbed through a trapdoor and onto the top of the pyramid. A storm brewed over Pergamos. Black clouds bulged and heaved, threatening to send a torrent of thunder and lightning down onto the city. The heavy, darkening air accentuated the contorted horror of the dead throne, sitting empty and desolate. Beside the throne, Princess Caeli knelt beside the motionless body of her father, Widukind. A *dead* Widukind.

Malphas has made his immortal sacrifice, thought Tom. *But where is Volerdie and his promised paradise?*

Germalian soldiers stormed the north and east walls, the female warriors swamping the battlements like moths drawn to a flame.

"Papa has left us," said Caeli as Tom approached.

"I'm sorry," he replied, placing a hand on her quivering shoulder.

"No time for sorry," said Dwarrow. "Let's get this over with."

"Volerdie may already be here," said Adalwolf.

Dwarrow marched over to Adalwolf and whacked him on the shin with his walking stick. "Where? Where is your beloved Divine Creator?"

Adalwolf shook his head.

"We're going to end this, one way or another," said Tom, pulling away from Caeli. "If we destroy the throne, Malphas becomes mortal."

"Look at him," said Adalwolf, pointing at the prostrate corpse. "Widukind was a fool. Believing Malphas will be mortal again is a fool's dream."

Tom bunched the front of Adalwolf's tunic in his fist. "Fool or no fool, we're going to finish it."

Adalwolf yanked himself away.

"Begin with the eyes of lost souls," Tom said to Adalwolf, taking a dark eye from the front pocket of his pants.

As he walked to the throne, the bleak sky cast a tremulous shadow over the petrified, twisted bodies and their frozen screams. Crowning the backrest, the eye sockets of the horned wolf glowed crimson like two demonic lighthouses guiding the path home for the eyes of lost souls. Tom reached up and placed an obsidian eye in the left socket.

He faced Adalwolf. "Now you."

Adalwolf heaved his shoulders, pulled the second dark eye from a pouch tied to his belt, and balanced it in the palm of his left hand.

"Hurry," said Dwarrow.

Adalwolf approached the throne, his hand poised in front of the wolf's right eye socket.

"Put it in," said Tom.

Adalwolf glanced at Tom, then reached up and placed the eye in the socket.

The throne's ossified bodies came alive. Skin, turned chalky white from suspended death, shone anew in hues of blush pink and buttermilk. The two hands at the ends of the armrests flexed their fingers. Feet at the bottom of chair legs scuffed the flagstones. Faces once set like ice moaned with the ache of generations of harrowing existence.

Dwarrow took the pouch of bone dust from his belt, loosened the tie cinching the opening together and spread the dust on the throne's seat. Twisted mouths screamed, and an acrid vapour wafted up from the chair.

"It's working," said Dwarrow, stepping back from the throne. "Now for the blood."

"You first," Tom said to Adalwolf. "Use your dagger to cut your right arm and drip blood onto the bone dust."

Adalwolf unsheathed his dagger. He hovered above the throne seat, keeping clear of the bony hands reaching for his clothes.

"Do it," urged Tom. "It has to be fresh blood."

Adalwolf clenched his jaw, sheathed his dagger and faced Tom.

"No," said Adalwolf. "I could be king again, and I need a throne. This throne."

A howling scream, louder than any coming from Volerdie's throne, exploded from the side of the pyramid platform before a blur of fury flashed past Tom.

Caeli, risen from her father's side, flung herself at Adalwolf. They crashed to the ground, rolling towards the edge and threatening to tumble down every one of the pyramid's three hundred steps. Adalwolf dropped his dagger and grabbed the pedestal of a stone pillar to stop his fall. Caeli thudded into him. They lay together for a moment on the precipice before Caeli lifted herself up. Then she dropped her knees onto his chest.

"*Arrrh!*" cried Tom, pain stabbing his heart.

"No!" yelled Dwarrow.

The werp rushed to Caeli. She flung her arm and knocked him aside. Then she pulled a bloodied dagger from Adalwolf's chest, stood, walked to the throne and let the blood drip onto the seat from the blade's tip. The long-suffering mouths screamed louder.

Dwarrow yanked on Tom's arm. "Get up. It's almost done."

Tom floundered on the floor, clutching his chest. "Feel...dying...."

*   *   *   *

Thaly burst through the kirika chapel door. Malphas raised an axe, ready to strike at Saskia trapped against the altar stage. Thaly unsheathed a throwing knife, took aim, and threw it at Malphas. It cannoned into the axe's blade, knocking the weapon from his grasp. Thaly sprinted down the aisle, bounded onto a pew backrest and leapt onto Malphas. He collapsed under her weight. She straddled his chest and pummelled his horrible face with her fists. Not a single punch left a mark.

Blood from Thaly's knuckles dripped onto Malphas' mouth.

He traced his tongue across his lips. "You taste so sweet, Athalee. I always knew you would. How wonderful we get to spend more time together."

Saskia chopped down across Malphas' neck with her cutlass. The blade passed through skin and bone and embedded in the timber floor.

Malphas kicked his legs and twisted his body, tipping Thaly off his chest.

He stood, yanking the cutlass from the floorboards. "It appears both of you are slow learners."

Saskia stumbled back towards Namu. In the chapel's aisle, Rosalie pulled an injured young woman close. Thaly drew her cutlass, prepared to battle Malphas until her death so Saskia and Rosalie had time to escape.

"That griffin must die," said Malphas.

He lunged at Saskia. Thaly threw herself onto the floor, knocking Malphas' legs out from under him.

"Run!" Thaly yelled to Saskia.

"My legs," said Saskia. "I can't run. And I won't leave Namu."

Malphas rose up again, sweeping the cutlass across Saskia's chest. The force of the blow split her ribs open. Shocked eyes pleaded for rescue as blood sprayed from her mouth. Then Saskia collapsed in a deathly heap, and Thaly's world crumbled.

*   *   *   *

Tom fought for air with short, shallow breaths. He tried to ignore the hurt, dragging himself along the ground. Dwarrow dropped his walking stick and pulled on Tom's arms, the little werp straining with all his might to get Tom closer to the throne. Caeli stood beside Adalwolf as if bearing witness to his final moments of life.

With the help of Dwarrow, Tom reached the throne's base. He grasped its legs and heaved himself up, resting his back against the front of the seat. Reanimated hands clutched at his shoulders, tearing his tunic. Tom drew a knife from his belt with his left hand, exposed his right palm, and slashed across the scars inflicted by his journeys as the birraman.

He faced the throne, reached his hand above the seat, and dripped his blood on top of Adalwolf's and the bone dust from Jean Anderson and Caeli Heine.

Then, he collapsed.

Adalwolf's body arched. His back curled in a spasm, forcing his bleeding chest towards the clouds. A last gasp rattled in his throat.

Dwarrow flung his hands over his ears as a hideous shriek erupted from Volerdie's throne. Vapour streams swirled up from the chair.

Animated bodies melted, faces, teeth, hands and feet churning together into a blurred, viscous mass. The werp cowered as heat pulsed from the disintegrating throne. Then he pulled Tom away.

The liquefying glob sizzled and hissed before, all at once, the silhouette of a grand chair turned to ash. Then a gust of wind scattered the alabaster dust into the gloomy sky, and two obsidian glass eyes clattered onto the flagstones.

Princess Caeli looked up as a cloud billowed overhead. To a fading, dying Tom Anderson, misty fingers appeared to reach towards her. Caeli breathed, then embraced the grasping sky. Reunited, her body and soul swirled together in a twist of silver light, lifting above the top of the pyramid and dissolving to become the cloud's lining.

* * * *

Manic rage swamped the pain throbbing in Thaly's wounded shoulder. She dived at Malphas. Pushed him back and back, away from Saskia's limp body. Namu sliced at the evil old man with her bill, but it passed through him. The griffin thrashed her head back and forth. Malphas snorted, then cut at Namu's face with the cutlass. Thaly knocked him off balance. Malphas nicked her arm with his blade.

It's no good, thought Thaly. I can't stop him.

Malphas raised the weapon above his head and swung down towards Thaly's face. Instinctively, she blocked the thrust with her cutlass. The edge of her blade grazed the back of his hand, and he flinched, dropping his weapon.

Everything inside the chapel stopped as if time itself froze solid. Malphas' eyes widened when a single drop of blood trickled across his knuckles, clung to the tip of his thumb, then splattered on the floorboards.

Blood. Warm, garnet, pulsing blood.

Malphas looked at Thaly. For the first time, the eyes of the self-proclaimed Worshipful Master showed fear. She clenched her jaw, drew her cutlass back, and plunged it into Malphas' chest. He gasped, clutching at the blade with flailing hands. Thaly withdrew the weapon, and Malphas crumpled to the floor in a pool of his own blood.

*   *   *   *

Tom lay beside the ashen remnants of Volerdie's throne, taking breaths that would surely be his last. Dwarrow knelt with him and rested Tom's head in his tiny lap, rocking back and forth and weeping. A fleck of ash wafted from the ground and floated across the pyramid platform to land beside Widukind's corpse. At the end of a splayed arm, as if trying to flick the ash away, two fingers twitched in a momentary spasm of resurrection.

~ Chapter 54 ~

"Goodness," exclaimed Dwarrow, "this is quite the ride. *Weeeeeee!*" Thaly glanced over her shoulder and laughed, then swooped Yagle down towards Malang Gunya, wheeling the griffin in a circle around the pyramid before skimming over the stone columns of the calendar of life.

"It appears we're late," said Dwarrow. "Everyone is already here."

Thaly nodded and spoke into Yagle's ear. The griffin slowed, hovered near the calendar, then alighted beside the pyramid base.

"How do I get off?" asked Dwarrow.

Yagle squawked, spreading his right wing like a ramp until the tip of the primary feathers touched the ground.

"You're light enough to slide down his wing," said Thaly.

"Slide?" asked Dwarrow. "How indignant."

"I could throw you off."

Dwarrow huffed. "Won't be necessary. I'll slide. I don't want to upset Malphas' assassin." He released his grip on the saddle, pulled his walking stick from a sheath normally used for a lance, pushed his shoulder satchel behind his back and sprang onto Yagle's wing.

"Too steep!" cried Dwarrow as he hurtled towards the flagstones.

A moment before impact, Yagle lifted his wingtip a fraction, slowing Dwarrow's descent.

He dropped from the wing, landing on his feet. "All good. Never any doubt."

Thaly smiled. "I'll join you in a moment."

Dwarrow scampered towards the calendar of life. Weald- and stone-grells stood together in a reverent gathering, heads bowed as they chanted a song of rebirth to the newly painted images of grell culture decorating the floor tiles.

"You are late," whispered Hanni as Dwarrow joined the crowd.

"Important dealings, Hannian stone-grell," said Dwarrow. "Too many important dealings."

"More important than this?"

"Well...no...but...it was the griffin's fault. I thought they flew faster than that."

Symian, the weald-grell leader, glared at Dwarrow, then cleared his throat. "Dwarrow mouldewerp has finally arrived. Did you bring it?"

"Yes, yes, yes," said Dwarrow. "Of course." He fussed around in the dozen pouches hanging from his twine belt. "Where did I put it? That's the more germane question. Where indeed?" He inhaled. *"Ahhh.* Here it is." He untied his favourite indigo-coloured pouch from the belt. "Couldn't smell it owing to the rancid emanation coming from...."

"Dwarrow!" hissed Hanni.

"Sorry. Old habits dying hard and all that." He handed the pouch to Symian.

The weald-grell uncinched the top and tipped an amber casing onto the palm of his hand. After returning the pouch to Dwarrow, he held the amber aloft, morning sunlight making it shine like merigold.

"Dwarrow mouldewerp has delivered the last seed of *ngayirr biyal*," said Symian. "The grell's most sacred tree." He walked into the middle of the calendar of life where a fire burned atop a hollowed-out rock no larger than a werp. Symian handed the seed to Mirrian.

"Her eyes are much improved," Dwarrow said to Hanni.

Hanni nodded. "The black is almost gone, and her skin begins to glow, though it will always be a pale yellow. And the scars on her face and in her soul will last until the end."

Mirrian took a sharp, pencil-thin piece of stone fashioned as a drill and twisted the tip into the amber casing until reaching the chamber containing the seed. Stone- and weald-grells laid green panalope leaves onto the fire until plumes of smoke wafted into the clear sky. After removing the stone drill, Mirrian held the hole in the amber casing over the smoke until a wisp became trapped in the seed chamber. She then placed her thumb over the hole.

"To the arboretum," said Symian.

Dwarrow and Hanni followed Mirrian and the crowd to Malang Gunya's garden, replanted and restored, and covering an area a quarter the size of the city.

In a patch of soil, tended with love to prepare it for seed germination, Wirrikow knelt and dug a hole with the wooden trowel gifted to Dwarrow by the weald-grell elders of Giigal.

"That's my boy," said Dwarrow, loud enough for most to hear.

Wirrikow stepped back. Mirrian handed the amber casing to Ayran, the oldest weald-grell elder. The smoke escaped from the drill hole as Ayran shook the sacred seed from the casing into her palm. She crouched beside the soil and placed the seed in the hole.

"Dwarrow mouldewerp," said Ayran. "Would you like to finish?"

Me? thought Dwarrow. What an honour. What an honour, indeed!

"Yes," said Dwarrow. "Most humbled."

He gave his walking stick to Hanni, pulled the trowel from Wirrikow's claw, stepped to the hole, knelt and shovelled a rich handful of dirt over the seed. Mirrian handed him a bowl of water, and he tipped it into the soil as the stone- and weald-grells hummed a soft, hopeful lament.

"Is it done?" asked Thaly as she stood beside Hanni.

"Most certainly," said Dwarrow, climbing to his feet.

"Now we must hope it grows," said Hanni.

Thaly smiled. "Griffin dung might help."

"As long as you collect it," said Dwarrow.

"They are ready for us," said Thaly. "In the nature precinct."

Thaly led Dwarrow, Hanni, Mirrian and Wirrikow to a secluded garden in the centre of Malang Gunya's nature precinct, where stone- and weald-grells studied the ecology of all Enthilen's creatures. On a lawned area, Nettie and Chloe arranged chairs in rows facing an arbour of twisting, climbing vines covered in white flowers.

Thaly skipped over to her lover and kissed her on the cheek.

Chloe smiled. "Did the ceremony go well?"

"Did you think it wouldn't?" asked Dwarrow.

"You might have mixed up the seeds."

Dwarrow crossed his arms. "Ridiculous. Well, where is everyone? I thought you were ready for us."

"You're not the most important guest here," said Nettie.

"I find that quite impossible to believe."

The sun rose to mid-morning, and guests began to arrive. Tilly helped a frail, hobbling Emelin to her seat. Genevea came with Zenais. Whibly limped up behind them, hanging off Melinda's arm. Stone-and weald-grells stood on the grass. Werps climbed into the remaining seats.

Thaly hugged her mother, then faced Dwarrow. "We'd better find the guests of honour."

They walked from the crowd towards an enclosed rotunda at the garden's edge.

Stepping inside, they found Rosalie cradling her infant son while Audie folded blankets and placed them in a cot.

Thaly put her arm around Rosalie. "How are you feeling?"

"Nervous," said Rosalie.

"Everyone's arrived. How's...."

"He's resting a little longer."

"The healing will take time," said Audie.

"No surprise," said Dwarrow. "The foolish boy almost died."

"I'm not a boy." Tom stood at the doorway, smiling down at Dwarrow. "Though, I'm probably still foolish."

Dwarrow leaned on his walking stick. "No. No, you're not, Tom Anderson."

Tom hugged Thaly, then kissed Rosalie as he pulled the wrap away from his son's face. "Most likely, he'll sleep right through it."

"Well, being a grell ceremony, I wouldn't be surprised."

"Dwarrow," said Thaly. "Behave." She faced Tom. "Are you sure you're up to this?"

"I came as close to death as anyone can," said Tom. "I still don't understand how I survived when Adalwolf didn't."

"I've been thinking," said Dwarrow. "When the throne disintegrated, it must have cleansed the eyes of lost souls of all their wickedness. Disrupted the path that leads one birth twin to another, and the blood connection between them."

"They are the Eyes of Relevation now," said Tom. "I guess that means they can't be used anymore to travel between worlds."

"Only one way to find out," said Dwarrow. "Hand them over."

Tom withdrew the glass eyes from his coat pocket. "I'm not sure about this. Rosalie and I have to return to Revelé. To guard the eyes and the Infinitas. If you disappear...."

Dwarrow snatched the treasure from Tom's hand. "Nonsense. No-one is disappearing. I'm almost certain."

"Almost?"

"Who wants to try?" asked Dwarrow, holding the eyes aloft. "I can't do it, of course. Enthilen wouldn't be the same without me."

Audie stepped forward. "I'll try. There's nothing for me in this world. I won't be sad if it works."

Dwarrow handed the eyes to Audie.

Sweat beaded on Tom's brow.

"Don't begin any of that counting nonsense," Dwarrow said to Tom.

"It's just...." started Tom.

"One in each hand?" asked Audie. "Is that right?"

"Yes, yes, yes," said Dwarrow. "Then wrap your fingers around the eyes."

Audie looked at everyone in the room, held a glass ball in each hand, then closed her fists. Nothing happened.

"Phew!" cried Dwarrow. "I was worried it might work."

Audie returned the eyes to Tom.

Hanni appeared at the doorway. "We are ready."

"Finally," said Dwarrow. "I'm excited about what's to come. Very excited indeed!"

The friends walked to the arbour. Tom, Rosalie and their son took their place under the archway. Dwarrow stood beside them, rubbing his clawed fingers over a vine leaf to feel the essence of life flowing through its veins.

Mirrian approached the young family, then faced the guests.

"Dear friends," she said, "this ceremony dates back to the time of the first grell ancestors, long before they set foot in Enthilen. As long as our history can recall. A new soul has come into this world. One born of the land we call home. We must announce this new life to the land, so it can comfort and provide for its offspring and accept the soul back into its bosom at journey's end. The *Ceremony of the Name* is the most important in all grell culture."

Mirrian faced the arbour. "Tom and Rosalie, step forward." The grell elder reached inside her possum-skin cloak and retrieved a smooth, clean totem of white swirls dancing across green softstone. She held the remembrance totem aloft. "This totem is ready to accept the story of your boy's life. All that remains is for you to announce his name to the land."

Mirrian unhitched a pouch from her coat and sprinkled soil into Rosalie's palm. Rosalie rubbed the earth through her fingers, then brushed it across her baby's forehead.

Tom cleared his throat. "Our homeland," he announced, "I speak to you now. Accept this new soul as one of your own. Care for him, as we will teach him to care for you. Protect him, as he will protect you. Cherish him, as he will cherish you. Our land, welcome into your heart this new life. Our boy, whose name is Grin."

"What!?" cried Dwarrow. "Surely a more appropriate name is Gwuendā-hæ Dwinë D'elch? I would have even accepted Dwarrow if your tongues are so lacking dexterity as to find my real name unpronounceable."

The congregation laughed, and Dwarrow felt his salmon-coloured face turn red.

THE END

Dramatis Personae

(Book III, main characters only)

For a complete dramatis personae of all named characters in the trilogy, visit my Blog at www.relevationtrilogy.com

Character	Culture ∞ First appearance	Relations/Notes
Adalwolf Heine	Erstürmen ∞ Sardis	Son of Ewald [disputed] and Romilda, known as the 'Absent King'
Anselm	Erstürmen ∞ Sardis	Hoch-Vater of Enthilen
Athalee [Thaly]	Dobunni ∞ Süden Forst	Adopted daughter of Emelin and Thane, adopted sister of Dayna, wind-rider of Yagle, senator of the Capri faction
Audie	Morundanian ∞ Laodicea	Cardinal healer in Gestade
Ayran	Weald-grell ∞ Giigal	Elder of the magu
Berard	Erstürmen ∞ Pergamos	Lieutenant in the Master's Shield
Berenice Atallum	Germalian ∞ Magna Avium	Wind-rider of Nia
Caeli Heine	Erstürmen ∞ Sardis	Daughter of Widukind, cousin of Adalwolf, Ewald and Genevea and siblings
Carian	Stone-grell ∞ Pergamos	Slave
Charmion	Germalian ∞ Portum	Sella of the Germalian Conventus
Chitti coin-tail	Mouldewerp ∞ Beitrag	Trader
Chloe Floriana	Germalian ∞ Portum	Thaly's lover

Character	Culture ∞ First appearance	Relations/Notes
Demetria	Germalian ∞ Magna Avium	Wind-rider of Eluji
Dwarrow	Mouldewerp ∞ Scaur Hills	Parent of Wirrikow
Elaine Anderson	Australian ∞ Littlehampton	Mother of Tom, wife of Bert
Elmbray	Unknown ∞ Slumstadt	Possible mage
Emelin Wallace	Dobunni ∞ Bagendon	Wife of Thane, mother of Dayna, adoptive mother of Thaly
Ende [the pale grell]	Tainted grell ∞ Breadelbane	Servant of Malphas
Erwin Brotmacher	Erstürmen ∞ Pergamos	Son of Wilfred and Adelina Brotmacher
Eudokia	Germalian ∞ Portum	Prime Lieutenant
Eutropia	Germalian ∞ Riverlands	Orator of the Arie faction in Germalian Conventus
Fullō	Draughoul ∞ Rārian Falls	Mother of Oldaric and Widukind
Genevea Stansfield [née Heine]	Erstürmen ∞ Sardis	Wife of Jurelle, mother of Jürgen and Saskia, sister of Ewald, Hadufuns, Widald and Gerulf, daughter of Oldaric
Grinnian [Grin]	Stone-grell ∞ Babir Birramal	Son of Frennan and Mirrian, brother of Hanni
Hál	Unknown ∞ Revelé	'Sage'
Hannian [Hanni]	Stone-grell ∞ Dalman	Daughter of Frennan and Mirrian, sister of Grin
Hartmut Adelmund	Erstürmen ∞ Gestade	Field Commander
Heron	Germalian ∞ Portum	Saskia's love interest
Hunger [the black grell]	Tainted grell ∞ Laodicea	Servant of Malphas

Character	Culture ∞ First appearance	Relations/Notes
Jean Anderson	Australian ∞ Littlehampton	Mother of Bert, grandmother of Tom
Julan	Weald-grell ∞ Pergamos	Slave
Jurelle Stansfield	Erstürmen ∞ Sardis	Husband of Genevea, father of Jürgen and Saskia, once leader of the Dobunni rebels in Bagendon
Kallisto Stratus	Germalian ∞ Magna Avium	Competitor in the Eligens
Krieg [the red grell]	Tainted grell ∞ Laodicea	Servant of Malphas
Lily LáDown	Dobunni ∞ Laodicea	Master of the Southern Vale, Hartmut's lover
Melinda Firebrace	Non-aligned ∞ Bramble Island	Daughter of Jameus and Lenora Firebrace, skullard and whale-master of the Grimart
Melitta	Germalian ∞ Portum	Orator of the Sagit faction
Mirrian	Stone-grell ∞ Dalman	Mother of Grin and Hanni, wife of Frennan
Nettie Barron	Erstürmen ∞ Sardis	Daughter of Yonna and Heady, sister of Rosalie, Petas and Allum
Oldaric Heine [Malphas]	Erstürmen ∞ Malang Gunya	Son of Alaric, father of Ewald and siblings, brother of Widukind, claimed father of Adalwolf
Puer	Germalian ∞ Portum	Handler of Yagle
Quenan	Weald-grell ∞ Dalman	Member of the Mulugan
Raf	Dobunni ∞ Desolate Mountains	Rebel
Rais	Pordillo ∞ Magna Avium	Qaysar [leader] of the Pordillo

Character	Culture ∞ First appearance	Relations/Notes
Roben	Erstürmen ∞ Gestade	Lieutenant to Field Commander Hartmut
Romilda Heine	Erstürmen ∞ Sardis	Wife of Ewald, mother of Adalwolf
Rosalie Barron	Erstürmen ∞ Sardis	Daughter of Yonna and Heady, sister of Petas, Nettie and Allum
Rostard	Erstürmen ∞ Sardis	King's soothsayer
Saskia Stansfield	Erstürmen ∞ Sardis	Daughter of Jurelle and Genevea, sister of Jürgen, wind-rider of Namu
Snick	Unknown ∞ Slumstadt	Assistant to Elmbray
Sonya	Dobunni ∞ Laodicea	Rebel
Symian	Weald-grell ∞ Giigal	Leader
Tilly Roebolt	Unknown ∞ Sardis	Daughter of Ella and Darius, granddaughter of Zaria
Tom Anderson	Australian ∞ Littlehampton	Son of Elaine and Bert
Tormil	Dobunni ∞ Desolate Mountains	Rebel
Whibly Horsars	Nordman ∞ Laodicea	Captain of the Grimart
Widukind Heine	Erstürmen ∞ Desolate Mountains	Son of Alaric, brother of Oldaric, father of Caeli
Wirrikow	Mouldewerp ∞ Bagendon	Son of Dwarrow
Wyan	Weald-grell ∞ Dalman	Member of the Mulugan
Yannus Rossingbird	Docklander ∞ Laodicea	Son of Dealhia
Yonna Barron	Erstürmen ∞ Sardis	Husband of Heady, father of Rosalie, Petas, Allum and Nettie
Zenais	Germalian ∞ Riverlands	Orator of the Capri faction in Germalian Conventus

Appendix (Book III)

A guide to ostamp

Abrolous Isles — a group of sparsely populated islands off Enthilen's east coast.

Afonwee River — the border between Germalia and Nordland, running from the Desolate Mountains through Ephesus and emptying into Elephai Bay.

Al Mōr Sŭrl — watchtower built by the Dobunni in the old settlement of Iglund (an island in the middle of the Anchep River). The watchtower was renamed the Sunrise Keep by the Erstürmen and incorporated into Sardis' inner circle.

Anchep River — major river running through the north-west of Enthilen and surrounding Sardis.

Babir Birramal — expansive forest covering the southern region of Enthilen, occupied by stone- and weald-grells.

Bagendon — a town built in the Scaur Hills by Dobunni rebels pledged to overthrow the Erstürmen Kingdom.

Barbarians — invaders/marauders from the lands of Morund, Oder and Sexton.

Bargan — the name of one of the two moons in the sky above Ostamp.

Bay of Deception — a bay in Nordland where King Giltbert made his last stand against barbarians.

Bay of Fires — a deep, protected bay surrounded by the Abrolous Isles and often used by barbarian ships for anchorage.

Bay of Marrumin — a bay on Enthilen's south coast surrounding Giigal.

Beitrag — trading post south of Pergamos.

Bellum cornu — also 'cornu'. Horn used by the Germalians.

Bethesda — the Dobunni name for Laodicea.

Bilawi tree — a tree with needle-like foliage found in Enthilen.

Bindari — secret location of the graveyard for stone- and weald-grells.

Birraman — stone-grell name for travellers from far-away lands.

Birth twins — two individuals born at precisely the same time, one of them on Earth and the other in Ostamp. Birth twins usually don't look alike and can be of different genders. However, they will always have the same birthmark, which persists until death.

Blood compass — gold pentagram that spins of its own accord after a single point of the star is dipped in the blood of a birth twin when their twin occupies the same world. There were once five compasses; only one remains.

Blue book — a book left for Tom Anderson that translates the Erstürmen language to English, and tells stories of Erstürmen culture.

Bramble Island — a popular fishing destination off Enthilen's east coast.

Breadelbane — abandoned village in the western Dambay Plains near the Scaur Hills.

Bullroarer — implement used by Dwarrow to call up his steed, Xaviary, the giant lizard.

Bunbili weed — tobacco-like plant smoked by the Erstürmen.

Calendar of life — the most sacred place in Malang Gunya. An open, circular temple surrounded by marble pillars with paintings decorating the tiled floor depicting essential aspects of grell culture.

Carcer — Germalian word for prison.

Cathedral of the Elders — room at the highest point in the enormous tree, *yurrubang*.

Centure — rank in the Germalian army akin to 'Sergeant'.

Classem — Germalian navy.

Conventus — ruling body of Germalia comprising two hundred and eighty-eight senators and the Sella [chairperson].

Carborupem — slow-burning powder used by the Germalians in their street lamps.

Crest — facial tattoo worn by all free grells. Each crest is unique, representing a plant or animal that the grell is responsible for protecting.

Curate — a holy man [priest] in the Erstürmen culture.

Curmudgles — dwarf-sized, human-like creatures living in Grauberge.

Dachlos — old, homeless people living in the ossuary in Pergamos.

Dalman — a secret location in Babir Birramal where stone- and weald-grells hold the sacred ceremony called garrabari.

Dambay Plains — vast grassland region in the centre of Enthilen once occupied by mouldewerps and stone-grells.

Dangal — shelter made by grells from branches, sedges, sticks and leaves.

Da Und Sepcarture — ancient name for the First Scripture.

Deeping pits — Erstürmen gaol adjacent to the outer wall of Sardis.

Desolate Mountains — an extensive mountain range in the north of Enthilen, marking the border between Enthilen and Nordland.

Detranté — narrow pass through the Desolate Mountains connecting Nordland with Enthilen.

Dhawura — grell name for the season of strong winds.

Divine Creator — another name for Volerdie.

Dobunni — settled Enthilen after the stone-grells and built Bethesda, Iglund (a village on an island in the middle of the Anchep River, now the location of Sardis) and the watchtower of Al Mōr Sŭrl. Came as peaceful settlers rather than invaders. Ousted from much of Enthilen by the Erstürmen and were confined to Bagendon and the Southern Vale in Laodicea before the settlements were attacked.

Dobunni rebels — those Dobunni pledged to overthrow the Erstürmen Kingdom.

Docklands — one of the four quarters in Laodicea. Wharf area next to Traders Bay.

Docklands Guard — soldiers tasked with keeping the peace and defending the Docklands from enemies.

Domina — title used by male Germalians when addressing a female.

Domina-homines — Also called 'lady-men.' Germalian male prostitutes often dressing as women (and servicing mostly men). Most work in brothels in Gustium, a suburb of Portum.

Dorfisch — fishing town on Enthilen's east coast near Gestade.

Draconarius — Germalian word for a person carrying a banner or standard.

Draughoul — a creature that has had its soul captured by the eyes of lost souls. They exist in a state of almost suspended animation but aren't 'undead' as such. They can be killed or, over time, their body will wither away to nothing. However, a natural demise can take hundreds to thousands of yarles [years]. Only human-like creatures can become draughouls.

Dreadwerp — relative of the mouldewerp (and the same size). Lives under the sands of Magna Avium and often rides slider serpents.

Dwell — name for both a specific hole in the ground where a mouldewerp lives and the collection of holes in a given location. Akin to 'home'.

Elephai — Germalian name for tufted goliath.

Elephas Tusk — tavern in Ephesus.

Eligens — a series of challenges faced by apprentice wind-riders vying to become the next person to ride their own griffin.

Elagear — person in charge of supervising the election of the Dobunni rebel leader.

Embruisia — also called **cerulean honey**. Mind-altering substance used by the Erstürmen.

Enthilen — land in the eastern half of Ostamp occupied by Erstürmen, Dobunni, stone- and weald-grells, mouldewerps and others.

Ephesus — border city between Germalia and Nordland, straddling the banks of the Afonwee River.

Erstürmen — settled Enthilen after being ousted by barbarians (the ancestors of Nordmen) from what is now called Nordland. Came as invaders and conquerors, claiming Enthilen for themselves regardless of other inhabitants.

Eyes of lost souls — two obsidian glass eyes with flaming pupils. One of the seven treasures from the throne of the dead.

Felsie — also called the pool of reflection. A lake in Laodicea located at the bottom of Hansen's Bluff.

Field Commander — rank in the Erstürmen army usually bestowed on those commanding one of the Erstürmen outposts or significant battles. This rank is immediately above lieutenant and below General, although many in the military view General and Field Commander as equivalent ranks. The Dobunni have also adopted the rank of Field Commander.

First Scripture — also known as *Da Und Sepcarture* in the old language of Pergamos. Ancient parchment believed to be written by Volerdie in his own blood, documenting his lore and secrets.

Flüsse — the central, most fertile and densely populated region of the Riverlands.

Gadhang — vast ocean to the south of Enthilen. Crossed by the first stone-grell settlers.

Gaping hollow — deep chasm that breaches the cave floor leading to the secret passage into Sardis.

Garderobe — small room off the throne hall in Sardis that houses the royal robes.

Gari yala — the speaking stone used to denote permission to speak during grell meetings.

Garrabari — ancient stone- and weald-grell celebration involving dancing and singing, telling stories and sacred ceremony. It happens in Dalman when both Seena and Bargan, the two moons, are full.

Gawimarra — grell name for the harvest season.

Germalia — region in the western half of Ostamp occupied by the Germalians. Main city, Portum.

Gestade — Erstürmen outpost on the central east coast of Enthilen.

Giagan — the revered panalope tree on the edge of Babir Birramal.

Giba — a stone sacred to stone- and weald-grells that casts its own light.

Giigal — weald-grell city on an island in the Bay of Marrumin.

Grauberge — cold, mountainous region east of Nordland. Home to the curmudgles, most of whom live in the city of Karlik.

Grimart — name of Whibly's ship.

Grōz Forst — Erstürmen name for Babir Birramal.

Grōz Wüste — large desert in the western half of Ostamp claimed by Germalians (who call it Magna Avium), but includes disputed territory claimed by both Germalians and the Pordillo.

Gulba — the peace stone given to Dwarrow by the stone- and weald-grells, signifying the alliance between grells and werps.

Guma — grell name for the storm season.

Gustium — seedy suburb of Portum.

Hansen's Bluff — limestone cliff to the north of Laodicea and overlooking the city.

Heilig-jün — twenty-four disciples that follow the teachings of Enthilen's Hoch-Vater.

Heine Empire — name for the unbroken reign of kings from the Heine family, beginning with King Giltbert Heine.

Hoch-Vater — a title meaning 'high father' and used only by the most respected curate in Erstürmen culture.

Homage march — march from Babir Birramal to Malang Gunya undertaken every yarle during the long dark by stone- and weald-grell pilgrims to honour the grells who died trying to protect Malang Gunya from the Erstürmen invasion.

Hurna — a horn used by the Erstürmen to rally troops in battle.

Hurst — tall pinnacle of rock in the Nordargen Sea where Erstürmen kings of old would hide treasures and jewels, and where legend has it, griffins used to nest.

Iglund — Dobunni village, built on the island in the Anchep River that is now home to Sardis.

Infada — Qaysar Rais' personal guard of twelve elite fighters who are armed with daggers infused with a deadly poison.

Infinitas — a silver jewel in the shape of a lemniscate. When combined with the eyes of lost souls, the Infinitas is the key to unlocking the wisdom of ancestors [and transforms the eyes of lost souls into the Eyes of Relevation].

Kamel — same as 'camel'.

Khorsal — cross between a camel [kamel] and a horse. Mount favoured by the Pordillo.

King's Quarter — one of the four quarters of Laodicea occupied by the Erstürmen.

King's Shield — elite Erstürmen soldiers who have vowed to protect the king with their life.

Kirika — building in most Erstürmen settlements containing a chapel for worshipping Volerdie, and other rooms. Often built underground and above the dungeon.

Koken — cooking/eating area in a typical Erstürmen family home.

Laodicea (Bethesda) — port city on the northeast coast of Enthilen at Traders Bay. Divided into four quarters (King's Quarter, Southern Vale, Docklands and The Terraces) and occupied by Erstürmen, Dobunni, and others. Dobunni settlers built the city and named it Bethesda.

Lata Via — main thoroughfare in Portum.

Legatus — military rank in the Germalian army akin to 'General' or 'Commander'.

Leichenhalle — room where the Erstürmen keep corpses before burning or burial.

Leviathan — enormous statue of a monstrous and mythical sea creature spanning the heads of Traders Bay.

Levit — young boy or girl tasked with assisting curates.

Lieutenant — rank in the Erstürmen army immediately above sergeant-at-arms and below Field Commander. Some armies also use **Prime Lieutenant** to denote a rank above Lieutenant.

Lokan — a cursed woodland in the foothills of the Desolate Mountains.

Lost Sisters — natural stone columns in Nordland located near the entrance to the road under the Desolate Mountains.

Lufu — Dobunni word for 'lover'.

Lumina — Germalian name for the twelve 'daylight' hours.

Lupanar — a brothel in Portum.

Magna Avium — Germalian name for Grōz Wüste.

Magu — name of the four weald-grell elders.

Malang Gunya — ruined stone-grell city in the middle of the Dambay Plains in Enthilen.

Marduk — life-size statue of an ancient man believed to have travelled between worlds and become a god. Considered by sea-farers as the God of the Ocean.

Marradir — a boulder in the middle of Dalman on which the stone- and weald-grells wrote and signed the truce that marked the end of tribal conflict between the groups.

Master's Hall — largest building in each quarter of Laodicea used by the quarter's master to conduct various business.

Meduz — grainy, milky alcoholic beverage found throughout Ostamp.

Meladoor tree — barbarians use the timber from this tree to make their ships.

Mendeal herbs — herbs found throughout Enthilen and used for medicinal purposes.

Milbi — small stone shelter used by stone-grells.

Miyan — the name for the grell custodians that tend the graveyards in Bindari.

Mons Harena — tallest sand dune in Magna Avium [Grōz Wüste].

Morund — a landmass situated east of Ostamp, across the Veiled Occyan, and home to people the Erstürmen and Dobunni call barbarians.

Mouldewerp — long-time inhabitants of Enthilen. Previously lived in the Dambay Plains until ousted by stone-grell settlers who used to hunt mouldewerps for food and sport. Now live in small and secretive groups, mostly in the Scaur Hills.

Mr Prickles — Widukind's pet dodo.

Mulugan — the group of stone- and weald-grells tasked with decision-making and guiding the two tribes during the garrabari.

Mumbal — grell name for the season of blossoms.

Murdark — name of a barbarian ship.

Muwin — a ground spider. Grin's facial crest [tattoo].

Needle — a narrow passage connecting the inner circle of Sardis with the second circle. The only [widely known] way to access the inner courtyard.

Ngayirr biyal — the most hallowed tree in stone-grell culture.

Ngulubul — meeting place on the edge of Babir Birramal where grells gather before undertaking the homage march.

Ngurung-ginya — grell name for the season of the long dark.

Nocturna — Germalian name for the twelve 'night-time' hours.

Nordargen Sea — sea to the north of Nordland.

Nordland — land to the north of Enthilen occupied by Nordmen (descendants of barbarians).

Nordmen [Nordman] — nomadic [mostly] people living in Nordland.

Occidian Sea — sea off Germalia's west coast.

Oder — a landmass situated east of Ostamp, across the Veiled Occyan, and home to people the Erstürmen and Dobunni call barbarians.

Ölblut — liquid extracted from the throne of the dead by Malphas and used to taint the skin of his four tainted grells.

Ossuary — underground graveyard found in Pergamos. Once used by the stone-grells to bury their children in, now home to the dachlos [homeless].

Ostamp — landmass that includes Enthilen, Germalia, Nordland, Grauberge, Pordillo Territory, Grōz Wüste and Babir Birramal.

Overseer — leader of a group of twenty grell slaves.

Pallaxium — largest building in Portum housing the ruling Germalian Conventus.

Panalope tree — a favourite tree of stone- and weald-grells used for various purposes. The largest tree species in Babir Birramal.

Pergamos — a lost and ruined city lying underneath the foundations of Malang Gunya. Believed by some Erstürmen to once be occupied by their ancestors. Also believed to be Volerdie's seat of power when he ruled over Ostamp and other lands. Malphas rebuilt the city when he ruled Enthilen.

Plainalope — goat-sized antelope.

Pledge Feste — name of the ceremony in which the Dobunni ask for citizens to pledge allegiance to the Dobunni rebels and their cause.

Pordillo — nomads living in the deserts of Magna Avium. Sworn enemies of the Germalians.

Pordillo Territory — land in the southwest of Ostamp occupied by Pordillo nomads.

Portum — main city of Germalia.

Praefecti — rank in the Germalian navy, akin to 'Commander'.

Proclaimant of the King — title bestowed on Lothar by Malphas.

Qaysar — title of the leader of the Pordillo, akin to 'king'.

Rārian Falls — where the Anchep River tumbles over the Riverlands Escarpment, west of Sardis. The Erstürmen maintain guardhouses at the top and bottom of the road that zig-zags down the escarpment face next to the falls.

Remembrance Totem — [also called 'family totem']. Softstone about the size of a taper candle. Grells etch the story of their life on its surface, and totems are handed down to next-of-kin or buried with the grell.

Rephaim — the corrupted grell soldiers, trained by Krieg and loyal to Malphas.

Revelé — small town in the northern foothills of the Desolate Mountains.

Riverlands — fertile farmland wedged between the Scaur Hills and Groz Wüste. Occupied by unaligned farmers and villagers.

Riverlands Escarpment — steep, sheer cliff running along the western edge of the Scaur Hills.

River Lousse — a river running from the Desolate Mountains south into the Dambay Plains and on towards Gestade.

River Milawa — river in the Dambay Plains and the closest river to Malang Gunya.

Rufous — small town on the outskirts of eastern Babir Birramal.

Sand Bēċe — small town on Enthilen's east coast.

Sardis — royal city of Enthilen, occupied and built by the Erstürmen, comprised of seven concentric circles. Each circle of the city is occupied by Erstürmen of different status; the closer to the inner circle, the higher the status. The inner circle is occupied by the royal family and trusted court. Left to ruin during Malphas' reign.

Satch — name for a troop of twelve Rephaim soldiers.

Scaur Hills — a rocky range running along the western edge of Enthilen, marking the border between Enthilen and the Riverlands and eventually Grōz Wüste.

Scripture verses — also called *Polus Sepcarture* in the old language of Pergamos. A black book believed to be an interpretation of the First Scripture. Only curates are typically permitted to read and interpret the scripture verses.

Seena — the name of one of the two moons in the sky above Ostamp.

Sella — chairperson of the Germalian Conventus and most powerful person in Portum.

Senatorial Dictum — the book of laws governing Germalia.

Sergeant-at-arms — rank in the Erstürmen army immediately above soldier and below lieutenant.

Serpent oil — highly combustible liquid.

Sexton — a landmass situated east of Ostamp, across the Veiled Occyan, and home to people the Erstürmen and Dobunni call barbarians.

Silver tausen — very rare and valuable coin. Value varies depending on which Erstürmen king is depicted on the coin.

Skullard — the title of a first-mate on a merchant ship.

Slider serpent — horse-sized snake that lives in the deserts of Magna Avium [Grōz Wüste].

Slumstadt — shantytown/ghetto on the fringes of Sardis.

Slyencia Bay — Portum's main harbour.

Softstone — stone used for grell remembrance totems.

Southern Vale — one of the four quarters of Laodicea occupied mostly by Dobunni.

Steward's Shield — soldiers sworn to protect Hunfrid, Steward of Sardis.

Stone-grell — [grell] early inhabitants of the land now known as Enthilen. Built Malang Gunya and occupied the city until being ousted by the Erstürmen.

Süden Forst — Erstürmen outpost in the south of Enthilen on the edge of Babir Birramal.

Sunrise Keep — Erstürmen name for Al Mōr Sŭrl; one of two keeps in Sardis' inner circle.

Sunset Keep — one of two keeps in Sardis' inner circle.

Tainted grell — a stone-grell whose skin has been tainted by Malphas using arcane, evil arts. There are four tainted grells with four different skin colours: Eroberung (white), Krieg (red), Hunger (black), and Ende (pale).

Terraces — one of the four quarters of Laodicea occupied by wealthier residents.

Testament of Fire — a ceremony used by the Dobunni to select rebel soldiers for critically important missions.

The Feign — the southern foothills of the Desolate Mountains.

The Hive — Portum's wharves.

The Ravage — a fatal disease that spread through Enthilen (mostly Sardis) during the final days of King Ewald's reign and the rise of King Adalwolf.

Throne of the dead — believed to be Volerdie's throne. Made from desiccated, ossified bodies. Also called the 'dead throne'.

Thyatira — ruined city in Nordland, once occupied by the Erstürmen before they were expelled by barbarians.

Traders Bay — bay neighbouring Laodicea, where the city port and docklands are located.

Tufted goliath — woolly, elephant-sized creature with tusks and horns living mostly in Nordland. Germalians call them 'elephai'.

Turma — Germalian name for a troop of camel [kamel] riders usually numbering thirty.

Tu'sok — sacred dead tree at the centre of the mouldewerp dwell in the Scaur Hills.

Umbo — title bestowed on the figurehead/commander of the King's Shield. Rarely participates in actual battle.

Undred — giant, horse-like creature with a single, curved horn protruding from its forehead.

Vater — a title given to the tainted grells, meaning 'Father.'

Veiled Occyan — ocean to the east of Enthilen.

Vertraúlich — dressing room for curates.

Vestium — Germalian word for wardrobe/closet.

Vigilum — law enforcers in Germalia, akin to 'Police'.

Vinum — Germalian word for wine.

Volatal Vexil — name for the twelve griffin riders [wind-riders].

Volerdie — a god worshipped by the Erstürmen. Also known as the Divine Creator.

Volerdie's Lore — another name for the scripture verses.

Volerdie's Wrath — seismic events that can occur in Enthilen from time to time.

Vulking — merchant ship owned by Captain Adcock.

Walar Rock — rock overhang near Gestade.

Weald-grell — [grell] once identified as stone-grells until the tribal war that saw them abandon Malang Gunya and settle on the south coast of Babir Birramal at Giigal.

Weregrim — large, blind hound residing underground in the tunnels connecting to Pergamos.

Whale-master — person in charge of guiding the whales that pull ships.

Wilay — furry, arboreal, cat-sized animal eaten by grells; skin used for clothing.

Wind-rider — a person who rides a griffin.

Wonchulus — an oasis in Magna Avium containing water.

Worshipful Master — preferred title of Malphas [Oldaric].

Wurloin — a whale-sized arthropod that makes funnel nests in the sands of Magna Avium.

Xaviary — horse-sized lizard ridden by Dwarrow.

Yarle — Erstürmen word for a time period covering six seasons/three hundred and sixty days.

Yirany — yellow tuber eaten by grells.

Yirra — grell name for the growing season.

Yulumbang plant — medicinal shrub used by the grells to treat sore throats and coughs.

Yurali bush — common shrub in Babir Birramal.

Yurrubang — an enormous tree at the centre of Giigal housing hundreds of weald-grells.

Zōdiakos — name of the room inside the Pallaxium where the conventus hold their meetings.

Acknowledgements

Many people helped the characters of *She Will Rise* reach their final destination. Thanks to my wonderful beta readers: Margrit Beemster, Raf Freire, Ian Boyd and especially Gayle, who endured another 18 months of life in Ostamp. During the last year and a half, I've enjoyed collaborating with fantasy artists Angel Munro, Belinda Morris and especially Jessie S. A'Bell, who all created amazing images to match the words on the page and the pictures inside my head (see my blog: https://relevationtrilogy.com/ for examples). Luke Harris from WorkingType Studio did another professional job of the cover and typesetting. Jessie S. A'Bell designed the brilliantly creepy throne of the dead adorning the cover.

Finally, thanks to you, for seeing this journey through to the end. It took longer to get there than I expected, but the best voyages are often like that.

About the Author

G. W. Lücke shares a small part of Tasmania with his partner, a mischievous border collie and a menagerie of animals and plants. He has no spare time, but when not writing, he fills the days with gardening, growing food, forest and beach walks, and being healed by nature.